Tinman

By

Jason Glover

This book is a work of fiction. Places, events, and situations in this story are purely fictional. Any resemblance to actual persons, living or dead, is coincidental.

© 2006 by Jason Glover. All rights reserved.

No part of this book may be reproduced, stored in a retrieval system, or transmitted by any means, electronic, mechanical, photocopying, recording, or otherwise, without written permission from the author.

First published by AuthorHouse 02/17/06

ISBN: 1-4184-6757-X (e-book)
ISBN: 1-4184-4972-5 (Paperback)

This book is printed on acid free paper.

Prologue

"Son, I promise that this move is the best thing for both of us," Debra Saxton expressed persuasively as she gently laid one of her young looking, smooth hands on one of her son's knees, and gave it an affectionate squeeze. "We just have too many bad memories in Marietta. I really believe that we need a fresh start," she continued as she rolled up the window of her black Lexus, finally having enough of the constant pounding of the interstate wind as she found herself constantly fighting her long, soft, beautiful sandy brown hair from slapping across her face. "You'll see," she concluded more comfortably. "And you'll agree that moving to the sandy beaches of Florida will be the best thing we have ever decided to do."

"Mom," Billy began a bit agitated. He was growing tired of being told that the move was the best thing for both of them. He was nineteen years old, fresh out of high school, and felt that he was at the age where he could make life altering decisions on his own. But his mother was adamant about this move, and showed no interest in his opinion on the matter. "Maybe this move is the best thing for you," he continued, clearly voicing his disapproval as he gazed into his mother's beautiful scorching blues eyes with crystal clear, ocean blue eyes of his own. In fact, the only characteristic that set he and his mother apart was the fact that he had blonde hair. His mom was forty years old, yet didn't look a day over thirty. She was an attractive woman, consuming a perfect slender figure, and a soft voice that could win anyone's heart with ease. Billy himself could have entered a beauty pageant and actually have a strong chance of winning. "But I just graduated from high school mom, and I was looking forward to spending the summer with my friends before I go away to college," he decided to add before dropping the subject.

"Son, I'm sorry," his mother continued hesitantly as she tried to think of something to say that would make her only child understand where she was coming from. "But it's just too painful in Georgia for me. Your father scarred my heart darling, and I don't think that it's ever going to heal unless I get a fresh start somewhere. And I want you there with me Billy. I don't think I could manage without you."

"Why did you let him get to you anyway?" Billy asked about his abusive father. At the very mention of his father's name, he couldn't help but to recall the loud, late night fights he'd heard his parents having after his father had returned home intoxicated, usually in the early morning hours. His drinking buddies had always seemed more important than his family. "He wasn't a good husband, and he damn sure wasn't a good father."

"Don't say that about Tom," Debra broke in. She couldn't help but to defend the man that had caused her so much pain. She remembered a few times when she had actually gathered the suitcases from atop their closet and was ready to leave him. Nevertheless, she had always stayed. "Your father wasn't always an alcoholic. Before he let that poison take over his body, he was the sweetest, kindest man that made every waking moment worth remembering. He used to be so good to the both of us."

"Maybe," Billy slightly agreed. "But the past ten or so years have been nothing but pure hell now haven't they?" he continued harshly, letting his emotions get the best of him. "And I know you don't want to hear this, but I'm not afraid to say it. After what he did to you, and after the way he treated me, neglected me, and called me nothing but a little piece of shit, I feel no pity for what happened to him. I don't feel any remorse for his death Mom. In fact, it was rather obvious that we didn't make him a happy man, so to be honest, he's probably happier now to be gone from this world. And to tell you the truth, I'm glad the son of a bitch is gone too. As far as I'm concerned, alcohol should have caused that massive stroke years ago. Would have saved us both a lot of pain." As those repugnant words left his aperture, he saw the hurt in his mother's eyes and somehow wished there was a way to retract his last few statements. "I'm sorr-," he began, but was cut short.

"No," Debra interrupted her son. "I'm sorry you feel that way about your father, and I understand that you don't want to have any memories of him. I may even understand why you won't claim him as your father. You have that right. However, no matter how hard we try, he has been a big part of our lives, and he will always be with us. Yes," she agreed. "He changed. You can even say that he turned into an evil man, but he would have never intentionally hurt either of us. No matter what he said to you, or did to me, he did love both of us very much. He had a disease son, nothing more, and it all caught up with him in the end."

Deciding that it wasn't critical or necessary to continue the argument with his mother, he simply decided to drop the subject of his father. Although he didn't believe that leaving his hometown was the answer, he knew that right now, his mother needed him more than anything in the world, and he loved her very much. He wanted nothing more than for her to be happy, and if moving to Destin, Florida was the answer, then he was all for it. "Mom," he finally decided to speak up once again, placing one of his hands on top of her own. "I love you."

Smiling, Debra squeezed her son's hand before continuing. "I know you do baby. Believe me, I know. And I know that it's going to be hard for you to get adjusted at first in this new environment. But you're really going to love it there. It's one of the most ravishing, comely, and exquisite beaches in the world, and I don't think I need to tell you about all the pretty girls that will be there," she threw that last part in with the intention of embarrassing her son.

"Trust me," Billy began, showing no signs of being embarrassed, yet feeling his mood suddenly become filled with a rapture of pure joy. "That's one area of the beach that I intend to explore until every avenue has been ventured, if you know what I mean?" he concluded laughing hysterically.

Then, turning up the radio, the two of them drove watching the road ahead as they headed Southbound along I-75 towards the sunshine state of Florida. Looking for a clean, fresh start at life, Debra Saxton was intent on leaving her past in Marietta, Georgia behind. She greatly longed for happiness, yet, she knew that if it weren't for Billy, she wouldn't have any impetus, or incentive to smile at all.

Billy, on the other hand, just wanted what was best for his mother. Every so often he spoke of his displeasure, but in the end, he knew that it was a battle he was destined to lose. He just couldn't bare the thought of leaving his mother alone right now. Not after her past, and not after the death of his father, even though he was desperately trying to forget all about Tom Saxton. In short, Billy wasn't willing to leave his mother until he was sure that it was safe for her to be alone.

Then, staring at the yellow lines of the interstate in front of him, even though they appeared to implement a detectable blurriness in his eyes, Billy finally decided to close his eyes and try to enjoy a nap. Yawning, he realized that sleep was something a road trip always seemed to allow him to catch up on. "That's right," he heard his mother's voice from the other seat. "Get yourself some rest, and when you wake up, we'll be in Florida."

"I can't wait," Billy replied in a sweet, yet sarcastic tone.

As Debra watched her son settle down into a gentle sleep, a smile crossed her face. She knew that in the end, and as soon as the two of them got settled into their new home, everything was going to be all right. The two of them were going to be just fine. She would make sure of it.

After all, she wouldn't have it any other way.

* * *

Meanwhile, in Starke, Florida, where the infamous Florida State Prison could be found housing the state's worst criminals.

Curtis Rains had been held in complete lockdown within the solitary confinements of cellblock C for the past ten years. Cellblock C was strictly for inmates awaiting the death penalty, and was also known, as death row. Rains was convicted in a court of law on eleven counts of first-degree murder. All of his victims never knew he had been watching them. They consisted of loving families; a wife, loving husband, and children. Many people tried to get inside his head as the years crept by, but to this day, no one had been able to get very far, and many questions still remained unanswered. No one knew what made him tick, snap, or turn into the madman that had leashed out at society with an evil so terrifying, it would never be forgotten.

Now, however, Curtis Rains's time was running out.

In three days, his stay on Florida's death row would come to an abrupt end and his execution would be carried out. In three days, justice would finally be served and his bloodthirsty, merciless soul would be laid to rest forever. He was a cold-blooded man, and his evil acts had been so cruel and brutal, that they were simply unforgivable. Everyone in society agreed that the death sentence was warranted in the case of Curtis Rains.

Yet, even though he was now looking death in the eye, a smile could still be found across his hardened face.

Curtis Rains was not afraid of death.

In fact, he welcomed it with open arms.

Tinman

Chapter 1

Destin, Florida.
As the black Lexus turned onto the rather secluded road of Sandy Point Lane, Debra began counting the houses until she found the one she was looking for. Looking over in the passenger seat she saw Billy still sound asleep, completely oblivious to the fact that the car had deferred to a slower speed as they exited the highway and entered a residential section. Finally she came to the eighth house on the right, and pulled into the driveway of her new home, 736 Sandy Point Lane.
She sat there in awe of the magnificent house towering in front of her. Until this moment, she never realized how big the place actually was, and for just two people living among these headquarters, it would be prodigious. However, Debra felt that the space would come in handy, as she knew that both of them greatly depended on an adequate supply of privacy.
She took in the whole magnificent scene at once. It was a beautiful white stone two-story house, complete with cellar, attic, three bathrooms, four bedrooms, huge kitchen, dining room, living room, den, and a study. Along the borders of the ancient, yet magical looking house, were rows of dandelions and roses, with three palm trees on each side of the cement driveway. The wooden front door stood massively in the center of the home. A dozen windows were scattered in an ancient harmony, giving even more life to the wonderful setting. Even though she couldn't see it from the front of the house, Debra knew that in the back a gigantic wooden deck could be found, with a patio leading down to the ocean itself. To this day, she still had no clue as to how she was able to get such a place for the

little amount of money she had to put forth. It was one of the biggest houses on the block; however; she had discovered it hadn't been lived in for over ten years.

That was almost impossible to believe. In ten years no one had been willing to pay the stunning price she had paid for this absolutely enchanting home. She just didn't understand, but considered herself lucky to have found a beach house at such an affordable price. She had just simply been browsing through the real estate market when her eyes suddenly stumbled across this home. Instantly, she had known that this was where she and her son, Billy, would live.

Putting the car in park, she turned the ignition off and shook her son's leg, awaking him from his obviously ravishing state of reverie.

"Billy," she whispered softly, yet showing large amounts of excitement. "Billy, honey, wake up. We're here. We're at our new home."

Rubbing his eyes, Billy stretched his back and neck, reacting as his mother had at his first glance of the home. It was a marvelous scene around him, almost breathtaking. He couldn't believe the mesmerizing house that stood before him. He never in his life dreamed of living in such a place. "Holy shit!" he blurted out, not realizing what he was saying. "Is this really our place mom?"

Debra nodded with a smile, showing her son that his foul language was of no significance to her at the moment.

"It practically looks like a mansion for crying out loud," Billy baffled, still stunned at the sight in front of him. "You didn't tell me we were going to be living like kings," he added with a smile. "It's just beautiful."

"Well come on then," Debra said climbing out of the car. "Let's go see the inside."

Following behind his mother, Billy swiftly chased her to the front door, and although he beat her to the handle, his luck inevitably ran out. Blushing, he turned around to face his mother, who was purposely lagging behind, and with a smile, she strolled with ease jingling the keys to their new home in her hand. "Come on," Billy began impatiently. "Why must you do this? I want to see the inside."

"Do what?" Debra answered with a chuckle. Then, she tried to fit every single key into the keyhole, and sure enough, the very last one was the one that unlatched the lock, and opened the door to their magic kingdom. Steadily, she held her hand tightly on the knob, gave it one extra squeeze, then with one last glance back at her son, whose eyes were still filled with anticipation, she pushed the door open.

The two of them walked inside the foyer and gazed around the incredible space around them. The inside was huge, and right in front of them stood the master staircase leading to the second floor. Without saying a word, Billy watched as his mother quickly headed off through the living room towards the other end of the house. "Where are you going?" he asked a little befuddled. Then, before his mother even had time to answer his rather ignorant question, it came to him. She was headed for the kitchen. Billy pinched himself for not knowing the answer before hand, because if there was one thing he was fully aware that his mother knew how to do, it was cook. Debra knew her way around the kitchen all right, and when he finally caught up with her, he found her rummaging through the cabinets and refrigerator, a constant smile extended across her beautiful facade.

"And you will be cooking what this evening?" Billy questioned permissively.

"Isn't this just the biggest kitchen you have ever seen in your entire life?" Debra returned her son's question with one of her own. "I mean, we could practically live in here if we really wanted to. We have about two dozen cabinets, and a huge refrigerator. I tell you, if we ever fill all of these cabinets up with food, the supply should last us until winter. And to answer your question," she paused momentarily to look into her son's eyes. "We will be cooking pasta tonight, and we might whip up a salad as well," she closed, putting emphasize on the word "we."

"Well, does it matter which room I pick out?" Billy asked quickly changing the subject. "I bet there's quite a selection to choose from upstairs."

"I don't see why not," Debra answered. "I'll be happy with anything. So why don't you run on up the stairs and explore your heart out until you find the room that best suits your needs. Then afterwards, maybe we can take a little stroll down the beach and check it out a little bit. I'll pick out some good lookin girls for you."

"Please," Billy hollered as he scampered on up the stairs. Then yelling. "I think I can handle that last part on my own."

Jason Glover

* * *

Meanwhile, back at the Florida State Prison.

Curtis Rains sat quietly on his single bunk, located along the right side of the wall within the small confinements of his cell. The cell was only eight feet long, and five feet wide with the single bunk, one stainless steel sink and one cold porcelain toilet taking up most of the already limited legroom. Nevertheless, Curtis just sat on the edge of his bed, staring at the pale stonewalls before him. He had been staring at the same wall for ten years now, with no engravings, pictures or written artwork to help him feel more at home. Now, however, ten years later, as he stared at the same bleached clean wall of his cell, he knew that his time was coming.

He was finally going to be taken from death row. His time to do the "walk," was finally drawing near. His era in American history was finally coming to a close. However, no expression of any kind was seen disseminated across his stern face and his eyes remained wide open, not letting any blinks ease the nerves within them.

Yet, the man himself didn't look like the type of person to be afraid of. Standing only 5'10 in height, and weighing only 160 pounds, not even half of which consisted of muscle, he just looked like your average everyday working man. His cell was probably the neatest within the entire prison, not showing any signs of dust or trash. His thick black hair was parted neatly to the right. His ever so shiny white teeth glistened within the holding cell, which was lighted by a single florescent bulb. He had a clean-shaven face. Everything about him seemed so normal, so humanlike. Everything except one thing. His eyes.

They were the only physical aspect of Curtis that could scare the life out of you, paralyze you with one single glance. There was a harshness about them that could make the hair on the back of your neck stand straight up. It was as if you stuck your finger in a light socket and left it there even though mounds of jolting electricity poured into your body. Only, the strength to remove your hand is not there because the electricity has paralyzed your instincts. That was the power of his eyes. No matter how much you wanted to turn away, you couldn't. Fear always took control as the presence of a deep evil was detected.

Curtis Rains was a man you would desperately try to avoid making eye contact with. It was almost as if his dark brown, almost blackened eyes, with pure white trimmings, could mesmerize you. They penetrated into the depths of your soul, ripping away at every essence of being, only to eventually strip you of your last few breaths.

And being a well-educated man, his psyche was very complex and his brain always at work. Ten years ago, he would have been at work trying to place his next victim, and how he would go about striking out at them. Or, how he could unleash the evil within himself, showing to the world what a man without a conscious or soul could do.

His drudgery, and his exertion in his acts of violence simply weren't heard of in today's society. Never showing any signs of remorse for the lives he had taken from this earth, he was more in tune with the ones he never had a chance to viciously rip apart. The pain and suffering he inflicted on his victims could make a heart skip a beat. However, every act of murder he portrayed appeared to be a work of art. A masterpiece, if you will, skillfully crafted and designed to never leave behind a single trace of his existence. Except for the bodies and the massive amounts of blood left behind every time his work had been completed, nothing had ever been found to link him to the crimes.

Curtis Rains was a man simply compelled to kill. It was the only thing he ever considered himself to be even remotely proficient at, and would give anything to have the opportunity to show the world his final work of art.

Unfortunately, he was beginning to realize that his time was running out.

The clock seemed to be ticking at an enormous speed as his final hour approached steadily and without prejudice. Even the electric chair, he knew, was waiting patiently to destroy every ounce of life he had left.

However, as the visions of his death came pouring in, no signs of impact were shown on his face. He was as calm as he was the first day he had arrived at the gates of hell, or at least the closest thing to hell the sunny State of Florida had to offer. Still, not a single glimpse of fear could be seen on the Tinman's face. It was almost as if he were mocking or not taking seriously what was coming to him. In fact, as the thought of his death came to mind, only one thing sprang from his ghostly face.

A smile.

* * *

Jack Reynolds, a guard assigned to the evening shift on death row, was simply walking throughout the cells counting the inmates and making sure everyone was where they were supposed to be, tucked neatly within the caveman comforts of their bunks. Day after day, he spent his time among the most notorious criminals in the state of Florida, interacting with pure scum who seemed to be spawned directly from hell. He did like his job, however, and was strong enough to never really let anything get to him. And under no circumstances did he ever let himself become emotionally attached to any of the inmates.

Finally, as he neared the end of the hallway, he came to the second to last cell. Inside he knew was the ever so quiet Curtis Rains. Every time he walked past the cell, he always tried to get a word out of Curtis, and up to this day, he had never succeeded. "How about it Rains," he spoke with an authoritative tone, once again, not expecting a response. "Cat still got your tongue? Or are you just nervous about the big day you have coming up?"

Still, nothing.

"So, you having any last minute thoughts about what you've done, wish you could change, or start over? Do you regret anything you've done in the past? Or are you still as fucked up as you were when they brought you in here Mr. Tinman or whatever the hell your nickname is? Tell me," he paused. purposely trying to get under the skin of the man in front of him. "What's it feel like to live without a soul? Huh? Answer me boy!"

Then, to his surprise, Curtis turned to face him. And a smile spread across his face. Then, a laugh. A gentle laugh, but an evil laugh.

"You think this shit is funny Rains?" Jack asked in a demanding tone. "Well, let's just see how funny you think this shit is when you're strapped to that electric chair awaiting death? And I can promise you, not a single tear will fall from anyone's eyes."

"You can't hurt me," Curtis declared, standing up and taking a towering tone. Then, staring into the guard's eyes in front of him, he continued. His voice, deep, and gruff. "And you can't kill me. I can reach any soul I want right here in this cell. It's been ten years and people are still talking about me. And they will continue to ten years after I sit in that chair. My soul will never perish, my spirit will never die."

Then, just as abruptly as he had stood up, Curtis seated himself once again on the edge of his bed and turned to face the wall once again. His laugh died away, his smile disappeared and his expression returned to its blank state.

"We'll just see how you feel about that in a couple of days now won't we," Jack concluded as he continued on his way around to the other inmates. "After all," he paused briefly. "You have less than 72 hours remaining."

* * *

"Isn't this all just so breathtaking?" Debra asked her son as they sat beside one another on one of the many sand dunes in front of their new home, deciding to pause for a minute before returning inside after their long walk down the beach. "I sure could get used to taking those long walks everyday," she added as she recalled her bare feet digging their way into the soft granule and remembering the tingling sensation she felt each time a dying wave managed to reach her feet splashing water on her legs. She couldn't help but smile, and so far, Destin had lived up to its reputation. She thought it was simply extraordinary, and was sure to bring the two of them nothing but happiness.

"Yeah, its not so bad," Billy replied. "I think this place might actually grow on me yet," he concluded with a smile.

"See," Debra replied climbing to her feet, wiping her body free of the sand that had managed to find its way upon her elegant body. "I knew you'd start to see it my way. Now come on inside and help me unpack some of the things we brought with us. I could use your help decorating you know, and the movers will be here first thing in the morning."

"All right," Billy agreed. "But can I come in a little while? I want to stay out here a little longer and listen to the waves for a few minutes. It seems to help me clear my head," he added refusing to make eye contact with his mother, and hoping that she wouldn't be able to see through him.

"Right" Debra chuckled. "You're nineteen years old for crying out loud. What do you care about the refreshing sound of the waves? The only thing that strikes you as being attractive and breathtaking is a long legged blonde with an above average breast size," she continued giving her son a hard time. "But by all means, don't let me stand in the way. You sit right here and wait for the girl of your dreams to come passing by, and then go sweep her off her feet."

"Mom!" Billy interjected, his face blushing slightly.

"I'm only teasing you," Debra said starting to walk away from her son. "Seriously, take all the time you need. Just pick one you know I'd like all right. I don't want you to bring home some half wit bimbo," she concluded still laughing at her sarcastic remarks.

"Mom!" Billy said once more, embarrassed at his mother's choice of words. "Will you just go inside please?" he asked with a smile. "I think I have this under control."

"Oh I bet you do," Debra replied, completely intent on getting the last word.

Billy watched over his shoulder until his mother disappeared into the safety of their new home, and then turned his head back around and concentrated on the beach laid out in front of him. Every so often, a person would pass by; some nice enough to wave, while others, usually couples, probably didn't even know he was there.

However, one thing was for sure.

In the short amount of time he had been sitting on the beach, Billy himself had never seen so many attractive women. His mother could get used to the comforting sound of the surf pounding against the shoreline, but he would love nothing more than to find himself surrounded by hundreds of beautiful women everyday. As his grandfather used to say, "plenty for the pickin!" That phrase, he thought to himself, could never be truer than it was right now.

Then, a startling movement from behind his left shoulder caught his attention, and he found himself spinning swiftly around to see what was there. At first glance he saw nothing. But the closer he looked; he swore he could make out the shape of a little head trying desperately to remain hidden behind a sand dune. Undecided if he should approach or not, he finally decided to turn back around and ignore whatever was there. As time passed, however, he found this task becoming increasingly more difficult.

He could feel the eyes of whoever it was surveying him, and it was quite uncomfortable. He found himself continuously glancing over his shoulder trying to get a glimpse at whatever was making him feel uneasy. Each time he went through this motion someone's head ducked quickly from site. "What in the hell?" he asked himself still not piecing together what was going on. Does this person really not think I know what they are doing?

Finally, getting tired of the bewildering situation he found impeding on his nerves, he climbed to his feet, and not even taking the time to wipe himself free of the clinging sand, he raced over towards the sand dune before the little head even had time to arise once more and see him coming. Scaling the dune, as if it were an Olympic challenge, he surprisingly found himself staring into the eyes of a terrified little girl, and one of her friends. Obviously, neither of them was over the age of eight or nine.

Speechless, he began with the first words that came to mind. "What are the two of you doing? It's not nice to spy on people you know?" He asked in a rather harsh tone, and one he knew he could have kept to himself. Then, seeing the fright in the little girls' eyes, he began again. This time, putting on a slight smile. "I'm sorry," he apologized. "I didn't mean to scare you kids. I knew something sneaky was going on." Seriously, he paused, trying to win their trust. "What are you two up to?"

Not answering Billy's exact question, one of the girls finally captured enough courage to speak to the stranger in front of her. "Do you live in that house?" she asked bluntly, and held her hand high, pointing to the house Billy and his mother just moved into that afternoon.

Billy nodded. "Why?"

Then, before he could continue, the two girls let out a devastating shriek, and they sprinted away from him screaming at the top of their lungs. "Wait!" Billy exclaimed trying to call the girls back. "Do you live around here? What are your names?" he asked trying to comfort the girls and bring them back. The last thing he wanted was for his next-door neighbors to be scared of him.

Needless to say, however, there was no sense in trying to call them back. And soon, the two girls had vanished completely from view. With his mind wondering, Billy decided to call it quits on his quest for the perfect woman for the night. "How strange," he said to himself as he began making his way to the back door of his house. Instead of meeting some blonde bombshell that would magically fulfill every desire he deemed possible, he ran into two little girls, who seemed to have nothing better to do than to stick their nose into someone else's business.

Their eyes, nonetheless, kept resurfacing in his head. They were truly scared of him, and it seemed to be because he said he lived in the house he now found himself entering. He didn't understand what was going on, and knew he probably shouldn't take such childish antics seriously. But he couldn't help it. There obviously had to be a reason for them to be afraid of the house.

And if he ever saw them again, he was going to find out exactly what it was.

Chapter 2

The following morning.

Opening the blinds, Debra let the sunrays come flooding into the room, and within seconds, she saw her son come alive. After moaning a rather humble growl, Billy stretched his body, and then sat upright on the couch he had slept on the previous night and stared sleepily at his mother. Rubbing his eyes, he struggled to get them accustomed to the sunlight that had so abruptly filtered the room.

"Wake up sleepy head," Debra began, knowing her screechy voice was absolutely killing her son's ears. "The movers will be here any minute and I have breakfast waiting for you. Just think about it, after today, we will be completely moved in."

"Great," Billy managed to say as he slowly lifted himself up and made his way into the kitchen. "And tonight, I'll be able to sleep in my own bed huh?" he added groggily. Then, he quietly seated himself at the counter and began enjoying the wonderful breakfast his mother had prepared for him. "Wow," he began with a smile. "What has gotten into you this morning?" he questioned as his teeth bit into a savory piece of bacon. "Do you plan on cooking breakfast every morning?"

"I don't think so," Debra answered with a grin. "I'm sure you'll have some gorgeous woman cooking and cleaning for you later on in life. But as long as you're with me, you can most certainly take care of yourself."

"Enough with the girl business already," Billy moaned, still a tad bit cranky from being woken up against his will. In his mind, he never acquired enough sleep. "What time is it anyway?"

"8:30," Debra answered. "The movers said that they'd be here by nine, and I wanted you up and ready to go give them boys a hand while I supervise and make all the decorative decisions that are going to need to be made. After all, this is such a big place, and we have so little stuff, if things aren't put in the appropriate places, the whole house won't look right. But I wouldn't expect you to understand that sort of thing."

"As well you shouldn't," Billy agreed, finishing up the last couple of bites on his plate, then with his drink in hand, headed for the backdoor, which led to the veranda. "Cause I don't know a damn thing about decorative designing or whatever it's called, nor do I care to learn," he added with a smile. Then, opening the door, he stepped outside and gazed out at the ocean and beach below.

Surprisingly, the beach was already swarming with people. Most of them just taking their morning stroll down the beach. Then, about twenty yards out in the ocean, he saw a few fins coming up and down through the water. Watching more closely, he saw one of them jump entirely out of the water, and then disappear back into the ocean blue hardly making a splash. "Mom," he hollered still amazed at the wonderful sight. "Come take a look at this."

Stepping out onto the back deck, Debra herself came just in time to see another porpoise jump out of the water, as if it was showing off to the world what a beautiful creature it was. "Wow!" Debra exclaimed. "I bet you've never seen that in real life before have you?"

Billy shook his head. "Nope." Then, down below, on the beach, and just in front of their home, he saw the two little girls he had seen the foregoing evening running about along the beach, as full of life as ever. Then, almost as if they felt his presence, the two of them stopped in their tracks, looked up at him, and ran off in the opposite direction. Once again, obviously afraid of something.

"I wonder what that was all about?" Debra asked as she too saw the two little girls running in disarray. "That's kids for you though."

"I don't know," Billy began as he recalled what had happened the night before. "I saw the two of them last night, and," he paused trying to choose his words carefully. "I was just sitting on the beach and the two of them were watching me from behind a sand dune. I had no idea it was two little girls until I ran up on them and surprised them. I know I scared them actually, but when I asked what they were doing one of them did the strangest thing."

"Go on," Debra spoke up wanting to hear the rest of the story.

"Well instead of answering my question, she just pointed at our house and asked if I lived here," Billy continued. "I told her yes, and then just like that the two of them starting screaming at the top of their lungs and ran home. I don't know," he paused. "It just seemed rather odd to me."

"I bet it did," Debra agreed. "But children will be children and they do have huge imaginations. And if I recall correctly, you weren't the most normal child yourself. You used to do some crazy things. In fact, on a number of occasions I thought about taking you somewhere to have your head examined. But look at you now. You turned out all right." Then, before Billy had time to reply, the ringing of their doorbell interrupted the two of them. "So that's what it sounds like," Debra changed the subject with a smile referring to the sound of the doorbell. "Looks like the mover's are early. You ready to make this move official?"

"Why not," Billy agreed as the two of them returned inside and made their way across the house to the front door.

* * *

Jennifer and Mary Anne ran as fast as their little legs would carry them until they got to the fifth house down from the Saxton's. Running until they reached the back patio, where they finally paused to catch their breath. From inside, the girls mother, Elizabeth, saw the two of them gasping for air, and wondered what had happened this time to bring the two of them back in such a hurry. Making her way onto the porch, she pushed her long wavy brown hair out of her face, and looked down at her two lovely daughters, their hair and dark brown eyes taking after their mother.

"What have the two of you gotten yourselves into now?" she asked with a smile as she leaned down and hugged the both of them tightly. "You two haven't been causing any trouble around here have you? There are too many nice people here. So," she paused. "What's going on in those two mischievous little heads of yours?"

"Nothing," Jennifer answered too quickly. Jennifer was nine, and two years older than her sister. "We were just racing to see who was the fastest."

"Uh huh," Elizabeth continued knowing she was trying to be outsmarted by her daughter. "You wouldn't be telling me a tattle tale now would you? You know it's not right when you don't tell the truth." She paused and watched as Jennifer nodded her head, her big eyes desperately trying to win her mother over. So, she turned to Mary. "Is your sister telling me the truth?"

Mary wanted so much to stick up for her sister, whom she took after and looked up to dearly. But as her mother's authoritative stare buried its way into her own little eyes, she knew she wouldn't be able to get away with it. "We were just scared mom," she blurted out of her little mouth, her rosy red cheeks blushing in the sun. "Scared of the people in that house."

"What house?" their mother asked confusingly.

"The old Haas house that has been empty for 10 years," Jennifer answered not letting her younger sister do anymore of the talking. "People live there now. A boy and a mom."

"I see," Elizabeth continued finally letting all the pieces come together. "And why are the two of you scared of those people?"

"Because they live there," Jennifer blurted out in a tone that stated she couldn't believe her mother even had to ask that question. "You know what happened in that house mom. I heard all of those terrible stories from my friends at school. They say that the house is haunted and that no one should ever go in there."

"Well I don't know what your friends have been telling you, and I'm sure I don't want to know," Elizabeth responded boldly. "But I can almost assure you that it probably isn't true. And besides, what happened in that house happened many years ago, before either of you were even born and there is nothing wrong with that house. In fact, its one of the most beautiful houses on this road," she added trying to convince her daughters that there was nothing to be afraid of.

However, Elizabeth herself didn't even believe her own words.

She remembered the day it happened ten years ago just like it was yesterday, and it being only five houses down from her own, knew it could have easily been her house that experienced what the old Haas home had gone through. To this day, it still made her skin crawl, and before it ever happened, she was just beginning to become close to the Haas family. In fact, the whole thing seemed like a nightmare, too mysterious and dark to even be possible. However it had happened, and no one in Destin would ever forget about it.

Then, as she felt her daughters watching her in awe, she knew she needed to finish making her point before it was too late. "What's wrong mommy?" Mary asked pulling herself into her mother's arms.

"Nothing sweetheart," Elizabeth replied. "Nothing is wrong with mommy. I'm just a little disappointed in the two of you is all. You girls know how to behave properly and I expect you to do so. I'm sure the people who moved into that house are very nice people, and as a matter of fact," she paused as an idea popped into her head. "As soon as your father gets home, we're all going to walk down there and invite them over for dinner. How does that sound?"

The two girls quickly exchanged glances and the fear that had taken control of their young minds once again resurfaced, and Elizabeth, watching them closely, could see the fear in their eyes.

* * *

Debra watched closely as her son and the movers manipulated every piece of furniture until it was in the perfect location. Or at least the furniture was maneuvered until the venue was perfect for her. All of the pictures had to be hung neatly along the spacious naked walls, trying to make the rooms look smaller than they really were. It turned out to be one of the most difficult decorative tasks she had ever encountered, even though she enjoyed a sensational career in the art of interior decorating. Some of her customers had even flown her from around the country to design the interior of their homes, and she had always been able to deliver exceptional results with ease. Nevertheless, with this home, that simply wasn't the case.

She found herself pointing her finger wildly as her mind swirled rapidly. Being a quick thinker, she contemplated every inch of the house in an effort to decide which arrangement would prove to be the most homely. Although she felt that her first instincts and inclinations were the correct choices, she had the movers, and her son, drag the undoubtedly cumbersome furniture to different locations around the house. Most of the time, only to have it all put back in the original setting.

As the last load of furniture was being unloaded from the movers' truck, and as the hours of painstaking lifting and moving were drawing to a close, she saw her son progress passed her, sweat dripping from his face, and with one swift motion, managed to roll his eyes, letting his mother know what he was feeling without saying a word. "I'm sorry honey," she said pinching his shoulder. "I know I'm being a little difficult right now, but you know how picky I am. Everything has got to be perfect," she concluded trying to draw a smile from Billy's rather disgusted expression. "Just hang in there sport, it's almost over and hopefully, we won't have to worry about moving again for a long time."

"If this is what it's going to be like every time we move," Billy spoke, his words seeming harsher than they really were as he simply tried to catch his breath before speaking. "Then, we're, or you are going to be living here for the rest of your life. Hell," he paused giving a slight smile. "I'm surprised the movers' haven't just unloaded all our crap and left it on the front lawn. I know that's what I would have done."

"I know, I know," Debra agreed with her son. "I'm a little hard to get along with at times, and I know I'm just the type of person people can't stand to wait on, or the type of customer that everyone hates to have to work for. But I really can't help it sweetheart. It's just my nature. You of all people should know this."

"That I do," Billy agreed as he walked back outside through the front door to help bring in the last load of furniture. "I just can't wait to sit down and relax for a little bit."

"Well, I'll be sure to make you something extra special for dinner tonight," Debra yelled making sure her son had a chance to apprehend what she was saying before he disappeared out the front door and into the blazing Florida heat. "We'll celebrate making this move official, and it will be a token of appreciation for all your hard work and understanding. And of course, to new beginnings," she added under her breath.

Finally, within the next hour, the move had been completed. The movers had packed up their things and headed back to Georgia, graciously excepting the generous tip given to them from the hands of

Tinman

Debra Saxton, who was always willing to pay the extra price or go the extra mile to make sure everything was right.

Then, as she came inside through the foyer, she paused as she entered her magical new home and couldn't help but to survey every inch. As the beautiful portrayal of her home really captured its effect, she stared astonishingly at what they had been able to accomplish in such a sort amount of time. "Ya know what?" she asked her son, as she made her way into the living room and joined him on the sofa, where his attention had been completely transformed to the television. Television was something she knew he had deeply missed. "I think we did one hell of a job today son. Everything just looks so perfect. Almost makes us feel right at home doesn't it?"

Billy nodded, obviously too tired to have an in depth conversation.

Then, switching her attention from her son to the television, she watched as she tried to figure out what had captured her son's complete attention. Surprisingly, it was the evening news. "I didn't know you liked to watch the news?" Debra asked impressed at her son's interest in what was going on within the community and world today.

"I don't," Billy admitted with a yawn. "I'm just too tired to get up and change the channel."

"Oh," Debra replied. "You had me going there for a second. So, what's going on in the world tonight?" she asked, not expecting her son to answer. Then, as she watched the news anchor begin with one of the top stories of the evening, she immediately saw that it was something she had absolutely no interest in.

It was something concerning a convicted serial killer whose death sentence was supposed to be carried out within the following day. However, as the name of the homicidal maniac was revealed, Debra found herself a bit more intrigued. Curtis Rains was a man she had heard about in the past. In fact, as she recalled the numerous slayings the man was responsible for, she found her heart beating a little faster and fear suddenly seemed to seize her body. Furthermore, she knew everyone who was watching the same news program were having the same interchanging feelings she now found herself involved with. Together, the two of them watched in silence as the anchor continued with the story:

"One of America's most notorious serial murderers is finally going to meet his match. At the Florida State Prison, located in Starke, Florida, Curtis Rains will finally be seated in the electric chair after years of living in solitary confinement. Curtis Rains, also known as the Tinman, is responsible for over 11 counts of first-degree murder. All of them, however, involved loving families, and he is one of the few serial killers in history that targeted entire families, as opposed to single, specific type of individuals. His death sentence is scheduled to be carried out at Midnight tomorrow, and a large joyous crowd is expected to be on hand, cheering on the death of the man many Americans are still desperately trying to forget. We'll be back with more on the story. Please stay with us."

"Well, I don't know about you," Debra began getting to her feet and making her way into the kitchen to begin preparing supper. "But I've heard enough of this stuff. I'm going to go and start dinner; your help would be welcomed if you were offering. And after dinner," she paused briefly. "What do you say we take another stroll down the beach? The sun should be setting soon."

"Sounds good to me," Billy groggily replied making an effort to climb to his feet and join his mother in the kitchen. Only, he never made it half way across the room, when the ringing of the doorbell suddenly interrupted him. Mystified at who it could be, he motioned to his mother letting her know that he would take care of it, and then slowly, he made his way to the front door.

Clamping his hands on the door handle, he half expected to open it and see the mover's returning with some piece of furniture forgotten or left behind on the truck. To his surprise, however, he found himself starring into the eyes of the two little girls he had seen on the beach earlier that morning and the previous evening. Only this time they weren't alone, and obviously not going to be running away screaming at the top of their lungs. Their mother stood between the two, with one arm around each of them.

Their little hands were clinging tightly to their mother, and you could still see the fear in their eyes. But why? There was absolutely nothing to be afraid of here. Smiling at the two of them, trying to bring their nerves at ease, he spoke. "I never thought I'd see the two of you standing on my doorstep," he began with a smile showing the two little girls that there were no hard feelings. Then, looking at their mother he continued. "Hi."

"Hello," Elizabeth started, returning his generous smile. "My name is Elizabeth Anne, and these are my daughters Jennifer and Mary. We live five houses down and just wanted to come wish you and your mother good luck in your new home and to welcome you to the neighborhood."

"Well please," Billy continued, stepping inside and gesturing for the three of them to enter. "Why don't you guys come on inside. I'm sure my mother would love to meet you as well." Only, as the three of them made their way past him, he noticed something rather odd. Only this time, it wasn't just the two girls that had a fearful expression on their faces.

This time, he could have sworn, to see something within Elizabeth's eyes as well.

He couldn't quite put his finger on it, but as he motioned for them to enter, he saw the mother's eyes raise a little, and her mouth take on a frown of some sort. He almost felt as though none of them truly wanted to enter the house, and was only doing so in an attempt at politeness. Then, as he followed behind them, he found his mother appearing from around the corner and watched as she began to take over the conversation. Seeing that his presence was no longer needed, he returned to the living room, and returned to his beloved television.

Only, this time, he found himself almost reluctant to pay attention to what was on the screen in front of him. Something was truly bothering him about this whole situation. He no longer thought that it was simply the two young children whose fear was simply brought on by their young age. Now their mother even seemed a bit withdrawn and hesitant when he motioned for them to enter the house. He sensed that there was something he was inclusively unaware of and wanted nothing more than to find out exactly what it was. However, what was he supposed to do?

He couldn't just walk up to Elizabeth and ask her what was going on.

His mother would never forgive him for making such a blatant scene. Nonetheless, he knew his mind would not settle until he found out just what it was about this house that was so damn terrifying.

Then, hearing the front door close, he turned to face his mother who once again began making her way towards him. "Wasn't that just the nicest thing?" she asked with a smile, showing she was happy to have met a new friend in Elizabeth Anne. "I thought that was so nice of them to drop by and welcome us here. Oh, and by the way she loved the way we decorated. She said it looked absolutely wonderful."

"Yeah," Billy began firmly, his mind still wondering through space. "But did she actually mean it?"

"What?" Debra asked not seeing where her son was coming from. "I don't know what your talking about, but I do know that they have invited us over for dinner tonight and I for one am going. Will you please join me so I don't have to come up with some excuse as to why you didn't show up?" Seeing no expression from her son's face, she continued. "Please Billy? Just do this for me?"

"All right," Billy finally agreed. "But I'm telling you something isn't right here mom. I can't put my finger on it, but something is definitely wrong."

Chapter 3

    After dinner with their new neighbors, Billy Saxton walked home along the beach, leaving his mother behind with Elizabeth to familiarize themselves with one another. Billy himself knew that their friendship got off on a very good note. Throughout the entire evening the two of them could barely keep their mouths shut, blabbering on, switching from subject to subject like there would be no tomorrow. From Billy's understanding, he felt that this was just typical female behavior, reminding him once again how thankful he was for being born a male.
    Just an average good old boy from Georgia, with no doubts, and no worries. However, his soul did impound a few regrets, those of which he prayed daily would be forgotten in time. Nevertheless, as he made the rather short walk home, he pictured the evening he had just spent at the Anne home. Throughout the entire meal, he felt the stares of the two little girls bearing down on him like he was some kind of caged animal, the whole time making him feel utterly uncomfortable.
    Showing a little poise and class, however, he had said nothing.
    He let himself be looked upon as if he were a performer in a circus, taking the mind-boggling abuse, which he knew the two children had no idea they were giving him. Billy wanted to jump out of his seat, point his narrow fingers at the two children and give them a piece of his mind. He simply wanted to get some answers as to why he was being looked at differently.
    His mother, he knew, still had no idea of what was going on, nor would she even consider the obvious concept that something was

rather odd. If and when he did find out what he was missing, the task of forcing his mother to see it the same way were slim to none. Finally, deciding to worry about his mother another time, he knew what he was going to do when he returned home.

Somewhere in that house there had to be some type of entity that could lead to the answers to his questions. After all, it was a gigantic home; something was bound to turn up sooner or later. He was sure of it.

The more Billy found himself steaming over this inauspicious issue, the more untimely and nerve-racking it became. In the end, he was sure it would turn out to be no big deal, and he would wind up kicking himself in the shin for making such an ordeal out of something so insignificant. Then again, it wasn't too often that Billy contained or attracted such strong feelings or vibes, and in the past, his instincts usually prevailed and were rectified.

Finally, as his house approached in the distance, he found himself not even paying attention to the spectacular scene of the setting sun, but more with anticipation as he thought about what he could encounter within the closed doors of his new home. In a way, he felt like a spy who had just been requisitioned to secure secrets pertaining to National Security. In short, he was actually looking forward to spending some time alone within the privacy and safety of his new home. He just wanted to try and get acquainted with the house, and of course, try to uncover any secrets, which had obviously been left behind.

Then, as he neared his home, a movement caught his eye, and for a brief second, he found his mind drifting away from the brainwashing mystery behind his home, and transfixed on what he saw standing before him.

It was a girl.

As he slowed to a steady walk, he watched as the girl in front of him crawled about along the sand directly in front of his house, obviously looking for something of sentimental importance. With a smile, he made his way towards the beautiful creature ahead of him. He realized that an opportunity such as this was hard to come by. Hoping his appearance was in order, he approached the strange female, and with no hesitation, he spoke with sheer confidence. "Hi," he began in a smooth tone, taking in every inch of the girls figure before his heart suddenly began melting and the palm of his hands grew wet with perspiration.

The girl looked up from her squatting position and returned the smile, showing her perfectly lined, glistening white teeth. Her whole body was covered by a dark Florida tan that made Billy's eyes wince a little, and he couldn't believe how lucky he was at this very moment. Then, looking into her gorgeous green eyes, surrounded by beautiful strawberry blonde hair, he could have sworn he had fallen into the bottomless pit of love. The sight of the perfectly shaped girl in front of him was simply astounding, and he wasn't about to let her slip through his fingers without an attempt to achieve happiness.

Then, "Is something wrong?" He asked finally coming to grips with reality, and forcing himself out of his state of reverie. "I was just on my way home, and I couldn't help noticing you down there looking for something. Is there anything I could do to help.?"

"It's O.K.," the girl replied as she began searching uncontrollably through the sand once more. "I just lost my stupid bracelet. I'm sure it's around here somewhere. I noticed it right when it fell off my damn arm and I was standing right here in this location. It's almost like it just disappeared into thin air or something."

"Well, I don't mind helping you look for it," Billy continued, he himself now squatting along the sand and looking for the bracelet the enchanting female in front of him had lost. "Is it a gold bracelet?" he asked trying to get some sort of concept of what he was supposed to be looking for. "And my name is Billy by the way."

"Yep, it's gold," the girl replied. "And I'm Tracy. Do you live around here?"

"Just moved in yesterday actually. My mother and I came down from Marietta, Georgia. It's right on the outskirts of Atlanta, actually. Are you from around here?" he returned the question.

"Unfortunately," Tracy began managing to smile, although her mind was working furiously to find her lost treasure. "Born and raised. I've wanted to leave on numerous occasions, but somehow I always seem to wind right back where I started. I guess its pretty and all, but it's kind of a small place ya know? I've known the same old people for years, been hanging out at the same old places for even longer. I just want a change of scenery ya know? Something different, or something new."

"That's exactly why we moved here actually," Billy continued on with the conversation, enjoying at how smooth and pleasant everything was going. "We came here looking for a fresh start. I tell you what though, there's nothing like falling asleep to the sound of the waves crashing against the shore. In fact, that is probably the best sedative on earth."

"Yeah, your right about that," Tracy agreed. "That's probably one of the only things I haven't had enough of, and one of the only things I'd probably miss if I do ever get a chance to bail out."

Then, as Billy felt something buried beneath a slight amount of sand, he grasped it and pulled it out into the open. Sure enough, it was the gold bracelet. "I found it," he gasped rather excitedly, knowing she was going to be very happy. Holding his hand out, he graciously let her take it out of his hands, enjoying the feeling he felt as their soft hands collided, even if only for a brief moment. "Consider this your lucky day sweetheart, we could have easily been out here all night looking for that thing. It must be pretty important to you huh?"

"Yeah," Tracy replied enjoying the comforting feeling of her bracelet attached to her arm. "It's one of the only things my father gave me that I am still in possession of and the only piece of jewelry that I actually love to wear. God," she paused grabbing his hand. "Thank you so much. Really, you are a life saver."

"Don't mention it," Billy replied with a smile, once again looking into Tracy's eyes. "I'm just glad I was here to help you."

Then, as the sun began to set and darkness was surely drawing close, Tracy checked the time on her watch, and Billy knew she was about to be headed on her way. Forcing himself to do something he ordinarily wouldn't do, he decided to take a chance. "Hey Tracy, it was really nice meeting you. You are actually the first person I met since I've been here and if everyone here is as nice as you, I'm sure I'm going to like it here just fine."

Laughing, Tracy replied. "Not everyone around here is as nice as me. Trust me. In fact, most people here would have probably told you to mind your own business and denied you the opportunity to help them look for what they lost."

"Maybe," Billy continued. "But then again, I wouldn't have stopped to help just anyone either. But I had a feeling about you."

"And what kind of feeling might that be?"

"I don't know," Billy shrugged his shoulders disappointed he didn't have an answer. "I guess I was just attracted to you, and I'd really like it if you let me take you out sometime. My treat of course. Lord knows I could sure use some company right now, and besides," he paused briefly. "You said you were tired of the same old people. Well, I certainly ain't from around here."

"This is true," Tracy agreed, a wide grin stretched across her face. "And I really don't know why I'm doing this, cause I normally don't But," she paused hesitantly. "All right. I'll go out with you one night and sort of show you the town. Although, there really isn't much to see."

"Really!" Billy exclaimed half expecting to be rejected. "Great. You just name the time and I'll come pick you up."

"Or I could just meet you at your house," Tracy replied. "You do live along the beach right?" Billy nodded. "Well, which house is it, and I'll come by tomorrow night around seven."

"It's this one right here," Billy answered pointing to the home located directly behind them. Then, just as those words exited his mouth, he watched as Tracy's eyes followed his finger, and then saw her smile instantly disappear when she realized which house he was pointing at. The breathtaking smile, which had seemed to ignite an eternal flame inside Billy's heart, was no longer there. Instead, in front of him stood a shell-shocked woman, her eyes big with what he encoded as absolute fear.

The exact same fear he had seen coming from the Anne family.

Only this time, however, it was with someone he planned to have further contact with. "I'm sorry," Billy spoke up trying to recapture the girl's attention. "But is something wrong?" he asked, although already knowing the answer. As a matter of fact, the closer he looked at the eerie expression on the girl's face, it seemed as though she had just seen a ghost and she looked as if she were only seconds away from collapsing onto the soft sand the beach comfortably provided. Tracy was obviously terrified of something.

But what?

"You live there?" she asked, her voice cold with fear, as she pointed up at his house.

Billy nodded. "Why? What's wrong?"

Jason Glover

"Nothing," Tracy answered quickly a she looked away from the house and turned to flee. "I'm sorry," she added in a hurry. "Maybe this wasn't such a good idea. But you really are a sweet guy and thanks again for helping me find my bracelet." With that, and before Billy had a chance to respond, she was gone, sprinting away into the sunset not even bothering to turn around and give him one last glance.

"Son of a bitch!" Billy cursed himself out of frustration.

Now, more than ever, his mind was made up. Why was everyone so afraid of the Saxton's home? What was the big secret? Better yet, what was going on?

Tracy was the last straw. It was time for him to find the answers to the mysterious questions that had suddenly shadowed his conscious, and as he looked up at his new home along Sandy Point Ln., he knew that somewhere inside, was the key to it all. Somewhere inside that house, there just had to be something that could put his mind to rest.

Finally, with his mind made up, he stormed into the house.

He would rip it apart if he had to, but he wasn't going to rest until he uncovered the truth about this obviously disliked domicile.

* * *

Curtis Rains was lying peacefully on his tiny cot within his cell, staring somberly at the ceiling above him, gazing into the single florescent light bulb, which allowed his cell to receive more light than was needed. Annoying him at times, almost as if he wasn't allowed to live in complete darkness, yet completely invisible to the other inmates around him, and undoubtedly shielded from the rest of society.

He could feel the eyes of the other inmates staring at his flesh every once in a while, and at other times, he would listen as a few of them seemed to have some sort of conversation about him. Sometimes, when he felt the presence of their eyes surveying him, he would turn quickly around and return the glance. Obviously afraid, and as if somehow he would be able to reach out and grab their souls, they would turn instantly away, pretending as though they had never been watching him. Whenever this happened, a smile would always cross his face. Behind bars, he still had the effect on society God had blessed him with. Even the other death row inmates didn't have the courage to look him in the eyes. Each time, they were immediately stunned with a feeling which made their heart's beat faster, and adrenaline strengthen.

Fear.

He could feel the fear growing in the people he made eye contact with, and it pleased him. Curtis Rains had the ability to freeze you in your tracks with one simple glance and his presence could never be forgotten. In fact, he considered himself and his being as the single definition for the word, "fear."

In the ten long attenuated years he had been locked down inside the sickening walls of the Florida State Prison, he had hardly spoken a word. Rarely ever speaking to any of the other inmates, and not one, could he call or consider being a friend. Just like his childhood, he had been totally on his own, dependent only upon himself, and receiving orders from no one. Except, of course, from an occasional guard who simply needed to get their power trip in for the day. But even then, he would only smile, as they would refuse to look directly at him.

Then, from out of nowhere, the guard who seemed to get the most pleasure from disturbing him came around the corner and appeared in front of his cell. Feeling Jack Reynolds' presence in front of him, he didn't even bother to look up and acknowledge him. Curtis simply continued to stare blankly at the light above him, just waiting to hear what the guard had to say this time around.

"Hey Rains," Jack began in a tone that would have grasped anyone's attention. "Tomorrow's the big day huh? And guess what?" he paused trying to bring any signs of life from the inmate in front of him. "I have been assigned to the staff involving your execution. Isn't that great. I'm going to be the one to come and get your sorry ass, shackle you from head to toe, and then walk you to the chair. Can you believe it Rains? I'm going to be famous for being the man to walk the Tinman to his death." Then, with a laugh, and deciding his point had been made, Reynolds turned and continued on his way down the corridor.

As if the words spoken to him had no effect whatsoever, Curtis continued to stare at the boring ceiling above him. Only this time, a movement caught his eye. Squinting a bit to see through the piercing bright light, he realized it was a bug that had somehow gotten itself trapped inside the light. Fluttering about in a furry to stay alive, Curtis knew that there was no escape for the tiny creature. He watched as the insect struggled to hold on, hitting every inch of the tiny compartment trying to find any crease to slip out and into freedom.

Unfortunately, there was none.

And from the Tinman's face, arose a smile.

It was a smile brighter than the beaming light above him, and it was a smile that resembled the one and only thing almost everyone was afraid of.

Death.

The sight of the bug fighting for its seemingly meaningless life brought back memories Curtis had of his victims as they struggled to live through the pain he inflicted upon them. Closing his eyes, he remembered the screaming. The retched screams of pain, the terrifying screams of fear, which had always blistered into the night air, disturbing the stillness as horrifying sounds emerged from his victims. Always working slow, he seemed to experiment with his chosen ones, trying to see just how much pain they could endure before giving up all their rights to live, as if somehow wanting to die to be relieved from the suffering they were going through.

In fact, his parents, he recalled had begged him to kill them.

In the end, however, it was his ego that had put him behind bars. Never letting a single family member escape alive, he began believing that it was impossible for anyone to decamp from the event they all knew was drawing near. With the rest of their lives completely under his control, and most knowing that he was not going to let them live, he would always listen as they begged for life. Begging him to let them be, and always asking why he was doing the horrible things he did.

Unfortunately, he never answered any of their questions, and he never came across anyone he felt deserved to live.

Finally, as the last signs of life seemed to vanish from the small creature above him, just as it did from his unlucky victims in the past, he felt his eyes growing heavy. Once again, he closed his eyelids, preparing for another long nap from within his cell. Only this time he was smiling. He knew the dreams of his slayings would soon return, bringing back all the sensational feelings of controlling someone's life and putting an end to their desire to live. He missed it. He especially missed and yearned for the one feeling that seemed to beat all the others when he was performing his works of art.

Power.

* * *

A couple hours passed, and everywhere Billy searched, he turned up nothing that could help him in his quest to find out what he needed to know. He looked in every closet, in every bedroom, and still nothing turned up that could answer the many questions, which seemed to continually echo throughout his head. He found the whole situation to be utterly nerve-racking, but his desire and will power only pushed him harder, and he wasn't ready to give up just yet.

Finally, deciding to take a little breather, he collected his thoughts and asked himself where wasn't he looking? After all, it was a huge house, and he knew he couldn't have covered every square inch. "Think damn it," he cursed himself. There had to be somewhere he hadn't looked yet.

Then, it hit him.

The cellar.

He hadn't searched the cellar. Filled with anticipation of what could be down within the confinements of the shadowy room, he made his way back downstairs and across to the hallway.

At the end, he knew, was the door that led into the depths of the underground room.

Nearing the doorway, however, he found his feet slowing to a rather humble pace. He didn't know why, but for some reason, fear began to set inside. Basements were always pictured as being creepy, and spooky in the movies, and he didn't see why anything would prove otherwise in this case. Nevertheless, he knew what he had to do, and there was absolutely no way he was going to turn back now.

With an intensified expression scattered along his clear complexioned face, he placed his hand on the doorknob, and with one swift motion he twisted the handle, and pushed the door open. The door creaked as it opened fully for the first time in years and slammed into the wall. The whole scene sent alarming vibes into his conscious.

Jason Glover

"Just like the movies," Billy said aloud speaking of the creaking noise made by the door.

Then, staring ahead of him, he looked down into the cellar below. He couldn't even see past the third step as an uncomfortable darkness seemed to purposely hide everything in the room. Stepping into the doorway and down on the first step, Billy wildly felt along the walls searching for a light switch of some sort, or a string. Anything really that could make the blackness and the uneasy feeling within the pit of his stomach disappear.

Finally, after a few seconds of fidgeting with disappointment, his fingers came across what he knew was a light switch. Briskly, he flicked his finger in an upward motion. For a split second, nothing happened, and a frown crossed his face as he realized the light didn't work. He had absolutely no idea where to find a flashlight and he wasn't about to travel down the steep staircase without being able to see where he was going, or knowing what he might find once he reached the bottom.

Then, just as he was about to give up for the night and turn around, he saw a flickering motion from a light bulb in the distance. Watching with anticipation, he prayed it would spring to life. Finally, the electricity held sturdy and the light bulb brightly lit the staircase in front of him. However, the staircase was the only thing exposed to the light. Whatever was contained down at the bottom of the cellar still remained a mystery.

Yet, feeling a bit more at ease, he was sure that there would be another light switch at the bottom, which would ignite the rest of the cellar. So, fighting off the fear that had been dwelling inside of him, he continued down the staircase, listening as the old, splintery boards cracked as he exposed them to the weight he hauled around. He walked slowly, making sure the steps, which were taking him deeper below the ground, were going to hold.

Finally, after seconds of holding his breath, he made it to the bottom of the staircase, and as he set foot on the cemented blackened surface of the cellar, he felt the coolness it provided, and chill bumps began to sprout along his arms. Luckily, he noticed a string in front of him, which he was sure, if pulled, would produce another light source. Clamping his hands around the single piece of filament, he gave it a good tug.

Sure enough, the light sprang to life, and once his eyes became fully adjusted, he was able to see the space around him. The cellar itself seemed to be rather large. Against one of the walls stood an old antique looking washer and dryer, which obviously were no longer in use and hadn't been for some time now. There was a sparkling steel furnace, which was also obviously not under supreme working conditions. And other than the thousands of dust particles floating about everywhere, the cellar appeared to be completely empty. With a frivolous expression, Billy still decided to walk around the mysterious room, not searching for anything in particular, but something that might strike him as being a bit odd.

Although it appeared as though everything, which had been contained within the cellar, had been emptied years ago, he couldn't help but sense that there was something down here he simply was overlooking.

His instincts told him not to abandon the search just yet. Squinting his eyes, he outlined every last inch of the indifferent, dampen cellar. The dreary, wintry scene still seemed to produce a living feeling of uneasiness within the pit of his stomach. However, the silence is what astounded him the most.

It was a silence that simply could not be described. An almost unearthly, mesmerizing silence that could make you feel your heart pounding repeatedly inside your chest. The whole scenario told Billy to turn back and run back up the stairs and into the safety of his home, closing the door to the cellar behind him and locking it, never to return.

However, he knew that wasn't possible.

After all, there was absolutely nothing to be afraid of. There was no one, and nothing down there beside himself. He was all alone in this dark, enigmatic, cryptic type surrounding, where no one could hear him scream or cry for help.

Nevertheless, he continued on.

Along the walls, he searched for boards, which seemed to be loose for any signs of hidden valuables, or those, which were meant to be hidden and never to be found. Time and time again, however, Billy found himself coming up empty handed.

Then, along the far corner of the left wall, was the only corner not visible by the guiding light. Forgetting everything else, he changed direction and headed for the dark region of the cellar. The closer he came, the more visible the shadowy corner became, and it was there he noticed something he had been searching for all along. It was there he noticed a single board, the bottom half of it protruding from the wall. Scraping marks could easily be seen along the cement where the board had obviously been purposely jarred loose.

With excitement, and eagerness flowing throughout his veins, he grabbed a hold of the bottom of the boards, and with one zealous upward thrust, the old piece of wood easily gave away. Loosing his balance, Billy fell to the icy cold basement floor, the board still held tightly within the palm of his hands. Climbing to his knees he peered inside the black hole coming from the cellar wall.

Unfortunately, he could see nothing.

Determined, he picked himself up and courageously strolled over to the hole he had made in the wall. Bending down, he reached his arm into the hole as far as it would go. Realizing he wouldn't be able to look inside the darkish, hollow lair, he simply moved his fingers across the uneasy surface, hoping to find something.

He was about to give up, when he felt the tip of something, just out of his reach. Whatever it was, it had a handle, and once he got his fingers around it, he pulled it from its hidden compartment, and into the light. Not believing his eyes, he sat there staring at the awkward possession in front of him.

It was a box of some sort, and there was no telling what he would find inside.

Chapter 4

    Easily scaling his way back up the flight of stairs, Billy soon found himself back within the comfortable, livable surroundings of his new home. Closing the cellar door behind him, he raced to his bedroom holding the featherweight box tucked tightly between his arm and ribcage. Not even bothering to see if his mother was home or not, he shut his bedroom door, latched the dead bolt, and sat on his bed.
    Placing the mysterious box right in front of him, he just sat there for a moment. Half of him was scared to actually find out what was inside, while the other half of him simply tried to guess as to what its contents could be. He listened intensely as the air conditioner sprang to life once again in its continuous motion to keep his home cool. Then, composing himself, he tried to vent out all of the excitement and anticipation that had been mounting ever since his obscure fingers had stumbled across the box that had been hidden within one of the cellar walls. Finally, after taking a deep breath, he grabbed the handle. Closing his eyes, he unlatched the lock and with one swift, brisk motion, Billy opened the hollow cube. Slowly, one by one, he opened his eyes, and after leaning over a bit, he peered inside the box. Filled with joy, but still not quite sure what the contents within the carton would mean, he pulled the articles from its container. Staring at them with a confused expression, his mind began to spin in circles.
    Inside the box, were two encumbrances.
    A picture of a family, and a little doll.
    As he stared at the obviously patriarchal picture, he wondered who the people were. Then, as if a light bulb sprang to life inside his

head, he knew the answer to his own question. He didn't know their names or anything, but he was certain that it was the family that had resided in the house before he and his mother had come along. However, for some unknown reason, he felt as though he were being pulled towards the strange people he saw in front of him. Almost as if there was something he was missing.

But what could it be?

He had never seen these people before in his life. Didn't know the first thing about them. Needless to say, however, he wanted to know everything there was to know. No matter how meaningless it was, or how appalling and horrendous it may become, it was information that Billy yearned for. His mind simply wouldn't be able to rest until everything was revealed and brought out into the open. There was obviously something the people of Destin feared about his home, and until he found out what it was, or until he was able to understand where they were coming from, he knew he would never be able to survive in this so called lovely town.

As he gazed at the smiling faces of the family in the picture, a feeling of both contentment and bewilderment came over him. There was a lady, a beautiful woman, middle-aged, standing next to her husband, and in between, was their little girl, whose joyous expression seemed to warm Billy's soul. In fact, as he gazed into the little girl's beautiful blue eyes and watched as the light seemed to sparkle off her angelic blonde hair, he somehow felt a connection between the two of them. In the picture, the girl couldn't have been more than eight or nine years old, and Billy couldn't help but to wonder just how old she would be today?.

But what had happened to the little girl and her family?

And why was their family picture placed within the box and cleverly hidden inside the hollow walls of the cellar?

So many questions continued to pound away inside his exhausted brain, and he found an aggravating anger building inside because even though his quest hadn't left him empty handed, he still was no closer to finding out the answers that boggled his mind. Finally, as he tried to reason with himself, he decided to put the picture aside and wait until his mother returned home. He was sure that the Realtor would have told his mother something about the family that had lived there before them. After all, there had to be a reason that no one had bought the house in ten years time. It truly was a beautiful and amazing home, and if his mother did know something, surely she wouldn't have hidden it from him.

Or would she?

No, that was simply unthinkable. He and Debra had grown very close over the years, both agreeing never to hide anything from one another. Especially anything of any importance. And to Billy, this was important. He hoped that if Debra did in fact know something that she would have thought to let him in on it. He felt as though he had a right to know. After all, he was living there too.

Nevertheless, knowing that there was absolutely nothing that could be done right at that moment, he placed the picture back in the box, and picked up the other object he had found nestled inside. With the doll in hand, he noticed a striking resemblance to the girl in the picture. Obviously, it had to be the little girl's doll. But again, he wondered why someone would have hidden it?

Once again, almost as if there was no escape from the continuous bombardment of overwhelming questions, he returned the doll back into its hiding place, closed the lid and placed it on the floor. Throwing his hands over his face, he laid down on his comfortable mattress, and within seconds, Billy felt his eyes growing heavy.

Desperately wanting to remain awake until his mother returned home, Billy hoped that she would be able to answer a few of the many questions that kept resurfacing. However, as his mouth opened, a relaxing yawn exited, and he realized his hard day at work was finally taking a toll on him. Instead of fighting his exhausted body, he finally made an agreement with his ego and decided to postpone and forget about everything until the morning hours arrived.

Closing his eyes, he allowed himself to fall into the deep sleep he knew was coming. Pushing the thought of the box he had found in the cellar aside, he precariously tried to forget about what he had found. Finally, as the blackness of night seemed to soothe his soul, a smile crossed his face as he began remembering all of the good times he had spent with his friends in Marietta.

Although wishing he were back home right now, he was still glad that his mother was happy. Debra had to understand, however, that he wasn't going to be living at home forever. Soon, it would be time for him to get his life in order and make his own mark in the "real world." And although he knew that time was rapidly approaching, he wasn't going to leave his mother until he was absolutely positive she would be all right. He didn't like to think about it, but meeting another man was probably the best remedy or medicine that could bring his mother back around. Billy was anxious to accept life's journey, but he was willing to wait until his mother was healthy in every state.

Then, remarkably, Billy found himself at peace. The disorienting thoughts seemed to exit without a trace. Within seconds, he was asleep, unconsciously listening to the relaxing sound of the surf.

* * *

Elizabeth and Debra had polished off the bottle of wine, which had been provided by Elizabeth's husband, Murray, and then the two of them proceeded to grab a few wine coolers from the refrigerator and headed out onto the patio. As the two of them seated themselves along side one another, Debra found herself looking into the eyes of the woman seated across from her, and a grin crossed her face. She had positively enjoyed Elizabeth's company this evening, and it felt almost as if the two of them had known one another all their lives.

"Elizabeth," Debra spoke up breaking the silence that had fallen over them as soon as they sat down under the moonlight to listen to the crashing of the waves. "Thanks for everything you've done this evening. It was an absolutely lovely dinner and your home is genuinely beautiful."

"Please, don't mention it," Elizabeth replied smiling. "It's the least I could have done to welcome you to this neighborhood. Besides, it's good to see a new face every now and then ya know? Most people along this beach seem to keep to themselves. The teenagers around here though, sometimes tend to get a little wild with the beach scene and all."

"Have you lived here all your life?"

Elizabeth nodded. "Yep. I remember when I was growing up here in Destin. I didn't live along the beach like I do now, but all of my friends did, and boy did we ever do some partying. If I recall correctly, there was this girlfriend of mine, Susan, was her name, and we used to go out of our way to drive the boys crazy around here.

And ya know what?" she paused with a smile, followed by a giggle. "It seemed to work every time."

Debra laughed at Elizabeth's attempt to assemble a joke, neither of the two realizing they had obviously passed their limit on alcohol. "Not me. I probably only made it to the beach a few times my entire childhood. I guess that's why it's so hard to believe that I'm actually living on one. I tell you what though," she paused as the two of them listened to the waves. "That's something I absolutely love about the beach. The sound of the crashing waves seems to put you in a peaceful state of mind doesn't it?"

Then, before Elizabeth had time to respond, her husband came onto the patio and placed his firm hands on her shoulders. "I'm about to tuck the girls in," Murray began giving his wife a little squeeze. "And then I'm turning in myself. The girls wanted me to tell you goodnight though."

Turning around, she waved to her two daughters who were watching her through the sliding glass window. "Goodnight doodle bugs!" she spoke loud enough for the two of them to hear. Then, pulling her husband over her shoulder she gently kissed his firm lips. "And goodnight handsome," she added before releasing him. "I'll be there in a little while."

"Nonsense," Murray interjected. "You two ladies take all the time you need to get to know one another." Then, turning to Debra he extended his hand. With a smile, he gave her hand a charming squeeze. "And Debra, it was a pleasure meeting you. Just don't let my wife corrupt you." As he turned to walk back inside he found himself cheering silently as he heard his wife mock his attempt to make the two of them laugh. However, he had won, and it had worked.

"You have a good man there," Debra began politely. "And your two daughters are absolutely precious. You must be so proud of them."

"Oh yes," Elizabeth replied. "They can be a handful sometimes though and I just want to grab them by their shoulders and ring their little necks. But they can be the two sweetest children you've ever seen at the same time. They normally stay out of trouble, thank God. What about you?" she asked slowly, not wanting to overstep her bounds. "Are you divorced? You don't have to answer."

"No, actually," Debra began to answer rather hesitantly, trying to choose the best words for the predicament she now found herself faced with. "My husband was an alcoholic and he died not to long ago from a massive stroke," she blurted out, deciding the best way was to be direct.

Shocked, and completely speechless, Elizabeth looked into her new friend's eyes trying to think of something she could do to comfort her. "Oh," she paused still stunned at the answer she received. "I-I'm so sorry Debra. I had no idea or else I wouldn't have asked."

"No, no, it's O.K.," Debra assured her. "I would have told you eventually anyway."

"And your son," Elizabeth continued. "Is Billy doing all right?"

"Oh yeah," Debra answered with confidence. "As a matter of fact, he's been able to deal with it a lot better than I. He's been very comforting and supportive through the whole thing, and I know he's worried about me. I always tell him that everything's fine, but I know he can see right through me. And he didn't exactly want to make this move with me either, and that he only came for me. He's never actually said so, but I can tell he doesn't want me to be alone."

"He seems like a great kid," Elizabeth agreed. "Has he met any new friends yet?"

Debra shook her head. "I don't think so. He's been upset about something lately. I'm not really sure what it is because I haven't been able to sit down and talk to him about it. But," she paused as she turned to look into Elizabeth's eyes. "I think he mentioned something about our house. I don't know. He sounded so convinced about something, but it all sounded so crazy to me."

Then, just as soon as those words exited her mouth, she watched in awe, as Elizabeth's eyes seemed to rise. The wine cooler slipped from Elizabeth's hands, and crashed onto the patio below. As the glass shattered into hundreds of pieces, Elizabeth knew that she had reacted poorly, and now felt as if she had returned to the sensitive age of her youngest daughter. Debra, however, had finally seen the same fear in Elizabeth's eyes that her son had witnessed in the two little girls. Quickly, Debra tried to think if she had said something wrong, or something that could have startled the woman opposite of her.

After a few long seconds, she came to the conclusion that she had not. Then, what had frightened her?

"Elizabeth!" Debra exclaimed. "What is it? What's wrong?"

"Nothing, nothing at all," Elizabeth answered trying to regain her composure. She was fully aware that she wasn't going to be able to get herself out of this one. "You just surprised me is all."

"Surprised you? What are you talking about?"

"You mean you don't know?" Elizabeth asked the woman in front of her as she found it hard to believe that Debra had no clue as to what had happened in her house ten years ago. Then, seeing the blank expression scattered along her face, she knew that Debra really didn't know. "Oh my God!' she exclaimed. "You really don't have any idea do you?"

"No I don't," Debra answered finding herself growing a fraction angrier than she wanted to be. "I don't know what's going on here, and I don't know why you so suddenly started to freak out. But please," she pleaded in anguish. "Will you please tell me what it is? I think I need to know. Please!"

"All right," Elizabeth cut in, realizing Debra had become upset. "But I should warn you. You are not going to find this very pleasant, and you might even wish you didn't know about it. But you're right, you should know. However," she paused, as an idea seemed to establish itself in her alcohol-infested brain. "I truly thought the Realtor would have said something to you about it. I mean, didn't she tell you why no one even considered to buy that house for ten years?"

"No," Debra answered confusingly, her mind recalling every conversation she had ever had with the Realtor. "If she mentioned something I'm sure I would remember."

"Oh believe me," Elizabeth paused. "If she would have told you about this, you definitely would have remembered."

"So," Debra pressed on. "What is it?"

"Well, ten years ago, there was a family that lived there. In fact, as the years passed, I myself grew to become rather fond of them and we used to spend a lot of time together," Elizabeth began. "There was David Haas, he was the assistant DA at the time, his wife Charlene Haas, and their nine year old daughter, Carey. They were truly a happy family without a single worry in the world. Until," she paused letting her voice trail off into silence, not quite sure about how she should proceed with such a touchy subject. "Are you sure you want to hear the rest of this?"

Debra nodded ardently.

"Well, I'm not quite sure how to say this. But," Elizabeth paused once again. "But the Haas family was murdered in that house ten years ago. Both David and Charlene were killed very viciously, and their little girl, bless her heart, did manage to escape. But Carey had watched her parents die, she herself lucky to get away, and she still isn't the same person she used to be and will never be the person she could have been. To this day, no one knows why it happened to them, but it was the only time anything of that nature ever occurred here in Destin, and no one has forgotten about it. Hell, my two daughters hear stories about it all the time at school and they come home scared out of their minds."

Not believing her ears, Debra waited, hoping that Elizabeth would start laughing and tell her that she had just been kidding around. As the seconds slowly ticked away, however, she knew that it wasn't a joke. The story, which had obviously been cut down, sparing her of the gory details, was true.

The family that had lived in that house ten years ago had been murdered.

Debra tried to grasp everything at once, and suddenly found herself with an overwhelming sensation of nausea. Her body began to shake uncontrollably, and when she spoke, she found her tongue getting in the way. "I-I can't believe it!" she exclaimed, rising to her feet, trying to overcome the distressing feelings that were building inside. "I can't believe that I was not told of such a thing. That's simply preposterous, and I'll be damned if I'm going to let them get away with it," she added speaking of the Realtor company she had been working with, and her voice taking on a bold tone of hostility.

"I'm sorry," Elizabeth too, climbed to her feet and walked over to the railing of the patio. "Does this mean that you're going to move out?"

"I don't know what I'm going to do," Debra admitted. "When we first moved down here everything felt so right, and I was sure that I had made the right decision. But now," she paused. "Now I just don't know." Then, changing the subject, she asked. "Well, whatever happened to the killer? Did they ever find him?"

Again, an uncertain look crossed Elizabeth's face and she had to remind herself that Debra obviously knew nothing about this whole situation. Coming back to reality, she nodded. "Yes he was caught." Elizabeth paused not really sure if she should go on or not. However, as she looked into Debra's innocent eyes, she felt that it would be better for her to find out from her instead of someone else just blurting it out. "Debra, you're not going to want to hear this either. But, the killer was Curtis Rains. Ya know, that Tinman guy who's actually supposed to be electrocuted tomorrow?"

"Great!" Debra exclaimed as she recalled how she and her son had been watching the news earlier that evening and the man known as the Tinman popped up on the screen. Never in her wildest dreams would she have expected to move into a house, which had once been ripped apart by the notorious Curtis Rains. "Elizabeth," Debra continued motioning that it was time for her to leave. "Thank you for a lovely evening, and I'm sorry it turned out this way. But I really should be getting home. Billy's probably worried about me."

"Come by anytime," Elizabeth replied with a smile as her counterpart set afoot on the beach and began walking home. "And please, call me Beth, and call me tomorrow and let me know how everything is going."

Elizabeth continued to watch until Debra Saxton became completely engulfed by the surrounding darkness and her thin body was no longer visible. Then, taking one last glance up at the moon, she turned and walked inside taking a deep breath of her own.

* * *

In Birmingham, Alabama.

Jamie Walker squinted her eyes as she tried to challenge her vision to see through the pouring rain that splattered along her smeary windshield. This proved to be quite an endeavor as the windshield wipers had long been out of decent working condition. Nevertheless, she slowed her car to the minimum speed average found along I-10 as she headed from Birmingham, Alabama to Starke, Florida. Turning on the radio, she fought to take her mind off the powerful southern thunderstorm that cursed her traveling conditions, and seemingly would stretch for miles ahead.

However, she knew that there was no escape.

She wished she could simply pull over until the weather became a bit more appealing. However, she didn't want to be late getting to Starke. It had been hard enough making up her mind to go there in the first place, and she knew that it wouldn't take much to get her to turn her Jeep Cherokee around and return to the safety of her Alabama home.

Jamie was one of the leading doctors at the Psychology Institute of the State of Alabama. She had spent the past few years of her life trying to understand the way the brains of mankind worked. Trying to find possible links as to why certain people behave in different, and sometimes violent ways.

However, she hadn't taken an interest into this field of psychology until the man whom went by the name "Tinman," had come into her life.

In fact, before Curtis Rains had evolved into the terrifying creature he had become, or before the rest of society had blackballed him, she had been his lover. She had been the only person to listen to his problems, to understand what the man behind the slayings had been feeling or thinking. Never once, however, did she expect him to do the things he did.

She was aware that everyone had problems, and most people do tend to deal with them in rational, clear ways that helped themselves get better and overcome the obstacles they sometimes find themselves faced with. And that's what she thought of Curtis. She knew that he was a very intelligent man, which was one of the reasons she had fallen so hard for him when they were first introduced to one another, and she truly believed that he would find some constructive way to deal with the problems he had faced as a child. Unfortunately, she had never been so wrong before in her life.

Curtis Rains had murdered his own mother and father, and to this day, showed no remorse or sorrow for his actions. Then, a couple of years afterwards, he began again. Choosing families out of the clear blue, perfect families if you will, and then destroying them, stripping away every ounce of life that could be found within them.

And again, there was no remorse.

After his arrest ten years ago, she had learned from authorities that he would stalk the families before striking. Sometimes taking pictures. Sometimes calling the homes of the unfortunate victims and recording the voices that would pick up. In fact, every family he dissipated, he would watch for months. Getting to know their every move, favorite restaurants, and sometimes he would even break into their homes before striking to learn every detail of the house, and assure himself the protection from making any mistakes, and to allow no escape.

Then, when the time was right, he would strike and the family would be completely unaware that they had been watched and observed for months. Unfortunately, they would also be unaware that death had been waiting right around the corner.

She now looked upon Curtis Rains, the man she once loved, in a different mode. There were lots of fond memories with him that she would cherish until the day she died, and it saddened her to know that no one had ever tried to contact him since he had been locked down on death row. Including herself.

Jamie didn't really understand why she was wanting to go to the prison in Starke, Florida, but she felt in some way that Curtis Rains would want to see a familiar face before he left this world and moved on. He had been all alone for ten years, and she simply didn't want him to die alone. No matter how hateful, cruel, and evil the Tinman was, he was still a human being, although, not considered to be. She was aware that her conscious would never let her forgive him for putting her through such a mind-twisting ordeal, but if he needed to get anything off his chest, she would be there for him.

Finally, as she drove into a clearing, she cut her windshield wipers off and almost simultaneously, her car phone rang. Picking it up, she already knew who it would be, and sure enough as the familiar voice on the other end of the phone sprang to life, she immediately recognized it as her live in love, Travis McKinley. "Hey baby," he immediately began after hearing her pick up the phone. "Listen, I know we didn't get off on the right foot when you told me you were going to see that guy in Florida, and I still don't understand why you say you must go see that crazy son of a bitch. But, I just wanted to call and tell you that I love you, and I'll be here when you get back."

"Thanks," Jamie replied as she looked at herself through the rearview mirror, wiping away the sleep dust from around her exotic greenish blue eyes. Then, as she put her thick, wavy, beautiful brown hair up in a bun, she continued. "I love you too sweetheart, and I promise I'll try and explain everything to you when I get back."

"No," Travis declared. "Not only do I think I don't want to know, but I also think its best for our relationship if I don't know." Then, with a little chuckle, he blew a kiss into the phone. "But I got to run babe. A few of my buddies from work are here to pick me up. We're going out. I love you," he said once again.

"I love you too," Jamie managed to sneak in before Travis hung up. "Have fun, and be careful," she added too late.

Then, as she entered another patch of thunderstorms, she clutched the steering wheel tight, flipped her wipers back on and concentrated on the road. "Damn this weather," she cursed out loud as she couldn't read the road sign she just passed which told her how many more miles until she crossed the Florida State line.

* * *

As Debra eased her way into the house she was a bit alarmed at how quiet it was. Her mind still had not come to grips with the reality that a family had been murdered in this very home by the notorious Curtis Rains. Her anger continued to grow at the Realtors for not even mentioning it to her. This was most certainly not a minor detail they could have easily overlooked.

No, they had deliberately chosen not to enlighten her.

Well, she wasn't going to stand for it. She had been pushed around many times in the past and it was now time for her to start standing up for herself. She was tired of people taking advantage of her. Hell, if they had had the decency to let her know, she probably would have still bought the house. She may not have jumped into it right away, but she probably would have still agreed to move into this wonderful house located right on the beach of sunny Destin, Florida.

At this moment, however, there was nothing wonderful about it.

Finally, as she mounted the stairs, she found herself standing outside her son's bedroom. "Billy," she whispered softly. However, there was no answer. Opening the door, she found her son lying on the bed, sound asleep. With a smile she walked across the room, rubbed her fingers through his soft hair, leaned down and kissed him on the cheek. "Goodnight sweetheart," she whispered softly. "I love you."

Then, turning around, she left his bedroom and headed for her own. She hadn't even noticed the small box located at the foot of her son's bed. Nevertheless, closing Billy's bedroom door, she left him alone to dream in peace.

Jason Glover

Chapter 5

 As the Haas family sat quietly throughout their evening meal, the only person that seemed to be the slightest bit interested in talking was David and Charlene's little daughter, nine-year-old Carey Haas. The two parents laughed at one another as they simply sat there listening to their daughter's constant chatter, not speaking to anyone in particular, just anyone who was willing to listen. Mostly, however, she seemed to carry on a conversation with her favorite little porcelain doll, whom she had named Kat, and whom looked to be Carey's identical twin.
 "Isn't mommy's cooking good?" Carey asked her doll as she pretended to feed her little baby, her stainless, sparkling green eyes seeming to bring life to her peachy, glossy cheeks. Wavy blonde hair drifted from atop the doll, and along with long brown eyelashes, Carey had dressed her in an elegant, forest green dress resembling a scintillating emerald with white ruffles wrapping at the bottom. "Why don't you tell her how wonderful it is? I know she'd love to hear it."
 "All right little one," Charlene began as she picked herself up from behind the dining table and began to return everything to the kitchen. "Why don't you take Kat upstairs and get washed up and ready for bed. Daddy and I will be up in a little while to tuck you girls in." For a split second after she had spoken to her daughter, she thought that Carey was about to refuse and beg to stay put with her parents. Surprisingly, however, she scooted from her chair at the dinner table, and clinging on tightly to her best friend, she obeyed her mother and began heading for the staircase.

"*You guys don't forget to come and tuck us in,*" Carey said aloud as she began to climb up the staircase that was gigantic in her little mind. "*You know how scared Kat can get if you don't come in and give her a kiss goodnight.*"

"*We won't honey,*" David assured his little angel. "*We'll be up as soon as we finish cleaning the kitchen. I promise.*" Then, once he was satisfied his daughter wasn't within hearing distance, he turned his attention to his wife who was hard at work in the kitchen washing the dishes. "*Need some help?*" he asked as he leaned over her shoulder and gently nibbled on her ear. "*That is one hell of a daughter we have there. I've personally never seen a child as full of life as she is.*"

"*But of course,*" Charlene replied with a laugh. "*She's takes after me. Didn't you know?*"

"*Funny girl,*" David chuckled as he spun his wife around. "*Looks like I'm going to have to teach you a lesson,*" he added as he gazed into his wife's charming blue eyes, and began to rub his masculine fingers throughout her golden locks of hair. Then, he put his arms around her waist and pulled her close, letting their lips collide passionately. Both of them enjoyed the familiar, and comfortable feeling it brought on. "*God I do love you!*" he exclaimed with a smile before he leaned over to kiss her once more.

"*And I love you,*" Charlene replied as erotic images began to spring into her otherwise normal brain. She wanted so much for him to just take her right there in the kitchen, making even more of a mess than had already been made. However, with their daughter still awake and running about throughout the house, she knew it was simply impossible. Trying to push him away before she let the situation get out of hand, she continued. "*But I have some cleaning up to do, and I don't really feel like having to explain something on the concept of sex to our nine year old daughter, whom you know will be walking back in here any minute to get us to come upstairs to tuck her in.*"

"*Good thinkin,*" David agreed, quickly kissing his wife one last time before forcing himself to behave and leave the kitchen. Then, just as he reached the exit, he turned once more and winked at her. "*But as soon as our little one is sound asleep, I will return, and you will be all mine woman. You hear me?*" he asked jokingly.

Once out of the room, Charlene let herself relax and she began to discard all of the naughty thoughts that had entered her mind just seconds ago. "How did I get so lucky?" she asked herself about her nonchalant, but perfect husband, and her entire life in general. She had an absolutely wonderful husband and daughter, beautiful home, their family was financially secure, and she was lucky enough to have the constant sound of the surf crashing against the shoreline to listen to everyday. She truly had the perfect life, and the perfect family.

Simply put, her life was complete.

Then, from out of nowhere, a sound came that struck her as being rather odd. It was the sound of their doorbell as it echoed its way throughout the entire house. No one had called and mentioned anything about stopping by, and they weren't expecting anyone. Then again, with her husband's profession, there was really no telling who it could be. But, he hadn't been working on a major case for over two months now, and she didn't know of any reason that could even be remotely important enough to bring anyone to her home this late in the evening. With her mind wondering, she turned the tap water off from the kitchen sink and headed for the front door. Halfway there, however, her husband, who continued to smile and look at her with his very dark and observing eyes, stopped her.

"I'll get it," he motioned happily; finally glad to be able to do something instead of just sitting down watching the television. So, putting it all out of her mind, she returned to the kitchen and let her husband handle whoever was at the door.

"I'm coming," David hollered cheerfully as he reached the door. Then, he grabbed its handle, and mistakenly proceeded to open the door, not even bothering to look through the peephole to see if any dangers lurked outside. He stood there with a smile, prepared to greet anyone outside. Only, what he saw was truly strange.

No one was there.

Not a soul in sight.

Closing the door behind him, he dismissed it and found his wife just finishing up with the dishes. Before she could even ask the question he knew was coming, he answered it. "I don't know who it was," he began grinning just as Charlene's mouth opened to speak. "When I opened the door no one was there. Probably just one of the many punk kids we have in this neighborhood playing a prank on us."

"Awe come on," Charlene retorted turning to face her husband, and returning his inconceivable grin. "Punk kids? You mean to tell me you never did anything or misbehaved in anyway while you were growing up? Or has the DA image you are desperately trying to live up to totally brainwashed you?"

Before he could answer, and as expected, Carey came pouncing into the room. Her face rather ashen, and she looked rather disturbed. Still holding Kat tightly as if she was going to run away, she looked up at both her parents before speaking. "Who was at the door?" she asked in a rather resounding manner.

"That was no one honey," David answered as he lifted his little girl above his shoulder and began to carry her back up the stairs, followed by Charlene as the two of them prepared to tuck her in for the night. Then, just as the three of them reached the stairs, the sound of the doorbell trifled through the house once again.

Only, for some reason, it didn't sound like the normal, friendly ringing of the doorbell. It was more earth shattering.

This time, though, David wasn't going to let the disturbing kids get away. Placing his daughter down quickly, yet gently, he raced to the front door and flung it open. "Damn it!" he exclaimed in annoyance as once again, no one was there. Stepping out onto the front porch he looked around him.

No one was there.

Surveying every inch of his yard, and his neighbor's adjoining yard, he still found nothing. The neighborhood was as quiet as it usually was. However, he knew that whoever was getting so much pleasure in pissing his family off that evening was somewhere out there. Probably watching him right now.

Steamed, he returned inside and shut the door behind him. The expression on his face told Charlene that he had seen no one. Then, without even acknowledging their presence, almost as if they weren't even there, he brushed past them and picked up the nearest phone. "Who are you calling?" his wife asked arching her eyebrows. "Your not calling the police are you? Those kids will get tired of it after a while. Just don't answer the door the next time it happens."

"It's not like I'm going to have them arrested or anything," David shot back not showing his wife how truly irritated he was. "I'm just *going to have an officer drive through the neighborhood and scare them off. It's no big deal honey. Just don't worry about it."*

Then, as he held the phone to his ear, he heard a sound that made his heart skip a beat.

The sound was the forbidden sound of silence.

There wasn't a dial tone.

Quickly hanging the phone up on the receiver, he picked it back up and checked once again for the sound he knew should be there.

Again, there was nothing.

With his heart pounding, and his emotions spinning wildly out of control, he glanced at the phone as if it were going to answer his questions as to what was going on. An eerie feeling began to creep inside, and although he didn't know why, he sensed that something was terribly wrong. Dead wrong.

"What is it?" Charlene asked, seeing the fear in her husband's eyes as it enveloped its way across his orifice. Only, he didn't answer. "Honey!" she exclaimed making her ways towards him. "David. What's wrong?"

Then, from out of nowhere, the three of them heard a sound coming from the front door. Only this time, it wasn't the sound of the doorbell; it was someone knocking.

KNOCK, KNOCK, KNOCK!

No one said a word. They just stood there, their hearts racing and their minds wondering. They listened intensely for the knocking to return, and after a few seconds of hearing nothing, they began to think that maybe whoever had been there had finally decided to leave them alone. Then.

KNOCK, KNOCK, KNOCK!

It continued again after a few seconds.

KNOCK, KNOCK, KNOCK!

Fear had easily seized control of Charlene's body and she clinched her daughter's shoulders uncontrollably. Looking up and into her husband's eyes, she asked. "David who could that be? And what do they want?" Unfortunately, David didn't have an answer, and without saying a word, he could only shake his head. Then, the knock came again. Only this time, it was louder, bolder, and even more terrifying. "Who is it?" Charlene shrieked at the top of her lungs!

Then, almost as if her words had invited the stranger in, they watched in horror as the door flew open and crashed against the wall. Pieces of wood were sent flying around as they ripped themselves free from the wall. The sound of the door being kicked in seemed to echo throughout the entire house and left the three of them standing utterly still as all of them were too terrified to move. As they searched the doorway for any signs of life, however, panic sunk in as no one could be found. "My God!' Charlene stammered. "What is going on?"

Then, from out of the darkness, appeared a man. He stepped from the stillness of the pitch-black night with a comfortable ease, almost as if he was returning home from work. He was dressed completely in black, and was wearing a hat that would not allow them the luxury of seeing his face. To the Haas family, the man was a ghost.

Then, the moonlight seemed to cast down at him perfectly, as if he were the star of a Broadway play. He looked up at the terrified family in front of him, and allowed them to look into his deadly, cold-blooded eyes.

Then, smiling, he decided to enter the home.

Suddenly, Billy woke up.

Springing up from the bed, he began to breathe more steadily. As sweat dripped uncontrollably from his body, he couldn't believe the nightmare he had just experienced, and the realness of it was hard for him to ignore. It was as if he had been right there, listening to every word, and watching every action. And although he woke before it happened, he knew.

He knew that the Haas family had been murdered!

Then, with his nerves still shattered on the brink of no return, he crawled out of bed and looked outside the window. As he gazed into the stillness of the night, he decided to grab the box at the foot of his bed. Flipping on a light switch, he opened the box and pulled out the little porcelain doll and the picture of the family he had found in the cellar.

As he peered into the family's eyes, a piercing jolt wrenched throughout his head and sent his mind into an infuriating bliss. Billy closed high eyes tight as he desperately tried to push the phenomenal visions aside, and tried to assure himself that the painful sequences wouldn't be returning. Soon, the throbbing, excruciating headache disappeared, and the visions of the family vanished as well into thin air.

However, once again he stubbornly began to gaze back into the picture, completely oblivious to the possibility that the painful visions could resurface and shudder his mind with pain and agony. Nevertheless, as if some unseen force was pulling him towards the family inside the picture, he gripped it tight with both hands. Soon after, he was looking once again into their vivacious eyes.

Then, just as before, the piercing visions returned.

Flashbacks of the nightmare he had just experienced resurfaced promptly, lacerating every nerve in his brain. At first the pain was unbearable, and every time he squinted his eyes in obvious discomfort, the pain would ease a little. Once he reopened them, however, and continued to look into the picture, the pain and visions would return with more force.

Billy began hearing the voices of the Haas family and he quickly remembered the conversations he had witnessed in his dream. He remembered the fear in Charlene's voice, and the fear, which had been visible in all three of their eyes. Yet, in the picture before him, their eyes had been so full of life. They had been full of life in his dreams as well, until the mysterious knocking had came from outside their door.

However, his visions weren't in order.

They kept switching from the happy meal the family was having, to the sudden fear and anguish they had felt when their door had been abruptly kicked in. Then, finally, he saw the man in the dream he knew to be the killer.

As the man looked up at the family, it appeared as though the wicked man was looking directly into Billy Saxton's eyes that very second. Suddenly, Billy found himself experiencing the exact same emotion the Haas family had been forced to endure.

Fear.

Sheer, electrifying fear.

Finally, Billy had had enough. He placed the picture of the family back in the box and closed his eyes. Desperately, he tried to relieve himself of the numbing visions. Frenziedly, he tried to put the apparition of the evil man behind him. He cursed himself as he wondered why he had even let himself get involved in such a mesmerizing and horrifying ordeal. However, he knew that it was inevitable.

It was the house.

Looking around the room, he wondered whose room it had been ten years ago when the Haas family had occupied these quarters. In the dream, they were the ones who truly belonged here. It seemed as though he and his mother were there to tie up the loose ends, to try and bring the home's beauty back to life again after it had stood in utter silence for the past ten years.

But why was he seeing these visions of the past?

Were they real? Did they actually happen? Or were they simply nightmares his mind seemed to get pleasure in creating?

No.

Everything was real.

Becoming frustrated, Billy picked up the beautiful porcelain doll and looked into its tiny sparkling green eyes. Then, not really knowing exactly what possessed him to do so, he flipped the doll over and stared at the forest green dress it was draped in.

Then, finding his hand shaking incorrigibly, he dropped the doll to the floor and wished everything would just disappear. He wanted to forget everything he had found that night, and regretted ever setting foot within the solitary confinements of the cellar.

He wanted to just put the box back in the wall and forget that he had ever found it. That, however, wasn't going to happen.

Billy Saxton suddenly realized that he was in a terrifying predicament.

Crawling back under the covers, he leaned over and turned off the light, hoping that there were still a few more hours until daylight. With nothing else to do at the moment, he decided to try and get some rest. He wished he were back home in Marietta, where he wouldn't even be thinking about the dreadful place he came to know as Destin, Florida. He was supposed to be happy here, having the time of his young life.

So far, that wasn't happening.

Finally, as his eyes grew heavy once again, he was pleased to find that the painful, terrifying visions he had experienced just seconds ago had disappeared. Then again, he could only pray that the nightmare would choose not to reemerge. Feeling confident that they would not, he smiled as he yawned once again and prepared to fall back into a deep sleep.

Still, one thing remained.

It was the look of the man he had seen standing in the doorway of this very home. He remembered looking into the man's eyes, and for some unknown reason, he felt as though he knew the man, or had seen him somewhere before.

No.

Billy was sure of it.

He had definitely seen the man before.

* * *

Curtis could tell by the way his body felt that it was the middle of the night. His muscles ached as he tried to move them around, making him feel much older than he actually was, and his constant yawning let him know that he was usually asleep around this time at night. Then, looking at the cheap wristwatch he had been allowed to buy inside the prison walls, he found out that it was going on 3:00 in the morning.

Taking a deep breath, he realized today was the day.

Tonight at midnight, he would be strapped to the electric chair and his execution would be carried out. He could picture himself sitting straight up in the chair, and as if he were already there, he could feel the eyes of the observers watching his every move. They would be looking for signs of remorse, signs of sorrow, or pity for what he had done. Most, he knew, would want to see him beg for his life. Laughing to himself, he knew that he wouldn't dare give them that sort of satisfaction. None of that was going to happen.

He was going to walk in there as calm as ever, acting as if nothing was affecting his state of mind. He laughed to himself, as he knew he would be able to see the fear in the eyes of the observers. But he would only smile. He would give them what he felt they really wanted to see anyway.

His evil smile.

His smile normally meant death was approaching, and he could visualize the headlines of the paper the following day:

"Curtis Rains, more commonly known as the Tinman, was executed today inside the Florida State Prison by way of electrocution. And fittingly, he died with a smile, showing the world just how evil and carefree he really was."

"That's probably what it's going to say word for word," he spoke to himself, his hollow deep voice seeming to echo throughout the entire floor of the prison. Then, as if he sensed something awkward taking place from beyond the prison walls, and somewhere far away, he closed his eyes and let his brain waves take control of him.

He could feel something.

But he couldn't quite make out what it was. Then, it hit him. Someone was thinking about him.

But who?

Curtis strained continuously until his mind felt like it was going to collapse. Aggravated, he laid down as he prepared himself to get some sleep. He cursed himself for not being able to feel what was going on. However, the vibes he had felt were strong. It was almost as if he could feel himself in someone else's soul and although he didn't know exactly who had been thinking of him at the time; he had been able to grasp the feeling that he found within.

Fear.

Someone out there was afraid of him at that very moment. But who, and why?

For ten years he had been locked down, yet, people from all over still curled up at the slightest mention of his name. The trademark of the Tinman was so strong and overwhelmingly powerful, that even when his physical body would be buried six feet deep in the ground, people from all over the world would still be talking about him.

Curtis was even more certain that his presence would still be felt.

He was certain the world would still be able to feel the ultimate, dreadful feeling of fear, and was confident that no one, absolutely no one, would ever forget his face.

His smile.

No.

Jason Glover

    The legacy of the Tinman would live on forever, never perishing like millions would hope. Therefore, he himself would never die. Curtis Rains wasn't ready to fall into the flaming pit of hell. He wasn't ready to move on into another world, where there would be no more pain and suffering. In fact, as far as he was concerned, a world without pain and suffering was for the weak. As righteousness took over, he realized that the end was far from coming. Instead, he viewed this as a new beginning.
    The Tinman wasn't going anywhere.

Chapter 6

15 years ago.
     Curtis Rains traveled slowly as he returned to his hometown for a weekend visit with his family. He hadn't seen his parents in over ten years. Yet, as he passed through the only traffic light that could be found within the small town's city limits, he was quite certain his parents hadn't changed much. However, that was the way the people and the cozy little town of Whigham, Georgia were. Nothing ever changed. Small town values had remained in tact over the years, and Southern hospitality could be found behind every unlocked door. It was a place where everyone knew everyone. Crime was almost non-existent, and no matter whom you passed driving down the long stretches of blacktop, a friendly wave would appear from a passerby.
     However, as Curtis pulled off the gravel and onto his parent's dirt driveway, he knew he had made a mistake in coming. Curtis had never experienced or established a bond with his parents throughout his childhood. He had grown even more distant from them as a grown man. The truth was, they weren't considered to be a part of his life.
     He recalled his youth, going back to when he was a mere eight years old, and remembered all the trouble he used to get into. However, most of the trouble had seemed to stem from his parents' imaginations. He remembered the joyous smiles that spread along their faces as they punished him, almost as if multiple orgasms were being achieved at the same time. In fact, the more he reviewed his past, the more certain he became that his unloving parents never wanted him.

He had always been in their way, and never did anything right. Curtis had always felt more like a burden than a son, and to this day, he could still remember the icy cold stare his mother had given him one day long ago. The callous gaze had petrified Curtis as a young child. However, it wasn't until she finally spoke that Curtis's life began to change forever. The hateful words that poured from her mouth that day had ripped away at his youthful heart, and damaged his soul forever. He remembered running away from his mother, wishing he had never been born as numerous tears fell uncontrollably from his eyes. He recalled the day as if it had just happened yesterday, and he remembered he had just came home for supper. Sadly, however, he had been late.

"Why in the hell are you late this time boy?" Curtis recalled his mother speaking to him. It wasn't until he didn't respond that she continued. "What's the matter? Cat got your tongue?" Again, when there was no reply, she continued. Only, her voice had taken on a boldness he hadn't heard before. "Answer me when I talk to you!" she demanded as she grabbed his tiny little neck and forced him to look into her eyes.

"Mom stop," Curtis pleaded. "Please. You're hurting me."

"I'll do what I damn well please you ungrateful little bastard," his mother shot back harshly. "And just wait till your father gets home, he'll teach you a lesson or two."

"But I didn't do anything."

"Oh yes you did!" She declared looking deep into her son's eyes. "You were born, and ever since you came into our lives, you have brought on nothing but trouble. It seems as though you take pleasure in making my life miserable, and now it's simply my time to return the favor. You aren't good for anything. In fact, I regret ever bringing you into this world."

His mother's words had torn away every precious feeling he had accumulated as a young boy, and he didn't know how to respond to such a flagrant display of hateful words. However, what had eaten at his insides the most was the fact that his mother was speaking the truth.

She didn't love him.

Tinman

Then, Curtis remembered turning to hide the sobbing he had known was near. Seconds later, he had ran out the back door and yelled at his mother. "I hate you! I hate you!"

Now, however, was a different story.

He wasn't as naïve, or as stubborn as he had been as a child. He was a grown man now, and he expected to be treated as such. Curtis had somewhat raised himself throughout the years. He couldn't count or depend on his parents for anything. In fact, the only things he could ever remember his parents providing him with, were fierce beatings. Thus, he had turned to prayer. Every night, he would curl up in a tiny ball underneath his covers. Every night, Curtis would pray to God, begging for no beatings to come.

Unfortunately, most of the time, his prayers were never answered.

Then, as Curtis stormed out of his state of reverie, he turned off the ignition and stepped out of his car. Once his two feet were on the ground, he stared at the house that had caused so much pain throughout his life. It was a doublewide trailer, and the roof was in dire need of repair. The exterior of the home, which was once a rather sheik white color, was stained dirty brown. Except for a few patches here and there, the grass had long since died away and nothing but reddish dirt remained. Curtis didn't see any flowers outlining the mobile home and knew his parents didn't care about its appearance.

He hated this house, and the people he knew were inside. He blamed the house and his parents for paralyzing his soul. As if a wicked spell had been cast down upon him from inside the haunting walls of the home, Curtis would never experience the magical, sensational feeling of love. He simply didn't know how to love anyone or anything.

Hate, however, was a trait he had become affiliated with, and he had learned it well.

He rejected his parents for tormenting him as a child. He hated the blue skies and the beautiful stars that would come out at night. He loathed the tall pine trees that surrounded him on a daily basis. He detested, and despised everything life had to offer. What concerned him the most, however, was the fact that there didn't appear to be an escape from the hatred that consumed his body.

Or was there?

There had to be a way to escape the misery surrounding his world.

Then, it hit him. It was time for him to strike back. It was time to take a stand and prove to the world that Curtis Rains was somebody.

Revenge had finally called out to him, beckoning him to retaliate. He wanted to retaliate for all the heartache and suffering he had been through. It was time for someone else to feel his agony. It was time for someone else to pray to God for help, only to learn what it felt like to have his or her prayers unanswered. Finally, retribution was at hand, and he knew his vengeance would be fierce.

Curtis changed as he began walking towards his parent's house that day. It was at this moment that he first managed, or found a reason to smile. It was at this moment that he realized his destiny. It was at this moment, that he became the Tinman.

BANG!

Suddenly, Curtis found himself wide-awake, lying peacefully on the cot inside his cell. Looking up, he saw the familiar face of the prison guard, Jack Reynolds. He looked at the nightstick grasped firmly within the palm of the guard's hand and suddenly became aware of the sound that had awakened him from his dreamy state. Jack had slammed it into the bars of his cell, purposely trying to wake him up, and now smiled at the fact that he had been able to triumph over the legendary Tinman.

"Wake up Rains," Jack ordered, causally tapping the bars once again as if he was playing some sort of musical instrument. "I didn't think a day would come when I would have to tell you this. But," he paused. "You have a visitor."

Not expecting to hear such a thing, Curtis tilted his head a bit and looked into the guard's eyes. He was profoundly convinced that he would be able to detect any honesty that could be found inside Jack's soul. Surprisingly, he realized the guard had spoken the truth. Someone was actually there to see him.

But who could it be?

And why?

"Come on," Jack hurriedly continued as he motioned for Curtis to turn around and allow himself to be shackled from head to toe. "I

Tinman

haven't got all day, and you," he laughed aloud. "You only have a few hours left before it's all over," Jack concluded frankly as he clamped the cuffs harshly around the inmate's wrists that were bound behind his back. He then grew a bit agitated, as Curtis seemed to completely ignore the pain the cuffs induced as they twisted their way into his flesh. Nevertheless, after going through the motions one more time around the ankles of the Tinman, Jack began leading him down the corridor.

"And you still have a life time my friend," Curtis decided to offer as he listened to his cell slamming shut behind him. "A life time to experience all the pain and suffering the world has to offer."

"The only suffering I'm interested in experiencing is watching your sorry ass fry to death in the electric chair. You just don't know how many nightmares will finally come to an end after tonight," Jack replied coldly, not afraid to show he felt absolutely no remorse for the man who's life would be ending in less than 24 hours.

Then, the two of them fell silent, and Curtis willingly let himself be pushed down the corridor. His mind was on an inexplicable escapade as he wondered who had come to visit him? His first thought was of his attorney and his mind joggled the notion that perhaps a last minute appeal was in motion just hours before his execution. Quickly, however, he dismissed the notion, as he knew he hadn't asked for an appeal. Nor did he want one.

Nevertheless, someone was definitely there to see him, and he knew that whoever it was, would have to be brave at heart.

After all, he was the man that everyone feared.

* * *

As Billy woke up the following morning, he let his eyes adjust to the blinding sunlight that penetrated through the blinds of his bedroom window. He cursed himself for not remembering to close them the night before. Today was definitely one of those days where he candidly wanted to stay comfortably wrapped under his soft covers for a good portion of the day, ingenuously thinking of no reason to get up. However, as an overpowering yawn escaped from inside his body, he knew that there was absolutely no chance for him to return to his peaceful slumber. Realizing he was just going to have to make the best of the tiresome day ahead of him, he groaned as he threw the covers off his relaxed physique.

Then, feebly, he crawled out of bed and stretched the tension out of his aggravated muscles. Seconds later, he opened his bedroom door and peered out into the hallway as a familiar smell appeared to stem from the kitchen. Instantly, the aroma of sizzling bacon overwhelmed him, and he couldn't help but smile as he realized his mother had once again gotten up to make the two of them breakfast. However, before he stepped out of his room, he promised himself that he wouldn't get wrapped up in the horrifying events that had found him the night before. He didn't want anything to interfere with his well being on this particular day.

"Mom," he called instinctively to make sure she was there as he sleepily made his way down the stairs. Then, as he passed the computer desk in the living room, he saw something that not only captured his full attention, but also stopped him dead in his tracks.

It was a picture of his father, Tom Saxton. It infuriated him to even look at it.

As anger began to weld up inside his frigid body, he grabbed the picture with one hand and slammed it face down on the desk. He refused to look into the man's eyes and gladly appreciated the fact that he was no longer apart of his life. Then, listening to the soothing sound of his loving mother's voice, he proceeded across the living room towards the kitchen, not giving the picture of his father a second thought.

"I'm in the kitchen honey," Debra declared somewhat cheerfully. "Did you have a good night last night? Sorry, I got home so late. But something happened and I-" she let her voice trail off into silence, and forced herself to look away from her son's worried expression.

"Mom!" Billy exclaimed confusingly. "What is it?"

"Honey, please sit down," Debra continued realizing now was as good a time as any to break the news to her son. "There's something I need to tell you, and there's something I think we need to talk about."

"Good," Billy replied as he turned on the small portable black and white television, which had been placed on the kitchen table for reasons he had not yet learned. Then, seeing the news channel light up, he turned to face his mother giving her his full attention. "Well, there's something I think I should tell you as well. But by all means, you go first," he concluded as he wondered what his mother needed to discuss with him, and debated whether or not he should let her in on what he had found inside their home and what he had seen shortly afterwards. The whole thing didn't even make sense to him, and knew it would be impressively difficult to understand. The last thing he wanted to do was get criticized by his mother if she didn't believe him, or have her think that he was losing his mind. However, he knew what he had seen the previous night, and felt quite strongly that it was best to get it out in the open instead of keeping it locked inside.

"All right," Debra proceeded, once again picking up the conversation where her son had left off. "But prepare yourself to hear something that you probably don't want to hear. And I'll do my best to try and explain everything. I don't know the whole story yet, but believe me; I'm going to find out as soon as possible.

Billy nodded as he began to realize his mother had stumbled onto something rather important. "I'm listening."

"Well-" Debra tried to continue.

However, before she could even muster another sentence, something appeared on the small television that caught the two of them off guard. The two of them became completely transfixed on the tube as the news once again began with a story concerning the egregious Curtis Rains. As the newscaster first began speaking in the common intellectual tone, the name of Curtis Rains, nor the name Tinman, meant anything to Billy. Debra, on the other hand, sat completely dumbfounded as she recalled the conversation with Elizabeth Anne. Suddenly, she found her heart speeding up, and she began looking around the room to see if the evil man was anywhere to be found around them. Billy, still utterly involved in the news program, didn't even notice his mother's panicky nature. In fact, it wasn't until a picture of Curtis Rains was displayed on the tube that Billy grew uneasy. The eyes of the man on the screen triggered something inside of him.

At that moment, he knew.

Billy knew that Curtis Rains had been the mysterious, evil man he had seen in his nightmare the previous evening. Without warning, every muscle in his body grew tense as the gripping sensation of fear took control. Billy just sat there in amazement, not believing the message his eyes were sending. Many questions began to form inside his head as he ostensibly ignored his promise to forget all about what had happened the night before. Now, however, that apparently wasn't going to happen.

He struggled to fight off the terrifying images of the Haas family as they desperately tried to reenter his mind. Quickly, he shut off the television and faced his ashen mother. "Mom!' Billy exclaimed breathing a little harder than he needed to be. "Mom," he continued trying to get her undivided attention. Then, as he paused for a moment, he noticed the fear in her eyes as well.

Had she known all along?

Never minding that question for the moment, he tried once more to talk to his mother. This time, however, he snapped his fingers beforehand. Surprisingly, Billy watched as his mother's eyes shuffled a little before making their way back to reality. "Mom!" he exclaimed once again. "That man," he continued pointing towards the television screen. "Curtis Rains. He was the man I saw in my dream last night," then he paused, realizing Debra wasn't going to understand what he was talking about. "Well. He has been here before."

Then, not allowing his mother any time to respond, he suddenly darted from the kitchen and headed for his bedroom to retrieve the puzzling box he had found hidden within the darkness of the enigmatic cellar.

* * *

Jamie Walker sat nervously in the colorless visitors room of the Florida State Penitentiary. There were two chairs behind a mahogany table, which had selectively been placed next to the only window inside the small, gloomy room. As time appeared to standstill, she waited patiently for her ex-lover to be brought into the room. She glanced out the window that overlooked the prison's courtyard and was shocked to find that of the hundreds of inmates that could be seen, a handful of them had already noticed her presence. Jamie began to feel uncomfortable as the stares of the inmates bore into her soul. She couldn't help but to turn away, forgetting that she was four stories above the men below her, and locked safely behind a heavily guarded door.

Nonetheless, the prison made her feel utterly powerless, and her head jerked upwards every time she heard one of the heavy doors from within the prison slam shut. She listened to the constant buzzing sound of what she guessed were guards letting certified employees into different sectors of the prison. Every time she heard one of theses jolting noises, however, she had expected to see Curtis standing in the doorway. She was expecting to see his cunning eyes looking down at her, and even though she wasn't expecting him to say anything, she knew she would be able to tell what was on his mind.

Jamie brushed her fingers through her hair as she tried to find an activity to put her nerves at ease. Everything she tried seemed to work for a few split seconds, when suddenly the nervousness would replenish. Only each time it returned, she found the butterflies in her stomach growing more robust than before. Jamie found this hard to believe as she had always thought of herself as being a rather stalwart person.

However, this was different.

After years of ignoring his existence, she had come to visit the serial killer known as the Tinman without asking his permission. Not once had she phoned or wrote to him to let him know that she had been thinking of coming down from Alabama. Therefore, she didn't know how Curtis was going to react to her impromptu stopover. After all, he had never asked her to come and see him. But if not her, then who would?

She knew the answer. No one.

If it weren't for her, Curtis Rains would be denied the chance to speak to a familiar face one last time and would ultimately die alone. She was offering him a chance to repent and ask for forgiveness for his sins. She was offering him a chance to say goodbye to someone he had once been close to. Truthfully, however, Jamie felt that she owed Curtis at least one visit and knew that her conscious would have troubled her for the rest of her life if she had not tried to visit him before his execution. Hell, it was offensive enough that she had waited until the last minute to come and see him.

But at least she came.

Now, she couldn't say that she didn't try.

Then, as she heard action coming from outside the door to the room, Jamie jerked her head upwards and gazed at the huge metal door in front of her. Slowly, the door opened, and after what seemed like an eternity, a couple of guards strolled casually into the room. Then, as the guards stepped aside, Curtis Rains appeared in the doorway, and was led into the room. He was completely immobilized as shackles dangled from his wrists and ankles and it became obvious that the guards weren't willing to take any chances with the Tinman. There was no margin for error, and no chance of escape.

Nevertheless, as Curtis came walking into the room, his head hung low. He didn't even bother to look up and see who had actually taken the time to come and visit him before his body was discarded from the rest of society. The shackles made it hard for Curtis to walk under his own strength, and he stood there dressed in a light gray prison issued uniform, his figure was just as Jamie remembered. She observed the smooth cheeks of the man she hadn't spoken to or seen in ten years, and could tell that he made it a point to shave on a regular basis.

Then, from out of nowhere, and catching her completely by surprise, one of the guards turned and spoke directly to her. "All right miss," he stated sarcastically, his expression easily showing that he didn't understand why she had come to visit the man everyone despised. "He's all yours for a little while. We'll be right outside the door here listening to everything the two of you talk about. If he decides to give you any shit, just scream and we'll be in here so fast neither of you will have time to blink. I'll rush right in here and the party will be over. Understand?" he asked the both of them. Then, turning to Curtis, he asked again. "You got that Rains?" he whispered. "Don't make me come in here and beat the living shit out of your sorry ass. You know I'll do it too. We could call it a special goodbye present from me." Then, laughing to himself, he turned once again and faced Jamie. "Good luck in getting this man to talk miss. He's hardly said a thing since he's been here."

Nodding her head, she waited until the guards had left the room before she decided to speak. However, before any words could come flowing from her usually talkative mouth, she stopped herself and continued to gaze at the figure of the man before her. Curtis had still not lifted his head to acknowledge her presence and Jamie got the impression that he didn't care that she was there. In some eerie, unnatural kind of way, she thought that perhaps he was unconscious, or sedated. Yet, the silence frightened her. Then, it was at that moment that it hit her.

She was alone with Curtis Rains.

Jamie knew he wasn't the same man she had been in love with ten years ago and was aware that the structured living environment he had been locked down in for the past few years had changed him immensely. Consequentially, however, she realized that Curtis Rains had never been the man she had once thought him to be. He had fooled her, just like he had fooled everyone else that had opened their hearts and given their trust in welcoming his desirable charm, only to feed off of his filthy lies. For the first time in her life, she realized that Curtis had never really changed. He had always been different from everyone else.

Curtis Rains had always been diseased.

Then, although never looking up to see the person sitting in front of him, Curtis spoke. His voice seemed rather dreary, and its deep content bounced uncontrollably off the naked walls. It was one word.

"Jamie."

Shell-shocked, Jamie didn't know how to reply. She fought down the lump that had risen in her throat, and when she spoke, she tried to sound as unafraid as possible "Y-Yes," she struggled to begin. "It's me Curtis. It's Jamie. How did you know?" she asked, as she felt herself relax a bit.

"Well, who else would even think about coming to see someone like me?" Curtis answered smartly. His non-sympathetic tone showing her that he wasn't looking for, nor would he receive any sympathy whatsoever. "Plus," he paused finally looking up. "I can smell your perfume. Hard to believe you still wear the same brand after all these years Jamie. And I bet you thought I would have forgotten by now?"

Amazed, Jamie found herself smiling as she realized she actually was wearing the same perfume. Then, as Curtis struggled to sit in the only other vacant seat across from her, she couldn't help but to gaze into his eyes. Anyone else would have turned immediately away and ran for safety. But with Jamie, it was different.

She wasn't afraid.

For some reason, she felt that Curtis wouldn't hurt her.

"So," she continued calmly. "How have you been Curtis?"

"Is that the best you can do?" he answered her question with one of his own and laughed at her attempt at breaking the ice. "How in the hell do you think I've been?" Curtis asked calmly, his tone still a bit icy. "For ten years I've been following the same daily routine. I've eaten, showered, slept, and jerked off at the same time everyday for the past ten years. But overall, I think I've been doing pretty damn good." Pausing briefly, he continued. "How about you pumpkin?"

"Never better," Jamie truthfully answered as chill bumps sprouted along her smooth arms after the word "pumpkin" slivered out of Curtis's mouth. It just didn't feel right to be called anything sweet by the man whom had put her through so much agonizing pain and emotional distress.

"And why are you here?" Curtis demanded, rather than asked. Then, as he watched the hesitance in her attempt to reply, he quickly spoke again. "And don't lie to me Jamie. You know I can tell when you lie to me. So?" he asked, finally deciding to give her enough time to answer.

"I don't know," Jamie hated to admit. "It was just something I felt I had to do. But if you don't want me here, I'll gladly leave," she boldly added trying to convince the man in front of her that she wasn't afraid of him and that she wasn't going to be pushed around. "And don't start complaining about your living conditions. You brought that on yourself Curtis, when you hurt all of those innocent people. And you hurt me you son of a bitch," she mistakenly added on a personal note as a tear welled inside her eye.

"I know I hurt you," Curtis replied showing no emotion. "And for that, I am sorry. It was never my intention to hurt you Jamie. You were the only person who ever really cared about me. But not to worry," he paused. "After tonight, I will be gone forever, making everyone's life easier and undoubtedly making everyone in this country happier. Myself included."

"Are you saying you want to die?" Jamie asked drying her eyes.

"Die?" Curtis questioned inquisitively. "I'm not going to die," he continued as his evil laugh filtered the room. For the first time, Jamie noticed just how evil his laugh sounded, and how carefree his conscience truly was. There was no remorse stemming from the man in front of her, and Jamie knew that there never would be.

Not believing her ears, she gleamed into his eyes. "Curtis, I have to ask you something," she paused, hoping it would come out the right way. "If you didn't get caught in Destin, Florida. Would you have continued to hurt people?"

After a brief hesitation, Curtis nodded coldly.

"Did you really like doing all of those violent things to those people? Including your parents?"

Again, Curtis nodded.

Finally, she realized that the man before her was not worth her time and effort. She should have never left her loving home in Birmingham, Alabama, where she had a decent man in Travis McKinley waiting for her, and who loved her very much. She now agreed that Curtis Rains deserved to die a horrible death. All of the sorrow, and pity she felt for him simply disappeared. Jamie wanted him to experience the same kind of pain, and endure the same kind of suffering he had forced his victims to savor. She wanted him to cry out in agonizing pain when the electric chair sprang to life. Climbing to her feet, she headed for the door, not even bothering to say goodbye.

"Where in the hell do you think you're going?" Curtis asked coming to his feet. Once he realized she wasn't going to answer, he continued. "I asked you where you were going?" Jamie said nothing, and Curtis began to realize that she didn't care about him anymore. She was leaving him. The only person he had ever felt close to was walking out on him.

"I'm getting the hell out of here and away from you," Jamie declared. "I'm sorry I even bothered to come here and I'm sorry we ever met."

Jamie's heartbreaking words seemed to slice through Curtis's already battered soul, just as his mother's words had many years ago. Jamie had been the only person he had ever cared for, and whom he thought cared for him. Now, however, it looked as though his supposition had been wrong. Then, suddenly, a vision of his parents came flooding back to him, and he knew what he had to do.

At that moment, just as though she were one of his victims, Curtis began to feel anger towards her. He wanted to lash out at her and rip away at her flesh. He wanted to hear her scream in pain as he began the process of ending her joyous life. Then, a familiar rage loomed over him as he began trying to free his hands from the cuffs.

Impossible.

Then, just as Jamie was about to reach the door, he jumped in her way. As the unspeakable evil sprang to life inside the Tinman, he managed to ram her into the wall, even though the steel shackles deprived him the luxury of using his arms and legs.

Jamie screamed as her head slammed into the concrete wall, and she could feel the blood ooze from the wound that had formed in the back of her head. As she grew lightheaded, she collapsed to the floor and was barely able to remain conscious. Just as the guards had instructed, she desperately screamed for the help she knew was right outside the door. Then, opening her eyes, she watched in fear as Curtis continued to try and inflict more pain upon her. She knew that if his hands and feet had been released of the cuffs, she would already be dead.

Then, without warning, the door opened and five guards came storming into the room. Jamie was thankful that they had heard her cry for help and looked upon them as if they were angels of mercy. Then, without hesitation, four of them ruthlessly grabbed Curtis and manhandled him to the floor. Afterwards, the beating commenced and the four guards continuously slammed their clubs over Curtis's pinned body while the other escorted Jamie Walker to safety. As she willingly let herself be led down the corridor, she heard the sound of Curtis's voice screaming in pain as the guards beat him severely. The nerve-racking sounds that trickled down the hallway made it appear as though they had no intention of stopping.

Surprisingly, however, she didn't care.

She wanted him dead.

However, as Curtis lay there and was forced to endure the physical beating he tried to push the excruciating pain aside, even though it throbbed throughout his entire body. As he lay there, he recalled Jamie's hateful words, and anger continued to boil inside. He could tell that his rage was stronger now than ever before and once the tortuous, painstaking beating came to a halt, two powerful thoughts entered his mind as the guards struggled to capture their breaths.

As he lay motionless on the floor, he wanted revenge, and reckoning.

Midnight was vastly approaching, yet Curtis had no intention of being laid to rest.

* * *

Placing the ancient box in front of his mother, Billy pulled back the metal lever and opened it. He pulled out the mysterious doll, and the family picture he had found and handed them to his mother. Billy purposely hadn't allowed himself to gaze into the scrutinizing photograph. He just didn't want the piercingly painful headaches he had encountered the previous night to return for another episode.

"I think this is the family that lived here before us mom," he spoke up with sound excitement. "And I know why no one has lived here for the past ten years," he paused watching his mother as she sat and looked confusingly into the picture, obviously not understanding where he had been able to find such belongings "It's because they were murdered mom. Right here, in this very house. And I know who did it."

"Curtis Rains," Debra quickly answered before her son could finish. "I know. I know all about it Billy. Elizabeth explained everything to me last night and I was going to talk to you about it today. Apparently though," she paused as she looked into her son's eyes. "You were able to figure all of this out on your own." Then, picking up the absolutely enchanting doll, she instinctively turned it over. "Oh my God!' she screamed as the doll fell from her hands, slamming into the linoleum of the kitchen floor. Debra realized it had belonged to the little girl in the picture. Terrified, she looked at her son for answers. "Where exactly did you find all of this stuff?"

"It was hidden behind a wall down in the cellar," Billy answered putting his arms around his mother at an attempt to comfort her. He realized now that he should have at least warned her about what he had found. "I told you something was wrong mom," he continued as he leaned over and picked up the doll. "Oh and by the way, her name is Kat."

"What!" Debra exclaimed not understanding anything, but wanting all the answers. "How in the hell do you know what the doll's name is? Better yet," she paused. "How did you know about Curtis Rains?"

"Well, I dreamed about the Haas family last night," Billy shyly admitted and watched as his mother's eyebrow arch a bit as he once again surprised her in knowing the names of the family members in the picture. "And in my dream, Carey, the little girl in the picture, called this exact same doll Kat. I know it all sounds crazy, but I'm serious mom," Billy paused taking on a convincing tone. "It was like I was reliving what happened to them so many years ago."

"And you saw Curtis Rains in your dream as well?"

Billy nodded. "Yeah, I saw him bust down the very door that now stands in perfect condition on the other side of this house. I woke up right after it happened though. As soon as his eyes became visible, I woke up. It really scared me mother. It was like I had been in the same room when it happened."

Debra found it increasingly difficult to understand everything her son was telling her, and although her realistic nature was telling her that it was impossible, she could see the honesty in Billy's eyes, and knew that he was telling the truth. "I believe you," Debra sympathetically replied. Then, picking up the picture she pointed to the parents. Just out of curiosity she wondered if he knew their names as well. Not realizing what she was doing, she held the picture up and catching Billy off guard, she forced him to glare into the eyes of the Haas family once again.

Almost immediately, the visions returned.

Billy clutched the sides of the kitchen table as he struggled to remain on his feet. He screamed in sheer pain as the vision of the past came flooding back inside his head. He heard the voices of the family and saw the elevated look of fear in their eyes. He pulled his hands away from the table and grabbed both sides of his head as he desperately tried to discard all of the repelling images that had resurfaced. "No!" he screamed before his vision was completely lost.

Then, loosing his balance, he tumbled forward. Billy extended his arms in a desperate attempt to reach out and find anything to break his fall. Unfortunately, his hands found nothing.

As his feet came out from under him, his head slammed awkwardly into the refrigerator, and he could hear the uncomfortable cracking sounds coming from his neck. Within seconds, an overwhelming pain seemed to diminish every ounce of consciousness he had left and he had no choice but to simply lay there, and wait for the surrounding darkness to close in.

Seconds later, Billy lay motionlessly on the cold kitchen floor as blood drained from the laceration on his head and warmed his body.

In an instant, blackness had found Billy Saxton.

Chapter 7

11:15 p.m. at the Florida State Prison facility.
Once again, Curtis found himself standing outside his parent's front door. He knocked three consecutive times before waiting patiently for either his father or mother to appear. After a few seconds, no one came, so Curtis repeated the knocking sequence once again. He slammed his fist into the door three times and as each knock passed, Curtis grew hungrier. The knocks became stronger, more powerful, almost as if he were trying to knock the door down, when suddenly, the door swung open and he found himself staring into the eyes of his father.
"What in the hell are you doing?" the old man in front of him asked. "You trying to break our damn door? The son of a bitch was unlocked. All you had to do was come on inside."
Then, something uncanny happened at that moment.
Curtis didn't respond to his father's intentional penurious outburst. He simply said nothing. He just stood there in the doorway and looked into his father's eyes. Only, for the first time in his obvious arrogantly lived life, he did not feel the fear and unwanted empathy usually brought about by the intermediacy of his parents. Curtis was no longer affected by the coldness found in his father's eyes.
No. He wouldn't stand for it any longer.
It was time for him to show his parents how it felt to become unloved and to feel unwanted. He wanted them to know what they had put him through. He wanted them to know what it felt like to live a life feeling nothing but pity and sorrow for oneself. He wanted them

to feel what it was like to blame oneself for all the world's bewildering downfalls. But now Curtis realized, he wasn't at fault.

His parents were.

Society itself was at fault.

No one had ever come to save the day while his parents tried to cudgel the life out of him. Throughout his childhood, whether the pain came from their own hands, feet, or some foreign object that seemed to rip the skin right off his bruised and battered body, they continuously struck out at him. There had been no escape from the monstrosities he was forced to endure as a child. No one ever came to his rescue when he would scream out in the middle of the night in unbearable pain, begging for help. Then, as the years passed, he remembered asking why?

Why had he been born in hell? What had he ever done to deserve the beatings that continuously collated around the mid-evening, or late evening intervals? Unfortunately, he knew now, that the answer was nothing. He had never done anything wrong, and he had never done anything that would have given his parents the right to treat him like a caged animal. Curtis Rains had been born human, but had been alienated as soon as the sun had risen the following day.

Now, however, Curtis was no longer afraid. He smiled at his father who still stood at the door, holding it open, and watched as his refinished face was suddenly overcome with an expression of confusing uncertainty. George could tell that there was something different about his son, whom had just casually walked passed him, never speaking a word. However, what had really captured his attention was the eye contact that had been made.

Curtis had never been able to look him in the eye before.

George grew scared as he could feel that something was wrong. But there was absolutely nothing he could do. He could only watch in unconditional fear as an evil smirk appeared along his son's face.

Then, as soon as the door closed, Curtis found himself immediately approached by his mother, Gretchen. "Well hello there stranger," her rather deep, crackly voice began as she put out a cigarette, only to light another one right behind it. "What's wrong with you? You think you're too good for your own parents? It's been several years since you've come this way. Shit, as a matter of fact, who knows how long it's been since we've heard a peep from you. No

Jason Glover

phone calls, no cards, nothing. You wouldn't even have come today if we wouldn't have called you I bet."

Again, however, Curtis didn't respond.

He suddenly found himself with the power to tune everything out. He could ignore everything his parent's said to him, almost as if he had never even heard or listened to a word they had said. Then, still silent, and still staging his evil smirk, Curtis brushed passed his mother and entered the kitchen. Speechless, Gretchen turned to face her husband. Surely he had witnessed what she had just seen.

George Rains was an elder man of sixty-five and stood a meager 5'10" in height. A thin layer of gray hair covered his entire body, and a big shiny bald spot could be found at the center of his head, as he was only partially able to cover it up. His face bore many wrinkles, especially under his eyes, and his nose was rather large, perhaps disproportionate from the rest of his facial features. It looked as if he hadn't shaved in days, and from the dirty pair of Wrangler jeans and the sleeveless blue flannel shirt he wore, Curtis could tell that he hadn't bothered to shower in days. He also sported thick bottleneck glasses that seemed to add to his age. In the end, the sickening sight of his father infuriated Curtis. George Rains was nothing more than poor white trash that lived in the isolated foothills of Georgia. He had aged into a weak man, and a man that Curtis himself no longer cared for.

His mother, Gretchen, wasn't in any better shape. Her hair remained dirty brown throughout the years, but just like her husband, her face was outlined by a storming encore of wrinkles. Her voice cracked when she spoke and an annoying cough would always follow due to her years and years of smoking. The sight of his mother was pathetic, and Curtis found himself wondering how the two of them could have survived all these years living in the shambles before him.

"Is something wrong with him?" she asked her husband about her son. "I don't think he heard a word I just said." George could only shrug his shoulders in awe. "Should have known. What would you know anyway?" Then, turning away from her husband, she slowly followed Curtis into the greasy, grimy kitchen, having to grab something every once in a while to retain her elderly balance. "Son," she tried once again to capture his attention. Then, getting a little annoyed she tried once again with more authority. "Curtis!"

Tinman

Nothing. "Damn it! What in the hell has gotten into you? Jesus Christ. You haven't changed a bit since you were a little snot nosed brat have you? Still the same old Curtis huh? You never could show your father and I the proper respect."

"Oh believe me!" Curtis exclaimed emotionally as he turned to face his mother, her eyes showing the shock she received as soon as he had spoken. "I have changed. I am not the same "little shit," you once thought I to be. And respect? You have the nerve to talk to me about showing you respect? Just get the hell out of my face mother," Curtis ordered. "I hate you!" he purely directed at his mother. Then, turning to his father as well, he spoke again. "I hate you both."

With that, he turned and fled from the kitchen, darting past both of his parents as he headed for the front door. He wanted to escape from his past once and for all, wanted his parents gone from his life forever. Then, as he opened the front door, he listened as his father desperately tried to call him back. Refusing to give him the opportunity to finish what he was saying, however, Curtis walked outside and slammed the door behind him as he suddenly found it hard to breathe.

Curtis walked quickly back to his car, and soon after twisting the key in the ignition, his car sprang to life. Placing his hand on the gearshift, he was about to put the car in reverse and speed away from his devilish home leaving his unworthy parents behind, when his breathing suddenly became calm and his head began to clear. Squinting his eyes and gripping the steering wheel so tight his knuckles turned a pale white, he thought about the encounter he had just experienced with his parents. Frowning, he knew that simply walking out on them wouldn't be the end to his problems. The fact that they would still be around was heart-drenching enough to drive him crazy.

No.

There had to be another way to get rid of them for good.

Then, as if a sign had been sent down from heaven above, something in the distance caught his eye. Forcing his vision to travel beyond their normal perimeters, he recognized the object as being one he remembered all too well. It was an ax. It's blade glistened ever so brightly in the sun as it's rays beamed off the stainless steel *sending them in numerous directions through the air. It practically looked alive as it balanced itself along the tall, wide-bodied pine tree.*

Not knowing exactly what he was going to do, he turned off his ignition, stepped from behind the wheel of his car and slowly strolled over to the ax. Once he approached the deadly object, he stared at it for a minute with rage seen easily through his dark, horrifying eyes. Grabbing it by the handle, he lifted it into the air and with one hand, reached out and felt the blade. Seconds afterwards, his finger was bleeding, and as the blood flew freely from the blistering wound, he watched in amazement as his hand was soon covered with the thick, rich, bright red liquid.

Finally, he knew what he must do.

Turning, he began making his way back towards the front door of his parent's home with the splintering ax held tightly within the palm of his hands. As soon as he reached the steps, his face began to take on an awkward look.

Crazed.

Then, not allowing his eyes to blink, he stood at the front door for a moment allowing his breathing to become severely heavier, and allowing the anger to continue to grow inside him. Veins began to sprout up along his sweat-drenched forehead, and as all the bad memories of his childhood began to come back to him all at once, he felt an adrenaline rush he had never experienced before. Finally, as if he was no longer in control of his actions, he knocked on the door three times with the heel of the powerful blade, deciding it was time to finish it once and for all.

KNOCK. KNOCK. KNOCK.

No answer.

KNOCK. KNOCK. KNOCK. He tried again.

This time, within seconds, the lock on the door was unlatched and soon the door opened and he once again found his weak father staring at him. Only, his attention wasn't focused on his son. Rather, it was at the ax that was still wedged tightly in the middle of his hand. Then, as George spoke to his son, he couldn't help but wonder what was going on, all the while never letting his eyes drift away from the mind-twisting object in his son's hands.

"Curtis?" he asked, his voice showing a significant amount of fear. "What in God's name are you doing?"

Curtis didn't respond.

"Please son," George pleaded, feeling his knees growing weaker. "What is going on here? Why do you have that ax in your hand?" he continued finding it increasingly more difficult to remain upright.

Again, there was no answer.

Then, as if Curtis had somehow transformed into a monster that crawled directly from the flaming pits of hell, he forced his father to look deep into his bloodthirsty eyes. Instantly, George knew what was happening. The netherworld of Hades had finally brought on the perdition that until now had been sleeping peacefully within the once terrified soul of his son. Only now, it had been brought out in the open, and unfortunately there was no turning back. The evil that grew inside the raging Curtis Rains could no longer be concealed and George knew that he was going to be the first to experience the terrifying wrath that had been waiting on him for years. Now, it was finally time for him to succumb to all of the wrong doings he had performed in the past, and as he slowly backed away from the door, he knew that he was staring death in the eye.

Then, as he slowly crept away from his son, George tripped over a nick in the grimy carpet and fell wildly onto the bright green sofa found against the living room wall. The sofa seemed to suction his buttocks to the cushions as his son entered his home, and after Curtis witnessed his old man's tumble, a ferocious smile spread across his face. George could feel the evil surrounding him, and as he realized that there was nowhere to go, he began praying to the one man he had taken for granted his entire life.

Shivering in pain, George Rains prayed to God.

"What's wrong DAD?" Curtis asked harshly, purposely trying to scare the life out of his elder father. "You're not scared are you? Impossible! Big bad George Rains scared of the son he used to love to torture and beat up on," he added as his temper began to flare. Then, vigorously, he grabbed his father by the throat, pulled him to his feet, and threw him into the nearest wall.

"Oh God please!" George pleaded as he managed to speak before he tumbled to the floor. The impact his body sustained as it slammed into the wall was too much for his jagged body to withstand, and as the bookshelf started to collapse on top of him, he had just enough time to raise his hands to his face as items began to fall heavily on top of his head. "Gretchen!" he screamed in obvious pain. Never before had George called on his wife for help, and although he sensed that his chances for survival were slim, he knew that Gretchen might be his only hope.

    Gretchen had been lying down in the bedroom, completely clueless as to the commotion going on in the other room until she heard a loud crashing sound, followed by her husband's cry for help. Angrily, she picked herself up and made her way into the living room all the while scolding her husband for bothering her. Then, as she rounded the corner, she saw George lying helplessly on the ground and her son standing over him with a smile stretched across his face. "What in the hell is going on in here?" she demanded as she helped George to his feet. Then, as she faced her son, she looked deep into his eyes as she tried to gain control of the situation through her evil stare. As her mouth opened, however, she hadn't even noticed the ax her son still had grasped firmly in the palm of his left hand. "I thought you were leaving?" she asked harshly, still completely oblivious to the anger and rage that had built up inside her son. "What made you decide to come back? I sure as hell wasn't going to stop you. Ya know," she paused. "I thought you would have gotten this hint a long time ago. You aren't wanted, nor are you welcome around here. So, why don't you just leave," she ordered, rather than asked.

    With one swift motion, Curtis closed his mother's mouth. His fist swung wildly as it connected to the bottom portion of Gretchen's jaw and Curtis watched in awe as the powerful blow sent his mother sailing to the floor. Then, Curtis walked on top of his mother, and once he reached her face, he placed the heal of his boot neatly between her throat and the bottom of her chin. He pressed down hard, making it impossible for her to breathe and laughed as her arms swung uncontrollably, pounding into the side of his leg as she desperately tried to soak in some air.

    Then, looking around the disgusting kitchen, Curtis began speaking to his mother as he recalled all of the times she forced him to clean the kitchen spotless, although he had never seemed to perform a good enough job. "Mom!" he hollered devilishly. "Why don't you get your sorry ass in that kitchen and clean it up? Huh?' he questioned harshly. "What's the matter, you can't speak? Answer

Tinman

me when I talk to you!" Curtis demanded. "Wait until your father gets home. He'll teach you a lesson yet."

Then, as his attention suddenly switched back to his father, he took his foot off of Gretchen's throat and listened closely, pleased as he heard her gag furiously as she struggled to get oxygen. Meanwhile, George had been watching his son manhandle his wife, and knew that there was absolutely nothing that he could do to protect her. Completely speechless, he could only wait to see what his son was going to do next.

"How many times did you beat me?" Curtis asked his father, demanding an answer. "How many times did you strike me for no other reason than because that bitch laying on the ground told you to. Huh?"

"Curtis," George pleaded. "I-I know w-we were hard on you. But," he paused. "But believe me, it was for your own good. All of it."

"No!" Curtis screamed, raising the ax high in the air. "You're lying."

Screaming, George closed his eyes as he saw the bulk end on the ax coming towards him. With all his might, Curtis flung the ax towards his father. He heard the powerful thud as it connected with the old man's shoulder and as the light weighted body of his father flew to the floor, he could tell by the disfigurement that his shoulder had been dislocated, and his arm severely broken.

"After what you two put me through you don't even have the guts to admit that you were wrong in doing what you did to me," Curtis continued walking towards his father once again. "All the other children around here grew up in perfect little families, none of them having to deal with what I went through. None of their lives ruined at such a young age. I was scared to go home. But ya know what," he paused raising the ax once again. "I'm not scared anymore."

George watched helplessly as his son turned the ax to where the blade was now facing him. Then, closing his eyes, he prayed silently to God one last time, as he knew the end was near.

Then, with one hard swoop, it was over.

Blood splattered inadvertently all over the furniture, the walls, and Curtis himself as the great impact ended George's life in a matter of seconds. As mounds of blood began to flow along the floor, Curtis *pulled the ax from his father's splintered, shattered cranium. Then, he faced his mother once again, whom was screaming in absolute fear as she witnessed the gruesome death of her husband.*

"What is it mother?" Curtis asked soothingly. "You're not sad that he's dead are you?"

"Please!" she pleaded as Curtis forced her to her feet and threw her up against the kitchen counter as numerous amounts of plates and glasses were knocked to the floor bursting upon impact. "I'm sorry for everything."

Curtis only shook his head. "I really wish I could believe that." Then, surprisingly, he dropped the blood-drenched ax to the floor, only to grab his mother by the neck with his bare hands. "Unfortunately," he paused. "I don't."

As the strangulation began, Gretchen fought with all her strength and will power to overcome the rage within her son. To this day she never imagined something like this would come back to haunt her. But it was happening. She had already lost her husband, and she knew that she was next. She was powerless against her son's overwhelming strength, and she could tell by the look in his eyes that there was nothing she could do to make him stop and spare her life.

She was going to die.

The only question was how much suffering was her son going to force her to endure?

Then, with one hand still around Gretchen's neck, Curtis reached into the sink and after a brief moment of fondling different silverware, he finally pulled out a knife. Holding it underneath her eyes, he let her see what was about to happen. "MMMMMMMMMMM!" is all he could hear his mother screaming as his hand hovered over her mouth. His grip was so tight she could feel her teeth gnawing away at the slippery flesh from the inside of her cheek, and she could taste the small droplets of blood as they filtered from the painful sores.

Then, with the knife in hand, he ripped off her blouse, and held the sharp, cold blade under her breasts. As if playing with her, he began moving the tip of the knife over her bare upper body, feeling the shiver as the benumbed blade hit her in different spots. Curtis held her head in a position that forced her to make eye contact with him the entire time, and as she watched all of the color drain from Curtis's dark, evil eyes, she knew what was about to happen.

Then, as Curtis's wicked grin turned into a horrendous smile, Gretchen watched in utter fear as his eyes seemed to penetrate right through her soul. A single tear fell from her eyes and ran down her cheek as she realized that he was about to strike. Seconds later, like a flash of lightning piercing its way through a blackened night sky, she yelped in pain as she felt the blade penetrate into her flesh, eating its way into her insides. Grunting, Curtis gave the knife one forceful upwards thrust and he watched in excitement as blood spilled from his mother's mouth, and he could feel the warmth of the thick fluid as it bled from the wound onto his own skin.

Finally, he pulled the knife from the wound, and stepped away from his mother. She fell immediately to the floor, choking violently on her own blood. Gretchen would have taken her last breath just a few short moments from that point, but to Curtis it hadn't been enough.

As he mounted his mother, he raised the knife high in the air, and then repeatedly slammed it down into her flesh, each time forming a new wound. After a while, her screaming died away, but Curtis couldn't stop. His anger, his rage was too strong. The only thing he was able to think about was slicing up his parents until there was nothing left for him to manipulate. In the end, he didn't relax from penetrating the blistering blade into Gretchen's blood-laced skin until his arm had grown tired.

Climbing back to his feet, he wiped the blood free of his hands and face, and then looked over the small portions of the house where the two lifeless bodies of his parents laid. Smiling, he considered the gory scene to be a masterpiece of some sort. He had created a work of art.

And their blood?

He had never tasted anything so sweet.

The floor of the small home was completely covered with pools of bright red blood. However, he felt no remorse, and regretted nothing. In fact, he wished he had grown the nerve that allowed him to destroy his parents sooner. Better late than never, he thought to himself as he waited until the sun went down to discard of their motionless bodies.

At nightfall, he carried their corpses into the welcoming woods that surrounded their home. Curtis knew the woods well as he remembered this was where he used to run as a boy whenever he felt *afraid. The woods had always been a safe haven to Curtis Rains, and now, they would prove to be the final resting place of his parents.*

Then, with an ax and shovel in hand, he tore them apart piece by piece, burying every part of their bodies in different sections of the forest. Finally, when everything had been taken care of, not a single trace of his parent's left behind, he casually strolled out of the woods, changed clothes, and casually climbed back behind the wheel of his car.

Cranking the engine, he backed out of the driveway, and left the livid scene of his parent's home behind, still joyous about everything that had transpired earlier that night. Finally, after all of these years his fear had subsided, and his true being had finally been able to seek out revenge, completely satisfied that no one would be able to find their unrecognizable bodies for months or years to come. Leaving his parents house that night, Curtis Rains became a different person.

He had become, the Tinman.

"Rains!" the voice kept calling out to him, over and over again. "Damn it! Don't make me come in there and repeat the lesson you received earlier. Haven't you had enough beatings for one day?" Suddenly, Curtis found himself lying wide-awake inside his tiny cell. As he looked wearily into the guard's eyes, he knew it had been the guard that had woke him up from the extraordinary dream of his parents' death. Then, placing his index fingers on the sides of his head, he tried to force the headache out that was supposed to have been taken care of by the pain killers provided to him by the pharmacist inside the prison, whom had so carefully examined him after the beating had been ceased hours ago. Blood coils, lumps, and scabs still remained all over his body.

"What is it?" Curtis asked, his voice showing an awkward state of weakness. "Is it time?" he asked, wondering if it was finally time for him to face death like a man, look it in the eye just as he had forced his victims to.

"No," the guard answered. "Not yet. You still have just over thirty minutes. The warden sent me down here to see if you wanted anything. You can have whatever you want you know?" Curtis only shook his head. "And a priest is hear to see you if you want," the guard continued expecting to receive the same response as before. Sure enough, Curtis forcefully refused. "I told the father that you would say that, so he asked me to send you a message."

"I don't want to hear a damn thing some stupid ass prison chaplain has to say," Curtis angrily protested. "Why can't you people just leave me alone?" he asked, his tone returning to its normal state.

"Fine," the surprisingly pleasant, likable guard continued as he turned to walk away from the cell. "But if you need anything Curtis, just give me a holler, I'll be right down the hall."

Curtis agreed.

Then, turning back around, the guard spoke one last time.

"It's never too late to ask for forgiveness Rains," he spoke aloud. "It's never too late to be saved. Not even for you."

* * *

Jamie Walker blared the radio as she sped her way down the interstate, cursing herself over and over again for coming down to Starke, Florida to see the notorious Curtis Rains. At one time he was a man she had once opened her heart to and loved with every ounce of calenture that could be found within the warmth of her steady beating heart. Somewhere along the lines, however, she realized he had changed.

Curtis wasn't the same man she used to be so fond of.

He was now a cruel, rude, and violent man, and he shouldn't have been allowed to stay alive the past ten years, even if they had probably been the loneliest years of his illuminating, sick-minded life. She now agreed with everyone else in America, who for years had been waiting to watch the soulless man be strapped into the electric chair, and agreed that he should have been killed the minute he was found guilty on all counts.

The Tinman needed to die.

It was the only way to set the wrong things right, the only way to bring peace to the many families who had been forced to live through the suffering anguish brought upon them by the evil man. Jamie no longer possessed any feelings of sorrow for the man, whom had chosen to travel down the wrong path, whom had lived through a troubled childhood, whom to this day had no excuse for what he had done. Nor, did it appear that he was going to try and find one.

Then, looking at her clock, excitement stood clearly out of her welcoming eyes as she noticed it was now going on 11:45. Smiling, she began to relax as she put her car in cruise control as she continued Northbound on her trip back home to Birmingham, Alabama. Jamie began singing loudly inside her vehicle as she realized that the end to one of the most devastating chapters of her life was drawing to a close.

In fifteen minutes, it would all be over.

* * *

Destin Memorial Hospital.

Debra Saxton sat next to her son, holding his hand firmly as she waited anxiously for him to regain consciousness. She still didn't understand what had made Billy collapse in their kitchen that morning. Debra recalled the two of them looking through the small box Billy had presented to her, saying he had stumbled across it down in the cellar. They had been talking about the unfortunate family whom had lived in their home before them, when all of a sudden, he began screaming in obvious pain and he threw his hands to his head, pressing down hard. It looked as though her son was truly loosing his mind, when his footing jolted loose, causing him to lose control, and sent him flailing into the air. It wasn't until his head roughly slammed into the refrigerator and Billy went plummeting to the kitchen floor that the screaming had subsided.

After a few short seconds of panic, Debra had managed to call 911, and soon help had arrived. She had been told that it was nothing serious, and that her son may have received a minor concussion from the startling blow. Nevertheless, as the hours slowly passed by, and her son remained condemned to a sturdy hospital bed, her mind simply couldn't help but wonder off into an emotional bliss, often seeming a world away, as she prayed continuously for her son to awaken.

"Come on sweetheart," Debra spoke soothingly as she gave her son's hand an affectionate squeeze. "I'm so sorry all of this had to happen. If I had known we would have never moved out here. I swear." Then, as if Billy had actually listened and took in his mother's words, a tear slipped out from under her eye as he unexpectedly returned the squeeze on his mother's hand. "Billy!' she exclaimed in awe standing up, hoping to see his eyes open.

Unfortunately, there was nothing. His eyes remained shut and his expression blank.

"It's all right," she continued, once again finding a seat next to him. "You take all the time you need to recuperate. I promise I'm not going anywhere and I'll be here as soon as you decide to come out of it."

Suddenly, her eyes darted quickly from her son to the hospital room door as it slowly opened. A nurse came pondering into the room and looked over her son's chart, obviously just coming in to check on his vital signs. "Ms. Saxton," the nurse spoke with a smile acknowledging the concerned mother who continued to watch her closely. "How's he been doing since I last came in here?" she asked calmly placing her hand underneath Billy's gown and then turning to survey the monitors that continued to beep continuously at the same rate.

"The same I guess," Debra answered not exactly knowing how to answer. Then, looking into the warmth of the nurse's eyes, she added. "Why hasn't he woken up yet? The doctor said that it was really nothing serious, and that I shouldn't be too concerned about it. He assured me that everything was going to be fine."

"Everything is going to be fine," the nurse assured her once again. "Sometimes head injuries take a little while to heal. Your son has no swelling of the brain, which is a very good sign. He has no internal bleeding. According to his x-rays, everything still seems to be intact, nothing out of order. Matter of fact, he doesn't seem to have any major complications whatsoever. Trust me," she paused walking over to place her hand on Debra's. "Billy is going to be just fine. He's just waiting until his mind tells him it's all right to wake up." Then, removing the comforting hand, she picked up Billy's chart and began heading for the door. "I'll be back in a little while to check on him again. But please, come and get me if he starts to wake up all right?"

Debra nodded. Then, just as the door was about to close, she saw a movement in her son's left leg. Standing up, she looked into her son's eyes. They were still shut, but his eyelids seemed to be pacing back and forth, wildly in disarray. "Nurse! Nurse!" she called exuberantly. "What's going on?"

With a look of uncertainty mounted along her young, smooth face, the nurse reentered the room and made her way over towards her new patient. Looking at the movement inside Billy's eyes, she knew immediately what was happening, and chuckled to herself as she looked up at the paranoid woman beside her.

"Ms. Saxton," she began with an encouraging smile. "There's absolutely nothing wrong with your son. He's perfectly fine."

"Then what's that flickering in his eyes?" Debra asked confusingly.

"He's dreaming," the nurse answered with a smile.

"Dreaming?"

The nurse nodded. "Billy is dreaming peacefully. It's a good sign really. It means his mind is working well. Besides, that's what he needs to be doing right now," she paused once again as she prepared to re-exit the room. "Happily dreaming."

* * *

Curtis looked at himself through the single piece of glass that hung in his bare cell as he viewed his new and improved appearance. His head had just been shaved, along with spots on his chest, and his legs and arm had been depleted of any hair. In fact, he hardly looked like the same person at all, hardly even recognizing himself.

Except, for his eyes.

They still concealed the lust and hunger that had been growing inside him for the past ten years, just waiting for an opportunity to strike again, wanting and craving the familiar odorless liquid of blood. Then, looking away from the bald scene in the mirror he glanced down at his watch. "Almost time," he said to himself, his chest taking on a heavier breathing ordinance. "Almost time to leave this place once and for all," he added speaking of the prison.

Then, he heard a noise coming from behind him. It was a voice. Only, not one he recognized as being among the guards. It was someone else.

Spinning around, a frown quickly shot across his stubborn face as he found himself staring into the eyes of one of God's merciful

Tinman

messengers. It was the chaplain, or priest of the prison, whom for ten years he never once had asked to see, or had a decent conversation with. In fact, the man of God himself had never tried to contact him until now. And why?

Because he was about to die.

Coming over to the bars between himself and the priest, he took on a cold stare, and gazed boldly into the minister's eyes. Courageously, the pastor withstood the inevitable urge to turn away and flee from the crazed man. Instead, being the righteous man he had always been, he tried to talk to Curtis. He tried to reach out to the hurting, lost soul in front of him. Lastly, he tried to welcome Curtis with open arms.

"What is it father?" Curtis demanded harshly, breaking the silence that had fallen over the two of them. "I thought I specifically asked not to see anyone."

"You did," father Jacob's answered calmly. "I just thought I'd stop by on my own to see if you had second thoughts." Then, pausing, he waited for the slightest motion to come from the prisoner. He looked for any signs that might tell him that Curtis truly wanted him to stay. Over the years he had grown accustomed to chatting with inmates right before their death sentence was fulfilled, their death warrants finally tucked away forever, and he had grown accustomed to almost every situation that could entail. Most of them, hadn't asked him to stay and pray, but in their eyes, he could see that they truly wanted him to do so.

Looking into Curtis Rain's eyes, however, he saw nothing.

Just a cold, dark evil that made the hair on the back of his neck stand straight up, and he felt his muscles began to shiver in fear, even though he was safe on the other side of the cell.

"I'm sorry father," Curtis continued. "But you wasted a trip. I don't have anything to say to you. Never have, never will."

"But son, please," the priest pleaded, trying to make his soul at peace with the almighty God above. "Just let me pray with you. Repent for your sins. God will forgive you."

"To hell with God!" Curtis exclaimed angrily. "If there ever really was such a person, why wasn't he there for me when I was a boy? If he had been, I bet you I sure as hell wouldn't be in the mess I'm in now. Can you answer that father?" he continued harshly as spit flew out of his mouth. "Or does he only comfort and love a select few? Maybe I wasn't good enough for him. Screw all of this "God will save you," talk. Ya know why?" he paused catching his breath. "Cause I don't want to be saved."

"But you-" Jacobs tried to persuade the Tinman.

"Enough!" Curtis ordered, silencing the man in front of him. "Listen up father cause this is something you might want to think about every night before you go to bed. You hear me?" Curtis paused and waited for a nod of respect. None came. However, he knew the priest was listening. "Some people might call me a coward for doing some of the violent things I did. But you know what I realized? I am not a coward. I'm one of the most powerful people on the face of the earth. I can reach out to who or whatever I damn well please and scare the life out of them." He paused briefly as his emotions began to boil inhumanly and he aggressively grasped a hold of the metal bars. "Everyone father. And I repeat, everyone has the capability or competency within himself or herself to become a Tinman. Everyone has the ability, the strength, and the mind power to take another human being's life without remorse for their actions. I'm even willing to bet that practically everyone in the world has thought about taking someone's life at one point in time or another. But they are the cowards father," he paused again. "They are the cowards because most people don't have the guts to act upon their precious thoughts and acute instincts."

"No," Father Jacobs tried to speak up, only to find himself cut off once again.

"I do not retreat, and I do not kill the weak!" Curtis continued loudly. "I kill the strong because it makes me stronger. I have the guts to do things to people some can't even imagine. And I don't want forgiveness father cause I'm not sorry for what I have done, or the pain I have caused. The only thing I want, and it's something you can't provide me with, is blood. I want more blood. I want to hear more terrifying screams from the families before I butcher them, slicing their heart alone into a thousand pieces. Now why don't you turn around and go back the way you came. You don't have any business down here with someone like me."

Dropping his head, the father turned and walked away, disappointed in himself that he hadn't been able to reason with Curtis

Rains. He knew that Curtis was going to be denied access to the most talked about land in the cradle of humanity. Heaven. Sadly, there was nothing he could do about it.

Curtis watched as the priest disappeared down the corridor, smiling and pleased with himself at the way he had handled the situation. Then, as soon as the big metal door buzzed loudly, and slammed shut, it opened once more and he listened intensely as numerous footsteps began clamping on the floor, almost sounding like a military team, as it headed towards his cell. Anxiously, he sat on his bed and stared one last time at the blank wall in front of him. Curtis knew they were coming for him.

"Rains!" he heard the familiar voice of Jack Reynolds call out to him as they began to unlock his cell.

Smiling, he looked up at the guard, not a trace of fear lingering inside his eyes.

"It's time."

Chapter 8

The door burst open.

The Haas family, incorporated with fear, stood silently, and said nothing as they clung onto one another for safety. They watched helplessly as the man entered their beloved home unannounced, uninvited, and obviously for unfriendly purposes. David looked down at his loving wife and daughter, and knew that their lives were in jeopardy. With his own conscious stricken in blatant fear, he realized he had to do something. He couldn't just stand there and watch as the stranger before him made his way towards his family. He had to do something.

But what could be done?

He simply wasn't prepared for something of this nature, and never once thought that anything like this would ever happen to his family. Grabbing his wife's shoulder, he spun her around and looked deep into her eyes. "Take Carey and the two of you go upstairs. Now," he ordered. His wife didn't speak, or reply to his instructions. She simply gazed into his eyes, her mind obviously entranced on the fact that death was reaching out to them. "Damn it Charlene!" David continued bravely as he began shaking her, forcing her to snap out of the death-defying phase. "Listen to me. Everything is going to be all right. I won't let anything happen to you or our daughter. But you have to go now. Take our daughter upstairs."

Without saying a word, Charlene grabbed Carey, whose tense body told her that she was terrified. Picking her daughter up, she sprinted up the stairs and disappeared down the hallway and into a bedroom locking the door behind them. Then, as she held her *daughter tightly within the palm of her hands, she forced herself to begin thinking clearly as she desperately tried to figure out a way to get out of this.*

Facing the stranger alone now, David looked the man in the eye and spoke as the man continued to slowly walk towards him, a smile still varnished across his dark, cold face. "Who are you?" he asked strongly, trying to hide the obvious fear he felt inside. "And what do you want with my family?"

There was no answer as the man continued towards him.

"Do you know who I am?" David continued as panic began to seize him. "I'm going to be the next DA of this town and you my friend picked the wrong house to break into. I'll make sure they lock your ass up and throw away the key." The man laughed at David's mute attempt at a bluff, and he realized that the man before him hadn't come there to rob his family. There had to be an ulterior motive for the man's presence and David furiously tried to remember if he had ever ran into the man in front of him before. He hadn't. The man before him was a stranger to David. But for some reason, David could tell that he wasn't a stranger to him. "Do I know you?" he asked, letting his courageous voice slip.

The man shook his head. "No," he answered as he came within ten yards of David Haas. "But you'll never forget me after tonight."

"What!" David exclaimed confusingly. "What are you talking about?"

"You'll always remember me as the man who killed your family," the man continued boldly, his deep cracking voice sending chills throughout the man in front of him. "You and your family live a life without worries, without fear," the man went on harshly. "You have the perfect life, the perfect everything, and I bet until right now you had never given your life a second thought have you?"

David fell silent, not knowing how to answer.

"Well, you are frightened now aren't you?" the man asked as another evil laugh escaped from his orifice, raving throughout what was once a glorious evening in the Haas home.

"Why?" David pleaded as he forced himself to begin backing away from the man in front of him. "Why are you doing this?"

This time, the man in front of him once again fell silent, and the smile faded away. Every step David took backwards, the man doubled forwards, and the distance between the two of them grew closer and closer. The darkness in the man's eyes seemed to disseminate throughout the entire home he had once felt safe and secure in. Then, David watched intensely as the man reached into the black cloak that sheltered the rest of his body.

Suddenly, David Haas's movements came to a halt as a shiny, silver knife appeared from underneath the shawl. Now grasped firmly within the palm of the man's hands, David watched as a smile returned to the man's face as he lifted the knife into the air. The man smiled, as he knew that David realized his life was about to end and there was absolutely nothing he could do to save himself. Pointing the piercing blade in the direction of the man in front of him, it's smooth, beautiful silvery surface allowing David to see his own lifeless expression that had clouded his high-spirited evening. Then, like an owl on the verge of capturing its prey throughout the darkened sky, the man lashed forward, extending the knife towards David's chest.

For a moment, David seemed paralyzed, unable to move or block the knife from penetrating into his silky flesh. Then, realizing his life was in the balance, he mustered enough strength to spin out of the way, just as the blade sliced through his shirt. He felt the blood drip from the flesh wound he had received from the knife, but had managed to escape from the blade that had been meant to sink deep into his torso.

However, the man quickly recovered and spun around once again to face his victim. David, realizing he had the man somewhat caught off guard, knew that this could be his only chance. Grabbing the man by the wrist, not allowing the knife to be brought back up within striking distance, he used his free hand to strike out at the intruder's midsection. Hearing the man gasp for air, David swung again, this time connecting with the man's lower jaw.

Then, with both men screaming in rage, and as cold-blooded fury took control of both their bodies; David picked the man up and began backing him into the wall. Before he had time to regain control, David lost his footing and the two of them tumbled through the sliding glass door and onto the back patio overlooking the moonstruck ocean. Pain was absent from both men as they crashed through the glass *portal, shattering it into thousands of pieces, some of the tiny particles finding their way into their flesh.*

As their strong bodies slammed into the wooden deck, David's fatal mistake came when he allowed the intruder to position himself on top. Now, he was no loner in control of the violent struggle he found himself tangled in. Lifting his fist, the stranger angrily began to pound away on David's countenance. Repeatedly, and with each massive blow, David felt all of his prestige and dignity slipping away, until at last, he was no longer able to even try and guard himself from being flailed upon. He just lay there in silence, absorbing the powerful blows from the man on top of him, his mouth so swollen, he couldn't even scream out in pain as blood drained into his eyes and the burning sensation began to take over.

Finally, the beating stopped.

The man looked down at the man he had been slamming his fist uncontrollably into, and once again, whipped out the knife, holding it high above David's body. Looking at the enlarged areas around the man's eyes, he knew that David probably couldn't even see what was about to happen. Then, as the man began speaking, the face of David Haas seemed to transform into that of his father, whom he had killed so many years ago, and suddenly he found the furious rage inside of him growing once again.

"How dare you fight me!" the man yelled into the night like a coyote howling at the moon. "How dare you strike me!" he continued harshly. "You can't deny the forces of evil when I choose to unleash my horrid sentiments on you," he began preaching like the devil himself. "You can't escape death when I am here. You should learn to accept it and die in peace, instead of with a fight you know you will lose in the end. Well," he paused gripping the knife with both hands. "The end has arrived for you my friend, and now it's time to finish what I came here to do."

Retching out into the night, the man forced the blade downwards. He didn't stop pushing the blade until he felt his own hands surrounded by the warmth of David's blood. Then, stepping back, he watched as the helpless man in front of him begin to try and stop the intense bleeding, as the wound lay open, his insides exposed. David coughed in spasms as he tried mercifully to stop the blood from clotting in his throat, denying him the right to breathe. Each time blood spurted from his mouth, however, more seemed to flow inside, and it seemed as though it wouldn't end until his own blood won the battle in choking him to death.

The man stood there smiling, watching the gory scene, completely satisfied at the way things had manifested. Then, from behind, the shadow of something moving inside the Haas home caught his eye. Spinning around, he watched as the little girl, Carey, he knew her name to be, ran down the stairs and across to the hallway, which led to the basement.

Turning, he left David to die and he made his way towards the little girl.

David, his vision blurry, saw what was about to happen, and with his last burst of adrenaline, and his hand still covering the wound that would eventually lead to his death, he crawled to his feet. Slowly, he made his way towards the intruder.

Slowly, he tried to save his little girl.

Moments earlier.

Charlene, still panicking and wondering how her husband was holding up downstairs as he tried to fight off the man who had suddenly decided to enter their home, and spread fear throughout their lives, left her daughter sitting on the bed as she raced to the window. Unlatching the lock, she lifted it as far as it would reach. Doing the only thing she realized she could do to save her family's life, she put her head through the open window and began screaming at the top of her lungs for help. "Help!" she screamed loudly throughout the star filled night, hoping and praying that one of her neighbors would be able to hear her cries for help. "Would someone please help us?"

Then, suddenly she heard a noise coming from behind her. It was the sound of the bedroom door closing shut. Stunned, she wondered if it was someone coming in the room shutting the door behind them or, was it someone leaving the room? Fear seemed to grip control of her body and she found herself shaking uncontrollably as she pulled herself back inside from the window and slowly, began to turn around.

"No!" she cried as she realized she was now the only one in the room. Carey, her beloved daughter was nowhere to be found. "Carey!" she screamed as she raced to the bedroom door, flung it open and stepped out into the hallway. Now, exclusively concerned for her daughter's safety, completely forgetting about her own, she raced down the hallway. Although her daughter was nowhere to be found, her motherly instincts told her to head towards the staircase as the presence of her only child could be felt heading in that iniquitous direction.

As she reached the top of the stairs she gazed down across the living room. Not believing her eyes, she stopped in her tracks. She could hear her own heart beating vigorously as it seemed to vibrate throughout her entire body, and the entire scene in front of her left her utterly speechless. She found her daughter trotting fearfully across the living room and towards the hallway, which led to the cellar. The man, who had came thrashing through their front door was walking towards Carey, a blood stained knife gripped tightly within the palm of his gloved hands. And then, behind the wicked man, she found her husband.

It was clearly obvious that David was hurt as he clutched his chest, which continued to pour blood like a faucet left on as water began running over the boundaries of a sink. She wanted to run to him, comfort him, and rush him to the hospital. But she couldn't move. She didn't know what to do.

Then, as her husband gained on the monster who had stabbed him, she watched in vain and in disbelief as the end of her husband's life unfolded right before her very eyes. "Leave my daughter alone," she heard David struggle to say as he grabbed the man's shoulder with his free hand, leaving the other one pressed tightly against the deep wound the knife had easily formed as it sliced it's way through his muscles and into the pits of his abdomen.

As Charlene watched in horrific suspense, it happened.

Without saying a word, almost as if the man hadn't even acknowledged or listened to what David had said to him, he spun around, released the grip the wounded man had on his shoulder and lifted the knife once again high in the air. The man looked deep into David's eyes as if mocking him for his brave effort in his attempt to save his daughter.

Before David could mutter another sound, the man brought the blade down once more. Only this time, he thrashed it forcefully across David's neck, slicing his jugular vein. Immediately, David felt a bitter weakness inside his body, and as his heart rate slowed down, he collapsed to the floor one last time. Closing his eyes, David prayed for the safety of his family, and within seconds he was gone. His heart stopped beating, the constant movement of his chest as he continued to breath came to a stop, and before he had the chance to say goodbye to his wonderful family, it was all over. David Haas had perished from existence.

Darkness had closed in, seizing control of his body for all eternity.

Watching from atop the stairs, Charlene cried out for her husband's safety. "No!' she screamed as her husband fell to the floor, blood pouring from both of the death defying wounds the man had inflicted mercilessly upon him. Charlene never imagined her life without the man whom had meant everything to her. Her worst nightmares were coming true tonight, and as the thought of never being able to see her husband again came flooding in, she felt as though she had just been struck by a semi. Loosing her breath, she felt her knees buckle from under her, and she too fell to the floor. Her hands grabbed the bars on the stairwell stopping her from plummeting downwards, towards the murderer who had just stripped her husband of his last breath.

As soon as the man cut open David's throat he turned away, knowing fully well that he would die within a matter of minutes, and began on his quest after the little girl, whom had scattered away down another hallway and into the cellar. Never once thinking about what he had done, or about how he had already destroyed the Haas family, his only thought was of Carey Haas. What he had done to her father would be nothing compared to what he was going to do to her.

Then, as he began passing the staircase and was prepared to cross over and into the hallway, where the little girl had fled, Charlene from above called out to him. "Why?" she begged to know. "Why are you doing this to us?" she asked again. "You killed him! You killed him!"

For a moment, it seemed as though the man was about to turn away from her and continue on his journey towards the prized little girl. But something drew him back, and his stance changed. He knew *the little girl wasn't going anywhere, and he knew he couldn't leave Charlene alive at the top of the stairs. Turning away from the hallway, he faced the woman at the top of the stairs and spoke, his tone cruel and evil, and his words lashed throughout the night like a thunderstorm, the electricity of his remarks sparking their way into the depth's of his next victim's soul. "Yes I did kill your husband," the man shot back at Charlene. Then, gripping the knife tightly once more, he looked into her terrified eyes. "And you're next."*

Then, smiling, he began mounting the stairs.

In a massively cold sweat, Billy jerked awake.

He grabbed his heart and felt it's steady beating sequence return to its customary, methodical pattern, and fought off the churning his stomach wouldn't let him escape. Adjusting his eyes to the dimly lit room, he surveyed his surroundings. Looking around him in a daze, the nightmare he had just experienced still fresh in his mind, he didn't know where he was, or how he had gotten there.

The room was dark, except for the drifting moonlight that was able to creep inside from a single window, from which the blinds had been drawn. The moonlight seemed to make the walls appear to be a bluish sort of color, although Billy knew fully well the real color of the walls were off white. Then, he looked at the gown he had been wearing, and felt the electrodes sticking to his skin. Finally, he realized where he was.

He was in the hospital.

But why? What happened?

Turning his head to the left, he felt a splintering headache form from within the depths of his brain, and for a split second he thought the visions he had been experiencing were about to return. He tensed his muscles as he prepared to endure the painful sequence once more as visions of the Haas family continued to play with his mind, leaving him utterly confused and somewhat terrified as he still did not understand just what was going on. Finally, however, his breathing eased and his veins found their way back into the depths of his body and he then fully realized the Haas flashbacks weren't coming back at that moment. Opening his eyes once again, he found his mother sleeping in an undoubtedly uncomfortable position on a single chair, the only other piece of furniture in the room.

"Mom," Billy whispered in an attempt to awaken his mother. "Mom, mom," he continued. Finally, he saw her head jerk upwards and soon their eyes met. An immediate smile protruded along her non-pomaded face. All of the cosmetics must have been worn off as her head constantly was pressed on a pillow or her own shoulder as she patiently waited for her son to regain consciousness. "You look so damn uncomfortable," Billy continued with a smile. "Why didn't you ask one of the nurses to bring you in a cot or something?"

Debra only shrugged her shoulders as she lifted herself off the chair and sat on the edge of her son's hospital bed, smiling at her son's question. It was good to see that he hadn't changed a bit. "How long have you been awake? Is your head feeling all right?"

"I just woke up," Billy answered, and with a puzzled expression began to answer his mother's second question. "My head?" he asked inquisitively. "What should be wrong with my head? How did I wind up in this hospital anyway?"

Debra quickly began replaying the events that had transpired earlier that afternoon and explained to her son how he had lost his balance for some reason or another and slammed his head against the refrigerator, which had knocked him completely unconscious and left him with a slight, minor concussion. "I was so worried about you," Debra flushed as she leaned over and pecked her son on the forehead. "For a split second, I thought I was about to loose the only other man in my life that meant anything to me. I'm still confused as to what happened though Billy. I mean, I remember you looking at the picture of the Haas family and then all of a sudden you started to freak out or something. That's when you lost your balance."

Billy began trying to explain to his mother about the awkward and sometimes incomprehensible visions and nightmares he had begun experiencing the night he had found the picture in the cellar. He could see clearly through his mother's grotesque eyes and knew that she was having a hard time believing what he was saying. "Mom, I know all of this sounds a little weird, but I'm serious. It's like I was right there in that house when they were murdered." He continued to tell her about the nightmare he had just awakened from, and the one that ended with the death of David Haas. "I know that Curtis Rains killed David Haas first, and from what I could gather, he was going after the wife next."

Debra didn't how to respond to her son. Reality told her that he was simply loosing his mind and that it just wasn't possible. Her motherly instincts, however, and the fact that he had been able to describe everything with such fine tuned detail and finesse told her that her son was telling the truth. If so, the only question was what were they going to do about it? Or, what exactly did his nightmares and dreams represent? Unfortunately, the answers to those questions weren't going to be found in a hospital.

"Mom, I have to talk to Elizabeth," Billy blurted out breaking the silence that had fallen over the two of them. "I don't know why, but for some reason I have to know everything. It's like something is drawing me towards the Tinman and the murder of the Haas family ten years ago, and I can't stop it. I really, really wish I could mom. But I can't."

"It's all right sweetheart," Debra replied soothingly as she rubbed her soft fingers through her son's hair. "We're going to be all right. I promise we'll get through all of this together. You'll see. Everything is going to be fine." As those words left her mouth, Debra herself had trouble believing them, and she was almost certain that her son hadn't taken them to heart as well.

"What time is it?" Billy asked, somewhat getting off the subject.

"Five till midnight," Debra answered and immediately knew what her son had been referring to by asking that question.

"So," Billy continued slowly hoping nothing out of the ordinary was about to happen. "In five minutes, the Tinman, or this Curtis Rains character will be laid to rest once and for all."

Debra nodded. "That's right. Soon, Curtis Rains will be dead, and maybe then we can finally put all of this behind us huh?"

"I hope so mom. I really hope so."

* * *

Curtis Rains walked calmly, and swiftly into the execution chamber where the electric chair had been waiting for ten solemn years to take his life. He felt the presence of the viewers in the audience, whom he was sure, would have been willing to pay top dollar to witness his death. Closing his eyes, he took a deep breath to clear his head as the shackles that bound his wrists and ankles together were removed and he was seated fittingly in the hardwood chair.

Opening his eyes he looked through the tainted glass, and glared into the eyes of the people before him. Many of them looked instantly away, terrified of looking into the eyes of the man they so desperately wanted to be dead, completely removed from the face of the earth. The one's whose brave souls allowed them to continue to look at him truly felt no remorse for what was about to happen to the wicked man before them. Giving them one last thrill, Curtis grinned at them, smiling cheerfully just as he always had done before he claimed the life of another innocent soul.

Then, as the leather straps were strapped tightly around his wrists and his neck was clamped tightly to the back of the chair, completely immobilizing him, his cheerful smile changed into an ice cold glare and he felt nothing but hate. He hated the world, hated everyone and everything, and blamed society for doing such a thing to him. Humanity was no longer an issue, and repenting not an option. However, Curtis didn't want to die. He simply wasn't ready to go.

His bloodthirsty rampage had not yet been completed.

Then, he was interrupted by the sound of the warden's voice. "Have you anything to say Mr. Rains?" he asked the inmate before him. "Any last words?"

Curtis didn't respond. His vivid expression told everyone in the room that he wasn't about to apologize for any of the acts of violence he had committed. He really was not sorry for what he had done, nor did he wish to be forgiven, although the preacher was hard at work in the corner of the room begging the Lord to take his soul and purify it, wishing him a happy, joyous life in the enchanting world of Heaven above.

"Very well," the warden concluded giving the guards the O.K. to continue with their procedure of locking and securing Curtis to the electric chair, as he himself continued to read the death warrant issued by the Governor of Florida. When he finished, Curtis found his mouth strapped shut, assuring his tongue would be held in place, as massive jolts of electricity entered his body. Another sheet was placed over his eyes to prevent them from popping out of their sockets.

As the closing remarks ended, Curtis listened as the low, hollow drumming of the electricity began to build up inside the room, and then the guard, who undoubtedly had the toughest job in the world, prepared to pull the final lever down, which would end his life forever. After a few seconds passed, but after what seemed like an eternity, it was over.

Curtis's body jerked spasmodically as the electricity poured into his body without mercy. His fingers, which had been clutching the arms of the chair flew wildly into the air, and after a few seconds, fell back down. That was the sign that all life had been drained from inside the body of one of America's most notorious and vicious serial killers. Never again would he be able to interrupt the lives of perfect families; families that were devoted to living in peace and harmony.

The Tinman had finally received the gravest penalty for all crimes. The Tinman had finally been laid to rest.

After ten years, Curtis Rains was finally, and fittingly dead.

* * *

12:02 a.m.

Jamie Walker flipped through the radio stations as she neared her home in the great state of Alabama. Completely oblivious and unaware of what time it was, she listened to the end of one of her favorite songs. The radio announcer's voice came on, as she was about to change the channel, when something caught her attention. Pulling her finger back, and resting her hand once again on the steering wheel, she listened to the news flash.

"It's a couple minutes past midnight people and for those of you who are driving somewhere along Alabama's beautiful highways, or back roads, it's time for you all to wake up cause I have some pretty damn good news. That psycho freak, Curtis Rains, has just been electrocuted to death in Starke, Florida after spending the last ten years on death row. For those of you who don't know who I'm referring to, maybe the name Tinman will spark those late night

memories for you. He was the serial killer who slaughtered families instead of individual people, and was truly the ambassador of pain and suffering. If the death of this guy brings you guys as much happiness as it does me, honk right now as you're driving to your place of interest. Matter of fact, I'll open up some lines right now for anyone who wants to call in and give us your opinion of the man everyone loved to hate. So call me now, and we'll discuss the Tinman one last time before we put him out of our minds forever. Caller number five will win brunch for two at your favorite restaurant. So call me now at 575-WXRY. This is "Smokin Steve," playing all of your country favorites in the Birmingham area, and we'll be right back with more from the brightest stars from today and some closing thoughts on Curtis Rains. So stay with us."

As the commercials began playing through her speakers, Jamie turned the radio off and took in a deep breath. She rolled down her window and breathed in the cool, Southern midnight air Alabama offered every once in a while. Was it actually true, she thought? Was Curtis Rains actually dead?

Of course he was.

A smile crossed her face as she realized the man she had once loved, but also the man that put her through mounds of heartache and pain would no longer be able to reach out to her and put her through such agony and suffering. Curtis Rains would no longer be a part of her life and now, she could finally concentrate on spending the rest of her life with the man she loved in Travis McKinley. Realizing she was within 20 minutes of her home, she pictured the loving arms of her soon to be husband graciously waiting to pick her up and carry her off on a golden chariot and into the world of enchanting calenture. Her lustful craving for his kiss and touch would all come out in one fiery outburst, sending the two of them in a daze as they concentrated totally on one another.

God she missed him.

Picking up the phone, she decided to call him and let him know that she was almost home. After dialing the number, and after listening to only one ring, she heard his gruff, familiar voice come on the other line. "Hi honey," Jamie spoke cheerfully, finding it hard to believe that she was wide-awake after the long drive she was about to complete. "I'm almost home. I'll be there before you know it."

"Good," Travis spoke clearing his throat. "Did everything go all right?"

"Sure did," Jamie replied. "Did you watch the news? I just heard over the radio that they had just finished with the execution."

"Good," Travis replied, wondering if that was the right thing to say. "I know you don't like me to say it sweetheart, but that psychopath should have been killed the second he was convicted."

"Say whatever you want," Jamie breathed hoping an argument wasn't about to ignite. "To tell you the truth, I'm glad he's dead too. Now," she paused deliberately about to change the subject. "I've done a lot of driving today, so why don't you go into the bedroom and get everything comfortable for the two of us."

"I'm laying in bed right now."

"Good," Jamie concluded. "That's exactly where I want you, so don't move. I'll be there before you know it."

Hanging up the phone, she took her eyes off the road for a brief moment as she troubled herself with fidgeting once again with the radio. Finally finding a station she wanted to listen to, she glanced back up at the dark road, and the long stretch of blacktop in front of her. For a second, she couldn't believe what she was seeing.

Screaming at the top of her lungs, she grasped a hold of the steering wheel with both hands, and panicking she slammed on the brakes, trying to steer the car clear of the object in the road.

It was a child.

She couldn't believe it. A small, naked boy was standing in the middle of the road.

And he was staring at her, not even attempting to get out of the way, until it was too late.

Closing her eyes, Jamie knew that she wasn't going to be able to avoid the contact that would shatter the small child's life indefinitely. But she had to try something. With one hard, swift motion, she veered the steering wheel to the right. Watching in retched silence, she winced in fear as her Jeep plowed through the small boy. She hadn't been able to miss him.

Then, realizing she was headed off the road, she tried to fight her way back on the highway. However, her tires touched the slippery grass that was still wet from the thunderstorms that had shot through the area just a few short hours ago.

It was too late.

She was driving too fast.

The traction on her tires had long since been overused and no matter how hard she fought, she wasn't in control of her vehicle. Hydroplaning, she gained speed, and as her headlights caught the darkness of the woods on the side of the road, her eyes grew big with fear as she focused on the large pine tree that now stood in her path.

Seconds later, it was all over.

Her Cherokee collided head on with the massive tree. The Cherokee was ripped apart from the impact, bits and pieces of debris could be seen flying hundreds of yards away, and smoke rose from her severely damaged engine. However, the tree itself didn't budge. Her head smashed harshly into the windshield, shattering it into a thousand pieces, and before Jamie Walker knew what hit her, darkness closed in.

Trapped inside her car, Jamie laid in an awkward position in the passenger seat, completely unaware of what had just happened. With no other cars passing along the Southern highway, the night fell once again into the decaying silence it was used to, everything ostensibly returning to normal, as if nothing had ever happened.

With the moonlight shining beautifully down from above, cascading along the premises of the accident, Jamie Walker lay motionless in the cab of her car, in a pool of her own blood.

Chapter 9

Two days later.

Finally, after days of relaxing in the hospital, Billy Saxton was glad to return to their new house along the sandy coast of Destin, Florida. Although the visions of the events that took place on this beautiful piece of property some ten years ago still lingered fresh in his mind, he was still glad to get away from the hospital and the ungraceful aroma of sick people. He had grown used to the annoying stench, as time seemed to pass all to slowly during his stay in the sanitarium retreat. The doctors and nurses had been very nice to him and treated him well. In fact, it appeared as though they actually cared about him and were doing nothing more than looking after his best interests when they asked if they could keep him for one extra night to run some more what seemed to be useless tests. Billy knew they simply wanted the assurance his brain was out of danger before releasing him from the hospital.

Nevertheless, he was glad to be out.

As soon as his mother opened the front door, he stepped inside. Taking one long look around him, he took a deep breath and decided he wasn't going to let anything get in the way of this glorious day, and suddenly he felt the urge to escape into his room and fall into a deep, peaceful sleep. Ever since he had come across the picture of Haas family in the cellar a few days ago, he hadn't been able to consume one night of sleep where he wasn't awakened by the screams and cries of death. But now he supposedly had nothing to worry about, nothing to fear.

Jason Glover

Curtis Rains had been laid to rest two days ago, put in some unknown, isolated cemetery, buried alone and without a headstone. Therefore, Billy felt everything should come to an end and return to normal. He wanted to be the same person he had been before he and his mother had made the move from Marietta, Georgia. Eagerly, he started towards the stairs, at the same time speaking to his mother. "I'll be in my room asleep if you need me mom."

"All right sweetie," Debra replied to her son, then reached into the depths of her pocket book, which she knew contained way to many items than were really necessary. Finally, her hands came across what she was searching for, and within seconds, she pulled out the bottle that contained the medication that doctors had prescribed her son. "If you're still sleeping in an hour I'm going to have to come up there and wake you up so that you can take your medicine all right?" Billy turned and nodded. "And I'll get something going for the two of us in the kitchen after while."

"Great," Billy replied, ending the conversation as he disappeared down the hallway and into his bedroom.

Debra waited until her son disappeared completely from view and listened as his bedroom door snapped shut. Then, she walked into the kitchen, placed his prescription drugs on the counter where they could easily be seen and not forgotten about, and then stumbled over to their answering machine. Not expecting to see the blinking light, which told her that someone had called and left a message, she was a bit surprised to find three un-played messages on the machine. Pressing the button that would bring the voices to life, she helped herself to a nice glass of White Zinfandel, a sparkling blush wine from California by Robert Mondavi. Twisting the wooden cork from the chamber of the bottle she poured herself a glass more than half full and sipped it gently.

Still waiting for the machine to spring to life, she walked over to the window seal that overlooked the patio and the beach beyond, and glanced at her array of African violets. Finally, the first of the three messages came on after a rather hollow, loud beeping noise.

The first message was a hang up. Undoubtedly, someone had dialed the wrong number.

As the second message sprang to life, she immediately recognized the voice of Elizabeth, her neighbor. "Hey Debra, I heard about what happened and I was just calling to make sure everything was all right and to see if there was anything I could do. Please give me a call as soon as you get this message. Bye." Smiling at the voice of her new friend, she already had the cordless phone in hand and was about to return the call when the third message beeped in. The familiar sound of a man's voice began speaking deeply, and she realized that it wasn't someone for her. It was for her son. Someone she knew Billy would have absolutely been thrilled to hear from.

It was Blaze Brookshaw, Billy's best friend from back home. "Hey Billy, and Mrs. Saxton," Blaze spoke excitedly on the answering machine. "I was just calling to check up on you guys and wondering how things were going at the beach and all. I've got some vacation time coming at work, and I'm not going to class this Summer so I was just wondering if it would be all right if I came to visit you guys for a few days. So, just give me a call whenever you get a chance. Later buddy."

Deciding Elizabeth's call could hold off for a little while longer, she walked steadily up the stairs and entered her son's bedroom. Although she already found him dead asleep on his bed, she shook him until his eyes were wearily opened and looking directly at her. "I'm sorry for waking you up," she began apologizing for her intrusion. "But I have some good news for you."

Handing her son the phone, she told him to call his best friend.

* * *

Elizabeth walked slowly along the beach, running her toes through the warmth of the sand as the sunrays played down along her tanned skin. She kept looking downwards at the trail of footprints she left behind, but every so often, she would instinctively look up and watch her two daughters, Mary and Jennifer, who giggled their way down the beach, every so often running and jumping into the gorgeous blue ocean next to them, only to scream as they came running out in fun. "You two don't run off too far now," she called to them as the distance between them seemed to grow larger and larger as every second passed. While Elizabeth's energy seemed to be draining from her still very functional body, the animation and efficacy of her two daughters seemed to continue to build. "Where does all their energy come from?" she asked herself as she realized her daughters either hadn't heard, or simply didn't pay attention to anything she had said.

Realizing that if she didn't quicken her pace, her children were going to be out of her sight in no time, she began to speed it up a little. Her pace, which had been nothing more than a leisurely stroll, suddenly advanced wickedly as she soon found herself half jogging after her two radiant little girls.

Sweat began to drain from her pours, and if it weren't for the constant coastal breeze that swept across her silky skin, Elizabeth was sure that the Florida heat and humidity would have gotten the best of her. Then, she suddenly stopped to catch her breath as she realized her daughters had stopped ahead and were waiting for her to catch up with them. As she approached them, she recognized the mocking smiles that were laid bluntly across their two innocent faces.

"What's the matter mom?" Jennifer asked grinning. "You getting too old to keep up with us?" she concluded as the two of them burst into a laughter that could brighten anyone's spirits on any given day.

"No," Elizabeth replied to her daughters still panting from the short exercise she was forced to endure. "I am not too old to keep up with the two of you, but why don't the two of you slow it down a little huh? I thought I was about to fall down and pass out chasing after you guys. You wouldn't want that to happen now would you?" she concluded with a half hearted grin knowing that she had been able to manipulate them.

"No," Mary answered lovingly as she came to her mother and placed her arms around her, her young innocence shining powerfully through her beautiful eyes. "I'm sorry mommy. I guess we just weren't paying attention."

"It's all right pumpkin," Elizabeth assured her daughter, who once again seemed to take things more seriously than needed. "Are you guys about ready to go home and let me fix you up a snack."

Mary looked at her older sister for the answer, not wanting her younger years to make a mistake in front of her role model. "Not yet mom," Jennifer spoke gracefully. "Just a little while longer all right? I promise we won't run off too far. We won't leave your sight."

Elizabeth was about to protest, as she truly wanted to get out of the raging heat that continued to drift down from the skies above. But her children were having too much fun and she shouldn't ruin it for them just because she wasn't in the mood to frolic around in the surf and sand. Then, as she looked over her shoulder, she found herself standing in front of the Haas home, now occupied by her new acquaintance, Debra Saxton. Surveying the perimeters of the unearthly home, the uneasiness and fear she continued to feel each time she passed by or glanced at the house returned once again, and she immediately drew her eyes away and back towards her daughters.

"What is it mommy?" Mary asked her mother, her young intellect telling her that something was wrong.

"Nothing is wrong sweetheart," Elizabeth tried to assure her little girl. Then, she forced herself to turn once again and face the home that had given her nightmares for years. Peering through the sliding glass door of the home, she noticed a movement from inside. Although she was momentarily blinded by the rays of sunshine that seemed to beam off the smooth glass door and thrash directly into her own eyes, she was sure she had seen something. Squinting, she spoke to herself. "Debra must be home." If so, she wondered, why hadn't she bothered to return her call?

"All right you two," she once again began speaking to her daughters. "You guys have half an hour to run along. I'm going to go right up there and visit with Debra for a little while. I'm going to be watching from her patio and if the two of you leave my line of vision I will ground you both for a week. Understand?"

The two of them nodded quickly, both eager to continue on their journey down the beach, neither knowing just what hidden treasures or creatures they would stumble across.

"All right then," Elizabeth spoke once again. "Go ahead, run along. But remember, be back here in thirty minutes." With that, she watched as her two perfect little angels ran away from her, both so full of life and energy, that neither looked back at her to wave goodbye. Elizabeth knew that the chances of them returning on time were slim, and she also knew that she wouldn't have the heart to actually punish them for disobeying her. They weren't actually causing any trouble or doing any harm. They were just acting their age, and who was she to stand in their way?

Feeling safe to take her eyes off her daughters, she courageously began walking up the deck to Debra Saxton's home, and soon found herself knocking quietly on the sliding glass door. Exhaling a deep breath, she waited for her friend to come and answer the door.

* * *

"Come on in," Debra gestured to her new friend, as she let the obviously exhausted woman outside her sliding glass door inside her home. "Why Elizabeth, you look as if you just finished running in a marathon or something. Is everything all right? Would you care for something to drink?"

"That sounds good," Elizabeth replied excepting the woman's offer for some liquid to replenish her system. "And everything is perfectly all right with me. I've just been chasing my two little girls all over the beach this afternoon and it's finally taking its toll on me I guess. How about you?" she paused not wanting to start a conversation her counter part didn't feel like having at the moment. "How is everything with you? Is Billy all right?"

Debra nodded enthusiastically as she ushered her guest a glass of wine from the very bottle she had just opened moments ago. "He's got a slight little bump on his head, and a nasty looking cut, but it looks a lot worse than it really is. He did hit his head pretty damn hard though and it scared the life out of me," she paused taking in a deep breath. "The doctor says that he has a minor concussion and that he shouldn't be on his feet for a while, and that he needs a lot of rest. It's going to be a tough task, but he'll get through this I'm sure."

"Yeah, he does seem like he's a pretty strong kid," Elizabeth added warmly about Debra's son. "So," she paused sensing the look of uncertainty that somehow gleamed through Debra's eyes. "Are you sure everything is all right?"

"No," Debra hated to admit as she felt her eyes tear up a bit. Then, she began at the beginning of how her son had somehow stumbled across the picture of the Haas family and the little doll, which he had been so sure, was named "Kat," given by the little girl she had come to know as Carey. She tried to explain the eerie, uncanny events that had taken place afterwards. Including how her son had been complaining of sleepless nights filled with deadly, horrific nightmares pertaining to the tragedy the Haas family had been subjected to some ten years ago. She even tried explaining the visions her son swore to be having each time he glanced at the family photograph. All of this, Debra knew was hard for Elizabeth to accept, as she herself had trouble understanding her son's arguments. However, as she finished, she saw a concerned look in her neighbor's eyes, and it comforted her in some way, as if she no longer felt alone.

When Elizabeth spoke, she chose her words carefully. "I really don't know what to say," she sadly admitted. "I personally have never believed in that sort of thing. However, my optimistic side tells me that anything is possible. So tell me," she paused eyeballing Debra. "Have you spoken to anyone other than me about this?"

Debra only shook her head in disgust. "I told the doctor at the hospital and he gave me a few phone numbers of some doctors that might be of some help. We just returned home today from the hospital though and I haven't had the chance to call any of them."

"Well from one mother to another, I think you should," Elizabeth continued seriously as she finished off her glass of wine.

"Care for another?" Debra asked climbing to her feet as she too found the need for another drink. Extending her glass towards her host, Elizabeth graciously accepted the woman's offer to refill her glass of wine, and waited patiently for her to return. As Debra stepped back outside on the patio she watched in silence as her neighbor searched the long sandy beach ahead, her eyes obviously searching for any sign of her daughters. When there was none, she recognized the concerned look that now encompassed her facial structure as wrinkles bore out from her forehead. "Don't worry about them," Debra began reconciling Elizabeth about her two daughters. "They'll be all right. I'm sure their not causing any mischief anywhere. They probably just lost track of time."

"I know you're right," Elizabeth breathed heavily as she took the glass of wine handed before her. Then, sipping it gently, she realized drinking wine in the sun probably wasn't the best thing to be doing knowing she still had to walk back home. But what the hell, she had a long day and it was time for her to kick her feet up and relax a little bit. "I just don't know about the two of them sometimes. I've never really been hard on either of them." Then, pausing, she continued. "I just don't know if that's a mistake that will come back and haunt me later on or not."

"Well, both Jennifer and Mary seemed to be in good health and normal if you ask me," Debra added half jokingly as she tried to bring a smile to Elizabeth's rather ashen face. "I really don't think you have anything to worry about. Billy, on the other hand," she paused not wanting to bore her friend with stories full of sorrow from her anything but perfect past with her husband Tom Saxton. "I'm still not sure about. He had a rather rough life growing up, and although he puts up the front of a sweet innocent boy, and pretends that nothing is wrong, I can tell that he's not telling the truth. In fact, I'm pretty sure he has a lot of anger built up inside and I know he'd feel a lot better if he would just get it off his chest."

"Have you tried to talk to him about it?"

"I used to try," Debra answered in a tone letting Elizabeth know that it hadn't been done in a while. "But every time I tried, we would wind up in some kind of argument and he would refuse to even mention his father's name. I can't blame him really though. But," she paused once more to take a sip of her wine, which as each sip passed, she found herself drowning gingerly into a relaxed state of mind, and right now, she felt as though she could tell Elizabeth anything. It had been a long time since she had been able to trust anyone. Her husband had left her feeling utterly helpless, useless, and with a sense that she wasn't worth a dime. "I haven't tried to speak to him in a while. I know if he ever needs to talk he'll come to me. So I guess I'm just waiting until he's ready."

"Well, I think Billy will be all right," Elizabeth assured Debra placing a caring hand on her shoulder. "But what about you? Have you met any lucky men around here in Destin? There are a lot of single men around here just looking for someone like you. Most of them like to fish all day and night, but they're all right."

"Nope," Debra sadly admitted. "I haven't even had the chance to get out of the house yet. I know Billy wants me to meet someone else. He's never actually given me the approval or anything, but I know he only wants what's best for me. I guess it'll happen when the time is right. After everything that's been going on, however, I'm not sure that moving here was the best thing for me, or my son. I know what I told you before sounded strange, but Billy has changed. And for some reason," she paused. "I believe everything he has said. About the nightmares, the visions, the headaches. Everything."

* * *

As the two women sat outside on the patio, talking amongst themselves as they sipped wine waiting patiently for Elizabeth's two little munchkins to return, they were completely unaware and oblivious to the fact that Billy had been upstairs, in his room, sleeping. Only, it wasn't a peaceful siesta. His slumber was full of numerous amounts of tossing and turning, his head every so often wildly thrashing into the headboard. Never awakening, Billy had no idea what his body was being put through, the trance he was in too powerful to overcome. At least, not until the phantasmagoria of illusions had once again subsided for the evening.

Once again, the incubus nightmares engulfed Billy Saxton.

Little Carey Haas sat on the cold cellar floor listening intensely to the events that were taking place in the home above her. Her father, she knew had been hurt badly. She had glanced at him as she crossed the living room heading for the basement, and had noticed him pressing his stomach inwards, desperately trying to stop the large amounts of blood from drifting outwards, staining the white carpet below. She now sat in silence, letting the darkness of the room hide her from the evil man she knew to be lurking about above her. She didn't know what exactly had drawn her to the cellar in the first place, and her mind never wondered why she had left the safety of her mother's arms in the upstairs bedroom. Now, she found herself alone in the blackened room, with nothing more than a picture of her family, she had somehow managed to tote with her, and Kat, her beloved porcelain doll.

Her body shivered uncontrollably as the damp, coldness of the room seemed to infiltrate right through her young, soft skin, and as the silence loomed over her, she could hear her teeth chattering together. Her young years wouldn't let her understand what was going on. However, she could sense the presence of danger, taste death, and smell the anguish. The man, whom had come from out of nowhere in the stillness of the night, came flooding into her home in a homicidal rage, obviously with nothing but deathly persecution on his mind.

As fear overwhelmed her very essence of being, she found herself clouded with doubt, and wondered if she would ever see her parents again? Clutching the doll tightly in the palm of her left hand, and grasping the picture tightly with the other, she felt her way, like a crippled blind person whom had just fallen out of their wheelchair, around the damp floor until she reached the spot she was looking for. It was a corner of the cellar, a corner in which she knew a board to be loose in the wall.

Working quickly, she jarred the wood loose even more, squinting slightly in pain, as splinters seemed to etch their way into her flesh. Finally, she first placed the picture of her family in a box she had been lucky enough to stumble across. Then, pulling the doll close to her one last time, a tear slipped from her eyelids, ran down her face, and splashed onto the cemented floor below. As if her heart knew she would never see Kat again, she kissed the doll's cheek, and then placed it too in the safety of the box. Finally, she shoved the box into the hole she had single handily formed. Once both prized possessions were secure, she quickly put the piece of wood back in place. Or at least, as good as she could make it fit. Then, once again, blindly feeling her way across the floor of the cellar, she crawled to the stairs, found a tight little spot underneath, just big enough to consume her small body, and hid terrified of what the night had yet to bring. Shivering in fear, and from the cold, Carey Haas closed her eyes and prayed silently to the one person she believed could save her and her family.

Praying to God, another sob left her fine cheek.

As the minutes rumbled along all too slowly, however, Carey felt as though the night would never come to an end. She hadn't heard a single noise from upstairs in what seemed like sempiternity, and as the seconds of dreaded everlasting horror continued, she found herself wondering if the intruder had finally decided to leave?

Then, right at that moment, something happened that answered her question.

There was a scream coming from above.

Carey immediately recognized the sound of her mother's voice, squealing in retched pain and anguish as she begged for her life.

"Please!" she heard her mother cry out in vain, only to be followed by another grisly outburst of pain as the man continued to hurt her. "No!" her mother continued to wail into the night as if someone was actually going to come from out of nowhere to help her.

For the next few twinkling minutes, Carey threw her hands over her ears, trying to cover them from the uncomfortable sounds of her mother being slaughtered to death. She was protecting her innocence, which until tonight had been so securely pure, never once falling victim to anything that might be considered lurid or of inhuman nature.

However, no matter how hard she tried, she couldn't escape the cries of her mother as she continued to beg for her life over and over again, struggling to stay alive and protect her daughter from the maniacal rage the man had been pursuing on herself. Charlene's screams pierced through the night, echoing throughout their lively home, and vibrating along the hollowness of the cellar walls.

Then, all of a sudden, there was silence once again.

Carey listened for any sound that might mean her mother was still alive, and half of her wished she could hear her mother scream in pain one last time, just to let her know that she was still there, still alive.

Unfortunately, nothing came.

Only silence. A dead silence, that made the tiny hairs on the back of her soft, genuine neck curl methodically upwards, and forcing her eyes to grow large, even though the room she had confined herself to was pitch black. She couldn't even see her feet below her as she buckled her head between her legs, hovering a hand over mouth, terrified the man above her might be able to hear her heavy breathing and be able to locate her.

As her emotions began to run out of control, she didn't know what to do. She wanted to call out to her mother and father and have them rush in, take her gently in theirs arms, where she could peacefully lay her head on their shoulders, leaving this dreadful nightmare behind.

That's it! A nightmare, she thought to herself.

She suddenly began pinching herself over and over again, hoping that she would instantly find herself laying wide awake on her bed, her comforting mattress below her as her tiny body sunk down into the depths of the sheets that would consume her entire body, *protecting it from the cool draft she had always felt first thing in the morning. The tips of her toes, however, had always seemed to be able to find the slightest opening in the sheets and would accept the cold air as it crept under the covers and sent chills throughout her tiny body.*

Unfortunately, even as her skin began to peel away, leaving blistering red marks behind, Carey found herself in the same place she had been before. She was still underneath the stairs of the cellar, continuously praying for herself and for her parents to come out of this alive and well.

Then, something happened that compelled her to hold her breath all together, as if constraining or constricting her lungs from breathing. With her whole body shaking in blatant fear, she listened as the door at the top of the stairs squeaked open.

For a moment, she heard nothing.

Then, a footstep came.

Someone was coming down the stairs and she knew that whoever it was, would be at the floor of the cellar in no time, and her precious hideaway would be revealed. Remembering her mom's screams, she knew her body would be exposed to the same type of rapid torture and punishment her parents had been forced to endure.

But, how did anyone know where she had gone to hide?

Then, as the footsteps came to an end, she realized whoever had come down to the cellar had reached its planking. Then, as the feet continued to shuffle around the still darkened room, they suddenly came to a stop.

What was going on?

What was about to happen?

A light sprang to life after a few short seconds of flickering on and off, the bulb obviously not ready to make up it's mind as to whether it wanted to work or not. Terrified, Carey squinted her eyes in a furious fashion, trying to get accustomed to the blanched light that had so abruptly disoriented her. Finally, she was able to see.

From her hiding place she was able to make out his black leather work boots, splattered with dried blood.

Unfortunately, she knew it was her parents' blood.

The man wasn't facing her, however, and as his feet once again began working along the parterre of the cellar, it appeared as though he was walking away from her. Carey was smart enough to realize that the instant the man decided to change directions and turn around, her presence would be revealed. She realized it was now or never. She had to try and escape the deadly wrath the man was planning to brutally force upon her.

Not allowing her young mind to think of the consequences that would happen if he caught her trying to escape, she began to edge her cradled body from the tiny compartment underneath the stairs, praying that her knees wouldn't make their usual popping noise as she moved them from a fixed position. Closing her eyes, she tried to climb quietly to her feet.

However, as her legs extended upwards, her knees popped.

Immediately, she opened her eyes and suddenly found herself staring into the eyes of the man who had broken into her home. Without saying a word, the intruder showed the little girl the blood-splattered knife he gripped tightly within the palm of his hands, and began walking slowly towards her terrified frame. He didn't expect a girl of her age to run from him as he felt she would be consumed with more fear then her heart could muster. Surely, he thought, she would be too frightened to move.

"Why Carey," he spoke soothingly, and saw the glimmer in the little girl's eyes as she became confused as to how he had known her name. "Don't be afraid of me. I'm not going to hurt you. You're such a pretty little girl."

Luckily, however, Carey hadn't been like all the other children the man had taken the pleasure of slicing up. Without responding to the man's kind words, she turned and fled up the stairs, careful not to lose her balance. Opening the cellar door, she ran from the deadly room, only to enter the living room, or the room of death, leaving the man, her family picture, and her doll behind.

As she sprinted for her life through the family room, she found her father's motionless body lying on his stomach to her right. Blood poured from all around him and she found no signs of life. Then, looking over towards the couch, which was now lying on it's back, she found her mother's wounded, raped, and battered body lying face up, her eyes still open, but not looking in her direction.

Carey couldn't believe what she was seeing, or what her young mind was witnessing. She wanted to stop running. Wanted to rush *over to her parents who loved her very much and see if they were all right. But she couldn't. She could feel the presence of the man behind her, barreling down on her. And for a second, she swore to have felt his hot breath shoot down the back of her neck.*

Finally, as a little voice in her head told her to keep running, she let out an earth-shattering scream and ran through the smashed sliding glass door. Running down the deck, which led to the ocean, she never bothered to look back and see how close the man was to catching her.

Reaching the ocean, she realized she needed to make a decision, and fast. Should she go right, or left towards the Anne home, where she knew her mother's friends Elizabeth and Murray would welcome her with open arms and protect her from the evil man that was chasing her. But then she remembered something.

Her parents hadn't been able to protect her.

Confused, she had to stop running.

What should she do?

Where should she go?

Then, a voice came from behind her. "Carey!" the man called after her trying to get her to stop. "Please stop. I'm not going to hurt you," he tried to assure her.

As each second passed, the man continued to gain on her.

As each second passed, Curtis etched his way closer and closer to his precious victim.

Finally, she realized she was running out of time. She had to get away from him! It took a while for her feet to sink into the soft sand the beach had lain for her, but after a few seconds, she picked up speed and was once again sprinting away from her death. Her path took her straight ahead, and she soon found herself colliding with the powerful ocean before her.

She ran as far as she could into the ocean, but as the water level reached knee high, she fell head first into the salty water and suddenly found her mouth being consumed with the bitter taste it provided. Swallowing half of what had seeped inside, she jumped out of the water gasping for air.

Still, with her last burst of adrenaline, she continued on.

Her weak, young body was no match for the powerful current the mighty ocean displayed, but she had to go on. Every once in a while, she would get pulled under and have to endure another feast of the salty ocean water, but each time, she would regain her breath and continue to swim out to sea.

Carey was swimming away from danger.

She didn't know how far she had traveled, but a noise from behind her, back towards her home suddenly made her stop wading through the water and she shifted her position. For the first time since she had been on the run, Carey looked back towards her home. All around the front of the house, she saw flashing blue and red lights.

It was the police.

They had come to save her and her family.

She checked the shoreline and the waterfront for any signs of the evilness that seemed to be destined to take her life.

There was none.

Finally feeling safe, Carey stopped swimming and took some time to catch her breath.

Carey Haas was finally out of danger.

Soon afterwards, Curtis Rains had been captured and taken into custody. Carey, his only surviving victim, had been left behind to actually live the life God had intended her to live.

Slowly, she began paddling herself back to shore.

* * *

Elizabeth and Debra watched, a little intoxicated, as Elizabeth's two little girls came strolling along the beach, their cheerful expressions could easily have been seen miles away, lighting up the path of any person in front of them. Glancing down at her wristwatch, Elizabeth shook her head. "I say thirty minutes, they take fifty."

"Well, between you an me," Debra added friendly. "I'm glad they stayed gone a few extra minutes. I absolutely enjoyed spending this time with you and you have to promise that we do it more often."

"If you keep serving me this absolutely divine wine, you'll probably see more of me than you'd want to," Elizabeth concluded climbing to her feet. Then, she handed her host the glass she had been using, taking the last inkling sip from the chilled chalice, and began to meet her children halfway as she remembered how uncomfortable they felt about coming up to the house which had withstood the horrible tragedy of the Haas family years ago. "Again Debra," she breathed. "Thank you so much for everything."

"It was my pleasure," Debra reassured her guest.

Then, before Elizabeth had been able to take her first step across the deck, the two of them froze in silence as a noise came from within Debra's home. It was an alarming scream.

And it was Billy.

Without hesitation, the two women barreled their way into the house and ran up the stairs. If it wasn't for the railing along the edge of the stairwell, both women would have lost their balance and plummeted to the hardwood floor below. Nevertheless, within seconds, they reached Billy's bedroom door just in time as another scream pierced through their eardrums. With their hearts racing, they shoved the door open and peered inside.

Billy was asleep on the bed, yet he was throwing his body around wildly, like a madman in a violent rage. What Debra was seeing was new to her and for a split second she didn't know what she should do. Finally, after a few brief seconds of staring in awe at the awkward scene in front of them, Debra snapped out of her state of reverie and rushed to her son's aid. Shaking him riotously, she desperately tried to awaken him.

"Billy!" she screamed. "Billy, it's O.K. You're just having a nightmare."

Suddenly, he jerked awake in a cold sweat and found himself gazing into the eyes of his mother. Crying, he let himself be wrapped up in his mother's loving, sheltering arms as he tried to vindicate himself of the horrific illusions his mind had once again created while he slept.

"They won't go away," he cried childishly. "They just won't go away."

"It's all right sweetheart," Debra assured her son. "Just tell me what happened."

Then, as if something came over him, his mood suddenly changed. The tears dried up and an anger he had never felt before seemed to surface, and he unwillingly decided to unleash it on the two women before him.

"Just get out!" Billy ordered coldly towards both of them. "Both of you. Just go away and leave me alone."

Stunned at her son's remarks, Debra slowly picked herself up off her bed, and as her eyes began to water, she hurried out of the room.

Chapter 10

    Travis McKinley walked with a slow pace and without the certain gracefulness he once carried wherever he roamed, as if showing to the world that he was the most important man in the world. His cockiness, however, was forgotten for the moment as he once again found himself walking with his head down and out of the Birmingham Memorial Hospital cafeteria. Once again, he forced the lump back down his gullet, and fought roughly to hold back the tears that desperately wanted to pour freely from his eyes. Once a man full of life, energy, animation, and happiness, he now found himself lingering into the depths of sadness and grief, as he slowly walked back towards the hospital room, where he would find his girlfriend, live in love, Jamie Walker lying motionless, almost lifeless on the hospital bed.

    Clutching the doorknob fittingly in his hand, he hesitated before opening. He hoped to find Jamie sitting upright in her bed with an enthusiastic smile crossing her gorgeous face as she held out her welcoming arms, wanting him to come between them, where he would once again be able to feel the warm embrace the two of them shared. It was an embrace that always seemed to remind the two of them how truly in love they were. Finally, closing his eyes, he prayed once again, and twisted the door open. Only after walking inside and hearing the door automatically shut behind him, did he open his watery eyes and peer ahead.

    Unfortunately, nothing had changed.

    Jamie was lying in the exact same manner as before, when he had left the room to try and eat something, which once again had proven to be an unsuccessful attempt at filling his nerve racked paunch. Sighing to himself, he shrugged his shoulders, took in a deep breath, and walked to the edge of her bed. Softly sitting himself next to her, he could no longer brace himself or hold back the emotional tears that were fighting to free themselves from inside his eyes. As the unrelenting tears exploded from inside his weary soul, he instantly knew that they would never stop.

At least, not until Jamie Walker awakened.

Which, of course, the doctor had explained to him that it was a very touchy situation and that there could be no guarantee on how long it would be before she snapped out of her coma and thrust back into reality. "It could be a couple of days, a couple of weeks, a couple of months, a couple of..." he remembered the doctor telling him. All of the internal bleeding had at this point been held under control and was not causing any damage that could prove in time to be fatal. She had received many cuts and abrasions that were treated in no time and bandaged securely. Her hip had been displaced. That too, had quickly been taken care of. A couple of her ribs were shattered and her left arm had been broken, the bone of her elbow actually penetrating through her skin as if showing off it's presence to the rest of the world. This injury had needed surgery as quickly as possible to prevent any infection, which could have lead to more serious illnesses or injuries. Then, there was her brain. Her head had shattered the windshield with such force that the doctors were surprised that she had even been brought to them alive. Nevertheless, at the beginning, her brain had been swelling rapidly. Almost miraculously overnight, however, it had settled and now the doctors had told him as long as the swelling didn't return, there was a good chance of her coming out of the coma with no physical disabilities.

It wouldn't have mattered though.

Travis would have loved her just the same. He was thankful that perhaps she had been spared the sorrow of knowing when she awoke that she could never be the same again. But it truly would not have changed the way he felt for the girl laying in front of him. With her breathing normal, he looked at the gash that lay on her forehead. That too, had no effect on his perception of her. She was still the most beautiful woman he had ever laid eyes upon, and always would be.

Finally, choking on the sobs that continued to pour from inside, he took her hand in his own and began speaking softly. "Please baby," he begged sadly. "Please hang in there and come back to me soon. I swear I'll be here whenever you decide to wake up." Then, pausing for a moment, he squeezed her hand affectionately, leaned over and pressed his lips, which were wet with tears, on her forehead. "God I love you!" he breathed as he pulled himself away.

Then, something happened.

Something he didn't understand.

All of a sudden, he jerked himself up and away from the bed and began uneasily looking at all of the monitors around him. They were beeping crazily. Something was happening to his angel. Once again, looking at the life form in front of him, he watched in awe as Jamie's arms jerked spasmodically out of control, and her eyelids shook harshly. As the monitors continued to pound their beeping sounds into the depths of his confused brain, he found himself backing away from the hospital bed.

"Nurse!" Travis yelled as his mind fell completely into a daze and he immediately began thinking the worst. "Someone please help!" he pleaded falling to his knees, tears streaming numerously from his ashen, pale face. Panic had seized him, and not knowing how to help her, he simply looked away and waited for help to arrive.

After what seemed like eternity, a team of nurses and doctors stormed into the room, rushing past him, not even acknowledging his presence as they set to work on Jamie Walker, the woman Travis one day intended to marry. Now, watching in silence, he prayed that the love of his life wasn't slipping away from him forever.

She simply couldn't die.

He couldn't live without her.

Nevertheless, like the sand washing away from the shore as the water forced its way back into the constantly churning sea, Travis McKinley watched in sorrow, as his love appeared to be slipping away from him.

"I love you," he managed to say in agonizing pain. "Please don't go," he added before being rushed from the room, and forced to leave the woman he treasured behind.

* * *

"Mom," Billy spoke as he finally came downstairs after showering, and found his mother messing about in the spotless kitchen. The aroma of Italian pasta lingered fluently in the air as he walked over to the pot and dipped his finger inside the simmering spaghetti sauce. Licking his finger, he turned to face his mother, just as she was finishing up a bottle of wine. "Mom," he tried again after not receiving a response the first time. This time, although no words were spoken, Debra actually turned around to face her son, whom had spoken so harshly to her and Elizabeth earlier that evening. "This is pretty good," he continued with a smile as he stuck his finger in the bowl a second time.

"Well good," Debra replied rather shortly as she turned away from her son again, not really sure how to speak to him at the moment. "I'm glad you like it," she added refusing to make eye contact with him. "I'd hate for you to snap at me again because my cooking wasn't up to par."

"Your cooking is absolutely wonderful," Billy assured his mother as he came behind her, placed his hands on her shoulders and spun her around, forcing her to look into his big blue eyes. "And it always has been." Then, as the two of them stood speechless for a moment, Billy knew he was going to have to apologize for what had taken place upstairs in his room a short time ago. "Look mom," he began blushing, not really sure how to begin. "I'm sorry for the way I spoke to you earlier. I was just having another nightmare and it scared the hell out of me is all. I'm sorry. You know I would never intentionally do anything like that."

"I know sweetheart. I know," Debra began soothingly as she accepted her son's trivial apology. "You really scared me though Billy," she continued letting a tear fall from her face. "For a second there you weren't the same person, and you reminded me of your fath-." She stopped herself short, not wanting to finish her sentence.

"I reminded you of who?" Billy asked directly, wanting his mother to finish. "My father?"

Debra nodded truthfully.

"Tom!" Billy exclaimed about his father as anger flashed throughout his body and he suddenly found himself being consumed with an internal rage that had been secretly living inside his soul since he was a small child. "Awe mom how could you?" he asked turning away from his mother. "How could you ever compare me to that man?"

"Honey I didn't mean anything by it," Debra tried to say as she sensed the hurt in her son's voice as he turned away from her. "I wasn't accusing you of becoming your father or anything. Believe me," she paused picking her voice up a bit. "I know you're nothing like Tom was, and I know you aren't the kind of man he was. You just really scared me sweetheart."

"And I'm sorry for that," Billy concluded, ending the conversation by walking out of the kitchen and through the patio door. Walking to the edge of the deck, he clutched the wooden posts firmly with both hands as he gazed down at the beautiful sandy beach and the ocean below. Couples strolled lovingly up and down the shoreline, never letting the water splash past their knees as they walked peacefully through the sand. Some couples just sat in silence as they gazed up at the enchanting crepuscular. And as Billy too stared into the reddish sunset, he felt that it had to be one the most beautiful assets mother nature provided.

However, his mind wasn't allowed to wonder off too far. Soon, he was once again staring straight ahead into the mighty ocean below, watching enthusiastically as each wave crashed powerfully along the shoreline. Then, from out of nowhere, an image appeared inside his head. And it seemed so real.

It was an image of Carey Haas.

She was swimming relentlessly into the ocean ahead, letting her small body be consumed by the overwhelming waves as they tackled her and carried her beneath the surface. Only seconds later, she would come thrashing out of the water, gasping for more air to filter through her lungs. Then it hit him. As he continued to look into the welcoming ocean ahead of him, he realized that right in front of him was where the small child in his nightmares had fled into the ocean and swam away from her attacker, Curtis Rains.

And she was alive.

Her parents had been murdered, but she had somehow managed to escape, Billy remembered.

The only questions now was:
Was she still alive?

Tinman

And if so, where could she be found?

Billy himself wasn't sure why he needed to see this mysterious girl. She had obviously been through more at such a young impressionable age than he could ever imagine as she had actually watched her parents being slaughtered to death. Nevertheless, he felt as though something was drawing him towards her. He didn't know why, he just needed to see her.

Turning away from the ocean he walked back inside his home, and as he passed the desk, which contained his father's picture on it, he found it once again sitting upright, his father's smile and cold brown eyes once again looking directly at him. Wondering why his mother even bothered to leave the picture up, he once again slammed it face down on the desk and entered the kitchen. As he spoke, his tone showed his mom that their quarry before was forgotten, and that now more important things were on his mind. "Mom," he began quickly, immediately able to capture her attention.

"What is it Billy?" Debra asked confusingly, seeing the wide-eyed expression written along his face. "Is something wrong?"

"I don't think so," Billy answered hurriedly. "But I need a favor."

"Go on."

"I need you to call Elizabeth and ask her if I may come over and speak with her for a while." Then, pausing for a split second, he looked into his mother's eyes once again and continued. "I think she may be able to help me."

"Help you?" Debra asked still confused, but now slightly intrigued as to what might be going on inside her son's head. "Help you with what?"

"My nightmares," Billy answered firmly.

✞ ✞ ✞

Murray Anne wiped the sweat away from his face as he finished up the final touches on polishing his Explorer. Every week he slaved in the constant heat of a Florida afternoon cleaning his vehicle to a tee. He would always do so, however, underneath the stilts on which his beach house stood firmly, never letting himself get exhausted in the baffling humidity the beach seemed to provide year in and year out. Finally, taking one last glance at his now sparkling vehicle, he figured there was absolutely nothing more that could be done, and made his way up the stairs, located right on the side of the house, and soon found himself on the back deck. He found his two little girls playing with their dolls; their attitudes seemed almost reluctant to let the heat and humidity bother them as they sat there looking carefree. "You girls aren't getting too hot out here are you?" he asked them with a grin.

"Nope," the elder Jennifer answered, never letting her eyes drift away from her doll as she tried to change its swimsuit.

"Didn't think so," Murray replied as he pushed the sliding glass door open and walked inside his home, letting the cool air from the air conditioner cleanse his soul and dry away all of the sweat that had absorbed in his shirt and shorts. "Jesus," he groaned as he found his wife in the kitchen. "I swear it's getting hotter and hotter every summer. I can't take the heat like I used to," he added as he sat on the sofa and switched on the television. The second his tush sank into the depths of the cushions on the couch, a yawn immediately escaped his mouth and he knew a nap would be coming on soon.

"Would you like some tea?" Elizabeth asked from the kitchen, already making an effort to pour him a sweetened glass of tea, and watching with a smile as her husband removed his shirt and laid his head to rest on another pillow. She could tell he was about to drift away into dreamland.

"Please," Murray managed to speak before yet another yawn came along. "Oh man. Right when I walk outside, I start sweating. I don't see how our two little girls can handle it," he continued once again peering at his daughters through the glass door.

"It's called being young," Elizabeth replied as she walked over to the couch and handed her husband his glass of tea. "And dinner should be ready in a few minutes so don't you fall asleep for long."

"I won't," Murray tried to assure his wife as he leaned his head back along the back of the couch and closed his eyes momentarily. "I probably won't even fall asleep," he added with a grin, knowing his wife wasn't going to believe what he was about to say. "I'm just resting my eyes for a little while."

"Sure," Elizabeth replied returning his fake grin, and returned to the kitchen just in time as the phone rang loudly throughout the house, bouncing along the walls until it was finally able to drown weakly into silence. "Hello," she answered politely just as the second baffling ring was about to go under way. "Hey Debra," she instantly spoke as she recognized the voice on the other end of the line. Then, she recalled Debra's son, Billy, and how he had so harshly spoken to the two of them earlier that day after awakening from another, what must have been torturing phantasm. "Is everything all right?"

"Oh yeah," Debra replied in a confused tone. "At least I think so. It's Billy," she paused not exactly sure how to use her vocabulary. "He says he needs to talk to you about something and he asked me to call you and see if it was all right if he came over for a little while."

"Hold on a minute," Elizabeth began not understanding just what was going on. "Let me get this right. Your son says he needs to talk to me? About what?"

"I'm not sure," Debra admitted. "He seems to think that you might be able to help him. I think," she once again paused, not wanting the wrong word to slip from her tongue. "I think it has something to do with his dreams, and the family that lived here before us."

"Oh," Elizabeth ushered quietly, not quite sure how to respond. At any rate, although she felt uncomfortable, if she could be of help, she knew she couldn't refuse her friend's favor. "Well," she paused almost about to say that it wasn't a good idea. "I don't know of how much help I can be, but I'll listen to whatever it is he has to say and go from there I guess."

"Thank you Elizabeth."

"No problem," Elizabeth finished the conversation. "Tell Billy he can come on by anytime he's ready." With that, the two women hung up the phone. Elizabeth, however, didn't turn away from the telephone and continue on about her business in the kitchen in getting supper ready for her deserving family. Instead, she stood there, staring at the phone in some sort of unearthly trance as if the hard object was going to be able to answer the questions that suddenly sprung inside her head.

What did Billy want to talk to her about?

Why her?

Something simply wasn't right, she could feel it in her bones. Finally, freeing herself from the reverie that had transformed her state of mind, she came back to reality and immediately began finishing up her home cooked meal. Try as she must, however, she couldn't put the thought of Billy Saxton out of her head, and for some reason, she felt as though she was going to regret ever agreeing to meet with him. After all, she didn't know how she was going to be able to help him in the first place.

Most importantly, however, she didn't like drudging up the past.

* * *

Travis McKinley sat tearfully out in the waiting room, as he patiently waited for Dr. Kennedy to return with the bad news that his girlfriend had passed away. The thought of never being able to see her, hold her, or kiss Jamie again continued to play over and over inside his drowsy head as his brain tried to picture a life without the one and only true love he had ever known.

Undoubtedly, the picture was blank.

With his hands trembling, he placed them firmly on the brink of his knees as he also tried to stop his legs from clapping together forcefully. There was no use. He couldn't stop the overwhelming sensation of sadness that the death of a loved one always seemed to bring. It felt as though the whole world was weighted upon his broad shoulders and he just didn't have the strength to accept the challenge God had so suddenly sprung on him. There had never been anything but pure happiness when the two of them were together. Sure, they had their minor disagreements that would lead to a few petty arguments. However, they would always end with a kiss.

The two of them belonged together, and they knew it from the first time they had met a few years ago when they just so happened to be shopping for the exact same camera, in the exact same store, at the exact same time. Only no words had been spoken then. It was later, when the two of them left the mall, undoubtedly at the same time, and wound up unintentionally pulling into the exact same fast food restaurant for a quick bite to eat. Both had noticed and acknowledged each other's presence, but again, no words were spoken. It was even later, when the two of them had received invitations to the exact same banquet, both without an acquaintance, and the two of them wound up talking and dancing into the late evening hours, neither taking for granted at how their paths had somehow managed to cross earlier that day.

That had truly been a day Travis himself would never forget. In fact, he would treasure it for a lifetime. He would never forget the first time he had ever laid eyes upon his beautiful princess. If today were the last day to see his loved one, he would never forget this day either. "Why?" he asked himself as he buried his head into his hands, and tears continued to stream from his face.

Why? Why? Why?

That was a question he knew he most likely would never find the answer to, but he also knew that it was a question he would never stop asking until he was lying on his deathbed. Thousands of beautiful memories began to churn inside his brain, and although the tears never ceased, he could feel a smile trying to lift the melancholy atmosphere that had sprouted up uninvitingly all around him. Then, his head lifted upwards at a slightly askew angle as he recognized the sound of the doctor's voice calling his name.

"Mr. McKinley," Dr. Kennedy began coming into the waiting room, his facial expression showing no signs of bad news, or good news. However, his mellifluous voice always seemed to bring a twinkle to his eye, as if somehow assuring him that everything would turn out all right. Then, as the bald headed figure approached him, his thin glass frames enlarging the pupils of his soothing brown eyes, and with his large white coat hiding his blue buttoned up shirt, he spoke again. The assiduity in his tone assured Travis that for the past hour or so the doctor had done nothing but look after Jamie. "How are you holding up?"

Travis shrugged his shoulders. "I guess as good as I can be," he replied with a certain hint of asperity in his voice. Then with an askance expression locked onto his face, he prepared himself for the bad news he was sure to come. "What happened in there?" he asked the doctor as he recalled the mind jarring beeping noises the monitors made as his girlfriend pounced uncontrollably around in her bed, her eyes falling back into their sockets. "Is it over? Is she." he cut his words short not wanting to finish his sentence.

Suddenly, the bland expression from the doctor changed into a confused glare as he tried to figure out what Travis was trying to ask him. "I'm sorry," the doctor continued placing a firm hand on the man's shoulder in front of him. "But I think you were mislead by what happened in Jamie's hospital room."

"What!" Travis exclaimed swallowing the lump that had formed in his throat. "I don't understand. What are you saying?" Then, pausing briefly, he continued. "Is she dead?"

Then, confusingly, Travis watched with uncertainty as a smile crossed the good doctor's face. "Dead?" the doctor asked letting a slight chuckle escape. "I don't think so. What you saw in that room was Jamie waking up from her coma. Sometimes people come out of it calmly, while others don't, like Jamie for instance. However, all she was doing was waking up. She was a little confused but we took care of that. She's back and she's perfectly normal, and the first thing she asked for was to see you."

Wiping his face free from the tears of sadness, Travis welcomed with open arms the tears of joy. Jamie hadn't died. She had come back to him. He was about to hurry past the doctor and enter her room, when the firm hand was once again placed on his shoulder. Spinning around, he looked into Dr. Kennedy's eyes. "Thank you so much."

"You're welcome," Kennedy responded. "But it's not quite over yet. She's got a lot of recovering to do. Now, she's very weak, tired, and probably in a lot of pain, so don't keep her up to long. And don't worry about her falling asleep, she's not going to fall back into another coma I can assure you," he added seeing the questioning glare coming from the man's eyes in front of her. "But she does need her rest, so don't push things all right?"

Travis nodded in agreement.

After turning away from the doctor, within seconds, he found himself standing outside Jamie's hospital room. Once again, clutching the handle tightly, he paused to wipe the tears out of his eyes.

Then, with a smile, he opened the door.

* * *

As Billy walked along the beach, nearing his neighbor's home, he still wasn't quite sure just exactly what it was he wanted to ask Elizabeth, or just exactly what it was he was trying to get

Tinman

accomplished. He just had the feeling that everything was starting to come together. He had come to grasp the fact that he was experiencing the nightmares and hallucinating visions for a reason.

But why was all this happening to him?

It wasn't just by chance that he stumbled across the family portrait and Kat! the beautiful porcelain doll that had been so cleverly hidden in the hollow walls of the cellar. No, there was a reason all of this was happening. There was a reason for Billy himself to get involved and he had to find out just exactly what that reason was. It truly seemed as though everything was coming together, and for some reason, he felt that Elizabeth Anne was somehow, or in some way, just a missing piece to the puzzle he so desperately wanted to put together. He only hoped that she would have some answers.

As the stars twinkled provocatively in the Southern sky, Billy finally approached the Anne home, and from a distance he could clearly see Elizabeth sitting patiently on the outside patio awaiting his arrival. As he neared the steps to the deck on which the woman was sitting, he could feel her eyes on him, watching him like a hawk, and he knew she was thinking about the volatile outburst he had unintentionally shown earlier that day when he awoke from yet another virulent nightmare. His mother and Elizabeth herself had simply been in the wrong place at the wrong time, catching the end of his unexplainable illusion. Nevertheless, he didn't return the uncomfortable stare until he reached the top of the steps and seated himself next to his neighbor. It was then, when Elizabeth realized her tormenting gaze and turned away from Billy only to look once again up into the clear, beautiful night sky.

"Thank you," Billy began breaking the uneasy silence that had befallen the two of them. "Thank you for giving me a few minutes of your time. And believe me, I don't want to intrude, and I don't exactly know what is going to come from all of this. But there are some questions that I need answered, and right now, I think you are the only one that can help me."

"Well," Elizabeth paused, glancing once again at the nineteen-year-old boy sitting next to her. "I can't promise you anything. But I'll most certainly try to help you anyway I can." Then, returning to stars, she spoke again. Only this time, she used a softer, gentler tone as she changed the subject. "It's a beautiful night isn't it?" she asked her counterpart, only to begin speaking again before allowing him the opportunity to answer. "Nights like this make me wonder if there's anywhere else on earth that's more beautiful than right here."

Billy didn't respond, he simply followed the woman's gaze into the atmosphere above them and then for some reason, found himself trying to make out some of the magnificent constellations he knew to be shining brightly above. Frustratingly, however, he could not. "Where's your husband?" he asked, taking his eyes away from the glorious stars. "It's Murray right?"

"Yep, and he's probably asleep by now. He had a rather long day for an old man. Now," Elizabeth paused turning to face Billy directly. "What is it you would like to know?"

"It's about Carey Haas," Billy boldly stated, seeing no reason to avoid getting directly to the point. Suddenly, however, he noticed a slight twitch of uneasiness pass through Elizabeth's body as she shifted uncomfortably in her chair. Her eyebrows arched, and as her eyes widened with an uncertain anticipation of what Billy was going to throw upon her next, she waited for him to continue. "All of those bloody visions, and nightmares I have been having are about the Haas family," Billy continued. Then, he went on to try and explain to Elizabeth about the doll and the picture he had found down in the basement and how he had actually seen how they were murdered, almost as if he himself had actually been present that horrible night. "I know it all sounds crazy Elizabeth, believe me I do. But it's the truth. I swear it's the truth."

"I believe you," Elizabeth spoke with a scratchy voice as she placed a relaxing hand on his thigh. "But I still don't understand. What does all of this have to do with me? What is it you want to know about Carey?"

"I know Carey didn't die that night," Billy stated boldly. "I saw her parents murdered, but she somehow managed to get away. What I need to know," he paused, not exactly sure how his neighbor was going to respond to his next question. "I need to know if she is still alive, and if so, where can she be found."

For a long time, the two of them sat in utter silence, never turning away from one another, but never speaking a word. As the memories of what happened long ago began to resurface, Elizabeth wanted to turn and flee into her home, closing the door and locking it on the

Tinman

person who now sat across from her. Nevertheless, as the memories of the past continued to dredge up from beneath the finer layers of her brain, she couldn't see a way out. She wished she could just put the Haas family out of her memory once and for all. In fact, it had been a long time since she felt the blood coiling sensation she now felt, twisting the insides of her intestines into a knot. Finally, forgetting the questions that had been laid before her just moments ago, she just sat there in a daze, staring at Billy as she waited for him to repeat the question.

"Is she?" Billy asked again, taking the woman's hand in his own. "I know this must be hard for you, but I really have to know." Pausing once again, his tone suddenly became rather gruff as he tried to snap Elizabeth out of her reverie. "Is Carey Haas still alive?"

"Yes," Elizabeth voiced sharply.

"Does she still live here in Destin?"

Elizabeth nodded, her hands trembling. "The last I heard of her, she just graduated from high school. I think she's your age actually, and she's been living with her Aunt and Uncle, Carol and Rick Goodman ever since her parents were murdered. I used to keep in touch with her quite often, but that slowly came to an end, and I haven't heard from her or her relatives in a few years now."

"Do you know where they live?"

Again, Elizabeth nodded, not really sure if she should be answering anymore of Billy Saxton's questions.

* * *

A short time later, Billy found himself jogging back towards his home after finally ending his conversation with Elizabeth, and now his mind was wondering in escapades of both excitement and fear. He still wasn't exactly sure what it was he was going to do, or even why he needed to see Carey Haas in the first place. However, he could feel himself being drawn towards the little girl he had been seeing in his sleep, almost as if he were in some way being beckoned to her.

Why?

She wasn't in any danger, and neither was he.

Jason Glover

To no avail, however, he had to go to her. Reaching into his pocket, he pulled out the piece of paper on which Elizabeth had taken the liberty of writing down the address of where the girl could be found. Satisfied that it hadn't fallen out, he placed it once again back into the depths of his pocket and continued on his late night stroll towards his home. He found himself growing increasingly tired, as the short jog seemed to take forever, and as his brain waves began working at a pace faster than normal.

Finally, slowing to a brisk walk, he took a deep breath and looked up at the stars above. He let his body relax as the moonbeams cascaded down along his shiny skin, giving it a glowing, bluish type color. He couldn't wait to crawl beneath the cold sheets he knew were waiting for him in his bedroom, only to give in to the comfortable warmth as a few minutes passed and his body began to accumulate it's heat. He only wished that sleep would come in peace. The nightmare had come to an end earlier that day when Curtis Rains had been taken into custody, so he wasn't quite sure what was left.

What else hadn't he seen?

What was missing?

Again, the overwhelming amount of questions began to rock his brain, and he once again began to feel the lightheadedness that came along with it. None of this would have ever happened if he and his mother had stayed in Georgia where they belonged. But no, they had to move to Destin. They had to reach paradise.

And what happened?

As soon as they stepped foot into what was once thought to be a lovely, and enchanting home, the nightmares had begun. Only his mother, Debra, for some reason had managed to escape all of the blood-lined events Billy had been forced to endure. He was sure, however, that there was a reason for it. He just couldn't figure out what it was.

Why him?

It was as if some unseen force from a power he would never be able to understand and come to know had chosen him to find the doll and the picture in the cellar. His mother had looked at the picture and she wasn't overcome by any mind shattering visions. Why was he? Billy couldn't know for sure, but he felt the answers he was looking for were close at hand. There was simply something he was missing.

There was just something he hadn't been able to put his finger on. But it was there, he was sure of it. He just had to look in the right place.

Finally, he stopped along the beach as he reached the front of his house. There he stood for a few moments just staring at the magnificent structure in front of him. What was once one of the most beautiful homes he had ever seen now appeared in a different manner. It was no longer beautiful and full of life. The house had consumed the blood of an innocent family, leaving behind a history Billy was just now beginning to understand. No lights were on in the house giving it a gloomy, empty, hollow appearance, and for a split second, Billy thought about grabbing a blanket and sleeping near the waters edge. The house in front of him was now looked upon as the house of death, and Billy no longer felt safe and secure, the feelings a home was supposed to give a family as it sheltered them from any dangers that may lurk beyond its doors.

It was getting late and Billy knew that he would have to get up early the next morning if he was going to try and locate the address Elizabeth had given him and be back at his home in time to meet Blaze Brookshaw, his best friend from back home, who was supposed to be arriving by noon. Reluctantly, he slowly made his way through the sand and headed up the steps to the back deck.

That's when it happened.

As soon as his foot touched the first wooden step of the deck, he felt his hand clench the railing as a familiar feeling came along. Then, suddenly, like a bolt of lightning flashing throughout the darkened sky, a piercing jolt of pain shot through his head and the headaches returned. Images began to sprout inside his head and he could hear the screams of a woman as she begged for her life. Only, it was no longer the sounds of a little child, he knew to be Carey Haas. It was someone else screaming bloody murder.

"No!" Billy screamed trying to force the images aside.

But it was no use.

Letting go of the railing, Billy began pressing harshly at his temples on both sides of his head as he tried to force the pain to subside. It was unrelenting, however, and visions of the strange woman stayed. As the screams continued to echo throughout his head, the pain only increased. Squinting, he tried to recognize the figure of the woman in front of him. She appeared to be no older than he, and her long, wavy angelic blonde hair reminded him of the little girl he had seen in the picture. Her blue eyes enlarged and drenched in fear looked upon him as if begging for his help. She wore nothing more than a red satin nightgown; single stranded above her shoulder, and cut off half way up her thigh. On any other occasion she would have been the most beautiful woman he had ever seen. Now, however, she had a look about her that didn't appear from this world.

It was the look of death, as if the woman knew she was going to die.

Then it hit him.

He knew who the girl was. It was Carey Haas. Only she was no longer the little bright-eyed nine-year-old girl he had seen before. She had become a woman, but the look of fear in her eyes had grown as well, and only took him back to when she was a child as she ran for her life from the Tinman. The look she had given so long ago hadn't changed in the last ten years. She was still terrified of Curtis Rains, and could never forget the *Tinman.*

Finally, loosing his balance, Billy fell backwards, landing without harm on the softened sand below. As the unbearable, torturing pain continued to sweep through him, he knew his consciousness was about to be consumed once again by darkness. "Please," he continued to beg to be left alone. "Please."

Nothing changed.

Once again, as the horrifying visions consumed Billy Saxton's spirit, darkness surrounded him, closing in with a grip so tight, he often wondered if it would ever be released.

* * *

The creature traveled gracefully through the space, which had been so ironically provided for him. At last, he could roam wherever he wanted and do whatever he wanted.

At last, he was free.
Free to kill.
Free to torture.
Free to harm anyone that dared to stand in his path.

It had already begun. Yet, no one would ever know just what was going on, or what was about to happen. For all intents the creature was dead. Dead and forgotten by all who hated it. However, it hadn't forgotten. Its anger and rage had only grown with time, only now to become so powerful it would never die. It couldn't be stopped, and its presence would be felt for all eternity.

Soon, it would be time.

A couple of days ago, it had made its presence known to the unlucky Jamie Walker, whom had suffered massive injuries in a single car accident. However, it was the creature that had spared her life.

Soon, however, it would strike again.

And soon, it would be time to unleash the unholy terror it held within.

Chapter 11

    As the morning sun crept through the hospital window, it seemed to sprout life all around the room, giving certain completeness to the dozens of flowers that had been placed decoratively around what must have been a rather dull, gloomy room before Jamie had graced it with her presence. Glancing in slight pain, she tried to peer out the window at the marvelously blue sky above. Unfortunately, she couldn't capture the slightest glimpse. It didn't matter. Her high-spirited mood told her that it was gorgeous outside. A few clouds were probably scattered high in the atmosphere, not threatening Birmingham with any signs of precipitation. Birds were lingering about carelessly in the trees, as a few simply flew freely throughout the sky until something came along that captured their attention long enough to land and investigate. She couldn't wait to get back outside.
    She could imagine it now…a nurse wheeling her out of the professional hospital building, and away from the constant smell of sick people, into the bright sunlight, where she would find Travis waiting with the passenger door open to his car, anxious to return them to their home where they belonged. She could almost feel the warmth of the sunrays as they belted their way across her suddenly pale skin, washing away her worries, assuring her that everything was going to be all right. Although she would be helpless, almost crippled and confined to a wheelchair, she would welcome the therapeutic warmth of the sun on her battered and bruised body.
    She had been briefed on the seriousness of the accident she had been in, and many people had already spoken to her, all of them saying the exact same thing. "You are lucky to be alive," or, "we

didn't think you were going to make it," or, "it's a miracle sent straight from the heaven's above that kept you alive." Maybe they're right, she thought. Maybe she was lucky to still be alive and kicking. This near death experience changed Jamie in many ways. She intended to live the rest of her life without taking anything for granted from this day forward. It was now time to actually live life to the fullest.

Jamie had already committed herself to the long recuperating period she knew she was going to have to endure before she could get back on her feet, and was well aware that it would be a while before her strength would return, and her pain disappeared. Nevertheless, it was just another obstacle she was going to have to overcome. She was not going to give up. She felt she was given another chance at life, and made up her mind to improve each and every day with a positive attitude and strong faith to return to normal.

Jamie Walker was glad to be alive, almost feeling as though her soul had been cleansed while sleeping peacefully in the coma her body had been thrown into. She felt like a new person, as though she was somehow starting over again, venturing out into a new life with nothing but wonderful journeys ahead to experience. And she couldn't wait. If she was getting a second chance, or a new start, she was ready for it to begin. She was ready to get out of the hospital, flee to her home, and into the arms of the man she knew loved her more than anything in the world.

Then, almost simultaneously, just as those thoughts entered her mind, the door to her hospital room opened and Travis McKinley appeared with more flowers in his hand, and a charming smile lurched across his tear free face. "You ready to get out of here sweetheart?" he asked soothingly as he handed her the flowers and leaned over to kiss her cheek gently.

"You have no idea," Jamie answered smelling the beautiful roses she was sure he had purchased from within the hospital gift shop. "Thank you," she began again running her weak fingers through his soft brown hair. "They're absolutely beautiful. But I swear if you spend anymore money on flowers you're going to go broke."

"For you, it'd be worth it," Travis assured her giving her one last peck before stepping away from her. "Now, let's see if I can't find a nurse to come in here and scoop your fragile little body into a wheelchair so we can get you home."

Jamie nodded and looked away as Travis neared the door, only to find herself staring up at the florescent light bulb flickering on and off above her bed. At first she thought nothing of it. Then, for some reason, her passive gaze into the light, turned into a magnetic stare and she couldn't turn away. It was as if something was forcing her to look into the light, and as every second passed, the light grew brighter and brighter, until she found herself squinting as she continued to gaze up at the ceiling above. Soon, nothing could be seen around her, only the bright piercing blue light the bulb gave away. She couldn't even see Travis, although she knew he hadn't left the room and was standing only a few feet away.

There was nothing, only the light.

Her palms became greased with sweat, and she felt her forehead begin to boil, as the heat seemed to intensify instantly. Clinching the sides of her bed harshly, she closed her eyes for a moment, hoping that when she reopened them the room would be back to normal. Counting to three, she tried to relax.

"One, two, three."

Nothing changed.

The light was still swarming around her, the heat absorbing into her skin until it felt as though she were going to meltdown completely, disintegrating from existence, vanishing from the face of the earth without leaving behind a single trace of her noble permanence. Her fear became a reality as she found that there was no escape from the blinding light that was now swarming around her. When she had awakened that morning, everything had seemed so perfect. Jamie had been sure that a beautiful day loomed ahead and the thought of returning home excited her. But now, she didn't understand what was happening.

Then, from the center of the light, she saw something moving. Peering more closely into the light, she realized it was something coming towards her. It was a life form of some sort, and it moved with ease through the piercing light as if not affected by the stinging florescent rays at all, nor did it appear to be affected by the massive heat. Squinting in pain, Jamie was forced to watch helplessly as the body slowly strolled through the light towards her.

She tried to scream.

But nothing would come out. She began to panic as she slammed her hands over her mouth, struggling to find out why she couldn't call out for help. As her steamy hands ran along the edge of her chapped lips, she couldn't believe what they revealed. It felt like thread of some sort, and it felt as if it were coming through her lips in different areas, only to reenter and come out again. No, she said to herself. It couldn't be.

Her mouth had been sewn shut.

What was happening to her, she wondered? She didn't understand how this could be possible?

Completely terrified, Jamie focused once again on the person that appeared to be coming towards her through the light. Her eyes grew big with fear, as the figure now appeared right before her very eyes, allowing her to make out its physical features. Completely transfixed on the person in front of her, she let her fear die away a bit as it appeared to be nothing more than a little boy.

As the boy approached her, his young blonde hair sparkled fluently through the jolting light that continued to overwhelm her body with heat, and his dark almost blackened eyes gleamed at her. And then, as she watched in silence, he smiled at her. The little child was smiling at her, as if wishing to cause her no harm, his completely naked body seeming to enjoy the warmth the light provided.

Still, Jamie didn't understand what was going on.

What exactly did this small boy want with her? Did she know him, she asked herself?

Then, the smile quickly died away from the boy's charming small face, and his expression turned into a cold blooded stare that raised the hair on the back of her neck to it's fullest extent. The looks of a sweet, innocent boy had disappeared, and now it appeared as though the devil's son himself had graced her with his presence. Now, the boy looked angry, and his eyes began to fill with a certain hate and a vicious rage. In all her years of working in professional psychiatry, she had never seen anything like this.

Was he angry with her, she wondered?

Nonetheless, as the rage built within the small child, Jamie watched completely immobilized by her injuries as his mouth opened. At first, it appeared that he was about to speak to her, but as his mouth opened, it looked more like he wanted to eat her, rip apart her flesh like a shark sensing blood.

Then, the boy drew closer.

And closer.

Soon afterwards, with his mouth still hanging awkwardly open, he raised his right arm and pointed at her. No words were spoken, he just pointed accusingly at her, as if blaming her for something. Then, from nowhere, she saw something pour from the child's mouth. It was a shiny red liquid. As it poured from the small boy's mouth, at first it only covered his body. But then, it grew rapidly, like a river running wild throughout an everlasting canyon, and soon, it was forming all around her. As the red liquid splattered across her face, she felt it's warmth and immediately knew what it was.

It was blood.

Unable to scream, she tried to squirm away from the overflowing blood that poured freely from the boy's mouth. But she couldn't stop it. It was all around her, all over her. The light seemed to slowly fade away. Only now, it appeared as though she was going to drown in the boy's blood.

Finally, it came back to her.

She knew who the boy was.

She had accidentally run over him the night of her accident. She hadn't been paying attention to the road and when she looked up, she remembered seeing the boy strangely standing in the middle of the road. She had tried to veer away from him, not intentionally wanting to take his life. But her attempt to save him had failed and she remembered hearing the pounding thud sound his body had made as her Jeep trampled over his helpless body. She couldn't believe it. She had killed him.

And he was coming back from the dead to kill her, as now she was helpless from the car accident. He must have thought that she purposely ran over him, but it just wasn't true. It was an accident. She had tried everything to prevent her truck from slamming into the small child.

It appeared, however, that now it was too late. She hadn't even remembered what had happened that night until now, when the boy so suddenly, and without warning reentered her life. She wanted to apologize to the boy, take him in her arms and let him see that she hadn't run him over on purpose. Again, however, the thread held tight, preventing her from speaking. The blood was at her nostrils now, and it was becoming increasingly more difficult for her to breathe. This was it, she thought. She was going to die.

Finally, with one last attempt, she gathered all of the strength she could muster, and brought forth all of the adrenaline she could find from within her weakened, almost paralyzed body. One last time, she closed her eyes and tried to scream for help.

This time, amazingly, she heard the screeching sound of her own voice. Placing her hand on her mouth, she found that the thread was gone. Confused, she opened her eyes.

The blinding light was gone.

The blood was gone.

And, the little boy was gone.

Travis immediately rushed to her aid and looked into her terrified eyes, taking her shaking hands in his own as he tried to stop them from trembling. "Jesus sweetheart," he swore briefly. "What is it? What happened?" But Jamie couldn't answer. There was no sign of blood anywhere. Her clothes, her sheets, the floors of the hospital room, none of it were splattered with any blood. It seemed as though the boy had never been there.

"There was a boy," Jamie uttered, her voice still cracking with fear. "And there wa-was," she paused momentarily. "And there was blood everywhere."

"What!" Travis exclaimed his bleak expression vividly portrayed along his clean-shaven face. "What do you mean there was a boy and a lot of blood?" Jamie didn't answer. She just stared uncertainly into his eyes as if she didn't know how to answer his question, or not wanting to answer it. "Jamie!" Travis continued firmly, trying to snap his girlfriend out of whatever trance her mind had captured her in. "Please baby. What in the hell is going on?" he sort of demanded, rather than asked.

"My accident," Jamie finally continued, her eyes still heavy with fear as she recalled the events of what happened the night she traveled home along the blacktop of an Alabama highway. "I wrecked because I was trying to miss a small boy that was standing in the middle of the road. I didn't see him until it was too late. Oh God

Travis," she sighed as she pulled him close and buried her head into his shoulders. "I killed him. I killed that boy!"

Travis glared at the weak form in front him. She appeared to be talking in circles, tongue twisters that he simply couldn't understand. "What?" he asked soothingly, hoping she could gratify his need for answers. "What are you talking about?"

"I ran over a boy on the highway right before I crashed into a tree!" Jamie declared harshly.

"I'm sorry Jamie," Travis continued, still trying to calm the woman down in front of him. "But there was no boy found. No other body was recovered from the scene of the accident but your own, and you're alive. The marks your tires left on the road made the highway patrol think that you were swerving to try and avoid hitting a deer or something. But there was nothing found. There was no body of a little boy found, and there was absolutely no blood of any kind but your own."

"What..." Jamie let her words trail away. "That can't be possible."

"I promise you sweetheart," Travis assured her one last time. "You didn't kill anybody."

Jamie had no choice but to believe him. After all, he would never lie to her about something like that. But then again, her eyes didn't deceive her either. She had seen a boy on the road that night and was quite sure that she had hit him, and she was extremely positive that he had just came through the blinding florescent light that momentarily blinded her and covered her with his blood. Nothing made sense to Jamie Walker. Was her imagination driving her crazy? Was she losing her mind, she couldn't help but wonder?

Her mind began swarming with questions she could not answer, and suddenly she felt weaker than ever before. Looking into Travis's eyes, she spoke once again. "Please," she spoke softly. "Just take me home."

* * *

As Billy awoke the following morning, he found himself nestled tightly within the comforts of his bed, the cushioned mattresses seemed to try and swallow him whole. Lying on his back, he found

Tinman

himself sprawled comfortably across his satin sheets, one leg hidden beneath the covers, one out in the open, welcoming the cool air, which poured from the air conditioning vent directly overhead. His toned chest lay exposed, also accepting without argument the chilled breeze as it swarmed his tired, relaxed body. The sun had risen hours ago, and he had awakened right at dawn, only to fall back into a deep sleep, as if his body was tired of being kept awake at night due to the frightening nightmares that always seemed to plague him. It was as if somehow he was being forced to rest.

Now, however, he had to get up.

Blaze would be arriving shortly, and yet he still had to ask his mother if he could borrow her car to drive around Destin, until he was finally able to locate Red Fern Dr., which according to Elizabeth, was where Carey Haas now resided. He had never before been to Destin, so he was well aware that all of the terrain would feel like some sort of foreign territory in another land. But he was good with directions and he was sure he would be able to find his destination.

He would find her. He just had to. Failure was not an option.

Groaning as he climbed out of bed, he stretched his muscles, enjoying the crackling sound his bones gave off. Looking down at his bed, he prepared himself to make it up, only to turn away realizing it wasn't worth the effort. As he climbed in the shower, he remembered walking home last night, only to encounter another mind twisting headache, which was always followed by a violent vision from the past. A past from which he had not been apart of, experienced, or even knew anything about until he had set foot in the old Haas home. He didn't remember how he had even managed to get to his room last night. The only thing he remembered before loosing consciousness was the vision of Carey pleading for help. Only she hadn't been a small child as he remembered in the previous visions he had first encountered. She was now a full figured woman, his age, and absolutely one of the most beautiful creatures he had ever laid eyes upon. Her face, however, still possessed the soft, sweet, innocent look it had held when she was a child, as if refusing to go away.

Billy figured that Carey Haas hadn't let go of her past.

Then again, after what she had experienced, how could she, he asked himself?

Jason Glover

Finally, turning the shower off, Billy climbed out, quickly dried himself off, brushed his teeth, shaved, deodorized himself, and threw on some clean clothes consisting of a pair of blue jeans, black T-shirt, and working boots. Lastly, he threw on his favorite baseball cap, and then grabbed the piece of paper, which contained the address of his lost companion and headed downstairs. He found his mother relaxing outside on the patio, taking in the early morning rays and enjoying a book by one of her favorite authors. Stepping outside, he spoke quickly, showing his mother he was truly in a hurry. "Mom," he began instantly grabbing her attention. "I need to ask you for a favor."

"Well don't you look energetic this morning?" Debra asked intuitively with a smile. "Do we have big plans for the day?"

"I guess you could say that," Billy continued in a rush. "And I need to borrow your car for an hour or so. I have to do something before Blaze arrives today."

As Debra spoke, she chose her words wisely, not wanting to show her son that she could tell he was purposely trying to avoid telling her where it was he was planning on venturing that day. "Well all right," she spoke uncertainly, telling Billy where her keys could be found. Then, without saying another word, she watched in confusion as he turned away from her and darted off after the keys to her Lexus. The sliding glass door shut behind him and her son disappeared into their home without even saying goodbye.

Billy stumbled across the keys right away and quickly headed for the front door. He had his hand on the doorknob and was just about to walk outside when his mother called him back. He turned and found her standing right inside the sliding glass door. Meeting her half way, he waited for her to begin speaking. "Would it be too much to ask you where you are going?" Debra stated flatly, trying to set her mind at ease.

Billy said nothing for what seemed like eternity, not really sure how he should respond. "Look mom," he began, once again avoiding the question. Before he could continue, however, she cut him off.

"Why won't you tell me where you are going with my car?" she demanded.

"Because," Billy said firmly, holding his ground. "I don't think you'd let me go if you knew where I was going. But I'm damn near twenty years old, and I know you might not understand a lot of things that are going on with me right now. In fact, I think I'm just now starting to get a grasp on them. Just trust me mother. Please," he paused to gaze into her eyes. "That's all I ask. Just trust me."

"Billy," Debra spoke boldly, letting her son know that he wasn't getting off the hook. "Just tell me where you are going. I do trust you, and I know you always make educated decisions. If there's something you need to do, fine. I'm not going to try and stop you. I would just really feel better if I know where you are."

"Fine," Billy began making his way back towards the front door. "Do you remember Carey Haas, that little girl I showed you in the picture? The daughter of the family that lived here before us?"

Debra nodded. "What about her?" she asked, her son's agenda still a bit vague.

"Well if you must know," Billy continued, placing his hand once again on the door-handle. "She's still alive, and she's still living here in Destin, and I'm." he let his voice trail away into silence.

"And you're what?" Debra demanded her son to finish.

"And I'm going to find her," Billy concluded opening the door to their home, preparing to escape into the front yard before his mother could protest. "I don't know why, but I have to go to her. I have to find Carey Haas."

* * *

Carey Haas sat in silence on the back porch of her Aunt and Uncle's home, located just inside the Northeastern boondocks of the small sportsman city of Destin, Florida. Nineteen years of age, she looked every bit of twenty-four, and her maturity level made her seem even older. Her angelic blonde hair remained the same as she aged every year, never giving in to the brown roots that constantly threatened to take over. Nevertheless, her natural hair color remained the same, unchanged from when she was a child. Her skin was still as soft as ever, her colorful blue eyes giving new meaning to the phrase "full of life." However, with Carey, that wasn't the case.

She wasn't full of life. In fact, there was something missing, and it was something that hadn't been with her since she was a child. Something that had been taken from her without remorse or regret.

Jason Glover

Her parents.

She sat on the porch swing, rocking back and forth, enjoying the shady breeze that periodically flowed across her backyard, and watched as leaves silently fell every so often off of the tall oak trees that had been rooted into the soil of the earth for hundreds of years. Sitting quietly, she listened to the chirping of the birds, which although she couldn't see, she could hear and feel their presence nearby. Carey sat peacefully as she flipped once again through the photo album that contained the only pictures she had left of her parents. Always keeping it free of dust, she found herself flipping through its glossy pages at least once a day. It was a pleasure to remember the days she had been fortunate enough to spend with them on the beach the first nine years of her life, before the devil had come into their home one eerie night and destroyed the innocence and love her family had accumulated.

She remembered the beach.

She hadn't been there in years, and for some reason, never actually cared if she ever returned. The sun, the sand, the magnificent blue sky, the sea gulls, the crystal clear blue water of the mesmerizing ocean. All of the things she once cherished so dearly when she was a child were now nothing more than a mirage of the past. One in which she sometimes wished she could forget. The beach was no longer a place surrounded by fun loving families enjoying their time in the surf. To Carey, it had become known as a place of death, a place where everything seemed to turn into blood. A place where every dream was inevitably shattered, splintering into a million pieces, only to be washed away into a sea of oozing, churning red liquid.

No, if she could help it, she would never return to her home along the ocean, or the beach itself if possible.

Closing the album, she took in a deep breath and gazed at the backyard in front of her. The dark green grass glistened as if perspiring in some way as the sprinkler system worked it's way periodically back and forth. A wooden, maroon bird feeder stood alone in the center of the yard, only instead of birds dipping their tiny beaks in for a quick and easy bite to eat, she found a squirrel perched in command on the single rail, his head invisible as it uninvitingly helped itself to the treats the small house held inside. A fence, also accompanied by numerous rows of gigantic oak, and pine trees, as they shielded her from any harm that may be lurking beyond the contained area, bordered the backyard.

Climbing to her feet, she glanced around one last time at the yard where she seemed to have spent every afternoon since her final day of high school ended a few weeks ago. She wondered what her friends were doing today? But then again, she couldn't really call them her friends. She had never actually had someone she could call a true friend, because there wasn't anyone in her life she could trust. Except for her Aunt Carol, her mother's sister, and her Uncle Rick, she had no one.

She wanted to be able to trust people; however, for the past ten years she had been living in a world of loneliness, sorrow, fear, and without the satisfaction of feeling safe and secure. The tragic remembrance of her parents' death, and how her own life had been jeopardized, somehow forced her to become an angry soul. She wished she could change, but somehow, she didn't think that was ever going to happen. She saw her parents' mangled bodies every night in her sleep, and she pictured it daily, as if it had just happened yesterday. She still felt the man's presence swarming around her every so often, just as he had that fatal night ten years ago. To this day, she hadn't been able to forget about the notorious Curtis Rains. She had watched the nationwide news elaborating and saluting the death of the estranged serial killer that had taken the life of her parents and many others. But the Tinman's death hadn't been as satisfying to herself as it must have been for the other millions of citizens who wanted him dead.

It was almost as if he wasn't dead at all.

She continued to be afraid, continued to believe the Tinman was still alive somewhere out there, refusing to die. Sometimes, late at night, when she found herself unable to sleep, she knew that it was because of him. Her terrifying nightmares alone sometimes prevented her from sleeping. But most of all, it was the man's eyes. She could almost swear that sometimes Curtis was still watching her with the same vicious rage easily seen rooted into the depths of his eyes. He had successfully murdered her parents ten years ago, and she was well aware that his mission also included killing her. Her life was spared; yet she feared he would continue to seek out her existence until he accomplished destroying her life as well.

She didn't know why, and sometimes wished she would have died alongside her parents. Her life had not been the same without them. As every holiday passed, she felt the loneliness come on even stronger, and she missed them even more as she realized she would never get to share anything with them again. She would never be able to bring home a boyfriend for her father's approval, not that she intended on dating anyone. In fact, there had only been a couple of dates she actually remembered adventuring out on. She would always ask to be brought home. Her trust always seemed to collapse and fear would escalate into a tormenting phase of uneasiness and pain. She knew a lot of guys found her attractive, and it wasn't that she didn't find them attractive as well. It was just that none of them made her feel safe. She wondered if she would ever find someone that could give her the safety she needed to feel secure.

Finally, shambling inside, she tugged her daisy dukes down as far as they would go below her navel, the muscles clearly visible in every section of her tanned legs and shapely thighs. Then, fitting her bra more comfortably under her tightly woven green body shirt that was V-shaped and accentuated her astounding breasts, she entered her aunt's home and closed the door behind her. Passing her relatives in the living room, she waved accordingly, politely acknowledging their presence then headed directly for her room. Once inside, she collapsed on her bed and prepared to take an early afternoon nap. Closing her eyes, however, she knew that she was going to have trouble sleeping. Surrounded by a dozen teddy bears and stuffed animals, she was the only person in the room. Yet, she didn't feel alone.

It felt like there was another presence there.

It felt as though something was watching her.

Something she couldn't see.

And she knew that as soon as she gave into the deep sleep her body desperately wanted her to enjoy, she would once again be carried unwillingly into the world of horrifying nightmares that always seemed to come whenever she sensed another presence in her room. She hated the nightmares, and wished they would just go away, and leave her alone.

However, they always reappeared, reasserting themselves in her mind, until sometimes she actually felt as if she was going crazy.

Tinman

"*Crazy. She's crazy as a loon,*" she recalled some of her classmates whispering as she passed through the hallways at school, not exactly sure how they were convinced that their bickering couldn't be heard and wondering what she had ever done that made them come to such a conclusion. But then again, she was sure some of them wanted her to hear them. They wanted to make her feel uncomfortable. They wanted her to run away in tears, calling for the teacher to come and help. As of yet, however, she had never given them the satisfaction of watching her suffer. She never gave them the opportunity to understand the pain she felt inside, nor did she want to. All of the years she had spent in the public school system in Destin, Florida, she had been alone, having no one she could call a friend, having no one she could even call a boyfriend.

The funny thing was, she didn't care.

She was happy living in a world where at least her parents would never be forgotten. She missed them. She loved them. And she wanted them back more than anything in the world. Or, at least, if nothing else, just long enough for her to actually say goodbye.

Finally, not being able to withstand the sleep she knew was coming on, she leaned over and glanced at the picture of her parents on the blue wooden nightstand next to her bed. David and Charlene's fairy tale expressions in the picture showed nothing more than happiness and brought back the many happy memories Carey had been able to experience as a child. Smiles played along their happy faces, their arms around one another, and then there was Carey herself, standing right in between the two of them, a smile also seen dwindling carelessly from her young facial structure. The only difference now was she was no longer smiling.

She had nothing to smile about, nothing at all.

Then, before closing her eyes, and giving in to the clairvoyance she knew to be near, she let a single tear fall from her eye socket, her cheek feeling the cool wetness as it absorbed into her pillow. Her heart ached at times like this…each and every day of her life.

✦ ✦ ✦

Debra Saxton sat inside, her mind wondering in circles like never before. Concentrating completely on her son, who had been gone for nearly an hour now, she wondered just what was going on inside his head. She tried to put herself in his position, tried to force herself to understand the deadly nightmares and blood endued visions he had recently been complaining of. But it was no use. She simply couldn't understand, and wouldn't be able to unless she found herself in the exact same predicament. So far, it seemed as though the chances of that happening were slim.

Then what should she do, she asked herself?

Every so often, she found herself flipping through the pages of the phone book until she came across a listing of a few psychiatrists who specialized in "meaningful episodes," she liked to call it. She could somehow sense the anger her son would feel if she went behind his back, without his permission, and set up an appointment with some strange doctor who wanted to study his mind.

But she couldn't help it.

She had to do something.

She couldn't just sit there and do nothing while her son was obviously experiencing pain, and going through something that terrified him. Billy was undoubtedly hurting inside, and although he never spoke much about it, she could tell and sense that something was wrong with him. He was changing. In fact, he had changed in only a matter of days. Ever since they arrived in Destin something had happened to her son. Damn it, she cursed herself, she wanted him back. She wanted her son back.

Bravely, she picked up the receiver of the phone and dialed the first number on the page. Within seconds, a cheerful secretary picked up the line on the other end. "Dr. Richmond's office. May I help you."

"Awe, yes," Debra paused slightly, half expecting to hang up on the bright young woman. "Maybe you can. May I speak with Dr. Richmond please? I'm not a patient of his," she added before the girl could ask the question she was sure to come. "In fact, I'm new here in town, and my name is Debra Saxton."

"I'm sorry," the doctor's secretary responded, her voice showing signs of reluctance. "But he's with a client at the moment. Could I take your number and have him return your call, or would you simply like to set up an appointment with him?"

"Appointment?" Debra returned the question, really not quite sure if she was doing the right thing. Nevertheless, she followed her motherly instincts and continued. "Um, sure. When is his next available opening?"

"Let's see," the voice on the other end paused as she flipped through an appointment book. "We could squeeze you in later on this afternoon if you'd like. How does three o'clock sound to you?" she added after another momentary, professional pause.

"Great," Debra concluded before hanging up the phone. "See you then."

* * *

Meanwhile, back in Starke, Florida.

Jack Reynolds sat quietly in his living room on his blandly colored antique sofa, simply reading the morning newspaper, enjoying a bold cup of coffee, and not really watching, but listening to morning news coverage his television portrayed without interruption. The minute he rose from bed, he knew that this was going to be a glorious day. He had the day off from work at the Prison, and the thought of not having to put up with the filthy scum infested inmates he had to deal with day in and day out was enough to put his mind at ease. His wife, Gloria, was busily working at City Hall doing her administrative assistant duties he knew to be nerve racking as practically every evening, she would come home with a disgruntled look spread across her face, sometimes even refusing to smile. And his eleven year old daughter, Sarah, had spent the night off with friends not returning until long after the sun had fallen behind the few dusk of clouds that lingered in the sky.

Today was his day. His day to relax, and absolutely nothing was going to arouse his anger, stir his pleasant thoughts, or bring him down. He simply wouldn't allow that to happen. Not today.

Then, something came across the television screen that forced him to reluctantly place the newspaper aside for the moment. Giving the newscaster his full attention, he watched with a frown as another story of Curtis Rains began. "Why can't they just kill this damn story and lay it to rest? The son of a bitch is dead for crying out loud," Jack mustered harshly, although knowing full well that there was no one to hear him. Nevertheless, the story continued.

For the past few days, ever since he himself had gladly pulled the final lever down, which had sent the multiple currents of electricity into the Tinman's body, eventually ending his life, he had been sort of praised by the press. Jack himself had had the honors of finalizing many of the death row inmates' unworthy lives. Yet, until Curtis Rains came along, he had never actually enjoyed his job that much and had never been recognized by the media. He was truly thrilled, and ecstatic about the fact that he had been the lone assassin in putting an end to a man's life who had caused so much suffering, heartache and pain in the years he had been free to roam about the country, stalking and slaying innocent families who had so much to give. Curtis Rains disgusted him to the fullest extent, and not a bone in his body, not a cell in his brain ever once regretted killing Curtis Rains. In fact, the only thing he did regret about the entire situation was the fact that he wasn't sure if Curtis had suffered enough as he experienced his painful, undeniable death.

However, one thing was for sure, Jack hoped so.

But for some reason, he didn't think so. In all the years he had spent with the demented serial killer on death row, he found out one thing. Curtis wasn't scared of death. In fact, he cherished it, almost as if it was the only thing he could actually consider holy. Curtis, although never speaking more than a sentence at a time, if speaking at all, would always speak in a terrifying tone, letting everyone know what would happen if he were ever released from prison. Luckily, that never happened, because he would have killed again.

It terrified Jack sometimes as he wondered what Curtis must have been dreaming about when he slept at night. And when the days came along where Curtis would remain speechless throughout the entire day and night, he couldn't help but wonder what must have been going through the brightly educated mind of the monster criminal.

Surely, his thoughts were always focused on death and the dying.

Death. And blood.

Many times Curtis had threatened to kill Jack himself and his family. Jack would only laugh, however, and purposely antagonize the man held against his will behind the steel bars of the prison. If

Tinman

there was anyone at the prison that could get into the mind of Curtis Rains, it had been Jack Reynolds. If there was any guard, who even dared to try and speak to the man known as the deadliest, most gruesome serial killer in history, it was Jack Reynolds. And if there was someone out there who could honestly say that they weren't afraid of the Tinman, it was Jack Reynolds. Jack had even stared into Curtis's eyes many times, and never once would he look away as his body became flooded with fear, unless it was time for him to continue on his short beat down the hallway, just making sure all of the inmates were locked down securely without the slightest chance of escape.

Jack even remembered the morning he awakened knowing fully well that at the midnight hour of that very night, he was going to end the Tinman's life. Surprisingly, he found himself filled with excitement and anticipation. He even arrived at the prison an hour early, his mind completely enthused with the notion that he would always be remembered as the man who laid Curtis Rains to rest once and for all.

However, after the execution, he found himself rather bored with his job, almost as if Curtis Rains himself had been the sole reason he had shown up for work everyday. He truly took advantage of his power as a guard when it came to Curtis, beating him every so often, even though knowing that he did nothing wrong. Mainly, however, it was because he knew he could get away with it. No one cared about what happened to the Tinman. No one cared about the beatings, about the verbal abuse that had been laid upon the already pronounced dead inmate. In fact, if it were ever to come out in the open that Curtis had been physically and verbally abused within the solitary confinements of the Florida State Penitentiary, no one would scream bloody murder. No one would try to step in and make sure it never happened again.

No.

People would cheer in joy, only wishing that they had been the lucky ones who were able to inflict pain on the man who thrived on administering pain to others who never deserved it. Curtis Rains, however, no matter what kind of childhood he had unwillingly grown up in deserved to be beaten, called names, or even slaughtered. In Jack's mind, the electric chair wasn't the punishment that fit the crime. In his mind, the slicing of the Tinman's throat, only after puncturing his chest with at least a dozen stab wounds would have been justified. Legally, however, that could never be done.

If possible, Jack would have jumped at the chance.

He would have loved to see the Tinman's blood escalate all over his hands, and drain to the cemented floor found in the execution chamber.

Yes, the execution of Curtis Rains had been a day to remember for all eternity. However, it could have been a lot more commemorate, and exciting.

A lot more exciting!

* * *

The creature swam provocatively through the darkened space that had been provided to it as blackness closed in a few short days ago. It cherished the freedom that finally, after years of incarceration, was able to experience once again. And it truly enjoyed, and possessed more power now than it ever dreamed possible.

It was unstoppable, invincible against mankind.

And soon, very soon, another unlucky person would feel its presence and be confronted with a force that simply wouldn't be denied or reckoned with.

The creature had already dispensed of some of its internal anger after ever so slightly changing the course of Jamie Walker's happy life. It had spared her life for one reason, and one reason only. She had to suffer. The creature was a master of suffering, a master of destroying the meaning of life. And it would not fail until its mission was complete. Unfortunately, it already had another unlucky soul in mind.

Chapter 12

    Billy Saxton walked clumsily out of the Dixie Convenient Store found along Northshore Dr., carrying a city map he had just purchased from the cashier inside. Climbing back into his mother's luxurious Lexus, he twisted the key in the ignition, waited patiently for the engine to spring to life then turned on the air conditioner, not allowing the Florida heat to get the best of him. Finally, after eliminating the distracting noise of the complex car stereo, he opened the city map of Destin, sprawling it out as far as he could manage on the passenger seat. He suddenly found his vision becoming blurry as he tried to sort out and read the thousands of road names that appeared everywhere on the map. He never realized Destin was so widespread. Needless to say, it was much bigger than he had originally gathered, and the task of finding Carey Haas seemed more and more impossible as each minute passed.
    "Damn it," Billy cursed himself harshly as he finally admitted to himself that he was lost. Then, taking in a deep breath, he exhaled the warm air, and closed his eyes for a brief moment to clear his head. Finally, he reopened them and once again stared at the map before him, which at first looked to be nothing more than an excellently crafted maze, or a highly designed labyrinth where the end would never be found. However, Billy wasn't going to give up.
    Folding the map in two, he decided that the Northeastern portion of the map was the only section of the map he actually needed to see. Placing his rigid index finger on one of the roads he saw at the top right corner of the delineation, he began slowly making his way

downwards until the name of the road he clutched on the piece of paper in his other hand came into view.

Then, he saw it.

Alpine Ave.

Looking at the street sign of the road that sat directly in front of him, he quickly found exactly where he was on the map. A smile crossed his face as he realized he was only a few short blocks away from Alpine Ave., and depending on the traffic, he was only about twenty minutes away from Carey Haas. Then, as Billy began to map the course he was going to follow in his mind, he put the car in drive, and pulled out into the oncoming traffic. "This is crazy!" he thought, but he couldn't see any other way. Carey Haas had been in his nightmares and visions, which always seemed to cause blackouts, and he didn't have the faintest idea why? She was a mystery in her own right, but not one he considered dangerous. The only thing he knew was that he had to go to her. He had to find out what was going on once and for all. There simply wasn't another solution.

As the minutes slowly crept by, he knew he was going in the right direction because within seconds of crossing the Piedmont Bridge, he found himself making an immediate left onto the road next to a twenty four hour barbecue pit stop, leaving the populated urban area of Destin behind. That road was Alpine Ave. Driving past the restaurant, he found himself driving along a road full of sharp twists and turns. There appeared to be nothing but rigid wetland areas all around him, and these areas appeared to be surrounded by a terrain of thick forests, all of the ancient trees covered with thick masses of green leaves, and darkened brown bark. It was silent, except for all of the animals that crawled about, making occasional noises to warn other animals of their existence. every so often letting some defining noise loose into the air as they let other animals know their presence was there. The environment itself was spooky, and the thought of turning around and returning home to his mother had never occurred to Billy Saxton until now.

Nevertheless, he continued forward. He had come too far to turn back now.

Then, up ahead, he found himself coming into a clearing of sorts. To the left the forests disappeared for a moment, and he found himself driving beside a lifeless marsh. The mucky waters, and mushy surface gave it the look of an ancient graveyard. Very little green could be seen growing from inside the disturbing wetland, and the polluting smell that pulverized his nostrils sent his nose hairs flaring in anguish. He gassed the vehicle a bit to get away from the marsh as quickly as possible. "How could anyone want to live next to such a thing?" he asked himself out loud as the excruciating smell vanished back into the murky area he left behind.

He passed a few old houses along the way, all in major need of repair. The simplest designs had been used when the homes had been crafted years ago, and Billy could see that the architecture of the past was nothing compared to modernistic structures found today. All of the yards needed immediate attention as trash could be seen scattered about in every direction from most of the lawns. All of the homes stood in silence, however, showing no signs of life whatsoever. They all looked dull and spooky as if one day their destiny was to sink into the pits of the muddy surface, swallowing them whole, relinquishing their scarred presence from the face of the earth and putting the homes out of their misery. Billy knew the people who occupied these homes weren't the most respected people in the world, and probably didn't have a lot of money, but he couldn't find an excuse as to why they had chosen to let their homes rot and decay throughout the years, as if they didn't care about their appearance.

Then, as he passed a few other lifeless homes, he once again came into the trenches of the forests and their presence swarmed around him. For five minutes he drove along Alpine Ave., seeing no signs of life except for the enchanting, bewildering forests on both sides of him. No other car had passed him in either direction as he traveled down the road, and the thickness of the woods beside him stifled his vision, not allowing him to see more than two feet inside. It was eerie to think the creatures and animals of the forest were watching him. He found himself growing more and more impatient with his journey, and the uncomfortable feeling of perplexity came along in a rather insulting, provocative manner. Warily, however, he continued forward, until another home came into view.

As he approached this single home in the middle of nowhere, he realized it wasn't the same as all the other's he had passed just a few minutes earlier. This two-story home looked to be full of life. It was a brick home, the top story lined with a single row of four windows, all of them in a beautiful display of enchanting colors, relinqvishing a church cathedral appearance. Billy knew that part of it was the sunshine as it reflected off the stained glass, but if looking from inside the home, you would be able to see through it as clear as day. The burgundy color of the window shutters matched the brick structure perfectly, and beautiful green vineyards hung flawlessly from every window, stretching their way into a magnificent tangle of gracefulness.

The bottom portion of the home was more homely, however. The large white, wooden front door stood perfectly in the center of the home, it's brass handle undoubtedly locked and bolted from inside. Two windows were found on each side of the front door, displaying beautiful flowery curtains showing the ever popular V-shape insignia, and a gorgeous display of flowers could be seen along the window seal inside the home.

The front porch consisted of three wicker chairs, two on the left side of the front door with a neatly woven wicker table in front. The other sat at the far end of the right side of the porch, two lovely hardwood trees on both sides the chair. Large, thick bushes, just tall enough to reach the beginning of the windows, before they were so craftily, and perfectly trimmed short, covered the entire front of the home. The cemented walkway, which lead from the driveway, had been kept edged neatly, keeping it free of the baffling weeds that constantly tried to destroy it's beautiful nature.

No sandy spots could be found along the freshly cut grass, and a bed of roses were planted in an elegant circular pattern as the red beauties surrounded the single large pine tree that loomed overhead in the far right side of the front yard. A bird feeder sparkled with life in the center of the front yard, and from the sides of the house, Billy could barely make out the confinements of a large backyard, undoubtedly just as beautiful and taken care of as the front.

Then, looking at the piece of paper he still clutched in the palm of his hand, he read the address out loud. Checking the mailbox number on the house in front of him, a smile crossed his face as he realized he had finally reached his destination.

He had found the home he had been searching for.
He had found Carey Haas.

Tinman

Finally, realizing he had been parked mysteriously on the side of the road for quite a while now, he put the car in drive and began once again creeping down the deserted road in front of him. He traveled about two hundred yards down the road, before deciding to turn around and head back towards the house he had just discovered. Now that he had found the home, however, his mind began churning furiously with frustrating questions. What was he supposed to do? How was he going to actually talk to Carey? Was he supposed to just walk right up to the front door, knock and ask to speak with her, he wondered?

No.

That would never work. Her aunt and uncle wouldn't allow some stranger to just come walking into their home, and pull their relative aside to talk to her about the haunting events of her past. How was he going to handle this? He had to somehow find a way to approach Carey Haas alone, not wanting his presence to be known to anyone else. Crazily, he slowed his car some ten miles below the speed limit and watched the house as the distance between him began to close in once again.

Then, something happened.

It was a car, and it was backing out of the driveway. Slowing his smooth riding car down even more, he watched in awe as a black Lincoln turned the opposite direction, as if heading towards town. Billy waited patiently and watched the car carefully. He wasn't sure if the car had noticed him, and wanted to see if the Lincoln was going to turn around. Shortly, however, a sigh of relief flushed over him as the car soon disappeared into the distance and into the twisting maze of dangerous curves that lead into town. Now, once again Billy parked his car on the opposite side of the road. He left his ignition running as he gazed once again at the brick fortress in front of him. He had been able to make out two figures in the Lincoln that had just pulled away from the carport and headed down the road. He knew that one of them was a man, undoubtedly Rick Goodman, Carey's uncle. The other he knew to be a female. Whether or not it was Carey's Aunt Carol, or Carey herself, remained a mystery.

Nevertheless, the opportunity was too good to be true, and he couldn't allow it to slip past him. He may never have another chance such as this one again. Finally, after telling himself that what he was doing was crazy and simply unheard of, he turned his mother's car off. Then, leaving the doors unlocked, he slowly crossed the street and headed for the front door of the house. His hands trembled with nervousness, and they shook in an uncontrollable motion, as he suddenly found himself in need of a bathroom. "You can do this," he tried to assure himself. "Just knock on the door and see who comes to answer." Finally, he balled his right hand into a fist, and knocked on the front door.

Knock, Knock, Knock.

He knocked three times then waited patiently for someone to come and acknowledge his presence. Frowning, he let a few minutes pass before realizing no one was coming to answer the door. He thought that he had knocked hard enough for anyone in the house to hear him. Nevertheless, he tried once again. This time, he used a bit more authority.

KNOCK. KNOCK. KNOCK.

This time, he was sure if anyone were inside, they would have heard him knocking. Again, however, after a few seconds passed by and into forgotten, lost time, no one came to greet him at the door. Perhaps no one was home, he thought to himself as he secretively began looking into the windows along the front porch hoping to see any signs of life from inside the home. Unfortunately, there was none. All of the lights were off, and everything appeared to be dark and gloomy as everything sat dust free and neatly placed inside the home. Still, someone had to be home. There had only been two people in the car he had just seen pulling out of the driveway. Someone had to be there.

After thinking momentarily of knocking a third time, he decided to skip it as he left the front porch, rounded the side of the house and soon found himself standing in front of the fence that came up to his waist. Hesitating for a moment before climbing over, he cautiously waited to see if a ferocious dog was going to come from out of nowhere and chase him away from the home as it protected it's occupants. Finally, feeling secure enough to continue, he leaped the fence with ease and suddenly found himself standing alone in the backyard.

What was he doing?

Tinman

He was trespassing, breaking the law. And he still hadn't the faintest idea why? If anyone were to drive by they would without question call the police thinking that he was some kind of burglar. Or worse. Perhaps they would think of him as a kidnapper, rapist, or maybe even a killer? Billy knew that he wasn't any of those things. In any case, he knew the ignorance of today's society would bring about the wrong impression, and if he weren't careful, he would find himself behind bars with detectives questioning him as to why he had been there? What would he do then? Try and explain to them about all of his darkened nightmares, and illusions? Tell them that he knew exactly what had happened to the Haas family, that he had seen everything as it unfolded that dreadful night? No, he thought to himself, they would laugh in his face, call him crazy and lock him up in some mental institution where even if he were crazy, he was sure to come out with even more of his mind lost, left behind in the world of lunatics.

His instinct told him to simply turn around and flee from the area. His passion for finding out what was going on inside his head, however, made him continue, and soon, he found himself standing on the back porch of the Goodman home. Heading straight for the backdoor, he peered inside one the windows searching for any movement from inside. There was nothing.

There was only a stilling silence.

Finally, with his mind wondering in a state of confusion and excitement, he placed his hand on the doorknob and twisted it slightly to the left. Breathing slowly, he realized the door was unlocked. Now, really not believing what he was doing, he pushed the door slowly open and listened in reluctant fear as its squeaking noise would have given himself away to anyone inside the home. Still, he stepped inside and closed the door quietly behind him. He stood motionlessly for a second, as he waited for someone to peer from out of nowhere and accuse him of breaking into their home.

First trespassing, now breaking an entering.

What was he doing?

Was it even worth the risks he was now taking?

Things were undoubtedly getting out of control, and Billy suddenly found himself doing things he would have never done before. He had never in his life broken the law before, except of course for a few speeding violations as he sometimes felt the need to drop the hammer. Now, however, he had broken two laws that could very easily cost him one hell of a fine, and perhaps a short time in the county jail. Then, realizing he had already entered the home, he shuffled his feet nervously before exiting the kitchen he found himself standing in, and soon found himself in the living room area, the front door now visible. A staircase was directly to the left of him, and for some reason or another, without giving the first floor even a fraction of his attention, he began climbing the stairs ever so quietly.

Billy wasn't certain why he didn't investigate the first floor more respectfully. It seemed as though something was drawing him, or pulling him towards the second floor. Never giving it a second thought, he allowed himself to be pulled up the stairs. After passing a few rooms along the hallway of the upstairs portion of the massive home, he found himself standing outside the only one that had the door closed.

For some reason, this room, the room with the door closed, was the only room that captured his attention. Placing his hand on the handle, he checked to see if it was locked.

It wasn't.

Trying to relax, he prepared to open the door. He couldn't wait to see what he was going to find inside.

* * *

Rick and Carol Goodman drove rather hastily back down Alpine Ave. towards their lovely home in the middle of nowhere. Many times the two of them had talked of selling the place and moving somewhere a little closer to the heart of Destin. Every evening, however, as the two of them sat amongst the stars, listening to the crickets chirping away, and listening to the wonderful silence their secluded home graced them with, they knew selling was never going to happen. Their ears were always filled with the sounds of Mother Nature and the creatures stirring about in the surrounding wood and marshlands. A car would pass every now and then, but the muffled sounds of their engines would die away just as quickly as they came and the peacefulness of their home would soon be restored. Inevitably, they knew they would never move out of their home.

They had too many memories there. Memories they never wanted to forget. Anywhere else simply couldn't be referred to as their home.

As Rick, behind the wheel of their classy Lincoln, rounded the sharp corners with ease, he looked at his wife beside him, her everglade green eyes never leaving the road ahead. Her neatly woven black hair blossomed around her beautiful, soft face. Carol kept herself in shape, looked younger than forty-five years of age, and Rick often wondered how he had gotten so lucky? "What is this all about?" he asked Carol as she continued to tell him to speed it up. "Why are you in such a hurry to get home."

"I don't know," Carol admitted firmly. "But something's wrong Rick," she continued, pausing slightly to look into her husband's enchanting hazel eyes, which seemed to sparkle the dullness his brown hair provided. "I can feel it. Something is wrong," she concluded looking at his gruff chin, knowing fully well that Rick's lazy nature wouldn't allow him to take the time to shave unless she forced him to do so. The past few years, she noticed Rick sluggishly slowing down a bit, and his belly was just now showing the signs that came along with old age. But he was only forty-seven years old, and she knew that if he didn't watch himself and take care of his body, he would wind up aging a lot sooner than he anticipated.

"Say no more," Rick added half jokingly, not really understanding what could possibly be wrong at their home. They had been gone for only a short while, leaving Carey sleeping peacefully in her bed, snuggled comfortably under the covers, as they went for a quick stroll to the market to pick up a few supplies that were needed for the meal they had planned for the evening. Rick knew his wife all to well, however, and every time the two of them left the house and left Carey unsupervised, Carol had always seemed convinced that something had gone wrong. Nothing ever had to date, and Rick had tried many times to convince his wife she was overly protective about her sister's daughter. Of course what had happened to Charlene and David Haas some ten years ago was tragic indeed, but Carey was going on twenty years old, practically a grown woman who could most certainly provide and defend for herself if need be. She no longer needed the guidance and supervision that they had given when they had taken her under their wings when she was a small child. It was time for her to make decisions of her own, plan for her future, and it had long since been past the time when they could leave her at the house alone.

Carol, however, just couldn't let go. The past of her sister's gruesome death still haunted her just as it continued to rip away at Carey. As the years passed, Rick seemed to be the only one to get on with life and what was left to live of it. Living in the past had always seemed to cause more grief and suffering than happiness, and finding happiness is what Rick thought living was all about. It had long since been time for the two of them to get on with their lives, and find happiness within themselves. No matter where it took them.

Carol, however, was Rick's happiness. So, with a cunning grin, he pressed his foot harder on the accelerator, doing nothing more than pleasing his wife. As they rounded the last of the sharp corners, they both knew that they would be back at home within seconds.

Carol's hand was already clutching the door handle.

* * *

Billy Saxton opened the bedroom door an inch or two, and peered with one observant eye inside the room. The walls had been covered by a thick pink color, the top and bottom covered with wallpaper that consisted of white and yellow wild flowers. There was a white bookshelf that stood along the far end of the room, and a sofa right next to it, containing about a dozen or so stuffed animals, all of them with welcoming smiles spread across their cheerful faces. A single white dresser stood along the wall that was closest to him, a mirror placed perfectly on its center. Billy could clearly see that he was looking into a girl's room.

Then, his eyes fell to the bed. Only it wasn't neatly made like everything else in the room. Then, he realized something else that he hadn't been expecting.

The bed wasn't empty.

There before him, was the girl he had seen in his sleep as the nightmares came into his life. There before him, was the girl he had seen as a child, in his visions of her family being slaughtered to death. There before him, was the girl he had always thought of as being a young child. However, she wasn't a child any longer. In fact,

Tinman

sleeping in the bed before him was the most beautiful girl he had ever laid his eyes upon. Right before his very eyes, lay Carey Haas.

She was lying on her back, her breathing steady. One arm lay twisted behind her head, the other laid flatly along her stomach, which lifted every so often as she took in another breath, only to fall again as she exhaled. Her entire body was covered with a beautiful smooth tan. Her blonde hair was just as beautiful as it had been when he had seen her the other night, and although he couldn't see her eyes, he knew that they would be just as enlightening. She was more beautiful than Billy could have ever imagined. Silently, he just stood in the doorway of the sleeping beauty's room, not wanting to awaken and frighten her. After all, he hadn't come there to harm her. Then again, he didn't know why he had come there in the first place?

Completely baffled at how beautiful Carey was, he opened the door a little more and stepped inside the bedroom. What should he do? Should he go over to her and wake her up?

No. That was completely out of the question, he answered himself.

He wasn't even supposed to be there. He hadn't been invited in. He had taken it upon himself to enter at his own risk, well aware of the penalties and consequences he could face if found inside. Nevertheless, the more he looked at the striking creature in front of him, the more he realized he didn't care if he was caught. Carey Haas was stunning, and meeting her was worth any risk or misfortune that may come. After all, Billy hadn't been sent to her by accident. There was something about Carey Haas that had attracted or induced his attention ever since he had moved to Destin and found the picture of her and her family when she was a small child. He didn't quite know exactly what it was he needed from Carey; he only hoped that she would be able to help him find out.

Then, something happened inside the room that froze Billy completely. At first, as her body began to twitch violently, Billy thought that he had somehow awakened her and she was terrified of him. As the seconds passed, however, and as her head slammed over and over again into her headboard, he realized that wasn't the case.

She was having a nightmare. It was the same kind of episode he remembered being forced to endure every time he laid himself to rest. Feeling sorry for the girl in front of him, he went to her. Softly seating himself next to Carey on the bed, he placed both of his hands on her shoulders, not allowing her to throw her body around in a wild rampage of fear. Not awakening her, he waited patiently for her body to relax and let go of the tension it had accumulated. Finally, when her breathing returned to normal, he let go of her rather broad shoulders, safely knowing that the nightmare had dispersed. Then, staring in amazement at the wonderful person in front of him, Billy slowly lifted himself off her bed and began backing away from the room. He was a bit saddened at the fact that he knew she would never know how he had just comforted her while she slept, chasing all of the demons away that had entered her life at that moment.

Then, something else happened. Only, this was something that caught him completely off guard, and as an adrenaline rush of fear spread throughout his toned body, he fled the room and hurried down the hallway.

Someone else was inside the house.

Her aunt and uncle had returned home.

"Carey!" he heard a woman's voice call out with a hint of panic in her voice. "Carey!" he heard the woman call out again as the front door slammed shut. Then, as he himself neared the flight of stairs, he stopped in his tracks as he heard the thundering footsteps of someone coming upstairs. Shaking in fear, he knew that his presence had been sensed. They knew that he was in the house.

What should he do? Where should he go?

Looking all around him, Billy desperately tried to find a place to hide. But there was nowhere to go. Then, he saw a door. It was a small door, so he knew it couldn't be a bedroom, and although it was pretty close to the staircase, he knew that the people hurrying up the stairs wouldn't see it. Finally, running to the door, he opened it and luckily found that there was just enough room for him to fit inside. Closing the door slightly, he watched in complete silence as Rick and Carol barreled up the stairs, only to plow into Carey's room seconds later, obviously worried that something had happened to her. Once they disappeared into the bedroom, Billy knew this might be his only chance.

Quickly, he stepped from the closet, not even bothering to close the door all the way behind him, and sprinted noiselessly down the stairs. Bolting for the front door, he ran into the front yard and found his mother's car still parked across the street. Fidgeting with the keys in his pocket, he found himself sweating like an irrational psychopath. "Come on damn it!" he ordered himself harshly.

Finally, he seated himself behind the wheel of the Lexus and hastily placed the key in the ignition. Instantaneously after the engine sprang to life, he put the car in drive and sped away from the Goodman home. However, as he left the most beautiful girl he had ever seen behind, he realized that he hadn't gotten any closer to finding another piece of the puzzle he so desperately wanted to solve. None of his questions had been answered. Frowning, he concentrated on the road ahead of him.

He couldn't believe he had just broken into a home. However, if given the chance, he knew he would do it again. Carey Haas was somehow important to him. Billy asked himself why she was so important? Unfortunately, however, he couldn't come up with an answer.

* * *

Moments earlier.

As Rick and Carol neared their home, both of them quickly noticed the unfamiliar and quite disturbing sight of the sleek black Lexus that was parked across the street from their home. "Oh my God!" Carol shrieked in horror as Rick pulled the car into their driveway and abruptly brought the vehicle to a stop. "I told you," she continued climbing out of the car and running towards the front door. "I knew something was wrong Rick. I just knew it."

"Just calm down sweetheart," Rick tried to control his wife's sudden fearsome outburst. "We don't know for sure that anything is wrong. Someone may have simply broke down or something."

"Don't tell me to calm down," Carol ordered harshly, not realizing the sting her words put on her husband's gentle heart. "I know something is wrong damn it. I can feel it," she added twisting the handle of the front door, only to become angrily frustrated as she realized it was locked. "Just open the door," she ordered rather than asked as her trembling body stepped aside allowing her husband in front of her. Saying nothing, Rick calmly unlocked the door, and as soon as he pushed the door open, the two of them burst inside, his wife stampeded ahead of him and headed directly for the stairs, desperately wanting to get to her niece's bedroom. "Carey!" she yelled panicking as she entered her home. "Carey!" she called again as she began climbing the stairs.

Rick followed closely behind his wife as the two them reached the top of the staircase. He wasn't quite sure just what exactly his wife thought had happened, but he refused to think of the worst until he had seen it with his own eyes. Finally, the two of them reached Carey's bedroom, neither of them noticing that her door was slightly ajar, and not shut tightly as it had been when they had checked on her before leaving the home. Nevertheless, he watched as Carol relaxed as they found her sleeping peacefully in her bed, just as she had been when they left.

Turning to face her husband, she spoke before he could say anything as a scorned look now took the place of fear along her naturally beautified facial structure. "Don't say anything," she whispered holding up her index finger. "I don't care what this looks like. I know I was not overreacting. Someone was in here Rick, and still might be. I just know it," she concluded trying to regain the poise that had left her, and trying to make herself believe that she was brave. Within seconds, however, she found herself burying herself into her husband's chest as he cradled her in his arms. Then, sobbing, she continued. "I'm sorry honey. I don't know why I get like this sometimes. It's like ever since Charlene was kille-" she never finished her sentence knowing that Rick knew what she was talking about.

"It's all right baby. It's all right," Rick assured his loving wife. "I know what you're going through and I understand." Then, before either of them could muster another sound, both of them stood in complete silence as they heard the familiar sound of their front door closing. "Stay right here," Rick ordered as he quickly departed from his niece's bedroom and hurried back downstairs. Running to the front door, he opened it and stepped outside just in time to see the Lexus speeding away into the distance. It was too far for him to make out the letters on the license plate. "Son of a bitch!" Rick said aloud as he realized that someone had actually been inside his home. Even when he and his wife had come home and went up to Carey's room, someone had been inside.

Suddenly becoming a bit frightened, he felt a bit responsible for not providing the protection his family deserved. Something serious could have happened to Carey as she was left home alone. Carol had been right all along.

Finally, as anger suddenly took the place of the fear that had momentarily seized his body, he came back inside his home, closing and bolting the door behind him. Walking back up the stairs, he knew he would find his wife sitting on the bed next to Carey, sheltering her from any danger that may be approaching. Reaching the top of the stairs, however, something caught his attention before he could reach Carey's room. It was the closet door. Only instead of being shut, it lingered halfway open. Not knowing exactly what he was going to find inside, he jerked the door fully open and peered inside.

There was nothing.

Then, as he began to shut it, he glanced at the floor. Pulling his forward motion back a bit, he stared at something on the floor. Bending down, he reached into the closet and picked up the piece of paper that looked out of place as it lay by itself on the brown carpet of their home. It was crumbled up, but as he opened it, his eyes grew wide with confusion and concern. There, on the piece of paper before him, his address had been written. He noticed the handwriting. He tried to familiarize himself with it, but it was no use. The handwriting was unrecognizable.

With the piece of paper clutched in the palm of his hands, he never thought of the possibility that he may be destroying any fingerprints that may have been left on it, and headed for the bedroom where he was sure his wife could be found. He knew that whoever was in their house had left it behind accidentally. Finally, entering the bedroom, he found Carey sitting upright in her bed, a startled look on her face, and his wife Carol sitting beside her. Both of their eyes came to rest on him. "Carey," he began hiding the piece of paper from view as he walked towards the girl he had raised as his own. "Are you all right?"

"I'm fine Uncle Rick," Carey answered brightly not sure what was going on. "I was just having another nightmare that's all. I'm all right though. Why?" she continued asking a question of her own. "Is something wrong?"

"No, no sweetheart," Rick assured the girl in front of him. "Of course not," he added half-heartedly, not feeling right about hiding the truth from his niece.

"It was weird though," Carey continued capturing their attention as she once again began speaking of her nightmare. "My nightmare, it," she paused struggling to find the right words. "It was different this time. It wasn't like all of the others when I wake up in a cold sweat. Something strange happened. It's like," she paused once again not quite sure how to continue.

"It' O.K.," Carol assured her running her brittle fingers through the girls hair. "What happened?"

"That's just it," Carey continued. "Nothing happened. It's like all of a sudden it all went away. Then I saw a face," she fell silent once again seeing the concerned look on her relative's faces. "It was like an angel or something, coming to protect me. I don't really remember what the face looked like. But I can still feel his presence. Like he's watching over me or something."

A few minutes later, Rick and Carol left Carey alone in the room and found themselves alone in the hallway. Shutting her door behind them, Rick took the piece of paper he had found in closet out of his pocket and handed it to his wife. "You were right," he began, watching as his wife's eyes turned to disbelief as she read the contents of the paper. "Someone was definitely here."

Throwing the piece of paper into the air, she headed downstairs for the phone. "That's it," she replied harshly as her fear too suddenly gave way to anger. "How dare someone come into our home? I'm calling the police."

* * *

Moments earlier, when Carey Haas was sleeping in her bed, the nightmares had come to her.

Carey saw herself walking through the home she had once resided in along the sandy coast of Destin. Only, there was nothing inside. No furniture, carpeting, nothing. Only stainless white walls surrounded her, and there was absolutely no sign of her parents. She

Tinman

remembered the feeling of safety this home once occupied, and the shelter it once provided when she was a child. But now, there was nothing.

Only silence, which made her realize that she was alone.

Then, a voice came. An evil voice, and it called out to her, beckoning her to come up the stairs.

"Carey," the evil voice echoed throughout the house, although no one could be seen. "Carey, come to me."

She wanted to turn around and run out the front door, never returning to the home that still haunted her soul. But something forced her to continue, and soon she found herself walking up the stairs. The voice continued to call her name over and over again, each time becoming more demanding of her presence. Then, she suddenly found herself standing outside the door of what used to be her old room. It was shut, but she knew that the voice had been coming from inside. Tears began to stream from her face, as she feared what she would find inside. But the voice continued.

"Carey," the evil voice whispered loudly. "Open the door Carey." For a few seconds, she didn't move. She simply placed her hand on the handle and refused to move. "I said open the door Carey!" the voice demanded harshly and she suddenly found herself terrified of what would happen if she didn't obey the order placed upon her. Finally, she reluctantly opened the door and stepped inside.

Shrieking in fear, she no longer found herself staring at the unblemished whiteness of the walls inside her home. The walls of her room were covered in a thick mass of blood. A pool of the red liquid had formed at the base of the wall as it continued to run down freely, not being blocked by any foreign objects. Then, looking up, she realized where the blood was coming from.

It was coming from her parent's lifeless bodies.

They were there. The two of them, David and Charlene, were side by side, nailed to the wall in a crucified position. Their heads hung low, and blood flowed freely from the wounds. Their naked bodies were exposed for the world to see and their insides vividly dangled from their mangled flesh.

She turned away and was about to flee from the room, when the door shut right before her eyes and locked itself. She tried to unlock it. She wanted to be free from the horrifying room she had entered against her will. But it was no use. There was no escape.

Cradling herself in a corner, just as she had done when she was a scared child, she placed her head between her legs and began bobbing back and forth, praying for help to come and take her away.

The evil voice she had heard suddenly turned into a horrendous roar and she knew that he was laughing at her. The voice seemed to get pleasure from the pain he was able to bring to her. As the laugh continued to pound away inside her head, more tears began to fall from her ashen face as she refused to look up and see her parents lifeless bodies nailed to the wall.

Then, from out of nowhere, something happened.

She felt relaxing hands on her shoulders, and although her first instincts were to turn away from the strange touch, she allowed it to continue. The hand soothed her soul, and soon the evil laugh disappeared into the world of the unknown. Opening her eyes, she watched as the blood-drenched room began to fade away, as if it had never been there at all. The horrifying images of her parents vanished from view, and soon, she found herself walking through a field of wildflowers that seemed to have no end.

The hands were still on her shoulders, and as she looked to her right, she saw one of them. It was a smooth hand, its gentle touch making all of the fears from within her subside, and she found herself relaxing. Smiling, she closed her eyes and enjoyed the touch the strange person was giving her. For the first time in a long time, she felt safe. She wasn't afraid.

Turning around, she tried to catch a glimpse of the angel that had come to her aid. As she turned, however, she felt the hands fall away from her shoulders and she couldn't make out any physical feature on his face. Except, for his eyes. They were the most beautiful scorching blue eyes she had ever seen.

Then, just as quickly as the angel had come to comfort her, he too disappeared without a trace.

"No," she tried to call the angel back, wanting to feel the warm embrace she hadn't felt in a long time once again. "No," she pleaded. "Please don't go. Please."

But it was too late.

The angel was gone.

His gentle-hearted touch, and his illuminating eyes, however, would never be forgotten.

Chapter 13

    Billy drove back into the driveway, slowly pulling his mother's car back into the same spot from which he had removed it a few hours earlier. Pulling the keys out of the ignition, he set the emergency brake and climbed out of the car. Seconds later, he barreled into his home, closed the door behind him and found his mother sitting in silence in the living room. Neither the radio nor the television was on. There was complete silence in the house. He didn't see a book in his mother's hand and knew immediately that she had been waiting for him to return home. As he watched his mother's gaze shift from the wonders her mind had been entranced in, he slowed his pace as her eyes bore into the depths of his soul. It was obvious that she was upset with him, and perhaps a little disappointed. He had been gone a lot longer than expected, and he himself knew that he should have at least called to let her know that everything was all right. However, everything had just happened so fast, and it simply slipped his mind.
    Nevertheless, he knew there was no escaping the lecture that was sure to come. He didn't even try to flee upstairs into his bedroom and avoid the onslaught of his mother's obvious anger. Her words would soon enough be slashing through him, and he knew she probably wouldn't allow him to explain where he had been and why he hadn't called. Billy knew he had to face the consequences of his actions like a man, and accept the punishment he knew his mother had every right to give. Even if he was almost twenty years old, he still lived and depended on his mother for survival. Needless to say, slowly, and somewhat reluctantly, he strolled over to her. Her stern gaze never

Tinman

left his eyes as he handed her the car keys and sat on the couch directly in front of her.

For what seemed like forever, neither of them said a word. Billy was waiting for his mother to jump on his case, and it appeared as though Debra was waiting for her son to try and begin with an explanation. However, neither seemed to know how to begin. They just sat in an uncomfortable silence, Billy knowing that his mother was disappointed with him, and Debra sensing that her son knew he was in the wrong. Finally, Debra decided to speak.

"Look Billy," she began, pausing slightly as she jiggled her keys in her hand. "I know you had something very important to do, and damn it I really hope you got everything squared away. But you have been gone a long time, and I have been sitting here in this exact spot for well over an hour now, worrying that something had happened to you and waiting patiently for a phone call, or anything just to let me know where you were and if you were all right."

"I'm so-," Billy tried to speak, but was instantly cut off.

"No," Debra jumped in holding a hand in the air. "Please, just let me finish." Then, after waiting for Billy to nod giving his mother his full attention, she proceeded. "This kind of behavior is just not like you, and I know I raised you better than that. Growing up, I always thought that you had matured well beyond your years, and I can only remember a few times when you showed me any form of disrespect. We have always had a close relationship, which was probably the only thing that got us through the rough times in our life. We have always been honest with one another, never hiding anything of any kind, never even attempting to do anything that would cause either of us to worry about the other. But," she paused. "It's like ever since we have moved here, things have changed. You have changed Billy, and I don't like it."

"Mom-" he was cut off again.

"It's like we don't even talk anymore son. It almost seems as though you're living in your own little world and I'm just slowly passing through your life. It obvious to me that something is on your mind and troubling you a great deal, but you're shutting me out and you have never done that before. Never. You've all of a sudden started hiding things inside and I'd hate to see you get yourself into anything that may cause you harm. I'm worried about you Billy. I'm truly worried about you."

"What is it you want me to do here?" Billy asked, somewhat surprised he had been able to complete a sentence.

"I want you to quit avoiding me and talk to me when there's something bothering you," Debra shot back emotionally. "I want you to be able to talk to me like you used to and trust me with anything. I don't like it when you hide things from me cause I can see right through you and I can tell that something is eating you up inside. I just want to help you Billy. But most of all," she paused momentarily once again staring straight into her son's eyes. "Most of all, I just want the old Billy back."

"Damn it mom," Billy began feeling a bit selfish and just plain terrible about himself after his mother had finished with the guilt trip she had unintentionally scorned upon him. "How can I explain something to you if I don't even understand what is going on myself? But I haven't changed mother. I'm the same old Billy as before. But you're right about something. There is something going on inside my body that's eating me alive. Ever since we moved into this damn house I don't think I've had one peaceful night's sleep. I've grown restless, groggy, confused, and I really don't understand just what is happening. But after today, I think it's all starting to fit together. I think I have found a piece of the puzzle, but I just don't know what is going to happen next."

"What are you talking about puzzle?" Debra asked, not believing the gibberish that flowed from her son's mouth, and hating the fact that it didn't make any sense to her whatsoever. "Damn it Billy!" she exclaimed. "What in the hell is going on here? What am I missing?" she demanded harshly.

"I don't know," Billy answered truthfully. "I wish I could answer that question mom but I can't. And don't think I asked for this to happen. I wasn't even expecting to move into a house where ten years ago a family was murdered by that serial killer. I wasn't expecting to find that picture and that damn Kat doll in the basement-"

"You see," Debra interjected. "How do you know that doll's name is Kat?"

"Because I just know," Billy continued shrugging his shoulders. "You have to believe me mom. You're just going to have to trust me

Tinman

through this no matter what happens because I'm going to need your support. In fact, you might be the only person that doesn't think I'm crazy. But you have to understand mom. I wasn't expecting to start having nightmares about the Haas family or experiencing these blackout episodes every time I see that picture. I wasn't expecting to relive the past and watch a family die. But it all happened. I know it sounds crazy, but for some reason, all of this is happening to me, and there's just got to be a reason. I don't know what it is or what I'm supposed to do, if anything at all. But there's got to be a reason for all of this, and I have to find out what it is before I really do go out of my mind."

Debra could only nod, not really sure of how to respond to her son's heartfelt words. She knew that he was telling her the truth. After all, he really had no reason to lie to her in the first place. Then, opening her mouth, she found herself about to tell her son about the psychiatrist she was going to see a little later on and that in the future she would be making him an appointment. Realizing, however, that it really wasn't the time to bring it up, she quickly found another topic that suited her just as well. "Very well," she began. "Can you at least tell me where you've been all this time?"

Only after a very long silence, did Billy speak. His face suddenly fell to an ashen appearance and Debra could easily sense the discomfort her son felt. "I tracked down Carey Haas, the little girl who was the only survivor when Curtis Rains trampled through this home ten years ago. She's still alive mother, and I found out where she lived."

"Did you talk to her?"

"No," Billy admitted. "But I did see her, and let me tell you this," he paused as a sudden smile stretched along his weary face. "She was absolutely the most beautiful girl I have ever seen. It took me longer than I thought to find the place, and when I did, well," he paused letting his words drown into silence. "Well, let's just say that I probably hung around a lot longer than I should have."

"You mean you spied on this girl?" Debra asked in a rather accusing manner.

"No, it's not like that mother," he grunted defending himself.

"Then why did you feel that it was absolutely necessary to go to her?" Debra continued to pound on the questions she knew her son would have trouble answering.

"I told you, I don't know," Billy pressed forward becoming a bit agitated at his mother's untrustworthy words, and at the nuisance she had become. "I don't know what Carey Haas has to do with anything. But damn it, I know she plays a role in whatever is going on inside my head, and I can't let it go. I don't know if she means anything or not? But I have to find out mom," he paused running his fingers through his softened hair. "I just have to find out."

Then, before either of them could continue, both of them were silenced at the sound of the doorbell. "That must be Blaze," Debra began changing the subject as she climbed to her feet. "Consider this your lucky day. You've been saved by the bell." Then, turning, she headed for the door to welcome her son's best friend inside their home. "But don't think that you're off the hook," she called back to her son. "We're not done yet. There are still a lot of things we need to discuss."

"Mom," Billy called just as her hand reached the doorknob and she was about to pull the door open. Finally, after she spun around and looked directly into his eyes, he continued. "I'm sorry about today. I really wasn't planning on being gone that long and you're absolutely right. I should have called."

"Apology accepted," Debra concluded with a smile as she opened the door.

* * *

Rick Goodman and his beloved wife Carol sat fidgeting on the sofa in their living room as they waited for the county Sheriff, Gabriel Burnham, also known to the community as "Gabe," to show up at their home and listen to what had happened. Not many people in the rapidly growing city of Destin would have been blessed with a personal visit from the Sheriff himself. Rick, however, had grown up with the muscle bound Sheriff, who didn't look a day over 37, even though he had just reached the half-century mark, and their relationship had grown even stronger as the years passed. As soon as Carol had called the Sheriff's office, Gabe immediately took the call

Tinman

and told them that he would be right over. Half an hour had passed before they heard the friendly honk of the Sheriff's 4 x 4 GMC Silver Yukon as he pulled neatly into their driveway. Dressed in street clothes, his badge hung from the belt buckle that was nestled around his perfectly fit blue jeans, and his .32 caliber revolver was holstered provocatively on his side. Before Gabe could even ring the doorbell he found Rick standing at the door, quickly ushering him inside.

"Good to see you again Gabe," Rick began extending his hand to his longtime friend as the Sheriff entered his home. "It's been a while hasn't it?"

"Yep," the dark haired, towering figure in front of him admitted. "Sure has. A lot of shit has been hitting the fan lately at the office and all. I didn't realize how much stress came with this job. The two of you would be highly surprised at all of the politics surrounding law enforcement, especially around a man in my position. It's almost not worth it to tell you the truth. If one minor thing slips up, an entire investigation could go to shit, and then I got every damn city official in Destin looking to harp on my ass until it's dead if ya know what I mean. That's why I came out here to see what was wrong with you guys. I just had to get out of that damn office," he began immediately taking control of the conversation, and his foul verbal exuberance was one in which the Goodman's themselves were used to after years of knowing the man, and understanding the stress of his job as county Sheriff.

"Well, do you plan on trying to get re-elected next term?" Rick asked with a smile already knowing the answer.

"Hell no," Gabe admitted without blushing. "I'm getting to old for this shit and I'll be damned if I'm going to let a bunch of unappreciative citizens in Destin kill me by way of a stroke or heart attack. No sir," he paused looking at both of them with his lightly colored brown eyes, his eyebrows connecting smoothly in the middle of his forehead. "After this term my ass is retiring and I plan on relaxing in the sun, and doing a hell of a lot of fishing. Perhaps take up golf and anything else I can find. Like maybe a wife," he added jokingly, momentarily recalling the two previous wives that had left him because his job kept him away from home. Then, coming to the subject at hand. "Now Carol, just what in the hell was that all about when you called my office a while ago? You were talking so fast I could hardly understand a word you said." Then, he paused briefly to glance around their home. "So, you guys seem to think someone was in here today."

"No," Carol spoke up. "Someone was definitely here," she concluded handing the Sheriff the piece of paper her husband had found in the upstairs hallway right outside a closet door. "Rick found it upstairs," she continued. "It was on the floor inside the closet and it's not any of our handwriting. Oh, and there was a black Lexus parked across the street and we are the only house around here. I don't know what it was doing there, but it definitely didn't belong there."

"Did you see anyone with the car when the two of you pulled into the driveway?" Sheriff Burnham asked skeptically, his professionalism forcing him to look at everything from every direction and to consider every possibility without ruling anything out.

Rick shook his head. "No one was with the car Gabe. But once we came upstairs to check on Carey, I heard the front door shut. I immediately ran back downstairs and opened the door, but by the time I got outside, the car was speeding away. And no," he answered before being asked the common question. "I didn't get to look at whoever was driving that car. He was too far away for me to even get the license plate number."

"I see," Gabe continued listening to every word put before him as he climbed to his feet and began pacing the house. "Have you noticed anything missing, anything at all? Jewelry? Money?" Rick and Carol shook their heads in puzzling formation as they realized nothing had been stolen. "Nothing was missing from the closet where you found this?" he asked Rick holding up the piece of paper.

"Not a thing."

"All right," Gabe moved forward. "Here's what I can do. I can send a team in here to dust for fingerprints if you like. But to tell you the truth it probably won't do any good. Between the two of you and Carey, I'd be willing to bet practically every surface in this house has your fingerprints all over it. Even if the person that were here wasn't wearing any gloves, well, it would still be hard to make a match if they overlap any of your set of prints. But we could give it a try if you'd like." Both the Goodman's agreed. "In the meantime," the

Sheriff started up once again. "I want you guys to keep your doors locked at all times, and try not to leave anyone out here alone if possible. And if anything strange happens again, or if you see that car again, don't hesitate to give me a call all right?"

"Why would someone who can afford to drive a Lexus want to break into a house is what I don't understand?" Rick spoke aloud what was on his mind.

"Who knows," Gabe could only shrug his shoulders. "You never know. The car could be stolen. But it was probably just some punk neighborhood kid, however, with nothing better to do and I bet the two of you scared him half to death when he heard ya'll come inside. I honestly wouldn't worry about." Then, as he was about to head for the door, the three of them were stopped in their tracks as they heard Carey's footstep's coming down the stairs. Soon, she was joining them in the living room, a brightly lit smile lingering across her face. Only, as she noticed all of their eyes falling over her, she could sense that something was wrong. "Carey!" Gabe exclaimed extending his hand to the girl he regarded highly, and felt was strong for having to battle the ordeal of growing up without her parents all of these years. He had actually been apart of the team to bring Curtis Rains to justice ten years ago and could still see the fear in Carey's eyes as she swam back to shore from the ocean that had provided shelter and saved her from death. "It's so good to see you again. How are you?"

"I'm fine," Carey answered firmly, then looked into her aunt's eyes. "What's going on here Aunt Carol? Is something wrong?"

"No dear," Carol answered, silently cursing herself for lying to the girl in front of her. However, she just didn't have the heart to let her know that someone had been inside their home while Carey had been sleeping in her bed. It would terrify her for days, maybe even weeks. "Everything is positively all right. Sheriff Burnham here was just in the neighborhood and decided to drop by and blow off some steam. We didn't wake you did we?"

"No," Carey answered, smartly realizing there was more than she was being told. "You didn't. I just heard Gabriel's truck pull into the driveway so I decided to come down and say hello."

"Well that was mighty sweet of ya," Gabe admitted squeezing her arm affectionately. Then, moving past her, he headed for the door. "Well, I guess I'll be getting back to the office before they find some sort of crime to charge me with and impeach my powers as Sheriff. Rick buddy," he paused to shake his friend's hand. "It was damn good to see you again. All of you." Then, lowering his tone, he continued. "Call me later all right?"

Rick nodded, and soon, Sheriff Gabriel Burnham disappeared out the front door, climbed into his truck and with one final honk, sped away from the Goodman home.

"All right guys," Carol immediately picked up the conversation capturing their attention. "How about the three of us take a long walk through the woods and then, when we come home I'll whip us up something nice to eat? After all, it's turned out to be such a wonderful day and it's almost gone. Let's enjoy what's left of it shall we?"

* * *

Meanwhile, back in Birmingham, Alabama.

Jamie Walker and her extravagant boyfriend, Travis McKinley, were enjoying the surprisingly rainless afternoon indoors, doing nothing more than spending quality time with one another. They didn't even want to exit their beloved home and enjoy the day outdoors, as both of them were well aware the heat and humidity would swallow them up. Instead, Jamie, with her wheelchair at her side, laid comfortably on her back, her head propped up on three soft pillows as she enjoyed a book her boyfriend had brought to her earlier in the afternoon. The ceiling fan, along with the highly powered air conditioner sent a relaxing, comfortable cool breeze floating about through the room, and she loved the warmth her sheets provided as they wrapped themselves gracefully around her partially, but not terminally paralyzed physique.

She could hear Travis watching television in the other room, every thirty minutes or so, however, he would appear in the doorway to check up on her and see if there was anything she needed. Each time, she would only shake her head and assure him that there was nothing more she needed to survive. She had his love, the entire king size water bed to herself, enough pillows to lend a helping hand to the largest homeless family in the world, a tall glass of sweetened iced tea at her side, and a wonderful book about the love of two strangers who never knew their souls were meant to combine and remain connected forever. What else could she possibly need? Nothing, she answered herself silently.

"Everything all right in here?" Jamie heard Travis's voice once again speak up as he entered the room. "Are you comfortable enough? Can I get you something to eat? Anything? Anything at all pumpkin?"

Laughing, Jamie glanced up from the book she had been enjoying and looked into Travis's enchanting brown eyes. Shaking her head in a manner telling him that she had no idea what she was going to do with him if he kept coming in to check on her every half hour. "Travis you are so sweet," she spoke as the giggles died away. "But really, you don't have to keep coming in here to check on me every ten minutes. I truly am fine. Everything is alright" Then, seeing the fake look of hurt in Travis's eyes, she smiled, forced herself not to laugh, and with one finger, motioned for him to come to her. Once he was seated next to her, his expression became more and more believable, and Jamie continued. "Well, on second thought, maybe there is something you can do for me."

"Name it," Travis quickly cut in, excitement igniting throughout his appearance, as his body suddenly seemed to come to life. "Anything you want angel I can get. Drugs, money, jewelry, cars. You can have it all if you stick with me babe," he added jokingly as the two of them burst into a laughter that allowed the love between the two of them to be felt thousands of miles away. They were truly a couple meant to be together.

"No, I don't think I need all of that sweetheart," Jamie responded with a smile as she ran her curvy fingers briskly throughout her boyfriend's hair. "However, how about a kiss? Do you think you can handle that?"

"Why madam I would be honored and it would be a privilege to complete the compelling task you have set before me. And although you may beckon the warriors to take me away and throw me into the lion's den after we are done, and although my body might be ripped to shreds as the vicious creatures hungrily attack my torso and rip their fangs into my flesh, it will be worthwhile. It may very well turn out to be the most painful death in the history of meaningless murders, but kissing your lips will get me by without feeling a single scratch. You see your majesty, I have been in love with you since the first time I laid my eyes upon you, and kissing your soft, but firm, beautiful lips will feel like a dream come true. It would truly be a journey I would have no choice but complete," Travis answered in a Scottish tone, mocking the fluent language of his for-fathers and mothers.

"Just shut up and kiss me damn you," Jamie replied as she silenced Travis's acting ability and pulled him close to her body. Then, finally, their lips connected as one and the passion that filled their souls momentarily escaped from inside and made its presence out in the open. After seconds of what felt like an hour-long escapade into ecstasy, Travis backed away and the two of them said nothing, but looked strongly into one another eyes.

"You are so beautiful," Travis genuinely began, as he leaned over once more and lovingly kissed Jamie's forehead. Then, climbing to his feet, he planned once again to depart from the bedroom, only to resume the daily chores his new household position entitled him to do. "Now, it's time for you to take your medicine. I'll be back in a minute to give it to you. And afterwards I want you to try and get some rest all right?" Jamie nodded in approving fashion. Then, before Travis could disappear down the hallway, she called him back. "What is it sweetheart?"

"I love you," Jamie sighed passionately.

"I love you too," Travis returned the heart warming words with a smile as he disappeared down the hallway and out of sight.

Just as soon as he returned with the medicine and then after she gulped down the gagging taste of the prescription drug, he left the room once again and Jamie suddenly felt the need for sleep. Her bones began to ache a bit, and she suddenly felt herself growing weak. Yawning, she placed the book aside and clicked off the light next to the bed. Moving one pillow from behind her, she placed it on her chest and clutched it tightly. Yawning once more, she closed her eyes and let the blackness close in around her.

Soon, Jamie Walker was sound asleep.

* * *

As soon as Blaze Brookshaw entered the Saxton home, Debra greeted her son's best friend with a warm smile and hug, only then to leave the two of them alone as she had an appointment of her own to keep. She didn't want to keep Dr. Richmond waiting. For all she knew, he could be her only hope in helping her son get over whatever phase he suddenly found himself going through. As soon as Debra's car disappeared down the driveway, Blaze closed the door behind him, passed through the towering foyer and entered the family room where he found Billy anxiously awaiting his arrival. "What's up dawg!" Blaze shouted with a smile as he raced over and grabbed his best friend. "How ya been man? Do you like it down here in sunny old Florida or what? Things damn sure ain't been the same since you left Georgia man."

"Well let me be the first to say that I wish I was back there again," Billy spoke up as he looked into the light brown eyes of the muscle bound figure in front of him. Blaze's hair was slightly shaved all around, only a beige baseball cap covered the top of his head. His face was cleanly shaven, and he sported nothing more than a pair of blue jean shorts and a plain black T-shirt. Hanging from around his neck was a classy, sparkling gold chain with a gold plated cross charm dangling freely from its center. "Good lord man," Billy spoke up as he took his eyes off his friend in front of him. "I know you like to work out but you sure have bulked up a bit since I've last seen you." Then, as Blaze flexed jokingly for his buddy in front of him, he let out a false grunting noise of sorts as he pulled his arm behind his neck. Then, he found Billy's eyes falling on something else. There, colored nicely on his triceps, was a tattoo. "Holy shit!" Billy exclaimed not believing his eyes. "When did you decide to go and have something like that done?"

"Not too long ago," Blaze answered with a smile. Then, stepping closer to Billy he pulled up his sleeve allowing him to take a better look. "Why? Do you like it brother? If not, say you do anyway."

"It's different, and I never would have expected you to go out and get such a thing. But," he let his voice trail off into silence as he viewed the work of art on Blaze's arm. It was a picture of a head, a dead mule carcass, such as one you would expect to find out in the middle of a dessert somewhere rotting peacefully away, and free of any scavengers that may be lurking about as all of the meat had long since been worn or eaten away. Its two horns were still intact, yet both of them appeared to be eroding away at a slow pace, and one was definitely shorter than the other. "But I like it," Billy finally finished as he returned to make eye contact with his buddy in front of him. "And it suits you."

"Shut up," Blaze spoke up. "Now come on, show me around this here house of yours and show me where I'll be sleeping if you don't mind."

"Oh, well by all means," Billy added as he picked up the single bag Blaze had brought into the home. "Right this way lad. Right this way." Laughing, the two of them mounted the stairs where Billy planned to give his friend a tour of the home from top to bottom. Finally, after dropping Blaze's stuff off in the room directly across the hall from his own, Billy continued with the tour of the Haas home. He showed his best friend all of the spacious, yet what used to be luxurious rooms the gigantic house held with dignity, and all of the bathrooms, which were beautifully decorated in light blue, and white colors. Finally, on the first floor, he went through the motions again, only this time walked him through the kitchen showing Blaze exactly where different kinds of food could be found. "And that's it," Billy concluded.

"Wait a minute," Blaze postponed the end of the tour as he captured Billy's attention. "What's down that hallway over there," he added as he pointed to the hallway directly across from the family room.

"Nothing," Billy admitted rather uneasily as he felt his hands grow clammy. "It just leads to an old basement. Nothing's down there. I've already checked it out."

"Well damn this place sure is huge man, and it's right on the beach too. How can you actually wish you were back home when you actually have the opportunity to live on the beach, surrounded by hundreds of beautiful women, and in a house of this size and stature? I'll bet this is the most beautiful house on this whole strip."

"It is," Blaze's counterpart admitted as the two of them headed for the back door to step out on the patio and gaze out at the ocean below. "But trust me, things aren't always what they seem, and in the case of this house, looks can really be deceiving." Then, before Blaze could even think of a response, he found himself standing out on the patio and looking down at the crystal clear blue ocean below, and accepting the slightly cool ocean breeze as it swept across his body.

"I don't know what you are having trouble with," Blaze spoke up loudly. "But I sure as hell could get used to this." Then, down below, he saw a family of four walking gracefully along the ocean, the two little girls every so often running wildly into the water and splashing about only to return seconds later to their parents side, who did nothing more than dip their feet into the water every couple of seconds. As he watched them frolic around in the surf, and sand, he noticed the husband and wife look up, acknowledge their presence and wave in a friendly manner. "Who are they?" he asked Billy just as he returned the gesture.

"My neighbors," Billy answered instantly recognizing the Anne family. "They seem to be pretty cool, but those two little girls, Jennifer and Mary are scared of this house."

"What!" Blaze asked confusingly. "Why is that?"

"I'll explain everything to you a little later on." Billy concluded in a way that told Blaze he wanted to change the subject if at all possible, and wishing he had never mentioned it at all. "Right now, what do you say we hit the beach?"

Nodding, Blaze replied. "Let's do it."

* * *

Jamie saw herself sleeping peacefully in her room, almost as if she were staring into a mirror, vividly visualizing her reflection as she slept the pain away from the wounds she had suffered in her automobile accident. Only as she shadowed her own body in front of her, her eyes were closed, and her mouth lay open automatically taking over the breathing exercises that were essential to continue living, instead of suffocating to death as she slept and as her mind fell into its unconscious state of being. The whole picture seemed all too awkward to Jamie as it felt as if there were actually two parties in the room. Only, both of them appeared to be her. However, one was sleeping worry free, her chest delicately moving upwards, only to fall back down seconds later as she exhaled the oxygen it had absorbed moments earlier, and her heart beating steadily to a dignified rhythm, pounding away the fluids her body needed to survive. The other, she couldn't see, but it seemed to be watching over her.

Instantly, Jamie knew that she was dreaming.

Then, just as sudden as the heart warming image of herself appeared sleeping on the bed, a blistering, blinding white light pierced through the room, and a booming sound of thunder echoed throughout the bedroom, sounding as if the sky was going to collapse right on top of her. Panicking, she looked up at the ceiling to see if any damage had been done. Surprisingly, no damage had been done as the quaking roar of thunder shook the house harshly. Finally, returning her vision to the image of herself sleeping on the bed, she saw something outlandishly perilous.

What was once a vision of her sleeping silently in her bed was now a vision of her sitting upright, her mouth gaping wide open as it held an expression of blatant fear. It was obvious that she sensed a dangerous source near by. Her eyes twitched as her pupils enlarged themselves to get adjusted to the white light that continued to pour into the room from an unknown, and unseen force. Jamie saw her own hands clutching the sheets of the bed with a grip so tight, it could have crushed a human skull if given the opportunity. Jamie wanted to run to the image sleeping on the bed and put her arms around the woman she knew to be herself, as if assuring her that everything was going to be all right. She wanted her to realize that this was nothing more than an ordinary nightmare that had chosen to come at an inopportune time. She wanted to force the image of herself to see that there was nothing to worry about because soon she would awaken and realize that everything was all right and that nothing had changed.

Only, as she tried to move her feet, she realized that she was completely immobilized, as if trapped inside some glass case of some sort, being forced to watch what was going to happen to herself next. Confused, Jamie suddenly found herself trembling slightly with fear as she realized she couldn't run to the bed and save herself. "Jamie!" she shrieked loudly, desperately trying to get her own attention. "Jamie, wake up! Please wake up!"

As she watched herself on the bed, however, she realized it was no use. Whatever had stopped her from moving, was now keeping her from hearing her own voice. Jamie watched herself on the bed as she *stared fluently into the white light, her whole body perplexed in fear. Then, from out of nowhere, a figure appeared from the light, and stepped into the room, eagerly making his presence known.*

It was the boy.

The boy she swore she had run over a few nights ago.

And the same boy she had visualized in her hospital bed as he tried to drown her in his own blood.

Terrified, Jamie watched helplessly as the boy, whose face bore an expressionless monolith, made his way towards the image of herself on the bed, his blackened eyes traveling into the depths of her soul. Then, suddenly, the corners of the boy's lips tilted upright, and a smile loomed about. Only, it clearly was not a friendly smile. It was more of a mocking smile, a smile that seemed to blame her for every wrong doing that had come into the boy's short-lived life. "Why?" Jamie tried to ask the child in front of her. "Why are you tormenting me? What do you want from me?" she begged precariously for answers.

Saying nothing, almost as if the boy hadn't even heard a word she had said, the naked boy continued towards the bed, his hand extending towards the sleeping Jamie, not even bothering to turn and look in her direction. Finally, Jamie was forced to watch as the hand of the child caressed the side of her cheek. Then, with an unimaginable burst of strength, the child was able to pick Jamie up, hoisting her body up on his shoulders. Slowly, the endurable child with monumental strength turned and headed back into light.

"Wait!" Jamie called nervously as she watched her body double disappear into the light.

But it was too late.

Soon, she could see nothing but the blinding white light.

Then, the light began to change. At first, she couldn't be sure as to what was actually happening. But as minutes dragged by, the white light turned into an orange color of sorts, and it began to move. Suddenly, immense amounts of heat began to blister her smooth skin, and she realized what was once nothing more than a piercing white light was now a burst of flames. Screaming in fear, Jamie realized her room was on fire. "Help!" she screamed into the ablaze she knew to be around her, praying to God that someone would hear her and come awaken her so that she could be saved once again. "Please, somebody help me!"

Unfortunately, however, no help arrived, and the flames continued to grow as they ate their way selfishly through the walls and floor of her bedroom, destroying everything in its path.

Then, she heard something.

It was a voice, and it was calling her name.

"Jamie...Jamie," the voice repeated, whispering through the crackling sound of the flames. "Jamie...Jamie," it continued, the tone of the voice becoming more legible and harsh. "Look. Look into the fire," it commanded. Obeying the order set before her, Jamie took a deep breath and stared into the hissing fire in front her. "Do you see me?" the voice asked as an evil laugh escaped shortly after. "Look hard Jamie. Do you see me?"

"No," Jamie answered as a tear rolled down her cheek. "Who are you?"

"Do you really have to ask that question?" the voice answered her question with one of his own. Then, from within the flames before her, appeared the child she had just witnessed kidnap herself off the bed and disappear into the white light that had once taken the place of the flames. A smile was still written across his face and as she looked into his eyes she couldn't help but to feel a connection between the two of them. "Do you know who I am now?" the boy asked, his voice much deeper than normal for a person of his age. Jamie only shrugged her shoulders in confusion. Then, right before her eyes, she watched as the boy began to grow.

Inch by inch, the small child in front of her began to rise into the air, his body parts forming as if he were aging at the speed of light. As the blurred image of the boy came to a halt, Jamie now found herself staring into the dark, evil black eyes of a grown man. Only, it wasn't just any man. It was a man she immediately recognized. The realization of whom it was now standing before her, amongst the retched flames as they coiled around his unburned, or scarred body, sent a numbing sensation of fear flowing throughout her body. Finally, she understood just how helpless she truly was.

Terrified, Jamie Walker found herself staring into the eyes of Curtis Rains.

Tinman

"I bet you thought I was dead didn't you," Curtis asked in a mocking tone as another evil laugh echoed throughout the room. Then, when no answer came from his lost love, he asked again. "Didn't you, you little bitch?" Jamie nodded forcing the lump down her throat. "Well surprise," Curtis continued. "If you could only see the look in your eyes right now sweetheart. Its like one eye is filled with surprise, and the other consumed with nothing but pure, mind-boggling fear. Just like the night you thought you ran me over. Oh man, am I brilliant or what? I came up with that one all by myself by the way. I'm surprised you didn't recognize me though after all of those times we used to cuddle up next to a cozy fire and look at all of our baby pictures. I guess you never really did care about me did you?"

"What do you want from me?" Jamie asked, her voice trembling.

"What do I want from you?" Curtis returned the question with another laugh. "I want you to suffer until you beg me to kill you. I want your fucking brain to shut down because your nerves simply can't absorb all of the tormenting pain I plan to put you through. You see," he paused as the smile faded away. "You really shouldn't have crossed me sweetheart. You were the only person in my life I actually cared about, and I never once planned on hurting you. But then I realized, you're just like all of the rest of the people out there who wanted nothing more than to see me die. However, I told you and a lot of other people but no one ever listened to me. Do you remember? Do you remember what I told you? Damn it, answer me!" Curtis ordered realizing his victim wasn't going to speak willingly.

"No, I don't remember," Jamie finally mustered enough strength to answer.

"I told you that I could not be killed. I told you that the Tinman would live forever because there was still some unfinished business left for me here in reality. And unfortunately," he paused momentarily. "Those plans didn't include you until you walked out on me at the prison. You really shouldn't have done that Jamie."

"I'm sorry," Jamie begged for forgiveness realizing her life was at stake. "Please don't hurt me."

"It's a little late for that now isn't it," Curtis responded coldly. "God I feel so powerful. I'm on top of the world sweetheart and there are absolutely no limits as to what I can accomplish. I can do *anything I want to anyone I want, and there is absolutely nothing you or anyone else can do to stop me. I'm untouchable. And you know why? My God your going to love this,"* he paused once again as another smile crossed his face. *"Cause I'm not alive, and it feels great,"* he added with a laugh. *"But you know what I like best?"* he asked, instantly doing away with the smile as his face took on a hardened look of death. *"I'm once again free. Free to kill!"*

"Please-" Jamie tried to interrupt.

"You're going to die in my hands Jamie," Curtis continued cutting her short. "And I personally am going to watch the life drain from your body." Then, extending both hands outwards he began walking towards her. "The Tinman is coming for you."

"No!" Jamie screamed desperately wanting herself to wake up. "Please someone help me!"

To no avail, no one heard her screams.

* * *

Carey Haas sat once again outside on the back porch as her aunt and uncle were inside happily preparing the evening meal the three of them would soon enjoy. The walk into the forests surrounding their home had helped in putting her mind at ease as she recalled the nightmare she had just experienced. The hollow sounds of the birds chirping back and forth, undoubtedly letting other critters know of their presence, always seemed to bring a smile to her face. Only now, there was something else that brought on a smile.

It was the feeling of no longer being alone.

It was the feeling of the two hands she had felt on her shoulders in her nightmare, also the hands that had come to comfort her, and rescue her from the horrifying vision of her parents lifeless bodies. She remembered feeling safe, almost as if nothing bad could ever happen as long as those hands were placed along her shoulders, clutching her tight, and leading her away from danger.

And then, there were the eyes.

They had been the most beautiful blue eyes she had ever seen, and they too, sent chills throughout her body.

To Carey Haas, they had been the eyes of an angel.

Her guardian angel, she thought silently inside.

However, she couldn't help but wonder if she would ever see them again?

Perhaps tonight, when she fell asleep again, maybe her angel would return and encompass her soul forever, not allowing her to be tormented by the horrible man in her dreams or by the horrible man whom had changed her life dramatically when she was a child. She wanted nothing more than to feel the warmth and compassion of those hands, and to look into the enchanting blue eyes once more. Just once more, Carey Haas wanted to believe that everything was going to be all right.

Chapter 14

"Wake up," Travis McKinley yelled as he rushed into the bedroom to find his girlfriend, Jamie Walker, perspiring furiously. A pool of her own sweat formed in the midst of the bed sheets as her body thrashed harshly across the bed, tangling her arms and legs tightly within the thin sheets, looking as if she were trying to escape from the grasps of an immobilizing straight jacket. "Jamie!" he yelled as he pounded on the bed and placed her in his arms, his strength enabling her unconscious body to continue to torment itself. "Please sweetheart, wake up!"

Then, suddenly, Jamie's motions ceased, and her dreadful screams drowned away, leaving the room as silent as it had been minutes before she had befallen to the deep sleep that had turned into a horrifying nightmare. Loosening his grip on his girlfriend's arm, Travis changed his positioning and looked into Jamie's eyes. He found them open, and knew that she had finally snapped back into reality. However, it was also obvious that whatever she had seen or experienced as she slept had not been forgotten. An abhorrent expression was still playing across her slippery face, and fear still loomed throughout her eyes. Grabbing her hands, Travis noted that they were still trembling uncontrollably.

"Jamie," Travis breathed soothingly, forcing her to look into his eyes. "What happened? What's wrong?" There was no response, and Jamie turned away just as quickly as she glanced into his eyes, almost as if she were scared of him. "Sweetheart," he continued softly, trying to convince his loving girlfriend that everything was all right and that she was safe in his arms. "Everything is all right sugar.

Nothing is going to hurt you. I'm not going to hurt you," he added, although wishing there wasn't the need to even say such a thing. "I'm here to help you baby. But you're going to have to help me. Please," he sighed squeezing her hand affectionately. "Please tell me what's wrong?" Again, however, there was nothing but silence and Jamie continued to refuse to make any form of eye contact with him. "It's only me, Travis," he continued finding himself growing a bit impatient, however managing to keep his composure, and stick with the calm, soothing tone he spoke with. "You know you can trust me. I would never do anything to harm you in any way, and you know that. So please tell me what is going on. What happened to you?" he asked once again, praying that his sincerity had gotten through his girlfriends thick skull. "There is nothing here that's going to hurt you Jamie. I would never let anything happen to you."

"I saw him," Jamie spoke suddenly, her tone enriched with terror as the words trembled out of her mouth, the chattering of her teeth clearly heard throughout the room. However, she still did not attempt to make eye contact with Travis. "I saw him Travis," she continued as she let a tear fall from her cheek. "He was com-, coming for me and he took me into the light, but then came back again for the real me."

"What?" Travis couldn't help but to ask as the words that poured from Jamie's mouth sounded like nothing more than a twisted ensemble of a troubled, and tormented soul, which was still lost in an unspeakable oblivion of retched evil and horror. It sounded like she was describing two different individuals as herself. Nevertheless, he vowed to try and understand just what she was trying to tell him. "Who was coming for you sweetheart?" he asked with an intriguing tone. "You just said you saw someone. Well, who did you see Jamie?"

"Him," Jamie breathed heavily closing her eyes as if trying to put everything she had just experienced aside. Then, opening her eyes, she finally turned to face her boyfriend. "I saw Curtis Rains."

"Awe honey," Travis continued soothingly. "It was just a nightmare. He can't hurt you now. He's dead."

"No!" Jamie shrieked with a faltering consternation. "He-" she shuddered at the possibility. "He's not dead Travis," she tried to make him believe her words. "Curtis is still alive and he's come for me. He's never going to leave me alone until I am dead. It was him I saw that night on the road when I got in my accident."

"What are you talking about sweetheart?" Travis asked still utterly confused at the whole situation. "You said that it was a small boy you saw out there on the highway. Not Curtis Rains."

"It was a small boy!" Jamie breathed. "But it was him. It was Curtis as a child. Don't you see what he's doing to me? He's driving me crazy, and it's never going to stop Travis. He will never quit until I am dead. He's come back to kill me."

"Honey would you just listen to yourself," Travis ordered as he loomed himself over her. "What you are saying is just not possible. When someone dies, they're dead and that's all there is to it. There's no coming back to haunt people. He is dead Jamie. Curtis Rains died in that electric chair a few nights ago and where he's at, he can never hurt you again. It's just not possible. All you had was a nightmare sweetheart. Nothing you saw was real."

Jamie desperately wanted to believe that Travis's words were true. But she knew that they were not. Deep down inside her, from a place that could never be touched or seen by anyone, she knew that her nightmare had in fact been a reality. The Tinman had come to her, and in all the years she had known Curtis Rains, he was one to never break a promise, and she knew that he spoke only of the truth. He had been one of the most honest people she had ever met and that fact alone was enough to make her realize that he had not been kidding when he said that he was going to kill her. She knew that Curtis would come for her again. She didn't know how, or when, but she knew that he would return. And no matter what Travis said to comfort her, she realized that there was absolutely nothing he could possibly do to save her. In fact, there was nothing anyone could do to save her. She couldn't even save herself.

Then, as she glanced behind the man in front of her, she caught a glimpse of the dresser along the opposite wall, with a one-way mirror sitting peacefully on its surface. She saw the terrified image of herself in the mirror. Yet, there was something else that captured her attention. There, along the stainless glass surface of the mirror, was a single word written. It was written in a red liquid of some sort, undoubtedly her own carmine lipstick, which could have been found in the top drawer of the hardwood dresser.

It read, in big letters:

TINMAN

* * *

Sheriff Gabriel, "Gabe," Burnham of Okaloosa County sat behind his desk inside his recently redecorated office. Leaning back in his chair, he stared at the screen saver on his computer monitor and watched as the colorful fish moved gracefully across the screen. Air bubbles moved slowly upwards from their mouths, and sea grass of green and yellow swayed peacefully on the ocean floor as the invisible current of the massive body of water instructed them. Taking a deep breath, he turned away from the computer screen and glanced around his rather empty room. His office had recently been repainted to a more relaxing white color, rather than the old stained white he had been forced to look at the first few years he had taken office in Destin. The floors had just been carpeted in a beautiful homely brown color, matching the large oak desk that was placed directly in the center of the room. An American Flag was placed in both of the back corners of his office, with two large windows looming between them. His office was empty except for the four tall file cabinets standing untouched along the walls, and the two cushioned chairs in front of his desk.

Gabe had a lot of empty space, which was how he liked it since it kept him from feeling trapped inside some small room with no escape from the mounds of paperwork that seemed to stream across his desk. He remembered the days before he had been elected Sheriff when his office had been a pigsty, and he remembered the feeling of being lost and confused. He had tried everything over the years to lose some of the stress that had mounted as more and more cases of homicide and narcotics came his way. He enjoyed putting the scum of the earth behind bars, but in no way did he ever expect to realize or believe just how bad society was. He took pride in removing criminals from the streets and locking them away from society.

Taking another deep breath, he began rubbing his temples along the side of his head. Then, closing his eyes, he mumbled aloud. "Just a few more months Gabe. Just a few more months and you'll be out of this hell hole," he spoke gingerly, finally able to admit that nearly thirty years with the Sheriff's office of Okaloosa county was finally taking a toll on him. Exhaling a deep sigh of relief, he moved his mouse beside his computer, which immediately forced the screen saver to disappear and began staring at the screen in front of him when his concentration was suddenly interrupted by a knock at his office door. "Come in," the Sheriff spoke professionally, already expecting his office door to come flying open any minute now and see one of his deputies standing their with a report he had requested earlier.

"Sheriff," the young deputy spoke up as he entered the room energetically and walked to the front of Gabe's desk. Then, extending his hand, he gave his superior a vanilla envelope. "Those are the test results from the fingerprints we retrieved from the Goodman home sir. The lab just finished with them."

"Thank you Jensen," Gabe replied nodding his head and calling his deputy by his last name. Then, waiting for the door to close once again as the deputy exited the room quietly, he opened the envelope and pulled the papers aside. Just as he had habitually foreseen, the fingerprints found inside the home couldn't be matched to anyone in their computer. The only traceable fingerprints found matched Rick and Carol Goodman. Sighing, he picked up his phone and dialed his friend's number. Within seconds, and after only a few short rings, he recognized Rick's voice instantly as he answered the phone with a polite hello. "Rick, hey it's Gabe," the Sheriff immediately began. "I did what you asked. I sent a team to your house to dust for prints while you and your family went for a walk through the woods behind your house. And unfortunately I have some bad news buddy. I just got the results back from our lab and they couldn't find anyone's prints but your own, and your wife's. I'm sorry man," he concluded.

"Don't be," Rick spoke up cheerfully trying to change his own mood. "It's not your fault someone broke into our home. It just gives me the creeps ya know? Cause I can't be here every second of the day and I don't know if Carey would be able to handle staying home alone if she knew someone had broke in. I mean she's home alone a lot, and what if this asshole comes back?"

"I know what you're going through," Gabe tried to reassure his lifelong pal. "And damn it, I really wish there was something more I could do. But until this guy comes back, or if this guy comes back I should say, there really isn't much I can do. I can have a near by deputy drive by every so often to see if he can spot the car you described to me. But other than that, just take the normal safety precautions and keep your house locked safe and secure. To tell you the truth though Rick," Gabe paused slightly trying to make his voice sound a bit more convincible. "I wouldn't worry about it. When you came home you probably scared the shit out of whoever was in there or they wouldn't have left in such a hurry. I very seriously doubt they'll return."

"I hope you're right," Rick replied uneasily. "I really hope you're right."

* * *

Debra Saxton left Dr. Kevin Richmond's office with her head down, not wanting the people moving about in the adjoining parking lot to see her face as she exited the psychiatrist's facility. Climbing in her car, she took a deep breath and turned the key in the ignition. As her forehead beaded up with sweat she turned the air conditioner up as high as it would go and then just sat there in her car thinking about what had just taken place behind the closed doors of Dr. Richmond's office. He seemed to be an admirable man with a modest or demure way of presenting himself. The many awards he had draped around his office walls indicated he was a man of great intelligence and that he took his vocation very seriously. Even as the casually dressed, forty year old man sitting behind his desk began to greet her as she had entered his office, she could tell that he was a man of honor, and a man she could trust. His hair had been grayed before its time, and although cleanly shaven, his large blooming green eyes hid behind some bloated, ample lenses, which were so thick it was easy to figure that his eyesight was far from being perfect. He spoke softly, yet his tone was very deep and his eyes never left her own when speaking to one another, making her feel a bit uncomfortable at first, but as time passed, she felt more relaxed and at home.

For almost an hour, Debra had tried to explain to the doctor what was going on inside her son's head. That task was more difficult than she had ever imagined as she realized she didn't understand it herself.

Nevertheless, she tried as best as she could to tell him everything. Dr. Richmond would hold up his hand ever so often, stopping her so he could jot down a few notes he felt to be of significant importance. Starting from his childhood and the death of Billy's father, she moved to all of the events that had happened ever since they had moved to Destin just a few short days ago, and when she had mentioned their living in the old Haas home from which the serial killer Curtis Rains had performed his final acts of violence, she noticed the slight arch in the doctor's eyebrows. Nevertheless, he had managed to keep his equanimity and stoicism and was able to listen carefully as Debra began describing the visions her son had been complaining of, and of the terrible nightmares she herself had bore witness to.

Finally, when she found herself running out of things to say, Debra listened eagerly as Dr. Richmond smiled and said that he would do everything possible to make sure everything was all right with her son Billy. However, when asked if she had told her son about her visiting the psychiatrist, Debra could only shake her head, telling Dr. Richmond that she hadn't mentioned it to her son. Before she left, Kevin had told her to set up an appointment as soon as she and Billy reached an agreement.

Now, however, as she sat behind the wheel of her Lexus, she wondered if she had made the right decision in coming to see Dr. Richmond without her son's consent. For even if Billy refused to agree with her actions, she knew that she should have at least mentioned it to him. Nevertheless, Debra had only done so because she was worried about her only child, and there was no way she was going to let anything sinister happen to Billy. She simply couldn't allow that to happen.

Putting the car in reverse, Debra backed out of her parking space and began the short journey back to her beachfront home. Quickly, she changed her frame of mind, and found herself thinking of something special she could prepare for her son and his guest. Only when the time was right, would she mention the psychiatrist to her son.

* * *

Billy Saxton and his favorite amigo, Blaze Brookshaw, returned home from the beach and when Billy realized his mother had still not returned home, he couldn't help but wonder where she was. Then, before his mind could even muster a guess, he noticed Blaze hovering over the computer desk staring at something. Now, finding his own mind intrigued and filled with curiosity, he made his way over to the desk to see what it was Blaze had found so interesting. As he looked over his friend's shoulder, Billy suddenly found his emotions exploding into anger, and his soul was suddenly consumed with a powerful rage, which could undoubtedly stretch across the vast ocean found in the back of his home. It was the picture of his father, Tom Saxton. He knew his mother had replaced it in its upright position after he had shunned it down. "Son of a bitch," he mustered out loud, as he brushed past his friend and once again slammed the picture flat down on its face, a smile accumulating across his face as he heard the glass crack that protected the photograph of his father from dust and other particles that may be damaging to its oily surface.

"I'm not even going to ask what made you do that?" Blaze interjected, stepping aside and moving into the kitchen.

"Good," Billy continued with the conversation. "Because I think you already know the answer."

Nodding, Blaze took a seat at the dining table and dipped his hand into the fruit basket retrieving an apple his stomach so desperately wanted to devour. Then, as he took his first bite into the precious fruit, his eyes fell upon a porcelain doll that lay in silence on the dining room table. Picking up the doll, he looked at it for a moment and couldn't help but wonder why it was there? He hadn't known Debra to consider these dolls as collector's items, and he felt pretty comfortable in presuming Billy was not the proprietor of such an article. Then, he was about to turn towards Billy, who was busy in the kitchen fixing the two of them something to drink, when his eyes fell on the picture, which had been left underneath the doll. Picking it up as well, Blaze looked into the happy eyes of the Haas family, and could tell from its quality that it had been a rather old picture. Finally, he turned to face his friend. "Billy," he began capturing his attention. "Whose doll is this?"

Jason Glover

Billy began to take a sip of water as the question was so suddenly sprung at him. "What?" Billy exclaimed as he almost choked while drinking the cool liquid.

Realizing he had struck a nerve, Blaze proceeded with caution. "Whose doll is this?" he asked once again holding the doll high in the air. "And who are these people in this picture?" Then, not understanding what was going on, he held the picture up as well, giving Billy a clean visual path to see just what he was talking about.

Once again, as Billy made eye contact with the photograph, the pain began to swirl inside his brain. Feeling the darkness close in, he dropped the glass of water onto the floor. The glass shattered into hundreds of pieces, which were anxiously waiting to sink deep into his flesh. "No," Billy screamed as he grabbed the sides of his head, once again trying to force the pain to go away.

To no avail, nothing departed.

Visions began to flow inside his head, and squinting his eyes, Billy knew that he wouldn't be able to hang on much longer. "No!" he screamed once again as he fell to the floor.

Then, seconds later, Blaze sprung himself from the table and stood over his friend. "Billy!" he called out hoping to get a response from his best friend, and not understanding what had just happened. "Billy what happened?" Unfortunately, there was no answer.

Billy Saxton once again lay in unconscious silence, his entire body tormented with the mysterious pain.

Blaze Brookshaw, on the other hand, was left without the knowledge of understanding what had just taken place, and felt absolutely helpless as he did not know how to help his friend. "Billy!" he tried once again as he felt a certain degree of panic escalate inside his body and his adrenaline began to flow like a river running over a magical waterfall. Feeling completely helpless, Blaze could only try and shake his friend back into the conscious world, and retrieve him from the blackened bliss in which he had momentarily fallen.

* * *

Travis McKinley worked vigorously to clean off the mirror, which loomed above the dresser drawers right in front of the bed he shared with Jamie Walker. The red lipstick only seemed to smear as he sprayed window cleaner across its cool, smooth surface, and he found it taking a lot longer than first anticipated to clean the mirror free from the agonizing word that had somehow been written in bold red letters. "I told you it was real," Jamie spoke up, her voice still a bit shaky. "He was here Travis. Curtis Rains was here."

"Nonsense," Travis interjected boldly, as he made his way back over to the bed finally able to rid the mirror from the mind-jarring shibboleth. "Honey, would you please listen to yourself? I know you might be going through a rough time right now, but it's just not possible that Curtis Rains came into this room and wrote out "Tinman," across the mirror. It can't happen honey. That son of a bitch is dead. He's dead Jamie!" he repeated stressing his point. "And he can never, ever hurt you again. People coming back from the dead is something that does not and can not happen."

"No!" Jamie hollered still curtly following her instincts, and believing that she was mentally stable enough to differentiate between fact and fiction. "You're not listening to me!" she cried as her emotions once again began to overflow with a rhythmic syndrome of fear and anxiety and soon she felt the free flowing teardrops once again dispense from her eyes and run down her soft, flaky cheek. "I know you can't possibly understand this Travis," she sighed in grievance, giving her boyfriend the benefit of the doubt. "But I know it was real. And I know he'll return."

"How do you know you didn't sleepwalk over to that dresser and write it up there yourself?" Travis asked not realizing his mistake.

"Is that what you think I did?" Jamie shot back, pulling herself free from his arms. "Do you think I'm crazy now or something? Fine," she paused momentarily trying to subdue to anger that was aggressively progressing inside. "Don't believe me if you don't want to." Then, she rolled over and turned her back on Travis. "Can you go now?" she asked casually. "I kind of feel like being alone for the moment."

"No," Travis replied strongly, realizing he had upset the one person he cared about more than anything in the world. "I don't ever want to leave your side sweetheart, and I'm not going to now if it's all the same to you," he added jokingly, although not expecting to hear a laugh in return from the beautiful woman beside him. "Jamie," he continued soothingly, as he tried to evoke some sort of eye contact or response. "Jamie," he tried once again showing that he wasn't about to give up. "Please talk to me." Without saying a word, Jamie rolled back over and looked into her boyfriend's eyes, waiting for him to continue. "I'm sorry sweetheart," he continued sympathetically as he rubbed his fingers through her hair. "I love you Jamie. You know I love you."

Nodding, she replied. "Yes, I know you do," Then, pausing briefly, she added, finally surrendering to the loving arms of Travis McKinley. "And I love you too."

* * *

Sheriff Gabriel Burnham sat patiently at one of the many red lights along Highway 98, which was most often referred to as the "Strip," in Destin, as was the case in Panama City, which was only 30 minutes East from where he now found himself grid locked in traffic. He had his air conditioner running full blast, and found a relaxing oldies station to listen to as he waited for the light to change colors and he could resume his homebound journey. Opening his mouth, a yawn escaped as he gripped the steering wheel with both hands, pushing himself backwards, stretching his aching muscles. Without speaking to himself, Gabe knew that tonight was going to be a short one as he planned on turning in early.

Suddenly, a car sped from the intersection heading in the same direction he was traveling. There was something about the vehicle that captured Gabe's full attention and sprouted his instincts with an undefined suspicion. That's when it hit him.

The car had been a black Lexus.

Stepping on the gas, Gabe purposely exceeded the speed limit as he attempted to catch up with the suspecting, dubious car that had just crossed his path. He knew that making a connection between the Goodman's home and the black car in front of him was a very difficult, it not impossible task, and he was also aware that there were probably hundreds of cars matching Rick Goodman's description of the Lexus he had seen parked clandestinely across from his wooded, isolated brick home. Nevertheless, he had always trusted his instincts, and right now, they were drawing him closer and closer to the car in front of him. As each second passed, he found himself gaining on the vehicle, and within no time, he knew he would be close enough to visualize the license plate number.

Just as he suspected, within two minutes, Gabe had been able to weave his way through traffic and found his stealth Yukon right behind the back bumper of the black Lexus. Picking up his radio, he began speaking with the dispatcher. "Dispatch," he began professionally, yet with a bit of skepticism as he easily made out the figure of a woman driving the car. "Sheriff Burnham here, I'd like for you to run a quick license check on a black Lexus I have in front of me."

"Go ahead with the number sir," the dispatch directed.

"MAT-NNI, on a Georgia plate," he returned, knowing that it would be a few seconds before the dispatch came back online with the information he had requested. As he waited for the female voice to return, he watched the car in front of him discreetly, yet his mission clear inside his head. Like the eyes of a hawk, Gabe waited patiently for his chance to catch his suspect off guard and fruitfully find out if this was indeed the car that had been seen parked across the street from the Goodman home. His presence completely unknown to the driver of the car, he simply followed the Lexus carefully, turning left when it turned left, or right when it turned right, never once dropping more than a few car lengths behind. Finally, with his aggression mounting, and his intelligence already asking himself questions he could not answer, he heard the dispatchers voice come back over the air. "Sheriff Burnham here. What have you got?" he asked filled with anticipation and hoping to hear anything that would cause reasonable suspicion and allow him to pull the car over.

"The vehicle is registered to a Debra Saxton of Marietta, Georgia. Vehicle was bought in Cobb County. She's a white female, 39 years of age-"

"Any priors, warrants, unpaid parking tickets? Anything?" he asked cutting the dispatcher off short, hoping to get to something that would allow him to evoke his power as a law enforcement officer.

"No sir," the dispatcher proceeded. "The woman doesn't have a record at all and never been in trouble with the law it seems. Her husband, Tom Saxton is deceased and she has just purchased a house on Sandy Point Lane."

"Address?" Gabe inquired, and listened intently as the dispatcher immediately said the address over the radio. Just as it was completed, Gabe felt every muscle in his body tense up, and his adrenaline began to devour itself with an energy level he had not felt in sometime. The address he had just heard sounded all too familiar to Gabe, and it instantly began to bring back memories he himself had tried long and hard to forget. The woman in front of him, driving the black Lexus had purchased a house along Sandy Point Lane. Only, it wasn't just an ordinary beach house. It had long ago belonged to the Haas family, where David and Charlene Haas had been viciously murdered, and little Carey Haas, at the time, had been the only one able to escape death from the hands of Curtis Rains. Carey Haas, he very well knew, now lived at the home of Rick Goodman; therefore, this had to be the right vehicle. It just had to be.

Contiguously, Gabe Burnham flipped the switch that evoked the blue and red lights, and switching on his PA system, he ordered the car in front of him to pull over and come to a complete stop. Surprisingly, the driver without hesitation began to pull off the road, and once safely out of traffic, came to a complete stop and shut off the ignition.

"Dispatch," Gabe spoke up once again getting the woman's attention. "Burnham here," he continued before hearing the woman's voice on the other end reply and tell him to proceed. "I'm pulling the car over. Stand by."

"Would you like me to send another unit?"

Pausing for a brief second, he eyeballed the car in front of him carefully searching for any signs that his life may be in danger. "That's a negative for now," he answered feeling the courage inside him build up. "Just have a few standing by. I'll be back on in a second."

"10-4 sir," the dispatch concluded. "Standing by."

Finally, taking a deep breath, Sheriff Gabriel Burnham stepped from his immense Yukon and approached the black Lexus in front of him. His hand, ever so slightly, rested peacefully on his holstered revolver.

* * *

Carey Haas sat in her bedroom, doing nothing more than gazing out the window on the second floor overlooking the tall pine trees that were scattered everywhere in the surrounding forests around her home. "Home," the word itself just didn't seem to fit the setting she found herself trapped safely inside. Even though she had lived in these quarters for over ten years now, the Goodman home was one that simply was not her own. And it simply was not where she belonged. Her home lay along Sandy Point Lane, and to this day, she hadn't heard of anyone taking it in and redecorating it as his or her own. Although Carey herself knew that she would never return to the home which held so many wonderful, yet so many dreadful memories of her past, she still considered it to be her one and only home.

It had once been the happy setting of her youthful life with her parents, eating every meal together at the dinner table, only to be followed with herself running up the stairs when she was little, proudly giving herself a bath knowing that shortly afterwards, both of her parents would come sneaking up the stairs and lovingly tuck her in bed, wishing her sweet dreams and saying her prayers with her. She remembered their smiles as they would lean over and peck her forehead, and sometimes place their hand under her armpit and tickle her acutely until she couldn't hold her laughter inside and soon the whole room would be filled with an unconquerable joy as the three of them would burst into a laughter which could have been heard around the world. Sometimes, in her sleep, she could see the smiles on her parent's beloved faces and hear her own laughter as they tickled her small body.

However, every time the pleasant memories would come flooding inside her tender, emotional body, the horrid images of their death would come storming in, throwing everything in disarray, and tormenting her lost soul. Then, her laughter would disappear and give away to another sound that made her body stiffen, and her heart momentarily stop beating. It was the sounds of her parent's screaming before they died. To this day, she still hadn't figured out the answer as to why something of this nature or magnitude could have happened to her family?

Why would God allow something like this to happen?

Why had Curtis Rains laid his rage upon them that unforgettable evening?

Why? Why? Why?

Over the years, however, Carey had been able to deal with the fact of knowing that she would never see her parents again. Not once, though, could she find enough strength to forgive the Tinman for what he had done to her parents and what he had put herself through. It was simply unforgivable. She had been happy the morning she had awakened and read in the paper that the notorious serial killer had finally been executed. It even gave her greater pleasure to read that no one had attended the burial service. Stunningly, however, the fact alone that Curtis Rains was no longer alive in this world didn't put her mind at ease.

It was almost as if Carey herself could still feel his cold eyes on her, and feel his warm breath beating down the back of her neck as he chased after her down the beach, fully intending to rip away at her flesh and consume her soul as she screamed in an earth shattering ensemble of pain. Even though Curtis Rains was pronounced dead, it was if he still was not gone. To Carey Haas, the Tinman was still alive.

And still coming for her!

* * *

The creature wondered ominously throw the widening and gaping prairie and felt its body relax as the feeling of freedom once again consumed his emotions as it drifted worry-free through space. Smiling, he recalled how he had just evoked his powers on one of the unlucky recipients of his evil. There were so many people he wanted to reach out and touch with the hand of death, and no one could escape his bloodthirsty rage that he knew was about to come.

For the past ten years it had been lying untouched, and hidden inside. But soon, it would be released and everyone would realize his power. And once again, everyone would fear him. Leaving his first victim lying on the bed, sobbing in fear as her mind wondered what had happened, he now found himself traveling in another direction. He was heading for the last place his mind could remember. It was unfortunately the place where his bloody masterpieces had came to an abrupt end.

He was heading for the Haas home, in sunny Destin, Florida.

Tinman

Only, as soon as he arrived, he knew it would no longer be looked at as sunny Destin. As soon as his presence would be witnessed and his mission complete, darkness would close in and swallow his victims like a tidal wave sinking a massive ship into the ocean, where it wouldn't stop until it reached the ocean floor and disappear from existence, possibly never recovered and no one ever knowing what had actually happened to the seemingly indestructible structure.

Finally, he felt a rage flicker inside, and opening his eyes, he found himself floating through a white plastered hallway. His senses instantly recalled the smell of death. Gracefully, he moved silently down the stairway, his presence unseen and completely unknown to whoever was in the home. Then, coming to the bottom of the stairs he gazed out at the living room in front of him. Smiling, he knew that this was where it had happened.

This was where he had sliced David Haas's throat and left him to die, and he remembered his hands had once been covered with the man's blood as he bravely tried to save his family.

Then, looking back upstairs he remembered walking upwards and lashing out at the woman he knew to be Charlene Haas. He felt his pants rise slightly, and realized he was developing an erection as he recalled the pleasure he had received from raping the defenseless woman in front of her deceased, or exanimate husband. Touching himself gently, he closed his eyes and relived the scene that had formed inside his head. Charlene had screamed for him to stop, but she hadn't been able to stop him as he forced himself inside her, ripping away at her vagina, her screams only pushing him harder as the sweat dripped from his body. He remembered grunting with a homicidal rage as his saliva exited his mouth and fell freely on Charlene's lips. Only, as he finished the first time, he found that his satisfaction hadn't been met, so he maliciously forced himself on her again and again. Repeatedly he bruised and raped his victim, accepting the joyous pain her helpless fingernails enhanced as she tried to rip away at his face and flesh.

Finally, he had beat her to a bloody pulp, consuming himself with her charred blood, and then stabbed her wildly like a lion attacking it's prey. Finally, after ripping off her fingernails, and cutting away at her genitalia and her reproductive organs, he left nothing for the investigators to find and link him to the scene of the crime. Then, zipping up his pants, he headed for the hallway, which lead to the cellar, where he knew he would find a scared little child. As he had reached the door, he opened it carefully, and knew he was about to start all over again and repeat the encounter he had just experienced with Charlene on her daughter, Carey Haas.

Only, things had not gone as planned.

He had been outsmarted by a nine-year-old demoiselle, and the lass had escaped his hands of death. Carey Haas had been the only one in all the years of his heartless rampages that had managed to escape, and run away even after making eye contact with the man everyone had once suggested as having the face of evil.

Thinking back on how Carey had slipped away from the pulsating grips of his hands, the creature suddenly found his blissful mood turn utterly sour, and anger once again began to boil in his veins.

He couldn't forget that Carey Haas had escaped.

And fortunately, it was something that he could make right.

Chapter 15

Starke, Florida.

"Honey, do you think we should be doing this?" Gloria Reynolds asked as her husband threw her gently on their bed and began unbuttoning her checkered blouse, only to remove the bra from her chest immediately afterwards, leaving her breasts exposed to the chilly draft coming from the AC vent. "Sarah is going to be home any minute now and you know the first place she'll come is up here to our bedroom to see if we are home." Her words didn't seem to penetrate through her husband's thick skull, however, as he only removed his own shirt, climbed on top of her and placed his hand on her firm leg, gently moving its way down her thigh and into the depth of her skirt. As he kissed her a few times, Gloria found herself overwhelmed with a passionate desire, almost yearning for love, and she didn't want Jack to stop touching her. Nevertheless, an image of their eleven year old daughter walking in on them as their bodies connected in a fury of love making kept creeping inside her mind and she simply wouldn't subject her daughter to something of that provocative nature. "Jack," she tried once again, finally forcing him to look into her eyes. "I'm serious. Sarah will be home any minute."

"No she won't," Jack Reynolds tried to assure his wife's good nature. "She called a little while ago before you got home sweetheart and explained that she wouldn't be home until a little later. I think she's going out to eat with her little friend. Which is fine with me," he paused as he breathed down her neck and placed one of his hands across her firm, astounding breasts "Because this is my day off Gloria, and I've been waiting for you to get home all day. So come on my buxom beauty," he continued with a smile as he began removing her underpants. "Let's have a little fun shall we?"

Saying nothing else, and pushing the thought of her daughter aside, Gloria gladly let her husband take advantage of every aspect her gorgeous body exhumed, and within seconds found herself lost, drowning away into a steamy, hot desire and thirst for love. Giving herself away to the passion she felt inside, she craved for her husband to be inside of her.

"Besides," Jack continued jokingly as the foreplay came to an end, and he prepared to make love to his beautiful wife. "The door is locked." Then, laughing, the two of them closed their eyes, locked lips and enjoyed the time alone they hardly ever were allowed to accumulate anymore. "I love you Gloria. I've loved you since the first time we met and I'll never stop."

"Just shut up and kiss me," Gloria ended the conversation as she grabbed her husband around his neck and pulled him close to her.

Half an hour later, both of them laid side by side on the bed, it's moist, silky sheets thrown off. Both of them completely nude, they just laid there and looked into each other's eyes. Cooling down, Gloria still found herself a bit out of breath as she spoke with a rather frigid tone. "Damn," she paused with a smile. "You need to take more days off. I could get used to coming home to this."

Before Jack could respond, the two of them were interrupted by the sound of the doorbell. Climbing to his feet, Jack threw on some clothes and prepared to exit their bedroom to let their daughter inside. Kissing his wife once more before departing from her view, he opened their bedroom door and stepped out into the hallway. Before closing the door behind him, he glanced back and spoke. "I told you we wouldn't get caught," he said with a smile, pretending that he was a teenager once again. "Now you go take a relaxing, long, hot bath. And when you get out, I'll have dinner ready. How does that sound?"

"You're too good to me Jack Reynolds," Gloria replied, returning her husband's warm smile "Too damn good."

Seconds later, Jack found himself unlatching the dead bolt of his front door, and with the casual notion of twisting the knob, he smiled as he gazed into the cheerful eyes of his eleven year old daughter, Sarah, her brown hair tightly woven into a gorgeous French braid, with her blossoming hazel eyes matching perfectly. "Welcome home

Angel," he greeted his daughter warmly stepping aside and allowing her to enter only after she gave him an amicable embrace. "Did you have a good time at your friend's house? You behaved yourself didn't you?"

Nodding, Sarah replied, her soft tone still displaying her buoyant nature. "Of course I did daddy, and yes I had a good time." Then, pausing briefly, she turned her smile into a false frown and continued. "I missed you guys though," she began speaking of both her parents. "And I'm glad I'm home. Where's mom anyway?"

"Upstairs taking a bath," Jack replied as he began leading his daughter into the kitchen. "But you can come and help me prepare dinner for the three of us. I'll cook whatever you like as long as you promise to help me. I'm not very good in the kitchen you know."

"All right," Sarah spoke agreeably. Then, changing the subject. "Hey dad. I saw you on the television again tonight. You know? When you were being interviewed by all of those reporters about that Tinman guy. What was his real name again?"

Freezing, Jack turned and faced his daughter sternly. "Damn it Sarah!" he shouted harshly, showing his anger a tad too much. "I thought we had this discussion a few nights ago and we both agreed that we wouldn't talk about that ever again. I don't want you to go around talking or even thinking about that evil man. You're too young and precious to have your mind consumed with such images. That man hurt a lot of people, and if given the chance, he would have hurt many more. But he's dead now, and the whole world might be wanting to talk about him. But I don't, and I don't want this family to as well. Now that's final Sarah. No more." Then, bending down he watched as his daughter tilted her head downwards, obviously upset that she had angered her father. "Oh, it's all right pumpkin," Jack willingly changed his tone to comfort his most prized possession. "I didn't mean to get so upset with you. I just don't want to hear that man's name ever again. Can you just do that for me?"

Nodding, Sarah brushed the sobs aside and looked up to face her father, accepting the warmth his soothing eyes seemed to scatter inside her body. "I'm sorry daddy. I won't do it anymore."

"Let's just forget all about that immoral man, go into the kitchen and make some supper shall we?" Then, taking her father's ample hand in her own, she pulled him towards the kitchen. Before the two of them could actually set foot in the fruitful environment, however, something happened that forced Jack Reynolds to stop in his tracks. Coming from the backyard, the two of them undeniably heard a thunderous sound that seemed to amplify throughout the entire house. The vivacious sound echoed throughout Jack's mind, just as it had his home and he found himself silently wondering just what it was that had caused such a ruckus? It had been an earsplitting, tumultuous timbre that had intrigued, mystified and shocked Jack all at once. Finding himself rather afraid of whatever could have made the racket, he released his daughter's hand and slowly walked over to the nearest window that displayed every inch of his backyard. Seeing nothing, he turned once again to face his daughter, whose face was ashen with fear.

"What was that daddy?" Sarah asked obviously a little scared and confused.

"I don't know sweetheart."

Then, from the bathroom, he heard his wife's concerned voice. "Jack? What was that awful crashing sound?"

"I don't know," Jack shouted back. "It came from the backyard and sounded like it came from the shed." Then, pausing he forced the lump of fear back down his throat. "I'll go check it out." Almost instantly, he picked up a metal prong standing near the fireplace and made his way towards the backdoor. "Stay here Sarah," he commanded his seemingly terrified daughter.

"No daddy," Sarah pleaded thinking of running over to her father and flinging herself upon him. "Please don't leave me in here."

"I'll be right outside sweetheart and your mother is right down the hall," Jack assured his princess. "Everything is going to be all right sugar bear. You'll see. Probably something just fell off the wall in the shed and crashed into something," he concluded although knowing full well that his daughter hadn't believed a word he had spoken as she plainly eyeballed the sharp object he grasped in the palm of his hands. Jack wondered if there was anything in the shed that could have evoked such a terrifying sound. It almost sounded as if a thunderbolt had escaped from the heavens above and landed directly on his home. "Trust me Sarah. I'll be right back. I promise." Then, saying nothing else, Jack exited his home through the backdoor and soon found himself standing alone in the hinterlands of his backyard. The sun hadn't set yet, and there was still plenty of daylight for him to see where he was going as he took his first steps towards the old, raggedy wooden shed that was located in the far left corner of his fenced in backyard, and was in dire need of repairs. If there was anything out there, he was sure that he would find it.

* * *

Meanwhile, at the Saxton home.
"Damn it!" Blaze continued to curse himself as he hurriedly tried to awaken Billy Saxton from the abysmal subterranean sleep he had witnessed him fall into, just seconds after showing him the odd picture that had been placed on the kitchen table. Blaze had struggled at first, but in time, was able to remove his friend from the kitchen floor and transfer him to the comfortable sofa in the living room. "Come on Billy!" Blaze exclaimed still not quite sure what had happened as he slightly shook his friend. "Please man. Wake up."

Finally, he saw a flickering motion come from Billy's eyes, and soon his arm moved upwards and clutched the top of his head. Billy's eyes were open now, although squinting a bit as if relieving himself from whatever hidden pain was still living inside his head. He tried to sit up, but still felt a bit lightheaded, almost as if he had been unable to intake any oxygen from the time he lost consciousness, and he fell back onto the soft cushions closing his eyes once again, accepting the fact that he needed more time to recover. "How long have I been gone?" Billy asked his best friend sitting at his side, a confused expression enveloped along his face.

"I'm not sure," Blaze admitted finding himself stumped and a little more flustered at the calmness Billy was able to speak with. It almost appeared as though Billy was used to the chaotic blackouts, and that was simply something that left Blaze's mind in an utter state of disorientation. "I suppose about a half hour or so. What in the hell happened man?" he asked unable to keep his questions inside. "One minute you're in the kitchen fixing us something to drink, and the next your lying unconscious on the kitchen floor in a maze of broken glass."

In good faith, and realizing his friend couldn't possibly understand everything that had been happening to him over the past few days, Billy managed to smile and let out a weak, evasive laugh, obviously abstracting humor from this turmoil situation. "If you only knew my friend," Billy managed to say, finally regaining his strength and was able to sit upright. "If you only knew."

"If I only knew what?" Blaze floundered back harshly, not seeing anything funny about what had just happened. "Why don't you just tell me what in the hell is going on?"

Nodding, Billy was about to give in and let his friend in on everything that had been happening ever since he and his mother moved into the house the two of them now found themselves sitting in, even planning on giving Blaze all of the details concerning the death of the family that had lived there before them and before their lives were cut short by Curtis Rains. Only, before he could begin, the two of them heard something that forced them to turn towards the front door. Seconds later, Debra walked inside with an angered expression placed along her face.

"Mom," Billy spoke weakly, his concern obviously falling to his mother who had entered their home in an obvious unfriendly mood. "Is something wrong? Why do you look so upset?"

"Why don't you tell me?" Debra shot back angrily at her son, her eyes never even glancing in another direction.

"I'm sorry?" Billy questioned not understanding what was going on. "Did I do something wrong?"

"Breaking and entering Billy!" Debra exclaimed harshly reliving the conversation she had been forced to endure from the county Sheriff, Gabriel Burnham. "I'd say that would qualify as doing something wrong. Am I ringing any bells in that head of yours? I knew I should have never let you go off in my car. I should have known you would be up to something. God!" she paused moving closer to her son. "Damn it Billy. How could you be so stupid?"

"I'm sorry mom," Billy tried to hold his ground, not knowing if a guilty expression was written along his face or not. "But I haven't the slightest idea of what you are talking about."

"Well don't explain yourself to me," Debra interjected, shrugging her shoulders carelessly. "Why don't you save your excuses for Sheriff Burnham. He's outside in our driveway and he wants to have a word with you."

Shocked, Billy couldn't believe at the sudden turn of events, and found himself feeling completely trapped without any means of escape. "What!" he continued, trying to delay the inevitable confrontation with the county Sheriff. "Am I under arrest or something? I swear I did nothing wrong."

"Well, that's not for me to decide now is it," Debra retorted, holding her ground strongly, relaying to her son that whatever he had gotten himself into, he was going to have face the consequences and find his own way out. "Now why don't you go outside and talk to that man before he thinks something is up."

"All right," Billy spoke firmly, walking past his silent friend Blaze, who found it best to just mind his own business for the moment. "I'll go talk to him," he added as he reached the front door, pausing slightly as he desperately tried to gather enough strength to face the authority figure with a clear head. Seconds later, he was outside his home, and walking towards the gleaming Yukon that was parked directly in front of his mother's Lexus. The older man stood at the hood of his truck, eyeballing him suspiciously as he walked across the driveway, a blank expression looming heavily over his facade.

With his hands trembling, and his eyes darting from side to side, not allowing himself to make eye contact with the man before him, Billy Saxton knew that he had lost his innocence.

* * *

The rusted hinges on the old shed squeaked grimly as Jack Reynolds pushed the doors open, listening closely as it slammed against the wall. The walk from his household to the termite-infested hovel seemed to take forever, and he couldn't count the times he thought about turning around and returning to the safety and shelter his beloved domicile provided. After all, the mind boggling, loud crashing sound hadn't returned, and it didn't appear that anything serious was wrong. Nevertheless, Jack found himself trembling with fear, and although he couldn't quite put his finger on it, he could sense that he was not alone as he hesitated before entering the dangerous shed.

A cool, swift breeze crossed his path, and he listened calmly as the trees swayed, rocking back and forth, almost giving him a slight feeling of safety as they unconsciously pushed him forward, beckoning him to enter the run down hut in front of him. The sun was clearly starting to disappear into the sky, and Jack was well aware that without a flashlight, and without the shed being able to generate any electricity, if he was going to be able to take a look around inside, he had to do so before the sun completely disappeared and gave way to a beautiful, clear night sky.

Then, desperately trying to rid himself of the uncomfortable psyche that had sprouted unexpectedly, and invited itself into his soul, he shook the last of the jitters aside and stepped inside the dust filled environment. It wasn't until he was actually inside the creepy setting that Jack suddenly realized that it had been a few years since he had even given the shed his slightest attention, even longer since he had actually gone inside. He found all sorts of useless objects from his past that he knew were far from operational. There was not one, but two old fashioned lawn mowers, dust completely covering their surface, not allowing the naked eye to even attempt to guess as to what their actual color was. Old yard tools, such as a hand pushed edger, bush trimmers, rakes and shovels covered the walls, most of the handles broken, and what seemed like massive amounts of nothing more than ordinary junk were piled up in an unorganized fashion, scattered everywhere around the small confinements of the shed.

Nothing appeared out of the ordinary, and there was absolutely no sign of anything falling down and slamming itself into the wall which could have made the rather disturbing booming sound Jack and his family had clearly been able to hear just a few short minutes ago. There had been no sign of severe weather approaching the area, as clear skies gave evidence of that. Feeling completely confounded, he gave way to the perplexity that was lingering about inside his brain. He couldn't find anything that could explain the bewildering, almost unearthly explosive sound he had witnessed just a short time ago. Shaking his head radically, Jack turned and prepared to exit the shed, when something happened that forced him to stay where he stood.

The fear he had felt moments before, quickly resurfaced and captured his soul. The feeling of being in danger followed closely behind and returned in an uplifting demeanor.

A cool breeze once again swept across Jack Reynolds's path. Only, it wasn't an ordinary breeze that had crept inside the shed, seeking its way through the open door and blistering his moistened skin from the environment outside. No, this windy sensation was far too powerful to come from Mother Nature, especially from the hot and humid Florida atmosphere where most of the time you had to remind yourself to breathe through the thick mass of intensifying air. This breeze almost swept him off his feet, and Jack at first struggled to balance himself as the wind speed stretched into a furious rage. Then, suddenly, the powerful gale died away, the blast almost forgotten.

Again, however, Jack Reynolds felt as if he were not alone.

He could feel it within the tightening pits of his stomach, and sensed someone's presence as the hair on the back of his neck came to a standstill. He felt unconditionally helpless, and was afraid to move any fragment of his now shaken physique. Without a doubt, he felt another presence around him, swarming over him, hovering around him unseen, and unheard.

Terrified, he began looking at everything around him, trying to find some clue that might give away the presence of whatever was watching him. Nothing. Whoever was there seemed to be just as invisible as the wind, and he still felt helpless as he failed in navigating where the outburst of wind had come from.

Eyes.

Jack could feel the presence of eyes watching his every move.

And silence.

The terrifying silence only seemed to strain his brain even more as he tried to make sense of what was happening. But he couldn't make sense of it. He didn't understand any of it, wanted to believe that the whole scenario wasn't real, and blame his imagination for making it up. But even as that thought entered his brain, Jack Reynolds didn't believe it. Whatever was happening was real. In fact, it was almost too real and he wished that he had never left his home. He should have stayed inside with his beloved wife, Gloria, and his darling child Sarah, whom was probably looking out the window this very instant to see if he was all right.

That's it. He had to get back inside. He couldn't take it anymore. His hands trembled uncontrollably with a fear his body was unaccustomed to, as he had lived the vast majority of his life not afraid of anything. Then, finally, with his eyes darting in a wild array of intrigue, they searched for any signs of danger that may be lurking about as he stepped forward and prepared to exit the shed once and for all.

Jack was within four feet from the door, when it happened.

Suddenly, and unexplainably, the door slammed shut, trapping him inside.

Unable to move, Jack once again found himself thunderstruck. Looking around the darkening shed as the sun continued to fold into the night; he told himself there had to be someone in the room. The door simply couldn't slam shut that forcefully without the help of a human being, he thought to himself as a surge of panic began to form.

But no one was there.

Save for himself, and all the junk, the shed was completely empty, and the staggering silence remained.

Sweat began to drip from his forehead, and without thinking, he loosened his grip and dropped the metal prong to the ground as he ran for the door. Forgetting that he had left his only means of protection behind, he grabbed the doorknob and jerked wildly at the handle as he desperately tried to free himself from the shed.

It wouldn't budge.

What was going on? The door had no locks on it. How could he possibly be locked inside? Then, as soon as that question evaporated into his conscious thinking, he figured out the answer. Someone had to be on the other side holding it shut, purposely not allowing him to exit. "Who's there?" he found himself asking in a shaky voice. Then, after seconds of hearing no response, he tried again. This time, however, using a bit more authority, ordering whoever it was to set him free. "Let me out of here!" Jack demanded furiously as he let panic sink in and once again began pulling harshly at the door.

Again, it didn't move.

Stepping back, he looked at the door for a moment. The wood was old and he knew that it wouldn't be too hard to splinter the door into thousands of pieces. Especially, if it meant being able to once again take command of his own life. Finally, Jack began to search around him for any tool that would be handy. It wasn't long before his eyes suddenly fell upon an ax. It was an old, rusted ax, but sharp nonetheless. Taking in a deep breath, and pausing briefly to wipe the sweat from his eyes, he once again brushed the fear aside for the moment, then picked up the ax and raised it into the air as he prepared to take his first swing into the rotten lumber.

Before he released the sharp blade, however, a voice called out to him.

It was a voice he was sure he had heard before, yet it was still unrecognizable. Although knowing that he was alone in the shed, he once again found himself searching its parameters to see if he could see who or what had spoken to him. Nothing. Brushing the voice aside, however, and thinking that he was simply hearing things, he raised the ax in the air once again and prepared to take his first swing.

The voice returned.

This time, however, there was no mistaking it.

"Jack!" the voice echoed throughout the increasingly dark room as the sun was almost completely out of view. *"Jack,"* the uncanny voice continued, obviously receiving pleasure from playing with his mind. *"I'm sorry we have to meet like this my friend. But I'm afraid I have some pretty bad news for you."*

"What!" Jack exclaimed ominously wishing he could see just who it was that was carrying on a conversation with him. "Who are you? And what do you want with me?"

"I've come to warn you Jack," the disguising voice answered immediately. *"I've come to warn you, and help you my friend."*

"Where are you?" Jack demanded bravely. "Why won't you let me see your face?"

"I'm afraid that's impossible Jack."

"Why?"

"Because it just can't be done!" the voice answered harshly, obviously becoming impatient and angry at Jack's tone of voice. *"Now listen to me. If you want to get out of here and return home to your so-called loving family, then I suggest you shut up and listen to what I have to say. Besides, it involves you Jack. You and your family. Especially that sweet little wife of yours,"* the voice concluded chuckling at himself. *"You are so blind Jack."*

"What?" Jack questioned finding himself completely in the dark. "What in the hell are you talking about? What about my family?" he demanded, finding himself giving way to the frustration that had been mounting inside. "What about my wife?"

"*Gloria!*" the voice spoke calmly, yet with a tone of accusing suspicion as he showed that he knew her name. "*Gloria, Gloria, Gloria,*" the voice repeated over and over again, once again finding humor in the fact that Jack was about to go out of his mind, leaving the sane world behind.

"What about my wife?" Jack demanded once more, now anger being the only emotion his body consumed. "What about Gloria?" he shouted raising the ax high in the air as if worshipping some unseen God.

"*She's a whore Jack!*" the voice finally answered coldly. "*She's a fucking whore.*"

"No!" Jack refused to believe a word spoken. "You don't know what in the hell you are talking about. My wife is not a whore you son of a bitch. Now why don't you stop being a coward and show yourself. Come on," Jack pleaded growing increasingly violent as each second passed, completely unaware that his behavior was exactly what the man behind the voice was expecting, and counted on. "Come on and let me see you. Face me like a man you son of a bitch and let me out of here. Or I swear, I'll kill you."

As Jack bravely let those words leave his mouth, he felt his courage slip away into the unknown as the only response he heard was laughter. It was an evil laugh, and he knew that he had been unsuccessful in pinching any of the man's nerves. Whoever was out there wasn't afraid of him, and obviously wasn't planning on going anywhere until his agenda had been complete and his job consummated.

"*Oh Jack,*" the voice spoke up, letting the evil laugh pass into the darkness that now conveyed the entire setting. "*Do you really think that it's you who has the upper hand here?*" Then, without giving his captive any time to reply, he immediately answered his own question for him. "*I don't think so Jack. You see, you're locked inside that shed, and I could tear it down, forcing it to collapse on your aging, weak body. Or I could just set it afire, watch you burn to death and not be able to differentiate between the crackling sound of this rotten wood, or the crackling sound of your bones as they heat up and disintegrate into ashes. Or,*" the voice paused again, making sure

Jack was taking in every option available to him. *"Or you can just relax and listen to what I have to say. And soon, I promise you will be able to see that I just might be telling you the truth. You see Jack, I'm here for one reason, and one reason only. I'm here to help you out. I don't have anything to gain from you by telling you this truth, even though you may choose to take it for granted and not believe a word I speak. But it is the truth Jack. And I'm telling you this so you aren't left in the dark anymore, and so that bitch will not continue to sleep around behind your back, and then come home to you and your daughter like nothing ever happened. She's a whore Jack."* Then, pausing concisely, to evoke more emphasis he added. *"Gloria is a dirty whore, a trollop if you will, and she needs to be punished. The only question is Jack, are you willing to punish her?"*

"No!" Jack screamed refusing to believe anything he had heard. "I don't believe you. Gloria would never do such a thing. Never."

"Fine," the evil voice shot back brutally. *"Believe what you want. But when you go back inside that house of yours tonight, and you lay down to bed with your wife, I want you to look into her eyes and then I'll come back and you can decide for yourself whether or not you want to believe me."*

"Fine!" Jack pleaded. "Just let me out of here."

"All right," the voice spoke up agreeably, and calmly. *"You can go back to your beloved family Jack. But remember one thing. Your wife is an untrustworthy, unfaithful bitch and she deserves to be punished. You can't let her off the hook Jack. You can't let her get away with it."*

Then, before Jack could reply, he felt the presence disappear, and no longer felt as if he were being watched. He could finally tell that he was alone. Finally, taking a deep breath, he moved towards the door and tried to open it once again. A wave of relief passed through him as he felt the door give way and easily open. Stepping outside into the fresh, night air, he found it completely dark and wondered just how long he had been outside in the shed. He glanced around him intensely, but saw no signs of anyone fleeing from his backyard. It was as if no one had ever been there at all.

But someone was there all right, that was one thing in which Jack was certain.

And as he made his way across the lawn and approached his home, the last words that were thrown upon him lingered inside his head and he couldn't help but to play them over and over again. No matter how hard he tried, he couldn't push them aside, and he simply couldn't forget them.

"Your wife is a whore," he remembered the voice saying. *"And she deserves to be punished."*

* * *

Carey Haas found herself standing outside of her relative's bedroom door. They had seemingly forgotten to securely close it all the way, allowing her to listen in on their conversation. Ordinarily, she would not have allowed herself to be this nosey. However, as she came from the bathroom and passed by their door, she heard her name mentioned, and decided to silently stand by and see just why they were discussing her.

"The only fingerprints they found in here belonged to us," she heard her uncle Rick tell his wife. "Gabe said that he would have a police officer drive by here every so often to see if that same car that was seen parked in front of the house reappears."

"Well what about Carey?" Carol found herself asking the inevitable question. "Should we tell her that someone broke into our house earlier today when we went to the store and left her here sleeping?"

"No," Carey once again recognized her uncle's voice. "There's no point in doing that. It would only frighten her. And who knows, perhaps Gabe was right. Maybe we did scare the hell out of whoever was in here and maybe he won't return."

"Maybe," she heard her aunt's voice carry on the conversation. "But what if they do come back? What'll we do then?"

Deciding she had heard enough, Carey decided to walk away and let her relatives finish their conversation in privacy. Walking into her own bedroom, she quietly closed the door and soon found herself sprawled comfortably out on her bed. Closing her eyes, she remembered the nightmare she had been having at the same moment her aunt and uncle must have been coming home from the grocery store. She remembered feeling terrified, only then to feel warm and safe as the hands grabbed her shoulders and soothed her body. Now, more than ever, Carey believed that her guardian angel wasn't a dream at all.

Someone had been inside her room while she was sleeping and was watching her twist and turn in her sleep. Only, whoever it was, they hadn't harmed her in any way. Instead, they had come to her, and without awakening her, soothed her soul, and forced her to feel safe in the most terrifying situation, which she seemed to experience everyday. Someone had been inside her room, Carey knew that now.

However, she wasn't afraid of him.

In fact, she wanted him to return.

She wanted to look into the beautiful eyes and feel the strong hands of the man whom had come to her as she slept and for the first time in years, made her feel safe. Her aunt and uncle were obviously upset at someone being in their home, and she knew that her overall safety was fresh in their minds. However, she didn't want whomever it was to be arrested or harmed in any way.

Carey Haas wanted to meet her guardian angel.

Then, closing her eyes, she decided to call it an early evening in search of the comforting sensation she had felt before. She prayed, and hoped that her guardian angel would return in her sleep, washing away any nightmare she knew to be lurking close by, just waiting for the right moment to enter her mind and turn her night into a living hell.

* * *

Earlier.

"Well look here son," Gabe spoke harshly to the nineteen year old in front of him. "Unless you can give me one good reason as to why you were at the Goodman home earlier today I'm going to have no choice but to place you under arrest. You see," he paused, his serious demeanor obviously controlling Billy's nerve-racked reactions. "I'm generally a very easy person to get along with. But the Goodman family, and their niece Carey Haas, are personal friends of mine and when their safety is at risk, I don't play around. So tell me son, why were you there?"

"I wasn't!" Billy continued to lie, adamantly denying any connection to the Sheriff's accusations. Billy could feel himself falling into the hands of the man in front of him, and knew that sooner or later he was going to make a mistake. But what was he supposed to do? Tell the man everything he had recently been put through?

No.

Then, he would be sent away to some mental institution and people would start thinking that he was as crazy as Curtis Rains himself. Billy refused to let that happen. He hadn't done anything wrong. He had done nothing but go to Carey Haas, not to harm her in anyway, but to perhaps help her, and perhaps better understand just what was going on inside his obviously twisted brain.

"All right then," Sheriff Burnham continued as he began to make his way towards the younger suspect in front of him. "Perhaps down at the station house you'll better be able to answer my questions. You should've just cooperated with me boy. It would have saved you a heap of trouble."

"All right, all right," Billy pleaded backing away from the officer, almost refusing to let himself be taken into custody. "I admit it. I was there. But I wasn't doing anything wrong. Carey needs my help. Curtis Rains is still-" he found himself scrambling for words, not once taking the time to breathe appropriately between sentences and everything streamed out in a confusing jargon which was almost impossible to understand.

"Son," Gabe interrupted, as he finally was able to make the teenager in front of him confess to his wrongdoing. The very mention of the name Curtis Rains was enough to force the Sheriff to reach for his handcuffs. "I think you better come with me."

"No!" Billy shouted, once again backing away from the authority figure in front of him. "I'm sorry, but I can't go with you. Carey needs me and I am not going to let her down."

Not knowing exactly what it was that made him do it, Billy Saxton suddenly found himself turning away from the Sheriff and running with all his might towards the ocean behind his beloved home. He heard the officer shouting at him to stop and even felt the barrel of the revolver pointed directly at him, it's sights nestled on his back. But he couldn't stop.

For some unknown reason, Billy Saxton found himself running from the law.

"I need backup!" Sheriff Gabriel Burnham yelled into his radio. "Suspect is fleeing on foot. I want a dozen units after this asshole," Then, pausing momentarily, he didn't allow the dispatch to reply before continuing. "Now damn it. Get some people over here now."

* * *

The creature laughed his evil laugh as nightfall fell on everything around him, swallowing everything into darkness. It was almost time to release his powers to their fullest extent. It wouldn't be long until he revealed himself to his victims as their final breath became expelled from their lifeless bodies.

He had already momentarily interrupted Jamie Walker's magical relationship with Travis McKinley.

He had already lit a flame inside Jack Reynolds's head, just waiting for the right moment to make the small fire turn into a massive, uncontrollable blaze that would change his beloved family life forever.

And although nothing drastic had happened thus far, he knew that he was never too far from Carey Haas's mind. And with her being his most valued, and prized possession, he would wait until the last minute before coming for her.

Her death, would have to be special.

Chapter 16

    Billy Saxton blindly tumbled his way along the beach, running as fast as his legs would carry him. Sunlight had long since fallen, fading into night, and save for the partial moon looming overhead, there wasn't a substantial source of light. Billy found himself squinting into the night, desperately trying not to lose his balance and descend to the sandy terrain below. He didn't want to allow the police officials anytime to catch up with him. He was well aware that right now, every second counted.
    For a split second, Billy found himself growing weaker and weaker, his stomach began heaving gusts of air that his body simply couldn't produce anymore, and he knew that he wouldn't be able to stay on his feet much longer. Then, as he closed his eyes briefly to wipe the stinging sweat away from them, he took one final deep breath as he continued to try and beat the pounding, unrelenting Florida humidity, when his feet stumbled across a sand dune and he lost control. Caught completely off guard, Billy extended his arms in front of him to break his fall, and suddenly found himself laying head first in the soft sand found everywhere along the beach. Spitting the minor particles out of his mouth, he heard the sirens in the distance. As he climbed back to his feet and was about to continue running wildly into the night, away from the Sheriff and his team of deputies, he paused once more, wasting valuable seconds, and looked behind him.
    Billy saw the beams from the dozen or so flashlights everywhere in the distance. Quickly, they were gaining on him and he knew that they wouldn't stop until they had found him. As intelligent as he was,

Tinman

Billy knew that running only made him look 100% guilty. He couldn't allow himself to be arrested. He could do more good on the outside, rather than being locked up like some caged animal, and if anything would ever happen to Carey while he was incarcerated, he just wouldn't ever be able to forgive himself.

Needless to say, Billy Saxton had no choice but to continue running.

Unfortunately, as he tried to pick up the pace once more, and continue impetuously along the ocean shore, he realized that he wasn't going to get too far. At the rate he was traveling, the deputies behind him would catch up with him in no time. He had to find cover. Soon, he knew patrol cars would be covering the area around every corner. He had to find somewhere safe, a place where he could rest, catch his breath, and allow himself the time to think rationally about what his next move should be. Billy knew that he couldn't go home, as cops would undoubtedly be swarming the place. Forcing his brain to work instantaneously, only one other place came to mind.

The Anne home.

Billy didn't know why he thought going there was the right thing to do. But for some reason, he felt that Elizabeth would take him in and hide him from the authorities. He trusted her, and felt that she would be the only person right now that may understand what he was going through, what he was trying to do, and why he was running from the law. He only prayed that the deputies weren't waiting for him there.

Then, turning around, he realized that he had long since passed the Anne home along the beach and if he tried to backtrack, he would undoubtedly run right into the welcoming arms of the deputies as they briskly surveyed every inch of the beach their piercing flashlights allowed them to see as they combed the area. "Think damn it," Billy ordered himself as the sound of sirens and the deputy's voices lingering in the distance began to close in. Closing his eyes, Billy brushed everything aside, cleared his head, and listened for an answer to come to him. Surprisingly enough, the answer came as he blocked everything out of his mind and listened to nothing else but the crashing of the waves. Facing the ocean, Billy knew what he had to do. He had to swim far enough out into the ocean where the men hunting him wouldn't be able see him, and then swim back to the Anne home. It was truly his only option.

Finally, deciding that he had wasted enough time, he forced another rush of adrenaline into his body, and hurled himself into the encompassing waves. With the help of the blackened night, Billy knew that he could swim right past the deputies without fear of being seen.

Soon, he knew that he would be in front of the Anne home. Billy only hoped that his instincts about Elizabeth wouldn't betray him. He knew his buddy Blaze was left behind in absolute bewilderment.

* * *

Elizabeth Anne found herself climbing out of bed, leaving her husband sleeping peacefully next to her, as she heard the taunting sound of the police sirens echoing throughout her neighborhood. The red and blue flashing lights came flooding into her bedroom numerous amounts of times, yet her husband slept soundly. Feeling a bit intrigued and curious as to what all the commotion could be about, she left her bedroom, checked on her two sleeping children, and then went to the nearest window. She saw patrol cars passing by her home, their spotlights swinging rapidly from side to side as they searched the area around them. Elizabeth could tell that they were after somebody.

Feeling a bit afraid, she stepped away from the window and made her way to the back deck. Checking the sliding glass door, she made sure that it was securely locked, and was about to turn away and return to the safety of her husband's arms, when something from outside caught her eye. Hesitantly, Elizabeth opened the door and stepped outside on the patio. Looking into the night, she could see at least a dozen deputies with their flashlights making their way along the beach. The whole scenario reminded her of the dreadful and unforgettable events ten years ago when the manhunt for Curtis Rains had taken place.

Then, as soon as the thought of the Tinman entered her mind, she couldn't help but to turn right and face the old Haas home, now purchased and in the hands of the Saxton's. Completely baffled, Elizabeth squinted her eyes and immediately recognized her new

Tinman

friend, Debra, standing on the back porch surrounded by police authorities. One, being Sheriff Burnham, whom she had recognized immediately. "Oh Jesus," she whispered allowed, but to herself as she tried to make sense of what her eyes were seeing. Then, as she watched in awe, she continued to try and make sense of the situation, when something caught her attention. It was the sound of a sternly voice, almost as if whoever it was, was in some kind of hurry. The voice itself caught her off guard, and clutching her chest, she found her hands trembling profusely, realizing that she was not only in a state of shock, but in an undeniable state of fear as well.

"Excuse me mam," the voice called out to her from the ground below the patio from which she stood. "Could you come down here for a minute? I'd like to ask you a few questions."

Taking a deep breath, Elizabeth realized it was a Sheriff's deputy. "Certainly," she replied clearing her throat, then proceeded to make her way down the seemingly short staircase, only to soon find herself facing the young deputy, baring nothing but her nightgown, which barely covered her cleavage. "What can I do for you officer?" she asked with courtesy.

'Have you seen a young adult white male come through here this evening? His name is Billy Saxton and he lives right down the beach from you. Perhaps you know him?" the deputy immediately questioned, not wasting anytime, and jumping right into it.

"Yes," Elizabeth answered truthfully. "I know Billy. Has he done something wrong?"

"Mam, I really can't comment on that right now," the deputy refused to answer her question. "But please mam, have you seen him?"

"No-No I haven't," Elizabeth continued to answer honestly. "I've only been on the porch a few seconds. Your sirens woke me up and I just wanted to see what was going on."

"Well if I were you, I'd go back inside with your family. It could be dangerous out here," the deputy continued, although not fully briefed on the situation. "But if he tries to contact you or if you do see him, call the Sheriff's department immediately. All right mam?" Then, only after Elizabeth nodded her head in agreement did the deputy turn to leave. "Sorry to disturb you mam. Have a good evening."

"You too," she called out and watched as within seconds, the deputy vanished into the night. Turning, she was about to head back up the stairs and into her home, when another voice captured her attention. It was coming from the carport, underneath her home, which stood on stilts. Only, it sounded more muffled, and she instantly knew that it was not another deputy trying to get her attention. "Who's there?" she ordered loudly, clutching the railing of the stairs, totally prepared to flee back inside.

"It's me," she heard the voice whisper. "It's Billy."

"Billy!" Elizabeth exclaimed, releasing the last of the fear from inside and hurriedly walked into the carport. Searching for any signs of Billy, she saw nothing. "Where are you? You can come out, I'm the only one here."

Then, she watched in amazement as Billy crawled out from underneath her Explorer and climbed to his feet. His clothes were soaking wet, and the look in his eyes told her that he was terrified, lost, and had absolutely no idea what to do. "I'm sorry for coming here Mrs. Anne. But I really have nowhere else to go. Please," he pleaded for her to assist him. "I need your help."

"My God Billy," Elizabeth continued placing a concerned hand on his shoulder. "What has happened to you? What have you done?"

"Nothing," Billy tried to get through to the woman in front of him. "They want to arrest me, but I can't let them. Carey needs my help."

"What do you mean Carey needs you?" Elizabeth asked confusingly.

"I promise I'll explain everything to you later," Billy rushed, knowing that it wasn't safe for him outside. "I need for you to hide me Elizabeth. I promise I won't stay any longer than I have to. I just need a place to rest, and get some dry clothes while I think of something to do."

"Billy. Do you realize what you're asking me to do? If I take you in and hide you from the law I could get in trouble myself. You're asking me to jeopardize my family Billy. I don't kn-"

"Please," Billy cut her off. "I wouldn't have come here if there was somewhere else to go," he admitted foolishly. "And I know what I'm asking you to do. But I need your help Elizabeth. You're the only one that can help me. If I get arrested, Carey Haas's life could be in danger. Please. It'll only be for tonight."

For some reason, Elizabeth felt obligated to help him. Especially since it seemed to concern the safety of Carey Haas. And although she couldn't make any sense of what Billy was telling her, she believed his words to be sincere, and she trusted him. "All right," Elizabeth spoke up after a moment's silence. "But only for tonight. Now come inside and take those clothes off. I'll see if I can find something old of Murray's that may fit you," she continued speaking of her husband. "And you can sleep in the spare bedroom. But Billy, if they come to my door and ask if you're here, I don't know if I can lie to them."

"I understand," Billy agreed as they reached the sliding glass door and stepped inside Elizabeth's home. Then, before she could lead him into the bathroom, Billy grabbed her shoulder and spun Elizabeth around, forcing her to look into his eyes. "Thank you Elizabeth. Seriously, thank you. You won't regret this."

"I hope so," Elizabeth whispered with a smile as she turned around and disappeared into her bedroom to scrounge up some dry clothes for her secret, yet trustworthy guest. She knew that she was going to have to tell her husband about the decision that she had made to take Billy Saxton in. She only hoped that Murray would approve of her judgment. Sometimes, he just didn't have the same heart and compassion that she had grown to enjoy.

* * *

Meanwhile, back in Starke, Florida.

"Did you tuck Sarah in?" Gloria asked the manly figure of her husband as Jack came floundering into their bedroom, his head hung low, purposely not allowing himself to look into his wife's eyes. It was obvious that something was on his mind, and as stubborn as he was, Gloria knew that it was going to be a tough task to try and pry whatever it was out into the open. "What's wrong honey?" she asked gently, forgetting about the question concerning their daughter as he joined her on the bed, and nestled himself under the covers.

"Nothing," Jack answered quickly, yet his tone filled with a coldness that Gloria herself hadn't heard in a long time. "And yes, I did tuck our daughter in. She told me to tell you goodnight and that she loves you."

"Never mind Sarah right now," Gloria blurted out harshly, matching the smart and angry tone her husband had shot at her for absolutely no reason at all. "And don't you even think about lying to me either Jack. I know you all too well, and you can't honestly lie there and tell me that nothing is wrong. It's written all over your face. So," she paused once again allowing her husband the time to answer her previous question. Jack's ignorance, however, continued to shine, and the tension between the two of them grew stronger as each second passed. Frustrated, Gloria decided to continue. "What in the hell is going on Jack? Just a couple of hours ago, we were making love on this bed, and then ever since you went out to that shed and came back inside you haven't said one word to me. You haven't even acknowledged my presence for crying out loud and I haven't the slightest clue why? Did I do something to upset you? If so, I'd sure like to know what it was because I can't remember doing anything that could have possibly provoked you into acting the way you are now. Please," she paused once again, looking straight into her husband's eyes. "What's bothering you Jack? What is it?"

"It's nothing damn it!" Jack retorted cacophonously. "Please Gloria. Can we just drop this whole thing? I'm really tired, and I have to go back to work early tomorrow morning at the damn prison. Can we please just call it a night and get some sleep? I just don't want to get into it with you right now."

"Well excuse me," Gloria replied, completely stunned at her husband's revolting words. "Ya know what," she continued sitting up in the bed and looking down at Jack in front of her. "I don't care if you're tired. Enlighten me will you because I'm not tired, and there's obviously something on your egotistical mind. You see, we're supposed to be married here, and whenever one of us is feeling troubled, we're supposed to open up and tell each other just what it is that's bothering us. If something is bothering you, it's bothering me, and I have a right to know what it is."

"Stop it!" Jack ordered, not realizing his tone had just resembled the one he used in ordering the inmates around inside the prison walls. Then, seeing his wife's mouth drop in disgust and her eyes grow with an unspeakable anger, she turned her head away from the man she loved and began to sob silently. Realizing it was too late for reconciliation, and seeing that there was absolutely no way to recall

Tinman

his hateful words, Jack too, turned his back on his wife and the two of them simply laid there in silence.

Feeling completely unwanted, and alienated from the warmth her husband's arms usually brought to her at night when the two of them retreated to bed, Gloria reached over to the night stand, switched off the light and buried her head in the pillows. There was a good foot between the two of them, and she couldn't help but think about rolling over and apologizing to her husband. She hated it when they found it necessary to get into an argument. Usually, however, it wouldn't take long for one of them to apologize to the other and everything returned to normal.

Tonight, however, Gloria Reynolds didn't see that happening.

She had done nothing wrong. Jack should be the one to apologize to her, and she wasn't going to budge. As the seconds, then minutes slowly drifted by, however, she knew that the stiff figure lying next to her wasn't going to apologize. Closing her eyes, Gloria silently let one final tear leave her eye sockets, praying that when she awoke, she would find herself engulfed in the passionate arms of her husband. Calming her nerves, Gloria began forcing herself to fall asleep. Tonight, however, she could already tell, was going to be a restless one.

Jack, on the other hand, lay silently with his back to his grieving wife, his brain swirling rapidly, forcing him to think about the impossible. Was it really possible for Gloria to be having an affair? The whole image of his wife baring her nude body to someone else sent a rage flying throughout his body, and his temper flared out of control. Griping the bed sheets tightly, Jack struggled momentarily with his emotions as he tried to control the agonizing rage that seemed to be taking control of his every thought.

He had never felt the anger his body now endured, and he could sense that it wasn't going to go away. It was going to continue to eat away inside his body, until there would be nothing left of him, except for some psychotic maniac looming for destruction of the man his wife had been seeing behind his back.

No. She wasn't having an affair. It couldn't be true. It just couldn't, he tried to force himself to believe.

However, as he closed his eyes to fall into the hellish sleep he knew to be waiting, the voice he had heard out in the shed once again returned, accusing his wife of being unfaithful and convincing Jack that she needed to be punished.

"She's a whore Jack," Jack recalled hearing against his will. The five letter word, however, seemed to be the only one that stuck out in his mind, and he played it over and over again until he found himself on the verge of loosing control.

"Whore! Whore! Whore! Whore!"

"No!" Jack screamed aloud as he climbed out of the bed and rushed out the bedroom, slamming the door behind him, and leaving his confused wife all alone. Gloria wanted to get up and run after him, only to discard that idea as soon at it entered her mind. For some reason or another, she felt that Jack needed to be alone.

Gloria heard the backdoor slam shut as Jack obviously walked outside, and for some reason, she felt her heartbeat quicken up a bit. She was afraid, she couldn't deny that. But what was she afraid of?

Was she afraid for her husband?

Or was she afraid of her husband?

She didn't know, but as the silence began to close in and as she relived the conversation the two of them had just shared minutes ago, Gloria could easily sense that something wasn't right. For the first time, in a long time, she felt all alone and felt as though she was loosing touch with the man she had vowed to devote her life to. "It was only a fight," she told herself. "Just a little argument."

Gloria knew, however, that it had been much more than that.

She could only wait and see how things were going to be in the morning, and although she tried to force promising thoughts inside her head, she could sense an underlying danger inside her soul, almost as if she no longer knew who her husband was, or if she even trusted him. Within seconds, Jack had turned into someone she didn't know, nor did she want to. Gloria had no choice but to confront her fears, and conceded that she was truly afraid.

Displaying her own ignorance, however, she refused to run away.

* * *

The next day.

As the bright sunlight began to pour into the unfamiliar room, Billy Saxton found himself laying wide awake, his eyes long since adjusted to the bright light that entered the room freely as no drapes or blinds were hung that could have blocked the annoying rays. Taking in a deep breath, he recalled everything that had happened the day before, and how the day had unfortunately come to the tragic end where he found himself running from the law. Smiling, and feeling well rested, he knew he had the strength to fight another day. He had made it through the night, he hadn't been captured by the authorities, thanks to Elizabeth Anne, and now he knew he had to live out the promise he had made to her as she welcomed him into her home last night. He had promised that it would only be for one night. Billy had caused enough trouble for himself, and the last thing he wanted to do was bring any harm to the Anne family, whom had absolutely nothing to do with anything that was going on.

Finally, stretching, he climbed out of bed, feeling an unusual burst of energy that he simply was not accustomed to in the early morning hours. That's when it hit him. Last night, he had actually been able to sleep without experiencing any nightmares of the past. He saw no blood, heard no screams from the Haas family, but slept peacefully in the welcoming darkness of the night. Was it possible? Was he finally beginning to understand what was going on? Did he finally know how to cope with the illusive visions that came his way, forcing him to fall into an utter state of unconsciousness, blocking his memory and forcing him to relive a past that he simply was not a part of.

Then, his thoughts were disturbed by a knock at the bedroom door. He instantly recognized the voice of Elizabeth from behind the door, and he whispered that it was all right for her to come inside. She greeted him with a warm smile, and stepped inside closing the door behind her, not allowing the alluring eyes and the intrusive ears of her two young daughters to bare witness to what was about to be said. Even though the door was only open for a split second as Elizabeth squeezed her petite body inside, Billy himself caught a small glimpse of the two youngsters as they peered their small heads around the corner of the hallway and looked at him with curiosity gushing out of their intrigued eyes. The whole scene was quite cute, yet Billy knew that he had imposed a threat to the Anne family and already knew what Elizabeth had come inside to talk to him about. She was going to ultimately ask him to leave, which he completely understood. He just needed a few moments to collect his thoughts and think of somewhere to go. Billy needed a plan.

"Did you sleep all right?" Elizabeth asked as she sat next to him on the bed and looked into his blossoming blue eyes.

"Oh yes mam," Billy answered, returning her warm smile. "And I plan to get out of your hair as soon as possible. I just need to concentrate on a few things first and try to figure out what I need to do to get myself out of this hole I fell into. I really never meant for this to happen Elizabeth. None of this was supposed to happen. Especially to me for crying out loud. I mean I wasn't even living here ten years ago, and I have absolutely no connection to the Haas family except for moving into that damn house."

"I know, I know," Elizabeth tried to comfort the obviously upset neighbor in front of her.

"Elizabeth, you have to believe me," Billy continued, not letting his hostess finish. "When I went to see Carey yesterday, I swear I had no intention on hurting her in any way. All I wanted to do was help her Elizabeth. It's like I can feel her soul inside my own and I know she is lonely, and feels lost. And she's scared Elizabeth. Carey is scared, and I know this may sound crazy, but I honestly think she has every right to be."

"What are you saying?"

"I'm saying I think Carey Haas's life may be in danger," Billy concluded. "That's the only reason I ran away from the police. Not because I'm guilty of anything. Yes, I may have been wrong for breaking into their home. But I had to see the girl I've been visualizing in my dreams. It's like I had to make sure that she was all right. The Sheriff is completely off in hunting me down like I'm some sort of deranged lunatic who was trying to harm Carey or the Goodman family. I'm trying to save her for Christ's sake." Then, looking into the woman's eyes next to him, he sensed confusion in them. "Elizabeth, I don't expect you to understand any of this. Just, well, thank you for letting me stay here last night. And I know I should be going."

"Billy," Elizabeth said bluntly, purposely capturing the teenager's attention in front of her. "I believe you. I believe that you intended no harm at the Goodman home. And I also believe that everything is going to work out. I'm just glad I could help out. And I'll try to get in touch with your mom somehow, anonymously of course, and let her know that everything is all right. She believes in you too. You know that don't you Billy?"

"Yes I do," Billy admitted, hanging his head low, feeling his pride dwindle into the depths of a black hole from which it would never be retrieved again. "But I know I've disappointed her. I just wish I could make her see the truth ya know." Then, he changed the subject quickly as an idea popped inside his head. "Say, do you mind if I use your phone real quick? I think I know a way to get out of here."

"Sure," Elizabeth agreed as she jumped off the bed and exited the room, only to return seconds later with a cordless phone.

Suddenly, Billy remembered his friend Blaze. He could only imagine what must be going through his best friend's mind as his first night in town; he had witnessed Billy running down the beach from the police. He knew he would have some explaining to do, but he also knew that Blaze would be there to help him out. Billy only hoped that Blaze hadn't left town, and that the police hadn't confiscated his pager. Quickly, he punched in his friend's pager number, waited for the voice to tell him to enter his numeric message, and then punched in Elizabeth's phone number, followed by his secret code that would allow Blaze to immediately know who was calling. Then, after hanging up, he waited patiently for the phone to ring.

Within seconds, a smile arched across Billy's face as the phone sprang to life. Without even saying hello, he answered the phone and began talking. His instincts told him that it was Blaze. "Thank God it's you man," Billy began happily.

"What in the hell is going on?" Blaze demanded seriously. "Your mom and I have been up all night worried about you man. You don't know how pissed off that Sheriff guy was when they were unable to find you. You are in serious trouble man!"

"I know, I know," Billy agreed breaking in. "And I need your help. We've always been there for one another, and in this case, I don't think I can get out of it without you. Tell me first though, are the cops still there?"

"No," Blaze answered. "They just left, and they've got the phones tapped. I'm using my truck phone to call you back."

"What about my mom?" Billy asked suddenly concerned for his mother's welfare. "How's she holding up?"

"She's a little upset. Do you want me to tell her that everything is all right?"

"No, no," Billy answered wisely. "I can't deal with that right now. I need you to come and pick me up. Don't tell anyone where you are going." Then, quickly, he explained to his friend that he was right down the road and that he would be waiting outside. "And Blaze," he called out to his friend before hanging up. "Could you bring that doll you asked me about with you? I think I might need it."

"For what?"

"I'll explain everything in detail when you get here," Billy pressed forward making him see that there was really no time to waste. "Thanks brother. I owe you one man."

"Yes you do," Blaze replied with a slight laugh. "I'll be there in three minutes."

* * *

Debra Saxton sat quietly on the sofa in the living room when Blaze returned from outside. Eyeballing him suspiciously, she watched in silence, sipping her coffee as he made his way over to the dining room table and picked up the porcelain doll her son had found in the basement. Saying nothing, she simply watched as he walked away from the kitchen table, the doll held firmly in his hands, and then disappeared back outside. Seconds later, she heard the muffling sounds of his truck as his engine sprang to life. There was no question; he was going to pick Billy up.

Debra was still magnificently confused and stunned at the events that had taken place at her home just a few short hours ago. She knew her son wasn't a bad person and would never intentionally try to hurt anyone. He simply wasn't capable of such a thing, and the way the Sheriff made him out to be some sort of career criminal only upset her even more. She had agreed to let the Sheriff come and question her son with the assurance that nothing was going to happen to him. Well, she had come through with her part of the bargain, and look what had happened? Everything had turned sour, and now the only person in her life that actually meant anything to her was running from the law.

Alone.

Tinman

She had always promised to be there for him whenever he was in need. Well, Debra was well aware that he needed her help right now. Unfortunately, there was absolutely nothing that she could do to give it to him. For the first time, it seemed as though Billy was completely on his own, and she would just have to believe in him, and trust him to work everything out before thing's got worse. In a sense, she was glad that Billy had managed to get in touch with Blaze and that he had been willing to go to his aid. She made no efforts to stand in Blaze's way when he walked out of the door, and had no intention of telling the authorities that her son had contacted his best friend. She was sure that they would find out in due time, but hoped that when they did, either this whole thing would be resolved, or Billy would be somewhere safe, and out of harm's way.

Debra really didn't even care that her son may have done something wrong. His safety was her only concern at the moment. Above all else, she just wanted him returned to her loving arms where she could look after him once again, without a scratch on his body. She vowed to never let anything like this happen again.

She also vowed, that as soon as possible, the house was going back on the market, and the two of them would be moving out.

Their lives had changed almost immediately after setting foot in the blood-lined history of the Haas home. Especially her son's. She had never experienced the pain and suffering he had been complaining of, and again, there was absolutely nothing she could do about it, or could have done about it.

Now, however, she was left with nothing but an aching heart, and a sense of feeling lost without the graceful presence of her son. If anything were to ever happen to Billy, or if he was ever taken away from her, she knew she simply wouldn't be able to bare it. She would have to surrender all her strength, dignity, and pride, shriveling up into a lifeless form until she would be buried six feet beneath the surface, and her soul brought safely to the gates of Heaven.

Without Billy, there really was no point in living.

Then, as she was about to take another sip of coffee, she felt the fatigue consuming her worried body, and knew that she needed to get some rest. Forcing herself to her feet, she was about to walk upstairs and into her bedroom, when suddenly, she froze in her tracks as she heard a knock come from the sliding glass door, which lead to the back porch of her home. Turning to face whoever was there, she managed a weak smile as she recognized the figure of Elizabeth Anne, her newfound friend, standing there with a concerned look on her face. Weakly, she walked over and pulled the door open. Stepping outside in the warmth of the Florida sun, she let the woman drape her arms around her as she tried to comfort her and ease the pain that must have been showing right through her rugged appearance.

"Debra I'm so sorry," Elizabeth sighed showing her sympathy. "I know everything. I wish there was something that I could do."

"No I wish there was something I could do," Debra interjected sadly. "I don't even know where my son is. I just wish I could have prevented all of this from happening. I feel like it's my fault."

"It's not your fault, and trust me. There was absolutely nothing that you could have done to prevent this," Elizabeth continued. Then, feeling obligated to tell the woman in front of her about how she had taken her son in last night, and knowing that it probably wasn't safe for them to talk there, she motioned for her to follow her down to the beach. "Debra," Elizabeth continued cheerfully. "Let's take a walk shall we? I think we need to have a talk."

Following right behind Elizabeth, Debra knew the conversation she was about to encounter was going to involve her son. Needless to say, she couldn't wait to hear what her friend had to say. She was all ears.

* * *

Gloria Reynolds awoke the following morning to an empty bed. The prison uniform her husband invariably hung on the outside of their bathroom door, was missing, and she could feel herself alone in the house. Jack had gotten up early, without even bothering to wake her up, and left for work. Their fight the previous night had not ended, and her husband had stormed out of the house that morning just as angry and as ill-mannered as he had been last night when he fumed out of their bedroom, slamming the door behind him, and then crashed through the backdoor and into the backyard. Although entirely against her will, Gloria had succeeded in falling asleep before he had returned to their bedroom, and slept undisturbed for the remainder of the night. In fact, she really couldn't be sure that Jack had returned to their bed at all. For all she knew, he could have slept on the couch. Or stayed outside all night.

Nevertheless, she had a job to get to, and she would be damned if she was going to let her loved one's spoiled mood ruin her day. She didn't deserve to be treated the way he purposely ripped into her emotions the previous night, treating her like some sort of wild dog, who had done something that its master didn't approve of. Well, she wouldn't stand for it. She loved her husband, naturally, but there came a time when she had to stand up for herself. Gloria refused to let herself be pushed around, even if Jack himself was trying to push them away, denying her the right to know what was going on. She wanted to help him, wanted to listen to whatever it was that was bothering him. For some reason, however, Jack wouldn't open up.

And Gloria wasn't going to wait around until he did.

She would be hurting, and worried about him of course, but she wasn't about to let it be shown any longer. When the time was right, she knew that he would come to her and let her in on what was eating away at his soul. Until that time, however, he was on his own and Gloria fully intended to go about the rest of her work day without thinking about the spat the two of them had taken part in last night.

There was one thing, however, that continued to mystify her.

It was Jack's behavior. It was something that she simply was not accustomed to. He seemed almost homicidal, and for a brief moment last night, she actually thought that he was going to physically attack her. Thankfully, he had not. But the fear that he had instilled in her was something that she had not forgotten, and was something that she knew she might never be able to shred from her memory. Within seconds, it seemed as though his mood had changed into one of violent content, almost sublimely evil, and his personality was one that she was not familiar with, nor accustomed to. Almost instantly, Jack had become someone that Gloria feared, and she had never been afraid of him in all their years of marriage. His sudden temper change was ostensibly psychotic and appeared to have come from some dark secretive place deep inside Jack's soul. What had brought the sudden crazed outburst on, however, remained a mystery.

And something told her that it was going to stay that way.

However, maybe after a day back at work, Jack would return home and be the same person that she had long since grown to love, and return with an attitude she had come to expect. She wouldn't know that, unfortunately, until her workday was done. Finally, climbing out of bed, Gloria Reynolds went into the bathroom and turned on the shower

* * *

Jack Reynolds' pace was slow as he walked down the corridor of the prison, his position still pinpointed him along the depths of death row, circling the scum of the entire state of Florida, as some of them patiently awaited their execution, and other's cried out, preaching for their innocence, and obviously afraid of death. He truly pitied their diverse, intelligent souls, and some of them, if it hadn't been for the brutal attacks and homicides they had allegedly cast on society, he might have actually felt sorry for them. Over his years of service at the prison, however, his compassion for the troubled inmates had slowly but surely diminished into thin air.

It wasn't until he had come into contact with the now deceased inmate, Curtis Rains, that his views began to change. Yes, the man known as the Tinman was probably the most highly profiled serial killer the walls of the Florida State Penitentiary ever had locked down behind caged doors, but he also was by far the most talented, and intelligent. He had the ability to get inside your head just by looking into your eyes, and you could actually feel the evil boiling inside his bloodstream. There were never any signs of remorse for his victims. Just a wicked smile, that made you want to lash out at him and strangle him until his last breathe exploded from his mouth, and his eyes jarred loose and popped wildly out of their sockets. To Jack, it had been a great honor to be the one to see Curtis to his final minutes. He had not only been able to help in the strapping process of the electric chair, but he had been the chosen one to pull the final lever down, which ultimately ended the Tinman's reign of terror on society. Finally, all of his victims and their families could live in peace in knowing that the man who had taken away their loved ones was dead.

Dead, and never coming back.

Tinman

Even now, as he once again passed by the cell, which once consumed the humbling figure of Curtis Rains, he wasn't surprised to see another piece of filthy trash lying on the bed. The whole block known as "death row," never changed. Once someone was put to death, the very next day, another convicted criminal was put in his place. Shaking his head, and clutching his nightstick tightly, he stopped in front of the cell, and tapped gently on the bars. Looking up from his bed, the muscular white inmate wearily climbed to his feet and faced him. "Sir?" the inmate asked almost mockingly.

"What's your name inmate?" Jack asked calmly, forcing his eyes to barrel inside the taller figure in front of him. "Name inmate!" Jack repeated harshly, feeling that it was taking him too long to answer.

"Jones sir," the convict answered, tilting his head upwards. "Jacob Jones."

"Why are you here?" Jack continued to pound away the questions. "No," he cut in once more, not allowing the prisoner time to answer. "Let me guess. Mass murderer, right?"

Before a verbal response, Jacob Jones simply nodded. "Killed fourteen people. All of them under the age of 18, and all of them beautiful young women. It's funny though. I can still taste their soft, fragile skin in my mouth, and can still smell their hair, and elegant perfume. They were so sweet, all of them."

"Enough!" Jack ordered backing away from the cell, feeling an unorthodox headache coming on. "Trust me pal, you don't want to get on my bad side. I can make your stay here a living hell from which you will not be able to escape. Or, I can make your short stay here as comfortable as possible. It's your choice Jones. Let's just hope you don't make the same choice the inmate that was in here before you did. Matter of fact, do you know who was in that cell before you?" Again, Jack didn't let the jailbird speak. "Well I'll tell you who it was. It was Curtis Rains, I'm sure you've heard of him. But the point is, I took very careful measures and great pride in breaking his jaw every so often, and sometimes his ribs. His blood spilled on the very floor you're now standing on numerous amounts of times, and I won't hesitate to treat you the same way if I have to. Do I make myself clear convict?"

"Yes sir."

"Good." Then, turning to walk away, Jack didn't even realize how fast his temper had flared. The only thing he could think of was how nice it would feel to crack the inmate's skull. Walking away, however, he could have sworn he heard inmate Jones muster something under his breath. Turning around, his rage had gone out of control, and his eyes held an anger that Jack himself had never felt before. "What did you say to me you son of a bitch?" Jack demanded.

"I didn't say anything."

"The hell you didn't," Jack continued, fumbling around with the keys in his hand until he found the one that would open the cell. "Did you say something about my wife you son of a bitch? Did you call her a whore?" The inmate continued to plead his innocence, and in reality he truly did not utter a word, but Jack, not realizing that his mind was playing a trick on him, continued to search for the right key. Finally, he found it, and within seconds, was inside the cell. Before the convict even had time to defend himself, Jack raised the nightstick and lashed out at his head. Blood immediately splattered around the room from the first blow, and the convict's knees buckled under him. Helplessly, there was no escaping the massive, destructive blows Jack Reynolds laid upon him, relieving himself from the rage trapped inside his body.

Guards piled into the room, and pulled Jack off of the severely injured inmate, some of them almost loosing their balance as their boots slipped on the large amounts of blood found covering the cell floor. Some felt ill as they realized pieces of skin were missing from the man's head. They couldn't see the white of his eyes, or even the white of his skin as the gruesome scene unfolded before their very eyes.

"Jack, Jack," one of the guards protested as they dragged him out and called for a medic to enter the cell. "What in the hell is going on? What happened? You know we're going to have to tell the sergeant about this."

"He-he," Jack paused searching for an answer, his head still not clear, almost as if he had not realized what he had done. "He went for my baton," Jack replied. "It was self defense." Then, leading Jack down the hall, the other guard eyed him with skepticism outlining his eyes. For some reason, he didn't believe Jack's answer, and he felt that he had intentionally tried to hurt, or even kill the inmate. Unfortunately, as soon as it went before the sergeant, it would be out of his hands, and the inmate would continue to try and survive the powerful blows exhumed on his head.

From the significance of the wounds, the prison guard doubted that Jacob Jones was going to make it. Chances of him pulling through were slim, especially considering his brain could have slid out of the gaping hole that had formed on his head.

Apparently, Jacob Jones's execution had come early.

* * *

Carey Haas sat wide-awake on her bed in the early morning hours, and allowed the sun to come flooding into her bedroom, seeming to cleanse and warm her hungry body. She could smell the aroma of sizzling bacon as it escalated its way up the stairs from the kitchen and into her room in an attempt to lure her to the seducing fattening food. Climbing out of bed, she decided to join her relatives in a pleasant breakfast, where afterwards, she could go outside and swing on the back porch.

Then, something came to her like a bolt of lightning streaking through a troubled sky.

She could sense something.

She could feel it tingling inside her bones, and in the constant drumming of her innocently beating heart.

Someone was near, and coming for her.

But who?

In time, she knew the answer would come.

Pushing the thought aside for the moment, Carey gained control, stepped outside into the hallway, and prepared to greet her aunt and uncle warmly as she welcomed the luscious breakfast she was sure they had prepared entirely for her enjoyment. As soon as she sat at the table, however, the phone rang. Her uncle Rick ran eagerly to the phone and immediately began speaking into the receiver. Watching him like a hawk, she was able to apprehend the slight arch in his eyebrows, and she could clearly see that something was bothering him, although he tried his best to hide it.

Then, after muffling a few sounds, words that Carey herself had trouble hearing, she watched as Rick stepped into the living room, obviously to talk in private. What could possibly be going on that Rick didn't want her to know about, Carey wondered? Whatever it was, she was quite sure that she was the topic of conversation.

If that was the case, then she certainly had a right to know.

And she was going to find out just what was going on once and for all.

Chapter 17

It was truly amazing.
The creature was vigilantly stunned at how easy it was to determine Jacob Jones's fate through the hands of Jack Reynolds. His master plan was working beautifully, and everything appeared to be falling into place. The sequence of events that had been taking place was finally coming together and soon they would ultimately reach its climax and turn the course of his victim's lives around.

The creature had the haunting capability to bring out an evil potential in anyone he dared to see act in an eerie violent rage. Everyone had the ability to take another person's life. Everyone had the potential to reach inside someone's soul, tear down the barriers contained in the ego, and enjoy the pleasure everyone's id longs for.

The pleasure of the kill.

The thrill of listening to someone scream, begging for their life, and then embedding their soul in one's own.

The electrifying sight of blood gushing freely from an open wound.

The tingling sensation of numbness as you fight off their valorous, and courageous efforts to survive.

And finally, the enrapture of knowing that you could produce death.

To the creature, death was beautiful. Doom, demise, all of it, was art and should be looked upon with only the keenest of eyes, and approached aggressively without upholding any forms of internal fear.

Jason Glover

Everyone had the latent talent to kill. Only the strong, however, could actually act on their feelings and willingly take the life of another. And only the strong, could achieve the greatness that would remain inside them until it was time for them to pass on into the gaping pits of hell for all eternity. Fear of the devil, however, was for the weak.

The devil was the master of creating the fate of an unlucky individual. The devil had earned the right to be respected, and feared. All the while, however, he could be found hovering over your shoulder, his presence unknown, but his very existence felt in every bone in the body. The creature, self-proclaiming, considered himself to be the very archfiend everyone feared. Forgetting Lucifer, forgetting the term "Satan," as he considered these to be terms without enough omnipotence, hegemony, or browbeating intimidation to describe his own hate towards society.

The creature was more powerful than could ever be imagined, and could bring terror to anyone, at any given moment.

Right now, however, he was concentrating on a select few.

A few that would soon enough meet their own destiny, and taste the fear that he would produce as blood leaked from their mouths.

Undoubtedly, the creature's climax was on its way.

And the terrorizing destruction of life loomed in the darkness, just waiting for exposure.

* * *

Birmingham, Alabama.

Jamie Walker laid fully awake in her bed, listening to the joyful chirping of the birds that winged their way gracefully outside her bedroom window from one tree to another, obviously enjoying the care free lifestyle they had been born into. The ceiling fan above her twirled a cooling, comfortable jet stream of air down below as she heaved the covers aside, welcoming the frosty zephyr. The uncountable prescriptions of painkillers were definitely playing a role inside her head, as no form of pain could be felt anywhere on her body. Jamie knew that every bone in her body would be aching by now if she had forgotten to take her medication, so she kept them close to her bed, and set the alarm for every hour it was time to repeat the cycle of dosing up. Her brain was light, her whole body tingled with a numbness that made her feel as free as the birds soaring outside her window, and everything around her looked so rhapsodic. Completely overcome with a cavorting, felicitous feeling of intoxication, she closed her eyes and laughed heavily for virtually no reason at all, except that she knew that she was auspiciously fortuitous to be alive.

She opened up a book that lay next to her on the bed and quickly began thumbing through the thin pages. Only it wasn't until after she finished an entire chapter did she realize that not only did she not understand what she had just finished reading, but she didn't remember anything that had happened. Laughing at her impaired brain, she threw the book aside and just stared at the ceiling fan twirling swiftly above her head. It appeared to be impossible to concentrate on anything mind-worthy, or that required any intelligence on her part. She would have to wait a couple of hours until the drugs wore off a little bit and her body got used to the high they brought on.

One by one, she watched the blades of the fan twirl by, sometimes trying to focus only on one. She realized that this was just another alarming task her brain was unable to complete. It only intensified her already inebriated mentality. Feeling overwhelmed by a sudden attack of dizziness, she closed her eyes and clutched her stomach tightly, ephemerally fighting the urge to lean over the side of the bed and vomit. The thought of the sticky liquid streaming from her mouth only made the butterflies in her stomach continue to churn. The odor she was well aware it would produce seemed to twist tightly away at her intestines until the feeling was almost unbearable, and non-escapable.

Sweat began to form along her forehead and the more she wiped it away, the more rapidly it would return. The bedroom, which had been so cool and comfortable from the ceiling fan just seconds ago, now seemed to be a boiling room of sorts. She felt as though she were standing in the middle of a dessert, her wholesome body basking in the sizzling sun. Jamie tried to push the covers off her. However, as she extended her hands, she realized that the covers weren't on her body. As the heat seemed to deepen inside the bedroom and her body with an unimaginable extremity, and her helpless nausea augmented to its fullest extent, she knew that the excessive sickness her body was in a frenzy over could no longer be kept at ease.

Clutching the sides of the bed, Jamie leaned over, and opened her mouth, allowing the garbage a clear path to the bedroom floor below. Gagging, she found her vigilant efforts to regurgitate unsuccessful and found her throat growing meagerly dry. For some reason, nothing would come out. However, whatever was wrong with her did not go away. In fact, the sickness only seemed to continue to magnify inside her body, enhancing its power over her own willpower.

She couldn't stand it any longer.

Jamie felt as though she had to heave out whatever it was inside her stomach that was bringing on so much pain. She wasn't going to give up until she had accomplished just that. With her eyes becoming watery, and her vision blurred, she continued to gag herself time and time again. Each time she failed to produce anything to exit from her mouth. Sobbing, she tried to fight off the weakness and fatigue her body had so suddenly gained, and found herself cramming her index finger down her throat, slamming it repeatedly into her tonsils. The gagging continued, yet the excrement continued to yield, unwilling to exit her tormented body. She was finding it increasingly more difficult to breathe.

Then, closing her eyes, she foolishly let go of the bed with her only other balancing hand, and with the other hand crammed down her aggravated throat, she had no other means to hold herself up. Harshly, she fell off the bed and slammed into the hardwood floor below. The pain worsened and Jamie simply closed her eyes and prayed to God to help her through whatever it was she was experiencing.

Weakly, she tried to subdue her sickness, and for some reason, she felt that whatever it was, Curtis Rains had been involved. He was coming for her again, and she was certain that he wasn't going to stop until he got his wish.

Unfortunately, she knew that was her death.

"Help me," she uttered although knowing that no one was there to hear her whimpering words. "Someone please help!" she repeated, almost screaming this time as she felt darkness closing in around her. Then, from somewhere hidden in the darkness she could hear laughter of some kind. Only, it wasn't a friendly tone. It was one of evil statue, and the only person that could actually enjoy doing this to her was none other than Curtis Rains. He was there, and he was enjoying every ounce of suffering he was putting her through.

Undoubtedly, there was no escape from the Tinman.

Unwillingly, Jamie Walker fell unconscious as the pain became too great for her stamina to overcome. Once again, she fell into a darkened world, and right into the hands of Curtis Rains.

* * *

In Starke, Florida.

"What in hell were you thinking?" Sergeant Ray Shriver hollered into the face of Jack Reynolds, demanding an answer. "You almost killed that inmate, and the doctors say he still may not make it. You fractured his skull, almost busted right through his damn bone. That's not what you were trained to do and I have never seen anyone act so unprofessional in my life. So," the towering Sergeant of the prison guards demanded. "What in the hell happened?" Ray was a stocky black man, standing over six feet in height, had a bald head, dark brown eyes, and a no nonsense mentality and policy. Everyone in the prison was silent as he passed them, afraid of the harm his muscles and mean nature might evoke upon them. He simply was not a man to toy with, and should be taken seriously at all times. "I'm waiting for an explanation Jack."

"I already told you," Jack shot back, anger still found in his voice, but no sign of remorse from his actions found anywhere. "He grabbed for my club sir. I wasn't doing anything but trying to defend myself. I did nothing wrong."

"What!" his supervisor shot back. "You did nothing wrong? You may have killed a man mister, and all you can tell me is that he went for your damn nightstick."

"I went inside his cell to check something out," Jack continued fibbing purposely and cutting Ray off. "And when I did he caught me by surprise. I didn't see any other choice but to use force on him sir," he added, speaking of the inmate, Jacob Jones, he may, or may not have killed.

"Why couldn't you just hit him once?"

There was no answer.

Jason Glover

"It's too bad he can't give his side of the story," Ray continued harshly. "But if he survives this, you can be damn sure I'm going to get to the bottom of this once and for all. And until I do," he added looming over Jack. "You're on suspension until such time a hearing date can be issued. You may have crossed the line here Jack. And if you did, I'm going to take you down, doing everything I can to put you inside that very same cell so you can think about what you did. Now get your ass out of here. I don't want to see you on these premises again until this matter is resolved. Dismissed." Saying nothing, Jack Reynolds prepared to exit Ray's office, when he was sharply summoned to turn around, disgust still hovering in his boss's tone. "And Jack, one other thing," Ray added curtly. "You may want to hire yourself a good lawyer. I think your going to need one."

Slamming Sergeant Shriver's office door, Jack Reynolds stormed down the hallway, only to exit the prison a few seconds later, not saying a word to anyone who stood in his path, not even acknowledging their presence. Rumors of what had happened along the iron clad walls of death row had raced throughout the prison at what appeared to have been the speed of light, and he could feel everyone's eyes hovering over him, eyeing him suspiciously, and almost accusing him of doing something wrong. Jack felt like a prisoner in a way, and didn't relax until he found himself sitting behind the wheel of his pick-up truck. Twisting the key in the ignition, the truck sprang to life, and Jack Reynolds left the grounds of the prison without looking back.

Turning onto the highway, he picked up speed and tried to force the anger that had surged inside his body aside. However, it wouldn't budge. Ever since that night in the shed, Jack had changed. He no longer looked at life through happy, unflagging, enterprising eyes. Now, unfortunately, everything seemed different. He no longer trusted his family, and was beginning to loose faith in himself. He knew he was going downhill, but there didn't seem to be anything he could do about it.

Whatever was happening to him, he had no control over and couldn't stop it.

He appeared to be stuck in this depressing, acrimonious, enraged world where nothing appeared to be what it seemed, and everything seemed controlled by some deep dark force that only the devil himself could provoke. His body was unwillingly being swallowed up by an invisible anger that had come from somewhere Jack's imagination could not fathom.

Now, however, as he traveled along the wide-open, but inconspicuously lost highway, a smile was not spread across his ire expression, even though he was supposedly heading to the one place everyone wanted to be.

Home.

Jack Reynolds was indeed heading home. But to what? An irresponsible eleven-year-old daughter, and an unfaithful wife? There didn't appear to be anything glamorous about his family, and it was no longer a happy setting. Instead, darkness had stormed overhead, placing itself right over his home, deteriorating through the roof, and contaminating every living soul that could be found within. This home, his home, was the last place on earth Jack Reynolds wanted to be. He knew his internal rage would only grow, and he feared the possible actions and harm he could bestow on his wife and daughter.

Nevertheless, he had nowhere else to go. Nowhere else to turn.

Jack Reynolds was homeward bound, and although he didn't know it, the flame inside his blackened heart continued to burn rapidly, charring everything crisply black. And soon, everything inside his murky soul would be colored maliciously raven.

Slowing his car abruptly, Jack turned the steering wheel and drove slowly into the driveway. Pulling the keys from the ignition, he surveyed his home. Then, walking towards the front door, he was at least thankful that for the time being, he was the only one there.

That, however, was certain to change.

His daughter, Sarah, could come waltzing in at any moment, and his wife, would arrive home shortly after five in the afternoon. However, Gloria was the last person Jack felt like dealing with. Knowing her persistent nature, Jack knew there would be no way to get around it. He was going to have to face his wife sooner or later. It was only unfortunate that he knew it was going to be sooner, rather than later.

* * *

Billy Saxton, along with his companion, Blaze Brookshaw, whom had come to his rescue in picking him up unseen from the authorities at the Anne home, found themselves traveling down one of many back roads throughout the sportsman town of Destin, Florida. Billy himself sat in silence for the moment, trying to figure out just where everything had suddenly gone wrong and turned against him. Clutching the doll firmly in his hands, he thanked Blaze for remembering to bring it, and was grateful for the double limo-tinted windows, which made it virtually impossible for anyone to see inside. In any event, as Billy sat thinking of what he should do next, Blaze was the one who ultimately broke the uneasy silence that had fallen over them.

"You know we can't drive forever Billy," Blaze spoke up being a friend. "Now, I know that I don't know just exactly what is going on. But as soon as a deputy or someone passes your mother's home and sees that my truck is missing, they're going to come looking for us," he concluded wisely, already expecting to see blue and red flashing lights in the distance as he continuously checked his rearview mirror.

"I know man," Billy responded calmly, his eyes never leaving the road, and his expression showing obvious signs of deep concentration. "And I am really sorry for getting you involved in all of this. But I really didn't have any other option, and I knew that I could count on you. I just hope things don't get any worse ya know? The last thing I want is for you to get into any trouble."

"What's this all about anyway?"

Carefully, Billy began explaining to his best friend every last detail of all the events that had been happening to him since he and his mother, Debra, had moved into the lovely home along the beach. Even explaining the Haas home's history and watching as Blaze's eyebrows every so often raised in shock as he tried to explain all of the blackouts and hallucinating visions that had come to him as he slept unconsciously. Billy knew that hearing most of this was entirely too difficult for his friend to gather and take in all at once. Even Billy himself, had a hard time believing that what he was saying was possible. But it was possible, and it was happening to him whether he liked it or not. Billy didn't volunteer for this, he hadn't planned on forcing himself into Carey Haas's life. It was more like he had been chosen, and in that case, he simply couldn't turn the other cheek and walk away. It simply wasn't his nature.

Then, finally, as Billy finished, Blaze turned to face him. "So, you did break into that house then? The Goodman home?"

"Well, yeah I guess so," Billy admitted boldly. "But I wasn't trying to steal anything and I most certainly was not going to harm Carey. I just had to see her man. I know that sounds crazy. But I just had to see her, and I don't regret going there at all."

"So," Blaze continued picking up right where Billy left off. "You really think this girl's life is in danger? And you really think you can help her somehow?" Billy nodded, his serious expression easily telling Blaze that he actually believed he could. "All right then," Blaze continued. "I may not understand everything you've told me. But I believe you, and I'll be right by your side throughout the whole ride. If this girl needs you, then you should go to her, and I'll do everything I can to help you out brother."

"I know you will bro, I know," Billy added with a smile. "Never doubted that for a second."

"So, what are you going to do now?"

"I don't know," Billy admitted shrugging his shoulders. Then, eyeing Blaze's mobile phone sitting peacefully between the two of them on the seat, he immediately knew what he had to do. He had to call Carey Haas. He had to talk to her. "I'll call her," he continued picking up the phone and dialing Elizabeth Anne's home number, only to jot down the seven digits she gave him seconds later. Then, after hanging up, he turned to face his friend once again, butterflies winging their way inside his stomach as nervousness of what he was about to do began to sink in. "So, what do you think? Should I call her?"

"I guess you don't have any other choice," Blaze answered. "But what if someone other than Carey answers?"

"I'll worry about that if the need arises," Billy answered as he found the last leg of strength he had been needing, and finally punched in the seven digits to the Goodman home. Biting his upper lip, he waited patiently for someone on the other end to answer, as each ring passed, the more tempted he found himself to simply hang up and forget the whole spontaneous idea all together. Then, as he heard a voice on the other end, it was too late. Now, he had to go through with it. He stuttered at first, as the voice of a man was heard on the other end, undoubtedly that of Rick Goodman, Carey's uncle. In fact, Rick had to say "hello," a second time before Billy could even build enough courage to utter a sound.

"Yes, may I speak to Carey please," he was finally able to let slip calmly from his mouth.

"May I ask who is calling?" Rick asked suspiciously, skepticism easily found in his tone.

"An old friend from school," Billy continued trying to slip past Rick's question.

"Do you have a name friend," Rick continued harshly, demanding an answer, the protection over his niece growing even stronger.

"Yes," Billy hesitated briefly. "Adam," he spoke up quickly saying the first name that came to mind. "Adam Lourcey." Then, there was a long pause and Billy could hear Rick's breathing barreling into the phone. For a spilt second, Billy thought that he was about to get hung up on, and be left with nothing more than a dial tone. However, surprisingly enough, he smiled as Rick told him to hang on and put the phone down to go and get Carey. Almost a minute later, he heard her voice come on the other end. Just as she had looked, her voice was simply breathtaking, and without a doubt the most beautiful he had ever heard. Her voice was soft, yet joyful, and even though she only spoke one word, "hello," Billy could picture her smile, and hear her laughing as the two of them trampled off into the sunset walking hand in hand. Again, however, as Billy found himself completely nerve-racked, Carey had to speak again before he could even begin talking.

"Hello," Carey repeated confusingly, not quite sure who was on the other line. The last thing she expected was to receive a phone call, and the name Adam Lourcey was one that she certainly didn't recognize. She had never even met anyone that went by the name Adam. Yet, for some reason, when her uncle came and told her that she had a phone call and told her who it was, she put on a blank expression and went to the phone. It was as if something inside of her forced her to go and see just who was on the phone. For some reason, and one she herself did not understand, she felt that it was her *Guardian Angel*. And if his name was Adam, so be it.

Tinman

"Yes, Carey," Billy began speaking excitingly. "First of all, you don't know me and my name is not Adam. I just had to think of something really fast so you're uncle Rick would put me on the phone."

"How did you know my uncle's name then?" Carey asked completely mystified at what had just been thrown at her.

"Look," Billy continued firmly, pushing her question aside not seeing the importance of it. "My name is Billy Saxton and I just moved here from Georgia. But under no circumstance are you to tell anyone that you have spoken with me. Please, I know it's going to be hard for you to trust me. But can you promise me that? Can you promise that you won't tell anyone that we've talked?"

"I guess so," Carey answered. "What do you want with me?"

"I don't really want to go over any details with you over the phone," Billy continued. "But I have to see you Carey. I think your life may be in danger and God only knows how many other people."

"What!" Carey exclaimed, a bit of fear gleaming through the phone.

"I want to help you Carey," Billy assured her. "And no matter what you hear people saying about me. Don't believe them. I never intended on hurting you, and I could never do such a thing. All I wanted to do was see you, and talk to you."

"It was you!" Carey breathed as chills covered her body and a gleaming smile spread across her face. Now, she knew for certain that someone had been inside her home and now she knew why her uncle was keeping it a secret. "You were really here weren't you?" Then, from out of nowhere, she added. "I saw you. Or, at least, I felt your hands. You grabbed my shoulders didn't you?"

"Yeah," Billy answered in shock. "You were squirming around in your bed having a nightmare. So," he continued after a moment of silence. "Can I see you?"

"I don't know," Carey hated to admit. "I wouldn't know how to get passed my uncle. He's really protective. But I'll think of something. Let me get a number where you can be reached and I'll call you back." Billy couldn't believe at how eager and willing Carey was at meeting him. It was as if he had gained her trust without having to say anything at all. It almost seemed as though she wanted to meet him just as bad as he wanted to see her. Nevertheless, he

265

wouldn't have wanted it any other way. Finally, after giving her Blaze's mobile number, she continued. "Wait a minute. How do I know that you are the person that was here?"

"You need proof?" Billy questioned half jokingly not understanding how her mood had so suddenly changed. "Well, let's just say that I have a certain doll with me that you might remember. You hid it in your basement a long time ago in the house I now live in." Then, after giving her a few seconds to take in everything that was being said, he continued. "And you named it Kat."

"How do you know that?" Carey demanded not believing her own ears. "How did you know what I named that doll? How did you know that I hid it in the cellar?"

"I'll answer all of your questions later," Billy assured her. "Please try and hurry. I don't know how much time I have. The cops might be after me here shortly, and I don't have anywhere to go."

"I will," Carey promised. "I'll call you back in just a few minutes."

Then, before she could hang up, Billy called her back. "Carey," he began seriously. "I feel like I know you, so I'm going to be totally honest with you here. Some of the things I have to tell you will be hard for you to hear and you may not even want to listen to what I have to say. It's going to bring up memories of your past, including your parents, and I know what you've gone through. I just want you to know that I care about you and that I'm here to help you. I just want you to be prepared, and not be alarmed when I bring up what needs to be said."

After a long silence, Carey spoke. "All right," she breathed a little uneasily. "Thank you." With that, the conversation ended.

Throwing the phone back down to the seat, Billy faced his friend. "I think that went well," he spoke up. "Now all I have to do is wait for her to call me back. I can't believe this man. I simply can't believe it."

"Believe what?"

"I'm finally getting somewhere," Billy continued. "After everything I've been through as of late. I am finally getting somewhere."

* * *

Moments earlier.

Rick Goodman stood motionlessly, and silently, controlling his inevitable breathing as silent as possible, his back against the adjoining wall as he listened to his niece, Carey, carry on her telephone conversation completely unaware that he was selfishly and wrongly spying on her, listening to every word that she mustered into the phone. From the moment he picked up the phone and the guy on the other end told him that his name had been Adam, he instantly knew it to be a phony name. Nevertheless, he kept his cool, and went to get Carey. The look in her eyes told him all that he needed to know when he told her who it was on the phone, and added proof to the fact that whoever it was on the phone, certainly did not go by the name Adam Lourcey. Normally, Rick would have continued to question the person on the other line, even hanging up on whoever it was if he felt that he was being lied to. In this case, however, things were different, and he knew something that neither Carey, nor the person on the other end of the phone knew.

Sheriff Burnham had tapped their phone, and the call was being traced and recorded this very instant. Rick felt a bit of shame and regretted not letting Carey in on the secret before she actually got into a conversation. However, he was only looking after her best interests, no harm intended. Someone had broken into their home, someone they now knew to have some sort of strange connection with Carey, and who now lived in the very home she once occupied with her deceased parents. Therefore, it was no coincidence that he had broken into their home that day, and there simply had to be an ulterior motive somewhere down the line.

And with the help of the Sheriff's department, Rick was going to get to the bottom of it.

By any means necessary. Even if he had to go behind Carey's back.

After all, she would thank him in the end. He was only doing what was right. He was only looking after Carey, his loved one.

Then, as the conversation drew to a close, Rick stepped away from the wall, and escaped into the kitchen, disappearing from the hallway without a single drop of evidence that he had ever been there at all. Seconds later, Carey came walking into the kitchen and approached him just as he washed away any signs of guilt from what he had just deceitfully done. A smile was plastered exuberantly across her face, and for the first time in months, possibly even years, Carey looked securely happy. Needless to say, whoever had been on the phone had been able to brighten her spirits, and that was something Rick himself had struggled with recently.

"So," Rick began joining Carey with a smile. "Who is this Adam fellow huh? I don't remember him ever calling here before." He questioned discreetly, not giving away his objective in uncovering the truth.

"He's just an old friend from school," Carey answered purposely not telling her uncle the truth. "And he's having trouble with something. He asked if I could meet him and help him out. Do you mind if I take your car for a little while? I think I could stand for some fresh air outside of this house anyway. I would love to get out." Then, she paused looking him directly in the eye. "That is, if it's all right with you of course," she concluded firmly.

Rick couldn't believe it. After everything he had done for this child in front of him, she for some reason felt the need to lie to him. Both of them knew fully well that whoever was on the phone, was not anyone by the name Adam. Yet, he knew that this was information he mischievously stumbled upon, but he still did not understand why Carey felt the need to purposely deny him the truth. For some reason or another, however, there was something that she simply did not want him to know, and he could do nothing more than respect her wishes. He couldn't say no to her, that would only make everything even more obvious.

"All right," Rick agreed regretfully, his expression never changing. "But be careful with my ride all right sweetheart?" he added jokingly with a smile, pretending that everything was all right. "And be home no later than eight tonight all right?" Carey nodded, took the keys from her uncle, and then disappeared once again to call whoever she had been talking to.

Once again, Rick silently followed, and placed himself once again along the adjoining wall giving him access to listen to everything his niece would be saying. Then, after that, there would be only one other person to phone, and hopefully resolve this matter once and for all. As soon as Carey left the house, Rick would call Sheriff Gabriel Burnham.

If this was who he thought it was, he wasn't going to get away this time. Billy Saxton would be flushed from wherever it was he was hiding, taken into custody and escorted in handcuffs behind bars. From which, he would never be able to harm Carey, or play with her already abnormal head ever again. Rick himself didn't know why, but Billy Saxton appeared to be nothing more than bad news, and someone Carey didn't need, nor want in her life, no matter what she herself was feeling inside. And the simple fact that he had secretly broken into their home, only shot even more anger throughout Rick Goodman's worn physique.

At all costs, he was going to keep the two of them away from one another.

* * *

Back in Birmingham, Alabama.

Travis McKinley walked inside the loving home he had shared with his true love Jamie Walker for quite some time now, and instantly called out to her. Moving quickly into the kitchen, he put the few groceries he had obtained from the market away, and clutching the half dozen red roses firmly in his hand, he called out to his girlfriend one last time as he rounded the corner, walked down the hallway and prepared to enter their bedroom. He figured she wasn't answering him because she was sound asleep as her medication kicked in. Undoubtedly, however, he knew that a firm kiss on the lips and the luscious scent of six roses filling her nostrils with a wonderful aroma would do the trick in waking her up. Finally, smiling, he twisted the doorknob and entered the room.

As his eyes fell across the pale, ashen, almost lifeless body of Jamie Walker, Travis dropped the roses where he stood and ran to her aid. He couldn't believe it. This was the last thing he was expecting to see when he returned home. He had only been gone for about an hour, and now regretted ever leaving her alone in the first place. Guilt began to sink in as the realization that he should have never left her home alone trampled over his conscious and made him question just what kind of person he was.

"Jamie," he shouted picking her up and holding her in his arms. "Please sweetheart, can you hear me. Wake up Jamie. Wake up." His words seemed useless, and her body was stricken with a heat wave of some sort. She was burning up, and a massive, thick layer of sweat covered her whole body. Something definitely was not right.

But what should he do?

"Jamie!" he repeated, calling out to his loved one. Travis couldn't stand viewing her in this helpless state. Ever since the wreck, things had not been the same. No. Ever since she had left town and gone to visit Curtis Rains, things had not been the same between the two of them. Jamie appeared to be slipping away, not necessarily dying, but falling into an unknown world, where perhaps only she could understand or be apart of. Nevertheless, he was not going to give up, and was willing to do anything, and go the extra mile, if it brought them back together. He wouldn't rest until things were back to normal. Until the two of them were happy again. "Jamie can you hear me?" he continued to question, as he gently shook her body he continued to hold firmly against his chest as he fell to his knees. "Please baby, wake up."

Then, as if a prayer had been answered, Jamie's head jerked awkwardly sideways, and suddenly her eyes sprang open. She shuddered briefly, not recognizing where she was or who was holding her. Only, when she looked into Travis's eyes did she calm down. Still shaking uncontrollably however, she managed to whisper a few words. "He-he came back."

"What?" Travis asked, happy to have brought her back. "Who came back?"

"Curtis," Jamie breathed, nausea still controlling her every move. "He ca-came for me aga-" she let her words die away, not finding the strength to continue their conversation.

"That's it," Travis took command, as he climbed to his feet, still clutching her in his arms. "You have to get some help." Then, saying nothing else, he carried her out of the house, placed her in the passenger seat of his car and then went around to the driver side and placed himself behind the wheel. "It's going to be all right sweetheart," he continued as he backed out of their driveway. "We're just going back to the hospital is all. I don't know what they prescribed you, but I'll get to the bottom of this. I promise I'll take care of you."

Not even thinking about where she was being taken, Jamie couldn't even hold her head upright, and fell into another deep sleep, where darkness was the only thing that could ease her pain.

* * *

Debra Saxton sat nervously on her couch. She tried concentrating on the television in front of her, but as she flipped through the channels, she found nothing that could take her mind off her son. After speaking with Elizabeth Anne, she finally was able to place a few pieces of the puzzle together, and now better understood the entire situation. She knew from the beginning that her son couldn't harm anyone. It simply wasn't in his nature. He went to see Carey that day because he felt like she is in danger and he knows something that may help her.

Why he had run from Sheriff Burnham, however, remained a mystery?

Debra admitted that she was still left in the dark about a few things, most of which she probably could never understand. But there was one thing she was certain of, and that was that her son did not deserve to be arrested.

He was a good person, and was only trying to help Carey Haas.

With all the power God had given her at birth, Debra was going to do everything she could to protect her son. She would bring him safely home again. Somehow, she would make all of the naïve people in this town see the truth. As of now, however, there was nothing that she could do to help him. She didn't even know where he was, and sat patiently by the phone, waiting to hear his kind hearted voice on the other line.

Debra missed her son, and she wanted to bring Billy home.

Chapter 18

Birmingham, Alabama.

Dr. Kennedy calmly walked out of the examining room from which the completely distraught figure of Jamie Walker had been assigned, and continued down the hall, a clipboard pressed firmly between his arm and body, towards the waiting room, where he knew kind-hearted Travis McKinley would be waiting. As the doctor entered the quiet, worry-minded room, Travis immediately felt his presence and looked up from a magazine, which he had not been too involved with in the first place, and jumped to his feet. Within seconds, he was standing right in front of Dr. Kennedy, his bleak, low hung eyes showing obvious signs of weariness, and Kennedy could easily tell that the past few days of trying to take care of Jamie Walker had proven to become very tiresome.

Then, getting to the point. "How is she?" Travis immediately asked the obvious question. "How is Jamie?"

"Well I really can not say for certain," Dr. Kennedy hated to admit. "Whatever the problem is, if she has a problem at all, I can assure you that it is not a physical one, and she is not suffering from any illness that I can see through my examinations. As far as a side-effect to the drugs prescribed for her, she is not allergic to them in any way, and her body appears to be perfectly normal, adapting to her injuries, and the healing process appears to be working very well-."

"Wait a minute doc," Travis interjected rather grimly. "How can you say that? You've been her doctor longer than I've even known her. Can you honestly say that the person in that room is the same Jamie Walker you've known for a long time now? She-she's talking crazy. She's bringing up things from the past about that damn Tinman guy, and she even thinks that bastard is still trying to kill her. The guy is dead for crying out loud. His brains are fried."

"Travis please," Dr. Kennedy tried to comfort and calm the confused person in front of him.

"No," Travis continued growing angry with the fact that for some reason, he was unable to understand what his girlfriend was going through, couldn't help her through it, and now was being told that her doctor couldn't even help. "There is something wrong with Jamie Dr. I know it and you know it, and I don't care what it takes. I want to find out just what it is. She's loosing control and I can feel her slipping away from me. She's not getting any better doctor. She's getting worse. I-," he fell silent for a moment, trying to fight off the frustrating tears that lingered in the distance just waiting for exposure. "I just want her to come back to me. I want her to be the old Jamie again."

"And so do I," the gracious, compassionate doctor spoke up, placing a firm hand on Travis's shoulder. "Believe me, I want nothing but the best for Jamie as well. And I'm not in anyway saying that she is never going to be normal again. To tell you the truth, I can't even say for certain that she's acting the slightest bit abnormal. Sure, she might be talking in sudden outbursts about some pretty unbelievable commodities, but we have to consider everything that she has been through. This whole ordeal she now finds herself having to overcome came about suddenly and unexpectedly, and has probably turned into a very dramatic experience for her. She's probably going through a lot of trauma right now. The only thing you can do for her Travis is be there for her."

"What are you saying doctor?" Travis continued not giving up. "Are you saying that there isn't anything that you can do for her? What about her insisting that she ran over a child that night? You know as well as I do that there was no body of a child recovered at the scene of her accident. And what about all of those illusions of Curtis Rains, and her continuous efforts to try and convince me that he's coming to kill her? Damn it!" Travis paused as he ran his fingers through his hair, obviously showing signs of stress. "She actually believes that this guy is still alive."

"I understan-."

"No you don't," Travis cut Kennedy off harshly, progressing his anger unfairly on the helpful doctor. "I don't even understand what is going on anymore, and I don't think Jamie does either. Please Dr. Kennedy," Travis pleaded his case once more. "There's got to be something that we can do."

"Perhaps there is," Dr. Kennedy gladly began speaking again. "However, what she may or not be suffering from is simply not my field. Now Travis, I'm going to give you a number of a one Dr. Roberts. He's a very, very good friend of mine and an exceptional psychiatrist. I'll take the liberty of calling him and letting him know that you'll be coming, but it's going to be up to you to make sure that Jamie gets there. If anyone can determine if Jamie is going through any psychological problems, he's your man."

"Thank you," Travis responded calmly, taking a deep breath and accepting the piece of paper Dr. Kennedy handed him. "And look, I'm sorry for venting my frustrations on you. I know you-."

"It's quite all right," Dr. Kennedy assured him, without letting him finish his apology. "I understand you're going through a crisis right now in trying to take care of Jamie, and I know there's a lot involved. You are truly a brave man for dealing with this the way you are. Now," he paused as he checked his clipboard. "I have some more rounds to do. But you can go in and see her now if you'd like. I'll be back to check on her one last time before she leaves." Travis nodded. "And Travis," Dr. Kennedy called him back before he could disappear down the hall towards the room Jamie had just moments ago been examined. "Do keep in touch, and don't hesitate to call me if anything goes wrong all right?"

"Will do," Travis replied, forcing a slight smile. "And again, thank you."

* * *

Meanwhile, back in Destin, Florida.

Billy Saxton and Blaze Brookshaw sat inside Blaze's Chevrolet pick-up, the key turned backwards in the ignition as they listened to the radio, not allowing the battery the satisfaction of drowning away. Both of them sat quietly across from one another, Billy trying to overcome the impeding nervousness he felt deep inside the pit of his stomach as he knew the moment he had been waiting for was about to arrive. Soon, very soon, Carey Haas would come pulling up beside them, and he would be able to meet the most beautiful person he had ever laid his eyes upon. He couldn't wait to just look into her eyes, possibly take her soft hand gently in his own, and experience the magical vibration he was certain would be there.

The two of them had arrived early at the park, not having anywhere else to go, and for the last half hour had just been sitting there in silence, thinking about all of the events that had transpired lately, and both trying to figure a way out without getting themselves into any more trouble. Smiling to himself, Billy recalled what his best friend Blaze had said moments ago, "Man, we're just two good ole boys from Georgia. Why does trouble always seem to find us?" Billy hadn't answered his friend's question, only shrugged his shoulders in agreement. For the time being, Billy found himself at a loss for words. His mind was filled with anticipation and excitement of meeting the girl that had come to him in his sleep, dazzling and confusing him, all at the same time.

Now, however, Billy didn't want to run away.

He wanted to fight the sleepless nights, ward off whatever unseen force was out there and had so suddenly chosen to enter his life with extreme prejudice. Pushing everything else aside, including his own safety, the only thing that mattered right now was the protection of innocent Carey Haas, whom he knew now to be a lot older than what she had been in his hallucinating visions and in his tumbling nightmares. For whatever reason, Billy had come into her life, not by choice, but perhaps by destiny. Fate had somehow chosen him to go to Carey Haas, and now, there was no turning back. He could feel it inside his bones, inside his very essence of life that something was terribly wrong, and that the small girl he had seen in his dreams was in danger. He could sense danger all around him, perhaps watching his every move, perhaps watching him this very instant. But Billy didn't care. He was ready for any obstacle that came his way, practically already declaring victory on a war that had not yet been fought. If this was the beginning, it was surely to be the beginning of the end.

Nevertheless he sat there, next to his trustworthy friend, still as confused as he was the first night he experienced the staggering events in that house along the ocean shore. Billy still had no clue as to where all of this was going to take him, still didn't know exactly what the outcome was going to be, or what needed to be done to end the whole ordeal. However, the answers, he was sure, would come when the time was right. When that was going to be, however, was simply another question that he asked himself, yet could not answer.

They were parked in seclusion, completely isolated from all of the children that were hollering and roaming freely throughout the wooded areas of the park. They had followed Carey's detailed directions to get to the spot, and had crossed a very narrow, wooden bridge that went over a small creek, only to find themselves parked along an evergreen embankment, where about ten feet below, another stream could be found. Behind the stream, was another forest, and every so often, a child would appear, running into the creek, only to retreat back into the forest and return to the playground, which was filled with an assortment of swing-sets and merry-go-rounds, on the other side.

The terrain around them, however, was astonishingly beautiful. In the front of them, was the creek, followed by a wooded area filled with nature trails. Behind them, was another wooded area, along with the narrow bridge they had crossed to get there. But on both sides of them, was a wide-open grassy field, which stretched in both directions as far as the eye could see. For a split second, it reminded the two of them of their homes in Georgia, and brought back many memories, some they would have undoubtedly preferred to stay hidden in the back of their mind, never to resurface again.

Then, taking a deep breath, it was Blaze who broke the silence that had befallen the two of them a long time ago. "What is going through your head right now at this exact moment?" he asked Billy, who finally turned away from the creek below and made eye contact with him. Shrugging his shoulders, Billy didn't know how to answer. "Come on man," Blaze pressed forward trying to pass the time. "After everything that you've been going through, there's got to be something going through that thick skull of yours. What is it? What is on your mind right now?"

"I honestly don't know," Billy admitted. "I guess I'm nervous in a way about meeting this girl ya know? Maybe wondering if putting myself in the line of fire, and getting myself into all of this trouble is worth it? I wish I could predict the outcome of all of this man. But I can't," he paused tilting his head downwards. "Because I don't know what's going to happen next. Maybe I'm making a big deal over nothing. Or maybe I really don't have a place in this, and I'm making a mistake by getting involved. But I'm telling you Blaze, I feel some connection here. Lately I've been feeling a lot of things that I have never felt before and I think if I ignore them, then that would be the wrong thing to do. The last thing I want out of life is to live with regrets." Then, looking up again, he concluded. "I can't walk away from this man. I just can't."

"And I'm not telling you to," Blaze continued. "And my gut feeling tells me that everything is going to be all right and turn out for the best. Besides, no one is judging you here. You are the only person that can make the decision on whether or not you should be getting wrapped up in something like this. Granted, I don't understand any of it, and I do have a hard time visualizing everything you've described to me. But I can tell you this," he paused, getting a firm look on his face. "If I were in your situation, I would be doing the exact same thing."

"Even if it included running from the cops?" Billy asked with a smile, surprised that he was able to laugh at the situation that could put him behind bars.

Nodding, Blaze answered with a laugh of his own. "Yeah, I think I would have done the same thing. All you were doing was following your heart man. It might not be the right thing to do, but if this girl's life is truly in danger, your not going to do any good locked up ya know?"

"Yeah, and even when I try to explain what has been going on, I know they'll think I'm crazy and won't believe a word I say."

"I know," Blaze continued cutting Billy short. "Which is why you did the right thing."

Then, the two of them fell silent, as they both felt the presence of someone or something coming from behind them. Then, they saw it. Crossing the bridge, was a car, a Lincoln Town car and it was coming right towards them. Billy remembered the Lincoln he had seen pulling out of the Goodman driveway the day he had gone to the house, and knew that Carey was behind the wheel. Butterflies flurried inside his stomach even more now as the car pulled up beside the truck, and he realized he wasn't going to be strong enough to push his nervousness aside. Wiping the last bit of sweat away from his forehead, Billy Saxton stepped out of the truck.

This was it. This was what he had been longing for.

Finally, it was time to meet Carey Haas.

* * *

Moments earlier.

Carey Haas swerved her uncle's Lincoln perfectly throughout the windy road, veering between the massive pine trees that stood in her way on both sides of the blacktop. Soon, she knew she would be face to face with the one person she considered to be her guardian angel. She looked at herself through the rearview mirror and saw herself smiling with joy and happiness. She was excited, and had never felt this way about anyone before in her life. It was all so new to her, yet it was all so wonderful as well. She only hoped he would be as perfect in person, as he had been in her dreams.

It was crazy though; she had never met Billy Saxton before in her life. Yet it felt as if she had known him forever, as if he had always been there, watching out for her over her shoulder, just waiting for the right time to come to her and let himself be known. Then, she said his name aloud.

"Billy Saxton. Billy Saxton. Billy Saxton," she repeated over and over again childishly. The name itself seemed to rip into her soul, filling it with all the happiness the world had to offer. Carey simply couldn't let go of what she was feeling inside. It was all so powerful, and although it almost seemed theoretically artificial, she knew that her feelings were as true as the heavens above as they welcomed her parent's souls some ten years ago. Billy Saxton was real. And her feelings were real.

Carey couldn't let them go.

Didn't want to let them go.

And in a sense, refused to push them aside.

After all, there was no point in hiding your feelings. There would be no point in denying yourself the right to be happy. Carey hadn't been happy for a long time. As Billy entered her life in her dreams, rescuing her from the evil nightmare brought on by a source so dark and cold, she knew it could be none other than Curtis Rains himself. She could sense that somehow her life had changed. She was starting to look at life differently, perhaps giving the future a chance, and actually wanting to continue living and make the best of this somewhat confusing life the good Lord had offered her.

To Carey, there was a reason for everything. And there was a reason Billy had come to her. For some reason, the very thought of this angel in Billy Saxton brought out the best in her. He had the ability to bring out emotions she never even knew she had, or was willing to show. But there was just something about him that she obviously had been longing for, and had finally found.

With Billy Saxton in her life, she couldn't see anything going wrong.

Then, as she crossed the old, wooden bridge, she saw the pick-up truck parked above on the hill, sitting peacefully along the embankment overlooking the stream below. At last, it was time to confront the person whom had come to her in her sleep, and soothed her soul.

At last, it was time to meet Billy Saxton.

She pulled her uncle Rick's Lincoln slowly next to the towering Chevrolet, and waited to see what she should do next. The excitement was almost unbearable, and although she knew the conversation she was about to encounter might not be the most pleasant as the memories of her parents death were sure to be dragged up, she still felt weak, and eager to finally meet her guardian angel.

This was what she had been waiting for.

Then, she saw the passenger door of the full sized truck open and a pair of legs covered in blue jeans climb out. Closing the door behind him, she saw him as he made his way towards her car.

He was coming to her.

Billy Saxton was approaching her.

Opening her door, she stepped outside and faced him, a warm smile spread across her beautiful face, as her long locks of blonde hair dazzled in the sun. Carey Haas looked utterly breathtaking, and her counterpart was nothing short of perfection.

For the first time in ten years, Carey Haas had a reason to smile.

*   *   *

Meanwhile, in Starke, Florida.

Jack Reynolds stepped out of the steamy hot shower, and grabbed a big white, cottony towel from atop the flush toilet. He then wrapped his heated body comfortably with the softness, wiping away the remaining drops of water only for them to return in the form of perspiration. Walking through the steam filled bathroom, he wiped away the dew that had formed and covered the entire glass mirror, which hung peacefully above the sink, and stared at himself intensely. He was trying to understand just what had brought on the sudden mood changes he had been experiencing as of late.

Without blinking, Jack slicked his hair back with both his hands, and felt the water drain from his tress and swiftly drip down his back, mixing in with the thick gathering coat of sweat that had formed all over his body. As he gazed at himself in the mirror, however, he felt as though he didn't know, or recognize his own reflection. It was as if he were staring at someone else. Someone disguised in his own body, forcing him to act in violent manners he had never been associated with.

But that was impossible.

He was staring at Jack Reynolds. He was staring at himself for crying out loud. There was no unseen demon growing inside his soul, forcing him to act violently. There was no mischievous devil living somewhere deep inside, trying to destroy his life, and obtain gratification from bringing his family's life down in ruins.

No. It wasn't impossible.

There had to be a reason he was changing. Then, Jack remembered the voice inside the shed of his backyard when he went to investigate the strange and alarming noise he and his family had heard, shaking the interior walls of their home violently. Only, as Jack recalled the sequence of events, he remembered someone locking him inside, and speaking to him from outside the shed. Effortlessly he had tried to escape, and free himself from inside the unsafe, dust filled environment of the run downed shed. To no avail, however, it had been no use, and he had been forced to listen to what the mysterious voice on the other side had to say, forced to take it in, and for some reason, he still found the trespassers words embedded inside his soul.

But they were lies; he tried to force himself to believe.

It simply was not true.

His charming wife, Gloria did not have an affair. Her being unfaithful was merely impossible to believe.

Yet, for some unexplained reason, Jack couldn't dismiss it.

"She's a whore," he remembered the voice saying once again. *"She deserves to be punished. The only question is, are you willing to evoke the punishment?"* Only, as he remembered the voice, he remembered the single door of the shed finally coming free, and as he yanked it open, stepped outside into the humidified Florida air, he expected to see the face of the person whom had been speaking to him. Shockingly, however, there had been no one insight, and Jack figured that it would be undoubtedly impossible for anyone to flee the area in such a small amount of time. Nevertheless, no one had been there, and it almost appeared as though no one had ever been there at all. Not a single footprint could be found outside the shed, and the more Jack searched and hunted for any remote signs of anyone being there, the more convinced he became that his mind had been playing tricks on him.

And then today, at the prison.

He had purposely, and intentionally cracked the skull of an inmate, whether he would live or die remained an unanswered destiny. However, he had blatantly chosen to raise his weapon on an unarmed man and pound away at the defenseless prisoner, his full intention to strip him of his very last breathe, welcoming his pleads for mercy, but ignoring them with a furious smile. His intent to kill was so strong it could not be overcome or subdued by Jacob Jones's merciful screams to live.

And the blood.

There had been so much blood. However, it only seemed to force Jack to want to inflict even more harm on his defenseless victim. The sight of Jacob's pain only made his thirst for blood, and his hunger to kill even more potent. If the guards hadn't rushed in and stopped the beating, death would have been inevitable. Some people may have looked at his obsessive actions in a different light, perhaps stating that he was doing the state of Florida a favor and saving the state millions in tax dollars. Many people, however, would see this as something else. Something much more extreme, and something clearly unforgivable. In fact, Jack knew that if Jacob Jones did wind up passing away by the harmful cold-blooded wounds he had forcefully laid upon him, he would be looked at in the same manner as all of the other disgraceful inmates contained in the isolated walls of death row. He knew, that he would be called a murderer.

And he wouldn't be able to argue his way out of it.

He couldn't explain his actions.

He couldn't take back what was already printed out as clear as day in black and white ink. He couldn't return to the tiny cell, mop up all of the seemingly endless gallons of blood and forget that anything had happened there at all. For the first time in his life, Jack felt trapped inside an overwhelming situation where every which way he turned; he found nothing but a dead end standing in his path. He had done wrong, and now would ultimately have to face the consequences, and except whatever punishment was thrust upon him. Clearly, his job was on the line, and even if Jacob Jones didn't die, he was pretty sure that he would not be welcomed back on the prison grounds. This was a battle Jack couldn't win.

His home life had wrecked his profession.

And his cheating wife, Gloria, was to blame.

Again, as the very thought of his wife entered his mind, a rage of pure, hate-filled anger ripped inside his body from nowhere, and as he continued to look at himself in the bathroom mirror, he could see the fury growing in his eyes, and could still feel the blood boiling in his veins. His lips began shaking uncontrollably, and he clutched the sides of the stainless sink tightly with both hands, as if some magical force would come along and free his mind of all the presumptuous, intrusive thoughts of his wife. Realizing that was not going to happen, Jack let go of the sink, and continued to stare at himself in the mirror, desperately trying to come up with another solution that would allow him to release his underlying anger, and vent out his remaining frustrations, which although most were unseen, he was sure were there.

"No!" he screamed aloud at himself, feeling comfortable in doing so knowing that he was the only one inside his beloved home. Then, without thinking, and before he could even realize what he was about to do, he raised his fists in a fit of anger.

BANG.

Jack Reynolds slammed both of his crafty, noble, balled up hands into the yearning, ample glass mirror, and within seconds, watched as his clear image splintered into thousands of different directions. As the glass cracked, and shattered profusely, however, Jack didn't pull his injured hands away. He continued to drive them deeper and deeper into the sharp edged glass particles, welcoming the comforting pain, and watched his very own blood running down his arms and dripping off at his elbows only to fall into the sink. Grunting, he continued to penetrate into the destroyed mirror, until he had reached the ultimate end and realized he wasn't going to get any farther.

Finally, Jack pulled his hands away.

With a smile, he looked at the harm he had inflicted upon himself. He could see some glass still lingering about inside his flesh, practically all of the skin from his knuckles had been sliced off, and the open wounds poured blood freely outside. To Jack, the scene was beautiful, and the pain seemed to soothe his soul.

Wrapping a wet towel around his blood gushing hands, he walked out of the bathroom with at last a clear head.

Finally, it was all coming together.

Jack Reynolds knew what he had to do.

Smiling, he turned off the bathroom light, and closed the door behind him, leaving the bloody mess behind, without even so much as giving it a second thought, or even attempting to make an effort in cleaning it up. The only thing on his mind at the moment, was his charming, innocent wife, Gloria. Any minute now, Jack knew that she would be returning home from work, and would want to finish the little spat they had the other night.

Tonight, would be another story.

If Gloria really wanted to know exactly what it was that was eating away inside his soul, and if she really wanted to be confronted about her unfaithfulness, so be it. It was time for Jack to stop holding back. He had to face his fears, confront his problems, and overcome any adversities that may stand in the way.

It was time to end the madness once and for all.

Even if the truth was something that Jack truly didn't want to hear.

Jason Glover

Then, walking into his bedroom, his blood-lined hands still draped in towels, Jack prepared for the confrontation with his wife. Smiling to himself, he waited for his wife to come home.

Soon, his madness would cease, and he would be free of any demons lying beneath his precious skin.

Soon, it would all be over.

* * *

Back in Destin, Florida.

Debra Saxton stood on her back balcony that evening, watching as the sun slowly began to set, listening to the crashing waves, as they pounded the surf harshly. Families and lovers strolled casually along the beach, their lives obviously without any discrepancies, or if there were any, they were of minor stature, and didn't need any allotted time to actually sit down and think about. Right now, Debra Saxton wished that were the case for her and her family.

Billy was not only her son, but also the only person she had left in her family, and he was not with her. He was out there somewhere, running from the law and whatever trouble he had found himself in. Meanwhile, Debra was at their home, not knowing where he could be found, and forced to wonder if he was even all right. She didn't even know if he was dead or alive.

Her motherly instincts, however, suggested that so far, Billy remained unharmed.

Looking down at the wood that had been handily crafted into forming the back deck of this beautiful beach front home, she wondered at how something so spectacular could have once housed an innocent family that had been devilishly murdered. She blamed herself, in a way, for all of the madness and the unnecessary downfall of the relationship between herself and her son. She blamed herself for the pain and torment her son was undergoing ever since they set foot in the very home she now stood, alone, and wondering what was going to happen to Billy.

More than herself, however, she blamed the house itself. The awful secrets finally exposed, revealing all of the memories of the past. The worst mistake of her life was packing her bags, and forcing her son to move to Destin, Florida with her. They should have just stayed in Georgia and fought the staggering memories of her abusive, and alcoholic husband Tom Saxton together, knowing that the pain would ease with time.

Now, however, she didn't even know exactly how much time her son Billy had.

Things had gone terribly wrong.

Stress built continuously with every passing second she didn't hear from her son, and it was growing more and more unbearable.

Debra Saxton was loosing her mind, and she couldn't take much more.

Anything, however, was better than loosing her son.

Something, somewhere, had to give. She had to have her son back, free from whatever unearthly evil force had taken him away. She felt helpless in preventing whatever dangers lay ahead.

Whatever was happening to her son, she couldn't stop it.

She began to question if anybody could actually stop the evil that appeared to be floating around the air of Destin. Everything had happened so unpredictably, and came astonishingly from out of nowhere, without even giving Billy a chance to catch his breath.

She knew, however, her son was strong.

He wouldn't give up without a fight.

She only prayed, that in the end, he would come out on top and be crowned the victor in what seemingly appeared to be an unfair battle between good and evil. In the movies, the good guy always came out on top. This, she very well knew, was not the movies, but real life, and anything could happen. This was the world where people had to fight to make their dreams come true, taking chances each and every day to succeed. Unfortunately, bad things happen to many good-natured people, some doing nothing more than dedicating their life for the sake of humanity. In today's world, you were lucky to escape life without any regrets or scars. Some ultimately going to heaven, while others fall into the burning, crackling flames of hell.

But where was the boundary line between heaven and hell?

What was truly the difference between right and wrong?

These were questions Debra couldn't answer, and the more she continued to think about the safety of her son the more helpless she realized she was in this situation, and the more worrisome she became. Why hadn't Billy called her yet? Then, remembering that her phone lines were tapped, she knew that Blaze must have warned his best friend of this fact and that had been the reason he had held on contacting her.

Bowing her head downwards, she let a tear fall from her twinkling eyes, not even bothering to wash them away. All she wanted to do was hear her son's voice one time to make sure that he was all right. Right now, however, she was forced to wonder if she was ever going to hear Billy's voice again.

"Please God," she whispered aloud as she looked up into the beautiful orange, cirrus cloud filled sky. "Please bring my son back to me. Watch over him and keep him safe and unharmed. Please," she continued looking away, and burying her head in her hands as she prepared to loose control and be overcome with tears, as the misery of loosing her son began to sink in. "And Billy, if you can hear me," she added sadly. "I love you. I will always love you"

Then, disregarding everything she had heard about her son, she walked inside and threw herself on the couch, visualizing every last promising moment she had spent with her son in the past. She remembered every smile, every laugh the two of them had been fortunate enough to share, even during the sudden death of her husband when sadness prevailed. Nevertheless, the two of them had managed to show that they truly loved one another, and no matter how hard Tom had tried to take that away from them, their bond was simply to strong to destroy, and wound remain intact until the end of time. Her love for her son was everlasting, could never be doubted, and would continue to grow, even if death split them apart.

Sobbing uncontrollably, Debra did nothing to hold back her tears, longing to hear any news regarding her precious son. She would wait forever, if she had to. She wasn't leaving until she heard her son's voice, even if it perhaps was for the last time.

But God was on Billy's side. For some reason, that was something she was sure of. So whatever happened, it would be God's will, and no matter what, that was something she could not question.

Looking into the eyes of the beholder, Debra closed her eyes and tried to get some rest. At first it seemed like an impossible task to accomplish. But slowly, she felt her restless eyes growing weak, and knew it wouldn't be long until she drifted off into dreamland. Not expecting to rest peacefully, she still welcomed any sleep that her body would allow. And if anything happened to her son, hopefully, she would never wake up.

A life without her son was simply not worth living.

* * *

Billy Saxton was speechless. He found himself feeling like he had a large shoe put in his mouth, not allowing him to speak freely about whatever was on his mind. Carey had climbed out of her uncle's car and seated herself on the hood of the black Lincoln. She too, didn't know where to begin or how to start up a conversation. The joy of finally looking into the eyes of the person she had seen in her dream was still shifting her stomach in fashionable knots, although she did her best to conceal her excitement from the handsome guy in front of her. She peered down, unnoticeable at Billy's hands, and remembered how they had squeezed her shoulders, ever so gently, soothing her soul, and shedding her nightmare from the notorious Curtis Rains. And then, as her guardian angel began to disappear from her dreams, satisfied that everything was all right, she had looked into his sparkling blue eyes.

She had felt so loved, so wanted, so special. But most importantly, she had felt safe, and all of the fear her body had been subjected to for the past ten years had gone away, disappearing almost as if they had never been there at all, even if it were only for a short time. But, only recently, had Carey learned that it hadn't been a dream at all. It had been for real. Billy had actually been inside her room, watching her sleep, saw her tossing and turning in her bed and had come to calm her down, and wash away the evil that masked her soul. Even though she had yet to hear an explanation as to why he had been there, she didn't care, and wouldn't care if she never heard one. For some reason, she trusted him, and wasn't afraid of him.

Nevertheless, the rest of Billy's figure was just as perfect as his hands, and just as beautiful as the eyes she remembered staring at her in her dreams. She didn't even know him, yet, she couldn't remember the last time she felt this way before about anyone. Then again, she knew that she had never felt this way before, and probably would never feel it again for anyone else.

Undoubtedly, and unexplainably, Carey Haas was in love.

And if possible, she would cherish this feeling for the rest of her life.

Also, she would cherish the figure before her in Billy Saxton for the rest of her life as well. She could only ask herself, however, if he felt the same.

Billy Saxton tried to read what was going through Carey's head by looking into her eyes. He couldn't tell, and was sure that she was able to look right through him and see what he was thinking. Before him, stood an angel. Carey Haas was the most beautiful woman he had even laid eyes upon. The perfect girl, with a figure many models would die for. She had a long, wavy, semi-thick mass of golden blonde hair, and greenish blue eyes that almost appeared to be that of a colorful emerald sparkling in the sun. She had the perfect smile, glistening white teeth, eyebrows that separated perfectly in the center, the clearest complexion, and although Billy had not yet been honored to find out, he was sure her skin was as smooth as it looked.

He felt like he was in a daze, and simply couldn't take his eyes off the stunning sight in front of him. He couldn't stop looking into her eyes, and desperately just wanted to reach out, take her in his arms, and hold her forever, or until the end of time. He never wanted to let anything bad happen to her again, wanted to deliver her from all the evil in the world, and show her all the love he could possibly give. She was perfect in every way, and she was what Billy had been waiting for his entire life. Fate had brought them together. It had been his destiny to move to Destin from Georgia and see her in his nightmares, a scared child running for her life, forced to witness and hear her parent's death.

And now that he was here, he wasn't about to turn back.

If he could help it, he would be with Carey Haas forever.

"Well," Billy finally took control, and mustered up enough courage and bravery to speak first. "Thank you for coming Carey. You really have no idea what I've been through lately. But I just had to meet you. I know that what I'm about to tell you is going to sound crazy, but I swear it's the truth. I came to your house the other day. I guess I kind of broke in," Billy smiled, hating to admit. "But I just wanted to see you. I feel some connection between the two of us, and I just had to see you. But no matter what your uncle or that Sheriff

Burnham guy says, you have to believe that I did not go there to hurt you. I swear I would neve-."

"I know," Carey cut him off, returning a smile that seemed to instantly ease Billy's pain. "I know you wouldn't hurt me. I trust you; otherwise I wouldn't have come out here Billy. I saw you," she added cheerfully. Then, seeing the confused expression lingering across Billy's face, she quickly continued. "That day you came to my house and came into my room. I was sleeping, but I saw you. I felt your hands, and I looked into your eyes. You were in my dream."

"I don't know what to say."

"Don't say anything," Carey continued. "You made me feel something that I haven't felt in a long time Billy. You made me feel safe, and it was like you scared away Curtis Rains in my nightmare. When you came to comfort me, he just disappeared and went away, and didn't come back. And I could see something in your eyes. I could never forget the way you looked at me Billy. And my God, I'm really glad to finally meet you."

"The Tinman was in your nightmare?" Billy hated to ask and destroy the friendly atmosphere, and regretted it even more as the smile washed away from Carey's face. Carey nodded awkwardly; obviously not ready to remember any of her nightmares. "Well, I'm going to be honest with you, and this is going to be hard for you to hear and possibly understand. But please, don't be afraid, and just bare with me."

"All right."

"I live in the house you used to live in as a girl, and I know everything that happened to you and your parents that night. Christ, I even know what ya'll had for dinner. And ever since I moved in, I've been experiencing visions of you as a girl, almost like I was reliving everything through your eyes. I saw what happened that night, every last detail, and I don't know why any of this started happening to me, but then I saw you again, and I couldn't help to think that something is wrong."

"I'm sorry," Carey replied with a sense of uncertainty in her voice. "I don't understand. What do you mean something is wrong?"

"I think you are in danger," Billy answered firmly, taking her hand in his own. "And I think that's why I was seeing the past, so I could warn you or help you or something."

"Help me from what?"

"Curtis Rains," Billy answered directly, and momentarily, their eyes locked once again, neither saying a word, Billy letting Carey take in everything that was being said, and could see the fear growing in her eyes. Her eyes began to cloud, and his instincts forced him to draw her close, and shelter her in his arms. "I'm sorry," he whispered into her ear. "I know this is something you don't want to hear."

"But. I-" she let her voice trail off briefly trying to fight back her tears, and not attempting to pull away from Billy's welcoming arms. "I thought he was dead."

"I don't think he is," Billy answered boldly, realizing his talk sounded crazy. "I think his physical body is dead, but I don't think his soul died Carey. And if you think about it, I know you can feel his presence too. Deep inside, you can feel that he is still around can't you?"

Carey nodded. "He hasn't left me alone in ten years," she cried finally unable to hold back any longer. "Everyday and night he comes to me, forcing me to look at my parents bloody bo-bodies. He-," she began stuttering as her tongue began getting in the way of the tears. "He won't go away."

"I'm sorry," Billy tried to comfort her. "I'm so sorry all of this had to happen to you. But I can promise you something. I will be there with you every step of the way. I won't leave you alone ever again, and together, I think we can beat him. I promise Carey," he paused pulling away for a moment to look deep into her watery eyes. "I won't let anything happen to you."

Then, changing the subject, he turned away from Carey and opened the truck door, smiled at the wink his best friend Blaze threw at him, then picked up the porcelain doll he had found in the cellar of the old Haas home and turned once again to face the woman in front of him. "I think I might have something that belongs to you," Billy spoke up once again, hiding the doll behind his back. "Do you recall hiding something in the cellar of your home ten years ago?"

Without hesitation, Carey answered. "Kat!" Revealing the doll from behind his back, he watched as Carey took it from him and nestled it close to her chest, happy that a smile had once again returned to her beloved face. "I have thought about you a couple of times," she continued jokingly speaking to the doll that once meant the world to her. Then, looking up at Billy, she continued. "Thank you."

"Carey," Billy moved forward, pressed his hand against her cheek, and without warning, leaned in and kissed her on the forehead. "Everything is going to be all right." Then, once again he opened the passenger door to Blaze's truck. "Come on," he continued about to introduce the girl of his dreams to his best friend in the world. "There's someone I want you to meet."

Chapter 19

Gloria Reynolds pulled into her driveway that evening, and noticed her husband's pick-up parked in its normal spot in the driveway. Only, as she checked her watch again, she realized that it was far too early for him to be home. Jack should still be at work, watching the inmates of the Florida State Penitentiary, making sure they were behaving, and supposedly rehabilitating. But he wasn't. He was home, his truck parked in the driveway proved it. She knew her husband to be a man of dignity, and pride, and was never the type to knock off work a little early. In fact, normally he was the one to stay late, or pick up a double shift. There had to be an explanation for his early arrival home, and only one seemed to come to mind.

Something was wrong.

Walking up to the front door, she twisted the knob and found it unlocked. Stepping inside, she shut the front door behind her and slowly began making her way through the house. The bottom floor was completely empty, and it appeared as if no one had been there all day. The television set was turned off, the kitchen abandoned, and no lights were on, leaving the bottom story of the home with a rather dull, dark gloomy appearance. Normally, when she returned home from work and her husband had a day off, she would've either found him in the kitchen preparing supper, or casually sprawled out along the couch watching something on the television. But Jack wasn't in either of the locations, and the silence that had fallen over the house made Gloria wonder if he was even upstairs in their bedroom? She paused every so often after each step, listening intently for any signs of life rummaging around the house. But there was nothing.

Tinman

Only silence.

And the silence was the main instrument that captured her attention, and made her feel slightly uncomfortable, almost as if she were in some sort of danger. Finally, after turning on a few lamps to add a little color to the bottom portion of her home and to change the depressing atmosphere, she began to mount the stairs, taking them two by two until at last she reached the top. Taking a deep breath, she was stunned to see the upstairs just as dark and quiet as the bottom of the house. She sensed that Sarah was not home, and headed straight for her bedroom. Expecting to see Jack asleep on their bed, she pushed the door open and walked slowly inside.

Nothing.

No one was there.

The bed was made; in fact, the entire room was crisply clean without any signs of dust. Cutting on the overhead light, Gloria sat herself comfortably on the bed, and began brainstorming. Many people would have just shoved her thoughts aside and pretended that nothing was wrong, quite possibly even deciding to enjoy the peaceful silence her house was providing. But she couldn't dismiss Jack's truck parked in the driveway, and she couldn't forget the eerie silence her house had fallen into. Something had to be wrong. And her husband had to be somewhere. But where?

Then, climbing to her feet, she listened intensely as she thought she heard two faint sounds coming from outside, in the backyard. That's it. That's where Jack was. He was doing something in the backyard. Once again, she left her bedroom, trampled down the stairs and reached the backdoor. Peering outside, she saw her only daughter, eleven year old Sarah, laughing and carrying on with her father. Every so often, running around him in circles, giggling uncontrollably as she tried to get Jack to chase her around the backyard. She let a smile cross her face as she remembered how loving and gentle Jack could be at times, and from the looks of things, it appeared as though everything was going to be all right, and return to normal.

Gloria watched as her husband tumbled to the ground in his blue jeans, pretending that Sarah had won the battle, only to allow Sarah to jump on top of him and struggle to keep him down. The wrestling match went on for a few minutes, neither her husband nor her daughter knew that she was watching them, and wishing that she could simply walk out the backdoor and join them in the fun. Something, however, was holding her back. Possibly the tension she could still sense and feel between the two of them. They had not yet resolved their differences. Hopefully after tonight, however, they would be able to reconcile, and make-up, forgetting that anything ever happened before. She hated fighting with Jack. She loved him more than anything in the world, and wouldn't ever do anything to jeopardize their relationship. Gloria didn't want to lose him. More than anything, she just wanted things to return to the way they used to be.

Then, as if Jack had been able to feel her presence behind the backdoor, he turned away from his daughter for a moment, and looked back. Gloria fought off the urge to duck down, and get out of sight, but for some reason, she remained and let her husband's eyes fall over her. Jack didn't move. Sarah continued to climb all over him, but it was like he wasn't even acknowledging she was there. The look in Jack's eyes made chills explode up and down her spine as the hairs on the back of her neck stood tall. As Gloria watched, he didn't smile. In fact his expression was blank. The only sign of emotion was that of anger. Apparently, things hadn't gotten any better between the two of them since last night, whatever had been on Jack's mind had not been forgotten.

The look in his eyes was almost genuinely evil. It was as if he were looking right through her, his dark accusing eyes piercing their way inside her soul, as if searching for something. Finally, Gloria had enough. Turning away from the window, she walked away. She couldn't take it anymore. There was no reason at all for her to be afraid of her husband, but she was. For some reason, looking into Jack's eyes had brought on an incredible sensation of fear that couldn't be subdued.

Any minute now, she was sure the two of them would come pouncing into the house from the backdoor, Sarah, undoubtedly would come running over and drape her arms lovingly around her welcoming her home from work. Jack's actions, however, remained to be seen, and picking up her car keys hesitantly, she thought briefly about leaving before he could come inside and confront her. Another argument was bound to approach, and Gloria just wasn't sure that she was prepared to handle it. She didn't know what was coming, or how she should deal with the problems that faced them.

Then again, she didn't even know what the problem was.

Jack had kept her clueless, never once telling her what was wrong, and if he was unwilling to let her in, then there was simply nothing that she could do about it. More than anything, she wanted to help him through whatever was troubling him. But for some reason, Jack wasn't willing to open up. Finally, she placed her car keys back down on the table and went into the kitchen. Pretending that nothing was wrong, she cut on the stove and prepared to make her family a hearty meal for the evening. However, no matter how hard she tried to push it aside, the thought of her husband wouldn't go away. The look in his eyes remained as clear as day in her mind, and the fear wouldn't leave her alone.

Then, startled by the sound of a door slamming shut, Gloria accidentally dropped the bag of rice she was about to pour into a pot of boiling water. Bending down to pick it up, she heard her daughter's voice calling out to her. Without having to look up, she knew that Jack had come inside right behind her. Finally, just as expected, Sarah came trotting cheerfully into the kitchen and gave Gloria an affectionate hug, and after a few short exchange of words, she disappeared from the kitchen and ran upstairs to her room, following the obvious instructions of her father.

Climbing back to her feet, Gloria opened the bag of white rice and poured it into the boiling water. She knew that her daughter had escaped to her room, but could still feel the presence of someone behind her. Spinning around, she found Jack standing at the entrance to the kitchen. His expression still blank, and without saying a word, he just stood there, staring at her. Not feeling comfortable turning her back on her husband, Gloria managed to smile, and hesitantly, walked over and kissed him on the cheek. Again, however, no emotion was shown from her husband.

Jack accepted the kiss, but didn't bother to return the gesture or attempt to put his arms around his precious wife. Now, Gloria was certain that something was terribly wrong, and she desperately wanted to call out to her daughter and bring her back downstairs so that she wouldn't have to be alone with Jack in the kitchen. Thinking twice, however, she tried to start a conversation. "How was your day at work?" she asked casually, forcing another fabricated smile. "You're home kind of early aren't you?"

Jack nodded, using a gesture to answer his wife's questions, instead of opening his mouth. "I've been home all afternoon," Jack continued firmly, the expression on his face never changing. "Appears I ran into a little trouble at work today."

She knew it. Gloria knew that something had happened to Jack at work. She felt it as soon as she saw his truck parked in the driveway. "Want to tell me what happened?" Gloria asked, not wanting to step on her husband's feet as she remembered the argument the two of them had fallen into the night before.

"Well it's quite simple really," Jack answered coldly, fury blazing in his eyes as he continuously had to hold himself back from snapping at his wife. "I went to work today, received another inmate, and-." He let his voice trail off into silence.

"And what?"

"And I damn near killed the son of a bitch," Jack answered with an evil, snickering grin. "In fact, I'm not really sure. I guess he still might die."

Gloria couldn't believe her ears. What was Jack talking about? He had just admitted to her that he may have killed someone, and again left her without any inclination as to why he would have even done such a thing. Then, looking at the wicked grin that had sprang across his face, she couldn't believe that he could find humor in such a thing. And above all else, did he really expect her to laugh at something of this nature. No, Gloria told herself. It couldn't be true. It simply couldn't be true. "Are you being serious?" she bluntly asked her husband, trying to control the unbelievable amount of fear her body was consuming at a rapid pace.

Jock nodded.

"I don't believe you."

"Oh it's true," Jack assured his wife. "I probably killed another serial killer today sweetheart, and I'm pretty fucking sure I lost my job because of it." He paused to see the horrified look in his wife's eyes. She was afraid of him. "But you know what's funny," he continued laughing at himself. "I could care less if that bastard lives or dies. And if I had my choice, he'd die in a heartbeat."

"Jack stop it," Gloria pleaded, trying to hold back her fear stricken tears, and stop herself from running out of the kitchen to find safety somewhere else. "You're scaring me," she honestly continued, not wanting to be around her husband any longer. Gloria couldn't quite put her finger on it, but for some reason, she felt as though whoever this man was standing before her, it simply could not be her husband. His lucid nature, the coldness in his tone as he laughed at possibly killing someone, and devilish look in his eyes, made Gloria doubt him even more. It was someone else, trapped inside Jack's body. "Please Jack. Just leave me alone."

"Leave you alone?" Jack returned harshly, slamming his fist into the wall. "Who the fuck do you think you are ordering me around like that?" Jack questioned and watched as Gloria jerked in fear at his sudden outburst of anger. "I'm not going anywhere until we finish our little discussion."

"About what Jack?" Gloria questioned, an overwhelming feeling of entrapment taking control. "I don't know what you're talking about."

"I'm talking about you having an affair," Jack blurted out coldly, his accusing eyes watching Gloria's every move. "How can you do such a thing you bitch? After everything I've done and provided for you. Never once did I even consider sleeping with another woman, and here you are, with the nerve to come home every night pretending that nothing is wrong, and without the desire to be honest and tell me the truth."

Gloria couldn't hold back the tears any longer. She had come home to a madman. She had never had an affair, never even once came close, or was ever tempted into being unfaithful. She truly had no idea where Jack could have come up with such an outlandish idea. How could he have so little trust in her? She was in love with him for crying out loud. Couldn't he see that? "Jack, please," Gloria pleaded. "Will you listen to yourself? I have not had an affair. My God, have you lost your mind?"

Jack could feel his body heating up, could feel the anger growing inside as saliva dripped from his mouth, and his chest heaved in and out wildly, building the infamous rage expanding inside his soul. Balling his fists up, Gloria noticed the cuts on his hands. Now, for the first time, she feared for her life. Jack was crazy, and she could sense herself being harmed. Then, she watched as Jack closed his eyes, and could see his eyeballs rolling spasmodically in the back of his eyelids.

Then, the voice he had heard outside the shed that night, returned to Jack.

"The time is now Jack," the voice whispered inside his head. *"She's lied to you again. She thinks you're stupid. You have to punish her Jack. You have to kill her."* Jack grabbed the sides of his head trying to force the voice to vanish, but it remained. *"She's a whore Jack. Kill her. KILL HER! KILL HER!"*

"Liar!" Jack screamed at his wife as he opened his eyes, and reached out to grab her around the neck. Only, as he opened his eyes, he realized that Gloria was no longer in front of him. She was gone, and he was alone in the kitchen. But where could she go? Then, the voice returned once again. *"Quick Jack. Go after her. You can't let her get away. You can't let her get away with this."* Obeying the orders thrust upon him, Jack raced through the house after his wife like a wild maniac. He couldn't control his rage any longer. Gloria had to pay for the pain she caused him.

She had to die.

Gloria hid in the pantry of the kitchen for at least five minutes. She sensed that her husband was planning to kill her. Listening consciously, she heard both the front door and the backdoor slamming shut, along with other doors found inside the house as Jack searched recklessly for her. It appeared that he wasn't going to give up until he had found her. But then, instantly, the entire house fell silent. Gloria stayed put in the pantry for a few extra minutes, waiting to hear any more signs that would lead her to believe that her husband was still somewhere close by. However, she heard nothing.

Just as it had been when she first arrived home, there was only silence.

Then, a thought came to her mind. Sarah. Her daughter. She had been upstairs in her room. Surely Jack would have gone in there to look for her, and-. No she refused to believe that Jack would ever take out the anger he felt towards her on their daughter. After all, she had heard no screams, heard no signs of Sarah struggling to run away from her father. Nevertheless, her safety was in question, and Gloria had to go to her. She had to make sure that her daughter was all right.

Opening the pantry door as quietly as possible, Gloria slipped outside and found herself standing once again in the kitchen. Looking around her, she was sure that she was the only one there. Then, without looking back, she sprinted across the house, up the stairs, and found herself standing outside her daughter's bedroom door. As always, it was shut tight. However, she was hesitant to open it in fear of what she may find inside. Then, looking behind her one last time, and hearing again nothing but dead silence, she twisted her daughter's knob, and pushed the door open. Stepping inside, she saw no one. Sarah was not in her room. "No," she whispered to herself realizing that Jack must have gotten to her. Finally, she had nowhere else to go. Gloria didn't know where to turn, or what she should do next. Then, spotting the phone in the corner of her daughter's bedroom, she realized she truly only had one option.

She had to call the police.

Running over to the phone, she picked up the receiver and dialed 911 without bothering to check and see if there was a dial tone. Seconds went by without hearing a single ring, and there was no sign of a dispatcher's voice ever coming online. Hanging up the phone, she tried once more. Again, however, she failed.

Jack had cut the phone lines.

Gloria began to panic, and she felt lost in a maze, trapped with no means of escape, and with nowhere to go. She had to get out somehow. Standing there in the middle of her daughter's room, alone, she listened around the house for any signs of movement and half expected to find her husband standing in the doorway, an evil grin attached to his face. Her knees grew weak in blatant fear, and Gloria just wanted to collapse to the floor, hopefully to awaken and find that this had been nothing more than an elaborate nightmare. Smartly, however, she knew that was impossible. This was real life. Her life was really being threatened, and her daughter was obviously in a heap of danger. Somehow, she had to help her.

Courageously, Gloria found every last ounce of bravery left in her weakened body, and exited Sarah's bedroom. Running back down the stairs, she found her car keys and raced for the front door. Expecting to feel her husbands hands wrap tightly around her neck just as she reached the door, she closed her eyes and prayed to make it outside. Opening the door, she sprinted into the splintering Florida heat and headed for her car. Still, her husband and her daughter were nowhere to be found. As panic continued to set in, Gloria struggled to fit the right key in the door lock. Finally, it slipped in and with one quick turn to the left, she listened as her doors unlocked, and jumped eagerly inside, locking them all again. Fidgeting with the ignition, Debra dropped her keys on the floorboard and looked around outside her car as she reached down for them to see if Jack was coming for her.

Again, no one could be seen.

Finally, she fit the key in the ignition and tried to crank her car. It wouldn't start. Her car had never given her any problems before. No matter how hard she ground away at the starter her car wasn't going to spring to life. "No," she screamed. "This can't be happening. Please God." Unfortunately, it was no use. Then, looking down at the hood of the car, she could see that it hadn't been shut all the way. She knew that Jack had somehow tampered with her engine, knowing that she would try to drive away. Everywhere Gloria went, led to a dead end. There truly didn't appear to be any means of escape. She was running for her life, and was desperately trying to locate her daughter. But in every case, Jack had beaten her to it, anticipated her every move, and outsmarted her all the same.

Looking around the driveway, she saw no one, and knew she couldn't just stay locked up in her car. Leaving the keys in the ignition, Gloria climbed out of the car, and after taking a deep breath; she leaned up against her door, closing her eyes as she tried to get a clear head. Then, she heard a noise coming from behind her. Startled, Gloria stood motionless, preparing herself for whatever was making the noise. As she turned around her eyes bulged in shock of what she was seeing.

It was Jack.

He was running at her, holding an ax high in the air above his head.

Then, as he reached her he yelled out a furious scream in anger. She could see the coldness in his eyes as they glazed over into a sensuous evil, and he swung the ax violently at her head. At the last minute, Gloria ducked and listened as the powerful ax slammed into the windshield, shattering it into thousands of pieces. Running for her life, Gloria ran away from her husband without looking back, and ran back inside the house. Climbing the stairs quickly, she could feel Jack's presence behind her, running after her at a quicker pace. She could hear him grunting behind her, and knew she had made a mistake by returning inside their home. Finally, as she realized he was gaining on her, she ran inside the closest door she could find, and locked it behind her. Turning on the light, she realized she was in the bathroom.

Her mouth dropped in shock as she saw the bloody scene. The mirror hanging above the sink had been smashed, and blood could be found splattered across the floor and in the sink itself. This was how Jack had hurt his hands she realized. Then, hearing a muffling sound from the bathtub, she rushed over, pulled the shower curtain aside, and found Sarah lying in the tub, her hands and feet were bound together, a piece of duck tape wrapped around her mouth and the back of her head. "Oh my God!" Debra shrieked not believing her eyes. "What has he done?" she asked aloud referring to Jack. Finally, without hesitation, she reached down and tried to untie her daughter. The knots were too tight, however, and they wouldn't budge.

That's when it happened.

Debra heard a smashing sound from the door, and stood up to face the man who had kicked the door down. Still holding the ax firmly in his hand, Jack walked inside and gazed directly into his wife's terrified eyes, ignoring the innocent, confused stare of his daughter. He could see his wife trembling with fear, almost as if she knew that the end was near. Then, raising the ax in the air, a smile crossed his face. It was an evil smile, and a smile that Gloria herself recognized as belonging to the one and only Curtis Rains.

"Why are you doing this Jack?" she asked as tears began to stream from her face. "I swear I didn't do anything wrong. Why?"

"Don't listen to her Jack," the voice returned. *"KILL HER."*

Then, seeing the grip on the ax tighten, Gloria knew he was about to strike. "Please Jack," she pleaded once more for her life. "Will you just think about what you are doing? You don't want to do this. You don't want to kill me. You love me. I know you do."

"How can I love someone like you," Jack retorted coldly. "I do want to kill you," he added without showing any signs of remorse. "I want you dead you lying bitch." Then, just as Jack prepared to bring the silvery blade of the ax cleanly down across his wife's head, she ran towards him and knocked him against the wall, throwing herself on him with all her might. Losing his balance, Jack tumbled to the floor and dropped the ax. Gloria desperately tried to grab the abandoned ax, but couldn't make it.

Within seconds Jack was back on his feet, and she felt his hand close in around her neck. Jack, his veins splitting outside his forehead, picked his wife up off the ground by her throat, and slammed her into the wall, her feet dangling in a fight to get oxygen. Looking in his eyes, Gloria could feel death arriving. There was no escaping the evil torment her husband wanted to thrust upon her. Gagging, she could feel herself growing weaker and weaker. Every time she made a noise however, Jack only tightened his grip, loving every weak bit of struggle Gloria was able to obtain.

Then, all of a sudden, he let go, and she collapsed to the floor, choking uncontrollably, and gagging as she desperately tried to revive herself. Then, a shadow appeared over her and she looked up from the broken glass on the bathroom floor to see Jack once again hovering over her, with the ax held high above his head. "Goodbye Gloria," Jack spoke up coldly. "It didn't have to be this way you know."

And then, with one hard, vicious swing downwards, it was all over.

As the force of the blow sent the pristine blade penetrating directly into Gloria's cranium, she died instantly. Freeing the blood-dripping blade from his wife's skull, Jack continued to slam it downwards crazily into his wife's motionless body. Over and over again, he continued to mercilessly pound away at Gloria's battered, and hacked up body, welcoming her blood as it splattered along the walls of the bathroom, and all over him.

Jack Reynolds felt the power of the kill. He felt the intensity of taking someone's life, and was enjoying every minute of it. Finally, without remorse of murdering his wife, he turned to face his eleven-year-old daughter, Sarah, whom was still held immobilized in the bottom of the tub. Sarah's whole body felt numb as the shock of what she had just witnessed sank in. Sarah had just witnessed her mother's death, and now, her father, a man whom she had trusted since birth, loomed over her in blood stained clothes, obviously about to turn on

Tinman

her next. *"You can't leave any witnesses,"* the voice ordered Jack. *"You have to kill her too."*

"I'm sorry sweetheart," were Jack's only words as he raised the ax in the air once more. Then, with one quick thrust downwards, it was all over. The mayhem had ended, and Jack's yearning for blood had finally come to a standstill, without allowing his daughter the right to fight for her life, as she was helplessly tied up. Nevertheless, dropping the ax where it lay, he walked out of the bathroom, leaving the lifeless corpses of his wife and daughter behind, without so much as looking back to regret anything that had happened.

Walking into the kitchen, Jack found the liquor cabinet, and took three quick shots of bourbon, when, the voice came once again. *"You did really well Jack. They both got what they deserved. But don't get too comfortable. There's still a lot that needs to be done Jack. There's still so much more that needs to be done."*

"Like what?" Jack demanded with a grunt. "What more can I do?"

"You have to cleanse your soul Jack," the voice continued laughing an evil laugh. *"Trust me, I'll show you the way."*

"I bet you will," Jack replied. "I bet you will." Then, taking one last shot, Jack returned upstairs to listen to the rest of the plan that would be laid upon him by the mysterious voice he found inside his head. Unfortunately, however, the plans and goals that Gloria and Sarah made would never become a reality.

For Gloria and Sarah Reynolds, darkness had closed in permanently.

* * *

Billy Saxton, Carey Haas, and Blaze Brookshaw sat on the hood of the full sized Chevrolet watching the sun begin to magnificently disappear behind a mass of clouds. Blaze was influenced greatly by the person he saw in Carey, and now understood more than ever why Billy felt so obligated in helping her and protecting her. He felt sorry for her in a way, having to grow up and live a life without her parents. He knew that only a very strong and unique individual would have been able to deal with such a dramatic and frightening experience and move forward. Blaze could only imagine the numerous sleepless nights she must have gone through, and the pain of seeing both her mother and her father's lifeless bodies lying right before her very own eyes. Needless to say, Blaze was thankful he hadn't gone through such an ordeal, and he found himself wondering exactly what he would do, or how he would react if such a situation of losing someone close to him ever presented itself. Hopefully, of course, that day would never come. But he was also aware that the unthinkable could happen at any given moment, you just had to be prepared, and hope that you lived your life to the fullest extent, not letting the slightest opportunity pass you by.

"Isn't this beautiful?" Carey whispered into Billy's ear, referring to the magnificent sunset, and pulling his arm further around her back, only smiling as he gave her shoulder a loving squeeze of affection.

"It sure is," Billy agreed as he looked away from the sky and into her eyes once again. "And so are you Miss Carey Haas. Your beauty goes beyond the most astonishing sunsets," he added with a grin, enjoying the perfect moment where he had the opportunity to compliment the girl in his arms. Then, changing the subject. "Isn't this weird though," he continued speaking of the two of them. "I mean, here were are, the two of us together ya know? And this is the first time we have spoken to one another, yet it feels like I've known you my whole life."

"Yeah, it's a little weird," Carey admitted. "But I'm glad you came into my life Billy. Honestly, I've never been happier than I am right now with you. I just hope it doesn't end. It almost seems like this is too good to be true."

"It's not going to end," Billy assured his angel, as he continued to cradle her in his arms. "I don't plan on going anywhere."

"Good."

Then, their romantic moment was interrupted as Blaze jumped off the hood of the truck and walked right in front of the two of them. "I'm sorry to interrupt you lovebirds," he spoke up with a smile, showing him that he was only teasing. "But I'm getting a little hungry, and I don't think I have to remind you that we are probably being looked for this very instant," he added looking directly at his best friend, referring to the authorities he was sure were out hunting for them.

"I probably should be getting home," Carey hated to admit. "I'll talk to my uncle tonight and see if I can't get him to drop this ridiculous charge against you." Then, the two of them jumped off the hood of Blaze's truck and Billy began walking Carey towards her uncle's Lincoln. Kissing passionately before she climbed inside, Carey found it extremely difficult to let go of Billy. She wanted to stay wrapped in his arms forever, and knowing that was impossible, she would've at least settled for the night. The way he looked at her, what she saw in his eyes, the way it felt when their lips collided with one another, and the way Billy held her. Everything was just so perfect, and she could tell that he cared about her. "I don't want to leave you."

"And I don't want you to go," Billy assured her. "But right now, it's probably best that you did. I promise I'll be thinking about you every second we are not together and I promise that you'll see me before you know it."

"But how am I supposed to get in touch with you?" Carey asked sadly.

"Let me worry about that," Billy smiled as he closed her car door once she was nestled comfortably behind the wheel. Then, leaning over, he kissed her one last time before she departed and returned home. "I'll miss you Carey, and I promise you'll hear from me very soon."

"I hope so," Carey replied with a smile as the Lincoln sprang to life and she began to back away from Billy, turn the car around, and head back down the windy road, zig zagging her way through the forest of huge pine trees before she exited the park and made her drive home. Finally, she stuck her hand out the window to wave by, and accepted the encouraging smile Billy gave her in return.

Then, turning to face Blaze. "That's her man," he commented, speaking of Carey. "That's the girl I've been waiting for my entire life brother. But for some reason, I can still feel that something is wrong."

"What!" Blaze exclaimed. "There is nothing wrong with that girl."

"No," Billy recalled his words, realizing they hadn't come out the way he had originally intended for them to. "I know there is nothing wrong with Carey. She's perfect. It's something else though man.

Something I can't quite put my finger on. But I think it has something to do with all of those visions I've been having. She's in trouble. And I don't even think she realizes she's in danger. But I can feel something out there. Like something is watching her ya know? And I know it's that Curtis Rains guy," he paused as the very mention of the killer's name sent a numbing pain of fear throughout his body. "I just don't know how, or what to do to stop it."

"Trust me," Blaze continued with the conversation. "When the time comes, you'll know what to do. Like me for instance," he paused to smile. "Right now, I know I'm hungry and I know that means I need to eat," he concluded still smiling brightly, proud of the way he had been able to come up with a good example.

Then, suddenly, and from out of nowhere, both of their moods changed dramatically.

Carey Haas, once again appeared right before their eyes. She came speeding across the old wooden bridge with her uncle Rick's Lincoln and began pounding on the horn. Obviously something was wrong. Then, slamming on the brakes right in front of him, she stuck her head awkwardly out the window and began yelling at them. "Run!" she screamed trying to warn them of what was about to happen. "Run away. Run away!" she continued to order, trying to get passed their confused expressions, and make them realize what she was talking about. "They're here!" she continued to scream. "They're coming for you guys."

"Who's here?" Billy stubbornly questioned instead of simply taking her advice to take off into the forest beyond. "Who's after us?"

Then, within seconds, his questions were answered. All of a sudden, four police cars poured into the open field between the two park forests and surrounded Blaze's truck. A silver Yukon, Billy knew to belong to Sheriff Gabriel Burnham followed and pulled up directly in front of him, blocking his view to Carey. Deputies from all sides climbed out and raised their weapons. "Get down!" they ordered both Blaze, and Billy. "Get down on the ground and spread your legs. Place your hands behind your head." Blaze wisely hit the deck, while Billy momentarily refused their orders, and stared ahead at the silver Yukon. He was caught, but why couldn't they see what a huge mistake they were about to make if he were taken into custody.

Billy was the only person who understood what was going on, and perhaps the only person that could help Carey Haas live. Then, watching with an angry expression, he saw two men pile out of the Yukon. One, was the Sheriff, and the other, was Carey's uncle, Rick Goodman. "Get down!" the deputies continued to holler in his direction.

Finally, Billy gave in and jumped to the ground. There would be no running from the law this time, and there certainly wasn't a huge ocean, or a blackened sky to escape into. For the moment, Billy decided to give himself up. Then, standing above him, he heard the elder Sheriff's voice speaking to him. "You just made things a lot harder on yourself son," he spoke up gruffly, his tone obviously telling Billy that he disapproved of his actions. "Did you honestly think you were going to get away? Why did you run from me that night son? That was a big mistake. I didn't want to arrest you that night because I could tell that you were a decent kid. But now," he paused as he leaned down and clamped hand cuffs tightly around Billy's wrists, disregarding the wincing in as the cuffs jerked away at his free skin. "Now I don't have a choice. I have to take you in. And your friend as well."

Without fighting, Billy let himself be hoisted up and pulled towards the nearest squad car, where Blaze was waiting for him, a smile still spread across his face, trying to make the best of this situation. Finally, when both were in the back seat of the squad car, did they speak. "Don't worry about it," Blaze confronted Billy. "We probably won't even get arrested man. They're not going to press charges against us for trying to help Carey. So what if you made a slight mockery of the Sheriff's Department. Carey said she was going to get her uncle to drop the charges remember?"

"Yeah," Billy answered angrily. "But what makes you so sure he's going to?"

Carey was forced to watch as Billy was lead to a patrol car and placed in the back seat. No. This couldn't happen. She wouldn't let it happen. She saw her uncle speaking casually with the Sheriff and immediately ran towards the two of them. Grabbing her uncle Rick's shoulder, she spun him around, interrupting his conversation, and making damn sure she captured his attention. "What in the hell are you doing?" she demanded angrily.

"Protecting you," Rick replied boldly, not believing the way Carey was behaving. "That son of a bitch in the back seat of that squad car broke in our house the other day, while you were sleeping and would have hurt you if your aunt and I hadn't of come home when we did."

"No!" Carey stood her ground. "He didn't go there to hurt anybody. Can't you see that he was only trying to help me? Are you honestly that blind Rick? You have to let him go. He is not a bad person."

"I'm sorry sweetheart," Rick replied trying to comfort the obviously upset girl in front of him. "I'm only doing this for you. You'll thank me later. Trust me."

"No!-." Carey was cut off before continuing.

"Carey listen," Sheriff Burnham cut in. "I don't know what that boy has been telling you. But I bet there are a lot of things he hasn't. We are doing this for your protection plain and simple. There are a lot of things intervening here that may seem confusing to you right now. But he knows a lot about your past, and-."

It was Carey who cut the Sheriff off. "No!" she screamed as tears began to weld in her eyes as she watched the squad car carrying Billy away into the sunset. "None of you know what you're talking about. Please Rick," she turned to face her uncle. "I care about him. Can't you see that. He's made me happier than I've ever been in my life. And I know he knows about my past, but that is something the two of you could never understand. But I understand him," Carey pleaded finally being overcome with tears. "And he understands me. Please," she pleaded once more. "Let him go. I need him."

"Nonsense!" Rick interjected, holding his ground. "I don't know where these feelings of yours are coming from, but I promise they'll go away with time. He's gotten into your head sweetheart. That's all."

"No," Carey continued to scream. "He's trying to help me. Why don't you want me to be happy?"

"That's it!" Rick put his foot down. "I will hear no more of this right now. Your aunt is sitting at home right now worried sick about you. Now I suggest you go on home and we'll talk more when I get

Tinman

there. I'm too busy to stand here and listen to you tell me the difference between right and wrong. Billy Saxton is going away, and nothing you say to me is going to make me change my mind. Is that clear?" Then, without even giving Carey the chance to reply, he spun away from her, shunning her from the rest of the conversation he was bound to finish with his childhood friend, Sheriff Burnham.

Completely shocked at the way her uncle had spoken to her, she knew his ignorance yielded him from seeing the truth in the matter. Sobbing heavily, Carey climbed back in her uncle's Lincoln and buried her head against the steering wheel.

Once again, her guardian angel had disappeared from her life.

And she wondered if she was ever going to get a chance to see Billy Saxton again.

Somehow, some way, she would make that happen. Without Billy, she knew life would turn back into the way it was before, and Curtis Rains would dictate her every move, blistering her mind with horrifying images of her parents dead bodies. She wanted Curtis Rains out of her life once and for all, and the only person that she felt could possibly make that happen, was Billy Saxton.

He was the only person that seemed to understand her.

He was the only person that could make her smile, and feel happy.

He was the only person that made her feel safe and secure.

And he, unfortunately, had been taken from her.

Then, looking up into the serene evening sky above, she whispered three words aloud; sure that Billy would be able to hear her, wherever he may be.

They were three sentimental words.

They were three words Carey hadn't spoken in a long time.

They were: "I love you."

* * *

Jack Reynolds paced himself steadily, vigorously sweeping the blood-drenched towel back and forth along the pale white wall of the hallway, directly in front of the open door of the bathroom, where the lifeless slaughtered bodies of his wife Gloria, and his loving, innocent daughter Sarah laid, their eyes still open, preserving the unmistakable onslaught of fear. Jack had re-entered the bathroom minutes ago, drenched a clean, sparkling white towel into their blood that outlined the entire blue tiled floor of the bathroom. Soon, all of the white had washed away, and the entire towel was laced with a bright red display of blood, dripping off at it's edges, and hiding the original color of the towel so well that it would have been difficult to picture the towel ever being white at all. Then, as he exited the bathroom, never once glancing at the corpses he had so viciously decided to decorate the bathroom floor with, he continued to follow the instructions given to him by the annoying voice in his head, and began working the towel consciously back and forth along the wall, writing letters so big, it practically covered the entire hallway, which was fifteen feet in length.

Jack, following the instructions given to him by the person that had forced him to raise his hand in anger and lash out furiously at his loved ones, didn't even realize what he was spelling. Until at last, he was told to stop, as his task had finally been complete. *"Now step back Jack."* The voice ordered, with an evil laugh lingering in the distance. *"Step back and observe the masterpiece you've created, using your victims own blood. And tell me Jack,"* the voice paused, letting Jack back up against the opposite wall and take in every last detail of what he had spelled with his families blood. Laughing to himself, realizing Jack hadn't the slightest clue as to what he had just done. Then, seeing the distraught expression on the prison guard's face as his mouth dropped low, and as his eyes opened with a stunned expression, he laughed his evil laugh one more time, and continued. *"Tell me Jack. Tell me what you see."*

Jack couldn't believe his eyes. Jack couldn't believe what his hands had drawn along the hallway wall. Never in his life, did he ever think he would have created such a thing. Completely stunned at what was written in his family's blood, he dropped to his knees, suddenly overcome by an astonishing dose of confusion, as he began to realize what had just happened. He didn't understand.

"Isn't it wonderful Jack!" the voice continued with a laugh, so staggeringly evil, Jack finally was able to recognize it. He had heard that laugh before. He was sure of it. But where?

The prison.
Curtis Rains.

He remembered Curtis Rains's laugh, echoing throughout the corridors of the prison at night, or whenever he had said something to Jack as he was walking away, fully knowing that he had gotten inside his head, and loving every minute of it. Then it hit him. Finally, Jack realized what had happened.

It was Curtis Rains.

The voice was Curtis, coming to him from the dead. It was Curtis who had forced him to attack his family like a wild animal running after it's prey at night, aggressively stripping them of their last breath, and it was Curtis who had filled his head with all of those eccentric lies about his loving wife Gloria, whom had unfairly paid the ultimate consequence through his very own hands.

No.

This couldn't be happening.

"Remember what I told you not too long ago, while I was locked in my cell Jack?" The voice, now known to belong to Curtis Rains continued. *"I told you how powerful I was, and I told you that I could reach anybody anytime I wanted. It was me Jack. The whole time, everything you've done since my death was because of me. I made you believe your wife was unfaithful. I made you kill your wife and your sweet, precious little girl. But what's ironic Jack, is the fact that you really didn't kill them at all. It was me who took their lives. I merely used you Jack. Funny isn't it?"* Curtis paused briefly. *"After all these years, I've finally been able to kill again. Didn't it feel great choking your wife and knowing that there was absolutely nothing that she could do about it? You were in control Jack. You had the power. But I was the man behind that power. I made it happen."*

"No!" Jack screamed not believing his ears. "No. This is isn't happening." For the first time, Jack was grieving. For the first time, he realized what he had done. Climbing to his feet, he rushed once again into the bathroom and viewed the motionless bodies of his wife, and beloved daughter. "Please God! No!" he continued in remorse, although knowing that it was too late. Picking them up, he cradled them in his arms and began rocking back and forth, forgetting the blood that poured all over his body, simply wishing that one of them would come back to life.

"I won Jack," Curtis continued coldly. *"Now, you'll always remember me as the man who made you kill your family."*

"No!" Jack screamed once again, gently laying his family back down on the bathroom floor. Then, climbing to his feet, he rushed into his bedroom, briefly viewing the bed in which he and his wife used to sleep, only to pass it by and head straight for his dresser drawers. Pulling the top drawer opened, he shuffled through his underwear, until his hands felt the handle of his .38 caliber revolver. Brining it out into the open, Jack stared at the sleek, silvery surface of the barrel, viewing his own pathetic reflection. Then, returning to the hallway, he once again viewed what he had spelled out across the hallway wall with his wife and daughter's blood.

Jack couldn't go on.

He couldn't live with himself after what he had done, and he knew that there was no way to take it back.

He had killed his family.

Now, it was time to do the right thing.

"I hope you go to hell you son of a bitch!" Jack spoke boldly, knowing that Curtis Rains heard every word he had said.

"I'm sure you do," Curtis replied. *"But I am the Devil, and I've created my own hell."*

Then, without saying another word, Jack held the gun to his temple, and pulled the trigger.

BANG!

It was over. Jack Reynolds was dead.

Taking his own life, perhaps trying to make the wrong things right. However, Gloria and Sarah's life could not be retrieved. Dead or alive, Jack knew the guilt would stay with him forever.

Jack's body lay slumped over in an awkward, obscure angle in the hallway. And before him, was the six-letter word he had spelled out with his family's blood. There, in the bright red color of actual blood, was a word so evil, whenever found, it would bring on an outburst of fear that would remain until the end of time. Blood dripped from the bottoms of the letters, giving it a description and an appearance as if it had come directly from hell.

It was one word. One powerful word.

In the blood of the Reynolds family, in big bright red letters, read:

TINMAN

Chapter 20

Destin, Florida.
One day later.

Billy Saxton sat patiently in the interrogation room with his fingers crossed as he waited for the Sheriff to come and join him, where he was sure they would engage in another unsuccessful conversation. He couldn't believe how big a deal Carey's uncle and the stubborn, aging Sheriff Burnham were making this out to be. Could they honestly believe that he was up to no good? Did they really think he was nothing more than a common criminal who had never done anything that contributed to society, and didn't belong walking down the streets as an average law abiding citizen, he asked himself silently? All of it was so irritating, and ludicrous. The most stressing of all, however, was the fact that they actually believed he had some hidden agenda, and wanted nothing more than to hurt Carey Haas.

Never in his life would he even consider doing such a thing.

And never once had that actually crossed his mind.

Bullshit is what it was, he thought to himself.

Nevertheless, Billy now faced being charged with breaking and entering, with possibly the threat of the state trying to show his intentions to hurt Carey Haas as she slept peacefully in her home. He knew that the chances of prosecuting him for the intent to commit bodily harm was knocking at the door. Without a good case, the jury probably wouldn't believe anything he said in court and quite possibly convict him. It appeared that everyone was blind to what was happening, except himself and the incomparable Carey Haas.

Nobody would understand what he had been going through, many would not even be willing to listen. Instead, he knew they would probably choose to convict him of a crime he did not commit, instead of hearing the truth, excepting the truth, and setting him free.

Billy still had time. He didn't think he had been charged with anything as of yet, and he knew that if he were, his mom would come forth with the bail money that would allow him back on the street. He was sure, however, his every move was being watched. He didn't care. He just had to get back into Carey's life. All in all, her life depended on it, and he couldn't let anything happen to her. Billy had promised Carey that he would be there for her through thick and then, and damn it, that's exactly what he intended to do.

Then, as he stretched his back along the outer edge of the hardwood chair, he came down and rested his elbows on the wooden table he was seated under, when the door finally opened, and the gruff figure of Sheriff Gabriel Burnham strolled in casually after telling the guard to remain outside. Closing the door behind him, Gabe approached Billy with a bold gaze that forced Billy to swallow the lump that had been building in his throat since he first set foot in the county jail. He hadn't been arrested before, and only knew what the justice system was like from the entertainment displayed on the television. So far, it was just as horrid and he found himself always looking over his shoulder, knowing that he very well didn't belong in such an environment. Then, the Sheriff sat directly opposite of him, and just gazed into his eyes, not saying anything at all, just drumming his knuckles along the surface of the table casually, as if perhaps waiting for Billy to speak first.

Finally, when it became obvious that Billy hadn't the slightest idea of what to say, Gabe broke their silence. "I can tell you don't belong in here son," the Sheriff began sternly, seeing righteousness in the boy's eyes in front of him. "But I have to tell you, some of the things you have done, were quite stupid, and you could have gotten your friend in a lot of trouble."

"I know sir," Billy cut in. "But nobody understands-." He was cut off.

"Nobody understands what son?" Sheriff Burnham groaned deeply. "You see, I tried to talk to you the other night at your mother's house, but you ran away from me. That was a big mistake

Billy. If you say you didn't do anything wrong, that was not the way to go about showing it. Now, there had to be a reason why you were running that night, and I want you to tell me why you did. I could be the only friend you have on the inside right now, but you have to help me. Carey's uncle, Rick, wants me to push this thing to the limit. And I'll be honest with you, until you give me some answers that's what I intend to do. I can make this very hard on you, or as easy as possible. But you have to come clean now Billy. You don't have a choice anymore, and you have nowhere else to run."

"I have to get out of here," Billy broke in. "Why can't any of you see that Carey's life is in danger, and that I didn't do anything wrong?"

"Why were you at the Goodman home then?" Gabe shot back drastically, slamming his fist into the table. "Why were you sneaking around inside their home and in Carey's room?" Then, pausing briefly to let his anger sink in on the boy in front of him he regained his composure before continuing. "I'll ask you again son. Why were you there?"

"Because I had to see her," Billy shot back, admitting the truth. Then, went on to describe the events that had happened to him ever since he had moved into the old Haas home with his mother, Debra. He watched as the Sheriff's eyebrows shot open with curiosity and disbelief as he explained all of the tormenting nightmares he had been forced to endure, along the with paralyzing, hallucinating visions that made him blackout and fall into a state of unconsciousness whenever he viewed the family picture of the Haas family. He desperately tried to explain to the Sheriff that he had actually witnessed the murder of the Haas family ten years ago, knew every detail of how they all were murdered, and how Carey had managed to escape. Billy was well aware that all of this would be rather difficult to take in and believe, but he had no other choice. The Sheriff wanted the truth, and Billy was giving it to him. There wasn't much more that he could do. Then, when he tried to force the Sheriff to believe that Curtis Rains was still alive, everything turned sour, and Gabriel cut him off.

"This is not a game son," Gabe shot back at the accused Billy Saxton. "In all my years as a law enforcement officer of this community I have never heard such a ridiculous story. That man is dead, his brains were fried not too long ago," he added, referring to the serial killer Curtis Rains. "And there is absolutely no way he can harm Carey."

"You're wrong!" Billy tried to plead his case.

"I don't know who you think you are, or what you are up to," Sheriff Burnham snapped as he climbed to his feet. "But I promise you that I'm going to get to the bottom of this. I'm a personal friend of the Goodman's and nothing will ever happen to them as long as I can help it. Now, maybe another night in jail will do you some good."

"Please," Billy pleaded. "Just listen to me. It's the truth."

"I think I've heard just about enough for tonight," the Sheriff wouldn't have anything to do with the lies he thought were pouring from the teenager's mouth. "Now your arraignment is set for 9:00 tomorrow morning, and I'll notify your mother and tell her where you are." Then, turning to leave the room, he turned one last time and faced Billy. "You should get yourself a lawyer son, I think your going to need one. And one more thing," he paused glaring dead into Billy's eyes. "I'm sorry we got off on the wrong foot son. I could have helped you out."

Billy closed his eyes and listened as the door slammed shut behind the Sheriff, and was locked, barricading him inside the small interrogation room. As silence fell over him, he replayed the conversation over and over again that had just taken place between the Sheriff and himself. He had done exactly what was expected of him. He had told the truth. But just as he thought would happen, no one was willing to listen. He was branded a liar, and knew that no matter who he talked to, or no matter how hard he tried to convince someone that his story was true, no one was going to believe him. Then again, how could he blame them, he asked himself. He knew that if he were in their shoes, he probably would have a hard time giving his own story credibility. However, he would have at least been fair. He would have at least checked it out, instead of simply dismissing it. After all, a life stood in the balance, and to Billy, it was a life well worth more than his own.

Then, he heard the latch click from the other side of the door, and soon, it burst open once again. Two guards stepped inside preparing to escort him back to his holding cell. Billy, deciding not to put up a fight he was sure to lose, allowed himself to be dragged to his feet, shackled at the wrists and ankles, and then led slowly out of the interrogating room. Within minutes, he was amongst the other criminals who were being held at the county jail. Some waiting to be brought up on charges, others preparing to go to court, or sent back to a nearby prison facility. As Billy was allowed a cell all to himself, he sprawled out uncomfortably along the small cot provided for him to sleep on, covered his head with the single pillow found at the top of the stretcher, and blocked out all of the disturbing sounds coming from around the interior walls of the county jail. Closing his eyes, he desperately tried to convince his body to get some rest, knowing that when he opened his eyes it would be a new day.

And praying, that when daylight came, things would be different.

There had to be a way out of this. There had to be a way to convince people, Rick Goodman and Sheriff Burnham especially, that his story was true. There had to be a way to clear his name, at the same time, convincing people that Carey Haas's life was in danger.

There was definitely an unseen, unspeakable evil out there, roaming about in the darkness, watching and waiting for the right time to lash out from the night and destroy the weak and innocent. However, only Billy Saxton himself, and Carey Haas could feel it's presence.

Around every corner, they could feel the eyes of the demon.

* * *

Carey Haas stormed throughout her aunt and uncle's home, angrily awaiting their arrival. She was fed up with her uncle's stubborness, and wanted it all to end. Another confrontation with her uncle ended unpleasantly. The way Billy and Blaze had been tracked down outraged Carey. You would have thought they committed murder, or kidnapped a child, or at least something drastic. The charge of breaking and entering alone, just didn't appear to justify the way they were taken into custody.

Her uncle Rick simply had to stop treating her like some small, defensless child that couldn't tell the difference between right and wrong. She appreciated everything her uncle had done for her since her parents death. However, Carey knew that was in the past, and now more than ever, she wanted to start living for the future. She wanted to put the terrorizing images of her parents' lifeless blood-spattered bodies to rest once and for all and rid her conscious of the alarming memory of the Tinman forever.

Carey would be the first to admit it in realizing that she was a very small child when she had been subdued, or forced into listening to her parents being slaughtered as they fought with all their might to save themselves from the clouded firgure, whom she had come to know as Curtis Rains. He had maliciously ripped away at their flesh until nothing but their own blood could be seen scurrying across their skin, and draining fluently across the hardwood floor. And being at such a young age, her brain had in some way been forced to mature at a rapid pace as it tried to hide the horrifying images of her parents in the back of her head. She had hoped that they would never resurface, and she could go on living a normal and healthy life. Unfortunately, that never happened, and everyday, Carey was forced to remember and live the events of the past over and over again as countless sleepless nights came her way. Her uncle Rick and Aunt Carol knew what she had been going through, and had been there for her whenever she needed them. Always there to comfort her, to listen to her problems, and protect her from the evil she knew the world brought to life.

But Billy Saxton was an exception.

Why couldn't her uncle see that, she adamantly questioned herself?

She didn't need to be protected from Billy. In fact, she needed Billy for protection. Her entire life, Carey had been longing, perhaps yearning for someone as special as Billy to enter her life and enable her to live again. He seemed to create and bring out feelings that she never knew were there. He was bringing out the best in her, teaching her to trust again, but most importantly, teaching her how to love. And there was simply no way she was going to let her uncle take that away from her. She needed Billy Saxton in her life. She hadn't realized it until a couple of days ago, but there was a connection that could be felt between the two of them, a twindling emotion so strong, it seemed to instantly combine their hearts and connect their immortal souls as one, pushing them deep into the chambers of love, while at the same time, fighting their way from the devastating plight of evil that seemed to cloud their very lives. If there really was such thing as a guardian angel, Carey Haas was quite certain she had stumbled across her miraculous savior in Billy Saxton.

Then, two headlights darted into the driveway and filled the interior walls of the living room with a brief display of shadows as they came filtering weakly in through the blinds. Running to the window, Carey peered outside and saw her aunt Carol climbing out of the black Lincoln she had returned home about an hour ago. Carol had gone to run a quick errand, and as promised, returned home promptly. Unfortunately, her uncle had yet to return home, and Carey figured he was still at the Sheriff's department, doing everything in his power to convince Sheriff Burnham to keep Billy locked up as long as possible. Then, her thoughts were interrupted as the front door opened and her aunt stepped inside.

"I swear," Carol immediately began speaking to Carey. "The sun has been down for over an hour now and it's still blistering hot outside. I almost can't bare this heat. Is it hard to breathe for you?" she asked. Then, seeing that Carey was not even attempting to answer her, she continued casually, trying to break the tension between them. "I guess that's Florida for you though. Say, has your uncle been home yet?"

Carey shook her head. "Nope," she responded plainly, disgust obviously heard in her tone.

"Carey come on now," Carol tried to comfort her. "Are you really that upset with Rick for doing what he did? He was only trying to protect you. He wasn't trying to hurt you or anything like that. You know as well as I do that he would never do such a thing. He loves you to death, and only wants the best for you."

"Then why is he doing this?" Carey shot back. "Nobody around here will listen to me. Billy Saxton does not want to harm me in any way. The only reason he broke inside our home that day was because he needed to see me."

"Listen to yourself," Carol came over and sat next to her neice on the sofa. "You don't even know that boy. You don't know what he's capable of, or what he has up his sleeve Carey. You shouldn't just instantly trust people like that, because when you do, that's when you get stabbed in the back. Trust me."

"You see," Carey darted hostilely. "That's exactly what I'm talking about. You just dismissed everything I've said without taking

Jason Glover

anything into consideration. Why is it so hard for you or Uncle Rick to understand this? I care about Billy-."

"You don't even know him," Carol broke in, silencing Carey by cutting her words short. "Now you said the only reason he broke in here that day was because he needed to see you right?" Carey nodded. "And why do you think that is?"

"Because I'm in danger," Carey answered truthfully.

"Danger?" Carol questioned groing concerned at the tone Carey's voice had drifted into. "In danger of what?"

"Curtis Rains," Carey blurted out bravely. "I know this is going to sound crazy Aunt Carol. Just try to believe me, please." Carey paused for a moment to let her aunt relax just a bit, enabling her to take in everything that was about to be exploited. Carey knew once again she would be wasting her precious breath. However, her Aunt Carol had always been more open, and optimistic than the stubborn, iron-clad headed person she referred to as her uncle Rick, and if anyone would be able to take her story into consideration, and perhaps force her uncle to see it for what it really was, it would be Carol. Nevertheless, it was well worth a shot, and perhaps Carey's only hope. "He's not dead," Carey finally continued. "I know that's hard to believe, but I swear it's the truth. Curtis Rains did not die in that electric chair. His physical body may be gone forever, but his spirit remained for some reason. And I can see him in my sleep, and I can feel him watching me every second. And I know, I just know that,-." Carey let her words drown away into silence, feeling the hairs on the back of her neck stand tall as she was about to finish her statement.

"What?" Carol pressed forward, finding herself intrigued. "You just know what?"

"That's he's coming for me," Carey blurted out in fear. "I know Curtis Rains is coming for me, and that's why Billy was here that day. You see, he knows it too, and he was coming to warn me. That's all he was doing. He wants to help me and nothing more. Yet, Rick is trying to force people into believing that he's some kind of monster who was trying to hurt me. Believe me, Billy wouldn't do that."

"Wait a minute," Carol wanted to back up a bit. "You said that he knows Curtis Rains was coming for you?" Carey nodded in agreement. "Well," Carol continued, choosing her words carefully, not wanting to sound as if she were mocking the teenager she had practically raised as her own. "Haven't you ever asked yourself how he could possibly know such a thing?"

"Yes," Carey admitted. "But don't you see. He lives in that house. He sleeps in my old room. And he found my old doll in the wall of the cellar, exactly where I had hidden it that night when my parents were killed. I was trying to protect Kat from Curtis Rains knowing that there was nothing I could do for my parents. But I knew I could save my doll. And ever since he and his mother moved into that house, he's been having the same nightmares as I, and he could see me in them. He's been having blackouts, and practically reliving the events that happened ten years ago. He knows everything that happened, every detail, almost as if he himself had been there witnessing the entire thing," she paused, struggling a bit to talk about her parents death. "And he could also see Curtis Rains in his visions Aunt Carol. He knows that he's still out there somewhere, and that he's coming for me."

Carol was speechless. She didn't know how she should respond to such a story. It had been extremely difficult to believe or confide in. But Carey had just spoke of her parents death, and Carol knew that must have been difficult enough. She had done it trying to convince her that everything she had said was the truth. Carey truly believed that Curtis Rains was somehow coming for her. Moreover, however, Carey also believed that Billy Saxton was not in any way a bad person, and did not belong in jail. Was it possible, Carol wondered? Could they have gotten the wrong imprerssion of Billy, and jumped to an unreasonable conclusion?

"Honey," Carol spoke up taking Carey under her wing and pulling her close to give her a warm embrace. "I'm sorry. I-I really just don't know what to say to that. Have you tried to talking to your uncle about this?"

Carey nodded. "Yes, but he refuses to listen to me. He treats me like I'm still ten years old. He never lets me finish, and even when he appears to be listening, I know he's not. It's like my words go in one ear, and then directly out the other. And I know he won't believe me. I just know it. But you have to aunt Carol. I swear it's the truth, and if my parents were still around, they would know it too. As a matter of fact, I think they are the ones that brought Billy into my life, knowing that I was in danger. I think they sent someone to care for me, and protect me. You have to believe me," Carey paused momentarily. "When I look into Billy's eyes, it's like I'm gazing into the eyes of an angel. He's everything I've ever wanted, and I have never ever felt this way about anyone before. I've never let anyone get close to me, and as soon as I find someone special, Rick is trying to take him away from me, and destroy my only chance to be happy. Well I'm sorry, I simply can't let that happen. I need him aunt Carol. I need Billy."

"All right sweetheart," Carol spoke gently, feeling an outburst of tears coming on, but not wanting her deceased sister's daughter to see her weep, or whimper like that of a toddler. However, she could sense that Carey really cared about Billy, and could feel that she truly needed and wanted him in her life. And because of her husband, and her own stubborness, Billy was now locked up behind bars. Feeling a tremendous amount of guilt and sorrow, it was beginning to feel like a sob was inevitable. Nevertheless, she held her ground, and kept her guard up, forcing the tears to remain hidden inside. "It's going to be all right Carey. I promise."

"But do you believe me?" Carey asked firmly, gazing directly into the heart of her aunt's eyes. "I need to know," Carey pressed forward, obviously not willing to leave the subject alone until she got an answer. "Do you believe me Aunt Carol?"

Carol found her mouth laying open, yet no words seemed to escape from within it's wet chambers. It just hung low, as if not permitting her talk, or Carol wondered if maybe she just didn't know how to answer. Then, finally, as if a little dense light sprang to life inside her head, she spoke using a tone filled with love, compassion, and honesty. Most importantly, however, a smile was vacated across her once blank expression, giving Carey a confident feeling that everything was going to be all right.

"Yes," Carol finally answered calmly, returning the stare into her neice's eyes. "Yes, I believe you."

* * *

"What do you mean you can't keep him locked up?" Rick angrily asked his long time friend as the two of them talked earnestly amongst themselves in Gabriel Burnham's office. "You mean to tell me we went through all of this trouble to track this kid down, and you may not be able to hold him longer than twenty four hours? That's absurd Gabe, and you damn well know it."

"Maybe," the Sheriff spoke up. "But I also know this. That kid I have locked up in a tiny cell has no priors. I mean he has absolutely nothing on his record. It's as clean as a baby's bottom when a mother gets done cleansing it Rick. And in doing a background check on Billy Saxton, you know what I turned up?" Rick shook his head. "Nothing. Not a goddamn thing. He was a straight A student up in Marietta, Georgia, where he lived until moving down here and into that home your niece used to live in. His father died of a stroke a few years ago, but that appeared to be the only thing of any meaning on any of the documents I pulled up on this kid."

"So what are you saying?" Rick stormed, lashing out at the authority figure in front of him. "Are you saying that you don't think that little punk deserves to be locked up?"

"I don't know right now," Gabe shot back, forcing Rick to realize that he was in charge of the situation. "I don't know what I believe. I do know this, however. You are overreacting to this whole situation."

"What!" Rick exclaimed. "That son of a bitch broke into my home, and tried to attack my niece, and then comes up with some ridiculous story about that Curtis Rains guy, telling us that he's still alive. How could I possibly be overreacting? Damn it Gabe, when it comes to the safety of Carey, I will do everything possible to protect her."

"I understand that," Sheriff Burnham continued. "But how can you be so sure that he was going to hurt her? Have you actually ever tried talking to him," he paused referring to the caged Billy Saxton. Rick only shook his head. "Well I have, and I'll tell you something. He really does seem like a pretty nice kid, almost incapable of doing any criminal acts or random outbursts of violence. I think he's a pretty decent kid, who for some reason or another, cares a lot for Carey. And I also think that knowledge scares the piss out of you, making you instantly jump to the conclusion that there's something wrong with him, or that he's a bad person. Well Rick? What if he's not? What if we are wrong about this kid and we lock him up for nothing? Would you be able to live with that? Would be able to live without the respect of your niece Carey as well, cause you know damn good and well that she doesn't want anything to happen to that boy. She cares for him too. And that my friend is obvious."

"I tell you what," Rick began in a frustrated tone. "I can live with anything, or any outcome. Whether it's right or wrong. Now," he paused, trying to subdue the anger he felt deep inside. "Why don't you quit trying to change my mind and just do your job? This kid broke the law and I want him prosecuted for it. All right? Do you think you can do that Gabe?" Rick paused mockingly, climbing to his feet as he prepared to return home. "Do you think that you can just do your damn job?"

"I already have," Gabriel answered purposely smiling to anger his friend even more, although now they didn't appear to be close cronies at all, but worst enemies on opposite sides of the law, which in itself was always a dangerous place to be. "I have taken the suspect into custody and he is pending his arraignment, which is scheduled for tomorrow morning. It's out of my hands now, unless he escapes, which isn't going to happen, and has fallen into the hands of the DA's office."

Then, without saying a word, Rick turned to leave the Sheriff alone in his office, frowning, a bit choleric and incensed at the way his conversation had just gone. He was tired, it had been a long day, and right now wanted nothing more than to relax in a hot bath, and then fall asleep in his king-size bed with his adorable wife lying right next to him. Then, as he turned to knob, the Sheriff called him back.

"Rick," he began calmly, rising to his feet. "I'm sorry man, but I have to ask you to give this some serious thought. You know I care about you and your family a great deal, and would never let anything bad happen to any one of you if given the chance. But I have also learned to trust and even depend on my instincts in all my years as a law enforcement official, and I am seldom wrong when acting on my instincts. Yes, at first when you called me, I felt that maybe something was wrong. But now, it's different. Billy Saxton is a good kid. I can feel it. I tried every trick in the book to try and make him scared enough to talk to me and admit that he had done something wrong. And nothing."

"Why are you saying this?" Rick interrupted.

"Because I think we're making a mistake," Gabe admitted. "I think we're making a huge mistake, and the safety of Carey may depend on what actions we take. Just think about this Rick all right? That's all I ask." He paused briefly to sip at his coffee. "Trust me friend. You don't want to live a life with any regrets. Especially when they just might involve someone you love."

As Rick walked out of the Sheriff's department and signaled for a taxi to take him home, his mind began pondering over his friend's last words over and over again. For the first time since learning of Billy Saxton's unscheduled appearance at their beloved home, Rick Goodman was seeing a different picture. It was a picture of his niece, Carey, smiling because she had someone in her life that made her happy. However, there was also a picture of her frowning, because he had heartlessly decided to pursue charges against him.

Rick was confused. He didn't know what to do, and really had nowhere to turn.

Maybe, however, it was time to follow and trust his instincts.

After all, a little faith could last a lifetime.

* * *

Meanwhile, back in Birmingham, Alabama.

Jamie Walker found herself relaxing peacefully in a warm body of water, her stark naked body sunken into the large bowl shaped bathtub, completely immersed and covered in a country scented froth, the foam hiding her bare flesh from the naked eye. She could smell the aroma of beef stew swiftly generating itself into the bedroom as Travis McKinley worked adamantly in the kitchen, slaving himself over the stovetop trying to prepare the two of them a nice, hearty meal. Closing her eyes, she felt the perspiration form across her face drizzle down, disappearing into the bathtub, as the immense steam and heat from the water filled the bathroom and fogged the long, full wall size mirror.

She had fought hard to forget the events that had happened the other day, where she had so suddenly been routed with a powerful sickness, which could not be explained. Her body had somehow been preempted into a deathly illness, which for a minute, Jamie had thought that her life was about to end. Instead, it had fallen into a minor coma as her body was just not prepared and didn't stand a chance to fight through the unbearable pain the wicked sickness had brought on. Her stomach twisted into knots, and her body temperature had flown up in a fit of anger. Then, finally, when Jamie had awoken, she found herself back in the hospital, the sickness long gone, almost as if it had never been there at all. Her doctor repeatedly assured both Travis and herself that she was not sick, and showed no signs of a weakened immune system.

Then, when she returned home, she forced her weakened brain to blackout all of the terrible events that she had succumbed to ever since Curtis Rains perished from electrocution as the state of Florida finally carried out its death penalty against the inhuman psychopath. If Jamie was ever going to get through this, she knew she mustn't allow herself to fall victim to the fatal memories of the criminal she had once been in love with. She tried to convince herself that Travis was right, that nothing that had happened up to date had been real, and nothing more than a figment of her imagination. She wanted to believe that perhaps she felt guilty for not trying to help Curtis back when the two of them had been involved with one another, and maybe that had been the reason her mind decided to play these tricks on her. Once dead, there was no coming back. But for some reason, she found it hard to force herself to believe that.

It all seemed too real to be a figment of her imagination. Jamie could have sworn to have actually seen the notorious Tinman. She could feel his presence swarming around her, hovering all around her spacious environment, watching her every move, and patiently waiting until she was most vulnerable to let himself known. She felt that he was coming for her, wanting nothing more than to ruin her life before the inevitable punishment of death was laid upon her for the way she had treated him. Curtis wanted to extinguish her flame, take her away from this earth, continue to bruise her soul even in the aftermath of her death, and carry over into the afterlife.

No.

It wasn't real. It simply couldn't be.

Nevertheless, Jamie couldn't dismiss it. Even at this very moment, she could feel the eyes of the man she despised watching over her, almost feel his hot breath working its way over the back of her neck, stifling the tiny hairs into thin air. Then, taking a deep breath, Jamie opened her eyes as fear once again began to sink in. Looking around the steamy bathroom, she wished she hadn't decided to close the door, almost forcing her to feel like she was trapped inside her own bathroom with no chance of escape if the evil man decided to make his presence known once again.

Then, she heard something from outside the bathroom. It was a shuffling sound, almost like someone was scampering across the bedroom floor on the other side of the door, and making their way towards the bathroom. Then, there came a slight tapping sound on the door, and Jamie found herself sitting upright in the bathtub, water flushed over the side of the indestructible material and splattered along the black and white checkered tile floor. Saying nothing, she prayed nothing contrite was about to happen. Then, closing her eyes, she prayed to the heavens above to protect her from whatever evil wanted to attach itself to her shadowy anima. A lump formed in her throat, but Jamie refused to swallow, as she hesitantly waited to see what would transpire next.

Then, the tapping came again.

Still, Jamie remained silent, as if trying to hide her presence from whoever was on the other side of the door. Save for the hollow tapping sound, nothing but dead silence filled the room.

"Jamie!" A voice suddenly followed the third tapping sound. "Jamie, are you all right sweetheart?" The voice asked, and immediately Jamie accredited it to belonging to the man she loved dearly in Travis McKinley. Wanting to kick herself in the head for being so stubborn, Jamie felt speechless. She should have known it was Travis simply coming in to check on her as he took a quick break from his cooking. Instead, however, she had acted childish, and feared the worse possible scenario. Once again, it had seemed her mind wanted to play tricks on her, and she felt that the tapping was none other than Curtis Rains's spirit coming for her once again. Then, realizing she hadn't responded to her soul mate, she heard Travis's muffled voice coming once again from the other side of the door. "Jamie?" he questioned with a concerned tone. "Honey? Are you doing all right in there?"

"Yes," Jamie finally blurted after the lump died away in her dry throat. "Sorry, I didn't hear you. I was washing my hair," she purposely gerrymandered, not wanting to consequently start an argument between the two of them if she let the truth be known. Jamie smartly realized that if she shared her honest beliefs as to whom she actually thought was at the door, she sknew her loved one would squash her beliefs that Curtis Rains was still alive in spirit. "I'll be out in a few minutes. I promise."

"Are you feeling any better," Travis asked compassionately, and smiled as he heard Jamie's cheerful voice on the other end assuring him that there was nothing to worry about and that she felt fine. "Well good. But don't stay in there too long, or I'll have to come in after you," he added with a loving laugh. "Dinner is about ready though, and I'm not about to try and keep it warm for you," he concluded jokingly.

"I won't be long," Jamie reassured Travis. Then, listened intently as she heard his footsteps drown away and exit the bedroom. She could feel his presence gone, and knew that she was the only person, or only living being around the vicinity.

Nevertheless, she still didn't feel alone.

Someone else was there.

"Travis," she muttered in a voice incapable of assimilation. "Are you there?" she continued to question, although knowing that he had returned promptly to the kitchen to check on the comestibles he had been trying to prepare for the two of them. Then, suddenly, even without hearing a tapping sound coming from the door, Jamie once again began to feel a seizing terror that gripped the beating of her heart, forcing it to speed up. "Please God," she prayed in panic. "Don't let this happen again," she added remembering what had happened earlier that day. "Please God!"

Unfortunately, the uneasy feeling of her not being alone persisted, and only grew stronger as each second seemed to take minutes to pass. That was it. Jamie couldn't take it anymore. She had to get out of the bathroom and be around the comforting arms of the man she hoped to marry one glorious day. Gripping the sides of the bathtub, Jamie pulled herself out of the water, and bore her naked body to the humid, steam filled bathroom. Grabbing a towel, she began to wipe away the water that had smoothed her skin, and gazed into the bathroom mirror. She couldn't see a thing, as the foggy piece of glass denied her eyes any means of penetration.

Turning away from the mirror, she completely dried off and pulled her cherry red cottony bathrobe around her firm, once relaxed form. She quickly made plans to exit the bathroom and put the uneasy feeling of being watched to rest. Grabbing a comb, she turned around and prepared to brush through her tangled brown hair.

Upon turning around, however, she couldn't believe what her eyes fell upon.

The mirror that had once been completely covered in steam wasn't any longer. It had been tampered with.

No! Closing her eyes harshly, Jamie tried to squint away what she thought she had seen in the mirror. "No!" she told herself aloud. Her mind had to be playing tricks on her again. It just had to be. It was all her imagination and nothing more. Finally, feeling her whole body began to tremble in fear, she opened her eyes, praying that what had been written in the steamed mirror would be gone, assuring her that it had never been there at all. Finally, after mustering enough strength, Jamie Walker reopened her eyes.

It remained.

There, on the fogged glass mirror, was a single word:

TINMAN

But who could have written it, she frantically asked herself? She had undoubtedly been the only person in the bathroom. She was sure of it. Nevertheless, her eyes told no lie, and the word was there. Needless to say, her mind had not played any tricks on her, and she most certainly was not going crazy.

It had to be him.

Jamie knew it had to be Curtis Rains.

He had come for her once again.

Then, holding back the plight of fear that was about to sink in once again, Jamie lashed out of the bathroom leaving the disturbing word alone on the bathroom mirror, hoping to never see it again. Slamming the door behind her, Jamie fled from the bathroom, her mind twirling in a furious maze of death and destruction.

Jamie Walker felt helpless.

Jamie Walker felt that there was no escape from whatever evil was after her, and could feel the Tinman's hand resting firmly on her shoulder.

Most importantly, however, Jamie Walker felt her life slowly ending.

* * *

The boy ate silently, his eyes never leaving his plate, as he worked hard to get through his meal without his parents barreling down on him. He didn't want to give them any incentive to lash out at him with stinging words that sunk into his flesh and embedded themselves in his soul. He was nine years old, always trying to do his best to please his two parents. However, no matter how hard he tried, or what he did, it was never enough. He could never please them, and had in some way grown used to the emotional abuse they laid upon him day in and day out, hollering at him for not doing something, yelling right in his face as they call him names his youngster years weren't supposed to be subjected to. Nevertheless, the pain of their words still hurt, and he knew that they would never go away.

Then, there was the physical abuse.

His body was bruised all around, and he couldn't count the number of times he had to run and hide, scared that his father's hand was going to kill him. Blood excessively drained from his body, and yet, there was absolutely nothing that he could do about it. Everyday, he had to come home.

There was simply nowhere else to go.

Everyday, the boy had to come home to the abuse, and forced to except the maltreatment.

It was mealtime again, however, and so far, the boy had been able to finish over half his plate without seeming to cause a problem. He listened to his parents talking amongst themselves, not even paying him any attention at all, as he was not fully listening to just exactly what was being said between the two of them as well. He was concentrating hard, not necessarily on consuming his meal, but just trying to get through it without disturbing his parents so that he could quickly disappear into his bedroom for the remainder of the evening, safe from any harm.

Then, just as he was about to scarf down the last couple of bites, he took time out to sip his tall glass of sweetened iced tea. Gulping down a large amount of the tasty beverage, the boy instinctively went to return it to the coaster from which it had sat just moments ago. Losing his concentration momentarily, thinking that nothing was going to go wrong, he took his eyes off his glass, and he missed the table all together.

The glass fell quickly to the hardwood floor and shattered into hundreds of pieces. Closing his eyes, the boy tried to form the barrier, as he knew an onslaught was not too far behind. It was only a matter of time before his parents unleashed their wrath upon him.

Then, it happened.

"You little shit," he heard his mother's voice curse him. "Look what you've done now." Then, he heard his father remove himself from behind his chair and walk towards him. Grabbing him by the neck, the boy's father jerked him harshly from his chair and carried him into the next room. It was the one room the boy feared more than anything in the world. It was also the one room, where the majority of the bad things seemed to happen. Never once had he willingly gone into the room, and every time, his body would come out with pain and sorrow. It was the room his father always brought him to when he had been a bad boy. And once again, he knew he had been a bad boy.

Saying nothing, the boy allowed his father to drag him into the room. Refusing to open his eyes, the boy felt the leather straps grasp his wrist and ankles as his father sprawled him across the hardwood surface. The boy was strapped to the floor, preparing to accept the powerful blows he knew he was about to be forced to endure.

As the first rap slammed into his flesh, however, he only squinted in pain, and held his breath, knowing that if he screamed, it would only make his father hit him harder. Praying silently, the boy hoped it would all end as soon as possible.

As another blow pounded away at his back, however, the boy let a tear leave his eye, and slip down the side of his cheek. He hated his life, and wished for someone or something to come and deliver him from this unearthly evil.

But for some reason, help never came.

Was it because he truly was a bad boy?

The boy didn't know.

Again, as the boy lay there, another tear escaped from his eyes, and joined the other one along the hardwood floor. Soon, the boy found himself lying in a puddle of his own tears.

Nevertheless, no scream came from the boy's mouth.

* * *

The creature couldn't believe it.

Even though he had finally left the world that had caused him so much pain, the memories of his parents still lingered about in his mind. Their extensive abuse simply could not be forgotten. Even upon remembering that he had taken their lives in the end, getting revenge for his childhood, the fact that he had murdered his own parents was not enough to kill the pain.

The creature might have won eternal life, but the memory of his parents and all of the cruel things they had done to him remained as well. Just as a child, there was no escaping them.

However, this only enraged the creature even more.

He could feel another outburst of anger coming on, and knew that it would have to be subdued as soon as possible. For the first time since enjoying the freedom death seemed to bring along, the creature was growing impatient. He had toyed with Jack Reynolds's and his family. But it would soon be time to strike again.

Chapter 21

 Carey Haas was once again walking around the empty confinements of the oceanfront home that she used to reside in with her beloved parents. Only, just as before, things were different. The walls were unadorned, completely repainted in a brisk white color, without any pictures outlining the walls to give the interior of the home a more unpretentious mien. No chattels could be found anywhere inside the enormous, spacious home, and the back patio had been refinished, it's glossy coat shining ever so brightly in the Florida sun.
 Everything was gone.
 Even the blood stains she recalled being there, had long since been removed, almost hiding the fact that her innocent parents had been slain to death in this very home some ten years ago. As Carey once again slowly crept through her old home it seemed almost impossible that such a massacre could have ever taken place in what appeared to be a rather enchanting home. It was truly a magnificent and beautiful abode, where a family could live in peace and harmony throughout the remaining years of their life, with the impeccable ocean not more than a few yards away.
 To Carey, however, this home would never be beautiful again.
 It would always stand for and be remembered as the place where an evil man stormed in one night, and on a bloody rampage, tormented and sliced her parents to death. And also where Carey herself had barely managed to escape the man's death grip, running her small body into the ocean where it had been overcome and

trampled by the waves, which at the time, had seemed so huge to her young years.

Finding herself walking through the kitchen, Carey could almost picture her mother and father chatting amongst themselves as she sat quietly opposite of them at the dinner table, talking to her revered porcelain doll, Kat. It wasn't long after the cherished memories of the good times she was fortunate enough to have been able to share with her family appeared, when the haunting visions of her past would prevail, quickly preceding the humane ones. Then, her smile would quickly fade into freight, and the world would continue to feel as if it were coming crashing down directly upon her lost soul, misplacing her into a world without compassion, decency, mercy, and filled with a devilish darkness, which her eyes would not be permitted to penetrate. This was the world of the Tinman. This world belonged to the devil himself, created by someone so evil, his very being couldn't be controlled, and his actions unexplainable. It appeared to be a battle between good and evil. And unfortunately, it appeared to be a battle she was destined to lose.

Then, as Carey exited the kitchen and made her way through the family room, she noticed the staircase. Walking to the front of the massive wooden stairs, she peered upwards, her eyes incapable of visualizing what might lie beyond the pinnacle, or uppermost step. She stretched her hearing as far as allowed, and couldn't hear a sound coming from above. Surely, she thought the upstairs portion of her nightmarish home would be as empty and lonely as the bottom half. Yet, gripping the handrail tightly with her left hand, Carey took her first step, and began heading to the top of the staircase.

She took each step one by one, her eyes darting off sideways scared she might lose her balance and tumble to the floor below, shattering her weakened bones with ease, and trapping her in a bitter, painful state of immobilization, where no one would be able to hear her cries for help. Her every breath seemed to inhale, and exhale with ease, and she listened intensely for any signs of life coming from above. However, there was nothing. Only silence. Nevertheless, Carey continued to climb the stairs, convinced that there was something she was missing.

Then, she reached the top. Stepping away from the stairs, she gazed down the long, straight hallway. The walls were as bare as the ones seen below, and every bedroom she knew would be empty. Slowly, Carey crept down the hall, peering into each room as she passed them, never taking the time to enter, just enough time for one quick glance, until she reached the spot she knew her conscious must have been dragging her to all along. Finally, her footsteps came to a halt as she reached her destination.

Carey now stood directly outside her old bedroom.

And oddly, her door was the only one that was closed.

Placing her hand on the knob, she was about to twist and push it open as her mind raced with curiosity as to what could be inside. But furthermore, more curious as to why her bedroom door had been closed, and who could have shut it. Then, just as she heard it creak as the hinges were in far need of repair, she slammed it shut before she could even open it an inch. For some reason, Carey didn't want to see what was inside her room. She didn't want to open her bedroom door and step inside. Terrified, she began backing away from her bedroom door until her own back rested peacefully against the adjoining wall, where she stood looking completely dumbfounded at the closed door.

Then, a voice summoned her. "Carey," the voice began speaking calmly. "Carey why are you scared? You have nothing to fear sweetheart." As Carey listened to the voice, she wondered where it could have come from. She looked in both directions down the hallway, and saw nothing. But the voice came again, hence she knew where it would lead. Her eyes once again drifted to her closed bedroom door, and she could sense that's where the voice had come from. "Oh Carey, why don't you come on inside? There's something I want to show you."

"Who are you?" Carey asked aloud. "And what are you doing in my room?"

"I knew you would be coming here sweetheart, and I just wanted to surprise you is all," the voice continued to whisper in an indistinguishable tone. "I've been watching over you for a longtime now. You don't know how many times I've come to you while you were sleeping just to make sure that you were all right. Honestly, you don't have anything to fear of me. I could never hurt you. Never, Carey."

"But who are you?" Carey demanded an answer, feeling her knees grow weak, and her hands instinctively began to tremble with fear.

"Why I'm shocked you even have to ask such a question Carey," the voice replied calmly. "Why I'm your guardian angel of course. I've always been your guardian angel sweetheart. You might not have always known that I was there with you, but I've been there Carey. I've been right by your side everyday. Now come inside darling. Come inside your bedroom and see your guardian angel."

Billy. It had to be Billy Saxton. Only he could present himself as being her guardian angel. Suddenly, her fears disappeared into excitement, and without any further hesitation, she burst into her old bedroom, expecting to see the face of the man she had fallen in love with. Once inside, however, her expression once again changed.

No one was anywhere to be seen.

She was alone in the bedroom. Tricked. Carey knew that she had been tricked into coming into the bedroom and now wished she would have stayed out in the hallway. Actually, she wished she would have never came back to this home at all. Turning, she prepared to flee the bedroom, when right before her, the bedroom door slammed shut, and the lock latched. Running to the door, Carey began jerking wildly, trying with all her might to open the door.

It wouldn't budge.

Then the voice came again. Only this time no words were spoken. Instead, all she heard was laughter. Evil laughter. She was being laughed at for having been tricked into entering the room. "Hi Carey," the voice came again making the hairs on the back of her neck come to a standstill. "Why do you want to leave me in such a hurry? We haven't had any fun together yet." Saying nothing in return, Carey continued to work at the door, and each time, failed to get it open. She didn't want to turn around, didn't want to see the face of the man whom had locked her inside the room. Completely terrified, she knew to whom the phonation belonged to.

It had to be Curtis Rains.

"Please just leave me alone," Carey cried in vain, knowing her words meant nothing to the evil man. "Please let me out of here. I haven't done anything to you. Haven't you done enough?"

"Shut up!" the voice demanded sourly. "How dare you speak to me with such a tongue. I control you Carey. And the only reason you are still alive is because I have allowed you to live, and this is the thanks you give to me? Don't you get it?" he asked harshly, pausing briefly to let a tear roll off his victim's cheek. "You can't escape me. You should have just let me kill you along with your parents and you wouldn't have to go through any of this. Is that what you wish could have happened? Do you wish you would have died alongside your parents?" There was no response. "Damn it bitch!" the voice yelled into Carey's ear. "Turn around and face me. Turn around!" he ordered.

"No," Carey tried to hold her ground, falling to the floor. "I can't."

"Then you must die."

Clutching her head between her knees, Carey could feel the presence of the evil man coming towards her. Feeling his hot breath stinging the back of her neck, and his hands clutching the sides of her shoulders. Then, the rubbing began, and she just didn't have the strength to fight him off, or warding off the uncomfortable gestures he brought her way. Then, she felt his tongue touch the back of her neck.

He was licking her, his saliva sinking into her flesh, absorbing her innocence and putting in its place the venom of the devil himself. She wanted to run away, but had nowhere to go. Carey wanted to ward off her attacker, but knew that nothing was going to stop this man from destroying her innocence.

Then, his hands took a staggering grip around her neck.

And within seconds, she could feel her body growing weaker and weaker from a shortage of breath.

This was it.

The Tinman had finally caught up with Carey Haas.

After ten years, he was finally going to kill her.

Carey Haas woke up completely exhausted, sweat barreling down her forehead and forming a small, wet puddle of misery right next to her head. Her body jerked up into an erect position, and Carey experienced an uncomfortable sensation as she troubled with her breathing sequence, her mind trying to make her believe that it was only a nightmare and that she was out of harms way. Throwing her hands into the air, she grabbed around her neck, and assured herself that everything was intact. Taking a deep breath, she bowed her head and thanked the Lord above.

She was still alive.

Carey had once again made it through another night, where somehow, Curtis Rains had managed to come to her, and force her to remember the terrible tragedy of her parent's death. He was mocking her, and terrorizing her already tormented soul. However, it had felt so real. To Carey Haas, she honestly believed that she should be dead by now. After all, her life almost seemed to reach one inevitable end. How could she escape the reach of Curtis Rains, his lurid touch, and his spirit, which couldn't be stopped? It was impossible. He could come to her anytime he felt like it, and there was absolutely nothing that she could do about it.

Then, with herself being used to awaken in the middle of a nightmare, Carey went about her usual means of dissipating it from her mind, and climbed out of bed. Walking over to her dresser drawers, she glared into the mirror sitting upright along its back banister, and viewed herself carefully. She could easily sense and see the fear outlining her eyes as she noticed that her pupils were dilated. However, that wasn't what caught her attention all together. Looking further down her body, she saw something that made her freeze. It was her neck. All around it were red marks, as if someone had actually been choking her. But that was impossible? It had been a nightmare and nothing more, she tried to force herself to believe. This simply couldn't happen. It couldn't be real. Yet, there they were, resting peacefully around her neck. "No," Carey cried in a horrific shock. The Tinman had come to her many times before in the past ten years, haunting her in her sleep, and taking control of her life.

This time, however, it was different.

This time, he had left something behind.

* * *

Billy Saxton had been trying to repose all night long. However, he found himself continually tossing and turning from one side to the other as his body ached from the uncomfortable springs barreling upwards from underneath the worn out cot. His feet hung low over the bottom edge, and as he tried to stretch his arms, his fists constantly slammed into the cement wall behind his head. Fortunately, however, as soon as Billy had been able to block out the agonizing moans from the other unfortunate criminals whom had been scraped up off the street, he was able to gain control of his unlucky circumstance and catch a little shuteye. However, every few minutes or so, his body would jerk awake from the unbearable folding bed, its sole purpose seeming to be to prevent anyone who tried to sleep upon it to do so.

It wasn't until Billy could scarcely hear the faint sounds of birds chirping, which undoubtedly meant that a new day was about to begin and the sun was about to shine, did Billy fall into a state of bitter sleepiness, and he could no longer hold his eyelids open. Hopefully, it wouldn't be long until he was set free from the county jail, all of the accusations against him forgotten and he could escape into the loving arms of Carey Haas once again. Only this time, hassle free. Nevertheless, as his body continued to ache, Billy found it utterly impossible to stay awake. However, as soon as he closed his eyes for the last time, he knew he had made a foreordained mistake.

This wasn't going to be a peaceful sleep at all.

Just as expected, as soon as darkness swarmed around the innocently drained figure in Billy Saxton, he was once again engulfed in a furious tumble of abhorrent, detestable illusions, which forced him to escape into the depths of a fiery inferno of doom and destruction. Once again, his eyes were forced to experience a terrifying experience that would leave him feeling weak and utterly helpless. Unfortunately, Billy Saxton was coerced into visualizing a world through the eyes of the devil.

The Tinman was back.

Only, as Billy once again allowed himself to fall victim to the nightmares, he noticed immediately that something had changed. They were no longer of Carey, and her family being stalked by the seemingly immortal Curtis Rains. No. This time, just as the last time before the illusions appeared to be long gone, It was of Carey Haas. Only, she was no longer a child. She was grown up, nineteen years of age, her figure blossoming the way Billy had remembered, and her beauty overseeing even the world's most magnificent ocean.

But she wasn't alone.

Someone was there with her, watching her sleep. But she couldn't see him. The dark clad figure stood over her bed, watching her steady rhythmic breathing sequence, with an evil grin spread along the outskirts of his hidden face. Only his white teeth could be seen glistening in the night, as his cold-blooded, blackened eyes remained hidden in the darkness. Then, with a sudden turn of his head, the ghostly figure seemed to turn his head and look directly into Billy's eyes, almost as if he knew that Billy was there, watching his every move. His smile, however, told Billy that the man knew there was absolutely nothing that he could do to stop his madness.

"No!" Billy tried to scream. "No! Carey!" he called out in panic, although knowing fully well that it was impossible for her to hear him calling out to her. "Carey!" he begged feeling exhaustively helpless. "Carey, please wake up. Please. Wake up. He's there," he continued to scream powerlessly. "It's the Tinman, Carey. Please, wake up! He's there!"

To no avail Carey continued to sleep.

Then, Billy watched in a radical, undiminished state of shock as the man's hands stretched forward and reached down towards the defenseless Carey Haas sleeping below in her own bed. This simply was not happening. There had to be something Billy could do. He was locked in jail, not permitted to walk amongst the civilized. Yet, as much as he wanted to wake up and learn of what had happened later, he could not force himself to wake up, and he could not look away. He had promised Carey that he would always be there from here on out, protecting her from the hands of evil. As of now, however, he was not, and his promise was left unfulfilled.

"No!" Billy continued to scream. Only this time, his attention was drawn elsewhere. Now, he was trying to speak directly to the Tinman himself, forgetting his own safety as long as Carey was safe from any harm. "Please," he begged. "Just leave her alone. She's already been through enough because of you. Why can't you just leave her alone?" His words appeared to have no effect, as the man's bare hands, his arms also dressed in black, continued to slowly make their way towards his victim. "No!" Billy cried out into the early morning hours. "Come for me. Come after me you son of a bitch and just leave her alone."

Tinman

Again, his words were ignored.

Billy couldn't turn away. He had to watch with an intensity so powerful, he could feel himself sharpening the edges of his teeth as he ground them together forcefully, praying that the seemingly inevitable wasn't about to happen. Clutching the sides of his cot tightly with both hands, and completely drawn away from reality, Billy lived his illusion from within the Tinman's eyes, forced to watch every detail. It was obvious that the evil man was not willing to spare any torment.

Then, it happened. The man's hands closed in around Carey's neck and he began to squeeze harshly. Billy watched as Carey's eyes jerked open and the struggle began. Her face suddenly turned bright red, and her eyes began to loosen themselves in their sockets. This was it, the Tinman was going to strangle her. After ten years of being locked up inside the Florida State Prison, Curtis Rains had succeeded in dominating and ending the life of the one person that was ever able to escape from his killing spree.

"No!" Billy screamed.

But the choking continued. Billy watched as Carey threw her hands into the air, begging for her life, begging to be set free.

She couldn't die. She just couldn't.

Then, Billy heard a voice coming from a distant place. It was a voice calling his name. "Billy. Billy," the voice called harshly. "Hey Saxton get your ass up boy. You're getting out of here." Suddenly, Billy found himself lying wide-awake on the same uncomfortable cot from which he had fallen asleep. Instinctively, he jerked upwards and immediately began searching his tiny cell for any unwanted, or unexpected visitors. There wasn't anybody there except the guard delivering good news. "You must have been having one hell of a nightmare boy," the guard continued. "I could hear your ass screaming all the way down the hall." Then, he paused as if waiting for Billy to respond. When none came, he continued. "But come on, someone's here to pick you up. Apparently, the charges have been dropped against you."

Confused, Billy climbed to his feet and exited his cell. However, his mind worked in an integral, consummated state of confusion as he wondered not only who would have dropped the charges against him, but also if the nightmare he had just received had actually been a reality or a figment of his imagination? Even as the thought crossed his mind, however, he knew it had to be real. After all, everything else had actually happened. This, most certainly, couldn't be an exception.

Soon, Billy found himself being led towards the exit of the county jail, where he found his mother waiting for him, a concerned look spread across her face, yet a sympathetic scorn still lurked in the distance of her eyes. However, before he could reach her welcoming, sheltering arms, a hand came from behind and grabbed his shoulder. Spinning around, Billy found himself staring into the eyes of Sheriff Gabriel Burnham. "Look son," the elder man spoke in a gruff tone. "I'm going to be keeping a sharp eye on you. Wherever you go, or whatever you do, I'll be watching. And it's probably in your best interest to just stay away from Carey Haas. Rick hasn't been in the best of moods as of late. He's aching for a reason to try and get me to throw you back in here. All right?"

"But who dropped the charges?" Billy found himself asking tiresomely.

"Between you and me?" Gabe asked with a slight grin. Billy nodded. Then, finally, after a long pause, the Sheriff continued. "I tell you what. You can thank me later." Saying that, Sheriff Burnham turned away and headed off in the opposite direction, allowing Billy to go and see his mother. If nothing else, Gabe had seen no reason into trying to destroy Billy's life, thus decided to set him free. Now, however, he would have a bigger problem to face. Undoubtedly, Rick Goodman was going to be furious.

Then, Billy finally reached his mother. "Oh honey," Debra welcomed her son warmly, draping her caring arms around him as she ran her fingers briskly through his hair. "Are you all right? I'm so sorry you had to go through that."

"I'm all right mom," Billy responded returning his mother's hug. "But can we get out of here please?" he asked, not allowing his mother to see his concern for Carey.

"Of course we can. Besides," Debra paused as the two of them walked outside and into the early morning sunlight. Squinting, Billy allowed his eyes time to adjust before taking another step. Then, looking into his mother's eyes, he allowed her to continue. "There's someone here to see you, and Elizabeth Anne and her husband Murray have prepared a barbecue for you this afternoon. So,

Tinman

welcome home sweetheart." Approaching his mother's Lexus, Billy watched as the passenger door sprung open, and the recognizable head of his best friend, Blaze Brookshaw appeared.

"Damn brother," Billy greeted him with another bear hug. "I thought for sure you would have headed back up to Georgia after all of this, and be pissed as hell at me." Debra ignoring their conversation, climbed inside the car and started the ignition, simply happy to have her son returning home. "But seriously, it's good to see you man. And I'm sorry about all of this. I never meant for you to get in any trouble."

"I know you didn't," Blaze responded with a smile. "But come on now. I know you really didn't think I would go back to Georgia after something like this. Hell, it doesn't get any better than this. This is the most excitement I've had in a while. Who really cares about the danger?"

"Blaze," Billy's tone turned suddenly serious and his smile faded. "You know you don't have to do this if you don't want to?"

Blaze nodded. "Maybe not. But I'm not going to turn my back on you Billy. If you need me, I'm here."

"Good," Billy continued with a smirk. "Cause we got a lot of work to do."

"Oh man," Blaze broke in, taking in a deep breath.

"What is it?"

"I don't know," Blaze admitted. "I just really didn't like the sound of that."

* * *

Meanwhile, back in Starke, Florida.

"Well I'll be damned," Detective Ashley Selvaggio bluntly stated as she walked into the hallway of the Reynolds home and found the slumped over corpse of the deceased Jack Reynolds, whom had taken his own life after murdering that of his wife, Gloria, and eleven year old daughter, Sarah. Then, turning to her side, she looked up at the single word written in blood, covering almost the entire length of the hallway. "Tinman," she said aloud. "Just what in the hell is going on here?" she asked the two detectives who had called her to the scene.

"I'm really not sure myself madam," young Steve Johnson admitted to his senior investigator, not afraid to admit that his young eyes had never seen such a grotesque scene. However, that probably was because he had chosen to practice law in the small town of Starke, Florida, where the state prison was the main attraction. "A neighbor found the bodies."

"Bodies?" Ashley interjected.

"Oh yes," Steve continued. "The wife and kid are upstairs in the bathroom. Right now, it looks as if this guy here, Jack Reynolds is his name, murdered his family, and then took his own life. I don't know why. Your guess would be as good as mine."

"Where's this neighbor that found the bodies?" Ashley asked as her eyes surveyed every inch of the scene, taking in every detail, trying to put together the puzzle in her head of what had actually occurred in the Reynolds home. She was a very talented detective, known by her department to always catch her man, and although the violator in this case appeared to have inflicted justice upon himself, she was well aware that there were still many questions that needed to be answered.

"Kenneth is questioning her now," Steve replied.

"All right," Ashley sighed heavily, taking in a deep breath. "You know what to do here. I'm going to go take a look in the bathroom." Then, with a nod, Ashley made her way to the bathroom, every step trying to expect the unexpected on what was undoubtedly going to be a gruesome scene. Finally, she reached the bathroom door. Hearing examiners and other investigators working anxiously inside, she paused briefly before entering and resuming control of the investigation. "You can do this," she told herself in a whisper. "You're strong. You can handle this." Then, taking in one last breath, Ashley entered the bathroom and feasted her eyes upon the gore below.

There on the bathroom floor, were the lifeless bodies of a slaughtered wife, and a defenseless eleven-year old girl. "Not pretty is it?" she heard one of the other investigators speak towards her. "Look's like that son of a bitch just snapped and went berserk on his family before killing himself. What do you think that Tinman shit is all about though?"

"I'm not sure yet," Ashley hated to admit, bending down to look over the lifeless bodies below. "But I'm sure it means something." Gazing into the eyes of the small child, Ashley could sense the fear that must have been running throughout the little girl's mind before her life was taken by her own father. Ashley then placed her hand close to the bathroom floor, but stopped short just as it was about to reach the massive amounts of blood that had scattered in seemingly every direction, covering the entire bathroom floor, concealing its original color. Closing her eyes, she tried to picture what had taken place. However, she could see nothing. Her mind drew a blank.

"Yeah," another investigator spoke up. "Well, whatever happened here, I'm just glad that crazy bastard made it easy on us. Saved us a lot of paper work huh?" A burst of laughter filtered through the bathroom as the men tried to make light of the horrendous, distressing scene in front of them. However, Ashley Selvaggio did not join in the laughter. Taking one more glance, she prepared to exit the room.

"You guys make sure you let me know what you find all right," she spoke sharply, not showing her weakness.

"You got it."

Within seconds, Ashley found herself exiting the Reynolds's home and squandering back to her black, sleek Toyota 4-Runner. Once she climbed inside, she closed her eyes and began her critical thinking process. She wondered just what could have gone on inside that home to cause such a massacre. Opening her eyes, she gazed into the rearview mirror, showing herself her very own beautiful dark brown eyes. Only thirty years of age, she didn't look a bit over twenty-five. She was a single woman, never seeming to have any luck in finding the right man. She had dated plenty in the past, yet none of them appeared to possess what she had been looking for. Then again, Ashley wasn't quite sure what she was looking for. She was dedicated to her job, that perhaps being a factor in her unsuccessful search for love, and loved every minute of it. She was sure someone was out there for her, however, she had long ago given up the search. Her beauty scorned its way through both, good and evil, and her perky lips were as luscious as a splintering ice cream cone. Her gorgeous smile, made you melt instantly, almost forcing you to turn away before falling in love at first sight. Her hair was autumn brown, a bit wavy at times, yet smelt like that of roses, and was most beautiful in midday as the sun seemed to direct it's rays directly onto her head, showering her with a splendor and a pulchritude almost unimaginable. She had been a law enforcement officer since the age of twenty-two, yet has proclaimed herself as the top investigator, with an impeccable record for the last five years. And although she found herself swamped with an enormous overload of stress, her figure remained firm, stunning, and gorgeous, never once giving in to the urge to break down. She was a man's dream, but lived a life without happiness, and a life without love. Perhaps, however, she was simply too busy chasing the bad guys, instead of mister right.

Finally, turning the key in the ignition, she put her truck in reverse and left the scene of the crime. It appeared as if the case would quickly be closed, and Jack Reynolds's would prove to be the guilty party in taking his family's life. However, for some reason or another, Ashley wasn't convinced.

Something was missing.

Something she couldn't quite put her finger on.

Yet she could feel it. She could feel it deep inside her bones that this case wasn't quite as simple as it appeared. The surface remained clear. A family had been murdered, almost certainly at the hands of the father. Yet, there was something else. Something only the strong, optimistic eye could see. Leaving nothing out, Ashley wouldn't consider this case immediately closed, and whatever it was that she wasn't seeing, she vowed to find out. Sighing to herself, she knew the next few nights were going to be of a sleepless magnitude. It had been a long time since a case had instantly captured her full attention. She didn't even know all the facts, and was well aware that some would be increasingly hard to obtain. However, she couldn't turn her back on this, couldn't ignore her instincts, and simply could not walk away. It was all too easy. The pieces almost fit too perfectly. Even if Jack had taken his own life after that of his family, there was still something else. There was something between the lines that her brain simply wouldn't allow her to see for the time being. But she was smart, and in time, she knew she would find what she was looking for.

"Tinman," she said to herself as she couldn't get the word out of her head, clutching the steering wheel tightly with both hands. She could feel a staggering headache coming about, letting her know that she was pushing her brain too hard. Nevertheless, questions continued to tackle her, and many of them, she couldn't ignore. Again, the mystifying word remained as clear as day inside her head. "Tinman," she spoke again, as the questions continued to stream in. Why had it been written along the hallway wall in blood? What was the significance of the blood? Why? What did it mean? Again, Ashley didn't know, but was going to find out. At all costs, she was going to find out what actually took place inside that home.

Then, again speaking to herself, she added one thing that she was certain of. "The press is going to have a field day with this."

* * *

Birmingham, Alabama.

Jamie Walker was pleased to find a new day. The sunshine, partially blocked by the blinds covering the windows above her bed, still managed to find a few cracks to seep into the room, throwing curious shadows along the walls. She listened to the birds chirping from outside, doing nothing more than enjoying her carefree lifestyle. Then, rolling over, she placed her arms around Travis McKinley, who slept peacefully right next to her. She loved him, loved everything about him, and didn't want to lose him. She knew that it was hard for him to understand just what was going on, and Jamie really didn't expect him to. It wasn't his problem, it was hers. Curtis wasn't after Travis, he was after her.

Then, smiling, she realized that last night had been the only night since Curtis's death in the electric chair that she had actually been able to obtain a good night's sleep, without any distractions or haunting nightmares that forced her to liberate her mind, and lose all grips with reality. She had neglected to explain to Travis what she had seen the previous night in the bathroom, knowing fully well that he would only tell her that it wasn't possible and that it was a fabrication inside her head.

Only Jamie herself, knew that it had been real.

And the boy, she had seen in the middle of the road, forcing her to wreck her Jeep had been real, although everyone told her that no body of a child had been found. And then, the boy had come to her again in the hospital, and at her home. Only at her home, she was able to realize that it had been none other than Curtis Rains. And then there was her unexplainable sickness, which almost brought on death.

All of it, she was sure, was due to Curtis Rains.

However, no one believed her, and no one probably ever would.

Then, Jamie suddenly lost her thought, as Travis's gruff voice splintered the peaceful atmosphere. "Sweetheart," he spoke gently turning to face her. "What are you doing up so early? Are you all right?"

Jamie nodded. "Actually yes I am," she replied with a smile. "But don't act so surprised. I actually had a good night's rest. No nightmares, no nothing. And I feel great Travis. I really feel good."

"Good," Travis replied pulling her close to his body. "I'm glad to hear it. You really have made an incredible recovery from all of those wounds you received from your accident. I don't think I've ever seen someone heal as fast as you, and for that my love," he paused with a slight smile, kissing her on the cheek. "I love you Jamie Walker, and I want to be by your side forever. I promise I will never leave you sweetheart. Without you in my life, I don't think I could amount to anything. Just stay with me, let me know if anything is wrong, and I'll do anything and everything I can to help you."

"You've already done enough," Jamie returned the smile, and added a charming kiss on Travis's forehead. "And you don't know how much it means to me to hear you say those things. I don't ever want to lose you either. Thank you," she paused, looking deep into his eyes. "Thank you for being there for me thus far. I know things have seemed to be a little crazy lately. But I'm trying Travis. I'm truly trying to fight whatever is happening in my life. I just get scared you know."

"It's O.K. sweetheart," Travis broke in. "It's normal to be scared after going through what you've been through recently. Not everyone would have been able to hang on as long as you have. But you know what, I'm still here, and I'm not going anywhere."

"Oh yes you are," Jamie disagreed as she threw the covers off the two of them and slowly climbed out of bed. "We are going to go somewhere today and do something fun. I want to get out of this house."

Tinman

"Are you sure?" Travis questioned, his concern fully towards Jamie's condition. "You're not a hundred percent yet sweetheart, and you know you need your rest."

"No," Jamie disagreed. "What I need is some fresh air, and some excitement for a change. And I'm not taking no for an answer," she paused, heading for the bathroom to freshen up. "So get out of bed."

Travis watched as the bathroom door shut, and listened as the shower was turned on and water began to pound away at the walls. Smiling to himself, he climbed out of bed and headed for the kitchen to prepare the two of them some breakfast before they wondered off and out into the warm, Southern sunshine. He didn't really feel that going out today was the best thing for his loved one. Yet, Jamie had been adamant about doing something exciting, and he knew that there was no changing her mind. Besides, this was the first time in a while where he had actually seen her so full of life.

If the old Jamie wanted to come back, then he wouldn't do anything to stand in her way. In fact, he would welcome her with open arms, and put Curtis Rains behind them once and for all.

To Travis McKinley, the Tinman was as good as forgotten.

* * *

Back in Destin, Florida.

As Carey gathered her thoughts, she finally exited her bedroom and began heading towards the staircase. She could hear her Aunt Carol and Uncle Rick talking amongst themselves below, and knew the inevitable confrontation with her uncle was just moments away. She was tired of his stubbornness, his ignorance in denying her the right to speak her mind, and his asinine refusal to see the truth. Her life was in danger and the only person who could feel her pain and sense the evil around her was Billy Saxton, whom for some reason, Rick had it in for. It was time to put her foot down. Time to make her uncle view things through her eyes. She wasn't a little girl anymore. She was grown, and she had lived with her parent's death for ten years. It was time for Rick to let go.

Wearing a red, slip on, silk nightgown, Carey Haas made her way down the staircase, and leaving her golden, angelic blonde hair in a strew of knots, she found her two guardians in the living room, sipping peacefully on some coffee. Storming in, Carol could sense the anger in her niece's eyes, and knew that an argument was about to take place. Rick, steadily reading the paper hadn't even noticed Carey's presence in the room, and was caught completely off guard when she spoke.

"Can I talk to you for a minute?" Carey bluntly asked her uncle, not caring that she had disturbed him, and a boldness could be found in her tone that let everyone in the room know that she was not playing around. "I don't think you understand just what is going on here Uncle Rick."

"No," Rick interjected folding the paper calmly, then turning to look into Carey's eyes. "I don't think you understand. The decision has been made, and I'm not changing my mind about that Billy Saxton boy. Look," he paused once again, not believing he was about to repeat words he had just spoken earlier. "You may not see this right now. But I'm doing this for you. I'm doing this because I care about you."

"Well I care about Billy," Carey held her ground firm. "You have nothing to fear from him."

"How can you say that?" Rick questioned. "You don't even know him. How can you say that he won't hurt you?"

"Because he couldn't have done this!" Carey stormed as she made her way to her uncle. Then, pulling her hair back, she revealed the abrasions found around her neck. Rick's eyes stood wide-open, disbelief seen in his expression. Clearly, he could see that someone had been choking his niece. "Look at it," Carey snapped, letting the fear of the nightmare she had experienced slip away and turn into anger. "Do you think Billy could have done this? No," she answered for him. "And you know why, because you and your Sheriff friend had to lock him up. Billy is not responsible for this, or anything else that you have accused him of Rick. He wouldn't hurt me."

"I'm not going to listen to this," Rick tried to turn away.

"Yes you are," Carey ordered continuing to hold her ground. "Everything I told you is true Rick. Billy didn't do this to me. Curtis Rains did this to me. He's not dead. Why can't you just believe me?"

"Because listen to yourself," Rick replied harshly, finding himself growing increasingly angry. "Listen to what your saying. You sound just as crazy as that lunatic that murdered your parents," he added, not paying attention to his hurtful words, and wished he could've taken them back as soon as they left his mouth.

"Rick," Carol jumped in, not believing what he had just said, and seeing the hurt in Carey's eyes. "Now that's enough."

"No it isn't," Carey jumped in, not crumbling into tears. "You say what you want about my parents and me," she paused once again pointing to her neck. "But you can't say that Billy is responsible for doing this to me. And I'm not crazy. I know what's happening, you're just making this harder on everybody. And since you seem to know everything then tell me, who did this to me? Huh? Who tried to strangle me?" Pausing, she waited for an answer. When none came, she continued. "Well I know who did this to me because I saw him. I saw Curtis Rains. He's here and there's nothing you can do about it. In fact, I don't think there's anything I can do about it. But there is something you can do for Billy. You can drop those ridiculous charges against him and let us be together. He makes me happy Rick, happier than I've ever been in my life. For better or worse, I want to be with him."

Then, before Rick could reply, the phone rang and he jumped up to answer it, feeling speechless and not knowing how to respond to Carey's heartfelt words. Upon picking up the receiver, he instantly recognized Sheriff Gabriel Burnham's voice. "Rick, it's Gabe," the Sheriff immediately began. "I'm sorry to call you so early. But I think you need to come down to my office for a minute."

"Why? What's wrong?"

"Nothing," Gabe fabricated just a bit. "I just think there's something you should know."

"All right. I'm on my way." Then, returning to the living room, he once again faced his niece as he grabbed his car keys and headed for the front door. "Look, Carey," he paused taking on a more gentle tone. "I'm sorry about what I said. I really didn't mean it. But I have to go now. I promise we'll talk some more when I get home. All right?"

Saying nothing, Carey watched as her uncle darted out the front door and within seconds pulled out of the driveway. Turning to face her aunt, Carey looked puzzled. "That probably didn't go so well huh?" Laughing to try and enlighten the mood, Carol jumped up off the sofa and hugged Carey graciously, trying to assure her that

Jason Glover

everything would turn out all right. Then, the phone rang again, and Carey watched as her aunt disappeared around the corner to answer it. Within seconds, she returned, a slight smile arched across her face.

"Someone would like to speak with you."

Running to the phone, Carey had a feeling that she knew who it was. It had to be Billy. It just had to. "Hello."

"Carey!" Billy's voice sounded excited. "It's Billy. I need to see you."

Chapter 22

    Billy stood silently on the balcony of the Anne home, overlooking the magnificent view of the ocean as his ears easily picked up the whipping sounds of waves crashing against the surf and sand below. His best friend Blaze, ran around with the Anne children, Jennifer and Mary along the sand as the three of them tried to efficiently throw the Frisbee back and forth. They had been successful on a couple of attempts. More times than not, however, the cylinder object would dart downwards and plow into the soft sand below. Murray, Elizabeth's husband, worked patiently at the grill preparing hamburgers and hot dogs galore, the aroma filling Billy's nostrils and forcing his mouth to water. Every once in a while, their eyes would meet, and Murray would give him an encouraging wink as if to say that he believed in him. Behind him, his mother Debra, and the caring Elizabeth Anne, whom against her better judgment, had taken him in when he desperately needed her help. The two of them giggled amongst themselves, sipping their wine graciously as they tried to capture as many sunrays as possible.

    Billy was glad to be out of jail, but his mind couldn't free himself of the horrible illusion he had experienced just a few short hours ago before he was released. He had spoken with Carey, and now knew that she was all right. Yet, why did it still feel like something was wrong? Rolling up his sleeves, Billy tried to force the fearful thought out of his head and enjoy the beautiful, hot and humid Florida day. Unfortunately, however, he knew that there would be no escape.

    Then, he felt a hand on his shoulder. Turning, he smiled as his mother offered him a glass of wine. "You look like you can use this sport, if not something stronger." Then, as the two of them giggled amongst themselves, she pulled him close. "You know I can tell that something is wrong with you Billy. Please tell me what it is. I hate seeing you this way. You should be having fun down on the beach with Blaze."

"I know," Billy admitted. "But I can't help it. Something bad is about to happen. Something I can't explain. And-" he paused letting his words be cut off short.

"And what?" Debra questioned her son. "Please tell me what's wrong. I just want to help you sweetheart. But you have to let me."

"I'm scared mom," Billy admitted. "And I don't know what to do anymore."

"Scared of what?"

Then, before Billy could answer, Elizabeth came over and placed her arms around both of them, interrupting the two. "I'm so happy to have you guys as my neighbors," she spoke, the mixture of sun and wine obviously taking its affect. "It's been so lonely around here." Then, pulling Billy off to one side, Elizabeth left Debra and her husband alone on the porch. "What do you say the two of us take a little stroll on the beach." Billy couldn't disagree. "I think you should know something Billy," Elizabeth continued. "You're not alone in this."

"I know," Billy spoke up. "But no one understands what is going on ya know?"

"Maybe," Elizabeth admitted. "But everyone here has faith in you. Your mother loves you to death and believes in you. You know Blaze cares about you and would do anything in the world for you. I believe in you. My husband doesn't think anything bad of you. And then there's Carey, and apparently from what I've heard, you've definitely made an impression on her. You have so much going for you Billy. Just don't let anyone stand in your way. I understand that something is going on. Now, I may not understand exactly what it is. But I can see it in your eyes Billy. There's nothing but goodness inside you, and you are doing nothing but following your heart."

"That isn't what I'm afraid of," Billy broke in. "Look Elizabeth, I don't even know how I got trapped in this situation. But for some reason, I'm here, and there's only one other person that can understand exactly what it is that's going on, and that's Carey. But I promised her that I wouldn't let anything bad happen to her. And frankly," he paused taking a deep breath. "I don't think I can keep that promise."

"Why is that?" Elizabeth asked sympathetically.

"Because I don't think I'm strong enough," Billy sadly admitted. "But I don't want to let her down ya know? However, I can't even explain exactly what is going on because I don't even understand it myself. It's beyond me Elizabeth. It's more powerful than me, and I honestly don't think I can stop whatever it is alone."

"Oh but you can Billy," Elizabeth tried to assure the nearly twenty year old boy in front of her. "You can do it as long as you never lose faith. Don't ever sell yourself short Billy. Never. And by all means, always stay strong."

"I don't think you understand," Billy tried to cut in.

"No," Elizabeth cut him off, determined to get her point across somehow. "I don't think you understand. No matter what is going on, it can be stopped Billy. You just have to find a way to do it. But again, you're not alone. Everyone is here for you. But even if we aren't enough, there's someone who can conquer all, even your greatest fears, and will come to you in your time of need."

"Really?" Billy questioned with a slight look of disbelief. "And just who might this be, and why hasn't he helped me thus far?"

"Oh but I bet he has. He's probably helped you more than you know, you just can't see it." Then, with a slight pause, Elizabeth drank the last of her wine, devouring the sweetened liquid with a smile, enjoying the moment for what it is. Finally, she took Billy's hand in her own, and came to a complete stop. Forcing him to face her, she looked right into his eyes before continuing. "I'm talking about God Billy. He's on your side. And believe it or not, he is watching over you. But even more important than that, he believes in you."

Billy didn't know what to say. He knew Elizabeth was right though. God had kept him strong enough to make it through what had already grown into an obdurate, incorrigible situation. Many people could have easily fallen victim to the intangible predicament, letting the nightmares and the unholy spirit of the devilish Tinman take control of their very lives and fall into a ruthless, malignant state of insanity. However, thus far, Billy had remained strong, overcoming many obstacles he hadn't even seen coming. He had survived, and was still in the game. More importantly, however, Carey Haas was still alive.

He couldn't let go of the feelings he felt inside his restless soul towards his only love. He couldn't just walk away from this without regretting it for the rest of his life. He needed Carey in his life, she completed the big picture, was the missing ingredient his life had been living without, and brought his longtime search for happiness to an end. She was the closure he had been looking for, and would never let her go. Together, the two of them had to make it. And he simply couldn't let her down.

"Thank you," Billy finally spoke towards Elizabeth as the two of them once again found themselves walking back up on the porch. "Thank you Elizabeth for everything you've done for me. Without your help, there's no telling what could have happened before today. And I'm sorry if I brought you or your family any inconvenience. I never meant for that to happen."

"Nonsense," Elizabeth broke in, holding her index finger to her lips, letting Billy know that his words weren't needed. "I'm just glad I could help."

"Well thanks again," Billy stated firmly. "Seriously, thank you." Nodding one last time, Elizabeth turned away from her walking companion and went inside her beloved home to furnish herself with yet another glass of wine. Then, as soon as Elizabeth disappeared inside, it wasn't long before Billy's mother; Debra came over and once again took her son's hand in her own. Looking into his mother's eyes, he could feel the intense bond the two of them shared between one another. It was a bond so strong; he knew it would last until the end of time. Even in death, they would still be able to communicate. "Mom," Billy began, a smile lurking out of the corners of his mouth. "I love you mother. I hope you never doubted that. I've always loved you and I always will."

"I love you too sweetheart," Debra replied, trying desperately to hold back the tears of joy that were trying to exploit themselves. "Where is all of this coming from Billy?"

"I just don't want you to be scared mom," Billy continued seriously. "I don't know what lies ahead of me. But whatever it is, bad or good; I just wanted you to know that I love you. And if something were to happen to me, I don't want you to be sad for me mom because I'll always be with you. Always."

"Billy," Elizabeth cut in, not wanting to hear anymore of this nonsense. "You really shouldn't be talking like that. Nothing is going to happen to you. You're going to be all right. Everything is going to be O.K."

"I hope so," Billy replied throwing his arms around his mother, only to squeeze her affectionately. "But I have to go now mom. I need to go and see Carey. She needs me and I can't let her down."

"Do you think that's really such a good idea?"

Billy shrugged his shoulders. "It's just something I have to do mom. Please try and understand." Then, he was about to turn and walk away when he turned around to face his mother one last time. "Tell Blaze I went out for a while and I'll be back later on. I'll call you in a couple of hours." Then, without waiting for his mother to reply, Billy turned and began to walk down the stairs and onto the beach.

"Be careful," Debra called out and watched her son turn around and give her an encouraging wink. "Please," she repeated this time to herself. "Please be careful Billy. I love you."

* * *

"You did what?" Rick Goodman shouted angrily once inside Sheriff Burnham's office. Refusing the seat offered to him by the top law enforcement officer in front of him, Rick began pacing the room back and forth, sweat barreling down his forehead as he somehow managed to lose control of the situation. Gabe was his good friend, the two of them could trace their relationship back to childhood, so Rick couldn't help but wonder how he could have gone behind his back and done such a thing. "How could you do it?" Rick asked, his eyebrows arched high in the air, and his pace suddenly came to a complete stop. "How could you?" Rick repeated, demanding an answer.

"Please Rick, for crying out loud," Gabe calmly seated himself behind his desk and tried to calm his friend down, although realizing he had a right to be upset, and figured that he himself would be prancing around Rick's office in a furious rage if their positions were reversed. "Will you please just calm down, have a seat and listen to what I have to say?" For a moment, Gabe thought that Rick was going to refuse his subtle offer and continue his rampage throughout his office, refusing to listen to reason and unwilling to forgive him for his supposed wrong doing. Then, surprisingly, Rick wiped the sweat from his forehead and in an irrational manner, seated himself in the chair directly in front of Gabe's desk. "Thank you," the Sheriff continued, pleased to see his friend calming down. "Now would you like some coffee or anything?"

Rick shook his head firmly. "No," he said harshly. "I want you to tell me just what in the hell is going on around here. How could you go ahead, without consulting with me first, and release that Billy Saxton kid Gabe? I thought it was a cut and dry issue. I thought it was out of your hands. Or was that just some of your police bullshit jargon to get me off your back?"

"Look Rick," Gabe spoke calmly, although feeling his temper flaring, and his patience growing short as his tolerance of the verbal abuse he was receiving was quickly decaying and turning to dust.

"No, you look," Rick cut his friend off. "You shouldn't have done it. That son of a bitch kid should be in jail right now, or in court for his arraignment. And who knows, he's probably with Carey right now as we speak."

"I had a talk with him before I let him go."

"Oh, well that just makes me feel a lot better Gabe," Rick replied scurrilously, finding it hard to think rationally.

"That's it," Sheriff Burnham snapped, not allowing himself to be used as a punching bag any longer. Removing himself from behind his wooden desk, he now stood directly in front of Rick Goodman. Clinching his fists tight, he slammed them down on his desk, knocking his coffee mug to the floor, ignoring the fact that the brown liquid seeped its way into his carpet. "I'm not going to sit in here and take anymore of your childish bullshit Rick. I'm trying to help you out here. I'm trying to talk to you in a civil manner. But I swear I'll walk out of here right now and leave you to sulk to yourself. If you want an explanation, fine, I'll give it to you. But that means you have to listen, just keep your mouth shut and listen." Gabe watched as Rick momentarily looked away from him, a sorrowful expression forming along his reddened face as his anger appeared to be slipping away. "Now damn it Rick, you should know me better than that," the Sheriff continued. "You know I would have never released that boy if I thought your niece was in any danger."

"And just how do you know that?" Rick couldn't help but to question. "How do you know he's not going to hurt her?"

"I just know," Gabe tried to convince Rick.

"Oh," Rick mistakenly cut in, his sarcastic tone returning, and his anger rebuilding. "I'm supposed to feel better because you say so. Well sorry Gabe, but your word alone isn't good enough for me," Rick said in a derogatory tone, his rebuttal easily seen in his eyes. "You let that son of a bitch walk out of here a free man because you have a hunch that he is good kid. Well, if he was truly a good kid, he wouldn't have broken into my house in the first place, and damn sure wouldn't have sped away when my wife and I came home. Does that really sound like an innocent person to you Gabe?"

That was it. Gabriel couldn't take it anymore. He could actually feel steam rising out of his ears, and heading aloft into the air condition vents above. Finally, losing his temper, he grabbed the man in front of him by his shirt collar and lifted him out of the chair and into the air until their eyes locked. Not even realizing how hard he was squeezing Rick's shoulders, Gabe spoke furiously. "Listen to me you ignorant, stubborn son of a bitch. Goddamn Rick, you really have grown into one senile old bastard. Have you looked into the mirror lately? I almost can't stand to be around you anymore. Now," he paused taking in a deep breath. "Do you really want to ruin that kids life by throwing him in jail and having an unnecessary arrest on his record? That could ruin his chance to succeed in this world, and these days you know as well as I that kids need as many breaks as they can get. Just think about what you're doing Rick. It's wrong. It's all wrong, and I honestly don't want to have any part in it."

"But it's your job Gabe," Rick continued not backing down. "You have a duty and responsibility to uphold the law."

"And I believe I am," Gabe continued not backing down. "I believe I did the right thing, and in this business my friend, that goes a long way and saves me a lot of hassles in the end. Billy Baxton is a good kid who could have a bright future ahead of him. I don't want to be the one to take that away from him Rick. And deep down inside, I know you don't want to either. Now don't get me wrong,

I'm going to keep a close eye on him, and if he does anything out of the ordinary I will throw his ass right back in a cellar. But as of now Rick, there really wasn't any reason to take him away from his family, from the people that love him. He's been through a lot, and he doesn't need the two of us breathing down the back of his neck. If you could have only talked to him yourself, you'd see what I'm talking about."

"Damn it," Rick breathed realizing his friend was right. "I'm sorry man. I'm just looking out for Carey. I'd never forgive myself if I ever let anything happen to her after what happened to her parents. I vowed to take her in my home, under my wing, and look out for her. And I don't know, I guess I'm just scared that I'm not doing my job ya know? I just want to protect her Gabe. That's all."

"You've done an outstanding job," Gabe tried to comfort his friend, releasing his stern grip on his shoulders and allowing him to sink back down into the cushioned chair below. "But Carey is grown now. She'll be twenty in a couple of months, going away to college. It's time you let go, let her take care of herself, make her own decisions and so forth. You've done all you can do, and she's turned out to be a wonderful person, unique and beautiful on the inside and out. You've done your job Rick, and you've done it well. But even Carey can see the good in Billy. She wants to be with him, and she trusts him with her heart. And you should too Rick." Pausing briefly, Gabe couldn't believe at how the mood had suddenly changed. Finally, he had gotten through Rick's thick head, and his words of wisdom were finally sinking in. "You shouldn't stand in Carey's way Rick. You no longer have that right. Let her be, and if it's a mistake, let her live it and learn from it. If Carey is willing to give Billy a chance, then you should too."

"I don't know," Rick spoke gently, breathing heavily in and out as he calmed down. "I know you're right and all. But I just don't know. For some reason, I don't trust him. I think he's up to something. But then again," Rick paused as he recalled the events that had taken place at his home earlier this morning when Carey had come downstairs after waking up to confront him. He remembered seeing the red marks around her neck and wondering where they had come from. "After this morning, I don't know what to believe anymore."

"This morning?" Gabe questioned confusingly. "What happened this morning?"

Knowing this was going to sound crazy to the Sheriff, Rick at first hesitated to continue with the explanation of what he had seen around his niece's neck, and furthermore wasn't sure if he should mention how Carey herself thought the abrasions had gotten there. Nevertheless, Gabe had always been one of his closest friends, and he trusted him with his life, and with his family's life. So, taking his time, and without leaving out any vital details, Rick began telling the Sheriff, who watched with speculation and concerned eyes, listening carefully to every word as he tried to make sense of what was being laid before him. Going through the motions, Rick told his friend about the red marks found around Carey's neck. Then, with disbelief ringing loudly in his own eyes he began to recount his niece's words and how she had desperately tried to convince him that Curtis Rains was responsible and that he was not truly dead.

Finally, when he was finished, Gabe spoke. "I-I don't know what to say."

"Neither do I," Rick agreed. "And I don't know what to do either. It's crazy, but she actually believes that that psycho is still alive," he continued speaking of Carey. "But that's impossible isn't it?" he asked Gabe, hoping to find an answer. "I mean when you're dead, you're dead right?" Gabe could only shrug his shoulders. "It just doesn't make any sense. I mean, there is no mistake is there? Curtis Rains did die in that electric chair didn't he? We can be certain of that can't we?"

The aging Sheriff felt obligated to nod. "As far as I know. I mean I watched them carry his body out of the prison on the news. But," he let his voice trail off into silence as he remembered speaking to Billy in the interrogation room. "I mean, I don't know what any of this means, if it even means anything at all. But when I questioned Billy, he mentioned something of the same magnitude. I mean he came out and told me that Carey's life was in danger and that Curtis Rains was coming for her. He said that's the only reason he came to your house that day. To try and warn her, and try and help her. I didn't take him seriously though. In fact at the time, I thought he was lying to me. But I'm not so sure anymore."

Jason Glover

"Well, what do you think we should do?" Rick asked, obviously out of answers.

"I don't know," Gabe hated to admit. "I don't know if there's anything we can do. I think we should have a little chat with the two of them though. Maybe they know something we don't."

Then, before Rick could continue with the conversation, a deputy came crashing into the Sheriff's office, holding a manila folder tightly in the palm of his hands. Both of them sure it's contents were obviously of great notability and importance as the deputy entered without even the slightest knock. His hands worked quickly as the deputy approached the Sheriff and handed him the folder. "I'm sorry to interrupt sir," the deputy paused to catch his breath. "But this just came in over the wire. I'm the only one that's seen it, but it's going to be ran in tomorrow's paper."

"What are you talking about?" Sheriff Burnham asked, finding his curiosity growing strong.

"It's a breaking news story from Starke, Florida sir," the deputy replied. "And I know what's been going on around here and everything." Then, pausing, the deputy tried to sound serious, yet with an unmarked and high profile professional attitude. "Sir," he began again, his expression stern. "You'll want to see this. I think this is something you need to look at right away."

* * *

Back in Birmingham, Alabama.

Jamie Walker found herself, with the help of a hand-crafted, creatively designed wooden cane, walking through the gorgeous Alabama National Forest. It was late in the afternoon, and the top, polished edge of the swan shaped cane felt slippery as the hours seemed to pass quickly by, and sweat continued to emancipate from her palms. They had spent the entire day in the National Forest, simply hiking through the tall, immense pine trees until they had found the perfect spot to stop and enjoy the picnic Travis had taken the liberty to prepare for the two of them.

It had been a glorious day, one in which Jamie hadn't experienced in a long time. The sky had remained clear throughout, it's bright gaping blue appearance seemed to give off a feeling of joy inside her weakened body, giving her hope for a new day, with only a few white cirrus clouds hanging motionlessly at high altitudes. The whole day had been filled with laughter, as the two of them grew even closer together, and with the beauty of Mother Nature surrounding them in every direction, it was truly the perfect plan for the perfect day.

Jamie's mind remained free throughout, never once falling victim to the vicious memory of Curtis Rains, and her insistence that he was trying to destroy her life. Today, she had vowed to remain happy, and enjoy the company of the man she loved, not giving the evil man the satisfaction of getting to her. And so far, her efforts had proven to be successful. In fact, his name, and the strange events she had been through as of late weren't even mentioned. They acted as if they were the only people left on the face of the earth. They spoke with passion, holding one another with an embrace that made life appear to be worth living. They were the essence of love, the essence of life itself, and in the few short hours they had spent together in the forest, communicating with one another was the only thing that mattered. Everything else forgotten, hopefully never to return again. Instead of a cold distilling darkness, the day was filled with an overload of sunshine, and the evil man Jamie knew to be hiding in the darkness, concealing his blackened heart, was nowhere to be found.

Jamie had struggled at first, but after a while, the two of them managed to climb a steep, mountainous hill. Once they reached the top, Jamie found a boulder resting peacefully in the middle of a small clearing of trees, overlooking the valley below. It was one of the most beautiful scenes Jamie had ever laid eyes upon, and now found herself perched on top of the large stone, with Travis sitting right next to her, holding her close as the two of them enjoyed the picturesque, heavenly moment together. No words were spoken as the two of them sat in silence. They welcomed the comforting shelter Mother Nature provided and accepted the invariable down slope winds that cooled them down.

Nothing could beat this moment.

If Jamie could stay forever, she wouldn't even give it a second thought. It was like a slice of heaven had been handed to her out of the gracious hands of God, sent down from a beautiful winged angel and placed directly into the palm of her hands. It was peaceful, charming, and made her feel safe and secure. Then, turning her cheek, she looked into Travis's eyes. "I love you Travis. Thank you for taking me here today. It's so beautiful."

"Yes it is," Travis agreed. "And I'm glad you're enjoying yourself." Then, checking his watch, he continued although cursing himself for knowing that he was about to spoil the mood. "But we should probably be heading back soon. The sun's going to start to set soon and we don't want to be stuck in this forest at dark. We'll never find my damn truck. Especially since we didn't bring a flashlight."

"You're right," Jamie smiled taking his hand in her own. "But promise me we'll come back here real soon."

"I promise." Then, after kissing her gently on the cheek, Travis helped Jamie climb down from the top of the rock. Holding one another close for a moment, Jamie closed her eyes and wished she never had to let go. She didn't want to let Travis go. Didn't want to return home. She just wanted to stay right there, with him, for as long as possible.

Then, something happened.

It was something completely unexpected that caught the two of them off guard. It was a loud, crackling sound coming from the sky above. It was a booming thunderous roar that splintered its way through their ears and tingled their spines. But the sky was crystal clear. Slowly, Jamie released her embrace from around Travis, and turned the opposite direction. Looking behind her, up at the sky, she was shocked at what she saw.

Behind her, the sky wasn't blue.

It was pitch black, and she knew that a horrendous severe thunderstorm must have been approaching at a mesmerizing speed. Looking over the valley once more, the sky remained clear. She didn't understand what was happening. How could this be? How could half the sky be filled with beauty, while the other covered completely in a fiendish, treacherous black color? It was a weather phenomenon, obviously not a dissent from the heavens above, but from a land of darkness, where only evil could produce such a mystical, puissant scene.

Then, the thunder rolled once again, and a streak of lightning could be seen in the distance.

"What's going on?" Jamie asked Travis completely terrified.

"Looks like a damn storm is coming this way," Travis replied as he made the first steps to get them back to the safety of his truck. "I didn't think it was supposed to rain today." Then, pausing, he grabbed her arm and helped her move quickly back down the steep hillside. "Come on sweetheart. We really have to get out of here. A storm is coming so it's probably going to get darker quicker than we first anticipated. I'll cook us a nice warm dinner when we get home."

Speechless, and still dazzled in shock, Jamie let herself be lead through the mountain, still clutching her ebony cane with a strong grip. The day, which had been so splendid and wonderful, was no more. The mood had changed, the beauty gone and almost completely forgotten. And the feeling Jamie Walker had vowed to be rid of for the day, quickly returned. Once again, she was scared.

Once again, it appeared as if hell was coming for her. She couldn't escape it. She couldn't get rid of whatever was after her. Completely terrified, Jamie didn't want to leave Travis's side. Clutching his arm tightly, she closed her eyes, trusting that he would lead her on a smooth path and not allow her to lose her balance and tumble to the hard ground below.

Why was this happening again?

Was there truly no escape?

Everywhere Jamie Walker went, darkness seemed to follow. And slowly, it was closing in once again.

* * *

Starke, Florida.

Day had long turned into night, yet detective Ashley Selvaggio worked aimlessly at her desk behind a towering stack of paperwork. Brushing it all aside, her attention was focused completely on the case she had been introduced to first thing that morning. It was the Reynolds homicide case, and her eyes gazed upon one of the many dotted lines, where her signature would be needed to consider this case closed. Her superior had spoken with her earlier that day, telling her to make sure the paperwork would be on his desk first thing in the morning. And although she had agreed to do just that, it was only because she didn't want her Captain breathing down the back of her neck. Ashley knew she wouldn't sign anything until she was sure, and confident that the case was solved. She was positive that in the morning, the lab tests would arrive and confirm that it had been Jack Reynolds whom had chosen to take his own life after he viciously attacked his family and slaughtered them to death. Even more, she was sure test results would prove that the blood on the wall, from which the word Tinman had been written, would belong to that of Gloria and Sarah Reynolds.

And in knowing these facts, what else was there? What else could she possibly want to know?

Ashley was completely dumbfounded, yet her gut instinct remained strong.

She was missing something. Something of vital importance that could bring this mystery to an end. However, it appeared as though her eyes were the only ones looking past the obvious and into the world of supernatural suspense. Everyone around the department had long since put this morning behind them, almost forgetting that it ever happened at all, assuming this particular case to be open and shut. All of them, except for Ashley Selvaggio.

Ashley knew that by morning, she would have no other choice but to confront her Captain and explain to him that she wanted to be allowed more time to look into the intriguing case. There was always the possibility that he would recoil her plea for a continuance and demand her to hand it over, not seeing any reason for further media frenzy. However, for some reason, she felt confident, felt that maybe, just maybe, he would see things through her eyes and allow her a little space. It was a long shot, but it was there, and Ashley was going to take it.

She could feel her fellow officers now, looking down on her, watching her as she moved, wondering just what she was trying to prove. She could feel their eyes now, mocking her as she passed, their eyes alone trying to force her to call it quits. She had moved up in the rankings so fast, and with ease, many believed it had been due to her gender. The fact that she was a woman was the reason she had been granted the investigator position to many of the men in the department. Not her quick wit. Not her ability to see through the obvious, to almost appear to go beyond the level of humanity. It wasn't that she could look into someone's eyes and practically immediately see their level of guilt of innocence. Being men, that wasn't acceptable. It had to be her looks, her beauty, her figure, or the way she seemed to blossom in the smell of roses. Sure, Ashley worked vigorously to remain attractive. However, that had nothing to do with her success in law enforcement.

Looking at her watch, it was a quarter past nine o'clock. Yawning, she looked over the notes she had jotted down earlier, after making what seemed like twenty or so phone calls. She was amazed at the number of facts she had been able to obtain in such a sententious period of time. In a few hours, she had learned a lot about the Reynolds family. Mainly, however, she was concerned with learning as much about Jack Reynolds as she could. What kind of man he was, what did he like to do, she wondered? And surprisingly, she had found the answers after calling a few of his close friends, and a phone call to the state prison, where what she thought would turn out to be a quick conversation, soon became a lengthy one.

She now knew that Jack had worked in the prison, all of his time working on death row, overlooking the worst of the worst day after day. And she learned that before his death sentence was carried out, the man known as the Tinman, had been locked down for the entire ten years he stayed behind bars on Jack's death row. It was clear that they had been in frequent contact with one another. In speaking with a number of guards, she learned of many confrontations between the deceased inmate and the empowering prison guard.

"Jack was a cool character," she remembered one of the guards saying about their fellow crewmember. "He always showed up on time, and really seemed to enjoy his job. He was quick to put a prisoner in his place, but pretty much just watched them, making sure they didn't get out of line. He was really strong, and never let any of them get to him. There was always yelling on death row," she recalled the guard pausing briefly to obviously take in a puff on a cigarette. "Ya know, inmates calling us names, threatening us and stuff like that. But Jack was able to blow it off, and never paid any of them any attention. Except," he had paused once again. "Except for Curtis Rains. He was a real sick son of a bitch and was always tormenting Jack. Staring at him, laughing at him and saying that he couldn't be killed. Shit, I couldn't even stand to look in the motherfucker's eyes. He was really psycho, and scared the piss out of me. But Jack could do it. Only, more times than not, it would turn violent, and Jack would just go crazy over Rains. It took a couple of us to hold him back a number of times. But it was weird. It was like Curtis was the only one that could send him over the edge, and he thrived on it."

In listening to the guard's converse, Ashley found it hard to believe that Curtis was able to survive ten years in prison without dying from any powerful wounds inflicted upon him through the hands of Jack Reynolds. It was also clear that Jack appeared to be an ill-tempered person when it came to Curtis Rains, and would spring quite often into a violent rage, where blood was the only thing that could calm him down. Other than that, there appeared to be nothing wrong with him. His neighbors claimed that he lived a healthy family life, loved both his wife and daughter greatly and was always smiling and fun to be around. Even the other guards at work claimed he was a wonderful person who would stick his head out for you and be there for you whenever you needed him. Except, when it came to Curtis Rains. Somehow, Jack transformed into a different person when it came to the famous serial killer. "Jack really had it in for the Tinman," she remembered another guard saying.

Then, Ashley learned of the beating of Jacob Jones, the prison's newest addition to death row. Jones had moved into Curtis Rains's old cell, and was minding his own business when Jack Reynolds arrived at work and immediately came to his cell. "It was weird," another guard proclaimed. "It was like Jack came to work that day with something on his mind, anxious to get to the cell once occupied by Rains. I thought he didn't get a lot of sleep the night before because he looked tired, and had bags hanging under his eyes and all. Anyway, he just starts conversing with Jones, the new inmate, and the next thing I know he's just wailing on him. I mean he put a pretty good beating on him. Put a hole in his head the size of a baseball. I didn't think the poor bastard was going to make it, but the last I heard, he was in stable condition and was going to be all right."

This too, intrigued Ashley for some reason.

However, none of it was enough. She could almost sense Jack slowly changing into a homicidal maniac. But why? Something had gotten to him. Or was it someone? Needless to say, however, Ashley was convinced that something had drove Jack over the edge. This wasn't a case for the theory of biology and crime. There was no chemical imbalance in Jack's brain. This was something that couldn't be accounted for, and couldn't be seen with the naked eye.

But Ashley refused to give up.

And for some reason, although she would never come directly out and say such a thing, she didn't hold Jack Reynolds responsible for the death of his family. There was still something else she was missing. Something she had to find. To Ashley Selvaggio, giving up was not an option.

Then, yawning once again, Ashley checked her watch and realized she had accomplished everything that would be consummated for the day and decided to return home and try to obtain a good nights sleep. As her curiosity continued to ponder around in her brain however, and as her curiosity continued to roll, she knew sleeping was going to be a difficult task until her quest for the truth had been fulfilled. Leaning back in her chair, she listened as her back crackled as it gave way to its stiffness and her muscles tried to expand in order to relax. Finally, after she ran her perfect, brisk fingers through her gorgeous brown hair, she removed herself from behind her desk and made her way to the door.

Flicking off the light, Ashley exited her suite, and soon found herself standing outside the department's parking lot. Before climbing in her truck, however, she gazed up at the bright shiny stars above, not even realizing that they resembled her own beauty. Breathing heavily, she spoke to herself.

"Help me Lord," she prayed closing her eyes. "Help me find the truth."

Then, climbing inside, she placed her key in the ignition, opened her sunroof and in seconds found her Toyota 4-Runner springing to life. Pulling out of the parking lot, she glanced one last time at the magnificent, heavenly stars above. Then, turning her attention once again back to the road, she yawned once again and couldn't wait to crawl under her satin covers and fall into a peaceful deep sleep. It was as if her bed was beckoning her to come home and sleep. The only problem was, she would be alone and without the powers of love.

Lonely, Ashley Selvaggio lived life in search of the truth, instead of happiness.

Jason Glover

* * *

The creature was smiling.

It was time for yet another massacre, and another soul would be lost into the evil world he had created, he himself swallowing them whole and cherishing every moment as they screamed in vain. The memory and pain from his childhood still lingered in the distance, and the fact that there was still a couple of people left that had hurt him, was not going over too well. He had been having fun at first; enjoying the terror he was bringing to their lives.

But soon, it was time for it all to end.

Soon, it would be time to complete his bloody rampage once and for all, and continue to roam freely in the very hell he had created. He was untouchable, was no longer a part of society and had been released from the torment and pain his previous world provided for him as he had remained locked behind a cage. They had been mad at him for becoming what society had forced him to become. It wasn't his fault.

However, it was beyond forgiveness.

It was time for retribution. Time for revenge. Time to get even.

Soon, his name would be known once again, and everyone would realize that only his evil, horrifying spirit could evoke such pain and destruction with such force. Only he could bring on merciless screams into the night as blood clinched his thirst, and death made him stronger.

He could sense a number of people thinking about him.

He could sense their minds wondering in his direction.

He could smell their presence as they desperately tried to understand what was going on.

And he could taste their fear.

Needless to say, the Tinman was back.

And it was time to strike again.

Chapter 23

Nightfall.

Travis McKinley awoke in a cold sweat to the sound of rolling thunder. It had been raining nonstop since he and Jamie had returned home that afternoon from the National Forest. They had been forced to listen to the constant chattering of wind chimes as a vicious wind stormed through the area, as rainfall continued to pound away on their rooftop. Travis found it difficult to sleep, but occasionally was able to doze off for a couple of hours, only to awaken once again as a crackling, deafening burst of thunder would come flowing from the skies above and split through his ears violently. A lightning rod in the distance would illuminate their bedroom briefly, only to disappear seconds later and return them to an uncomfortable darkness. Every time the stentorian, clamorous sound of thunder would disturb his sleep, Travis would jerk wide-awake immediately, thinking that something was wrong. Checking on Jamie, he would find her sleeping peacefully next to him, obviously unaware of the storm around them. Feeling childish, he would desperately try to fall back asleep, only to awaken once again as another tumultuous roll of thunder splintered the night's peaceful atmosphere. Travis couldn't remember the last time such a powerful thunderstorm penetrated the Birmingham area. He could actually hear the trees cracking outside.

Finally, realizing his battle for sleep was a losing ordeal; he quietly climbed out of bed not wanting to disturb Jamie, and made his way into the kitchen to fix himself a steaming cup of coffee. As the kitchen light sprang on, Travis was surprised that his electricity remained in circulation. Any other time, it seemed as though his neighborhood was the first to lose its power. Nevertheless, he wasn't complaining.

It took only a few minutes for the coffee to become rich and dark brown, and soon Travis found himself nestled comfortably in his favorite recliner, using the remote control to move him from one channel to another until at last he found something that captured his attention. Deciding on the news, he wanted to find out just where this storm had come from and why there was no warning of a severe squall. The gales were so powerful Travis was certain a few trees would fall before the night was over.

Checking his watch, it was past midnight yet he wasn't tired, and the coffee he was devouring wasn't a solution to his problem. Hopefully, the storm would soon pass and he could return to his bed where his beloved girlfriend Jamie Walker slept peacefully. A thunderstorm had never denied him his sleep in the past, and Travis found his mind wondering just why he was having such trouble putting it behind him.

Nevertheless, there he was, wide awake, unable to sleep.

Finally, he found a channel that was discussing the weather and saw from the Doppler radar that the storm would be gone by morning. According to calculations, the skies would return completely clear by noon, with most of the rain gone by the early morning hours. Travis really didn't care about the battering rain; it was the constant thunder that was keeping him awake.

Then, something happened.

Travis listened acutely as the booming sound came echoing throughout his home. Only, this wasn't the sound of thunder. It was the sound of something reverberating, or fulminating into another object. His mind filled with amazement and curiosity as to what could have caused such a disturbing sound. Travis climbed to his feet and ran to the front door, still baring the hot cup of coffee in his hand. Turning the knob slightly, he could clearly hear the violent winds pulverizing their way across his lawn, destroying anything that was unstable enough to break free from its barrier and send it sailing into the night. Travis opened the front door of his home and stepped outside on the porch and was immediately pounded by gallons of raindrops, as the downpour appeared to form and move directly in his direction.

Part of him wanted to run for shelter and return back inside to the safety of his home. What he saw, however, kept him where he stood, his eyes fixed on the unbelievable scene in front of him. It was an enormous pine tree, and it had fallen directly on top of his neighbors home, its branches easily thrashing their way through the roof, a big gaping hole seen each time a streak of lightning lit up the night sky. No lights came on inside his neighbor's home, and he immediately wondered if they were all right? He watched momentarily for any signs of life. Unfortunately, however, there was nothing. No one appeared to be escaping from the home.

Running back inside, not realizing how soaked he was, he set his coffee mug on the bar and immediately picked up the phone. Preparing to dial 911, he became frustrated as he realized there was no dial tone. This was crazy. He had electrical power, yet his phone wasn't working, he grumbled silently.

"Damn it," Travis scorned his telephone as he threw on his working boots, grabbed a flashlight out of the hallway closet and returned outside, knowing what he had to do. The walk to his neighbor's home was virtually a short one. Yet, as he battled the rain and wind, he realized his decision to go out in the storm might not have been the smartest he's ever made. Nevertheless, he had to do something. He had to make sure the people inside that home were all right.

His feet squashed in the mud puddles, and he dodged small objects that the wind seemed to throw at him. Finding it hard to see just exactly what lay in front of him, Travis turned on the flashlight and was once again disappointed at how faint and weak the light was, practically unable to penetrate no more than ten yards into the darkness. Finally, however, after what seemed like an eternity, Travis McKinley reached his neighbor's home. A lightning flash briefly lit up the night sky once again, and Travis couldn't believe the damage the large tree had inflicted upon the home. In the front of the house, almost the entire roof had been dismantled, pieces scattered everywhere in the front yard as the wind continued to rip away at the loose shingles.

"Is everyone O.K.?" Travis screamed into the night, doubtful anyone would be able to hear him, and yet wondering if it was actually safe for him to try and enter the faltered home. Again, seeing no movement from inside, and hearing no screams for help, Travis stood motionless, wondering just what his next move should be? There was no other choice; he had to enter the home. Taking in a deep breath, he felt an enormous wind of adrenaline enter his body giving him the courage and strength to go forth. Taking his first step, Travis McKinley didn't look back, and entered the home through the unlocked front door, which surprisingly still operated perfectly and remained unaltered.

Once inside, Travis immediately shined the flashlight around the interior. Water continuously poured in from a large orifice the immense pine tree had formed in the ceiling. Slowly, Travis began making his way throughout his neighbor's home, searching every bedroom, bathroom, closet, and found nothing. "Is anyone here?" he called aloud into the night as another roll of thunder formed and exploded into the twilight. "Is everyone all right in here?" he asked pointlessly. Then, giving one last look around the entire core of the home, he decided to call it quits.

He had risked injury to himself and had traveled out into the heart of a massive, severe thunderstorm for nothing. No one was even home, and it appeared as though no one needed his help. Realizing he had probably overreacted to the given situation, Travis cut the flashlight off, knowing it was virtually not providing light for a distinguishable path through the storm as he headed back towards his beloved home. Once back inside, he planned to remove himself from the drenched garments his body bore, and settle once again into the warm, cozy bed to snuggle with the woman he treasured so much. Even if he couldn't sleep, he would much rather just be lying right next to Jamie, than darting off out into a robust, potent thunderstorm, looking to help people that weren't even home.

As of now, Travis McKinley welcomed his bed.

Then, reaching the steps to his front door, he stepped under the shelter and began to wipe his feet off on the mat placed directly in front of the wooden door. After taking his upper clothing off, Travis removed his shoes and was about to twist the doorknob, anxious to return inside and get out of the violent rain shower and into safety from the destructive winds, which had to be exceeding the twenty-five mile and hour mark. Pushing the door open, his body shivered for a moment, and he was about to step inside, when a sound captured his attention.

Turning back around, his face became covered in a flustered expression. Travis stepped to the edge of the front porch and listened keenly with both ears to see if the sound would return. He hadn't been convinced that he had heard anything at all, perhaps the storm delivering him a false message and was doing nothing more than toying with his imagination. For a moment, Travis didn't hear anything, and doubted the troublesome sound would come again. Motionlessly, Travis stood in complete silence, listening intently for what he thought he heard.

Finally, after a few chilling minutes of hearing nothing, and realizing that his body was once again becoming trampled by a furious rainstorm, he turned and was about to return inside to the warmth and safety of his abode. Walking back underneath the front porch, Travis once again started brushing the water off his muscular torso when the sound came again. Only this time, it was more distinct and clear.

It sounded like a person.

A person screaming for help. Could it be possible, Travis wondered? Could someone be in danger?

Stepping back outside and out from underneath the sheltering roof of the porch, Travis strained his ears once again to try and figure out exactly where the sound had come from. This time there was no mistake, and no dispute. He had heard something. Someone needed his help after all. Then, as soon as it appeared as though the sound was once again going to hide from the grasp of his eardrums, Travis became frustrated. Surprisingly, however, it came again, and this time, the words were clear as day.

"Help!" Travis could clearly hear someone crying out. "Please! Someone help me." Someone was undoubtedly in trouble, and Travis was sure he was the only one that had heard the dense, muffled cries for help. It sounded like that of a small child, sex not known, but the voice obviously terrified. He couldn't turn his back on a child. No. There was no way Travis could simply walk inside his home, return to bed, already not being able to sleep, and just forget that he had ever heard someone's cries for help. "Help!" the voice once again shouted into the night, overcoming the thunderous boom that simultaneously seemed to appear at the same time. Then, with the hairs on the back of his neck standing tall, Travis quickly ran inside his home, his mind already determining what needed to be done.

Quietly, he entered his bedroom and drew his twelve gauge shotgun from the closet not wanting to awaken Jamie, knowing she wouldn't approve of what he was about to do. But what other choice did he have? His phone didn't work, and it was too dangerous to try and drive for help. After all, by then, it could be too late. Then, exiting the room, Travis threw on a raincoat, put back on his soaked work boots and with the shotgun in one hand, and a single flashlight in the other, he headed back out into the night and into the storm, to try and find whoever had been calling out for help.

Travis placed three shells in the pump action implement of war, not knowing exactly what kind of situation he was about to confront, and wanted to be ready for even the most drastic of circumstances. Listening unwaveringly for the cry to come again, Travis prepared to follow his instincts, hopefully leading him in the direction from which the voice had come.

"Help!" he heard the weak voice call out again, and immediately headed towards the wooded area, located just to the right of his home, and extended for miles beyond. "Help!" the voice repeated with more frequency as Travis's pace quickened, his ears following the sound until he reached the entrance of the woods. Looking up at the copse of trees, Travis momentarily hesitated before entering, but knew there was no turning back. Then, holding the gun out in front of him with the flashlight directly underneath, Travis McKinley entered the woodland as the storm continued to swell and the terrain remained sluggishly rugged. Looking back after traveling only a few yards, Travis couldn't believe how dense the thicket of trees had become. Already, he couldn't see the clearing on which his house resided. Except for the weak flashlight, he was completely blind, and for the first time, his heartbeat quickened and a nauseating fear began to take over his body. Travis began to realize, that perhaps he had made a mistake.

Nevertheless, he wasn't turning back.

"Help!" the voice came again.

"Hang on!" Travis called back as loud as his voice would allow, praying that whoever was out there had been able to hear him. "I'm coming. Just keep screaming so I'll know where you are."

"Help!"

"I'm coming," Travis tried to assure the terrified child. "Just hang in there."

Jamie Walker couldn't believe her eyes.

Why was Travis running like a madman across their front lawn and towards the vicinity of the woods? What could he possibly be thinking? She remembered being awake when Travis had entered their bedroom just moments ago. Although not saying anything, she thought that he was doing nothing more than returning to bed after coming from the kitchen to catch a midnight snack. However, as the seconds flew by and she felt no movement on the bed, she opened her eyes just in time to see him depart from their bedroom with his shotgun grasped in between his two hands.

Becoming instantly alert, Jamie found herself wide-awake in bed, utterly speechless as her mind wondered what was going on? Then, hearing the front door shut, she couldn't believe he had actually gone outside in such a hounding storm, that didn't appear to be ending any time soon and moving nowhere fast.

Nevertheless, it had been too late to stop him. Then, sitting up in bed, she spun around and peered outside the bedroom window. She watched for a moment, as Travis appeared to be standing still in the middle of their lawn, in the middle of the storm, waiting for something. But what? Then, just as quick as a flash of lightning came darting out of the disturbed, electrified atmosphere, he was gone, racing in the direction of the woods holding the shotgun with one hand, and a flashlight in the other. He was after something, that was obvious, but Jamie had no idea what that something was.

Climbing out of bed, she once again grabbed her ebony swan shaped cane and made her way out into the living room. Jamie realized she wouldn't be able to return to sleep without Travis lying right next to her. Until Travis returned home, Jamie knew that it was going to be a long night.

A long, lonely night, where anything could happen.

Then, walking to the front door, she tried to turn the knob that would spring their porch light to life. Unfortunately, nothing happened and she saw not even the slightest attempt for the bulb to flicker on. Terrified, Jamie ran into the living room and checked another light, praying that the one found on the porch was nothing more than a dead bulb that needed to be replaced. Again, however, nothing happened. Frantically, she tried another light, and another, only to receive the same result.

The electricity was out.

Going to the nearest phone, Jamie picked up the receiver and pressed her ear firmly against the cold object. Nothing. Only silence. Only, it wasn't your ordinary comfortable silence. It was a dead silence that seemed to ring inside her ears for minutes after she slammed it once again back in its place. Jamie didn't know exactly what she was so afraid of, yet as panic kicked in, she desperately wished Travis were there with her. Why did he have to leave? What could he possibly be looking for? Or better yet, what could have possibly compelled him to run into the forest on such a disastrous night?

Feeling herself loosing control, Jamie slowly made her way back to the bedroom and searched her dresser drawers for a couple of candles. She found them exactly where she remembered placing them, and once lit, set each of them at the two ends of the oak headboard behind her head. She welcomed the comforting light, and she tried her best to dismiss the invigorating and evil shadows that formed and lurked about, covering the walls of her room. Closing her eyes, she tried to think of the wonderful day she had experienced before the chilling storm had inserted itself into their lives and ruined her perfect day.

The storm, however, felt different. It didn't feel like a storm brought upon by the hands of Mother Nature, but by some other unseen, driven force that could manipulate the gorgeous free-spirited skies above. The storm was a framework of a reckoning in the midst, where nothing but a flagitious evil could be found hiding behind the confining barriers of the blackening clouds, as they blistered the once blue skies above, diminishing its beauty. And to Jamie, the beauty could be lost forever. Now, she wondered if she would ever see another beautiful sky again?

Once again, she was afraid.

And sleeping, she well knew, was not an option.

Pulling a book out from underneath the bed, she opted to try anything to take her mind off the uncomfortable situation she found herself in. Closing her eyes, she prayed to God to see her through this storm and the little imprecations she found herself experiencing. Furthermore, she prayed for Travis's safe return home, where she hoped he would have a good explanation as to why he had left in the first place.

Lying on the bed, in her candlelit room, Jamie proceeded to read in a desperate attempt to forget about the evil spirit she knew to be lurking in the darkness.

Travis McKinley found himself struggling to walk steadily through the immense forests, and slipped on a number of occasions, tumbling to the hardened floor below, only to quickly climb back to his feet and continue on his expedition to find the person calling out for help. He knew that he was going in the right direction, as the voice steadily grew louder and louder and more distinct. Combing the area as best he could, Travis realized that if he wasn't careful, he himself might have a hard time finding his way home. Putting his own life in jeopardy, he well knew, was not worth that of another individual.

"Help!" he heard the voice again, only this time, he knew he was within thirty yards of whoever it was. "Help. Can you still hear me?"

"Yes, I can hear you," Travis replied, anxious to reach his destination. "I'm almost there. Hang on."

Piercing his eyes into the night, Travis took in a deep breath and began forcing himself through the heavily wooded area. Trampling over the evergreen bushes that stood in his way, and with each step taken, he made sure his footing was snug. He could feel his legs and arms being sliced by the thorns of the many unseen brambles, but ignored the slight pain his wounds seemed to convey. The deeper Travis traveled into the unfamiliar territory of the woods; however, the number of thistles seemed to grow rapidly. Until at last, it almost seemed as though his entire body would be covered in bloodthirsty abrasions, anxiously awaiting him to scratch away. Nevertheless,

Travis remained focused, and continued on his way through the woods, not giving the scrapes a second thought.

Then, Travis came to a large pine tree, and paused momentarily to catch his breath. The trees shielded him from most of the rain that continued to fall from the skies above, and briefly he found himself leaning against the bark of the tree. Shining his flashlight wildly into the night, Travis searched for any signs of life. He had to be close, he could feel it. He could feel the presence of another individual somewhere close by. From where he stood, however, he could see nothing. Travis wasn't even sure how far he had actually traveled into the forest, or for that matter, how he was going to retrace his steps and find his way home? Right now, however, his only concern was finding the lost individual and transport whoever it may be to safety.

"Hello!" Travis called into the night. "Are you still out here?" he screamed loudly. Then, still leaning against the large pine tree, and still grasping the shotgun tightly in the palm of his hands, he waited patiently for the voice to respond. When nothing came, Travis's body stiffened and fear once again began to take a staggering grip on his conscious. Had he gone the wrong way?

No.

That was impossible. He had been following the sounds, listening as he came closer and closer to whoever had been calling out into the night. He couldn't have traveled too far off course, if he had at all, and was sure that from where he stood, the child would still be able to hear him. Yet, as his eyes surveyed the darkened land in front of him, he saw nothing. And as he waited for the child to respond, his exhausted ears heard nothing. What was going on? "Hello!" Travis repeated obstreperously. "If you can still hear me, please say something."

"I'm over here," the voice suddenly wailed into the night, the child's high-pitched tone squelching throughout Travis's ears, almost piercing them with a sharp pain. Travis was close. "I'm over here," the voice repeated in the same tone, telling Travis there was a terrified child lurking in the midst of the thick forest, trapped in the storm.

"All right," Travis spoke up. "I'm coming. Don't be afraid. I'm almost there." Then, Travis waited for a burst of lightning to light up the area. When one came, Travis ordered the child to keep screaming until at last, he had reached his destination. Following the high pitched screams for help, Travis ran with surprising ease throughout the forest, his feet gingerly working their way over the soggy soil, while at the same time cautiously balancing Travis's body, making sure he kept his footing. Travis bolted throughout the forest, weaving in and out of the large pine trees, and pointing the flashlight directly in front him. Then, running atop a small protruding hill, Travis once again came to a stop, and surveyed the land below.

"Help," the voice bellowed once again in a clamorous manner.

Then, turning to the left, Travis shined the flashlight straight ahead. There, slumped over next to a large pine tree, and no more than five yards away, was a small child no more than eight or nine years of age. It was a boy, a small boy, his naked body glistening into the night each time a lightning rod shot down and reached the surface as the rain shower covered his body with a thick coat of liquid. Travis stood motionlessly for a moment, not believing his eyes. He had found what he had been looking for. He had found the person calling out into the night for help. However, he had never expected to see what lay right before his very eyes. Completely dumbfounded, Travis McKinley slowly walked towards the little boy, trying his best to hide the concern in his eyes, even though his mind was dazzling with questions.

Then, he approached the little boy just as another bright light illuminated through the blistering storm and came shrieking down from the skies above. Travis knelt down and tried to look the terrified boy in the eyes, but the boy sat sternly, seeming to refuse to make eye contact with the man whom had risked so much to come to his aid. It was almost as if the small child was trying to parry, avoiding the situation he found himself in. He was completely exposed, his ecdysiast covered in mud and rain. Bags outlined his eyes almost making the helpless child look as if he hadn't slept in days. His body shivered in the dampened area, obviously in need of warmth, as his conscious trembled with an unbearable fear.

"It's all right," Travis tried to comfort the small child in front of him as he slowly draped one of his arms around the boy. "It's all right now. You don't have to be afraid anymore. I'm going to get you out of here." As those words left his mouth, Travis himself began to wonder once again what was going on. How did the boy get there in the first place? What was he doing there? And why was he nude? Then, picking the boy up, hoisting him to his feet, the two of them slowly began making their way through the forest, Travis doing as best as he could in remembering which way he had came. His navigation seemed to turn into more of a guessing match, and he suddenly realized the entire setting around him looked the same. He didn't know if he was traveling along the same path that he had taken to get to the small, deprived boy, and now it appeared as though he was just as lost as the child had been. Travis knew, however, that he would never divulge his weakness.

As the two of them walked hand in hand through the darkened forest, the continuous rolls of thunder became prevalent, but its boisterous sounds never getting to them. Then, the boy's grasp on Travis's hand tightened profusely, and he could feel the boy's heartbeat vibrate through the palm of his hands. Critically, he knew he had to get the boy to safety. Kneeling down, Travis brought the two of them to a stop as another blast of lighting provided a momentary beam of light through the murkiness and obscurity of the forest. Travis looked into the boy's eyes, and immediately turned away. The child had brown hair, which was sobbing wet, but his eyes captured Travis's immediate attention. They were dark, almost completely black and the white of his eyes seemed to illuminate the blackness around them. Travis felt his own heartbeat quicken as he was forced to look away from the small child. Then, not knowing why he suddenly felt uncomfortable, he turned to face the boy once again, whom was still glaring at him.

Once again, Travis McKinley looked into the boy's eyes.

And once again, he sunk away with fear. What was it about the boy's eyes that forced him to turn away? Why was he afraid of such a little boy? There was nothing to be afraid of, he told himself. Nothing at all.

"Is something wrong?" the boy asked, still shivering.

"N-No," Travis replied falsely. "Nothing at all. How long have you been out here?"

"I can't remember," the boy answered. Then, sensing something in Travis's eyes, the boy continued to change the subject. "Are you lost too?" Then, he paused waiting for Travis to answer. When none came, he continued. "You look like something is bothering you. Is there something wrong?"

"I'm not sure," Travis hated to admit, still neglecting to tell the boy the truth. "I heard you screaming from my yard, and I just came out here to look for you. I'm pretty sure we're going in the right direction though. Don't worry. We'll get out of here and I'll cook you a nice hot meal and give you some dry clothes."

"You're a liar," the boy shot forward boldly. "You're lying to me aren't you? You don't know where you're going do you?" The boy paused and gazed into Travis's suddenly confused eyes. Travis couldn't believe what he had just heard. The boy's tone suddenly changed into one of anger, and his body was no longer trembling with fear. It was as if instantly the child's mood had changed. He couldn't believe how rude the boy had been, directly calling him a liar. Travis didn't know what to say or how to respond to such an accusation, even though it had been accurate. Then, before the boy continued, Travis watched in disbelief as a smile protruded from his face. The smile seemed to mock him as his black eyes continued to look through Travis's soul. "It's all right," the boy continued still smiling. "I know how to get out of here. Follow me." Then, letting go of Travis's hand, the child turned away and began heading throughout the forest.

Travis didn't understand.

How could the boy know which way to go? He had been lost, screaming for help.

What was going on here?

"Wait a minute," Travis called out to the boy. Then, he watched as the boy stopped in his tracks, and although he didn't turn around to face him, he could still see the ends of a smile coming from the sides of the boy's face. The boy was still smiling at him, obviously having some kind of fun in this caterwauling situation. "But how do you know the way out?" Travis asked expecting some answers. "I thought you were lost and needed my help?"

There was no response. The boy slowly turned around and once again faced Travis, baring his blackened eyes directly into Travis's own, neither of them no longer concerned with the horrendous storm that was taking place above them. Although no words were spoken, the smile remained on the boy's face.

"Listen here," Travis continued growing aggravated at the child's misbehavior. "I want to know what is going on here." Then, pausing, he thought of an even better question. "Who are you?"

"Let's just say," the boy began to respond. Only, his tone was no longer high-pitched and matched that of an eight-year-old boy. Now, it was deep, and the small figure in front of him sounded like that of an old man. "Let's just say," the boy repeated. "That things aren't always what they seem Travis."

"How do you know my name?" Travis demanded, feeling a bit uneasy. "Who in the hell are you?"

Then, along with the smile, came a laughter that seemed to splinter its way into the night and seep into Travis's head. Travis was scared; he didn't know what to do. Didn't understand what was going on. "Oh Travis," the boy continued gruffly, his tone deepening as each second passed. "You know who I am." Travis could only shake his head as his mind drew a blank. Then, right before his very eyes, the boy started to change. He was aging right in front him. He began growing taller, his bones thicker, his facial features becoming older, and soon, the boy was no longer a small child. He was a fully-grown man, dressed in scornful black clothing that matched his eyes, and a long black cloak was honing over his shoulders. Also, in his hand, Travis could see a glistening silvery knife that sparkled in the electrified air. Laughing, the man walked towards Travis, and looked dead into his eyes. "Now do you know who I am?"

This was impossible.

This simply couldn't happen. At least, not through Travis's eyes. Just seconds ago, the grown man now in front of him had been an unclothed little boy, who desperately needed his help. This just couldn't happen. It had to be a bad dream. It just had to. Nevertheless, each time Travis tried to look into the man's eyes, he found himself turning away as the hairs on the back of his neck stood tall, and his conscious grew overwhelmed in fear. Still, Travis now recognized who the man was. "B-But you're dead," Travis breathed, almost choking on his own words. "This can't be real."

Laughing, the man replied. "Oh yes I'm dead all right. But I've come back Travis. I've come back for Jamie."

"No."

Tinman

"Remember that little boy Jamie said she saw in the road that caused her to wreck her truck?" the man asked. "Well it was me Travis," the man replied before Travis had a chance to speak. "You really should have listened to her Travis cause then you might have had a chance to save her life. Now, however," the man paused letting his voice drown into silence. "Now, I'm afraid you'll never have that chance."

"No!" Travis screamed into the night, prepared to fight for his life. Then, raising the shotgun in the air, he aimed it directly at the heart of the man. The man, he now knew to be Curtis Rains. "You stay away from her."

"I'm afraid I can't do that," Curtis replied coldly, then with a wink, turned away from Travis and began heading off into the forest on his way back to Travis's house. "Let's just hope you can find your way home before it's too late."

"No!" Travis shrieked once again as he pulled the trigger.

BANG.

As the gunshot blast echoed momentarily throughout the forest, Travis pumped the gun once more and ran forwards to see if he had hit the man who had tricked him, and lured him into the forest with the sole purpose to get him lost. Travis moved the flashlight back and forth from the spot in which the man had stood, but found nothing. There was no way he had missed him. It was impossible. Yet, no body could be found anywhere. Travis McKinley was the only person around.

Frantically, Travis began to sprint through the forest. He lost his footing numerous amounts of times but continued forward. He didn't know if he was going in the right direction or not. The only choice he had was to follow his instincts. Hopefully, they wouldn't betray him. He had to get home before anything happened to Jamie. He would never forgive himself if anything happened to her.

Then, in the distance, a voice called to him, a chilling laughter following.

"Hurry home Travis," the Tinman said mockingly. *"I'll be waiting for you."*

Jamie Walker found herself earnestly browsing through the pages of her book, not really paying attention to the words. The only thing her mind seemed to elaborate on was her boyfriend, Travis McKinley. The storm continued to wail outside her bedroom window and the thunder continued to crackle in the night sky, sometimes so powerful it sounded as if her entire home was about to collapse and the steady light burning on top of both the candles flickered briefly, almost looking as if they were about to extinguish themselves. Jamie felt alone; none of the characters she had learned in her book were able to give her the companionship she desperately needed. After all, they weren't real. They were fictitious people made up from an author's imagination, each one supposedly designed to be unique in some way to capture the reader's attention. Well, the characters had been well formatted to Jamie, but she needed the real article. She needed Travis McKinley.

Unfortunately, he wasn't there.

He was running about in one of the many Alabama forests, carrying around a flashlight and a shotgun like he was pretending to be some kind of war hero. Surely, if he felt obligated to grab his gun, it was something of major importance. And something of major importance, Jamie felt, meant that she had a right to know as well. Needless to say, however, he had chosen to keep her secluded in the dark, and now her mind was a mess.

Sighing to herself, Jamie put the book down, climbed out of the covers and gazed once more outside her bedroom window and into the fuming, besieging storm. Listening closely, she could hear the upheaval outbreak of winds and the convulsion stifled hysteria inside her battered soul. An uneasy feeling began to shape inside her stomach, and after minutes of looking for any signs of life coming from the forests, she finally gave up and returned to bed. Deciding not to read anymore of the book, knowing she would have to read the pages all over again another day, Jamie pulled the covers up around her chin and simply gazed around her room.

It was quiet. Almost too quiet.

The electricity was out, the phone was dead, and the only thing that appeared to give off any signs of life at all were the two single flames burning atop the candles. They swayed ever so often as she moved about in her bed and jerked the headboard, only to return to

Tinman

normal seconds later and almost burn motionlessly as the wax continued to give way and diminish into a burning liquid, which would eventually turn cold and solid. A few shadows could be found on the walls, and Jamie found herself trying to see if she could name any shapes that may be found within.

For the first few tries she was unsuccessful.

Yet, she tried again. Finally, she was able to make out a cylinder shaped object. And then a bird, a cat, and the list continued. Jamie now smiled as she had finally figured out a way to pass the time until Travis returned home, and she didn't even have to leave the warmth of her bed. So, the game continued, and Jamie remembered back when she was just a child and she used to look up in the middle of a brilliant, beautiful blue sky day, and see how many shapes or objects she could visualize in the clouds. What she was doing now, undoubtedly, was a little different, especially since it was indoors and involved using the shadows of two burning candles, but it was effective, and Jamie cherished anything to take her mind off of the bedlam that seemed to swarm around her.

Laughing, she thought she saw a baby's bottom amongst the shadow's outlining her walls. Then, with a smile she focused in on one shape that had long ago captured her attention, yet she continued to look past it, unable to pinpoint in her head just what it was. It looked like something vaguely familiar, yet her mind could do nothing with it. Finally, however, she was confident she had named everything else there was to see, except this one shape. Now, she was able to concentrate fully on the object, putting everything else aside, bound and determined to figure out what it was.

The shadow in some way annoyed her, and left her feeling completely puzzled and distraught. It was bugging her, and she found herself concentrating harder than ever before, each time, however, not coming up with any answers. The intriguing shadow appeared to have a round shape in the middle, with a circle shape, or cylinder type pattern around it. "Damn it," Jamie cursed herself, desperately wanting to triumph. Then, it hit her.

A hat.

It was a hat, and it was a hat that she herself had seen before. It looked like one of those old black, leather, Australian bush hats. Finally, she had been able to figure it out, and conquered the game her mind had created. Now, however, it floated in a different direction. Now, she wondered why would the shape of the hat she was seeing in the shadows look so familiar? Where had she seen it before? And on whom? She knew that Travis had never owned such a hat, and she herself had never had the incentive to go out and purchase such an item.

Yet there it was on her wall, shaped by the flames of the candles, and looked so familiar.

Then, something happened.

The candle flickered, tampering with the shadow that had been seemingly frozen along the wall. The bush hat swayed momentarily, and then proceeded to fall back into its recent fixed position. Only this time, it had changed. Something else could be seen in the shadows. Now, underneath the bush hat, she could make out a head, and a neck.

Then, the candle moved again.

And the shadow grew once more.

Now, before her very eyes, Jamie could make out the entire upper body of an individual in the shadows, and as the flame flickered once more, she now faced an enormous shadow of a person on her wall, designed perfectly by the candles. What was happening? Was her mind playing tricks on her again?

Nevertheless, the bush hat remained, and the shadow of a person remained intact. Once again, Jamie Walker began to sink into an overwhelming state of fear and she began to shrink back into her covers, foreboding whatever was about to happen next. Panic set in, and Jamie could hear her heart racing out of control. She closed her eyes, yet for some reason, always reopened them and peered at the discomforting shadow outlining her bedroom wall. The game was no longer fun, and she desperately wished that it would end. Then, she had an idea. If she blew out the candles, the shadows would disappear.

Determined, Jamie prepared to remove herself from under the covers. Lifting her head up, she was about to throw the covers off and extinguish the flames when something happened. She couldn't move. She was trapped under her covers, completely immobilized. Frantically, she tried to remove herself from underneath the covers. But it was no use. From her neck down, her entire body was consumed by a single sheet, from which she could not retreat. It was like there was someone on both sides of the bed, pulling the sides of the sheets tightly, strapping her underneath. Jamie couldn't believe what was happening. No matter how hard she fought, she couldn't budge.

Then, a staggering voice came to her, echoing throughout her room. *"Jamie,"* the voice called out to her as an evil laugh pierced through her eardrums. *"What's the matter Jamie? I told you that I would be back."*

"No," Jamie screamed realizing it was Curtis Rains.

Then, she once again looked at the shadow of the man on her wall. Completely helpless, Jamie was forced to watch in tears, scared for her life as the shadow suddenly began to move on its own, coming off the wall and then standing directly in front of her bed. She could see right through the grayish, cloudy form in front of her, it's ghostly appearance chilling every bone in her body and tingling her spine all at once. What was going on, she asked herself? Jamie didn't know, but she feared the answer, and in one last attempt to remove the sheets, she knew that there would be no chance of escape.

Then, the shadowy figure began to change. Transforming right before her very eyes into that of a man. A man dressed all in black. He was clothed in black work boots, black pants, black shirt, a black coat that dangled to his knees, and also bore the black bush hat she had first recognized in the shadows on her wall. Then, lifting his head high in the air, she saw his dark, black eyes that could spread fear into the heart of the living. There right in front of her, stood the evil man she had long ago been in love with. There, before her, was Curtis Rains, his vicious smile sitting fearlessly on his face as his dark eyes bore into her soul.

"Oh Jamie," Curtis spoke up sympathetically. *"Don't look so surprised. You were just having so much fun playing your little game with the shadows; I just had to join in. I mean you looked pretty lonely, with Travis being lost out in the woods and all. I hope my company will do."*

"Travis?" Jamie questioned not believing her ears and feeling her heart drop at the sound of her lover's name. "Where is he? What have you done with him?"

"I have done nothing to him yet Jamie," Curtis laughed. *"Man, you really care about this guy don't you? That's too bad really,"* he paused as another depraved, immoral laugh escaped from his mouth. *"Too bad you're not going to get a chance to tell him goodbye. I told you I was coming back for you Jamie. You shouldn't have said those words to me in the prison and I would have left you alone. Don't you get it,"* he paused once again. *"You are the only person that I have ever cared about, and the only person to have ever cared about me. But I can't forgive you for what you said to me Jamie. There is no other way. Otherwise, I will never be able to rest in peace."*

"Go to hell you son of a bitch," Jamie screamed in freight as tears continued to storm through her eyes and run down her cheek. "I hate you Curtis Rains. I hate you."

"Shut up," Curtis demanded. *"Don't you know better than to speak to me that way? I am God compared to you. I can be anything I want to be, whenever I want to be it. I can touch anyone's life with one glance and change it forever. You, my dear, are an exception. The only reason that you are still alive is because I've let you live this long. You couldn't stop me. No one can stop me. God couldn't even stop me. Don't you get it Jamie?"* Curtis paused to laugh once again. *"I am the devil, and the world you've been living in the past few weeks has been the hell that I've created. And not you, or anyone can take that away from me. Nobody can hurt me anymore, and nobody can stand in my way. So to you Jamie, I am truly your worst nightmare. And unfortunately,"* he paused once again. *"It's time for me to end this little charade for good and steal your soul for all eternity. Look into my eyes Jamie,"* Curtis ordered. *"I'm sorry, but it's time for you to die."*

Then, suddenly, as Curtis Rains stood over her bed, Jamie felt her headboard begin to shake uncontrollably. Twisting her head upwards as far as it would go, she could see the candleholders moving closer and closer to the edge. Terrified, she tried to move out from underneath the covers. It was no use. She was still trapped. Panic began to sink in and Jamie Walker truly believed her life was about to end. Once again, she looked up at the candles, the bottom portion of the holder already hanging over the edge.

This was it.

He was going to burn her to death.

"Please God," Jamie breathed, still having faith in the almighty one. "Please help me."

"God can't help you," Curtis replied laughing once again. *"There is no use praying to a man that doesn't exist,"* he continued boldly. *"He can't save you Jamie because he's not alive, and he isn't powerful enough to conquer me."*

Then, it happened.

Both of the ignited candles fell over the edge of the bed and immediately set aflame the sheets. The fire started weak, but within seconds had grown rapidly and was working it's way towards Jamie. Again, she tried to move, but the sheets that remained on top of her and underneath her pinned her down to the bed. Crying for help, Jamie could feel the heat of the flames as they easily scorched their way through the cottony sheets and made their way directly towards her flesh. She inhaled some of the dark dense smoke that began to circulate throughout her bedroom and began choking spasmodically. This wasn't something that would pass in time. Curtis wasn't going to go away this time. This time, it was for real.

This time, the Tinman was going to kill her.

Then, closing her eyes, Jamie Walker knew the fire had reached its mark. Completely immobilized, she could feel her hair singeing down and disappearing into dust. She was going bald as the flames ignited her hair, diminishing everything down to her skin. Her entire bed had burst into one enormous flame, and now it was her nightgown that had sprang to life.

"No," Jamie screamed as her flesh continued to sizzle, and the pain grew utterly unbearable. She could feel the skin on her face being charred. In complete shock of what was happening, Jamie closed her eyes and let darkness cave in. There was so much pain. Jamie just wanted to go away, and be taken from this earth forever.

Jamie Walker no longer wanted to fight to live.

She would rather die than live in a world controlled by Curtis Rains.

Now, Jamie Walker welcomed the darkness, which was quickly closing in.

Travis McKinley finally reached the edge of the woods. Completely exhausted, he threw himself into the clearing, lying motionlessly on the ground to quickly catch his breath. Travis could tell that the storm was weakening, as the rain was no longer strong enough to block his vision. Then, standing up, forgetting about all of the cuts and bruises his body had accumulated in running throughout the forest, he ran towards his home. He had to get to Jamie before it was too late.

Running through the small field, he reached his front yard and saw that there wasn't any lights on in the house. Except, for his bedroom. It wasn't until he got close enough to actually peer inside the window, that he realized it was a fire. "No!" Travis screamed into the night, putting all his fears aside. "Jamie!" Then, busting through the front door, Travis immediately ran into the bedroom. Stopping momentarily in his tracks, he couldn't believe his eyes.

There, lying on the bed was his girlfriend, completely engulfed in flames.

He had to do something.

Running to Jamie, Travis picked her toasted body up and carried her into the bathroom. Grabbing as many towels as he could, and forgetting about the burns that had spread to his own flesh, he began to pound away at Jamie until the fire had at last been diminished. "Oh Jamie," Travis breathed not wanting to touch her charred skin. "I'm so sorry. I'm so sorry I wasn't here to protect you."

Jamie's entire body had been badly burned, Travis was sure there was no way for her to survive. Then, he heard something. It was Jamie, she was trying to breathe. "It's all right sweetheart," Travis immediately interjected. "Don't try and say anything. I'll go and get some help." Joyful that she was still barely alive, he knew that if he didn't get help fast, she would die before morning. Climbing to his feet, Travis spun around, exited the bathroom and was about to walk out into the hallway, when a dark clad figure appeared in the doorway, blocking his vision. He immediately recognized who it was.

"You should have let her die in those flames Travis," the Tinman scorned. *"All you're doing is putting her through more pain than is necessary. It's too late to save her Travis. You were too late and now she's going to die no matter what."*

"That's not true," Travis hollered, no longer afraid. "She's going to be all right."

"I don't think so," the Tinman continued. Then, as Travis tried to bravely walk past the evil man, Curtis removed something from his cloak that looked awfully familiar to his counterpart. *"You left this back there,"* Curtis laughed acutely at the joke he had made. There in his hands, was Travis's shotgun, and it was pointed directly at him.

"You can't kill me," Travis broke in bravely. "You're not even real. You're a ghost, and you can't pull that trigger."

Smiling, it happened.

BANG! BANG!

Two shots rang out into the night, and two shotgun shells fell to the floor. Curtis Rains walked through the blood that quickly scattered throughout the entire room and leaned over to look into Travis's McKinley's eyes. *"You should have stayed in the woods Travis. I would have let you live."* Then, placing the gun right next to the torn apart body of Travis McKinley, as the small shells spread out and ripped into his flesh with a furious passion, killing him instantly, Curtis Rains walked into the bathroom to check on Jamie. She wasn't dead yet, but he was sure that she would die within a matter of time.

Travis McKinley was dead, darkness quickly closing in around him. And Jamie Walker, wouldn't make it through the night.

For the two of them, the nightmare of the Tinman was at last over.

Then, after leaving his trademark on the bedroom floor, right next to Travis McKinley's deceased blood ridden corpse, Curtis Rains walked right out the front door, took three steps away from the porch, and with a smile faded into the night, lifting himself high up into the clouds above, devouring the fear he had been able to instill in his victims and enjoying the taste for blood. As Curtis joined the storm, a burst of electricity shrieked throughout the night sky and shattered the ground below.

Laughing, the Tinman disappeared from the face of the earth, where he would remain hidden until it was time to strike again.

To Jamie Walker and Travis McKinley, however, that time had been now.

Chapter 24

A new day.

The creature was once again flying freely throughout space, unseen to the human eye, but his powers able to reach beyond the limits of anyone's imagination. He could travel at the speed of light to anywhere he needed to be, and could with the snap of his fingers enter a life, destroying everything underneath the skin. His powers continued to grow as yet two more lives had been taken by his deadly hands, and their souls confined inside the creature for all eternity, forced to gaze into his eyes and live through them in a world-without-end.

His destination had already been charted, and the creature himself was simply following the violent, severe thunderstorm, which continued to head Southeasterly at an enormous speed. The creature enjoyed the storm, which seemed to destroy and demise anything that stood in its path, trampling over small towns and cities with no chance for mankind to bring it to an end. This was Mother Nature at its best, and the creature took pride in realizing he possessed the same powers as Mother Nature.

He had the power to do anything he desired.

He had the power to kill, and had already stormed back into the lives of many, since he was released into freedom after electrocution. Five more innocent people had died without the slightest mercy or remorse. Death was all the creature knew, and pain was the only lesson he knew how to teach. He had learned to become evil and strong at a very young age, and it had turned him into the man he was today.

The creature was the Tinman.

Only one target remained before he could call an end to his bloodthirsty rampage.

Soon it would all be over.

Soon, the Tinman's fury and anger could subside, and he could live peacefully in the comforting darkness he had created forever. His journey was coming to an end, his expedition to a close. Yet, he knew his name and his artwork would remain in the midst of society forever. Why he had ever chosen to do the things he did would remain a mystery for all time, the Tinman himself not allowing anyone to actually know the truth. Nor, would anyone ever find out on their own without him coming back.

He would be the reason small children woke up in a furious cold sweat scared out of their wits. Just the very mention of his name would make anyone shiver in fear. He was a legend in his own way, his marksmanship and his evil lasting forever. And he would always be there, drifting through space until a reason to strike again would prevail. He was the most evil man society had ever known, and he would live forevermore.

The Tinman couldn't be stopped, and his evil impossible to control.

And yet, soon, it would be time to lash out at his most prized possession. It was time to return to the person he had been waiting ten years to reckon with. She was the only person to ever escape his deadly touch, which made her strong. But the creature was going to make her weak, and she was going to suffer indefinitely before her death. No matter what, however, one thing was for certain.

There would be no escape this time.

At least, not until her heart was resting in the palm of his hands.

* * *

Meanwhile, in the early morning hours back in Destin, Florida.

Carey Haas jerked awake, and within seconds found herself sitting upright in the single bed found in the center of her bedroom. Looking out her window, she could see numerous brilliant rays of sunlight desperately trying to beseech their way into her room, obviously disturbed to find a barrier of blinds standing in their path. Yawning,

Carey climbed out of bed and slowly made her way to the window and with a single pull downwards on the string, watched as the blinds rose high in the air and clinched at the top. Squinting, Carey tried to forget about the disturbing nightmare she had just experienced and forced her mediocre eyes to get adjusted to the light. After a few seconds, they had done just that, and she found herself staring up at the immense sky above, hoping to find a beautiful day lying before her. Although she did find a substantial amount of Florida sunshine, a frown slid into place across her groggy face as she saw something that caught her eye, and within a few hours, she was sure the sunshine would disappear.

Unfortunately, clouds were rolling in.

And once again, Carey Haas was forced to remember the nightmare that had came to her in the early morning hours, and had continued to plague her mind until the moment her body allowed her to awaken.

As Carey stood there, in front of her window, with her golden locks dangling in the partial sunlight, she closed her eyes and allowed herself to succumb to the horrible nightmare.

Fearlessly, she relived it all over again.

The man had stood silently, hiding in the shadows of the walls, watching the woman keenly as she played her game in identifying shapes and objects from the awkward shadows that sprang to life on her walls, as the two candles found atop her headboard flickered ever so often forming new identities. Carey could clearly see that the game was quite addicting to the brunette woman that had come to her in her illusive dream, and that she was trying superlatively to finish the game successfully.

The woman looked rather injured, her movements short-lived and sometimes forcing the woman to grimace in pain. Yet she was soundly beautiful, her wavy brown hair glowing in the dim candlelight, and her nearly flawless figure shadowing itself above the darkness of the room, giving the gloomy scene a more enticing appearance. Yet, as the woman continued to play the imaginary game her mind had come up with to obviously pass the time, she not once noticed the man that was hiding in the shadows of the walls, smiling at her as he watched her every move.

The shadow of the man alone, even though Carey herself could not see his face, frightened her. How could the woman sit there peacefully, sometimes even laughing to herself and not even notice the man hiding along her wall? Better yet, Carey wondered, how could she not be afraid?

Unless, the unidentifiable woman couldn't see him.

That was it, the woman didn't even know the shadow was there, completely translucent to the very presence of the shadowy figure. But he was there, Carey could see him. He was right there in the shadows of the walls, looking over the woman lying on the bed steadily as if he were just waiting for the right moment to come to life and catch her off guard. Wanting to help, Carey tried to call out to the woman she didn't recognize and let her know what she saw. It was no use, however. The woman couldn't hear her, didn't even know that she was there. Feeling bitterly helpless, Carey Haas was forced to watch the scene in silence, waiting for the climax to happen, and waiting for the man hiding in the walls to jump out of his hiding place and trample over the poor, lost, and obviously wounded woman in front of her.

Carey couldn't stand it. Why couldn't she just wake up? She was tired of having nightmares each and every night she tried to consume some rest she knew her body desperately needed. Why couldn't she just be normal again, and put the past behind her? Nevertheless, she remained asleep, and in her nightmare continued to watch as the woman amused herself in the shadows along her bedroom walls. Upon looking into the woman's eyes, she could clearly see that she had never met the woman before. She didn't even know her name. But then, why was she there? Why was she in Carey's nightmare? Something definitely wasn't right, and everything about the nightmare felt fundamentally wrong.

Then, something happened.

"A hat," Carey could hear the woman say, finally able to name the shape that had kept her in awe and stumped her brain for so long. Then, Carey watched in dead silence as the shadow began to grow and before she knew it, the figure of a fully-grown man appeared in full view. Only this time, Carey hadn't been the only one to descry it. Finally, the brunette that had been forced into Carey's esteemed nightmare could see it, and now, she too could sense the danger and

taste the fear that the creepy shadow along the wall provided. Carey didn't want to watch what was about to happen next, yet she couldn't pull her eyes away. For some reason, she couldn't wake up, and she couldn't turn the other cheek. Just as before, she wasn't in control of her own nightmare, destined to see it to the bitter end.

The woman's eyes had turned briskly sour, and Carey could see her hands trembling with an overwhelming heap of fear. The woman was terrified, yet she too could do nothing to stop the immense shadow from growing. Raving in a frenzied state of mind, Carey watched as the woman tried to roll over in her bed, remove herself from underneath the warmth of the textiles, and frantically blow out the two candles, hoping to draw and end to the mysterious shadow that lurked along her wall. Carey couldn't believe what she was seeing. Listening to the woman's screams for mercy, she realized that the woman was unable to remove herself from the covers. She was trapped, almost as if someone had pinned her down underneath the covers and pulled them tight, strapping her down firmly, and rendered her completely helpless.

Then, the shadow began to change.

And soon, Carey herself knew who it was.

It was Curtis Rains, the same man that had come to her so many nights in the past ten years, looming over her destiny to live a peaceful verve, and constantly reminding her that he had been the one to take her parents away from her life, making sure she knew from who's hands their blood had been spilt. Nevertheless, Carey still did not understand why she was there? Curtis obviously wasn't after her this time, but after the woman whom Carey had never seen before in her life. What was going on? Who was this mysterious woman, and why was Curtis after her?

Before Carey could even attempt to answer her own questions, something happened that caught her completely off guard. Screaming at the top of her lungs, she watched as the two candles crept closer and closer to the end of the headboard, and then simultaneously both of them fell over the edge and almost instantly started a meager flame within the sheets of the bed. The woman tried desperately to escape, but something was holding her down.

Unfortunately, the fire continued to grow.

And soon, the defenseless woman's entire body was inundated in a furious onslaught of flames. The holocaust crackled in the night, and as the blaze continued to roar, Carey watched in horrific shock as the woman screamed in pain. But Curtis Rains only stood there in silence, a smile blistered across his face, enjoying the deadly inferno he had created. Carey couldn't take it anymore. She wanted to wake up and never be reminded of the gruesome conflagration again.

But she couldn't wake up. And the helpless woman continued to burn intensely. Until finally, there was no movement on the bed, and the woman's screams died away. Carey couldn't believe it. Right before her eyes, the Tinman had slain another person. And even though she didn't know who the woman was, she was sure the nightmare meant something.

Then, another person appeared in the room.

It was a male, and he was dressed horribly. His skin was tainted in mud and his entire body was covered in water. However, the man ran towards the burning woman, and never minding his own safety, picked her up off the bed and carried her into the bathroom. Seconds later Carey watched as the man reappeared, tears dripping down his face as he desperately tried to call for help. Only, as the man tried to exit the bedroom, Curtis was standing in his path, a polished shotgun gripped tightly within the palm of his hands, and the same evil smile pinpointed across his devilish face. At first, the man seemed surprised to find the figure of Curtis Rains standing in the doorway. Only, after a few seconds, the man courageously confronted the Tinman, and the two of them shared a few unfriendly words.

That's when it happened.

BANG. BANG.

Curtis had pulled the trigger his finger had been waiting anxiously to squeeze, and the man that had come to the woman's rescue now lay on the bedroom floor, his body completely motionless, and his life drained forever. Then, Carey was forced to watch as Curtis made his way to the dead body of the man, bent down and didn't come back up until both of his hands were covered in the man's bright red blood. Walking to the nearest wall, Curtis began spelling something. Once he stepped away, Carey could read what had been written in blood. It was one word.

It read:

TINMAN

Then, Curtis turned his head and faced her direction. Carey couldn't believe it. He had known that she had been there all along, and now was staring at her with his dark eyes reaching deep into her soul. Finally, a smile crossed his face and the unfavorable, yet recognizable evil laugh erupted from his throat.

That's when Carey Haas had finally woken up.

Then, when she finally was able to come to again, she still found herself standing in front of her bedroom window, and still staring up at the darkening sky as the storm she knew was quickly approaching. Shaking her head, Carey tried everything to put the nightmare aside. She didn't understand what it meant, and didn't want to find out. Talking to herself for a moment, practically forcing her to come back into reality, she was about to make her bed, when a knock suddenly came to her bedroom door. "Come in," she called out casually. Then, turning to face her door, she watched as it slowly opened and her uncle Rick stepped inside her room.

"I wasn't sure if you'd be awake or not," Rick began slowly. "I didn't want to wake you up or anything. I-." He paused not exactly sure what he was trying to say. "Well I know you went out with that Billy Saxton kid last night, and by the time you got home I was already in bed. Well," he paused once again. "I guess I was just hoping the two of us could have a little talk."

"I'm sorry for not telling you where I was going," Carey stated, sensing what the conversation was about to entail.

"Don't worry about it," Rick answered with a smile, and then watched as his niece looked up at him with uncertain eyes. She obviously couldn't believe that his mood had changed. "I'm not upset about you leaving last night, and not even that it was with Billy. I've been doing some thinking Carey," Rick paused as he came over and sat next to his bewildered niece on the bed. "And I think you're absolutely right. You're not a child anymore Carey, and not only do I have to stop thinking of you as one, but I have to stop treating you as one as well. You do have the right to make your own decisions, and

Tinman

it's not fair for me to try and stand in your way. I guess," he paused once again, not believing what he was about to say. "I guess all I'm trying to say is I'm sorry. And I really mean it Carey. I'm sorry, and I know that I was wrong."

Carey let out a deep breath. "I-I'm really not sure what to say," she began, but found no other words to follow. Then, grabbing her uncle's hand, she squeezed it affectionately and gazed up into his sincere eyes. "Thank you so much," she exasperated as a bright smile shot across her face. "Thank you for understanding Rick. You don't know how much that means to me."

"Good, I'm glad everything's O.K.," Rick broke in. "However," he continued returning her genuine smile. "Since I'm going to be all right with all of this, don't you think it's at least fair for me to officially meet Billy?" Then, he watched as another doubtful expression loomed over Carey's face, as she was once again unsure of where the conversation was going. "I'm just teasing you," Rick continued not wanting to ruin her mood. "We can meet when you're ready for us to meet. Deal?" Carey nodded. "However," Rick continued once again, only this time wishing that he didn't have to change the subject. "The sooner the better. You see, Sheriff Burnham and me have been doing some talking, and we've found out a couple of things. He thinks he needs to talk to the both of you."

"What's wrong?" Carey immediately asked.

"Nothing," Rick tried to assure her, although he himself didn't believe his own words. "Gabe just needs to clear up a few things is all. And I promise, Billy isn't in anymore trouble."

Then, before Carey could go on, the two of them were interrupted by a baffling sound coming from downstairs. It was her aunt Carol, screaming about something. They couldn't understand what Carol had yelled at first, but the second time, both of them listened closely. "You guys!" They clearly heard her screaming. "Come here quick. I think ya'll should see this." Suddenly feeling energetic, the two of them jumped to their feet and sprinted out of Carey's room, both heading for the staircase. "Hurry up," Carol screamed again unaware that they were on their way."

"What is it?" Rick asked as soon as he entered the living room with Carey, only to find Carol sitting upright in a recliner staring at the television. "What's going on Carol? You scared the crap out of us." Saying nothing, Carol only held up her hand and pointed at the television. Rick was about to say something, when his eyes glanced at a picture on the screen. Shutting his mouth, he turned up the volume, and the three of them sat silently watching the special news report. The news anchors voice was gruff, yet he spoke clear and his words passionate. Only, in the top right hand corner of the screen, was the picture of Curtis Rains. Carey's first instinct was to run away and escape back into the confinements of her bedroom, not wanting to hear anything that pertained to the evil man that had killed her parents. Yet, something made her stay, and along with her relatives, her eyes remained glued to the screen.

"Good Morning everyone, I'm Frank Dean and this is a special HYZ news report. Recently, the infamous serial killer Curtis Rains, also known as the nefarious Tinman, was killed in the electric chair after waiting ten years on death row in the Florida State Prison for his sentence to be carried out. HYZ had just learned, however, that although the man behind the myth is gone, his legend still remains behind. In Birmingham, Alabama this morning, the body of Travis McKinley was found dead in his bedroom, shot two times by a shotgun. His girlfriend, Jamie Walker, was found barely alive in the bathroom and was rushed to the nearest hospital. She was badly burned, as the bed in which she slept, was set afire. She is listed in critical condition, and remains in a coma. The doctors aren't positive if she's going to make it, and authorities are still baffled by the scene. However, the police were able to find single words written in blood on the wall of the bedroom. The single word spelled: Tinman. Authorities clearly state that there is no way Curtis Rains is involved. Yet, us here at HYZ has just learned that in Starke, Florida, a triple homicide was found two days ago in which Jack Reynolds, an employee of the state prison, apparently snapped and murdered his wife and eleven year old daughter before turning a gun on himself. At this scene as well, although miles away from one another, the single word Tinman was also found written in the victim's blood. From HYZ news, I'm Frank Dean and this has been a special news report. Join us at five for further details."

Tinman

Even after the news broadcast disappeared and a cheerful commercial came on the air, the three of them continued to stare at the television screen, none of them knowing how to respond. Rick couldn't believe such a news channel would come on so early in the morning and spread such horrendous news. Who really wanted to know about two murders that couldn't even be related or connected except for a single word? It was one big coincidence and nothing more. Were they actually trying to convince people that the Tinman was still alive, and still roaming around through society able to kill at freewill? That was impossible, and Rick was angry that the news channel would even suggest, much less broadcast such a statement.

Carol could sense her husband's frustration. "I can't believe they would say such a thing on the air." Then, turning to face Carey, she was all ready to ease her niece's pain, when the look on her face left her speechless. Carey's eyes had sunk low into their sockets and her hands were trembling dramatically. "Carey," Carol continued climbing to her feet and rushing over to the terrified girl in front of her. Rick too, turned to see what was going on. "Carey, honey. What is it? What's wrong?"

For a moment, Carey couldn't speak. She couldn't believe what her eyes had just bore witness to on the television. It had been real, she thought to herself as she remembered the nightmare once more. It hadn't just been a nightmare at all. It had been real, and the two people she hadn't recognized had been real. And just like her parents, she had watched them die.

"Carey," Rick jumped in, his strong voice seizing the moment. "Tell us what's wrong sweetheart. Please. We want to help you."

"I saw them," Carey stuttered profusely, as a strand of saliva escaped from the corners of her mouth.

"Who?" Carol asked confusingly. "What are you talking about?"

"Those two people in Alabama," Carey continued more rationally, finally coming to her senses and brushing most of the fear aside. "I saw them last night, in my nightmare. And-." She paused not wanting her words to come out the wrong way. "And he was there too, but they didn't know." Carey didn't realize it, but nothing she had said made any sense as both of her guardians looked upon her with confused expressions. She was rambling, couldn't find the right

403

words to say, and didn't know how to say them. Nevertheless, she continued, and both Rick and Carol did their best to follow. "He was there, and he killed them."

"Who killed who?" Rick asked boldly, trying to force the words out of Carey.

"It was Curtis Rains," Carey blurted out feeling a bit of nausea coming about. "And I saw him last night," she continued speaking of the people in Birmingham, Alabama. "He came to me while I was sleeping and he made me watch. He made me watch the whole thing."

"What did he make you watch Carey?" Carol asked calmly. "I don't understand."

"He made me watch those people die," Carey screamed in a fearful pain that tormented her entire body. "I saw him kill those people. It was really him. And now," she paused once again, trying to swallow the lump that had formed in her throat. "And now I think he's coming after me."

* * *

Detective Ashley Selvaggio couldn't believe what had just appeared on the news. She had already asked one of her assistants to phone Birmingham to find out as much as they could about the incident. She knew it might take a few hours to sort through the information being thrown at her from every direction. She was on to something here. She could feel it. And yet, thus far, she had nothing concrete to back her up. All she had to go on was her own hunches and speculations, and she knew that to many, that wouldn't be enough.

She had been placing many phone calls to the Birmingham area, trying to track down and speak with as many as possible that knew, or were close to the deceased, simply waiting for the police to fax her the information needed to try and figure out exactly what had happened last night. What was going on inside her head would undoubtedly sound crazy to anyone who refused to view things with an open mind. However, Ashley couldn't help it.

For some reason, she felt the murders were connected.

She didn't care that the Jack Reynolds case in Starke, Florida was miles away from the big city of Birmingham, Alabama. There was still something there that captured her attention and she wasn't about to let it go.

She had tried to sleep the previous night, but her brain simply wouldn't allow her to do so. Over and over again, she began contemplating what her next move should be. She really was a bit high strung, and didn't know how she should approach the mind-boggling situation she found herself in. So far, everywhere she had turned, only a dead end would surface, and she would once again be left empty handed, with nowhere to go, and the pressure of her Captain breathing down the back of her neck to quit wasting time and close the case. Sighing, she looked at the mounds of paper work on her desk, and sensed that she was getting nowhere. She knew her Captain wouldn't be in his office until the end of the day, and then, unless she had something concrete to show him, she knew he would order her to close the case. She had to find something, and fast. She was running out of time. And yet, as she once again stared at her desk, and glanced at the towering stack of paperwork, she was sure that none of the answers she desperately needed could be found anywhere in them.

What she was looking for couldn't be found in the paperwork.

It was something blind to the human eye. Yet, there had to be a way to find it. Something linked the murders together; it was just up to her to find out what it was. She was traveling in the wrong direction, yet didn't know which way to turn. Again, however, she wasn't going to give up without a fight. There had to be a place she forgot to look. Somewhere out there, maybe not even in Starke, Florida, but somewhere out there, she was certain someone knew something that could help her tremendously. The missing link was out there, and Ashley was close.

She only hoped she could find it in time.

* * *

Debra Saxton came strolling in from a long walk on the beach that morning, whistling slightly to herself as she came walking through the sliding glass door, exiting the warmth of the Florida sun only to render her body to a more comfortable fixture of circulated air. Once inside, she took off her headphones and placed them on the kitchen table. She was about to walk into the kitchen and fix herself a nice glass of wine, when she surprisingly saw her son Billy, and Blaze Brookshaw talking amongst themselves in the living room. Neither of them seemed to notice she had even entered the room, as their eyes remained glued to the television, and their voices too weary for her to make out anything that escaped from their mouths.

Taking a deep breath, Debra poured a full glass of sparkling white wine and then headed into the living room to spend some time with her son and his friend. Once past the kitchen, however, she found herself walking past the computer desk, where once again, she found the picture of her deceased husband Tom, sitting face down. Taking a sip of her wine, she looked in the direction of her son, knowing it had been he that had slammed the picture of his father to the hardened surface of the desk. However, Billy didn't look at her. Then, deciding not to mention it, Debra silently put the picture back in its upright position, stared into the once loving eyes of her husband one last time and then joined the two boys in the living room.

"You guys have anything interesting planned for today?" Debra inquired with a smile; sure she had surprised them with her sudden appearance. "It is a beautiful day out ya know? You two should be outside enjoying it."

"Mom," Billy immediately interjected seriously. "Did you see the news earlier by any chance?" Debra shook her head as her mind began to wonder where this conversation was heading. "There's been a couple of murders mom," Billy bluntly continued, he himself not sure how his mother was going to react. "Four people have been killed and one is barely alive."

"I'm sorry," Debra found herself cutting in. "And why do I need to know this?"

"Because," Billy was about to continue when he was once again cut off. This time, however, it was the annoying clatter of the telephone that had neglected him to speak. Jumping to her feet, Debra sprinted towards the phone and within seconds was holding it close to her ear, winking at her son assuring him that their conversation hadn't been terminated.

"Ms. Saxton," the voice on the other end immediately recognized her and began speaking. "This is Sheriff Burnham. I hope I am not disturbing you."

"No-no," Debra continued as a worrisome expression blanketed her face. She placed her glass of wine on the nearest surface; fearful she might deploy it to the ground below. "You are not disturbing me at all Sheriff," she went forward trying to hide her true feelings. "What can I do for you?"

"I need to speak with Billy," Gabe gruffly continued, getting to the point. "He's not in any trouble or anything," he immediately assured the worried mother. "A lot has happened around here in the last twenty-four hours and I think your son might be able to help us answer a few questions. Carey and her uncle have already agreed to meet with me at Pier 21 in about an hour. If you and your son could make it that would be wonderful."

"Sure, we can be there," Debra replied. Then, she grabbed a pen and began jotting down the directions the Sheriff gave her as quickly as possible. Before the two of them hung up, however, she asked. "Sheriff. Is there something wrong? I mean, should I be worried here?"

"No ma'am," Gabe answered, slightly bending the truth. "I just need to sort a few things out is all."

With that, the conversation ended and Debra rejoined her son in the living room with Blaze. Both of them instantly recognized the confused expression lingering freely from the corners of her mouth, and shallowly exposed deep in her eyes. Climbing to his feet, Billy rushed towards his mother. "What is it mom? Who was that on the phone?"

"It was Sheriff Burnham," Debra replied. "He wants to meet with us in an hour." Then, pausing she looked deep into her son's eyes. "He didn't say what this was going to be about, but it sounded like it was pretty important. Anyway," Debra continued shaking her head as she walked away from the two boys and headed upstairs to get ready. "You two just be ready to go in about half an hour. We'll take my car."

Once the two of them were alone in the living room, Blaze looked sternly at Billy. "What do you suppose this is going to be all about?"

"Beats me," Billy admitted truthfully. "I'm kind of nervous though."

"For what? You didn't do anything wrong did you?"

Billy shook his head. "Damn it man," he continued exhaling a deep breath as he took a seat next to his friend. "I just wish this whole thing would end you know? I'm tired of it. I'm tired of this house, I'm tired of all the nightmares, and I'm tired of living in the past man. It has to stop Blaze."

"And it will," Blaze tried to assure his friend although he himself didn't understand the slightest thing that was going on. "You'll get through this man. You'll see. And then you and Carey can live happily ever after," he added with a warm smile. "Seriously though," Blaze added putting his hand on his friend's shoulder. "You know I'm here for you right?"

"Yeah I do," Billy stated. "And thank you. Thanks a lot."

* * *

An hour later. At Pier 21.

Pier 21 was a huge fishing exhibition with enormous fishing fleets and sailboats stretching as far as the eye could see. It was located along the edge of a busy highway, and many of the towns tourists could be found boarding a charter boat preparing to spend the day fishing in the vast, beautiful Florida waters. The day was increasingly becoming cloudy and a vast wind continued to pick up each hour, assuring everyone that a storm was approaching. The Pier stretched at least two miles in width, with signs hanging every five to ten feet commercializing different charter boats and their Captains names, along with the mates directly below. Mini bars were located up and down the stretch of boardwalk, where flocks of fisherman hungered for beer. There was also a jet ski rental place in the northern most end of the Pier and few restaurants in between, all of them standing on stilts and overlooking the entire Pier, extending the view into the crystal clear blue waters of Destin, Florida.

As Debra, Billy, and Blaze walked the pier they were surprised to find the Sheriff sitting alone at a picnic table, to the left of the pier where nothing but a long line of boats could be found. Except for a few people walking up and down the pier gazing at all the different boats, the Sheriff was the only one around, leaving the large crowd of people in the vicinity of the restaurants and mini bars. He appeared to be looking out at sea, but he sensed their presence long before they ever approached him. Smiling, he stood up and welcomed them comfortably. Once the four of them were seated at the picnic table, the Sheriff spoke up.

"I'm sorry to drag you guys out here on a day like this. Sure looks like one hell of storm is heading our way. But I just didn't want for all of us to try and pile into my office. Seriously though," he paused. "Thanks for coming."

"Your welcome," Debra spoke up as both Billy and Blaze remained silent but watched the Sheriff with sharp eyes. "What exactly was it that you wanted to see us about?"

"I'll explain in a minute," Gabe assured them. "There are still a couple of people missing."

"You mean someone else is coming?" Billy asked, his expression blank. "Who?"

"Carey and her uncle," Gabe answered. Then, seeing the discomfort in the boy's eyes he added. "Don't worry about it son. I think Rick's had a change of heart." Suddenly, he saw Billy's expression turn to relief, as he watched him relax, releasing mounds of tension that had suddenly formed. "Its really you and Carey I'm concerned about," he continued speaking towards Billy. "And I want the two of you to tell me everything you know."

"But Sheriff," Billy spoke up seeing Carey and her uncle approaching in the distance. "I don't even know what I know and I already told you everything. But you didn't believe me before." Billy added with strengthening tone.

"I know I didn't," Gabe admitted holding up his hand. "And I'm sorry Billy. But now I'm here, and I'm asking for your help" Then, he paused briefly for Rick and his niece Carey to join them at the picnic table. Finally, he focused his eyes on both Billy and Carey before continuing. "Now I'm here to listen, and I promise not to take anything for granted. I'm here Billy and I need your help and yours to Carey. Just answer my questions as best you can and don't leave anything out. I don't know what's going on here and I don't think I can find out unless you can help me."

"But do you believe me?" Billy asked firmly, his eyes held firmly as he glanced in the direction of Carey, whom he just wanted to run to and place his arms around. "Do you believe in me Sheriff?"

Gabe hesitated for a moment, and for a second, it appeared as though he was not going to answer. Finally, however, he opened his mouth and stared directly at Billy. "Yes," Gabe answered honestly. "I do believe you Billy, and I want to help."

* * *

Back in Starke, Florida.

Sunset was vastly approaching and Detective Ashley Selvaggio couldn't believe the information she had accumulated. Her superior, Captain Gerald Armstrong, was waiting for her in his office with a not so glamorous look tattooed across his clean shaved face. A smile was stretched across Ashley's however. Finally, she had found something that made sense. Finally, she had been able to connect the two murders together. Not only that, she could also connect them to Curtis Rains.

Over the last three hours she hadn't left her desk in search of something to link the murder in Birmingham to the one right there in Starke. At last she had found it. She knew that Jack Reynolds was in constant contact with Curtis Rains, and often beat him. And now, she had learned that Jamie Walker was no stranger to the illicit serial killer. Before the authorities in Destin, Florida had captured Rains, Ashley had discovered that Jamie Walker was involved in a relationship of sorts with none other than Curtis Rains himself, and it was an intimate relationship at that. Furthermore, in talking once again with a few of the guards at the prison, she had learned of Jamie's visit to the prison just hours before Curtis's execution was carried out. What came as a surprise to her, however, was the fact that Curtis had tried to attack her while she had visited him, and the guards were adamant that he would have killed her had they not intervened. Surely, Ashley thought, Jamie must have provoked him in some way and made Curtis angry, the same way Jack's constant abuse must have enraged him.

Finally, the connection had been made.

Both Jack Reynolds and Jamie Walker knew Curtis Rains quite well, and both had died with the word *"Tinman,"* written near their bodies. It wasn't a coincidence, Ashley was sure of it. Whatever happened in Birmingham, was related to the mysterious death of the Reynolds family right there in Starke, Florida, even though it had already been confirmed by the lab that Jack Reynolds had taken his family's life before turning the gun on himself. Nevertheless, Ashley had pressed forward, and for some reason didn't hold Jack responsible for what happened.

Up until now, she had concentrated her efforts in trying to find as many people as possible that had in some way been in close contact with Curtis Rains in the past. Her ongoing search continued to bring nothing, but Ashley never gave up, and about an hour ago, something finally turned up. She had found someone that surely, Curtis Rains had remembered throughout his ten-year stay in prison.

It was Carey Haas.

The homicidal maniac had killed her parents, and her escape was the reason Curtis Rains himself had been caught. Yet, Carey Haas, Ashley learned was still alive and still living with her mother's sister in Destin, Florida, and for some reason, Ashley felt that Carey held the answers to her questions.

"Selvaggio can you come in here now," she was suddenly disturbed by her Captain's deep voice. "I haven't got all night."

"Yes sir," Ashley replied as she removed herself from behind her desk and within seconds entered Captain Armstrong's office, shutting the door behind her. She took a seat directly in front of his desk and faced him properly. Gerald Armstrong was a big man at forty-six years of age. He stood 6'5" in height and weighed over 240 pounds, most of it consisting of muscle. His dark brown hair and green eyes gave his facial appearance a boyish look if he kept it cleanly shaven. When not, however, and a mustache would protrude, he looked like an old man, incapable of law enforcement. However, everyone in the department respected him, and never questioned his decisions. Everyone, except Ashley Selvaggio.

"Can we get this over with please," Armstrong set forth as he let out a deep breath. "I really would like to get home. Do you have those papers signed like I asked so I can wrap this Reynolds shit up once and for all?"

Nervously, Ashley had to state the truth. "No sir, I haven't signed them yet."

"What?" Gerald groaned unpleased. "Why in the hell not? The lab results came back and it's quite obvious that wacky son of a bitch killed his fucking family and then shot himself," he spoke harshly of Jack Reynolds. "The lab evidence is precise and conclusive detective. How can you possibly want to hold off on closing this damn case? It's open and shut. Jesus Christ," he paused momentarily. "Please don't tell me you want to continue investigating this."

"Actually, yes I do," Ashley replied calmly. "I've found a few things I think you yourself might find interesting."

"What I'm interested in is closing this fucking case," Armstrong shot back. "Who gives a shit what you found. We already know who's guilty. We know who killed Gloria and Sarah Reynolds. Damn you Ashley," he paused once again to take a deep breath. "You're a damn good cop, and I'm happy you're a part of my team, but you have to learn when it's time to let go. You always seem to think there's something missing, or that there's some kind of conspiracy going on out there and that everything's one big cover up. Well I can't cover for you any longer Ash. I wish I could but I just can't. I've got the press and the Governor breathing down my back on this one, and both of them are satisfied with the answers. Why can't you be?"

"Because," Ashley tried to speak already prepared to receive another lecture. "Did you see the news today?"

"Oh no," Gerald immediately sensed where the conversation was going. "I know you're not trying to connect that shit in Birmingham with what went on here. No way, that's out of the question."

"No it's not," Ashley held her ground. "And if you'll give me some time, I know I can prove it."

"Bullshit!"

"Just listen to me Gerald please," Ashley begged. "I know I'm doing the right thing here and I have never let you down before. All I ask is that you give me a few more days on this. I'll keep it as quite as possible. No one else has to know I'm even working on the damn case. I just can't let go of this sir. There's something missing, and I know I can find out what it is."

"Listen to yourself. You sound crazy."

"Maybe I am," Ashley agreed sourly. "But I still want to find the truth."

There was a long silence before Captain Armstrong continued. Then, bowing his head, Ashley knew she had won the confrontation. "All right, you have three days to try and clear whatever your trying to prove up. But after three days, if you don't have anything to go on, it's finished, no questions asked. Deal?" Ashley nodded. "And you owe me one detective."

"I know," Ashley responded as she prepared to leave the room. "And thank you sir. I promise not to let you down."

"Oh you won't," Armstrong laughed hoarsely. "Because it's your ass if you do."

As Ashley left her Captain's office she decided it would be best to wait until morning before telling him that she would need to leave town for a few days. Perhaps he would be in a better mood by then, although his understanding might remain the same and she was sure that he would question her every move. Nevertheless, if she was going to get to the bottom of this she knew she would have to leave Starke, Florida.

Tomorrow morning, Ashley Selvaggio had another destination in mind.

Tomorrow morning, she would leave for Destin, Florida.

Chapter 25

The meeting with the Sheriff was over, and as Billy, Blaze, and Carey climbed into Debra's Lexus, they realized that nothing had been accomplished. Billy and Carey had tried to convince everyone at the picnic table what they felt was happening. But their words only seemed to bring on disbelief, except in the eyes of Sheriff Gabriel Burnham. He was the only one that actually listened to every word they said and try to make sense of it. It was hard to believe that Curtis Rains was still somehow alive, hard to believe that he still had the power to kill since everyone knew he had been pronounced dead while sitting in the electric chair in Starke, Florida. However, what no one realized was his power. No one could understand just how powerful and evil Rains really was, and it almost appeared as though no one wanted to believe that after ten years, the notorious serial killer still wanted to bring death to the last remaining member of the Haas family.

As the meeting had drawn to a close, the Sheriff had offered to return Debra to her nightmarish home along the sandy beach of Destin, Florida, as she granted Billy her car for the remainder of the afternoon. Debra realized Billy might want to spend some time with Carey and his best friend, and when surprisingly no objections came from the girl's uncle, the deal was done, and the meeting adjourned. Drizzle had begun to fall from the darkening sky above as everyone left for his or her separate ways. Debra, and the Sheriff climbed into his silver Yukon, while Rick and Carol allowed their niece to depart with Billy and Blaze, promising to pick her up later at a designated spot. As the three teenagers, all of them practically twenty years of age, climbed into the black Lexus, however, Billy and Blaze had no idea where to go.

    Carey, on the other hand, had an idea. She wanted to go somewhere she hadn't been in a long time, and knew that now was a good time to return. Perhaps her parents had a few answers to the many questions that stumped her brain. She knew that even after ten years of living a life without her parents, they had never really left her in this staggering world alone. Sometimes she could still feel their presence around her and her father's caring eyes watching over her. Although when the nightmares came to her, they didn't appear to be able to offer any protection. Curtis Rains was always present, as if he were bragging about being more powerful. In fact, it seemed as though the only time Carey was actually at peace and alone with her parents, was at the cemetery. It was always quiet there. Carey usually went alone unless her aunt and uncle decided to join her. Even when that happened, however, they allowed her time alone with her parents and waited patiently for her to return to the car.

    And now, as they headed for the burial place, Carey found herself in the company of Billy Saxton, and Blaze Brookshaw. She knew her parents would have loved to meet both of them, and now was their chance. She wanted to introduce Billy to her parents, let them know what he had done for her and how he made her feel. Although she had no doubt they would have approved of him, she was certain she would be able to feel it if they had not. Seated in the passenger seat, Carey looked over towards Billy every so often and smiled at his gorgeous face. He was so wonderful, she knew she was lucky to have him come into her life, and wished that he would stay forever. She had to give him directions knowing that he wasn't "from around these parts," smiling as she remembered his Georgia accent. Finally, when they arrived at a long stretch of highway they found the rain coming down rather hard now, and Billy squinted through the windshield making sure he could see the road ahead.

    "Damn," Blaze spoke up from the back seat. "This storm came from nowhere didn't it?" Both Billy, and Carey agreed. "I swear I'm going to stop listening to those damn weather people. If they ever actually get a forecast right, or a meteorologist who actually knew what he was doing, I would have known to bring an umbrella," he added jokingly, trying to keep everyone's good mood at its peak.

"I think my mom's got one in the trunk," Billy began with a smile. "But I doubt this storm is going to stay long. It's a thunderstorm, and they're almost always over after an hour or so. Especially the powerful ones." Billy added, not realizing he had been set up for a comeback from his best friend, and not seeing that Blaze's last statement had been a witticism, or a raillery, rather than common conversation.

"Shoot," Blaze went on with a smile as he caught Billy's eyes from the rearview mirror. "Sounds to me like you should go down to the weather station and put in your application buddy. I can see it now," Blaze paused before continuing. "And coming up next, an accurate forecast from our very own meteorologist, Billy Saxton," he concluded doing his best to sound like an anchor from an award winning news channel.

"No," Billy broke in, joining Blaze in the fun. "I think I'd purposely tell people lies about the weather, just to piss em off. I can see it now, it would be a clear day, not a cloud in the sky, and I'd go with an 80% chance of rain," he concluded snickering foolishly.

"And let me guess," Carey joined in the conversation a bit late as she took one of Billy's hands in her own as he steered the car with the other. "On a day like today, you would have said no chance of rain," she added with a charming smile, and already knowing how her country bumpkin was going to respond.

"Something like that."

Then, as the three of them laughed amongst themselves, and the rain continued to pound away at the windshield, none of them realized how close they were coming to their destination. Carey, opening her eyes, caught view of the entrance to the cemetery just as they approached it. "There, there," she pointed just as Billy was about to pass the two enormous brass gates to the cemetery. Billy slowed the car safely, aware of the driving conditions, and with ease, was able to make the turn and enter the peaceful cemetery, knowing somewhere inside, he was about the encounter the headstones of Carey's parents, David and Charlene Haas. As he squeezed his mother's Lexus through the rather tiny opening the gates allowed, the three of them noticed ivy vines growing immensely across the opening of the gates, twisting and turning their way around the brass bars giving it a more vivacious appearance.

The single road on which they traveled had been paved, and every so often another road would lead to the left or right, allowing one to travel deeper into the cemetery to get to their loved one. Billy, watching Carey's eyes, continued forward not veering until given the instruction to do so. The rain appeared to lighten a little, almost as if it had expected them to arrive there today, allowing them a peaceful atmosphere as Billy was able to switch his wipers entirely off. The grass was as green as imagined, the groundskeeper obviously good at his job, and few titanic oak trees had been left in sequestered places throughout the gardens. Moving his eyes from left to right, Billy was amazed at how many headstones could be found. Some of them extremely large, others small, but all of them lavishing the same benevolence, and marked ones sadness. Then, pulling off and slightly onto the grass, in case another car wanted to pass, Billy followed Carey's instructions and turned off the car.

"They're over there," Carey spoke of her parents calmly as she pointed out the driver's window and towards one of the few large oak trees found on the lot. As Billy surveyed the terrain, there was no other oak tree in sight, and with it's mighty branches extending in different direction, it had to be the largest of the bunch. "My parents are buried right in front of that tree," Carey continued letting out a deep breath, preparing herself to visit with her parents once again, and praying that she could remain strong. "You can see them from here if you really try," she added with a smile, speaking of their headstones.

Before Billy spoke, he squeezed her hand affectionately, and bore into her blue eyes with nothing but compassion seen in his own. "Carey, are you sure you want to do this? We can come back another time if you'd like."

"No," Carey remained strong. "I want to. I mean," she paused as she managed to smile. "I want us to."

With that, the three of them removed themselves from the vehicle and walked slowly across the green grass, making sure they weren't walking along anyone's graves. The rain had subdued itself into a weak drizzle that flushed over their faces in a cool manner, also helping them escape the humidity. Soon, they had reached their mark, and the three of them found themselves standing directly in front of Carey Haas's parents, David and Charlene. Billy was overcome with a moment of sadness as he stared at the beautiful marble headstones before him, and realized once again the greatness of Carey's loss, and couldn't help but to sympathize with her on this occasion. He wondered what her parents had been like as they lay beneath the ground, and it bothered him in knowing that he would never have the chance to meet them in person, never be able to get to know them and become part of their family. Nevertheless, as he took Carey's hand in his own, he had to tackle the tears that welled almost uncontrollably in his eyes. Leaning over, he kissed her on the cheek.

The headstones were addressed in a unique marble, the water from the rain running down the sides of the stones, sinking into the ground below. Flowers remained at the front of both graves, and inscribed in each were words of love, telling everyone that both David and Charlene's souls would be connected forever, and their love never lost. "It's beautiful," Billy whispered to Carey, as he couldn't take his eyes off of the headstones. "It's truly beautiful." Carey nodded.

"They deserved the best," Carey breathed, her voice a bit shaky.

Blaze, realizing this was a moment when the two of them needed to be alone, backed away from them quietly and began returning to the car. He was never one to show his emotions, never one to let anyone see him cry, and found it difficult when placed in a situation where he was supposed to comfort one that was in tears. Sometimes, he wouldn't say the right thing, sometimes he didn't know what to say at all, and making a mockery of one's emotions was something he simply didn't believe in. In Billy's case, however, it was different. The two of them had bonded on numerous occasions, both of them knowing more about the other than anyone else on the face of the earth. Every secret between the two had been divulged a long time ago, and more were sure to come. Billy was the only one to ever see Blaze engulfed in tears, and was probably the only one that would ever understand him fully. He would never turn his back on Billy. He would stick with him until the bitter end, and never back away from any compromising situation, even if it meant giving up his own life for the one person that meant more to him than anything in the world. They were truly best friends, brothers, and would continue to be whether in the hands of life, or death. Finally, reaching Billy's mother's car, he returned to the back seat and waited for Billy and Carey to join him.

"It's still sometimes hard to believe that they are gone," Carey continued back at her parent's gravesite. "I mean sometimes I can feel them still here you know, and it hurts to know that I can't be with them, touch them, hug them. All I have are pictures and memories," she concluded as she allowed herself to be wrapped in Billy's sheltering arms, knowing the inevitable was about to happen and she wouldn't be able to postpone her tears much longer.

"I know," Billy tried to ease her pain. "I know how hard it must be for you, and I am truly sorry you had to go through this. You didn't deserve it, and they most certainly didn't. I just wish I knew exactly what to say," he admitted. "But when my father passed away," he paused once again as he found himself entering a meaningful subject of his own. "I wasn't sad." He watched as Carey looked up and into his eyes with a confused expression. He could tell she didn't understand. "I didn't like my father."

"Why?"

"Because he wasn't a nice man," Billy went on, hiding his emotions well. "He hurt my mother and I a lot. He never hit me or anything like that, but he did hit my mother every once and a while. Probably more than she has ever admitted, and she was always crying. I hated him when he made my mother cry. And then," he paused once again to catch his breath. "And then he would always come and start in on me. He would yell at me constantly, call me names, and always try to confine me to my room. I wish there was something I could have done about it. But I couldn't. He was bigger than me, more powerful and I knew if I dared to stand up to him he would've tried to kill me."

"I'm sorry," Carey said compassionately. "I had no idea."

"Don't be," Billy continued strongly. "You couldn't have known unless I told you about it. But the truth is, Tom was an alcoholic," he paused after revealing his father's name. "And he loved to drink more than he did his family, and in the end, that's what eventually got him. And to this day, I am not saddened by his death because I know both my mother and I are better off."

Finally, Carey realized it was going to be up to her to change the subject. Still clutching his hand tightly, she motioned for the two of them to step closer to her parent's graves. Kneeling down, it appeared as though she was looking right through the headstones, and into the ground, where her parent's bodies lay motionlessly, and without life when she spoke. "Mom, dad," she breathed as a tear finally rolled down her cheek. "This is Billy Saxton. I wanted you to meet him."

For nearly half and hour, the two of them spoke to her parents, never once doubting that perhaps their words wouldn't be heard, and by the time they climbed to their feet and began heading back to the car, both of them felt like a huge weight had been lifted from their shoulders. They felt relaxed, relieved and had found an incredible amount of energy that had been stored away, hidden somewhere inside their bodies. As they reached the car, Carey's tears came to an end, and a smile resurfaced across her beautiful face. Billy walked her around to the passenger side, and was about to open the door for her to join Blaze, when she stopped him and kissed him unexpectantly.

"I love you," she spoke sincerely. "I will always love you Billy."

"And I you," Billy returned a kiss of his own and felt his heart landslide into fourth gear. Finally, once seated inside, he closed the door, just as the rain began to pick up again and hurried over to the driver side and climbed in. Cranking the engine, the smooth riding Lexus backtracked on the same road as they prepared to leave the cemetery. "I hope we didn't keep you waiting too long," he spoke to Blaze as he looked at his friend from the rearview mirror.

"No, no," Blaze assured them as a yawn crept from his mouth as he tried to speak. "Not at all. In fact, I needed to catch up on a little beauty sleep anyway." Then, changing the subject, he added. "So, where to now?" He asked seriously. "I mean, we can't let this absolutely wonderful day go to waste," he concluded jokingly as the rain once again stood in harms way and splattered profusely across the car limiting Billy's vision to no more than ten yards ahead.

"I don't know," Billy shrugged his shoulders. "What do you want to do?" He turned and asked Carey, whose eyes were watching the road ahead.

As Carey answered, she couldn't believe what she was about to say. "I want to go home."

"All right," Billy responded wondering if he had done something wrong.

"No, not my uncle's home," Carey stated matter-of-factly. Then, feeling her heart beat quicken a bit, she tried to suppress her emotions and limit the fear that mounted as each second passed. "I was talking about my real home. The home along the beach. The house where you now live."

Billy looked at her acutely. He couldn't believe what she had just said. He couldn't think of a reason that might explain why she would've wanted to go there in the first place. There was absolutely nothing there for her, except bad memories of her haunting past. He didn't want her to got through any emotional stress or shock that could harm her well being. "Are you serious?" he couldn't help but to ask.

"Yes," Carey replied trying to sound braver than she really was. She didn't know why she wanted to return to the place where her parents were killed, but it was as if something was drawing her there. She didn't know why, but she had to go, even though regrets were sure to come as soon as she walked through the front door.

"You're sure you want to go to that house?" Billy repeated the question.

"Yes, I am sure!" Carey blurted emotionally. "Trust me Billy. It's time I faced my fears."

* * *

The creature moved restlessly along with the powerful thunderstorm as its core neared his final predetermined, and preordained target. Soon after the robust storm passed through the Destin, Florida area, its purpose would have been served and it would eventually die, drowning out at sea. The creature smiled as he flew invisibly in the darkness of the clouds, knowing that the citizens of Destin had no idea he was returning. Soon he would leave behind another perfect exhilaration of blood and misery for the weak, as his rapture would bring sorrow and pain to the ones fortunate enough to elude his all mighty touch.

He was almost there, and he could sense fear in those that actually knew he was coming. Very few people sensed the danger, and could taste the fear he was about to instill. But even those, couldn't escape him. He was too powerful, could even be considered a figment of ones imagination, but he was real, and could touch the lives of others in an instant. The creature was moving at a speed that was unimaginable, and within the hour, he would glide peacefully to the place he had remembered day in and day out for the last ten years.

After ten years of being confined to death row, the creature was returning to the Haas home. It was his last mark of excellence before society began to forget his name and were without worry knowing that he was off the streets and out of harms way. But the prosaic town of Destin was about to meet the man they had desperately tried to forget one last time. This time, however, no one and nothing was going to be able to stand in his way.

His anger was boiling.

His blood bubbling like steaming water jetting from a hot spring.

He couldn't control his rage any longer, and it was finally time to complete what he had started so many years ago. It was finally time to tackle the one person that had been able to escape the Tinman.

Yet, everything had to be perfect.

His final meaningful execution would have to mark his excellence forever, and instill fear into everyone for all eternity. Everything had to be intact, every detail fit to perfection, and he would settle for nothing less. His victim was inevitably going to suffer before she died, almost wishing that she had died along with her parents so many years ago, instead of living in a world where she had learned nothing but pain, sorrow, and loneliness. In a way, the creature felt that he would be doing her a favor and set her free from having to live in a vicious world without her parents. Yet it was the fear he remembered seeing in her eyes. He wanted to see it again, wanted to hear her cry for help, although knowing none would come, and then at last, he would close the chapter on the Haas family forever.

The creature wasn't dull-witted, however, and knew of the few people who were expecting his arrival. Some, he was well aware would probably try and put an end to his filthy, blood-ridden rampage and silence his madness forever. He would welcome them to try, of course, all the while knowing it would be an unsuccessful attempt for mercy and in the end, their own lives would be taken as a result. In fact, he already had a plan in mind for a few people who he could *sense would be waiting for him, and he would take care of that in due time.*

Right now, he had to focus on his final target.

She was so beautiful, it would almost be shameful to destroy her and take her away from the many people that loved her on this earth. Her beauty even seemed to shine through the tenacious storm in which he now dwelled. However, when he was through, and the people of Destin witnessed her remains, her beauty would all but be forgotten. The fear in her eyes, however, would remain, and death in this sportsman town would once again rekindle in the night as everyone hovered over their children and locked their doors to try and keep him out.

It was almost time, and his excitement grew.

He found ecstasy in what most would consider vicious, and was meagerly turned on at any given site of blood. A pricked finger was something he loved to run over to and suck the warm blood into his mouth, feel it rolling down his tongue and into the back of his throat, cherishing every drop until there was no more. He was a madman, his greatest passion being death as he considered every act of violence a work of art, or something to remember.

Yes. Everything was going to be perfect.

There would be no escapes and no change in plans. He thought long and hard about what he would do if given a second chance at the little girl who had escaped him so many years ago, and now after waiting patiently for a good portion of his life, the time was rapidly approaching. Carey Haas was his biggest prize of all, and her blood would undoubtedly taste the sweetest.

She was weak, however, and he knew which buttons to push.

And in the end, he smiled to himself as the thunder rolled, that would be her downfall that would eventually cost her, her precious life.

The creature was his own prototype, and soon, very soon, the entire world would know of his return.

⸪

Back in Starke, Florida.

Detective Ashley Selvaggio pulled her Toyota 4-Runner into her driveway and soon found herself walking through the front door of her one story home. Tossing her badge and keys onto the coffee table, she quickly escaped into the kitchen and poured herself a nice mix of the ever popular Jim Beam whiskey and coke. Pressing the receive message button on her machine, she wasn't surprised to find it empty. Who in Starke, Florida was actually going to call her? She had made it quite clear a long time ago, when she had first arrived; that none of the men in the town fit what she was looking for. She was a beautiful woman, but she was a picky beautiful woman, and that was a hard obstacle for any man to overcome. Many had tried, none of them successful in stealing her heart.

Seating herself in a recliner, she flipped on the television, although not even taking the first glance to see what popped up on the screen. Closing her eyes, she reviewed all of the facts she had learned in her head, tried to piece together a puzzle everyone but herself doubted was there at all. Still, however, nothing made sense, and she only hoped her trip to Destin wouldn't turn up the same. She sensed that Carey Haas would be able to reveal something to her that she simply couldn't see. Carey was her last and final hope to bring proof that the Reynolds case in her hometown and the awful murder in Birmingham, Alabama were related. It was just a hunch, she knew, but it was a strong one. More than that, however, it was all she had.

If she came back empty-handed, Captain Armstrong would have no choice but to force her to call it quits, and she herself would have no choice but to comply. She was well aware that his reputation was at stake, along with her own. But she didn't mind what other people thought of her. She knew her job, and did it well, and would continue to do so even if it meant transferring out of the small town she appeared to be stuck in, and move somewhere else. Somewhere, where her beliefs seemed normal, and people would be more willing to let her explore a bit, and find the ultimate truth. Even if it meant she had to look in a forbidden zone of secrets and lies. The town of Starke, however, was dull, almost like a spider web that clung itself to her and wouldn't let go. Ashley sometimes felt like a fly, just waiting to be eaten by the taunting spider that anxiously waited for his hunger to approach and he could remove himself from the middle of the web.

She sipped her liquor beverage, and felt the cold ice cubes hit her luscious lips just as a meager sip of liquid escaped into her mouth and easily glided down her throat. The stiff drink appeared to be exactly what the doctor ordered, and she knew that after she had devoured the one in her hand, she would soon fix herself another, and then another until she could escape into a world without worry or confusion. If she was going to get through this, she knew she would have to find time for her brain to relax, and allow her body a good rest every so often. Otherwise, she would not only loose her full intelligence, but grow weak and weary, letting any distraction deter her from the focus she was accustomed to and was greatly required.

Ashley Selvaggio snapped off the television, growing annoyed with the noise, and simply enjoyed her time alone. She would have to eat something sooner or later. Right now, however, she wasn't getting up to fix anything in the kitchen. She was finally relaxed, and comfortable. The very spot in the recliner was probably where she would find herself waking up the next morning. Stretching momentarily, she soon finished her first drink, and only then did she climb to her feet and move once again into the kitchen. Pouring herself another hard drink, she was startled as her phone rang, destroying the peaceful atmosphere her home had welcomed her to. Wondering who could be calling her, she let it ring three more times before finally answering.

"Ashley," she instantly recognized her Captains voice. "This is Armstrong. If I'm disturbing you, good," he snapped angrily, obviously upset about something that she had done.

"I'm sorry Gerald. Oh, I mean sir," Ashley corrected herself. "What are you talking about?" She asked calmly, although tempted to simply hang the phone up and forget about her boss ever calling. She simply was not in the mood to be yelled at, and didn't feel like putting up with anyone's bullshit. She was off duty, and thought that surely whatever he had to say, could have waited until morning. Ashley waited for her superior to continue, however, aware that he wasn't going to let her off the hook. If she hung up, he would directly call back only to have something else to yell at her about and perhaps even threaten her job.

"I can't believe you," Captain Armstrong continued in a pissed off fashion, and Ashley found herself picturing him right now, sitting behind his desk with two red puffy cheeks as he clutched the phone so tight, his knuckles had long ago turned white. "Why would you possibly want to do such a thing?" he continued to ask, perhaps expecting her to understand just what was going through his mind. "You are so damn naïve sometimes, and irresponsible at that."

"Excuse me," Ashley jumped in growing angry now, and feeling a need to defend herself. She wasn't going to stand for any abuse from a man, at least not tonight, even if he was her boss. "But I am neither of those, and quite frankly, I'm sorry sir, but I don't appreciate you calling me at my home and treating me like some incoherent child. I deserve better, and I expect nothing less. Just because you disagree with some of my decisions doesn't mean that they are wrong. And I'm sorry sir, but if you truly feel the need to yell at me, it would be considerate if you at least let me in on just what this is all about."

"Are you through?" Gerald asked gritting his teeth.

"Are you?"

"Not in the slightest Detective," he continued harshly as if not even listening to a word she had just spoken. "I can't believe you were going to head over to Destin without letting me know. And this Carey Haas bit. What kind of shit is that? That poor girl has been through enough don't you think? Were you actually going to drive there and interrogate her?"

Ashley couldn't believe it. She first wondered how he could have known about her plans to travel to Destin, as she had known for a fact that she hadn't divulged that information to anyone. Then, it dawned on her. He had deliberately gone through her desk and ran his sneaky paws through her notes. And knowing Armstrong, and his snaky eyes, he probably jumped on it as soon as she left the department that evening. Her anger had finally reached the limit. He had invaded her workspace. "Sir!" Ashley cut in coldly. "Did you go through my desk."?

"Yes ma'am I did," Gerald sneered not hiding anything, and obviously feeling he had done nothing wrong and it had been his right to do so. "I was walking out of my office, in a pretty descent mood actually, when I saw this notepad on your desk. It indicated you were going to Destin to talk to Carey. Well I'm sorry detective, but your acting like your shit don't stink has got to stop, and if I have to be the one to stop it, I will."

"Are you saying I can't go to Destin?"

"You're goddamn right that's what I'm saying!" Armstrong stormed. "And don't even try to talk your way out of this, because I'm not going to change my mind. You have no business there detective. None whatsoever."

"Who are you to decide that?" Ashley questioned her Captain as her blood continued to boil and run cold in her veins. "People have been killed-." She was cut off.

"So what?" Armstrong interrupted her. "People die everyday. It's a sick world out there, and our job is to do what we can to get the bastards off the streets and lock them behind bars. We're not paying you to run around on wild goose chases, chasing after criminals who have already been killed. Jack Reynolds killed his family, and who gives a shit what happens in Birmingham, Alabama?"

"I give a shit, and I'm going to Destin," Ashley bravely held her ground.

"I am ordering you to stay put detective," Gerald continued trying to draw closure to the conversation. "And if you try to pull anything funny, just know your affiliation with this department is in question. Now damn it Ashley, I'd hate to jeopardize your future, you've got a good head on your shoulders sometimes and you've done a lot of good for this department. But I want your ass to stay put right here in Starke, and I'll expect to see you in here bright and early tomorrow morning with a nice smile glistening across your face. Are we clear?"

"No."

"Ashley, I'm warning you," Gerald continued to scorn. "Don't try me this time."

With that, the conversation was over.

Ashley slammed the phone down harshly, and found herself throwing the glass holding the alcohol in the sink, enjoying the crash as liquid splattered everywhere and glass scattered about. Closing her eyes once more, she tried to vent out all of her frustrations towards her Captain, and release the unnecessary anger she felt inside. There was no way she was going to let him get to her. She was too strong for it, and she certainly wasn't going to let him stand in her way.

Racing upstairs she entered her bedroom and threw open the closet doors. From atop, she retrieved a suitcase, and her mind had long ago been made up. She was going to Destin regardless. Only she wasn't going to wait until morning. Throwing clothes in left and right, she then proceeded out her front door, locking it behind her and climbed into the driver seat of her 4-runner once again.

There had been a change in plans.

Ashley Selvaggio was going to Destin tonight.

* * *

Sheriff Gabriel Burnham found himself nestled comfortably on the couch in Debra's home after accepting her gracious offer to come inside for a cup of coffee. Billy, Blaze, and Carey hadn't arrived yet, and the elder Sheriff doubted he would see them again before he left. Debra had just taken his coffee mug from him and headed for the kitchen to grab a refill when his mind began to wonder. His eyes had seen it all in all of his tiresome years masquerading around as a law enforcement officer, and sometimes he wondered if the job was worth the stress and torment his body was forced to endure. Everyday he grew closer and closer to retirement and a full pension was waiting. He had grown fed up with the scum society had to offer and would be glad when it was all over and done with. Looking back, he knew he had experienced a great career, and helped the lives of many. But it was time to turn it in, and hand his badge over to someone else. Someone who was as eager as he had been to sustain an impeccable reputation, and bring peace to the growing city of Destin, Florida.

Looking around Debra's home now, however, he realized he would never see it as belonging to the Saxton family. It would always belong to David and Charlene Haas in his mind, their ghosts constantly clinging to what was once theirs. His eyes visualized the remodeled and furnished living room, in which he now sat, but the haunting memories of blood remained, and he could still see David's bloody body laying on the floor, a deep gash in his throat, and Charlene, who had been raped repeatedly with her flesh sliced and carved in an articulate fashion. Charlene had been forced to endure as much pain as possible before Curtis had finally decided to kill her, it was seen in her eyes, and Gabe himself often wondered what it must have been like for her the few minutes before she died. Closing his eyes, he remembered the night when he was merely a police officer and he was called to the scene.

He remembered how he, along with two other officers, who unfortunately had died in the line of duty a few years back, had chased Curtis Rains along the moonlit beach before they eventually caught up with him and tackled him to the ground. He remembered looking into his evil blackened eyes as he placed the handcuffs on the serial killer, and then as another officer carried him away and put him in the back of a patrol car, he had ventured into the Haas home and absorbed the massacre. It was like nothing he had ever seen, blood was everywhere. And it had been moments later, when Carey's young body had floated to the surface and was recovered incredibly unharmed. He had felt her pain then, and could feel it now, ten years later.

Then, his thoughts were interrupted as Debra's hand came into view, holding another cup of coffee before him. "Thank you," he breathed heavily, the bags and wrinkles under his eyes showing his years. "So tell me," he went on. "You say you didn't know about what happened in this house before you moved in?"

"Certainly not," Debra assured him, anger in her tone directed towards the Realtor. "If I would have, you bet your ass I wouldn't have moved in."

"Can't blame you really," Gabe sighed tiredly. "You know the people that lived here before you, Carey's parents, they were good people. They really were, and they most certainly didn't deserve what happened to them. To this day, I still think it's a miracle that Carey is still alive. I guess you can understand why everyone around here is so protective of her. She's been through a lot."

"I know, bless her heart."

"I can tell your son will be good for her though," Gabe admitted rather plainly. "Billy seems like a good kid, and I think he's probably just what Carey needs right now. From talking to Rick and Carol, they both told me that she hadn't made all that many friends in school. I'm sure it was hard for her to open up or trust anyone."

"But she's such a beautiful girl."

"I know," the Sheriff smiled slightly. "I think that's what worried her uncle most. I just wish I knew what to make of everything that's been going on. I'm not exactly sure what it is," he paused climbing to his feet and began walking about the home, coming to a stop as he reached the sliding glass door and peered outside at the patio, only to allow his eyes to overlook the ocean below. "But I can definitely sense that something just isn't right, and I hate not being able to do anything about it."

"Sheriff?" Debra began to question concerned. "Do you think that Billy and Carey are in some kind of danger?"

"I wish I could say that they weren't," Sheriff turned to face Debra momentarily only to resume staring out at the gloomy day before him, watching as the wind knocked over the oats standing tall from the sand dunes, and the rather amusing display of rain as it splattered across the ocean. "But I honestly don't know what to expect. I guess all we can do is pray for the best, and hope nothing ever happens. But," he paused to face her once again. "I don't think it's going to be that easy. To tell you the truth, I don't like any of this at all."

"Sure is one heck of a storm," Debra changed the subject. "I didn't hear anything about it on the news."

"Well, if you can't trust your local meteorologist who can you trust?" Gabe spoke with a smile.

"Maybe the local Sheriff?" Debra returned friendly.

Saying nothing, Sheriff Burnham once again looked out the single pane of glass and stared out at the propelling storm above. He could tell it was intensifying every second, and knew the total package had yet to arrive. Sipping his coffee, he could see the steam rise from his mug and warm his forehead. "This is mighty good coffe-," his compliment was interrupted as his eyes fell across something beyond the patio and along the shoreline of the deserted beach below. He strained his eyes to reach the distance and fought to visualize a clear path through the storm. It looked as though someone was standing on the beach. It was a man, but he wasn't walking, he was just standing there, directly in front of Debra's home. Or as he knew it, the *Haas* home.

But where had the man come from?

He hadn't been there a few seconds ago.

Yet, there he was, standing directly in the middle of the thunderstorm, and staring at him through the sliding glass window. Putting the mug on the nearest table, Gabe pulled the sliding glass door open and stepped outside, paying Debra no mind as she asked him if something was wrong. Gabe didn't care that his body was soon trampled by what seemed like gallons of water as the winds splattered him with rain harshly. Walking to the rail, he returned the glare at the man, who seemed reluctant to leave.

As the Sheriff stared, however, he couldn't help but feel he knew the man.

The man was dressed in all black. Black work boots, black pants, a black trench coat and a black hat. Where had he seen this kind of attire before? It seemed so familiar to him. "No way," he said aloud as a thought came to mind and his conscious was immediately stricken with a fear so powerful, he could feel his muscles tense up and his elder heartbeat unhealthily quicken. "It couldn't be." Yet, as the man lifted his head and stared into his eyes, Gabe knew the truth. He could never forget those eyes. He thought that he would never see them again. But there they were, against everything he had believed in, those eyes had returned. Sheriff Burnham couldn't believe it. He was once again staring into the deadly eyes of Curtis Rains. "Son of a bitch!" he groaned as he quickly drew his six-shooter from his holster and his blood ran cold in retched fear. Carey and Billy had been right after all.

The *Tinman* had returned.

Jason Glover

Chapter 26

Debra watched the Sheriff draw his pistol and immediately ran towards the sliding glass door to see what was going on. He was standing in the middle of the patio, completely being trampled by the rain, as his eyes remained fixed on something in the distance. She could see a dark clad figure on the beach, simply standing there and looking up towards her house. She had no idea who the man was, but his very appearance made her entire body tingle and an insurmountable force of fear seemed to spread throughout her body like wildfire. Who was this strange man in front of her home? Where had he come from? And why was he there?

"Sheriff?" Debra called out into the horrendous storm. But he did not answer. Didn't even acknowledge her presence, for whoever was down along the beach succeeded in capturing his full attention, almost seeming to mock the elder Sheriff. But Debra couldn't take it. She had to know what was going on. "Sheriff!" she called out again, this time with more authority. "Will you please tell me what is going on? Who is that man?"

"It's impossible," the Sheriff snarled not answering her question directly or turning to face her. "That son of a bitch is supposed to be dead."

"Who?" Debra asked, although as soon as that question left her mouth, she knew the answer. It was Curtis Rains. The man dressed completely in black garments was Curtis Rains. "Oh my God!" she screamed as panic sank in.

"Do you have a flashlight?"

"Yes," Debra answered as she darted off from view and seconds later returned with two flashlights. Stepping out onto the porch, she handed the sheriff one and before any talk could continue, he slipped past her and began walking down the steps towards the beach. "Sheriff wait." Debra pleaded uselessly. "What are you going to do?"

"If this son of a bitch wants a confrontation, I'll give him one," Gabe yelled as his feet reached the soft sand and he slowly began walking towards the figure standing before him. It was unbelievable. It was as if Curtis Rains wasn't planning on running, or fleeing away from him. He was taunting him, practically daring Gabe to approach him. Nevertheless, with his gun held firmly out in front of him, he had the evil man in his sights, and ached for the opportunity to pull the trigger. "Go inside and call for backup," he yelled back at Debra, realizing he did not have his radio with him and knowing the danger he was about to encounter. Without looking back, he knew that Debra would comply with his order and he would have a team of deputies there in no time.

Sheriff Burnham was within thirty yards of Curtis Rains when he could completely visualize the man on which he had drawn his gun. Now it was certain. It truly was him, and his glistening white teeth stared at him as a smile formed across his protruded face. Something wasn't right, Gabe sensed with ease. This whole situation just didn't feel right. His instincts, which he practically trusted 100% of the time, were clearly telling him to turn around, and go back inside and wait for help.

But Gabe couldn't do that.

As if he had something to prove, he continued to move forward, and the distance between himself and the madman was drawing increasingly close. Gabe fearlessly tried to force every doubt out of his mind, and release all of the fear that had instilled itself in his brain. Every life form could be killed. There was a way for everything to die. But how do you kill something or someone that was already dead?

Unless, Curtis Rains never died.

Finally, however, the distance between the two was close enough to speak. "Don't you fucking move!" Sheriff Burnham ordered allowing the rain to continue to batter his body. "Stay right there Rains."

"Why I'm impressed Sheriff," Curtis replied coldly, still smiling as he raised his arms in the air pretending to surrender. "After all of these years you didn't have any trouble recognizing me." When the Sheriff made no effort to respond, Curtis let his smile drift away and an evil expression formed along his complexion. His eyes bore into Gabe's soul easily and he could sense that the elder man in front of him was afraid. "I suppose you know why I'm here don't you Sheriff?" Again, Gabe didn't reply. He continued to move steadily towards Curtis, the gun still raised into the air. "All right, you want me?" Curtis asked as a smile returned. "Well then come and get me."

With that, like a flash of lightning, Curtis Rains threw his hands back down to his side and began darting off down the beach, running away from the elder Sheriff, confident that he would follow.

"Freeze!" Gabe yelled into the storm, although knowing his orders meant nothing to the man he had just encountered. "Damn it," he scorned himself as he put his gun back in his holster and prepared to flee after the escaped serial killer. He knew that if he didn't tail him, and at least keep a close eye on him, then Curtis could get away. And simply put, Gabe couldn't let that happen. He had to go after him on foot, which was something he hadn't done in a long time. Gabe's bones ached as he first picked up speed, and he knew that his body was too old for this kind of vigorous exercise.

Nevertheless, Sheriff Burnham barreled after the notorious serial killer on foot as the storm continued to wail and day was quickly turning into night. Clutching the flashlight tightly in the palm of his hands, he vowed never to let the man out of his sight. It was time to put an end to this nightmare once and for all.

To Curtis Rains, however, this was just the beginning.

* * *

Debra's entire being was stricken with panic. Her hands trembled fearfully and she found herself having trouble picking up the phone. She waited to hear a dial tone before dialing, but wasn't the least bit surprised when she found none. Her phone was dead. Running back to the sliding glass door, she stepped out on the porch, clutching the flashlight in the palm of her hands. She could see Sheriff Burnham and Curtis Rains running down the beach as Gabe fought hard to stay

Tinman

in pursuit of the estranged killer, and knew that somehow, she had to find help. She couldn't allow Gabe to go after that man alone. She would never forgive herself if anything were to happen to him.

Then, it hit her. The Anne family. Surely, they were home and could help. Without thinking twice, Debra followed Gabe's steps down the back end of her patio and soon found herself slowly running through the soft sand of the beach and towards her neighbor's home. She didn't care that she was growing increasingly wet, she was just glad that the sun had chosen to remain strong for the moment and that nightfall had yet to arrive. She shivered, but it wasn't from the cold. She was scared, and wasn't sure exactly what to do. The thunderstorm itself had no bearing on why she was afraid. It was all due to one man, and it was a man that until now, she felt didn't exist. But her son, Billy, had been right. Curtis Rains was still alive and well, and he had some sort of unfinished agenda to uphold.

Finally, she found herself gasping for air as she reached the Anne home, and quickly climbed the balcony. Not wanting to scare Elizabeth's children, she knocked as calmly as possible on the back door, and saw the shock in Elizabeth's eyes as she ran to her aid. Pulling Debra inside, she took her to the nearest bathroom and handed her a towel.

"My God Debra!" Elizabeth exclaimed. "What's going on here?"

"I don't have time to explain everything now," Debra shot back quickly as she threw the towel off her soaked body knowing that she was just about to return to the violent storm. "I need for you to call the Sheriff's department and call for help. I think Sheriff Burnham may be in a lot of trouble." The youngsters, Mary and Jennifer tried with all their might to listen in on their mother's conversation, but she quickly sent them away, flushing them to their rooms. "I have to go after him Elizabeth, because if I don't, no one will know which way he went."

"Slow down," Elizabeth tried to calm the pale women in front of her. "Who do you have to go after? I'm sorry, but I'm afraid I don't understand any of this. Who do you have to follow?" She repeated the question just as her husband Murray appeared in the doorway and looked at the two women with a confused expression.

"What's going on?"

"Gabe," Debra went on answering Elizabeth's question. "We were at my house when we saw someone standing outside. It was-." She cut her words off knowing what she about to say was going to sound crazy. "It was Curtis Rains," she snapped not caring if her words were going to be taken seriously or not. "And Gabe went after him. They went running down the beach and I was supposed to call for backup but my phone doesn't work. You have to do it Elizabeth. You have to call for help." Then, saying nothing else, Debra knew she had little time if she planned to catch up with the Sheriff before it was too late. "He's in danger," she screamed as she reached the backdoor once again. "We've got to help him."

Elizabeth wanted to call Debra back, but knew that it was no use. There was no way she was going to be able to hold the woman back. Still in shock, she ran to the phone and followed Debra's instructions by calling 911. She couldn't believe what was happening. After ten years, it appeared as though it was all happening again. Curtis Rains was back, and ready to destroy even more lives. It was extremely hard for her to make sense of Debra's words, but she believed her, and knew that she was telling the truth. After hanging up the phone, she looked in the direction of her husband. "What should we do? We can't just let her run off into a storm like that all alone."

"I'll go after her," Murray spoke up, seeing no other option. "You stay here with the kids and I'll see if I can't catch her."

Elizabeth wanted to object, but knew that her husband was right. He appeared from their bedroom with a bright yellow raincoat, and a small pistol he had bought years ago when they had first arrived in their new home. The sight of her husband with a gun brought both panic and fear to her droning heart, and she imagined all of the dangers her husband was going to walk into. Then, he was about to walk past her, when she grabbed his arm and drew him close. "Please be careful," she begged not wanting to live a life without him. "Please come home."

"I will," Murray promised. "Just stay here with the kids and try not to worry."

"I love you."

"I love you too," Murray replied with a smile as he kissed her forehead warmly, then exited out the back door and headed after Debra, who thankfully was still in his line of sight. He too didn't understand what was going on, but Debra had been terrified when he had listened to her inside his home as she talked to his wife, and apparently Sheriff Burnham was in danger. They needed his help, and he couldn't just turn the other cheek. He had to go after them, and if at all possible, bring them back safely.

Elizabeth watched until her husband was almost completely out of view before she lost control. How could this nightmare be happening again? A stream of tears flowed freely from her eyes and she turned away from the horrifying beach and the immense thunderstorm that continued to roll throughout the area. "Please God," she prayed aloud as she reached her children's bedroom and twisted the knob. "Please watch over them and bring them back unharmed." Then, as soon as she entered their room, and sat on the bed, both Mary and Jennifer ran to her and cradled themselves in her arms.

"What's wrong mommy," the youngest Mary asked emotionally.

"Nothing sweetheart," she replied knowing her children could see through her lie. "Everything's going to be all right. I promise."

"Where did daddy go?" Jennifer asked having listened to their conversation moments ago.

"He had to go help some people honey," Elizabeth soaked in her tears. "But he'll be back in a little while." Elizabeth didn't know why, but she wondered if she would ever see her husband again. She hoped for the best, but feared the worst. Holding her two children tightly in both arms, she cradled them gently, knowing this was going to be a long night.

Debra ran as fast as her light feet would carry her across the hardened soft sand of the beach. Every once in a while, rain would slip into her eyes, and evoke a weak burning sensation. Nevertheless, she continued forward, unaware that behind her, Murray Anne followed her tracks. Gabe was nowhere to be seen in front of her, and there was no way she was going to be able to follow the hundreds of footprints embedded in the sand. Any one of them could have been his.

Panting, she could feel herself growing short of breath, and knew that soon she was going to have to stop for air. She could see the end of the homes along the beach, and knew that beyond there would be nothing but a wide stretch of sand ahead, with a wet woodland area to the left and the almighty ocean to the right. Debra had no weapons. In fact her only utensil, being that of a flashlight. She probably shouldn't have left her home, and simply stayed put to wait on her son to return home. But it was too late to turn back now. Her choice had been made. She knew that Gabe would never turn his back on her, and she owed him the same courtesy.

After what seemed like eternity, Debra paused momentarily and flicked on the flashlight as darkness quickly began to surround her. She had long ago passed the last house along the beach, and seeing no signs of life anywhere, she felt alone. Sounds of wildlife from the woods beside her came to life, some of the animal cries overcoming the resounding thunderstorm. Her hair flapped array in the mighty wind, and her clothes grew heavy as water continued to sink into the fabric.

Catching her breath, she flashed the light in the distance, and strained to see if she could see anyone ahead of her. At first, she saw nothing. Then, about a hundred yards in front of her, she was able to make out the shape of a person.

It was Sheriff Gabriel Burnham.

He was searching the terrain ahead, probably unaware that she had come after him. "Sheriff!" she tried screaming into the night although sure that he would be unable to hear her. So, once again she picked up her pace and headed in his direction. Keeping her eyes on his foggy appearance, she knew that she would reach him soon.

As Debra continued, however, her legs continued to grow weak, and the uneasy feeling in the pit of her stomach continued to grow. She could sense the danger, taste the unforgettable fear and saw the darkness closing in around her at a deafening pace. Soon, her flashlight would be her only source of light.

* * *

Gabe stopped at the entrance to the cove, knowing this was where Curtis Rains had entered the many tunnels and caves that had been off limits to the public years ago due to safety reasons. A few small children had drowned in the caves found alongside the grassy cove a few years ago as they wondered off from their families, and with curiosity explored the hidden treasures they felt could be found within. The rocks found inside the twisting caves were slippery, and some would slip and hit their heads before tumbling unconscious into the brutally cold waters of the grotto, a pool of red water always found around their discolored bodies. Others would manifest their way deep into the twisting caverns only to become lost in the underground chambers and die within days. Warning signs had been posted all about, and it was now illegal to trespass into the cove.

Now, however, Gabe himself had no other choice. Curtis Rains had escaped into one of the caves, and there was no other alternative but to go after him. Slowly, he drew his pistol into the air once again, and flicked on the beam of his flashlight. Walking down the edge of the cove, he passed many small caves that ultimately were too small for a grown man to enter. The largest cave, Gabe knew could be found towards the backstretch of the channel as the body of water silently entered the woods. His instincts told him that's where Curtis Rains could be found.

With his fearlessness overcoming the storm, Sheriff Burnham continued to hunt the man he had taken into custody so many years ago. And if he found him, he knew that he wouldn't hesitate before pulling the trigger. His feet sank into the murky waters outlining the cove, sometimes the mud seeming to try and pull his elder body into the soil, but he kept his balance and continued towards the opening of the large cave, which surprisingly no one had ever named.

It never occurred to him, however, that perhaps, he was the one being hunted.

* * *

Meanwhile, Billy pulled his mother's Lexus safely into their driveway and parked as close to the front door as possible. It was raining tremendously hard now, and he wanted their run to the house to be as short as possible. Billy turned off the lights and killed the engine as the three of them looked out the window, through the storm and stared at the beach home in front of them. Billy knew what must be going through Carey's mind at the moment, and desperately tried to assure her that she didn't have to go through with it if she didn't

Jason Glover

want to. Carey only refused, however, and was the first to open her door and step out into the rain.

As Blaze and Carey waited for Billy underneath the front porch, desperately trying to stay out of the rain, a little impatience followed as he fumbled the stack of keys found on his mother's key chain, searching for the one that would allow them to enter his home. "Got it," Billy said aloud as he quickly fit the key into the hole and with a single twist to the left, twisted the doorknob and pushed the door open. The three of them ran inside, Billy the last to enter, shut and locked the door behind him. The three of them easily noticed that there were no lights on inside the home as they stood silently in the foyer. Saying nothing, Billy couldn't help but wonder where his mother had gone? After all, he had her car, and a violent storm could be found displaying an aggressive amount of energy outside. He knew his mother wouldn't have gone out in such weather. Nevertheless, he tried calling out to her and no one replied.

"That's funny," Blaze spoke up. "Isn't that Sheriff Burnham's truck out in the driveway?"

Billy didn't respond, however, he felt that his friend did have a point. The Sheriff had given his mother a ride home, where she had undoubtedly invited him inside. But now, neither of them could be found anywhere. A worried expression hung shallowly over Billy's face, and suddenly he felt Carey's hand slip into his own. He looked into her eyes, as if searching for answers as to where his mother could be. It simply wasn't like her to just leave the house without leaving him a note as to where she was going and when she planned on returning. Billy couldn't help it. For some reason, he felt that something was terribly wrong.

"Are you all right?" Carey asked compassionately.

"I wouldn't worry about it man," Blaze interjected towards Billy. "She and the Sheriff probably went over to the Anne home. I bet Elizabeth invited them over for dinner or something."

"You're probably right," Billy spoke up not believing his own words, and pretty sure his two counterparts saw right through them as well. "I guess I shouldn't worry until there's something to worry about huh?" he added, trying to force a smile. Then, he left the two of them standing in the foyer as he escaped into the home to turn on a few lights. Blaze, immediately disappeared into the kitchen to subdue the hunger that had been building all day as Billy returned to find Carey standing motionlessly in the foyer, her eyes darting back and forth rapidly as she visualized the interior of the home she had lived in so many years ago. Rushing to her, Billy draped his arms around her and held her tight. "Are you all right?"

Carey couldn't answer the question thrown upon her as it appeared as though her body wouldn't allow her to talk. She felt her hands trembling profusely, and felt her knees growing increasingly weak. For an instant, she thought she was going to collapse right there in the middle of the foyer and fall to the cold, hardened surface of the white marble floor below, from which she could see her own reflection. Looking at herself in the marble, Carey instantly remembered her childhood and how she used to roam around this very house and pretend to be a dancer as she slid across the marble, and twirled about in a marvelous dress that could bring glamour to anyone that wore it. She used to stare at herself in the marble when she was a child after her imaginary performance and imagine herself standing on stage, receiving applause before she would dart off behind the stage curtain and out of view from the audience.

"Carey," Billy spoke up breaking her concentration. "If this is painful for you, we don't have to stay here. We can leave and go someplace together. Just you and me. I'll understand."

"No," Carey breathed as she stepped away from Billy's embrace and prepared to explore the rest of the home. "I want to stay," she paused looking back and into his eyes. "Just let me be for a little while. I promise I'll be all right. This is just something I feel I have to do alone." Billy, not knowing what to say or do, could only nod, and watched in sadness as Carey left his side and embarked into what was once her home. For some reason, he could feel her pain, and wanted to let her know that she didn't have to go through this or suffer alone. He wanted to run to her, and make her feel safe and secure. Nevertheless, he remained behind, remained strong, and did as she wished.

As Carey entered the living room, she didn't even realize how it had changed. Didn't notice the new furniture, the different wall painting, nothing, as her mind only allowed her to remember it as it had been ten years ago. She could feel her chest having trouble breathing, and could hear her heartbeat ringing through her ears as she closed her eyes and pictured her parents' lifeless, tortured, and mangled bodies laying in a pool of their own blood in the living room. Even now, however, there was nothing she could do for them. Nothing at all. Except, watch them die, and listen to their screams.

Once again, Carey could feel death all around her, and she knew that she had made a mistake in coming back here. She could feel tears forming in her eyes, as she felt once again like that of a child who had just witnessed her parent's death. Running up the stairs, she didn't even feel Billy and Blaze's eyes upon her as she darted off to the one place in the entire home she felt could take all the pain away.

Carey Haas was returning to her bedroom.

Opening the door, she quickly ran inside and slammed it shut behind her. Breathing harshly, Carey fell to the floor as her knees finally gave away and she sank her head between her legs and began to sob uncontrollably. What was happening to her? She was loosing her mind, she thought. This was entirely too much for her to handle. She wasn't strong enough to face Curtis Rains yet, and she knew that by coming here, he would win again. He wanted her to remember her parent's brutal murder. He wanted her to remember every last detail. How they screamed, how their bodies looked with holes sliced into their flesh. He wanted her to feel the pain he had had inflicted upon them, and how it had felt for them to know they were about to die. It was simply too much for Carey to take. She was loosing control of everything. And the memory of her parents was stronger now than ever. Crying loudly now, Carey sat motionlessly in the corner of what was once her room, wishing she had never returned.

Everything had come back with a vengeance, almost as if some unseen force was expecting her return. Carey was no longer the tall, perfectly figured woman almost twenty years of age. She saw herself once again as a child of nine, where she had been forced to grow up well before her time when a single knock at the door changed her life forever. Then, when Curtis Rains had finally decided to bust into her beloved home, everything she had considered so divine and electrically heaven had instantly turned into that of a bitter abyss, where her soul was constantly being thrust into the underworld. Her life had turned into a flaming hell, from which there didn't appear to be any means of escape.

Carey knew that Curtis Rains would never let her live a life of peace. He would always be there to remind her of his power. Always be there to let her know that he was the one to take her parents away from her. She couldn't beat him, she knew that now. She was completely powerless against this evil that knew no boundary, and wouldn't except defeat. Nor, she knew, would this evil ever perish.

Opening her eyes, Carey visualized her bedroom. Although it now belonged to Billy Saxton, everything looked the same. His bed, looked exactly like that of her own. In fact, her illusion was real. This was still her room. Climbing to her feet, she used the wall for leverage and began prancing about the room. Falling on the bed, she remembered how her parents would always come up and tuck her in, and not realizing what she was doing, Carey began calling out to them like she used to, and then looked towards the door, waiting for them to burst in and surprise her. It was almost as if she had forgotten that they were dead. Living in the past, Carey's conscious had blocked all of the horrible memories out, and she had completely returned to the milieu, or ambiance of a child. "Mom, Dad!" Carey screamed once again with a smile lingering across her face. Then, closing her eyes, something happened.

She saw someone.

Only, it wasn't her parents. It was their killer. It was Curtis Rains, and he was staring at her, evil pouring from his eyes, and his hands still covered with her parent's blood. "No!" Carey screamed in bewilderment. "Get away from me!" she continued to plead like a terrified child in the middle of a bad dream. "No!"

"Carey!" Billy's voice rang out as he burst through the bedroom door and rushed to her aid as her body shook out of control on the bed. "Carey, it's me Billy," he continued covering her body with his strength, not allowing it to move. He saw her eyes open, and for a moment, it appeared as though she didn't recognize him. She still looked scared of something. "Carey, it's all right. You must have fallen asleep. You were having a bad dream. It's all right though sweetheart. I'm here now."

Carey didn't understand.

Everything had seemed so real, almost like it was happening all over again. But now, she was back to herself again. The child that had momentarily been trapped inside of her was long gone; returning from wherever it had came. Perhaps, hiding once again deep inside her soul until another time would permit its return. Taking a deep breath, Carey realized where she was and who was sitting next to her. She was glad to see that she wasn't a child anymore, and even more delighted to find Billy before her, looking upon her with his beautiful blue eyes instead the darkened pupils that belonged to the demon. "Oh God Billy," Carey sighed as she threw her arms around him and pulled him close. "I'm sorry about all of this. I don't know what happened. I-."

"Don't worry about it," he cut her off with a smile and loving kiss on the forehead. "It's all right. I understand Carey. I just heard you screaming from downstairs while Blaze and I were watching television, and I knew you said you wanted to be alone. But I couldn't help myself. I had to come."

"I'm glad you did," Carey smiled as she sat up. "It was just so real ya know?" She paused as she remembered feeling like that of a child all over again. "It was like I was nine again, and reliving everything. I," she paused not exactly sure how to say what was on her mind. "I saw them again Billy," she continued knowing Billy would understand what she was talking about. "I saw my parents again. And they. They, were dea-," she had to end her sentence abruptly as the words of her parents death still hurt too much sometimes to speak of.

"You don't have to say anything Carey," Billy assured her as he tried to quiet her. "You don't have to say anything to me at all. Now," he paused, pulling her to her feet and forcing her to exit the room. "Let's go downstairs. Blaze is slaving in the kitchen trying to cook us a nice dinner."

"What about your mom?" Carey asked changing the subject. "Have you heard from Debra yet?"

Billy could only shake his head. "No I haven't."

* * *

Debra herself had reached the cove as the storm continued to batter her weakened body. She found herself walking along the edge of the marsh carefully, the beam of the flashlight clearing a path in the darkness as she desperately tried to search for the Sheriff's footprints.

Surely, he would have left some planted in the thick, soupy mud that stood in her way. Then again, she thought, it would have been easy for the rain to wash them away. Sighing to herself, Debra felt a bitter state of fear come over her body as she found herself standing in the middle of the cove, all alone, and away from the warmth of civilization. Her son, she knew would have been home by now, and was probably worried sick about her. She had made a mistake in coming after the Sheriff and knew now that her own life was in danger.

Yet, she didn't turn around.

Billy's life remained in question as long as Curtis Rains was still out there, and Debra wouldn't take any chances with her son. If there were anyway she could help, or assist the Sheriff in putting an end to this mayhem once and for all, she would do it without question. So, with the flashlight still held firmly in the palm of her hands, Debra foolishly continued to make her way through the marsh. Watching her every step, she tried to take every precaution possible to allow herself to remain standing and to not fall into the water of the bay, which appeared to be rising quickly.

She saw trees in the distance, and knew the bank of the cove was about to carry her into the woods. The trees, she hoped, would provide a little bit of shelter from the rain, and if it blocked a small portion of the powerful wind, it would be extremely helpful. The cover of the forest sounded real good to Debra Saxton at the moment, and she now found her pace quickening. Pushing the fear aside for the moment, Debra felt as though she was on a mission.

She had to try and save the Sheriff.

More importantly, however, she wanted to save her family.

She would rather die than loose her only child in Billy Saxton. He was the single reason she was able to climb out of bed each and every day and go on with life. Without him, Debra had no life to live, would have nothing to look forward to, and would have no one to love. Billy was the essence of her motherhood, and the essence of her existence, and nothing was going to take him away from her. Billy's seemingly Immortal soul was too precious and valuable to just be released into the hands of evil. If she had to, Debra knew that she would fight until her death.

For without her son, Debra Saxton was dead anyway.

Sheriff Gabriel Burnham had finally reached the entrance to the large cave that stood right off the embankment of the cove and was partially hidden in the trees of the surrounding forest. Wiping the rain from his face, he shined the flashlight in the vicinity of the darkened cave. The hole in the rock was simply too hard for the weak beam to penetrate from outside, and Gabe knew that he would have to enter the haunting sector in order to find what he was looking for. With his best intentions at heart, yet fear still doubling within, he climbed the few stones and stood at the entrance of the cave, it's gaping wide hole welcoming, almost beckoning him to enter.

Finally, clutching the gun tightly in the palm of his hands he took his first step into the cave, and immediately saw the two passageways from which he was supposed to embark. The tunnels were separated by a sharp edge of stone, both the same in height, and both allowing his body easy access. He didn't know which cave to choose, however, and bending down, he tried to find any signs of footprints that might lead in the direction of Curtis Rains. Finding nothing but a slippery, dusty cavern floor, he knew he would once again have to rely on his instincts. Shivering in the dampened area, he felt a cool breeze pass over his body.

Immediately, Gabe knew that he was not alone in this cave.

Choosing the cave on the left, he held both the gun and the flashlight out in front of him. Water dripped from the ceiling and a few sounds from predators could be heard within. Nevertheless, his courage remained strong. He was doing his job, and nothing more, even if it did run a little more personal than he would like to admit. Shining the flashlight all around, he saw nothing ahead except more cobwebs, spider webs and puddles of water. Surely, he knew that soon the cave would build on water and the area in which he was now confined would begin to breakdown and the spacious environment would become thinner. Never blinking, Gabe's eyes continued forward, surveying every inch, and just waiting for Curtis Rains to decide to make his presence known. Taking in a deep breath, however, he knew one thing.

Curtis Rains wouldn't have lured him into such a place for no reason. There was no way he was going to surrender or go away quietly. Although he feared the man he had long ago helped in capturing and putting away, he knew that another confrontation was going to be inevitable.

Of the two men that had entered the cave, he was sure, only one would come out alive.

"Rains!" Gabe found himself screaming loudly throughout the cave, trying to hide the fear his voice slightly possessed. "Rains I know you're in here. Now come on out you son of a bitch. I think we've got a score to settle." At first, there was no response. Then, in the distance, the Sheriff could hear laughter. Picking up his pace, he began darting around the sharp edges of the cave, following the weak illuminating path his flashlight granted him and soon found himself standing at another split off. He could hear water running straight ahead, and decided to remain in the same cave.

Seconds, then minutes passed and he heard nothing. Yet, he knew he was heading in the right direction. He knew the evil Curtis Rains was close, and there was no way he was going to let him walk out of this cave alive. He had to put a stop to this madness once for all. It was time to end the rein of the illusive serial killer forever, and bring justice to the pain he had caused for all eternity.

"God damn you Rains!" the Sheriff shouted harshly. "Come on out. I'm tired of playing your fucking games. Let's get this over with once and for all. It's just me and you in here."

Again, there was an evil laughter that echoed throughout the cave and shattered the Sheriff's nerves.

Then, he heard Curtis Rains speak.

"You really want me don't you Sheriff?" Curtis asked mockingly.

"You bet your ass I do."

"Well just a little farther then Sheriff," Curtis continued as his rage continued to grow. "I want you to come to me."

"Oh I'm coming you son of a bitch," Gabe shouted loudly throughout the tunnels. "Just don't run away from me this time you chicken shit."

"Oh trust me," Rains continued with a smile in the darkness as he realized the good old Sheriff didn't understand just what he was getting into. "It's time for me to stop running. I'm not going anywhere."

Chapter 27

    Ashley Selvaggio had just passed a road sign stating that the city of Destin, Florida was no more than 20 miles away. She was close, and knew as soon as she reached her destination, she was going to have to find Carey Haas immediately. She had already gone against her boss's direct order and had proceeded to travel to Destin against his will. Looking at her pager, Captain Armstrong had beeped her three times since she pulled out of her driveway in Starke, Florida, and she hadn't returned a single one of them. Obviously, he had expected her to go regardless of how strongly he felt about it, which could explain his continuous efforts to try and reach her. Yet, she no longer cared. She was working on a case, simply doing her job, and refused to accept the indisputable fact that Jack Reynolds had been the only killer that night at his home.
    She knew, however, that her job would undoubtedly be in question if and when she did return to Starke. Her Captain, she very well knew, was going to give her an ear full and call her an assortment of names in which many women might take offense to. If he did fire her, however, she knew it would probably all be for the better. Her personality didn't fit in with the small population of Starke, Florida. She wasn't happy there, and knew her skills could better be exercised somewhere else. Somewhere, where her own beliefs were more common.
    Nevertheless, as Ashley drove along the highway, she was forced to use her windshield wipers at full speed as she encountered a severe thunderstorm. The sun had long disappeared and the lights outlining the deserted highway were dim and provided very little light through

the storm. Her foot remained glued to the gas pedal, and she found herself driving her 4-Runner at least ten miles over the displayed speed limit. Clutching the wheel firmly, she was comfortable in knowing that she wouldn't loose control of her vehicle.

Another sign passed, and now she was within ten miles of Destin, and within ten miles of finding Carey Haas. She didn't know exactly what she was expecting to find here, but sensed that something was there. She felt that Carey's own life was probably in danger, if she had been right in concluding that the Reynolds case and the Birmingham case were connected, and at best, could at least warn her of the possible dangers. Completely at ease with her decision to leave her home behind, Ashley felt somewhat relaxed behind the wheel of her car.

About twenty minutes or so passed and she found herself driving along the main highway of Destin, Florida. Condominiums, and beautiful resorts outlined the beach side of the road, with nice restaurants, fast food joints and gift shops scattered along the opposite end for the tourists' satisfaction. This was her second time visiting the town known as a fisherman's paradise, and she was amazed at how much it had grown in the last few years. In no time, the city of Destin had blossomed into a money making metropolitan, and continued to bloom every year at an overwhelming pace. More and more people across the nation stormed into Destin every year to visit the beautiful coastal waters and to charter a fishing boat, with the assurance that their satisfaction was guaranteed.

Tonight, however, things were quiet and the streets were naked. She was traveling along the strip, and although there was virtually no traffic, she grunted to herself as she still found herself stopping at every traffic light. Listening to the radio, she had learned of a flood warning through the early morning hours and the thunderstorm was supposedly going to continue until daybreak as well, with possible gusts of wind along the immediate coast of up to fifty miles per hour. No wonder everyone remained indoors on a night like tonight, and Ashley herself wondered if she had used good judgment in choosing to travel on such a vindictive evening.

Nevertheless, it was entirely too late to turn around now. She was already in Destin, and in pulling out her notepad; she found the address to Carey Haas's aunt and uncle's home. In such weather, she knew it might become a bit difficult to follow the road signs, and she would be the first to admit that she didn't know where she was going. Pulling out her car phone she decided to call the local police station. After introducing herself and her occupation, she found herself talking to a sweet voiced female on the other end, which took a considerate amount of time in explaining how to find the road from which the Goodman home could be found.

Within seconds, Ashley was on her way.

Turning off the radio, she decided to enjoy the silence, except for the rain that continued to pound along her windshield. It was time to concentrate fully on the situation at hand, and rivet her attention amply in locating Carey Haas. Finally, she found herself turning off the highway and onto a two-lane bridge. Gripping the wheel firmly, she knew she was heading in the right direction, and soon, her destination would be reached. Smiling, she would just be happy when she could step out of her truck and stretch her stiffened back. She had been driving for hours, and needed a break.

Actually, she needed a stiff drink, she thought, teasing herself. But that could wait until time allotted.

* * *

Rick and Carol Goodman sat nervously in their living room, waiting patiently for Carey to call them and tell them where to come and pick her up. She was supposed to call long ago, and the two of them couldn't help but to think that something was terribly wrong. Rick had called Sheriff Burnham several times in the past two hours, both at home and at his office and each time, he got the same response. Gabe was nowhere to be found. He wasn't responding to his radio each time the dispatcher tried to reach him, and his machine picked up at his home. The storm that continued to intensify outside their beloved home only made the uneasiness grow even stronger as each minute slowly passed, and now the two of them were sitting helplessly on the edge of their seats.

"Rick, I'm worried about her," Carol spoke up of their niece, breaking the unbearable silence that had fallen over them. "This just isn't like her not to call or anything."

"I know," Rick replied, trying to remain calm. "But I don't know where she could be. I know the Sheriff took Debra home, but I can't reach him anywhere. His office doesn't know where he is and he isn't home."

"Do you think she's with him?"

Rick only shrugged his shoulders. "I don't know. But I don't like the idea of her being out in this weather either. It's too dangerous." Then, climbing to his feet, Rick decided to try one other place and cursed himself silently for not realizing to call this place long ago. Surely, if she had been with Billy this entire time, they would have returned to his home along the beach by now, and although it continued to anger him slightly that she hadn't been considerate enough to call and at least let them know that she was all right and safe, he placed his anger aside as he picked up the phone.

He was grateful to hear a dial tone as he picked up the phone, but as he pressed the numbers slowly, the memories of the beach home came flooding back with a force so powerful they simply couldn't be denied. He remembered the night he and his wife, Carol, had received the phone call from the police station explaining of David and Charlene's death and that they were needed to come to the station to pick up little Carey, whom had been the only survivor of the massacre. Surely, he thought to himself, her old house would have been one of the last places she would have wanted to go.

Then, his concentration was baffled by a busy signal coming from the other end of the line. Fear splintered its way through Rick's spine as he realized the busy signal didn't indicate someone was talking on the other end. There hadn't been a slight pause before the distracting busy tone amplified itself through the phone. Instead, as soon as he finished dialing the number the sound appeared, telling him that it was either off the hook, or not in service. Placing the phone back on the hook, he returned to his wife in the living room, who easily picked up on the disturbing look across his face.

"Rick?" Carol questioned, growing concerned. "What is it? Is something wrong?" At first, her husband didn't answer her. He just sat across from her in his favorite recliner and stared out the window. It was apparent to her that something was on his mind. "Rick!" she continued more decisively trying to capture his attention, and as his head snapped and turned to face her, she knew she had succeeded in doing just that. "Will you please talk to me? Who did you just try and call?"

"Carey's old beach house," Rick finally replied as his eyes once again moved to the window and the storm beyond. "You know where Billy lives now?"

"Of course I know where you're talking about," Carol snapped not believing he had been so naïve. Did he honestly expect her to be able to forget the place in which her own sister and brother-in-law had been murdered? "How could I forget?" Then, changing the subject, she added. "Well, was she there?"

"I don't know."

"What do you mean you don't know?"

"I mean the phone is out of service, or off the hook or something," Rick answered calmly knowing his words were going to upset his wife dramatically. "But she has to be there Carol," he continued firmly, trying to decide what needed to be done. "I don't know what it is, but I just know she's there. There is no other place they could have gone," he concluded speaking of not only his niece, but Billy Saxton and Blaze Brookshaw as well. "I mean none of them would have wanted to be out in such a storm. They probably just went there until the storm died down a bit."

Not saying a word, Carol removed herself from the sofa and went into the kitchen. Picking up the phone, she decided to try and call her sister's old home as well. Amazingly, the number was still memorized, and within seconds she was pressing the phone to her ear, desperately hoping to hear it ringing. Just as Rick had explained moments ago, however, there would be no such luck and the busy signal promptly appeared. Placing the phone back on the receiver, Carol felt her heartbeat quicken, and her hands began to tremble uncontrollably.

As a few minutes passed and she didn't return to the living room, Rick joined her in the kitchen and found her standing in front of the sink, her hands clutching the sides of the counter tightly. Moving behind her, he placed his hands warmly around her waist and gave her an affectionate squeeze. He kissed the back of her head, and then moving her hair aside, wet the side of the cheek briefly with his lips. "Are you all right?" he asked sympathetically, knowing she was worried about Carey, and if anything were to happen to her she would take full responsibility and beat herself up for the rest of her life.

"No," Carol admitted as a tear flowed from one of her eyes and ran freely down her cheek. "I'm worried about her Rick. I don't know why, but I just feel like something is wrong."

"I know," Rick agreed as he pulled her close. "I'm worried too. But, what do you want to do?"

For a moment, Carol said nothing. She just stood there and absorbed the comfort her husband's manly arms provided and welcomed the warm sanctuary that seemed to burgeon through his arms and into her soul, bringing her trembling hands to a momentary abate. Yet, the splintering thought of Carey being in trouble remained and continued to hound her brain without remorse. The last question her husband had thrown at her seemed almost unanswerable until now. "I know what we can do," Carol spoke up, knowing Rick might not approve of her decision.

"What?" Rick asked, not really sure if he liked the energetic, yet cold tone his wife had instantly evaporated to the surface.

"We should go there Rick," she replied firmly, desperately trying to dissuade the fear that continued to develop inside her numbed body. "I think we should go there. If something is wrong Rick, maybe we can help."

"But what if she's not even there?"

"Hopefully she's not," Carol admitted. "Hopefully we'll be wasting our time and she's somewhere else with Billy. But if she's there Rick, I don't know exactly why, but I think that something might be wrong. If she's there, and if what she's been telling us is true, she could be in a lot of danger."

"All right," Rick hesitantly agreed, although knowing there would be no way to change Carol's mind. "Just let me grab a coat and we'll be on our way."

"Thank you," Carol spoke softly. "I just want to make sure she's all right."

"I understand," Rick kissed her gently one more time. "But I'd try not to worry if I were you. I'm sure everything is fine. The storm probably just cut their phone off and she's been unable to call. Seriously sweetheart, everything is going to be O.K. I just know it."

"I hope so," Carol muttered to herself as her husband left her side to find his raincoat. "I really hope so."

* * *

Meanwhile, Sheriff Gabriel Burnham continued his relentless search for Curtis Rains as he continued to travel deeper and deeper into the unfamiliar caves found alongside the cove. He kept his flashlight steadily in front of him, and his revolver drawn sharply. Every once in a while, he grasped the stone walls of the cave to regain his balance as his feet every so often would momentarily lose their stability and he found himself almost falling harshly to the cold, wet, slippery cavern floor. Water could be found up to his ankles now, and the width of the caves continued to diminish in size. There was approximately two feet on either side of him, and he found himself running short of breath. Nevertheless his pursuit for justice continued.

Then, his lighting gave way to a large opening directly in front of him and sounds of running water could be heard thoroughly in the distance. Picking up his pace, he reached the opening in no time and found himself standing on a ledge. Peering down, he saw a large pool of water not more than ten feet below him. Shining the flashlight vigorously around him, he found a small waterfall coming from one of the stone walls of the caves and watched as the water escaped through the opening and plowed into the pool of water, sending ripples in a circular motion towards him. Any other time, this would have been a wonderful, exciting, beautiful encounter. Now, however, he had no time to take in the beauty before him. His mind could only focus on apprehending the killer that to his knowledge had been electrocuted to death days ago.

"Rains," Gabe spoke firmly, listening as his voice echoed throughout the open room the cave had led him to. "Are you in here? There's no other way out of here except through this opening. So come on out. You can't escape." For a brief moment, there was no reply, only the sound of the waterfall, and Gabe began to wonder if perhaps he had been tricked and if somehow Curtis Rains had been able to elude him only after leading him deep into the cave with the thought that he would become lost. After shining the flashlight around the entire spacious room one more time, he was about to retrace his steps, when something happened.

Listening intensely, he heard laughter. It was the same evil laughter the maniac was known for, and at that instant, Sheriff Burnham realized that he was not alone in the cavern. Curtis Rains was there with him, probably watching his every move, and anticipating his arrival.

"Well Sheriff I'm so glad you could make it," Curtis spoke softly, yet his voice still had the power to bounce off the walls and descend directly into Gabe's ears and send chills down his spine. "For a minute there I didn't think you were going to make it and that you were going to give up. But I'll give you one thing Sheriff," he paused as another mischievous laugh escaped from his throat. "You really are one persistent son of a bitch."

"Show yourself!" Gabe ordered, all the while doubting his counterpart would comply.

"Just open your eyes," Curtis whispered mockingly. "I'm right in front of you. Can't you see me?"

Gabe couldn't respond. Fear pounced through his body at an enormous speed and his tongue seemed to be lodged in the back of his throat. For the first time, he realized that Curtis Rains had the upper hand in this situation. He had made a mistake by coming into the caves alone, and knew that even if his men had been summoned and were tailing him, it would take them forever to locate him in the heart of the caves. He was alone, with hardly any protection, save for his gun. Gabe was alone with a known killer, whom he knew had no conscious and was condemned with an evil that held no boundary. Finally, for perhaps the first time his life, the Sheriff tasted real fear, and his courage began to fade slightly, shivering up into a ball and hiding in a corner. He didn't know what to do.

"Come on Gabe," Curtis continued to mock. "Don't tell me you're getting cold feet after all this? You've tracked me down. You've found me."

"Go to hell you son of a bitch."

Laughing, Curtis responded. "Oh I'm there Sheriff, and believe me, it's not as bad as everyone says it is. In fact I'm kind of starting to like it here. What about you?" he paused waiting for Gabe to respond. "How do you feel about knowing that you're standing right smack dab in the middle of hell?" he asked after hearing no response. "better yet," he paused once again to snicker at his prey. "How do you feel about standing in the same room, face to face with the devil himself?"

"Goddamn it!" Gabe yelled into the cave growing frustrated. "Quit playing games and show yourself you son of a bitch!"

"You are so fucking blind!" Curtis shot back coldly; rage could have easily been seen in the depth of his eyes. Then, with the snap of his fingers, the interior walls of the cave lit up brightly as a fury of flames erupted into the air. Despite the water dripping from all the stonewalls, the fire continued to burn powerfully, lighting up the entire area. "Is that better?" Curtis asked harshly. "Can you see me now?"

Gabe's eyes took a moment to get adjusted to the newfound bright light, but soon excepted it's warmth and he peered into the pool of water below him, still holding his gun tightly in the palm of his hands. There, before him, standing in the center of the pool of water and directly in the center of the flames, was Curtis Rains, his arms once again extended as if he were willing to surrender. Never taking his eyes off the mass murderer, Gabe quickly lowered himself into the pool of water and grasped a good foothold. "Don't you move you son of a bitch?" he ordered as he pointed the gun directly between the man's eyes. "I would love nothing more than to pull this fucking trigger and watch your brains scatter all over this damn cave."

"I'm sure you would," Curtis spoke rationally, and with a calmness that wasn't appealing to the Sheriff. Then, slowly, he lowered his arms and reached into the black cloak that was draped over his broadened shoulders. Knowing the Sheriff wasn't about to pull the trigger, Curtis kept a stern face and stared directly into Gabe's eyes. He could sense the man's fear in front of him, could hear his heart beating rapidly, and knew that he was afraid for his life. "You shouldn't have followed me Sheriff," Curtis whispered as he pulled a glistening silver knife from the depths of the cloak and twirled it between his fingers. "You could have lived ya know. I didn't want to kill you. All I wanted was Carey, and no one else. That's all."

"Over my dead body you son of a bitch."

"I figured you'd see it that way," Curtis continued to speak rationally, never once removing his glare into the Sheriff's eyes.

"That's why I let you follow me all the way out here and into this lovely cave. It's just the two of us in here sir. Kind of creepy isn't it? Staring death in the eye."

"Drop the knife!" Gabe ordered.

"Maybe you're not understanding me here," Curtis continued with a slight laugh ignoring the Sheriff's order to lower his weapon. "I am in control!" he barked harshly into the cave. "Your fucking life is in my hands now. So why don't you just shut up and show me some fucking respect before I cut your out of shape ass up like an ice sculpture. After all, I am aching to find out what your insides look like. They have to be absolutely tasty."

Saying nothing, Curtis Rains had crossed the line and without warning, Gabe fired three rounds at the serial killer. He watched as the bullets entered the man in front of him and then witnessed as Curtis Rains tumbled backwards and disappeared into the water. Still gripping the gun firmly, Gabe ran into the water and searched for his body. Seconds, then minutes passed and he had found nothing. Then, finally, he spotted him. His body floated to the top of the water stomach first. Grabbing Curtis by the shoulder, he rolled his body over felt a bit of relief as he found his eyes shut tight. Pressing his hands underneath his chin and along his neck, he searched for a pulse.

There was none.

Finally, Curtis Rains was dead.

Placing his gun back in his holster, Gabe pushed Curtis Rains body away and watched as it floated throughout the small pool of water, the whole scene ignited by the flaming stonewalls of the cavern. Finally, he reached the wall and began to climb back up and into the cave that would lead him out. He was tired and he needed some fresh air. He didn't understand what had just happened, didn't see how a whole nation could have been fooled of this man's death and certainly didn't see how he had been able to escape. Gabe himself had watched as Curtis's body was pulled out of the prison on a stretcher and placed in the back of a Hurst. There didn't appear to have been a mistake, and surely, the state of Florida wouldn't have electrocuted the wrong man. That was impossible. Yet, he had just been face to face with the man everyone loved to hate, and was a bit reluctant to realize that many questions would never be answered.

Then, he heard something, which made him freeze in his tracks, and the hair on the back of his neck stand tall. It was a voice. But it was impossible. Curtis was dead. He had shot him three times. He had no pulse. Nevertheless, Gabe slowly found himself turning around, and fear once again sprang to life as he found himself standing before the man he had just shot.

"Don't you ever turn your back on me!" Curtis snickered as he held the silvery knife firmly out in front of him. Now, however, there was no smile protruding across his grim face. Anger was etched across his entire face as he spoke with a rage almost unimaginable. "You really are one ignorant son of a bitch do you know that!" Curtis paused allowing the Sheriff to attempt to swallow the lump that had formed inside his throat and left him almost completely speechless. "Did you really think that you could kill someone that's already dead?"

"This is impossible!"

"Yeah that's what they are all going to say about me one day," Curtis broke in as he began to move towards the Sheriff, who slammed his back into the stone wall of the cave and was forced to watch in blatant fear as his assailant made his way towards him. Finally, Curtis was close enough to Gabe to taste his breath and he placed the edge of the cold blade underneath his chin. "Look into my eyes!" Curtis ordered harshly. "Look into my eyes and tell me what you see."

There was no response.

"You see death don't you?" Curtis continued as a fury began to rip through his body. "Right now, you know you're about to die don't you?" Gabe could say nothing. "I could spare your life, but I know you would try and ruin my perfect plan. You see, when I go after Carey, I don't want any distractions and I knew you would do your best to stand in my way. But don't you get it? It's fate. I was destined to kill her and there is absolutely nothing that anyone could do to stop it. My hands were meant to be wrapped around her throat, and cut into her flesh, devour the pleasure of touching her entire body from head to toe."

"You really are one sick son of a bitch!"

"That's right," Curtis mocked him as he teased the knife along Gabe's flesh. "But I am one powerful, immortal son of a bitch who is once again free to do as I please and destroy anything my desire yearns for. I am a God if you will, and my evil is more powerful than anything this world has ever seen or known. I cannot be stopped and only the foolish will dare stand in my way. Like you for instance. What makes you think you have the right to stand in my way? Or better yet, stand in the way of destiny?"

"I am not afraid of you," Gabe spoke carefully, feeling a small portion of blood drip down his neck as he desperately searched for a braver conscious.

"Yes you are!" Curtis shot back. "I can see it in your eyes."

"Why don't you just go ahead and kill me!" Gabe yelled into the demon's shaded eyes. "Your spirit might be powerful, but inside you're weak and I will forever more be stronger than you. Because my soul will go to heaven, and sooner or later we will overpower you and bring you down."

Curtis laughed loudly as his grip on the knife tightened. "Jesus you really are reaching aren't you? I'm surprised you were able to come up with that actually."

"Let's just get this over with damn you!" Gabe ordered bravely. "I don't want to look into your eyes any longer. And you're wrong about one thing, I am not afraid to die, and I am no longer afraid of you."

"Right now Sheriff," Curtis spoke calmly. "Carey and her two little friends are at the beach house. She's trying to face her fear to get rid of me. But I can feel her inside of me and I think she knows I'm coming. She's going to die tonight Sheriff. Granted, you're going to die well before her, but she's going to die. My mission is almost complete. It's just too bad you had to stand in my way. I respect you because you really are a brave man Gabe."

"Your compliments mean nothing to me."

Then, closing his eyes, Gabe knew the end was near. He had tried his best to fight the evil before him. Yet, he had failed and was accepting defeat. He knew that he was going to die, but he was going to die with honor. He refused to give the phantom the satisfaction of knowing his weakness and fear of him. Sheriff Gabriel Burnham was no longer afraid of Curtis Rains. Then, he felt the knife swiftly begin to move as Curtis spoke to him one last time.

"Goodbye Sheriff."

Then, with one fatal slice, Curtis Rains watched in amazement as Gabe's throat split open and blood began to spew from the open wound. Gabe's hands instinctively grabbed his throat and the usual choking noise could be heard echoing throughout the vast area now consumed with the darkness that followed death. Then, holding the knife before him, he watched as the Sheriff took his last breath and fell into the cold waters below. Curtis looked at his reflection in the knife awkwardly. Feeling his rage continue to grow a bit, he brought the knife forward and licked its silvery surface clean. The taste of blood made his insides churn with excitement, and now he realized it was time to finish what he had started some ten years ago.

Now, it was Carey Haas's time to die.

Walking back into the center of the flames, the *Tinman*, held his arms high into the air and he let out an evil roar that escaped into every cave found inside the cavern and seemed to bounce off the stone walls forever, perhaps never coming to an end. Then, in the blink of an eye, he was gone.

He disappeared without a trace, leaving the lifeless body of Sheriff Gabriel Burnham to be feasted upon by the carnivores he knew to be hidden inside the cave. Following its life, the flames disappeared along with Curtis Rains leaving behind no trace of his existence.

Once again, the cavern was quiet.

Quiet in death.

* * *

Debra Saxton finally reached the entrance to the large cave. Pulling herself out of the marsh, she fought hard to keep her balance as she scaled the slippery large rocks and then gathered herself in an erect position as she stood at the mouth of the cave. She was sure this was where Sheriff Burnham had entered and gone after the illusive Curtis Rains, yet as she peered down at the weak light her flashlight provided through the thick darkness, she hesitated before entering the crypt like atmosphere.

This wasn't a good idea she told herself, and knew of the possible dangers of entering such a confined space. Not only did it now house one of the most notorious serial killers ever known to mankind, but it was simply too dark and Debra was well aware that it would be easy to get lost in the darkness, perhaps never being able to find her way out or to be found by the search party she was sure was developing. And surely, she thought to herself, Gabe had been aware of the simple dangers her mind easily forced her to look into.

Nevertheless, Debra pressed forward and took her first steps into the cave. Almost immediately, the thicket of darkness seemed to swallow her up and hide her from society. The flashlight was weak, but it enabled her to see directly in front of her, and she made sure her feet weren't trampling over anything that might cause her to slip and fall to the hardened surface below. Slowly, Debra crept through the cave, sometimes using her free hand to clutch the sides of the cave, and sometimes sliding her feet gently across the surface. She found herself feeling a bit heavier than normal as rain had exceeded in soaking her clothing, and as she felt the water squish between her toes, she could still hear the fearsome storm cracking in the night outside of the cave.

Then, hearing something move behind her, she spun around wildly and through the light in the vicinity from which she had heard the noise. A rat scurried out of sight, and although the fear she had succumbed to disappeared in relief to the fleeing rat, she still had trouble calming herself. Everywhere around her, was darkness, and Debra couldn't even see the entrance to the cave. She didn't even know if she was going in the right direction. Gabe could have ventured into any one of the many twists and turns this cave provided. She thought about calling out to him, but decided against it knowing that she could very well give her position away, and instead of running into the Sheriff, she may very well encounter the man that had so suddenly turn her son's life upside down.

It was cold in the cave, and Debra found herself shivering uncontrollably as she watched her breath in front of her. A nice hot bath, and new set of clothes sounded too good to be true right now, and she couldn't help but to wonder if she would ever return home to her son. She was a single mother, and although she tried hard to stay in shape and keep her figure firm, she knew she had no business following the Sheriff into the cave. She should have waited for help. She should have stayed home, waited for her son to return, and then help the police any way she could assist them in locating Sheriff

Burnham. Now, however, it was too late, and she had no choice but to continue.

Time passed slowly to Debra, and she heard the sounds of more rats and bats living about deep inside the cave. And every few feet, she swore to feel the eyes of the animals on her, as if waiting on her to die so they could feast on her rotten flesh and devour her rich blood for an appetizer. Then, finally after what seemed like an eternity, she stopped in her tracks as she heard a sound in the distance.

It sounded like running water.

Straining her ears, Debra moved a little faster and soon found herself coming closer to the distinct sound as it grew more powerful and became even clearer. In the distance, her flashlight saw an opening of sorts, and soon, Debra found herself standing on a ledge, overlooking a small pool of water as a waterfall tumbled from one of the stonewalls of the cave. She shined her flashlight around the room, desperately searching for any sings of life, but found nothing.

She searched the walls of the room for signs of another cave appearing on the other side of the room. She didn't find one, and knew that she was going to have to backtrack and go another way. Thankful that she wasn't going to have to try and cross the small pool of water, Debra turned around and was about to retrace her footsteps, when she heard something from behind her. It sounded like a squealing noise of sorts, and quickly she spun back around and darted her flashlight into the pool of water. She saw another large rat climbing out of the water and then disappear into a hole just big enough for him to hide inside the cave. Throwing the light back into the water, she wondered what it had been doing there.

Then, she saw it.

Floating on top of the water was a body. It was a man, and he was floating on his stomach, only his backside visible to Debra as a pool of red liquid, which she knew to be blood, swirled around him. "No," Debra whispered as she immediately made the connection and knew who she was looking at. "No," she repeated backing away as fear enveloped its way throughout her entire body as she realized she had been too late.

It was Sheriff Burnham.

Debra didn't know what to do and she began to panic. Curtis Rains had been there, and he had killed Gabe. With her hands trembling, she searched the room one last time, half expecting to find Curtis standing before her as he waited for her to follow the Sheriff inside the cave. He wasn't there. Save for the deceased Sheriff, she was the only one in the room.

Backing away, she felt her lower lip shaking uncontrollably, and she dropped her dismal flashlight to the ground below. She didn't even attempt to go after it as it slammed onto the cold surface below and then rolled over the edge, splashing gently in the pool of water below.

Now, there was nothing but darkness, and Debra was terrified.

As she made her way back into the cave, she couldn't see her own hands in front of her, and she spasmodically tried to grip the sides of the cave with her hands, hoping to find anything to sustain her leverage. She was loosing control, and found herself growing short on breath. Crying, Debra wished she had never walked into the cave, or dropped her flashlight.

Then, something unexpected happened.

She lost her footing.

Her fingernails scratched at the walls of the cave, but she was too weak, and her arms couldn't hold her up. A terrifying scream pierced throughout the cave as Debra bellowed for mercy in the darkness. There was no one there to help her, however, and as her feet finally came out from under her, she closed her eyes and screamed one last time before her head slammed into the stone surface below.

The crash was solid, and she could feel blood ooze from the gaping wound on the back of her head. Her eyes were blurry, and she could feel herself slowly loosing consciousness. She felt a sharp pain in her neck, and knew that she was lying in an awkward position. This was it, she thought to herself as her consciousness slipped. It was her time to die.

Then, she heard something in the distance and could have sworn to see a weak light coming towards her. "Debra!" she heard a voice call as it echoed throughout the cave. "Debra where are you?" She forced a smile even though she could not reply, and simply thought that it was nothing more than a dream. No one had followed her into the cave. She was alone. Yet, the voice soothed her in a way, and she welcomed it to return.

Suddenly, the light was more intense and she saw the shadow of a person standing over her. She couldn't make out who it was as her vision remained blurry. "My God!" the voice breathed heavily. "Debra are you all right?"

She didn't respond.

The last thing Debra remembered before loosing consciousness and giving in to the preceding darkness were two hands. She felt two arms move around her body and pick her up.

"It's going to be all right Debra," she heard the voice say. "I'm going to get you out of here."

* * *

It didn't take long for Ashley Selvaggio to find the Goodman home, and she now found herself steering her Toyota into the cemented driveway. She switched off her engine and killed the lights as she surveyed the yard in front of her. The porch light was on, giving full view of the front yard of the brick home, yet there didn't appear to be any lights on inside. There were no cars parked in the driveway, and she immediately began to wonder if anyone was even home? Climbing out her truck, she made sure her gun was snug beneath her jacket and she ran through the powerful storm and found herself standing on the front porch. Ringing the doorbell, she knew her only choice was to awaken anyone inside the home.

"Hello!" Ashley tried yelling into the home as the pounding wind spun her hair wildly and rain splattered across the surface. "Is anyone in there?" Unfortunately, there was no response. "Rick. Carol," she continued uselessly as she remembered their names, although this time not expecting an answer. "Damn it," she sulked as she backed away from the front porch and began walking along the left side of the home. Climbing the small fence that stood in her path, she now found herself standing in a large backyard. It was a dark, stormy night, yet Ashley consented into realizing that on a beautiful sunny Florida day, this would have been a beautiful backyard surrounded by forests on both sides.

She found a screened in porch on the back of the home, and surprisingly, she found it to be unlocked. Stepping inside, she surveyed the swing, and luckily escaped the pounding storm that soaked her clothes. Not wanting to alarm anyone inside the home that she may be an intruder, she knocked on the back door calmly. When no answer came once again, she checked the doorknob.

It was unlocked.

Thinking this was a bit strange; Ashley pushed the door open and listened as it squeaked throughout the home. Drawing her gun from her holster, she slowly stepped inside the home and found herself standing in the middle of the kitchen. Immediately, she cut on the light and looked around. The phone was on the hook, and everything appeared to be nice and neat, and in the same place the owners had left them.

Walking into the living room, she stood in front of the staircase and listened for any signs of life from above. There was nothing. No one was there. Walking back into the living room, she felt like a common criminal, and safely put her revolver back in its holster. Taking a deep breath, Ashley felt herself stumbling once again into a dead end. Where could they be, she wondered of Rick and Carol Goodman and thinking of Carey Haas. How could anyone actually want to go out in such a storm?

She seated herself at the kitchen table, and stared blandly at the phone. Getting an idea, she removed it from the receiver and held it to her ear. Hearing a dial tone, she took her pointer finger and pressed redial. She listened closely as the numbers jingled in her ear, and within seconds she heard something that she found rather disturbing.

Instead of ringing, there was a busy signal, and she knew that the phone on the other end was off the hook.

Hanging up the phone, she pressed her hands to her temples and began to think. Ashley felt lost in a maze in which held no end. It was almost as if she were stuck in some game, a puzzle that was missing only one piece. However, she knew it could be found easily. Every time she misplaced something, it was always found in the last place she expected it to be, after she had spent hours, sometimes days searching in places where she should have known it wouldn't be. This was the same thing. The answers were right in front of her; she was just too blind to see them.

"Who's phone was off the hook? Where could they be?" she asked herself out loud. "Come on Ash. Think damn it. Think!" she ordered herself.

Then, it hit her.

The beach home. The home in which Carey herself used to live before Curtis Rains murdered her family and had tried to end her life as well. That's where she had to be. It just had to. Pulling the Velcro pocket of her forest green jacket open, the beautiful detective pulled out her notepad and searched for the address of the oceanfront home. She recalled writing it down a couple of days ago, doubting at the time that she would ever need it.

"Yes," she said aloud as she found the address.

Then, she locked the backdoor from which she had came inside and left through the front door, sealing it too behind her. Climbing back in her truck, she backed out the driveway and was on her way. Ashley didn't know why she felt so certain that Carey Haas could be found at the beach home. Yet, her instincts were pulling her there faster than she herself could drive.

After all, there was no place else to look.

Ashley Selvaggio was running out options. More importantly, however, she was running out of time.

Chapter 28

The creature was silent as he made his way through the storm, yet his rage could be felt miles away. He couldn't hold off any longer, as his conquest for blood was finally upon him. He had been waiting a long time for this very moment. He had spent the last ten years of his life playing with her mind, forcing her to relive her parent's death through his eyes as he showered her with bloody nightmares. Carey had never been able to forget him, and to this very day, she was still afraid.

He had made her weak, while he himself grew stronger as each day passed and another soul was consumed and conveyed into his blackened heart forever, with no chance of escape. To finally unleash his wrath on his most precious victim, sent sheer excitement riveting through his veins, and he himself couldn't believe at how conquering his query made him feel inside.

The Tinman had butchered many people in the past. All of them held a significant meaning to him and all of them made him feel powerful and somewhat Godly as he looked into their eyes right before the final moment and saw the fear he had been able to instill. None of them however, could compare or were even remotely compatible to what he saw in Carey Haas. The joys of finally extinguishing her flame would last forevermore inside him, and he would cherish every moment, and taste her blood with little scrutiny.

The Tinman was no longer apart of society, hadn't been since birth. But now, no one could reach him. No one could capture him and put him behind bars locking him away from the rest of society. He was the keeper of the darkness, a devil that had been granted everlasting life, while at the same time, still evoking the powers to kill, or to draw blood at any given moment.

His vengeance could not be escaped.

And his wrath, which was ready to explode, could no longer be ignored.

His grand finale, his final work of art was seconds away from coming to life. After ten years, he was finally going to be reunited with the one that got away. Every moment he had spent locked behind bars, he had thought about Carey Haas. He remembered how sweet, and innocent her young years had provided, and he still remembered seeing the fear in her eyes. The Tinman listened to his heart as it beat out of control and the anticipation he felt was almost unbearable.

Completely invisible to the human eye, he stood silently in the middle of the storm, beckoning it to grow even stronger as the night he had created was about to be filled with screams of terror. He stood in the driveway of the old Haas home and saw the lights on inside. The front door, which he had kicked down so many years ago, had been remodeled, its glossy wooden coat perhaps supposed to bring on an assurance of safety. Closing his eyes, he smiled his evil smile, as he knew that just beyond the front door of the old Haas home, Carey could be found. She was right where he had encountered her ten years ago, perhaps waiting for his return.

He remembered all of his victims in his past, recalled the names his parents used to call out to him, and winced in pain as he felt his father's hands gripping his neck. As his rage continued to grow he realized that they couldn't hurt him anymore. No one could ever hurt him again.

For the first time in his life, the Tinman was free.

Then, pulling the silver knife once again from underneath the black cloak, he took his first steps forward. As excitement continued to ripple through his fingertips like electricity running wildly through a power line, he knew that soon, he would reach the front door and the massacre would begin.

Soon, he would be reunited with Carey Haas.

* * *

Billy Saxton and Carey Haas sat close to one another on the sofa in the living room, while Blaze continued to work aimlessly in the kitchen to prepare the three of them a late evening supper. Billy could hear the sounds of pots and pans being scattered about, and every once in a while he would look towards Carey, who was smiling profusely at the whole situation.

"Do you think he knows what he's doing in there?" Billy asked Carey, directing her towards Blaze as yet another loud sound came booming through the kitchen. "Because, well I'm starting to wonder if perhaps we should be more worried about the storm in the kitchen than the one that's been going on outside," he added with a smile and slight chuckle to try and brighten the mood.

"Should we go in and take a look?" Carey asked, as she looked deep into Billy's eyes.

"No," Billy answered quickly as he pulled her close. "I'm scared to see what I might find in there. I think the best thing for us to do, is sit here patiently and wait for him to call us in. After all, he is working so hard in there." The two of them laughed out loud and knew that Blaze would be able to figure out that they had been discussing him and his seeming incompetence at cooking.

"Go ahead and laugh," Blaze called from the kitchen. "Just wait. Ya'll should know better than to piss off the cook."

"I'm sorry man," Billy interjected. Then, changing the subject, he glanced down at his watch and saw how late it was becoming. Still, he had heard nothing from his mother. Carey pulled his wrist towards her and freaked when she saw what time it was. Jumping up, her eyes darted off wildly for the nearest phone. "What is it?" Billy asked plainly, although sensing that something was obviously wrong. "Carey? What's wrong?" he asked just as she darted off and ran towards the phone, which was resting on the computer table.

"My aunt and uncle," Carey breathed as she quickly dialed their number. "They're going to be so mad at me for not calling. I know their worried sick." Then, holding the phone to her ear she waited patiently as she listened for the ringing to occur. A confused expression took hold of her face as she pressed her finger down on the hook, only to remove it again hoping to hear a dial tone. Unfortunately, there was nothing.

The phone was dead.

Billy saw the uncomfortable expression spring across her beautiful face and immediately climbed to his feet and made his way towards her. Holding the phone tightly in the palm of her hands, they began to tremble, as another shot of fear sank deep inside her body and seemed to implant itself directly on her soul. Approaching her, Billy grabbed her chin gently and forced her to look into his heavenly eyes. "Carey. Is something wrong? Why are you so suddenly upset?"

"The phone's dead," Carey breathed, a bit surprised at how bad her voice shook. "Something's wrong Billy. I just know it."

"Calm down sweetheart," Billy tried to comfort her, unyielding to her resistance. "There's a powerful storm going on outside. I'm sure everyone's phone is out of service right now. There's nothing to worry about sweetheart. I told you that I was going to take care of you, and by God that's what I'm going to do. I love you Carey," he soothed as he leaned over and kissed her precious lips. "I think I've always loved you. And I always will."

"We have to get out of here," Carey stated bluntly. "Please. Can we leave?"

Billy didn't know what to say. She was obviously terrified of something, and the phone line being out of service had triggered it. Not knowing how to object and not wanting to start an argument, he took the phone from her hand and replaced it on the receiver. "Sure," he spoke gently as he cradled her in his arms. "We can go anywhere you want to go O.K." Carey nodded as she felt herself growing increasingly weak. "I can take you home if that's what you want."

Carey couldn't speak. Her hands were shaking out of control and she sensed that something was terribly wrong. Nothing felt right anymore. Her old home, the home in which her parents had been killed, and the home in which she now stood made her feel increasingly weak and powerless. The setting wasn't right, and she sensed that something bad was going to happen. Finally, she grabbed a hold of Billy's hands tightly, and allowed him to lead her across the living room and towards the kitchen, where Billy planned to reveal his plan to take her home to his friend. Just as they were about to enter the kitchen, however, something happened that made both of them stop in their tracks. It was a knocking sound coming from the door. For a moment, the two of them froze, almost skeptical that they had even heard it at all. Seconds passed, however, and the knocking returned. This time, however, it was more powerful, and they knew that it had been real.

KNOCK. KNOCK. KNOCK.

The three knocks seemed to echo throughout the entire home, its booming sound piercing its way into their eardrums. Billy's mind grew flustered as he wondered who could be at his door at such an hour, and in the middle of such a storm. Carey, on the other hand, couldn't budge as another haunting memory of her parent's death came flooding back forcefully.

Once again, Carey remembered being that of nine years old, and enjoying what had appeared to be another magical dinner with her two loving parents. She had scampered off to get ready for bed, brushing her teeth and so forth, when she returned to the staircase and found her parents standing in the middle of the immense foyer. She ran to them, and not understanding what was going on, had followed their eyes to the front door, as if they were waiting for something to happen. That's when she had first heard the three loud, hollow knocks at the door, and at nine years old, she had immediately grown concerned and had known that something was wrong.

She remembered her father, David running to the door and pulling it open. No one had been there. He had stepped out onto the porch and searched the front yard, but no one had been there either. Then, he would close it and return to her and her mother, Charlene. Only, the knocks came again and again. Each time the beating would last of only three strikes. Each time however, they had grown more intense. She recalled her father moving to the nearest phone as he prepared to call for help.

Only, the phone had been dead.

That's when the door finally burst open, and her horrific nightmare officially began.

And now, ten years later, as Carey found herself once again inside the home in which she used to reside, the scenario was almost identical. The phone was dead, she had learned of this herself, and just moments ago, there had been a nerve-rackling knock at the door. She felt her knees growing weak and was sure that if Billy hadn't been holding her up, she would have tumbled to the floor below. Her eyes grew watery and whatever dangers could be found outside the front door, she knew she was entirely too weak to face them.

KNOCK. KNOCK. KNOCK.

The knocks came again, and Carey dug her claws into Billy's flesh without warning. She was terrified, and didn't know what to do. Billy grabbed her shoulders and forced her to look into his eyes. "I need you to be strong Carey," he breathed, although he himself didn't like the situation he found himself in. He knew it couldn't be his mother at the door, for she surely wouldn't have forgotten her key. He didn't like to think of the alternative, but what other choice did he have. He knew this day would come sooner or later. "Whatever happens," he continued firmly. "Just stay strong sweetheart and I promise everything will be all right."

Then, Blaze appeared from out of nowhere. "Is there someone knocking at the door?" he asked casually before seeing the concern in his best friends eyes, and how drastically Carey's entire body seemed to be consumed with fear. Not knowing what to do or say, he looked to Billy for the answers. "What's going on Billy?"

"I don't know," Billy hated to admit. "But the phone's dead, and some-." His words were cut off as the terrifying knocking came again from the front door.

KNOCK. KNOCK. KNOCK.

The knocking this time was louder than ever and the three of them couldn't help but to cower away in blatant fear. Blaze, leaving the two of them where they stood, grabbed a knife from the kitchen and cautiously made his way towards the front door. He listened as Billy and Carey tried to call him back, but ignored their wisdom and continued forward. He hoped to find someone standing outside who was simply lost in the rain or was experiencing car trouble. His instincts, however, told him something different, and as he reached the front door and clutched the knife tightly in the palm of his hands, the dangers had never seemed so real. Nervously, he placed one hand on the doorknob, and after fighting off his last line of fear; he sprang the door open and peered outside and into the storm.

No one was there.

"No one's going to be there," Carey spoke like a terrified child towards Billy as Blaze returned and told Billy the exact same thing.

"No one was there."

Billy looked down at Carey and steered his vision directly into her eyes. How could she have known that no one was going to be at the door? Everything seemed too intense for him, and he found trouble in understanding just what was going on. Of the three of them inside the home, Carey appeared to be the only one that could relate to what was happening. "Carey," he spoke gently. "I need you right now." Pausing, he gave her a moment to regain her composure before continuing. "Do you know what's going on here?" Carey didn't speak. She could only nod.

KNOCK. KNOCK. KNOCK.

The knocks came once again and they pierced their way throughout the home. Blaze, growing increasingly angry darted off away from them as he once again ran towards the front door. This time, without hesitation he sprang it open and peered outside. "Damn it," he scorned loudly as once again there had been no one there. Stepping out on the front porch he tried to survey the entire front yard through the storm. There was absolutely no one in sight, and he had no choice but to return inside and close the door, locking and bolting it behind him. As Blaze approached Carey and Billy, he once again could only shrug his shoulders in bewilderment.

"Carey," Billy spoke up once again. "Do you know who's out there?" Carey couldn't answer. It was like her tongue had been dragged into the back of her throat denying her the privilege to speak. "Please Carey," Billy groped, trying desperately to put the pieces together. "Do you know who's out there?" he repeated the question.

"Y-ye-yes," Carey struggled to communicate. "It's him," she screeched into the night as her body finally gave in to the fear it had obtained.

"It's who?" Billy questioned holding her firmly. "Who's out there?"

"Curtis Rains!" Carey exclaimed boldly. "He-he's come f-for me."

Both Billy and Blaze remained speechless. Neither knowing what to say or how to comfort the struggling Carey Haas. Billy stood up and stared in the direction of the front door. This was what he had been afraid of. All of his virtual fears were coming true and it appeared as though he was finally about to confront the man that had come to him in his sleep and forced him to live in a past he had not been meant to be apart of. He wished he could dismiss Carey's words and pretend that they were not true. However, he knew that she was right.

The *Tinman* was there.

KNOCK. KNOCK. KNOCK.

The knocks came yet again, and as Blaze was about to take off for the front door one last time, Billy grabbed his arm and pulled him back. Looking deep into his eyes, he forced a seriousness into Blaze, one in which he had never seen from his best friend. "Don't go," Billy ordered him as he realized Blaze did not understand any of this.

"What do you mean don't go?" Blaze questioned his friend. "This shit can't go on all night. Whoever is out there needs to be stopped."

"Blaze!" Billy spoke firmly, his eyes never blinking. "You can't stop whose out there."

"What are you talking about?"

Then, before the two of them could continue speaking to one another, something happened that forced both of them to fall silent. They heard a loud crashing sound, and as the three of them looked towards the front door, their eyes met just in time to watch as the big, wooden front door came crashing down. The door had been kicked in. Carey screamed in freight as she looked to Billy for protection. Holding onto his arm, the three of them watched in silence as a life form appeared in the doorway.

There before them, standing in the middle of the doorway, and with the storm twirling wildly behind him was a man, dressed in black. Wet, black work boots could be found covering his feet and a black cloak could be found hovering over his broad shoulders. A black bush hat remained glued to his head, which was tilted not allowing them to see his face. Carey knew from the moment she laid eyes on him that it was none other than Curtis Rains. She had feared this day would come for as long as she could remember, and now, it appeared as though that day was upon her.

Then, looking up, the man allowed them to see his face. A grim smile was smirked along the outside of his lips, and his blackened eyes coerced them into feeling the evil he possessed. Laughing into the night, his glistening white teeth sparkled around the room and he took his first steps towards them as he began making his way slowly through the foyer. He reached his hands into the cloak and retrieved the knife he knew Carey would remember as the one that had killed her parents.

As the evil man moved closer, the three of them stood completely silent. None of them able to move as fear gripped them with a magnetic shield that seemed almost impossible to penetrate.

* * *

Elizabeth Anne watched in awe as at least a dozen police officers and few K-9 units proceeded down the beach in front of her house and in the direction in which her husband, Murray, and Debra had galloped off after the honorable Sheriff Gabriel Burnham. The storm continued to roar outside and her two children remained snug underneath her arms as she sat quietly on the couch, gently rocking them back and forth as she desperately tried to assure them that absolutely nothing was wrong. But that wasn't true, and her children could sense it. In fact, everything was wrong.

Every since her husband had taken off after Debra Saxton, she had forced herself into subduing the tears that were aching to show themselves to the world. She couldn't allow that to happen, however. She knew she had to remain strong for her children. She didn't want to give them any reason to worry until time showed that there was indeed a reason for them to be.

Her youngest daughter, Mary, was sound asleep, and she eased her light body onto the couch. Jennifer opened her eyes at her mother's sudden movement, only to close them once again as she realized she was just making herself more comfortable. Then, without saying a word, Jennifer allowed her mother to believe that she was asleep and she watched as Elizabeth removed herself from the couch and walked to their sliding glass door to get a better look at the frenzy that was taking place outside.

Elizabeth watched the dozens of flashlights dart back and forth, surveying every inch of the beach as the deputies searched fearlessly for their glorious leader in Sheriff Burnham. She had instructed them moments ago that he had taken off after a suspect resembling that of Curtis Rains and that they had been heading towards the cove. So, the dogs had been brought in, and the search had begun. A dazzling helicopter could barely be heard as it twirled its way throughout the blistering storm, and if it hadn't been for the bright spotlight that covered a vast portion of the darkened beach below, she would have never known that it was there.

Then, something happened that captured her immediate attention.

Elizabeth could have sworn that she had heard a scream coming from somewhere in the distance. It had been faint, yet she was sure she had heard it. But, where had it come from? Opening the sliding glass door, she stepped outside and was immediately engulfed in a fury of rain. Ignoring the uncomfortable environment Mother Nature was momentarily providing, she walked to the edge of the balcony, and with a quick turn to the right, she faced the old Haas home.

Her vision could only carry her so far, but the deadly house was no more than a hundred yards away and she couldn't help but to remember the tragic events that had taken place there some ten years ago. She could only imagine what it must have been like for Debra and Billy to move into such a place without prior knowledge of the blood bath that had transcended there, and would always remain locked in the walls, until the womb was opened and they could resurface. Still, as Elizabeth looked towards the house, she saw a few lights on, yet she didn't know what had made her walk out into such a storm in the first place. Then, it hit her.

The scream she had heard, it had come from the old Haas home.

Then, how come no one else seemed to hear it?

"Mom," she was suddenly distracted as she turned around to face her older daughter, Jennifer standing at the foot of the sliding glass door. "Are you all right? What are doing out in this storm?" Elizabeth didn't answer her daughter's questions, and only smiled as she remembered being the age where questions seemed to pop up all day long. Getting annoyed, her daughter pressed forward. "Mom. I'm scared."

Rushing inside, she returned with her daughter to the couch, who refused her warm embrace due to the wetness her clothing had accumulated. "Sweetheart," she spoke softly, desperately trying to hide her fear. "I promise that everything is going to be all right. There's no reason for you to be scared sweetheart."

"Then why were you outside?"

"I thought I heard something," she honestly replied, although denying her daughter the full truth as to what she had really thought she heard. Then, deciding to change the subject, she picked the sleeping Mary up in her arms and was about to head for her bedroom when she turned once again to face Jennifer. "Come on you. Let me get the two of you in bed. And if this storm persists, chances are you won't have to wake up early and go to school tomorrow." The excitement of her child's eyes brightened her gloomy spirit momentarily and she willingly followed her from the couch. Minutes later, the two of them were tucked tightly in bed, and Elizabeth returned to the living room.

Pouring herself a full glass of wine, she quickly consumed it and refilled it seconds later. Walking once again to the sliding glass door, she gazed once again at the Haas home and felt a tingle overcome her spine. Something wasn't right, and she sensed the dangers the night had yet to bring.

"Please God," she prayed aloud knowing the man upstairs could hear her. "Please don't let this happen again."

* * *

"Blaze, take Carey upstairs," Billy ordered as the man in front of them continued to slowly move towards them. Blaze, following Billy's instruction, grabbed Carey by the wrist and proceeded to pull her upstairs, leaving his friend alone to face the madman that had so suddenly decided to come storming into this home. The two of them disappeared into Billy's bedroom and locked the door behind them. Neither of them, however, feeling safe and secure. Blaze began to panic and he didn't know what to do as Carey simply lay on the bed and sobbed loudly.

The man snickered as he watched the two of them elevate upstairs. Yet, he didn't take off after them. His attention remained focused on Billy, and his sharp, dark gaze bore into his soul. *"Billy Saxton I presume,"* the man spoke calmly as his breathing rhythm grew heavier.

"How do you know my name?" Billy inquired, trying desperately to by some time. He needed a plan.

"I know everything Billy," the man's voice continued in a baneful, bone-chilling tone. *"And I'm pretty sure you know who I am don't you?"* The creature waited for a reply. When none came, he gladly

continued as he stopped just short of striking distance. *"I'm the demon that's been coming to you in your sleep Billy. I'm the reason you wound up in the hospital with a slight concussion. I'm the reason you found that stupid fucking doll and the picture of Carey's family in the basement. And you know why?"* He paused again not expecting a reply. *"Because I wanted you to find them,"* he answered for Billy. *"I wanted you to be a part of this. I wanted to see if you were actually strong enough to stop me from harming our little precious Carey Haas."*

"You stay away from her."

"I'm sorry Billy," the man laughed momentarily, yet never shifting his poignant gaze. *"But I think you know I can't do that. I need her just as bad as you do to complete my life. I need to taste her blood and dig deep into her flesh. She has to die Billy, and if you really care about your family, friends, or yourself, you will do nothing to stand in my way."*

"You go to hell you son of a bitch," Billy yelled in aggravation. "You think you're so powerful don't you? Just because you are able to get into people's minds, doesn't make you invincible. And I am not afraid of you."

"Shut up you little fucker," the man ordered growing impatient and furious that Billy Saxton refused to grant him the respect he felt he truly deserved. *"You don't know what you're talking about. I am more powerful than your meager mind could even begin to imagine and you should fear me. If there's anyone in this world that you should fear, it's me. I'm the reason you can't sleep at night. I'm the reason you wake up in a cold sweat and your stomach feels empty and tied in knots. I am the real article Billy. And getting into people's minds is the least of my capabilities."*

"I know what evil is," Billy shot back, holding his ground, hoping his mind would give him an idea soon. "I grew up in a house filled with evil. My father was an evil man. But you know what, he could never hurt me. I wouldn't let him, and I'll be damned if I'm going to let you."

"Your father wasn't an evil man," the man continued as his grip on the sharp knife continued. *"He was an alcoholic, who slapped around your mother every once in a while."* He paused once again seeing the surprise in Billy's eyes that he was educated of his past.

"Your father was weak, who let the booze take him under. The fact that he didn't love you and had no trouble showing it doesn't make him evil. It just makes him honest. He couldn't have taken your life without feeling remorse. Now that would be evil. But you see, I can, and I will. I feel no pain and I fear no man because I have no conscious. I have the choice to let people live, or to let people die. And what if Billy," he paused yet again to make his point clear. "What if I gave you the choice? What would you do? Would you choose to die trying to save Carey, who's already dead by the way? Or would you be smart and choose to live. Because if you want to live, I'll let you walk right out the front door right now, and I promise to be out of your life forever."

"Fuck you!" Billy stated coldly, feeling himself growing angry as he listened to the man in front of him compare himself to his deceased father. "You don't know anything about me, or my family."

"You're not answering me!" the man lashed out impatiently. *"Tell me Billy. Do you want to live or die?"*

"I refuse to die by your hands!" Billy continued bravely.

"Well then," the man moved in closer feeling himself on the verge of attacking. *"I see you've made your decision."* Then, in the blink of an eye, the man lashed out and tried to slam the blade into Billy's midsection. Billy saw it coming, and quickly moved out of the way. He escaped into the kitchen and found a large butcher's knife. The man hadn't followed him into the kitchen, and Billy peered around the corner to see if he was still standing in the living room. He was nowhere to be found, seeming to vanish into thin air. Then, he could hear the man's voice. It was so distinct it almost seemed as if he were right behind him. Still, he was nowhere to be seen. *"Billy, do you honestly think you can kill me,"* the man retorted laughing evilly. *"In case you've forgotten. I'm already dead."*

Billy didn't respond, but he knew that the man was right. Once again, Billy felt powerless and he began to wonder if he would actually be able to keep his promise to Carey Haas. Could he save her life? Could he truly defeat the *Tinman?* Without having to rack his brain, he knew the answer.

No, he could not.

"Carey," Blaze spoke up. "I want you stay right here on that bed and lock the door behind me. Do not answer it for anyone. Not even me all right? I have to go check on Billy." Carey nodded and as soon as Blaze left the bedroom, she sprang from the bed and slammed the door shut, locking it tightly. Dropping to her knees, she realized it was happening all over again. Ten years later, the same events were taking place, and Curtis Rains was simply picking up where he left off.

Finding herself alone in the room, she was more terrified than ever before. Ten years ago, she had been young, and hadn't really been able to understand just what was going on. Fearing for her life, she had simply ran away from the evil man and had been fortunate enough to escape. This time, however, it was different. She had nowhere to run. She was trapped inside this home. It was a death trap, and now, more than ever, she wished she had never returned.

He had been expecting her to come back.

Blaze reached the staircase and peered down at the living room below. There was no sign of his best friend Billy, or the intruder anywhere. Everything was quiet, and that's what disturbed him more than anything. "Billy!' he called out foolishly, hoping to find a clue as to where he could be. "Billy. Where are you?" For a moment, he heard nothing. Then, coming from behind him on the second floor, he heard Billy's voice. Turning around, he faced him and forced an encouraging smile. "Damn man, don't sneak up on me like that. Where's that man?"

Billy shrugged his shoulders. "I don't know man. I lost him and then came up here to look for you and Carey. She is all right isn't she?"

"She's a little shook up," Blaze admitted. "She's in your room though. I told her to lock the door behind me and not to open it for anyone."

"Good," Billy replied as he placed a friendly hand on his friend's shoulder and gave it an affectionate squeeze. "Take me to her man. We have to get her out of here. I don't know when that crazy son of a bitch is going to return." Blaze was about to head back down the hallway and lead Billy to his room, when he heard something coming from the bottom floor. It was a voice. And it too, sounded exactly like that of Billy's. Completely astonished, he turned away from Billy and peered down below. Appearing from the kitchen, was someone that sounded and looked like Billy, and he was holding a butcher's knife in his hand.

This was impossible. Blaze was confused. How could this be? There couldn't be two of them. "What the hell is going on here?" he asked as fear gripped his soul and he remained motionless.

"Blaze!" Billy called from right outside the kitchen, or who Blaze thought could be the real Billy. "Get away from him. That's not me. It's him. That's Curtis Rains. He wants you to take him to Carey so he can kill her." Blaze didn't know what to say or what to make of the situation he now found himself in.

"Don't listen to him Blaze," the voice behind him continued harshly. "I'm the real Billy," he continued forcing Blaze to look into his eyes to see the truth.

"No he's not," Billy called from the kitchen. "Please get away from him."

Blaze didn't know whom to believe. The whole situation seemed impossible and he felt trapped with absolutely nowhere to go. Then, the impressionist revealed himself. The person he had first thought was Billy stepped away from him momentarily and was about to flee down the hallway, when he suddenly spun around and an evil grin crossed his face. Shell shocked, Blaze watched in horror as Billy's body began to grow, and transform right before his very eyes. Soon, he found himself standing face to face with Curtis Rains.

"Surprise!" Curtis yelled evilly as he removed the sleek knife and began walking at a furious pace towards the distraught Blaze Brookshaw. *"Look into my eyes before you die."* Curtis ordered as he raised the knife high in the air and proceeded towards his counterpart. *"I want you to see the evil inside me, and the reflection of your fear. Your blood is about to be on my hands!"* the *Tinman* stormed as he prepared to lash out at his latest prey.

Blaze watched in shock as the knife drew closer, the whole scene appeared to be developing in slow motion. He had never seen such a thing before. Curtis Rains was gaining on him, the knife sparkling in the dim light, anxiously waiting to plant itself into his flesh and rip him apart. The black cloak, the evil man was wearing seemed to flap in the wind as a slight breeze swept through the hallway, and Blaze found no way to try to defend himself, or ward off his attacker.

He was facing the devil, and this was a battle he simply could not win.

The man's face was hardened as his jaws seemed to stiffen and his muscles tightened, preparing for the acceleration needed to drive the knife deep into his flesh. Blaze wanted to run, but couldn't move. His legs wouldn't budge as fear held them firmly in place. The evil seen in the man's eyes was one he had never seen before, and was sure that he would never be able to forget such an expression.

Then, the man reached him, and forcefully tried to slice his chest.

Blaze moved backwards, forgetting that the staircase was there to avoid any contact with the knife, and lost his balance. Screaming in pain, the knife could only muster a flesh wound as it ripped away at it's shirt and designed a lightning bolt type scar beneath Blaze's skin, and he began to tumble down the stairs.

"No!" Billy screamed as he ran towards his friend, watching in anger as Blaze's body was thrashed around wildly, until harshly slamming into the hardened floor at the bottom of the staircase. Billy immediately saw the cut on Blaze's chest, but knew that it wasn't near as bad as it looked and definitely wasn't fatal. However, his body lay in an awkward, obscure angle, leaving Billy to wonder if anything was broken. His eyes were closed, and Billy was glad to see his chest slowly moving up and down. For the time being, Blaze was still alive.

Then, looking up, he noticed Curtis Rains peering down at him from the top of the staircase, holding the knife that contained Blaze's blood dripping off the edges. Smiling, his dark eyes peered into his soul and he licked the knife clean with his tongue. Billy didn't say anything, and could only watch as he disappeared down the hallway, knowingly after Carey.

Carefully, Billy moved his friend over to the couch and laid him upon it. "Damn it man. I'm so sorry," he sulked drawing back his tears. "You hang in there all right? Everything is going to be just fine."

Unfortunately, Blaze couldn't answer him.

Billy didn't take his eyes off his friend until he reached the edge of the staircase. Then, growing angry with the man for injuring his friend, he grabbed a hold of the railings and scaled the staircase with ease. Once at the top, he immediately headed for his bedroom, where he knew Carey could be found. Once he reached the door, however, his worst fears came to life.

Twisting the handle, he found the door to be locked.

Moments earlier.

Carey Haas was soaking in an uncontrollable state of fear. The man that had seemed to be living inside of her for the past ten years, never once letting her forget her parent's gruesome death, was back, and he appeared even angrier than before. He had forced her for the past ten years to live in a world without trust, and in a world full of fear. Perhaps he had been testing her, trying to make her strong as he prepared her for this very night. She should have seen it coming a long time ago. Now she knew. Curtis Rains had been inside her head earlier that day when she so suddenly decided to return to the home that still haunted her in her sleep. She hadn't wanted to come here. It had been him all along. And now, he had her right where he wanted her.

Then, a knock came from the bedroom door, and her body jerked with blatant fear. Her chest began heaving uncontrollably as she watched the doorknob twist from left to right. Whoever was outside was trying desperately to get inside. Then, a bit of relief showered over Carey as she recognized Billy's voice on the other end of the door. "Carey it's me Billy. Open up." Hesitantly, Carey steadily made her way off the bed and soon found herself standing in front of the door. "Come on sweetheart," she heard Billy's voice continue. "Open up. It's time to get you out of here."

Finally, ignoring Blaze's last words he had spoken before leaving the room, she unlatched the door and opened it slightly. Peering outside, she couldn't believe what she saw. There, right in front of the doorway, was Curtis Rains, a big smile standing across his face as he spoke to her using Billy's voice. She tried to slam it shut, but it was no use. He was too powerful.

Pushing the door open, Curtis Rains stepped inside and threw Carey to the bed, closing the door behind him. Almost immediately after he secured the lock, he heard Billy running up the stairs and then try to bust down the door. Carey kept looking towards the door, but Curtis ignored Billy's persistence and spoke to her directly. *"I've been waiting a long time for this Carey. You've been on my mind for the last ten years. Perhaps being the sole reason I have been able to survive."*

Carey couldn't reply. Her worst nightmare was standing right before her. After ten years, she had to face the man that had murdered her parents one last time. "Why are you doing this to me?" Carey begged, fearing for her life. "Why can't you just leave me alone?"

"Because you're still alive," Curtis replied coldly as he ran the cold, silver blade of his knife underneath her chin, toying with her desperation. *"I wouldn't move if I were you. One quick jerk and I could slash your throat. Kind of ironic if you ask me,"* he paused as a laugh escaped from his throat. *"This is the exact same knife that I used to kill your parents. I can only imagine what your blood tastes like Carey. If it's half as sweet as your mother's I'd say I'm in for a real treat."*

"You can't get away with this. People know where I am and they'll be coming for me," Carey spoke as a couple of tears ran down her cheek as she desperately tried to keep her neck fixed in one position.

"So let them come," Curtis replied bluntly as he shrugged his shoulders. *"And they too will die. I cannot be stopped this time Carey, and I cannot let you get away."*

"I'm tired of running from you! If you're going to kill me, why not just get it over with?"

"Because I'm just starting to have a little fun here Carey. You haven't suffered enough." Then, suddenly, Curtis grabbed Carey by the neck and jerked her off the bed. Holding her firmly in front of him he allowed her to take weak breaths, and could feel her body growing weak. Then, he brought her to a stop in front of the dresser mirror, and forced her to look into it. He licked the side of her cheek and smelled her hair fluently. Smiling, he continued. *"You really are beautiful Carey."*

"I've suffered all my life because of you," Carey blurted out, sensing that her life was about to be over. "I've regretted waking up each and everyday just knowing that you would still be there."

"That's not good enough for me!" Curtis shouted. "And if you're smart, you won't be as stubborn as your fucking mother. That bitch simply wouldn't quit fighting so I had to make her suffer drastically. Now, I do have to make you suffer Carey," he paused as he slid his hand underneath her shirt and began fondling her breasts. "But I promise to be gentle with you." Carey wanted to remove his hands from her body, but knew if she tried to resist him, it would only make matters worse. She had no choice but to stand there, and allow him to touch her body. *"My god Carey!"* Curtis exclaimed as his excitement grew intensely. *"It feels so good to be close to you again."*

"Just kill me you son of a bitch!" Carey ordered bravely. "I'd rather die than to have you touch me."

"Listen here you little bitch," Curtis shouted loudly through the room. *"You don't want to piss me off because bad things happen when I get angry. Do you really think for one minute I'm going to feel sorry for you? Do you want to test me? Fine,"* He paused as he closed his eyes to awaken his fury. *"Do you want to know what your precious little aunt and uncle are doing right now? There on their way over here to rescue you,"* he replied without giving her time to answer. *"Can you see them,"* he asked as he pressed the knife against her throat and forced her to look in the mirror. *"Look really hard Carey because you might be able to say goodbye."*

"No!" Carey screamed, as she was able to visualize her relatives through the mirror. Her uncle Rick behind the wheel of his black Lincoln, with her aunt Carol in the passenger seat as they drove throughout the storm down a deserted highway. "Leave them alone!" she ordered.

"I'm sorry," Curtis replied harshly. *"But I'm afraid I can't do that."* Then, pausing, he spun her around and looked into her eyes. *"I'm afraid they're not going to make it."*

Carey closed her eyes not wanting to watch was about to happen.

* * *

Rick Goodman and his wife, Carol, drove silently along one of the many deserted highways of Destin, Florida as they traveled through the storm. Their niece's safety was a great concern to them at the moment, and no matter how fast Rick found himself driving, it simply wasn't fast enough. They hadn't heard from her in hours, and the last time they had seen her, was at the pier when they had met with the Sheriff. Rick stared firmly at the road ahead, gripping the steering wheel tightly as he prayed his tires wouldn't loose traction with the road and send them spinning around out of control.

"Don't you think you should slow down?" Carol asked hesitantly as she saw the veins in her husband's hands sticking out copiously. "The roads are slippery out and accidents happen all the time out here in bad weather." When Rick didn't even bother to respond, she felt herself growing aggravated with her husband. "My God Rick," she continued moving closer to him. "I know you're worried about Carey. But I am too. And if and when we find her. Well, I just want to be alive is all."

"You're right," Rick spoke calmly as he let out a deep breath and removed his foot slightly from the accelerator. Watching the speedometer drop, he took one hand off of the steering wheel and affectionately slipped it into her own. "I'm sorry. I don't know what I was thinking."

"You were just being yourself," Carol spoke up with a smile, adhering to the fact that she knew her husband inside out. "Once you get an idea into your head, you just tune everything and everyone else out, and hardly ever admit that you were wrong. All I'm saying honey, is that we can't just jump to the assumption that Carey is in trouble. And I don't think we should worry until we have something to worry about."

"Once again," Rick took his eyes momentarily off the road to look at his beautiful wife. "You're right. And that's why I love you."

"Damn," Carol shook as she suddenly found herself feeling a little frisky. "I don't think I've heard you say those words to me in quite some time."

"Well I do," Rick continued squeezing her hand. "I do love you."

"I know. And I love you too."

Then, turning back to face the road, Rick was just in time to see the traffic light ahead suddenly turn red. "Damn it!" Rick cursed himself for not paying attention as he slammed his foot on the brakes. Instantly, the two of them listened as the tires began to squeal over the stretch of blacktop. Removing his hands from his wife's loving grip, he returned it to the steering wheel as he tried to regain control of the vehicle. Saying nothing, he knew Carol's eyes were fixed on the road ahead, and sensed that she was terrified. He too, didn't know what was about to happen. However, Rick realized he didn't have time to panic, and he simply followed the driving instructions he had learned years ago and turned his car into the direction he wanted the vehicle to go.

Almost miraculously, the Lincoln came to a halt, and stopped just short of the intersection as two cars began to pick up speed. Holding her chest, Carol looked to her husband with a baffled expression blanketing her face. Taking a deep breath, she allowed herself to calm down, feeling safe that the two of them were out of harms way. "That was close," she breathed, feeling her nerves still a bit shot.

"I'm sorry," Rick apologized realizing it had been entirely his fault. "I should have been paying attention."

Then, before either of them could carry on, the light turned green and Rick slowly eased his foot off the brake and cautiously began to cross the intersection after looking both ways. Once back on the road, Rick drove safely, never allowing his eyes to dart away from the road and traveling at a constant speed of five miles below the speed limit. Rick too, had somehow fallen into a state of shock as he realized just how close they had come to causing an accident and he desperately tried to calm himself down. Over and over again, he released deep bursts of air, yet nothing seemed to work.

His heart continued to beat rapidly, and sweat began to form along his forehead. A minor pain suddenly appeared in his right arm, and he felt his vision growing increasingly blurry. Rick felt uncomfortable and knew that he probably shouldn't be driving feeling this way. As he slowed the car down even more, he could hear his own pulse echoing throughout his ears.

Noticing her husband's uneasiness, Carol grew concerned. "Rick," she spoke firmly, glad to see that she had captured his attention. "Is something wrong? You don't look so good."

"I don't know," Rick spoke quickly as his chest began to heave and it hurt to speak. "I think I just need to get out of this car."

"Honey, what is it?" Carol asked suddenly growing afraid that Rick was about to have a heart attack. "Rick maybe you should pull the car over. Do you think I should take you to the hospital?"

"No," Rick snapped as the pain in his arm continued to grow rapidly. "I'm going to be fine."

Then, a sharp undetected pain shot through his entire body and Rick was forced to let go of the steering wheel as he clutched his chest, almost seeming to try and dig through his flesh and reach his heart. It felt like his heart was about to explode and Rick screamed loudly as the pain continued to grow inside. Closing his eyes, he never noticed how his car was changing lanes and traveling over the median and into oncoming traffic. He had trouble breathing, and he finally fell forward as his body gave in to the heart attack. Leaning over the steering wheel, his foot lashed down on the accelerator and the car began to pick up speed.

"Oh my God!" Carol screamed in panic as she realized what was happening. Her husband was having a heart attack, and she couldn't help him. Unbuckling her seat belt, she looked through the windshield just as their car hit the median and was seconds away from meeting the powerful cars coming in the other lane. "Rick talk to me!" she cried fearing that he was already dead.

Then, just as her hands clutched the steering wheel, she found that her actions had come too little too late.

The black Lincoln slammed head first into a semi, the driver of the eighteen-wheeler never having time to slam on brakes as the whole situation happened too fast. The smaller vehicle crumbled with the powerful impact, and their bodies were crushed instantly. Rick and Carol Goodman died in seconds and without warning. They had no idea that when they stepped out of their house that night that their lives were going to end. Yet, on this stormy night, darkness captured their souls for eternity.

They would never see their niece, Carey Haas again.

And they would never know, that the *Tinman* had been behind their demise.

Hopefully leaving the world for a better place, Rick and Carol Goodman perished unexpectedly this dreadful night, loving one another just as much as they had on the day they had first met.

Chapter 29

Carey couldn't believe her eyes.

As she stared into the hazy mirror, she felt a part of her life vanishing into thin air. She wanted nothing more than to turn away and pretend that this nightmare wasn't really happening and was nothing more than a figment of her imagination. Yet everything around her seemed so real. As Curtis Rains placed his hands upon her, they felt so real, as if his touch could easily seep past her flesh and into her bloodstream. And his lips, as they eased across her smooth, unblemished skin, sent the hairs on the back of her neck straight into the air as if she were half expecting him to start ripping away at her protoplasm with his sharp edged, glistening white teeth. Reluctantly, Carey felt as though her only choice was to surrender to the madman that had come to her through the darkness in his final plight to take her life. This nightmare was real.

Carey felt helpless. If she tried to remove herself from the staggering grip the *Tinman's* muscles had around her waist, clutching her wrists tightly behind her back, she was sure he would slice her throat as she continued to feel the bitter coldness of the blade pressed firmly against her neck. As tears continued to silently fall from her cheek, she wondered if anyone could feel her pain? She could hear Billy pounding away at her bedroom door, desperately trying to open it. Yet, as she visualized her guardian's death in the mirror, Billy's screams seemed faint, almost non-existent.

Almost as if she were not permitted to turn away, Carey watched in horror as her aunt and uncle almost skidded into an intersection and came to an abrupt stop just as cars began moving in the opposite direction. For a second, she knew that they were going to die. Nevertheless, the light once again turned green, and they continued on their way. She knew that they were coming for her.

Then, she saw her uncle grab his chest and his face shot forth and expression of agonizing pain.

She saw her aunt Carol, her face puzzled and terrified she tried to reach for him as the car began to lose control and drive onto the slippery grass of the median. Carol desperately tried to steer the car back onto the highway. But it had been too late, and the driver of the semi-truck had little time to try and stop his rig. Carey could tell that there was no chance for them to have survived such a jarring crash. They were dead, and all the while, she could hear Curtis laughing in the background.

Just like her parents, and seemingly everyone else in her life that she had ever cared for, the *Tinman* had taken her aunt and uncle away from her. As she listened to his evil laugh, she felt the blade of the knife beneath her chin, and now, more than ever, wished he would just get it over with. She was tired of suffering, and was tired of being alone. As long as she was alive, she knew that everyone she loved would die without mercy to the hands of Curtis Rains.

Save for herself, Carey Haas had no family left.

* * *

Detective Ashley Selvaggio sped along the highway, purposely exceeding the speed limit as she headed towards the ocean front home in which Carey Haas used to reside. She made her way out of the boondocks, from which she had found the Goodman home, and the rain continued to whip wildly across the glass in front of her. She was amazed at how quickly this massive storm had accumulated into such a destructive force.

She couldn't recall the last time the South had experienced something so devastating. Sure, thunderstorms were rather common in the great state of Florida, some of them even producing great winds that could easily spring trees from their roots and send them thrashing to the ground below. Yet, there was something about this particular storm that forced her brain to think on another level. And although her instincts told her to fear what the night had yet to bring, Ashley continued to glue her foot to the accelerator, and watched as the speedometer continued to creep its way up.

Then, as she found herself along a wide stretch of a four-lane highway, divided by a grass median in the middle, something in the distance captured her attention. She saw flashing lights ahead, and could make out at least one fire truck, two ambulances, and an astonishing number of patrol cars. There could only be one explanation. An accident had occurred.

As she approached the scene, she took her foot off of the accelerator and her eyes intuitively began to drift over the darkened terrain as she tried to visualize what had happened. Getting closer, her headlights easily allowed her to see two skid marks in her lane. She followed them and found that a few feet later, the tracks headed straight into the median. A semi-truck was stopped, and almost completely buckled underneath, was the remains of a crushed black Lincoln town car. A white sheet had been draped over a few openings; not allowing the passerby's to get a clear glimpse inside the vehicle. And Ashley knew, that hidden behind the white sheet was someone's dead body.

Finally, slowing down Ashley came to an abrupt stop in the highway after checking her rearview mirror and found no one to be traveling behind her. Immediately a patrol officer approached her, dressed in a poncho and holding two signal flares in his hands, the bright yellow light glowing in the darkness.

"Can I help you ma'am?" the officer replied as he threw one of his hands on his head as the vicious wind appeared to try and steal his hat. "It probably isn't safe to be out here tonight," the young officer continued before allotting her anytime to reply. "This is some pretty nasty weather we're having, and it's supposed to get worse before it gets any better."

"I know," Ashley replied with a smile as she grabbed her badge and ID, and began showing the officer her credentials. Then, not knowing why, she pressed forward. "You mind telling me what happened here?"

For a second, the officer looked puzzled, and she sensed that he was wondering why someone like herself would be curious as to what appeared to be nothing more than a routine traffic accident that unfortunately claimed a few casualties. His face was blank, and he almost seemed uncertain if whether or not he should reveal any information to her. Obviously he was a rookie, and didn't want to divulge any information to the wrong person that might coincidentally get him into trouble.

"Do you need to go check with your superior first?" Ashley was quick to continue with a smile as she realized the young officer didn't want to pull the graveyard shift his entire career. "Cause if you need to, I'll gladly wait."

"No ma'am," he returned her warm smile. "I'm sorry. I'm just new to this you know."

Ashley nodded in retrospect as she remembered her younger years as a peace officer.

"Unfortunately Detective," the bright-eyed policeman before her began. "What you see here is common around these parts. Especially on nights like tonight. Every time we get a storm like this pushing through this area we have accidents and fatalities. But what it looks like," he paused as he turned away from her to view the scene again. "A couple was heading in the direction you are now, when somehow, they lost control of their car, crossed the median, and slammed headfirst into the oncoming semi over there," he concluded pointing towards the eighteen wheeler.

"Was the driver of the truck injured at all?"

The officer shook his head. "No, but he's a little shook up. Kind of in shock I guess and can't really remember much about what happened. But the couple that was in the Lincoln, well, they didn't have a chance. Their seat belts weren't on when they crashed into the semi and their bodies were crushed instantly. If the license plate number hadn't been saved and if their id's hadn't been found inside the car, we probably wouldn't have even been able to identify the bodies."

"Have you notified the family?"

"I'm afraid they have no family," the officer went on graciously. "Except a niece that they've been looking after. But we haven't been able to get in touch with her yet ma'am. We are looking for her though and I'm sure we'll track her down in no time. She wasn't in the car so I'm sure she'll turn up somewhere. But to be truthful," he paused as if pretending to lower his tone. "I'm just glad I'm not going to be the one that has to break the news to her."

"Do you mind telling me the names of the people in the car?" Ashley asked casually as a light began to flicker inside her head.

"Not at all. It was Rick and Carol Goodman."

Ashley couldn't believe it. Suddenly, her heart began to beat out of control and she could feel her chest rising passionately as her body desperately tried to consume some air. Her body began to feel weak, and everything around her looked deadly. Glancing past the officer and into the wreckage along the other side of the highway, she began to theorize that what had happened had not been an accident at all.

But a work of evil.

"Ma'am," the officer continued making his way closer to her car. "Is something wrong?" he asked as he sensed her discomfort and watched as her eyebrows arch with apprehension.

"The girl," Ashley spoke almost illegibly. "The niece you said they've been looking after. Is her name Carey Haas?" she asked although already privy to the answer. She just wanted to make sure.

The officer nodded. "Yes ma'am. That's her name. Why?"

Throwing her truck in drive, Ashley slammed on the accelerator. Beforehand, however, she handed the officer a piece of paper that contained the address to the oceanfront home. "Dispatch as many officers as you can to this address as fast as you can," she ordered loudly as she began to drive into the storm and continue on her journey in finding the missing Carey Haas. "Get some emergency vehicles in route as well." With that, she was gone.

For a second, the young officer simply stood in the middle of the storm trying to understand just what had happened, and wondering just exactly who was this mystery woman he had just encountered, and why was she in Destin? Dazed, he watched until her 4-Runner was completely out of sight. Then, still clutching the piece of paper tightly in the palm of his hands, he followed his directive and found his superior officer on the scene to deliver Detective Selvaggio's message.

As Ashley drove throughout the storm, the speed limit had long since been forgotten. Carey Haas could be found at her old home, she knew that. She could feel it. And she was in danger. Gripping her hands on the steering wheel tightly, she only hoped that she could get there in time.

When she had departed from her home in Starke, Florida, she wasn't expecting to face such an undesirable situation. She knew that it had been more than a coincidence in finding the deceased bodies of Rick and Carol Goodman along the deserted highway. And she knew beyond a reasonable doubt that they hadn't been involved in an accident at all. Instead, they had been murdered.

And the killer was still on the loose.

* * *

Carey now found herself atop the bed in what used to be her room. Curtis Rains loomed over her, still holding the knife in his hands, and the same piercing smile hung across his face as he moved closer to her. Not resisting his touch, a tear rolled down her cheek as the knife split open her shirt and he ripped it off with his bare hands. Her bra was the only thing left in hiding her breasts from his eyes.

"You killed them," Carey spoke with feeling as the impact of her relative's death began to kick in.

Curtis Rains only nodded as he viciously began to undo her jeans. Minutes seemed to pass by as hours, and now Carey found herself naked, except for her underwear as she lay across the bed. Holding the knife once again against her neck, Curtis leaned in and spoke passionately into her ear.

"You are so beautiful," he whispered into her ear as his tongue slid out and touched her skin. *"You definitely have your mother's looks. I can't wait to see what it feels like to be inside of you. I have been waiting a long time for this, and I have been fantasizing about this since the day you got away."*

Carey couldn't speak, and she couldn't escape. She knew Curtis was going kill her. But first, he was going to rape her, and make her suffer before her death. No longer willing to fight, Carey Haas just lay there in silence, excepting his touch as his hands briskly made their way over her body. Shutting her eyes tight, she couldn't watch as his lips began to move across her body. Finally, after ten years, Carey Haas was no longer afraid of Curtis Rains. Instead, now, she had learned to accept death. Sobbing uncontrollably, Carey Haas simply waited to die.

Then, something happened, that caught her completely off guard. Opening her eyes, she watched as Curtis Rains jumped off the bed and looked towards the bedroom door. Her door lay askew against her wall and she knew that it had been kicked down. Sitting up, she saw Billy standing in the doorway. He hadn't given up on her. He had come to her yet again in what appeared to be another uncontrollable nightmare.

"Get away from her!" Billy ordered angrily as he stepped inside the bedroom and approached Curtis Rains.

Curtis, turning his back on Carey, let out a vicious howl into the night, and began slowly walking towards Billy. The smile had faded and disappeared from his face as his rage grew, and he held the pristine knife steadily in front of him. *"You don't know when to give up do you?"* he spoke coldly, and Billy could sense that he had upset the evil man by interrupting him. *"I've tried as long as I could to let you live. But you refuse to go away. Do you really believe that you can beat me?"*

"I'm damn sure going to try," Billy stated matter-of-factly, showing Rains that he had no intention of backing away, and was simply not going to go away without a fight. "If you want her," he continued looking towards the direction of Carey, who was desperately trying to put back on her clothes. "You're going to have to kill me first. I promised her that I wouldn't let anything happen to her, and that's exactly what I intend to do you son of a bitch."

"You really love her don't you?"

"Yes I do," Billy replied finding his question a bit out of place. "I love her more than anything in this world."

"And you are willing to die for this love?"

"If I have to."

"Then so it shall be," Curtis continued as he raised the knife high into the air and began backing Billy into the corner. *"How dare you look upon me with those detestable eyes,"* he continued to lash out at Billy as his anger continued to grow. *"I am the keeper of lost souls, and no matter what you pretend to be, I know you're afraid. I can see it in your eyes, and can smell it in the air you breath. How dare you test my fate, my power, and look past the honor I so rightfully deserve."*

"You have no power," Billy retorted fitfully, never once looking away from the madman. "You're an evil man. You think you're powerful because you can produce fear. That doesn't make you a man. It makes you a coward. Only cowards go after the weak. Only cowards kill."

"You can't even begin to imagine the powers I possess. And you can't pretend to know who I am or what I'm about because you haven't lived the life that I have lived. You haven't seen what I have seen, nor have you experienced the terror I've felt. All my life I have been nothing but a slave. A slave that was forced to endure pain. But at an early age, I learned to escape my fear and turn it into a living source. My powers came from my tears and years of pain. And now, it's my turn to show the world what they had forgotten about. I didn't deserve what happened to me. I deserved to live a normal life like everyone else."

"And what about Carey?" Billy questioned boldly. "She doesn't deserve to be treated this way. She has done nothing to provoke this madness inside of you. She's innocent just like you were. And she deserves to live a normal life just like you did. You were a victim," Billy paused momentarily as he saw a flicker in the *Tinman's* eyes. "But Carey doesn't have to be. For the first time in your life, you can do the right thing."

"Her death," Curtis Rains paused as Billy's back was now pressed firmly against the wall and their faces were locked up, no more than two inches separating the two. *"Is the right thing? She has to die Billy. There is no other way."*

Billy, sensing the opening, took his eyes away from Curtis and found Carey still sitting on the bed, watching the scene in horror. He could tell that she was expecting him to die. "Carey!" Billy shouted knowing this could be her only chance. "Run! Get out of here." For a moment, she just sat there, a dumbfounded expression lingering across her face, almost as if she didn't understand his words. "Damn it go!" Billy ordered, knowing their time was limited. "Run away!"

With that, Carey finally stood on her feet and without hesitation, ran away from her old bedroom, leaving Billy and Curtis Rains behind. Soon, she found herself standing in the hallway of her old home, and immediately began to head towards the stairs. Reaching them, she hesitated at the top and peered down below. She could see

Blaze lying motionlessly on the couch, a little blood dripping from an open wound along his chest. Finally, she fled down the stairs and quickly ran towards the one place that had sheltered her long ago when the *Tinman* had first decided to enter her life.

The basement.

As Carey fled from the room, Curtis Rains had no chance to reach out and grab her. Grabbing Billy's throat with his free hand, he watched as Carey escaped down the hallway. *"No!"* he shouted loudly, angry that she once again had managed to slip away from his grip after he had been so close in devouring her innocence. Nevertheless, he knew that it didn't matter. He wasn't like the man he had been ten years ago. He didn't have to run after her and fear that she might outrun him. Curtis Rains wasn't alive, and he was immortal.

No matter where she ran, or where she tried to hide, this time, there would be no escape.

Finally, he focused his attention back on Billy. *"How dare you try and stand in my way. I am the devil as you know him, and I cannot be stopped."* When no reply came from his prey, Curtis Rains gripped the knife tightly and his eyes grew large as his anger grew and his rage could easily be seen in his veins as they outlined the whites of his eyes. For the first time, Billy was truly afraid, and he now realized there was nothing he could do to protect himself. As he looked into the *Tinman's* eyes, he could see his life flashing before his eyes, and he knew that he was about to die.

"Please don't," Billy said firmly, although not showing any emotion in his eyes. "I have too much to live for."

But it was too late. Curtis Rains had already made up his mind and didn't want Billy around for any more distractions. His veins popped out of his right hand as he prepared to drive the knife deep into Billy's flesh, welcoming the pleasant sensation he would pick up as soon as he felt the warm blood of his victim oozing over his own oily skin. No longer smiling, Curtis Rains let out an evil cry into the night as he sent the knife whaling forwards.

Billy closed his eyes as the knife seeped into his flesh, easily passing through the barrier of his skin and finding his insides. He felt the blood drip from his stomach and his hands instantly drew towards the wound as he desperately tried to stop his blood from escaping his body. However, Billy didn't let out any cries of pain, and no longer begged for mercy. He wouldn't allow Curtis Rains to have that satisfaction.

Then, as Curtis removed the knife from Billy's stomach, he let go of his throat and looked deep into the teenager's eyes. A smile returned as he began to lick the knife clean. He watched as Billy struggled to keep his eyes open, and was not surprised to find him falling weakly to his knees just seconds later, his hands still battling the flow of blood. Kneeling down, he spoke softly.

"It's no use you know? You can't stop the bleeding and no one is going to be able to help you in time." Then, pausing, he lifted Billy's chin into the air with the edge of the knife, forcing him to look into his eyes. *"You are going to die Billy. So tell me, was it worth it?"*

Not waiting for a reply, Curtis Rains walked away from the badly injured body of Billy Saxton, satisfied that in time, he would die. Heading down the hallway, his nostrils flared wildly as he searched for the beloved Carey Haas. There was no one left to stand in his way. Finally, vengeance was upon him.

Fleeing down the stairs, he wisely headed for the darkened room of the cellar. He could feel her presence, and knew that she would've returned to the one spot where she had been able to elude him so many years ago.

This time, however, it wasn't going to work.

Reaching the door to the cellar, Curtis threw it open and listened as it slammed against the wall. He saw the foot of the stairs but the rest of the way was covered in complete darkness. Straining his ears, he heard nothing but silence. Yet, fear was in the air and he knew Carey was down below, hiding from him. Laughing, he slowly proceeded down the stairs, scraping the side of the wall with the jagged edge of the knife.

"Carey!" he spoke softly, almost whispering in the darkness of the room. *"I know you're in here. Why don't you come out? I promise I'm not going to hurt you,"* he added with another piercing laugh as he repeated the words he had spoken so long ago. *"I just want to talk to you."*

There was no reply.
Only silence.
Yet, the chilling fear remained.

As Billy looked at the staggering wound he had received just moments ago, he felt his vision becoming increasingly blurry, and knew his chances for survival were slim to none. He still hadn't heard from his mother, and figured that she could have fallen into the same fate he had just encountered. Perhaps, just perhaps, this was God's will, and this was his time to die.

As of now, however, he wasn't dead.

He coughed loudly, and listened as his voice echoed throughout the now dead silent home. Another cough soon followed, and this time, he spat up some of his own blood. Terrified, he knew he wasn't going to make it.

He blinked his eyes profusely trying to restore his vision. Then, weakly, he used the wall to climb back to his feet, leaving a bloody handprint everywhere his slippery hands touched. Groping in pain, he never let out a cry for help. If death were coming, he would let it take him gradually.

However, he still had a few breaths left, and as of now, Carey Haas still had a chance to survive.

It seemed to take forever to reach the staircase, and as an alarming amount of nausea began to sink in, he began to doubt that he could make it to the bottom. Nevertheless, he had to try. Griping the handrail as best he could, Billy Saxton slowly proceeded to make his way down the stairs. Taking it one step at a time, this journey appeared to be a never-ending circus, and with every step, he came closer to loosing his balance and fall to the hardened floor below.

To Billy Saxton, darkness was slowly closing in.

Carey sat with her head between her legs, shivering in the cold, almost dampened area of the cellar as she sat directly on the cemented floor hiding in the darkness from the intruder that was after her. She remembered hiding under the stairs ten years ago when she had been nothing more than a terrified child, searching for safety, and upon trying it again; she realized that she could no longer fit in the small space located directly under the staircase.

Settling for a dark corner of the basement, Carey simply sat there, and waited for the evil man to come after her. After ten years, she was once again running for her life, and was once again searching for safety in the empty confinements of the basement. Memories of her past began to flood her brains intensely, and she felt more tears dripping from her eyeballs. She couldn't stop them. And apparently, she couldn't stop her fate in that of dying through the hands of the person that had taken her parents away from her so many years ago.

Unfortunately, it appeared as though the *Tinman* had always been apart of her life. And would be, forevermore.

Then, the door at the top of the staircase flew open and she could see the shadow of the devil standing at the top. She listened as he spoke to her, and knew that soon her hiding place would be revealed, and her life once again in jeopardy. She began to shake uncontrollably, and did her best not to mutter a sound.

Not even wanting to breathe, Carey sat there in complete silence, hoping and praying that Curtis Rains would turn around and walk right back up the stairs and away from her.

Unfortunately, this was not the case.

"Oh Carey," she heard him call as he reached the bottom of the staircase. She listened intensely as he moved his black leather boots across the hardened floor. *"Come on out sweetheart. Why make this any harder than it needs to be. I know you're scared. And I know you're tired of running. Just come on out,"* he whispered with a laugh as his voice echoed throughout the darkened room. *"If you come out, I promise I'll be able to ease your pain. I can take you away from this world you hate so much. And I can deliver you from evil Carey. I have the power to take all your pain away."*

Carey said nothing.

Then, a light flickered on. Carey removed her head from between her legs and squinted until her eyes adjusted to the new environment. She saw him standing in the middle of the cellar, his hands still clutching the string that dangled from the ceiling. She was amazed that the light still worked. Yet, she removed herself from her crouched position and was thankful that her knees didn't begin to pop.

Curtis Rains was standing with his back turned to her as his sharp eyes surveyed every inch of the basement floor. She slowly began walking towards the staircase as she noticed his head turning in her direction. Carey was within ten yards of the staircase when he spotted her.

"*Gotcha!*" Curtis yelled as he instantly ran towards his precious victim.

Not looking back, Carey reached the stairs and began running with all her might. Just as it had been ten years ago, Carey fled from the madman, sensing his presence behind her and knowing that he was in hot pursuit. Once again, she felt his hot breath breathing down the back of her neck, and feared the worst.

"*Not this time you little bitch!*" she heard his evil words calling from behind her. "*You can't escape me this time.*"

Reaching the top of the stairs, Carey fled from the basement and soon found herself standing in the living room. Heading for the sliding glass door, her only other choice was to flee out into the powerful storm and along the beach. Gripping the sides of the walls, she spun around and was about to dart through the sliding glass door when she noticed Billy standing at the bottom of the staircase. He was holding his stomach, and a thick pool of blood could be seen at his feet.

He had been stabbed.

Carey had no choice. She couldn't turn her back on him and leave him for dead. Stopping in her tracks, she changed directions and headed for the only person she had ever loved. "I'm so sorry," she whispered into Billy's ear, not even thinking of looking back to see how close Curtis Rains was to reaching them.

"Y-you should g-go," Billy tried to speak as more blood poured from his mouth. "You can, st-still get aw-away."

"I'm not leaving you!"

"Y-you have to."

"No I don't," Carey remained strong having made up her mind, and feeling a new wave pass through her soul. For the first time, she was no longer afraid. In an instant, she had grown firm. "You're all I have left Billy. I can't leave you. I have nothing anyway if I don't have you."

Then, she felt the presence of someone directly behind them and she spun around to face Curtis Rains.

"*You really are one persistent son of a bitch aren't you?*" Curtis asked, speaking towards Billy. "*You really just won't give up will* you? *You should have been dead by now. But obviously you're a strong person. And for that, I respect you."* Then, pausing, he raised his knife once again into the air. *"However, I still can't let you live."*

"No!" Carey shrieked as she stepped in front of Billy just as Curtis Rains lifted the knife into the air and was about to strike.

"Get out of the way!"

"No!" Carey boldly replied. "Please, leave him alone. It's me you want. Not him."

"Carey!" the Tinman's tone almost didn't sound human, as his rage had finally reached its highest point. *"Get the fuck out of my way you little bitch! I'm not going to warn you again."*

"I'm not moving!" Carey remained strong.

Curtis had had enough as his blood began to boil, and his determination to kill had reached its limit. If Carey wanted to play tough, that was fine by him. Her flesh and blood would taste just as sweet dead or alive. After all, it was the pleasure of the kill that he was seeking, and this pleasure couldn't be found anywhere else.

Like a flash of lightning darting out of the darkened, black sky above, the *Tinman* raised his hand into the air. The knife sparkled in the twilight as his white eyes turned blood red, and his true being began to form. *"How dare you defy me!"* he retorted as his disfigurement began to take place. Suddenly, his normal appearance began to disappear and the devil began to form right before their very eyes.

Curtis Rains was turning into the creature.

His clothes disappeared, his hair, everything. The skin found around his body vanished and was replaced by a blackened almost charcoal surface that looked crisp and scaly to the touch. His eyes remained dark red, and his blood continued to boil. Juicy fangs began to form, and his saliva turned into poisonous venom. He no longer looked human, and now could easily be seen as nothing that could be found on the face of this earth. Right before their very eyes, Curtis Rains had transformed into his true self.

He had unmistakably become, the *Tinman.*

He was about to lash out his final fury of rage, when something happened, that even he could not understand.

From above, the ceiling appeared to be lifted from the roof and carried off into the powerful wind of the storm. Before Curtis Rains had the chance to slam the knife into Carey Haas's skull, he stopped in his tracks, and stared into the gaping hole of the ceiling above. Confused, he could feel his wrath weakening, and yet, he didn't understand why. What was going on?

Then, a blistering, piercing white light appeared.

Squinting his evil eyes, the Tinman stared into the light, and saw a figure standing before him.

"Who the hell are you?" Curtis demanded coldly.

"I'm the one person in this world that can stop your evil," a voice replied as a man appeared from the white light, and began floating to the ground below. "And I came here to do just that."

"That's not possible. No one can defeat me."

"You should have thought about that before you came after my son. You should have left my family alone, and you should have never tasted his blood," the voice continued as the mystery man continued to walk towards him, a white gown hanging over his shoulders.

"Son?" Curtis questioned confused. Then, before the man could respond, he knew the answer. The man standing before him was none other than Billy Saxton's father. And like him, he too had died. *"No!"* Curtis replied in a shocked tone. *"This can't be happening."*

Tom Saxton's bold gaze met the evil glare of Curtis Rains. "It's finally time for you to die Rains," Tom began boldly. "Because as long as you're alive, I'll never be able to rest in peace."

Carey didn't know what to make of it.

She didn't know what to do.

Yet, right before her very eyes, the *Tinman* was dying. The man that had come through the light walked straight towards Curtis Rains and extended his hand. His hand easily passed into the creature's flesh, and Tom began to squeeze the life out of the madman's evil heart. Confused, she listened as the *Tinman* began to scream out in an agonizing pain.

Soon, it was over.

The evil Curtis Rains was dissolving before her very eyes. It appeared as though her nightmare was finally over.

Looking up, she watched as the man knelt beside her. "Don't worry," Tom spoke gently. "It's all over now. That man can never hurt you again. He's gone to a place from which he will never be able to escape." Carey was speechless. She didn't know what to say. "Can you do me a favor?"

"Anything," Carey replied, still amazed.

"I need you to tell Billy that I'm sorry," Tom replied as he looked down at his unconscious son. "I need you to tell him that I'm sorry for never being there for him, and for the way I treated his mother. I never meant to ruin his life, and more than anything in the world, I just wish he could forgive me. I still love him and his mother, and I always will."

Then, just as quickly as he had come, Tom Saxton disappeared into the night sky, just as the rain began to slow down. Billy, near death, never had the opportunity to witness his father's heroic deed. More importantly, however, he never had the opportunity to hear his father send him his love.

* * *

Moments earlier.

Detective Ashley Selvaggio pulled into the old Haas driveway found along the beach just as a small portion of the roof was lifted off and sent wailing into the night. Leaving her headlights on, she killed the engine and without thinking twice, stepped out into the stormy night and began to run towards the front door. She could clearly see that someone had kicked it in. Or *something?*

Drawing her pistol into the air, she held it firmly with both hands, not willing to take any chances. Reaching the front door, she placed her back against the wall, amazed at how quickly she had become drenched in rain, and began counting to three before she entered the home.

"One. Two. Three," she counted aloud as she heard sirens coming in the distance and felt a bit of relief in knowing that they would be there in no time. Finally, she exhaled one last deep breath and stepped into the foyer of the home, with her gun armed and ready to fire, she pointed it directly in front of her.

Her eyes grew large in disbelief and her mouth dropped low as her eyes took hold of what was directly in front of her at the foot of the staircase. She saw who she felt must have been Carey Haas standing in front of a boy, as if protecting him from something.

Then, her eyes were fixed on the creature.

It was unearthly. The creature's entire body was crispy black, and his gleaming blood red eyes could be seen clearly from her standpoint. Ashley didn't know what to expect when she had entered the home. Needless to say, however, she never expected to see anything like this. Her imagination could run wild, but it did have limitations and she felt for sure a line had to be drawn somewhere.

Nothing in her imagination, however, could explain this.

And then, a light appeared from the opening in the ceiling, and a man appeared. Not knowing what to do, Ashley watched in silence, no one else in the room even remotely aware of her presence, as the man dressed in a white gown approached the creature and then reached into his flesh, looking as if he were about to rip out his heart. Completely mesmerized, Ashley realized that she had stumbled onto something she may not ever be able to understand. She had been right, nonetheless, in conceiving that there was more to the Reynolds murder case in Starke. Again, however, this was beyond even her most supernatural theories.

Walking closer to the creature and the man that had appeared from the darkened sky above, it appeared to be a battle between good and evil. Lowering her gun, she knew it was powerless against these life forces. Yet, her finger remained on the trigger, perhaps for safety precautions. The closer she got to the creature, the more afraid she became. As the evil life form howled into the night in pain, she felt her own heartbeat quicken a bit and she realized something.

She was staring at the devil himself.

Then, it was all over, and after the man exchanged a few words with Carey, he lifted himself back into the air and disappeared without a trace. Running over to Carey, Ashley replaced her gun in her holster and knelt next to the young woman. Reaching over, she placed two fingers underneath Billy's neck as she worked hard to try and find a pulse. She could feel Carey's paranoid stare on her and could tell that she was wondering if Billy was going to be all right.

"How is he?" Carey asked quickly, as a tear dwelled between the edges of her eyes. "Is he going to be all right?"

"I don't know," Ashley hated to admit. "He's lost a lot of blood. But an ambulance is one the way." Then, Ashley watched as Carey looked away from her and began staring up at the sky above. The storm appeared to be clearing out and the rain had slowed to almost nothing more than a slight drizzle. As she looked into Carey's eyes, however, she could immediately sense that she had been through a lot, and couldn't help but to feel anything but sympathy towards her. Carey Haas was truly a remarkable young woman, and was certainly lucky to be alive.

"Is it over?" Carey asked, hoping the woman before her would have an answer to her question.

"I don't know," Ashley again hated to admit. "I think so." Then, as a team of deputies and an ambulance pulled into the driveway, Ashley helped Carey to her feet and began leading her outside. "What about you?" she asked with a smile as she gazed once again into the incredible girl's eyes. "Are you all right?"

"Yes," Carey replied with a smile. "Actually, I am."

Chapter 30

It was a beautiful day. The clouds had finally disappeared and gave way to the welcoming warmth of the sun. Birds gawked flawlessly in the sky above, perhaps a sign that the sun represented a new day, a new beginning. Still, emotions ran deep within the large crowd of people that hovered over the coffin as it slowly began its descent into the earth below their feet. Carey Haas stood next to Debra Saxton, hand in hand, as tears rolled silently down their cheeks. Death was still around them, and even though Carey had already gone through the painstaking ordeal of burying her aunt and uncle one day earlier, she still found herself loosing strength as she gazed into the depths of a six foot hole once again. Once again, Carey had come face to face with Curtis Rains, and once again, she had escaped death. Her heart, however, would be scarred for all eternity as Curtis had managed to take her loved ones' souls with him. Carey had no family left, and she could only imagine the struggles her life had yet to bring.

The ceremony ended shortly, and Carey slowly, with her head hung low, followed Debra to her car. Looking back at the coffin of Sheriff Burnham, she silently said goodbye one last time and continued on her way, desperately trying to regain her strength. Somehow, she had to tell herself that her life was not over. She knew that there was still a lot left for her to do, to see, to experience. She knew that Curtis Rains would never be able to hurt her again. She knew she still had Billy Saxton to comfort her, and help her get back on her feet. The saga of the Tinman had finally come to and end, and even though she knew that she would never be able to forget her dreadful past, she knew she would have to fight to make sure that she didn't live in it. At all costs, Carey Haas was going to make it. She was going to be all right.

She was going to make her parents proud.

Then, from behind, Carey heard a muffled voice calling out to her. Turning around, she found Detective Ashley Selvaggio making her way towards her. "Carey," Ashley breathed as she finally approached the distraught girl in front of her. "How are you holding up?"

"I'm doing okay," Carey replied, refusing to make eye contact with the woman in front of her. "I know I've got a difficult road ahead of me. But I'll be okay. It's," she let her voice trail off as she forced herself to swallow the lump that had formed in her throat. "It's finally over. My nightmare is finally over, and my parents can finally rest in peace."

"I'm sorry for your losses," Ashley continued as she placed a loving hand on the girl's shoulder in front of her. "But I can see that you are a very strong young woman, and I know that you are going to be all right." Then, Ashley reached into her pocket and pulled out a piece of paper. "This is my cell phone number Carey," she continued as she placed the piece of paper in the palm of the girl's hand in front of her. "And I want you to call me anytime, day or night, if you feel the need to talk about anything."

"Thank you," Carey breathed as she forced a smile to cross her face. "Thank you for believing in me."

"There is no need to thank me," Ashley returned the warm smile. "I'm going to be leaving town as soon as I leave here. But I'm serious, I will only be a phone call away if you need anything, anything at all."

"All right," Carey replied realizing that the conversation was coming to an end. "Take care detective."

"Call me Ashley," Ashley returned as she started to walk away from the amazing girl in front her. "And you take care of yourself as well Carey."

With that, Carey watched as Ashley walked away from her. Her eyes followed her until she had reached her Toyota 4Runner. Before climbing inside, however, Ashley turned and waved one last time at Carey. After returning the wave, Carey met Debra at her car and climbed inside the passenger seat. Taking a deep breath, she looked over at the woman sitting next to her behind the steering wheel.

Leaning over, Debra put a warm had on the girl's thigh. "Are you ready to get out of here?"

"Yes," Carey answered firmly. "I'm ready to get on with my life."

* * *

As Detective Ashley Selvaggio pulled out of the cemetery and drove her Toyota to the nearest interstate that would lead her away from Destin, Florida, she couldn't help but to think about everything that had transpired the last few days. The reality of the Tinman forced her to question her own beliefs. She had never experienced anything of this nature before. Curtis Rains should have died in the electric chair. But he had not. He had come back, stronger than ever, for the one that got away. And Ashley knew that even though she was a law enforcement officer, and always carried a loaded revolver in her side holster, she knew that her bullets would have been no match for the evil she had seen that night at the old Haas home. There would have been nothing that she could have done to save Carey Haas.

Feeling helpless, Ashley reached into the middle console of her SUV and pulled out her pager. There had been four pages from her Captain back in Starke, Florida. Shaking her head, she knew that she was never going to hear the end of it when she returned to her supervisor. She also was well aware that the chances of him, or her fellow officers ever believing the story she was going to tell was slim to none. She could picture the snickering behind her back, and could feel the stares of all the men in her department as they accused her of being insane.

It didn't matter.

She knew the truth.

Then, just as she was about to place the pager back in the center console, it sprang to life and the vibration caught her off guard. Pulling the device to eye level, she frowned as she realized it was Captain Armstrong once again. It was apparent that he wasn't going to give up until she returned his call. Completely annoyed with the situation, Ashley rolled down the window of her 4Runner and let the coastal air come storming into her vehicle. It was at that moment that she realized something had changed.

She had changed.

She took her eyes off the road for a moment as she stared at herself through the rearview mirror. Looking into her own eyes, Ashley realized that she had been living a lie. She wasn't happy with her life. She wasn't happy with most of the choices she had made, and she knew that if she continued down her current path, it would probably only lead to the end of a liquor bottle.

No. She was certain. Changes needed to be made.

With her mind completely made up, Ashley grabbed the pager tightly in the palm of her hands and threw it out of the window. Seconds later, she found herself heading off the interstate and soon came to a red light at an intersection of a highway that ran North and South. She didn't know which way she wanted to go. But she knew that she did not want to return home to Starke, Florida. That wasn't her home anymore.

Then, deciding to travel North, Ashley decided to follow her heart. She wanted to start over somewhere. Start a new career, a new life, a new everything. She was still a beautiful young woman, and knew that wherever the road took her, she would be able to make a name for herself.

Ashley Selvaggio had reached a crossroad in her life.

Turning her back on everything she had accomplished up until now, she rolled up her window, turned up the radio, and placed her foot on the accelerator. As the speedometer slowly crept higher and higher, Ashley found herself singing along with every song that came on the radio.

Then, looking into the rearview mirror once again, she looked into her own eyes and realized that they didn't appear to be lost anymore. Then, she looked at her face. She couldn't believe what she was seeing. She was smiling.

And that was something that she hadn't done in a long time.

* * *

Jamie Walker lay motionlessly on the hospital bed. Her badly burned body had been wrapped tightly, and as the painkillers began to wear off, she could easily feel the menacing, uncomfortable pain from the wounds of the burns. As much as she wanted to scratch away at the pestering sensation, she held strong, and simply laid in agony, her mind constantly wondering if the hellish nightmare she now found herself in had come to an end.

She thought of Travis McKinley. She knew that he had been taken from her, and she knew that she could never love anyone the way she had loved him ever again. A tear silently fell from her eyes as the thought of never being able to see, or hold her beloved Travis again came crashing into her heart. Her weakened soul seemed lost. She tried to fight off the urge to give up, to wish for death. She knew that's exactly what Curtis Rains wanted her to do. He wanted her to give up, to beg for death, and as much as she didn't want to give the evil man such satisfaction, Jamie couldn't help herself.

She was alone, and she wanted to die.

Slowly, Jamie edged herself off the hospital bed. She could feel her flesh separate slightly as the movement seemed to catch the healing process off guard. She held her breath for a moment as her entire body appeared to be consumed with an insurmountable amount of pain. Nevertheless, nothing was going to stand in her way. Determined, Jamie Walker slowly took her first couple of steps in days as she headed for the bathroom. She scolded herself silently as each step brought more and more pain to her crispy skin. She hadn't even realized until this very moment that the bottoms of her feet had been burnt as well.

Then, finally after what seemed like an eternity, she reached her destination. Slowly, Jamie entered the tiny bathroom of her hospital room and after finding the light switch, she waited a moment until the fluorescent bulbs sprang to life before preparing herself for the sight she was about to see. Gripping the sides of the sink with each hand, Jamie gazed into the depths of the sink as her heart began to beat out of control. She couldn't believe it. She was scared of herself. She was afraid to see what Curtis had done to her.

"Stop it," she ordered herself. "You can't let him beat you," she added, speaking of Curtis Rains. "You can't let him see that he was able to get the best of you."

Then, after a few more seconds of building her self esteem, Jamie Walker took one final deep breath, and then slowly lifted her head from the sink and gazed into the tiny mirror that hung on the wall before her, directly in the center of the sink. Her head had been wrapped tightly with bandages, and a few bloodspots could be seen trying to penetrate through the cottony substance. She could feel her body shivering as she realized she didn't even recognize the eyes staring back at her from the mirror. Those couldn't be her eyes, she thought silently to herself. Her eyes had always been so full of life, so full of energy. Nonetheless, there before her were the eyes of a stranger. They were dark, cold eyes that would force anyone to take pity on her. They gave off the essence of loneliness, sadness and grief. Feeling almost hollow inside, Jamie let a few more tears escape from her eyes as she finally lost her composure and had to turn away from the dreadful sight in front of her. As she wept in the bathroom of her hospital room, she began to realize that she truly was alone. No one was there to comfort her, to let her know that everything was going to be all right, or to let her know that she was loved. Travis was not there, and would never be there again. It was at that moment that she realized her eyes were telling the truth.

She was alone.

Then, feeling a resurgence of anger begin to form inside her lost soul, Jamie stared into the glass mirror once more, and then carefully proceeded to unwrap the bandages from around her face. She had to know. She had to see what Curtis Rains had done to her.

Within minutes, her objective had been complete. Her eyes remained closed as she slowly removed the last of the bandages from her face. Then, as she felt her strength revive itself, she regained her composure, and prepared herself for the worst. Whatever she was about to see, she was quite certain that it wasn't going to be pretty, and she was quite certain that what she was about to see would change her life forever. Then, with one quick movement, her eyes fluttered open and her hands immediately covered her face as she took in the horrific scene in front of her. She didn't look human. No undamaged flesh could be found along any portion of her face. There was nothing but charred remains and blackened scabs that appeared to be putting forth a valiant effort in piecing her flesh back together again.

Jamie couldn't believe what she was seeing. No longer was she a beautiful dark haired girl with everything in the world seeming to be going her away. No. Curtis Rains had come for her, taken her loved one away from her, and then turned her into a grotesque monster that would be looked at and called names as she walked down the street. She had become a freak, a hideous creature that looked as if it should be locked up in a cage somewhere and kept from society. Now, Jamie Walker was certain.

Her life would never be the same.

Her facial scars were never going to heal.

No, they would always be there. Every time she looked in the mirror from this day forward, she was going to be forced to look into the eyes of a monster. Curtis Rains had changed her life forever, and he had scarred her flesh for all eternity. Now, she was certain, that she would never forget Curtis Rains. He would never be far out of her mind. Every time she looked in the mirror, her scars would remind her of him.

Remind her of how he slaughtered Travis.

Remind her of how he had managed to instill a part of himself inside her own soul. In an eerie coincidence, she was well aware that society had abandoned Curtis Rains many years ago. But as she continued to gaze at herself in the mirror, she was well aware that once released from the hospital, her disfigured face would be enough for society to abandon her as well. Curtis Rains had gone through life without feeling loved, and always feeling alone.

And Jamie Walker knew, that just like Curtis Rains, she would not be able to escape the loneliness. Furthermore, she also knew that she wouldn't be able to escape the anger she was going to feel inside once she became an outcast from society.

Then, as she turned away from the image of herself in the mirror and slowly began to make her way back towards the bed, she realized that she didn't have anything to live for. She had absolutely no reason to smile, to laugh, to continue on. She had put up a fight against the evilness in Curtis Rains.

Unfortunately, however, it was a fight that she had lost.

And now her soul, her spirit, and her very essence of being would be lost forevermore in a valley of darkness.

* * *

Carey Haas quietly knocked on the bedroom door of the Anne home where she knew Billy was sleeping soundly. When she heard no response, she slowly opened the door, and stepped inside. There, she found Billy exactly where she had left him before she and Debra had left for the Sheriff's funeral. As she watched his chest move up and down, she couldn't help but to smile at the gorgeous man in front of her. Billy had been her guardian angel, her soul mate, her true love. Not wanting to wake him up, she tiptoed over to the edge of the bed and then without saying a word, leaned down and kissed him on the forehead while holding her hair back in a ponytail.

"I love you," she whispered as she decided to exit the room and let Billy sleep for a while longer. She knew that the doctor's orders were to let him get as much rest as possible. Just as she reached the door and was about to let herself out, however, she heard his crackling voice call out to her.

"Carey!"

Spinning around, Carey couldn't help but to smile as Billy winked at her, and although she could tell that he was in a lot of pain, he smiled at her and held out his hand. Carey ran over to him and took his placed her hand in his. Billy managed an affectionate squeeze before his energy faded and he had to let go. Carey noticed his weakness, and ran her fingers through his softened hair. "You shouldn't be up Billy," she spoke with a mother's tone. "The doc told you to take it easy."

"I know, I know," Billy interjected boldly. "And I'm going to. But first, I need you to help me do something."

"What?"

"I need to go back to the beach house," Billy answered firmly, and immediately recognized the uncertain glare stream from his girlfriend's face. "There's just something that I have to do Carey. We won't be there but for a few seconds I promise. I just don't think that I could make it by myself is all."

Carey was about to flatly refuse, but as she stared deeper into Billy's eyes, she could see that whatever it was that he wanted to do was important to him, and she also knew that trying to change his mind was pointless. Besides, he had been there for her, believed in her, and almost died trying to rescue her from the monstrous Curtis Rains. Now, it was time for her to be there for him. "All right,"

Carey agreed as she began to help him dress himself, careful not to hurt the healing knife wound. "It's going to be tough sneaking you past your mother, and you know she'd go crazy if she knew you were doing this."

"Don't worry about it," Billy replied. "Together, the two of us can accomplish anything." Then, he paused briefly before changing the subject. "How is Blaze holding up anyway?"

"Blaze is all right," Carey answered happily. "He went to the store with Murray to pick up a few things. I think they were going to rent a movie too. Elizabeth seems to think that everyone could use a good laugh right now, and I for one can't disagree with her."

"Nope," Billy continued as Carey helped him to his feet and handed him his cane. "That sounds like the perfect evening." Then, drawing their conversation momentarily to a close, he opened the bedroom door and peered outside. No one was in sight. Motioning for Carey to follow, the two of them crept down the hallway and out the front door without making a sound. Debra and Elizabeth had been outside on the back porch with the two little girls, and neither one noticed the commotion going on inside the home. "All right," Billy started in once again as he grabbed Carey's hand and peered down the street at the old beachfront home that caused them both so much pain. "Do you think we can be strong enough to go in there one last time?"

"You bet your ass we can," Carey answered firmly, showing no signs of fear.

Ten minutes later, yet after what seemed like an eternity, the two of them had reached the front door of the old Haas home. Wasting no time, Billy twisted the knob, pushed the door open and stepped inside. Carey's mind began to race wildly as she wondered just what was going through Billy's mind? Why had he wanted to come back to such a dreadful place?

Within seconds, her silent questions were answered.

Billy knew exactly where he was going. With his cane in one hand, and Carey's hand in the other, Billy Saxton made his way over to his mother's computer desk located in the family room of the old beachfront home. There, he found what he was looking for.

It was the picture of his father, Tom Saxton.

It was still laying face down, exactly how Billy had left it the last time he had walked by it and noticed it sitting upright. Letting go of the cane, Billy reached over and grabbed the picture in his hand and brought it close to his face. It had been a long time, but Billy now found himself looking into his father's eyes once again. He had never noticed it before, but there was a smile spread across Tom's face as Billy gazed into the picture. He felt his hands begin to tremble, and his heartbeat began to quicken as he visualized what his father had done for him a couple of nights ago.

"He loved you Billy," Carey whispered as she gave his hand a sympathetic squeeze.

Billy nodded as he placed the picture back on the computer desk. Then, he was about to turn and walk away when he wiped a tear away from his eyes and spoke to his father for the first time in a year.

"I forgive you father, and I love you. I've always loved you dad, and I'-l" he let his words slip away as a lump formed in his throat and tears bean to stream more profusely from his eyes. "And I'll never forget what you did for me," he managed to get out as he found his body becoming increasingly weak, and he knew that he should get back to a bed as soon as possible. Clearing his head, however, Billy said one last thing. "Thank you!"

With that, Billy Saxton and Carey Haas walked out of the old Haas home one last time, and save for the crashing of the waves, everything was dead silent. As the front door closed behind them, both of them were sure that they would never return again.

THE END

About the Author

He was born and raised in Tallahassee, Florida and has had an enthusiasm for writing since high school. At twenty-five years old, **TINMAN** is his first published book that brings to life his gift for writing about the supernatural, and horror of this tale. His passion for writing includes unpublished poetry, and his writing style always blends with a sensitive approach to life, love, and friendship. **TINMAN** includes a love story and heroism; focusing on many different relationships throughout the story. Jason enjoys combining the all-American family story with horror and the supernatural; providing his readers with both reality and the surreal approach to the unnatural.

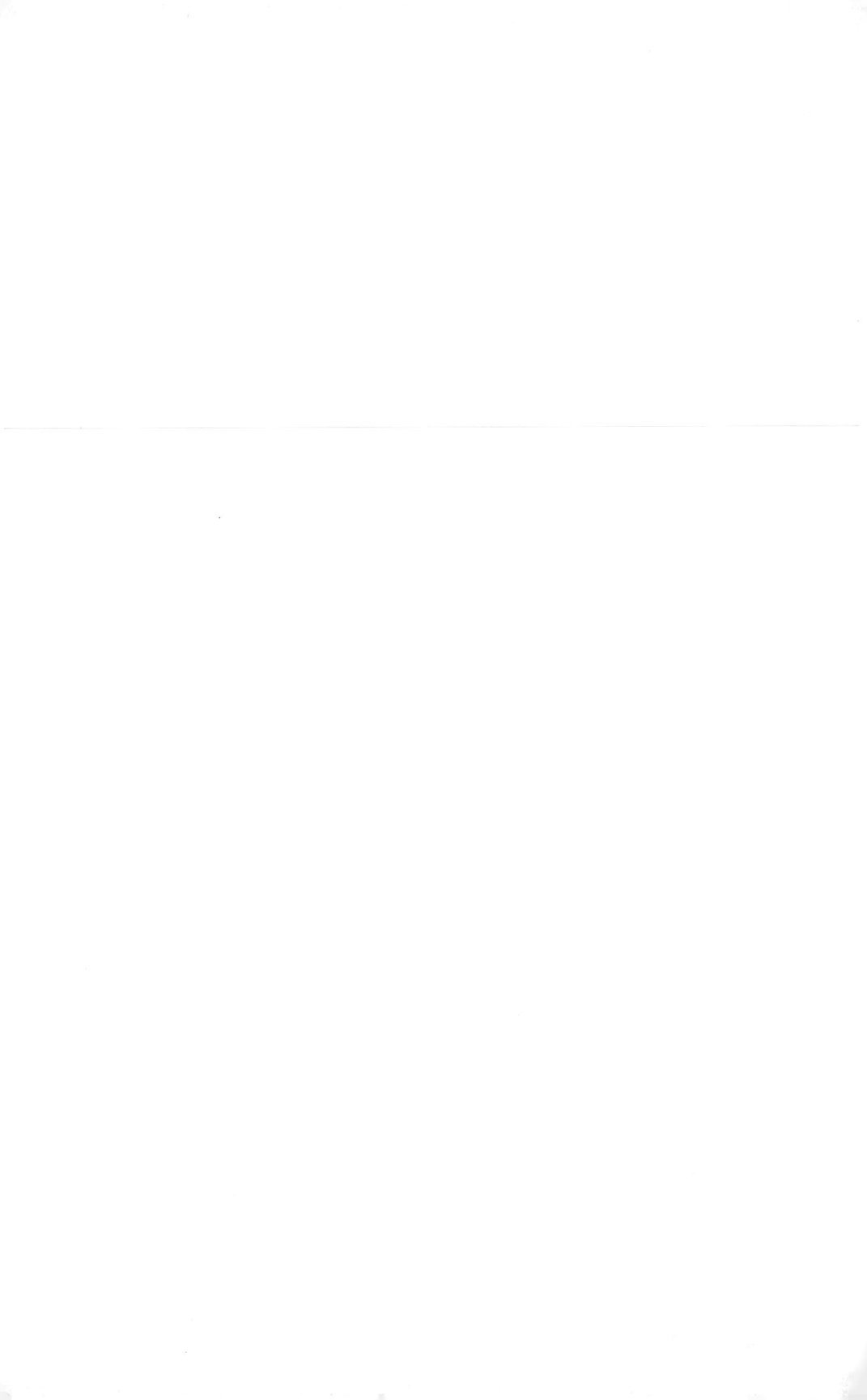

Printed in the United States
52661LVS00007B/22-24